SALAMANDER'S FIRE

Also in Legend by Brian Stableford

Serpent's Blood
Chimera's Cradle

SALAMANDER'S FIRE

The Second Book of Genesys

Brian Stableford

Published by Legend Books in 1997

1 3 5 7 9 10 8 6 4 2

Hardback edition first published by
Legend Books in 1996

Legend Books
Random House UK Ltd
20 Vauxhall Bridge Road, London SW1V 2SA

Random House Australia (Pty) Limited
20 Alfred Street, Milsons Point, Sydney
New South Wales 2061, Australia

Random House New Zealand Limited
18 Poland Road, Glenfield
Auckland 10, New Zealand

Random House South Africa (Pty) Limited
Endulini, 5a Jubilee Road, Parktown 2193, South Africa

Random House UK Limited Reg. No. 954009

A CIP catalogue record for this book
is available from the British Library

Papers used by Random House UK Limited are natural, recyclable products made from wood grown in sustainable forests. The manufacturing processes conform to the environmental regulations of the country of origin

ISBN 0 09 944361 9

Typeset in Sabon
Printed and bound in the United Kingdom by
Cox & Wyman Ltd, Reading, Berkshire

Part One

In the Narrow Land, Betrayed by Fear and Fury

There is no destiny; the future cannot be foretold, but the world is pregnant with many possibilities. Some will be given birth and suckled with nourishing milk, and the strongest of these will grow to be things which are new not merely in the world but in the universe. What will be new cannot be foreseen, but its shadow might be glimpsed in the fertile imagination.

There once came a Serpent into Idun, which brought the gift of a tree whose fruit had knowledge of good and evil, and the forefathers bought the tree with promises they could not fulfil.

'I will make you a gift of my blood,' the Serpent said, 'and hope that you will use it wisely.'

The forefathers accepted the gift, and made a further promise they could not fulfil. 'We shall return this gift a thousandfold,' they said, 'if only we can use it wisely.'

There also came a Salamander into Idun, which brought the gift of a tree whose fruit had knowledge of another kind, and the forefathers bought the tree with coin the Salamander could not spend.

'I will make you a gift of the fire in my heart,' the Salamander said, 'and hope that it might warm you.'

The forefathers accepted this gift, and gave the Salamander another unspendable coin. 'We shall return this gift a thousandfold,' they said, 'if we can only feel its warmth.'

Serpents die, and Salamanders too, and the people of the world brought death with them when they first descended from the sky, but if ever the world is devoid of Serpents or Salamanders men will have cause to mourn. Better by far that the promises their forefathers made might one day be fulfilled, and the coin they paid might one day be spent. Milk that is given to the nourishment of Serpents and Salamanders is already owed, and does not go to waste.

There is no destiny. The future cannot be foreknown, but the human mind is pregnant with many designs, some of which may be realised if only the necessary instruments can be devised and forged. We cannot know today what we might discover tomorrow, but the scheming mind should make what provision it can. Remember this, for it is a truth as vital as any in the lore.

The Apocrypha of Genesys

I

LUCREZIA DIDN'T SEE where the dragomite warrior came form, but she knew immediately that it wasn't one of those which had marched alongside the wagons – always at a respectable distance – for the last fifteen days. She didn't know exactly *how* she could tell, but she was in no doubt at all, and she didn't waste a second in turning to run.

She heard it moving after her, but she didn't look back to meet its huge, nearly-human eyes or consider the serrated edges of its horrid jaws. She ran, hoping that the urgency of her plight might compensate for weariness and hunger. The privations which she had suffered of late had reduced her body to a level of weakness and discomfort which seemed entirely unnatural to her aristocratic sensibilities.

The warrior was slow, by dragomite standards. Its six double-jointed legs had been adapted by millions of years of evolution and a whole lifetime of practice to the work of negotiating the mazy gullies and jaggedly precipitous slopes of the Dragomite Hills, but it was not in good condition. The crests of these southernmost hills had lately begun to regenerate in the wake of the plague but the creature was undoubtedly half-starved. It was also alone – and that was probably worse.

Lucrezia didn't imagine for a moment that she understood what went on in the alien minds of dragomites, but she had come to realise that a lone survivor of a devastated nest, bereft of the influence of queen and drone, had to be reckoned devoid of whatever passed for sanity among dragomitekind. She knew, therefore, that the thing that was coming after her was deranged. It was damaged and distressed, uncertain in its purpose, but no less dangerous for that.

She ran upslope and not down. She knew that downslope led to the riverbank; that was where she had been heading in order to fill a waterskin. It would not do to get trapped between the dragomite and the cold grey water. She knew, too, that her only hope of becoming visible to the sentries posted by the wagons was to climb up as high as was humanly possible.

In the meantime, she yelled for help, as loudly as she could.

Her cries echoed from the surrounding slopes, crazily compounded by the lunatic architecture of the carefully crafted mounds. She knew, alas, that the volume at which her words came back to her was no indication of the likelihood of their being heard a hundred mets away; the hills played tricks with sound as well as sight. They sometimes seemed to have been designed with the specific intention of violating all human intuition and expectation. She howled anyway, as lustily as her overworked lungs would permit.

As she bounded from one ledge to another she felt that she was moving with uncommon skill and efficiency, but she saw when she glanced around that the warrior was gaining on her. It was scuttling after her like a giant predatory spider, flowing over the uneven ground with a smoothness that seemed quite unnatural in something so massive. The rattle of its armoured feet was oddly subdued; the chitinous substance which made up the walls of the dead nests was not as hard as rock, and it muffled footfalls of every kind.

Lucrezia's head was unusually clear. She was afraid, but not panic-stricken, and the difference was sufficient to let her feel proud of her composure and resolution. It was not that she had grown used to the everpresent possibility of sudden death, and certainly not that she was past caring whether she lived or died, but simply that she had come to an accommodation with the pressure of necessity. She had learned to keep her head, even in circumstances like this. Had she been born wretched, perhaps she would always have known how to do that, but because she was a princess and had led a sheltered life she felt fully entitled to think it a marvellous achievement. She didn't credit it to the mysterious Serpent's blood which was rumoured to be surging through her veins, brought out of quietness by some mysterious trigger; she claimed it as her own achievement, her own triumph.

The slope was becoming so steep and so eccentrically pitted

that she needed her hands as well as her feet to propel her forward. She had dropped the empty waterskin.

The dragomite warrior was moving more slowly too, but it was still gaining ground. It was no more than a dozen mets behind her now, and that dozen mets represented no greater space of time than a couple of heartbeats.

'Help me!' she screamed again.

There were not so many echoes to scream back at her now, but she still couldn't see the wagons, and she was no longer certain that she had picked the right slope to climb. She knew how horribly easy it was to become disorientated among the mounds, and to lose one's sense of direction utterly.

She had lost her straw hat too, and the sun's midday heat beat down on her head, whose once beautiful hair was now close-cropped like Hyry Keshvara's, but sunburn was a trivial threat compared to the jaws that would soon be snapping at her heels.

She reached a high shoulder of the mound, fervently hoping that the wagons might come into view beyond it, but there was nothing to be seen but more precipitous slopes. She didn't mean to hesitate, but sudden uncertainty as to which way to turn confounded her movements, and for a moment or two she was utterly torn between this way and that – a pause which reduced the margin of her advantage over her dragomite pursuer to less than the space of a single heartbeat . . . and then, unluckily, she slipped and fell.

She went over the edge of the ridge at the steepest place, sliding into a narrow crevice which scored her ankles and elbows remorselessly as she fought to arrest – or at least to steer – her tumbling fall.

So total was her loss of control that the velocity of the descent took her well away from the dragomite's eager head, but she knew that the advantage thus gained would be very short-lived. When the fall ended in an ungainly crash, she would certainly be bruised and it was all too probable that the breath would be knocked out of her. She would be incapable of further movement, at least for a while – long enough, at any rate, for the dragomite to descend with all due care and finish her off with a casual swipe of its jaws.

Then, of course, it would eat her.

Dragomite warriors were specialist vegetarians when things

were normal, and would turn cannibal in preference to eating any other kind of meat, but when plague and madness upset the usual order of things a dragomite would eat almost anything. Lucrezia had been hungry for so long, and had forced down so much that was utterly unappetising in order to fuel herself, that she bore the creature no grudges on that score.

As the slope curved towards the horizontal she was able to slow her fall without paying too heavy a price in lost skin, but bruises were exploding all over her body. She felt fairly sure that none of her limbs was actually broken, but she knew as she finally rolled to a stop that she was quite helpless. She couldn't use her momentum to bring her to her feet; the best she could contrive was to finish sprawled on her back rather than on her belly, looking up into the sky.

For days the sky had been cloudless, but it was hazy now and there was a moistness in the warm noonday air that might – in calmer circumstances – have seemed delicious. She tried to lift her head to watch the dragomite warrior scuttling down the sheer side of the mound. She was paradoxically glad to find that she could.

The creature was thirty mets away and closing fast: two heartbeats; perhaps three. Its long legs were moving with great rapidity and an eerie grace.

Then, seemingly out of nowhere, another figure came hurtling into her field of vision, thrusting itself into the diminishing margin which separated her supine body from the moment of death. Lucrezia's heart leapt as she measured the newcomer's size, hoping that it might be Dhalla – and even when she saw that her would-be rescuer was only half the size of a true giant she felt justified in clinging to the thread of hope. She had seen Andris Myrasol fight dragomites before; she knew that he was no longer scared of them, and that he had a plentiful resource of that foolish recklessness which men of his stripe called bravery.

She watched the amber throw his javelin at the dragomite's head, and execute a curious capering bound as he continued his run, determined to attract its attention and draw it away from her.

The dragomite was unhurt by the tip of the javelin, which missed the orbit of its eye by a few sems, but the grace of its movements was utterly lost as it tried to stop in its tracks, confused by contrary reflexes. Its huge eyes – which were more like the plaintive eyes of a cow than the compound eyes of an earthly insect – lost co-ordination as it tried to keep both the humans in view.

Lucrezia's head was still quite clear, and her thoughts were relatively unconfused by pain. She marvelled at the fact that this strange and rather silly character would unthinkingly do this for her: for someone who had plotted to use him destructively, as if he were no more than a toy or a beast of burden. How things had changed in the last three tendays! *It's strange*, she thought, as she watched the monster turn its head first to one side and then the other, as if it were trying to restore order to its disorientated consciousness by shaking up its sensory input, *how amenable we are to change, once the order of things begins to break down. Perhaps the dragomite warrior isn't the only one here that ought to be reckoned mad.*

The warrior, poor stupid thing that it was, went after the moving target that was Andris Myrasol. Lucrezia guessed that its instincts gave it little or no choice in the matter. The nature and purpose of a warrior was to respond to threats; even desperation could not break such a deep-set resolution.

The dragomite followed Myrasol, and Myrasol – having dawdled a little until he was certain that he had his enemy's attention – broke into a run. First he ran directly away from Lucrezia, then jinked to his right. Lucrezia couldn't tell whether it was an arbitrary manoeuvre, or one forced upon him by the awkward lie of the land, or an attempt to lead the creature to ground where other friendly forces might be waiting. Painfully, but in no mood to be defeated, she lifted herself up on her elbows, and then sat up straight. She was determined to watch the final act of the drama, if it were to be played out within her line of sight.

She saw then that Myrasol hadn't come alone. He had been followed, evidently without much delay, by allies who were absolutely certain to defeat the rogue warrior.

No dragomite warrior in all the world was equipped to stand against two of its own kind; dragomites were not like humans and their heroism did not extend to feats of that sort. Myrasol must have known that Jume Metra's warriors were not far behind him, and that he only had to distract Lucrezia's attacker for three or four seconds to win them the time they needed. He danced between the newcomers with evident glee.

The rogue had no chance, but it didn't turn to flee. Nor, indeed, did it offer as much resistance as it might have. It seemed to Lucrezia, as she watched the butchery, that it accepted its fate. She wondered whether it was capable of welcoming the end of its hopeless struggle against adversity, of being grateful that the irresistible spur of instinct would finally be forced to let up. The creature was undoubtedly deranged, but Lucrezia couldn't help asking herself whether it *knew* that it was deranged, and was therefore ready to welcome the terminus of its now pointless existence.

When Jume Metra's warriors leapt forward with deadly efficiency to disable and kill it, the lone dragomite closed its large eyes and tilted back its head, as though to catch the furious rays of the noonday sun with its snaky palps. Lucrezia was still watching the victorious warriors dismantle her pursuer when Myrasol came limping back to help her to her feet.

'Anything broken, highness?' he asked, producing the title with the blatantly ironic note that had somehow become customary to him and to Checuti. She was not in the least discomfited by the sarcasm, given that it came from him. If such a teasing note had been sounded by Jacom Cerri, Aulakh Phar or Carus Fraxinus it would have been a different matter, but whenever they called her 'highness' – and they usually remembered not to – they always sounded as if they meant it. Merel Zabio always sounded as if she meant it too, and Ereleth certainly did mean it. The only one of her close companions whose tone was still uncomfortably and infuriatingly ambiguous was Hyry Keshvara.

'I don't think so,' she said. 'How about you?'

He looked ruefully down at the leg he was trailing. 'Twisted the ankle on the last turn,' he said. 'It'll be fine in a few minutes.'

'Thanks,' she said. As he opened his mouth to speak again she quickly raised a hand. 'Yes,' she said, 'I know. I'd no business going off to the river on my own in the middle of the midday. I should have been asleep, or conserving my strength, and I shouldn't have been thirsty – or if I was, I should have gone rooting around for somebody else's waterskin, no matter how many sleepers I had to disturb to do it. I know.'

The big amber had the grace to grin. He also had the grace to turn away, to look at what Metra's warriors were doing.

'Dragomite for supper again,' he said with a sigh. 'It seems to keep us going, along with the fungi Metra's mound-women scavenge, but it's not what I'd call *food*. If humans had been intended to eat dragomites, Genesys would surely have ordained that our tongues and bellies should find their meat more palatable. Let me look at that leg.'

'You've been listening to Carus Fraxinus,' she observed, hauling up her right trouser-leg to expose the worst of her bruising. 'Any ordaining that Genesys did was a very long time ago, and if what he and Ereleth have deduced is reliable – assuming that they have at last condescended to be honest with one another regarding their deductions – the whole point of whatever crazy plans Genesys set in train was that the order of things couldn't be relied on. The wonder is that we find *anything* palatable.'

'It's you who've been listening too attentively to Fraxinus, highness,' Myrasol countered, amiably enough. 'I try not to get too caught up in his flights of fancy – a feeble brain like mine overheats if it's fed too many insoluble enigmas and unanswerable questions. Your leg's been knocked about a bit, but it's not swelling – can you get up?'

Lucrezia knew that he didn't really believe that his brain was feeble. He thought that he was simply showing common sense in shrugging off Fraxinus's attempts to solve the mysteries of the lore by rational analysis.

'You've signed on for the whole trip,' she pointed out as she stood up, flexing her limbs experimentally. 'You know full well that Fraxinus isn't going south in search of new trading opportunities. It's curiosity that drives him on, and the more puzzles he identifies the more fervent he becomes.'

It wasn't strictly true; Fraxinus was far too calm a man ever to be described as *fervent*, but it was true enough.

'I'll be content to find out what's waiting for us at Chimera's Cradle if and when we get there,' Andris said. 'For the time being, I'm concentrating all my attention on getting out of these accursed hills. I don't care what horrors there are lurking beyond the horizon; I just want to see the last of this endless dungheap. Where are you going? The camp's that way.'

Lucrezia had begun to walk away from him, heading upslope. She tried to walk without a limp, but it wasn't easy. 'I need my waterskin,' she told him. 'Not to mention the water I came out to fetch. I'm even thirstier now than when I set out. I lost my hat too.'

He came after her, still hobbling slightly. She let him catch up.

'I'd better come with you,' he said, leaving out the title because he knew she didn't want him to use it and wasn't, for the moment, disposed to tease her.

'You don't have to,' she told him. 'That was a thousand-to-one chance. There can't be any more rogues about – the plague devastated this region two full years ago.'

'There's no way to know how many rogues might be about,' the amber said, in an annoyed tone. 'We're not the only ones travelling south from the war-zone. There are bound to be other parties of egg-carriers, with warriors in attendance – and they might be a lot quicker than the one you just outran. Anyway, you don't have to be so proud about accepting my help. We're all on the same side now, remember?'

'All right,' she said tiredly. 'Pick up your spear and stand guard over me, if that's what you want. Doing Dhalla's job for twenty minutes won't make you into a real giant, though. You'll never be more than half the man she is.'

The amber didn't reply to that, but his expression said that he thought it uncalled-for – as, indeed, it was. She wondered why she'd felt compelled to say it, given that he had just saved her life. She realised, somewhat to her own surprise, that she felt guilty and resentful about having to stand in his debt. She wanted things to be even between them, or at least to *seem* even.

'You're right, Prince Myrasol,' she said, trying to mimic his ironic tone as she pronounced the title. 'We *are* all on the same side – even Metra and her dragomite siblings. We have to be, if we're to stand the slightest chance of making something out of this grand folly. It's myself I'm annoyed with, not you. I'm trying to compound one stupidity with another, and you're right to stop me. I'm sorry.'

His parchment-coloured cheeks took on a slight golden glow. 'Well, highness,' he said, this time doing his best to suppress the sarcasm which normally transformed the title into a kind of sly insult, 'I suppose that's settled. Let's get the water and get back to the wagons. Now that you come to mention it, I could do with a drink myself.'

'Unfortunately,' she said with a sigh, as she recovered her waterskin, 'even the water tastes foul. You'd think the rain would have washed the slopes clean after all this time, but there's still that strange undertaste. Do you suppose the Soursweet Marshes are sweeter than they're sour, or will their water be just as bad?'

'If I had to bet,' the amber replied, 'I'd bet on the sour. But we have to keep hoping, don't we? We're owed a slice of luck, don't you think?'

'You might be,' she told him. 'I think I just had mine.'

2

FROM THE BACK of the small wagon Jacom Cerri caught sight of Princess Lucrezia and Andris Myrasol making their way down the gully in a somewhat laboured fashion. The bright light startled his eyes and he had to turn away to rub them. When he turned back again he reached down to help them climb up, gasping as he took the strain of the amber's unreasonable weight, which did not seem to have lessened much despite the hunger they had recently endured. He noticed the way that the princess flinched as she bumped her knee against the backboard while climbing over.

'What happened?' Jacom asked the amber anxiously. 'I woke up to find that you'd left your station, and that the two dragomite warriors had deserted theirs – I was on the point of raising the alarm when I saw you coming over the ridge.' Turning to the princess, he added: 'Aren't you supposed to be asleep in the big wagon, highness?'

'You don't have to call me highness any more,' Lucrezia reminded him, as she nowadays made a point of doing. 'I'm no longer a princess. And please don't tell Ereleth that I went off on my own and nearly ran into trouble.'

'*Nearly*,' Myrasol observed, 'is something of an understatement.'

Jacom looked at them impatiently, wishing that they'd condescend to tell him what was going on. No matter how often he told himself that he was being oversensitive he couldn't shake the conviction that he was always the last one to be told anything. He could understand that no one considered his opinions worth seeking, given that he found the endless discussions which went on in the big wagon quite beyond his comprehension, but even a hired sword – which was, admittedly, what he had been reduced to – needed to be kept informed of threats and dangers.

He looked around to make sure that Merel and Checuti hadn't stirred. They seemed to be sleeping soundly enough. Both had taken turns on sentry duty during the first period of the midday, so they were entitled to be tired, and they had long ago learned the art of staying asleep while people climbed in and out of the wagon.

Myrasol followed the direction of Jacom's glance, and nodded guiltily. 'I'd better get back out,' he murmured, replacing the wide-brimmed hat he had only just taken off. 'Who knows what might be lurking in the hills, ready to launch an assault on us?'

The princess was busy drinking from her waterskin; it wasn't until she'd had her fill that she removed her own hat, which looked as if it had been recently trampled underfoot.

'What happened?' Jacom whispered again, when the amber had lowered himself down and walked off towards his sentry-post, limping slightly.

'I went to get some water,' she said. 'These last few days have been so utterly uneventful that I took it for granted I wouldn't run into any trouble. I was wrong. Luckily, Andris and Metra's dragomites came to my rescue. He played bait while they provided the trap. He twisted his ankle because he was so pleased with his own cleverness that he turned round too quickly.'

While she was speaking she drew up the legs of her trousers to expose the shins. Jacom drew in his breath at the sight of several bloody bruises, but what he was thinking was: *It should have been me! I should have been the one to save her. I wasn't even properly asleep – I could have been out there with Myrasol, if it hadn't been for the sun's blistering heat . . .*

'I fell,' the princess said, by way of further explanation. Jacom watched her roll up her left sleeve to display more contusions about the forearm and elbow. Her clothes were loose, not because hunger had made her thin but because they had been borrowed from Keshvara. She had not had the opportunity to pack a trunk of her own clothes when Checuti's men had accidentally abducted her, but she'd never seemed in the least distressed by the necessity of borrowing. She took a perverse pride in her unsuitable attire.

'Let me see, highness,' he said, reaching out as if to take her arm. She drew it away from him.

'It's nothing,' she said. Then, relenting slightly, she added in a lighter tone: 'What fraction of the leakage is Serpent's blood rather than my own, do you think?'

Jacom sighed, wondering whether she would have let him take her arm if it had been he and not Myrasol who had heard her cries for help. 'You must be careful, highness,' he said, as solicitously as he could.

'Why?' she retorted, though not in an aggressive way. 'Are you still nurturing the hope that you might be able to take me back to Xandria, to buy your way back into my father's good graces?'

'That's not fair,' Jacom said, although he wasn't sure that it was entirely unfair. While the princess was alive and well, the possibility of returning to Xandria and reclaiming his commission remained open, and he couldn't put it out of his mind. He'd accepted the probability that his exile might well be permanent, but he was determined to keep alive the possibility that it might not. In any case, there was a matter of duty involved. He might be in reduced circumstances but he was still bound by honour to serve the princess as well as he could.

He felt a slight flush creeping upon his cheeks as he reminded himself of that last reason, because he was well aware of his own hypocrisy. He knew full well that he would have deserted Ereleth without a second thought, in spite of the fact that she was a queen, because she was old, ugly and evil-tempered. Lucrezia wasn't, and that had rather more to do with his continued loyalty than any honest obligation of duty. Fortunately, his golden skin had been darkened by exposure to the tropical sun, and he knew that the blush didn't show.

'Do you hate me, Jacom?' the princess said pensively, as she rolled her sleeve down again and shifted about in search of a comfortable position in which to sit, wedged between the casks and sacks which cluttered the wagon.

'No, highness!' he said. 'Why should you even think it possible?'

'Call me Lucrezia,' she said. 'I think it possible because I got you into this situation, and its's very obvious that it's one you don't relish. If it weren't for me, you'd still be marching up and down on the citadel walls putting on a bold show of being a soldier. You'd be eating regular meals, wearing a nice clean uniform, spending your off-duty hours in an endless riot of drinking and whoring in the quayside taverns. In fact, you'd be living the life you always wanted. If it weren't for my stubbornness, you might still be able to go back to it.'

'It wasn't *your* fault I lost my position, highness,' Jacom said uncomfortably. 'It was Checuti who blasted all those doors to smithereens with his barrels of plastic and seized the Thanksgiving coin. If you hadn't gone missing your father might have sent me to the wall – or even the scaffold – to make an example of me. Your abduction gave him an alternative, for which I'm profoundly grateful. Anyway, who'd want to be a fool in a uniform parading up and down on those desolate walls day in and day out, year after year, when he could be part of a great adventure like this one?'

'You really ought to practise lying a little more often,' she told him. 'It's obvious that your education in that particular art has been badly neglected. If you'd been born a princess instead of some lordling's son, you'd have been very thoroughly trained, I can assure you.'

'I'm not a lordling's son,' Jacom informed her stiffly. 'My father was a fruit-farmer. There's not much call for lying in that line of work. Just a little bit of haggling now and again.'

He looked out into the bright and hurtful daylight so that he didn't have to meet her gaze. The two dragomite warriors had returned now, and they took up their station outside the mouth of the tunnel into which their fellows had retreated – along with the three Serpents – to wait out the midday. Two mound-women came behind them, dragging sleds made from the dorsal plates of a dragomite. Each sled was fully loaded, but he couldn't see exactly what the loads contained, and he couldn't raise much curiosity.

'When I saw that Andris was gone,' he murmured, 'and that they had gone too, I couldn't help wondering . . .'

'They really are on our side,' the princess assured him. 'I don't know how the trick was worked, by Mossassor and his fellows or by Metra and the drones, but they've been educated to recognise every one of us. We're not actually established as nest-mates, but we're creatures to be guarded and defended nevertheless.'

'We're prisoners really,' Jacom said hollowly. 'They'll look after us until we're no longer useful – but what then?'

'I don't think they'll turn on us, no matter what happens,' Lucrezia said. 'It's difficult to get much sense out of the Serpents, because Mossassor's knowledge of human language is elementary and the others won't condescend to use it at all, but I've done my best to get to know Jume Metra. She's even worse at lying than you are, and I'm inclined to accept what she says. The drones really do know what it means to make a pact, and I think they'll honour it. I think we can trust them.'

'You're the one with Serpent's blood,' Jacom said resignedly. 'I'm just an ordinary human being. I'm out of my depth. I don't know what Fraxinus and Ereleth think they might find by reading between the lines of the so-called *Apocrypha of Genesys*, I don't know what Dhalla means when she says that she has Salamander's fire burning in her heart, I can't begin to understand Aulakh Phar's account of *paedogenesis* and I don't know why Andris Myrasol feels obliged to look after that horrible severed head which called him *brother*. But then, I'm just a fruit-farmer's boy who thought that a few years' education in the Arts Martial and a commission in the king's guard were all he needed to—'

He broke off all of a sudden. It would have been undiplomatic in the extreme, as well as absurdly fanciful, to conclude: *marry a princess of the realm and live happily ever after*.

'Perhaps you *would* understand if you tried a bit harder,' she said, rather brutally, 'instead of spending so much time brooding and sulking.'

'I don't brood,' he informed her stiffly, 'and I certainly don't sulk. I just don't say very much, because I don't like to make a fool of myself.'

He regretted the remark as soon as he'd made it, all too well aware of the fact that an unkind observer might easily judge that he'd done nothing *but* make a fool of himself since the moment he'd managed to arrest the wrong man for breaking Herriman's leg in the brawl at the Wayfaring Tree. If only he'd managed to grab Burdam Thrid instead of Andris Myrasol, none of this would have—

The princess cut off his train of thought by saying: 'If you *don't* hate me, Captain Cerri, perhaps you could bear it in mind that you'd be slightly more use to me – and to yourself – if you could overcome your fear of making a fool of yourself long enough to gain a sensible understanding of what it is we're actually trying to do . . . or what we *think* we're trying to do.'

'I'm not a captain any more, higness,' Jacom said defensively.

'And I'm not a highness, captain,' she retorted. 'I can't tell you why Andris Myrasol is so determined to hang on to that head he collected in the depths of the dragomites' nest. You were there, so you're probably in a better position to judge than I am. As to the rest of it, it's rather difficult to put it in a nutshell, but I'll try.

'Carus Fraxinus and my house-mother think that when the forefathers first came into the world, descending from the ship that sailed the dark between the stars, they tried to set things up so that the people they intended to leave here would be safe and well provided for. Genesys was the plan by which they intended to achieve that end, but it didn't work out the way they originally intended. Unexpected difficulties emerged – difficulties which they hadn't encountered in planting colonists on other worlds orbiting other stars.

'The *Apocrypha of Genesys*, according to Fraxinus, is something that was tacked on to the lore at a late stage, once the original plan had been modified. One part of it tells us that the forefathers took something from the Serpents, and something from the Salamanders, in order to repair the plan. The Serpents and the Salamanders evidently co-operated with the forefathers, and received promises in return, which some of them still expect to be honoured, even though Mossassor and his companions don't seem to know any better than we do exactly what it was that the forefathers took or exactly what it was they offered in return. Whatever it was, it has something to do with the metaphorical Serpent's blood that I'm supposed to have in my veins and the Salamander's fire that giants are supposed to have in their hearts.

'According to Aulakh Phar, we carry around within us millions of tiny creatures too small to be seen with the naked eye, and we stand in constant peril of invasion by others that might do us harm – the things which cause disease and infection. Some of the ones which live inside us all the time actually help us in one way or another. Phar thinks that both Serpent's blood and Salamander's fire are tiny creatures of that kind, but that they're usually inactive, doing nothing except reproducing themselves over and over again. At some stage, though – in response to some kind of trigger of which our conscious minds know nothing – those particular tiny creatures become active, and undergo some kind of metamorphosis. It's as if caterpillars were capable of reproducing themselves as caterpillars, only completing their life-cycle by changing into butterflies once in every thousand, or once in every million, generations. That's what *paedogenesis* means.

'Fraxinus thinks that the plague which destroyed the fungi on which dragomites feed is only one aspect of a more general upheaval which is gradually spreading through the plant and animal species we call *unearthly* – which means, in his opinion, everything which was already here before the ship arrived. He thinks that everything we call *earthly* is descended from things which the people of the ship made, as part of the Genesys plan. Fraxinus thinks that the plague is a symptom of some kind of crisis in the world's affairs – something which also involves us, simply because we're here. He thinks that Serpent's blood and Salamander's fire were given to us by the forefathers to help us through the crisis, and he thinks that we might be able to find out how, if only we can get together with the right kind of Serpents and the right kind of Salamanders. That's Ereleth's contribution, I think – her secret commandments tell her to seek out those Serpents and Salamanders which are also inheritors of arcane wisdom. She was hoping that Mossassor might be one, but he's – sorry, *it*'s – been a sad disappointment to her. Mossassor's just chasing rumours, like Fraxinus, and it doesn't know enough human words to give us a clear account of the little it does know.'

'He knows our language better than we know his,' Jacom murmured. He refused to be fetishistic about referring to Mossassor as *it*, although he was perfectly happy to accept that the Serpent wasn't a male. It was obvious to anyone who cared to look that the tiny loincloths which were the only things the Serpents wore – except for their hats, belts and backpacks – couldn't possibly contain a penis and scrotum; whatever they were hiding had to be much less obtrusive.

'That's true,' Lucrezia admitted. 'Anyhow, for the time being Fraxinus's determination to track down any relics of Geneys that might still be found at the Navel of the World and Ereleth's secret commandments both require us to go south – which seems to coincide with the dragomites' desires. We're agreed that it's best to aim for the place marked on Myrasol's map as Salamander's Fire, where we might find better informants. Mossassor says that Salamanders have better memories than Serpents, and that they learned more from the forefathers than his own kind – although he admits that he's never actually *seen* a Salamander.'

'Nor has any of us,' Jacom pointed out. 'Even Dhalla only says that *her people* know Salamanders. She pretends to be deep, but she's really rather stupid.' Jacom didn't like Dhalla. On the one occasion he'd asked for her help she'd treated him with naked contempt.

'She's not stupid,' Lucrezia retorted, as he'd known she would. 'And she doesn't pretend to be deep. She's a lot like you, in some ways – you just feel uncomfortable around her because she's twice your size.'

'If Mossassor's an *it*,' Jacom said, 'so's she. There aren't any male giants, are there?'

'She's a she,' Lucrezia told him frostily. 'Just as Jume Metra is a she. The fact that she doesn't know how giants get pregnant – or even *if* they do – doesn't make her a fool. Jume Metra knew nothing about her male equivalent until Andris showed her that head. Maybe we're the unusual ones because we *do* know how our reproductive system works. Ereleth thinks that Mossassor doesn't know how Serpents reproduce, although he may be just reluctant to talk about it.'

I couldn't blame him for that, Jacom thought. *I wouldn't want to have to explain the facts of life to Ereleth – and I wouldn't know where to start if I had to describe the process to a Serpent.*

'Do you understand all that?' Lucrezia asked, when he said nothing out loud.

What's there to understand? Jacom wanted to say. *It's a farrago of nonsense, all superstition and speculation. The lore of Genesys is just a story and all Phar's ramblings about creatures invisible to the naked eye is just magical mumbo-jumbo to make people believe in the efficacy of his medicines. There's not an ounce of clear meaning or common sense to be found in any of it.*

What he actually said was: 'I'm trying.' It wasn't much, but it was the best he could do. For a moment, he thought she was going to stare at him in open disgust, or make some remark about his parentage, but she didn't. He couldn't read the expression on her face at all.

After a pause, she said: 'Are you sure you don't hate me, Jacom?'

'Quite certain,' he said, honestly enough.

'What about Andris? Does he hate me?'

'He doesn't hate you either,' Jacom assured her. 'He's grateful that you gave him that stuff to kill the worm Ereleth made him eat. He knows that Ereleth would have kept him captive for a lot longer. He understands that the business with the bush wasn't anything personal.' He paused, glancing into the shadowed depths of the wagon to make sure that the others were sleeping before adding: 'Merel doesn't like you much, though. And nobody likes your house-mother at all.'

The princess didn't seem unduly disturbed by the fact of Ereleth's unpopularity, nor was she surprised by the news of Merel's attitude to her.

'I'm glad you're with us, Jacom,' she said soberly. 'I'm glad Andris is with us, and I'm even glad Checuti's with us. Ereleth's glad too, even though she doesn't go out of her way to make herself likeable.'

'Thanks,' Jacom said, without overmuch enthusiasm.

'Try to talk to Jume Metra,' Lucrezia advised him. 'Try to talk to the Serpents too, if you can bear it. You'll feel better if you can just make contact with them. We should be clear of the hills tomorrow or the next day, if Myrasol's map can be trusted, and we don't know what we'll find there, even though my all too brief encounter with Djemil Eyub gives us some cause to hope that it won't be anything very unusual.'

Jacom looked again at the two dragomite warriors standing patiently on guard. It was impossible to tell from their stance whether they were there to keep potential enemies away, or to make sure that their supposed friends didn't escape. 'I wish I could be as confident as you are, highness,' he said.

'Say *Lucrezia*,' she retorted impatiently. When he hesitated, she said: 'Go on! *Say it*.'

'Lucrezia,' he said obediently. 'I wish I were as confident as you, *Lucrezia*.'

'There you are,' she said. 'You only have to make an effort. That's all it takes.'

He would have liked to believe that she was right, but in his heart he couldn't. He just wasn't capable of it. He couldn't believe in Fraxinus's ship or Ereleth's secret commandments or Phar's bacteria or Dhalla's unearthly fire or *Lucrezia*'s magical blood . . . and he couldn't believe that all he had to do to set his mind at rest was to make an effort.

One day, highness he thought, *you'll run out of luck and pluck, and neither Myrasol nor the dragomite host will be there to save you. I only hope that I will.*

3

LUCREZIA PREFERRED TRAVELLING by night, provided that the stars shone brightly enough to light the way. It sometimes became quite cold, but the chill of the darkness could be kept at bay with extra clothing, while the heat of gaudy sunlight simply had to be borne. She liked riding under the glittering panoply of the heavens; it made her feel that she was somehow keeping company with the stars. She no longer suffered overmuch from saddle-soreness and thus found riding far more comfortable than sitting in the back of one of the wagons, and on horseback she could look up into the sky with renewed curiosity and wonder.

She had always known the lore of Genesys, of course, and had always believed it in a way that some commonsensical people – Jacom Cerri, for instance – clearly never had, but she had never before had occasion to give it much thought. Unlike the mysteries of witchcraft and the gossip which circulated constantly within the Inner Sanctum, that part of the lore had never seemed relevant, to her or to the world. It simply hadn't mattered whether its truth was literal or metaphorical. Now, however, the question of its exact meaning and significance had taken on a certain urgency. When she looked up at the stars that shone upon the Dragomite Hills she had abundant cause to wonder how many were suns orbited by worlds akin to – but subtly different from – the one in which she lived, and how many ships there might be floating between them, bearing cargoes of livestock and seed, and whether she might indeed be part of an infinite company of human beings which extended throughout the firmament.

But if the ships are free of the curses that afflict worldly life, she thought, *why should the people on board them be interested in worlds at all? If the ships are incorruptible, safe from all manner of decay and corrosion, why should the people who dwell there wish to condemn their children to suffer all the torments of rottenness?*

'Be careful!' said a warning voice, and Lucrezia lowered her eyes to the ground just in time to balance her weight as her mount skidded and scraped down a steep slope.

When they were on the level again Lucrezia looked back, and saw that it was Jume Metra who had spoken. Metra was also mounted. She was the only mound-woman who had taken the trouble to learn to ride, and although she had not yet grown used to spending long hours in the saddle she had become moderately adept in the art.

'Thanks,' Lucrezia said. 'I was daydreaming.'

'It isn't day,' Metra pointed out.

'I mean that I was lost in thought,' Lucrezia corrected herself, with a slight sigh. 'Do you never get carried away by tides of ideas?'

'Sometimes,' Metra admitted.

'There you are,' Lucrezia said. 'You're only human, after all.' She knew as she said it, however, that it wasn't true. Metra and her fellow mound-women might be reckoned more than human or less, but never *only* human. Jacom Cerri had told her exactly what he and Andris Myrasol had seen in the depths of the dragomite nest, and what they had inferred in consequence. Jume Metra and her sisters – human and dragomite alike – had been born from eggs laid by the dragomite queen. She had no navel, and the milk which had nourished her in infancy had been the dragomite queen's; her own breasts were vestigial, as devoid of function as those of a human male. And yet, her flesh was human flesh and the language she spoke was the language of humans.

'We are the true humans,' Metra said, with a slight glint in her eye that might or might not mean that she was being deliberately provocative. 'You are the estranged ones: the orphaned and the lost.'

'The orphaned and the lost! Is that what you call us?' Lucrezia asked. 'Is that what you think we are: descendants of workers or warriors who strayed from their nests?'

'Yes,' Metra replied. 'But . . .' She stopped, seemingly lost in confusion.

'But you're not sure it's true,' Lucrezia finished for her. 'Not any more. In fact, you know it can't be true. Mound-women who wandered away from the nest couldn't produce children – not unless there were human males already out there, and probably not even then.'

Metra said nothing, but Lucrezia felt sure that the mound-woman didn't regret starting the conversation and wasn't trying to end it. She wasn't devoid of curiosity, although she might have had few opportunities to exercise the faculty before the plague devastated the hills. There were thoughts she couldn't yet voice, but she was learning.

'It's an interesting conundrum, isn't it?' Lucrezia said affably. 'Whether your kind is descended from mine, or mine from yours, something very remarkable must have happened, must it not? If you were the original humans, how could it ever have come about that warriors or workers who strayed from your nests suddenly found themselves able to bring forth young without the intercession of the dragomite queen? How could those strays develop organs of reproduction if they had not been designed by nature to reproduce? But there are similar questions to be asked if we look at things the other way round. If *we*'re the original humans, and your ancestors strayed *into* the nests of which they became a part, how did it come about that the dragomite queen was able to give birth to their subsequent generations while their own reproductive organs became inactive?'

'We know no answer to that question,' Metra said.

'Like so many questions,' Lucrezia observed, 'it's more easily evaded, or left unasked, than answered. But I have seen a bush, which was said to be just as unearthly as the dragomite queen, which readily took root in the flesh of an earthly dog. As it grew, the two organisms became fused into one, although the bush wouldn't flower. A similar bush killed the human host in which it grew, but the host was weak; had it taken root in a strong and healthy man it might have completed its natural cycle, becoming a compound creature: a chimera. That's what you are, Jume Metra, although you bear no obvious dragomite stigmata: a chimera, part human and part dragomite. I mean no insult by saying so, because I think that I may be a chimera of sorts myself. The lore of Genesys says that we all are. According to the lore, that's why the garden which they made after their first city had crumbled into dust was named Chimera's Cradle.'

'There is no insult in calling us dragomites,' Metra told her, although that wasn't what Lucrezia had said. 'We are of the nest; we are all of one flesh, all of one mind.'

Not quite all of one mind, if we can place any trust in what Jacom Cerri heard Myrasol's head say before it detached itself from the flesh of the dragomite queen, Lucrezia thought – but that wasn't the line of enquiry she wanted to pursue.

'How do you see the future of the world, Jume Metra?' Lucrezia asked quietly. 'Will the day come when there is nothing to be found in it but warring hives of dragomites? If the hills recover from this catastrophe, will they expand again, swallowing up the Forest of Absolute Night and the Spangled Desert and every other region under the sun, until they have swallowed up *everything*? You know that the world is round, do you not, and that its surface is finite?'

'We know that the world is round,' Metra informed her stonily. 'We know that it is also hollow, or might be. But there are places where dragomites cannot go – places where tunnels cannot be excavated, where hills cannot be built, where queens cannot form their inner chambers. There will always be other kinds of earth and other kinds of creatures – both dwellers in the deep and crawlers on the face. It will always be possible for humans of your kind to find a place among the crawlers, to excavate your own hollows and build your own walls. You need not fear that our kind will ever exterminate yours.'

'But there are places where your kind and mine might compete, just as there are places – like the Spangled Desert – which are useless to both,' Lucrezia was quick to say, confident that the guess was good. 'If you were given space to do it, you could make new nests in the fertile plains of Xandria, and in the lands to the south of the hills – the lands from which the men you slaughtered in the forest had come.'

'Do people of your kind not fight for territory among themselves?' Metra countered. 'That is life. One nest contests with another, while either might make pacts with a third; it is the way of things. Are cities any different?'

'No,' Lucrezia admitted. 'They aren't.'

'Then your kind and mine are alike in this: we cannot avoid

the necessity of war, nor can we ever win a final victory. We do what we can and must to preserve our own nests. That is all.'

If that is all, Lucrezia thought, *then what am I doing here? What are Fraxinus and Phar and Hyry doing? What are Ereleth and Dhalla doing? Or are we just the orphaned and the lost, like that rogue which attacked me so half-heartedly?*

'That's a bleak view of existence,' she said aloud. 'To me, it seems less than human.'

'When there is abundance,' Metra said earnestly, 'pressure builds; then there is war. When there is scarcity, desperation grows; then there is war. Peace is a matter of balance; it cannot last long. When there is abundance, there are no alliances, but when there is scarcity, alliances become necessary. You understand that, as do we. It is the same for all of us, and for every living thing.'

Perhaps it's unwise and unkind of me to try so hard to make her into a philosopher, Lucrezia thought, *if that kind of understanding is the only reward that thought will bring her. But it may be fear and apprehension speaking. She knows that we'll soon be out of the hills, and that the balance of power between the nest and the true humans will shift. She must suspect that we'd welcome any opportunity to be rid of them – and rightly so.*

'There has to be something more than that kind of expediency, for your kind as well as mine,' Lucrezia said soberly, as much to herself as to the mound-woman. 'There has to be something more to life than a constant battle for living space – some kind of end for which to aim, some kind of purpose which our dreams and ambitions might serve.'

Metra didn't ask why, but nor did she utter some brief and dismissive denial. She was slowly becoming a new person, more complicated than the warrior-machine which had fallen upon Djemil Eyub's men in the forest and killed them with unthinking efficiency. She wasn't yet the kind of person who automatically asked *why*, but she was no longer the kind of person who couldn't. Lucrezia, on the other hand, had always been the kind of person who asked *why*, even before she had fallen under the spell of Ereleth's stern tutelage – so she asked herself the questions which Metra would not pose, even though she had no answers.

Why *did* there have to be any further purpose? Weren't life and multiplication their own reward? If there really were ships of some barely imaginable kind sailing the dark between the stars, what were they doing if they were not questing for new living space? Why would they have left the world which made them, unless that world had already become a single vast hive, or city, or whatever might be imagined in place of a hive or a city, which now sought to extend its petty empire to the bright-lit wilderness of the sky? What could the purpose of Genesys have been, if not to give the tiny handful of people who were to be ancestors of the people of the world the means to spread throughout that world and make every sem of it their own? Why shouldn't one believe that there was, indeed, nothing to life but a ceaseless battle for living space, in which one sometimes had perforce to form temporary alliances, but in which everyone – at the end of the day – was a potential enemy to everyone else, except one's own nest-mates?

On the other hand, if that were the case, would the people of the world before the world – the world from which the ship that had brought people to *this world* had first set out – really have taken the trouble to build such a marvellous device? Was a whole world not big enough to fight over, without extending the fight beyond its limits? Wasn't Xandria – the largest empire ever known in a world whose lore declared it inhospitable to empires – quite content with its present boundaries?

Lucrezia was awkwardly aware that she didn't really know the answer to that question. At any rate, she didn't know what her father would have said in reply had it been put to him. She had a strong suspicion, however, that any king of Xandria who found a way to extend the boundaries of his empire would greet the possibility as a glorious opportunity, without pausing for an instant to ask *why*.

'There *is* more to human life than life itself and the struggle for territory,' she finally said to Jume Metra. 'If there were nothing more than that, no one who had a secure and comfortable place in the world would ever leave it – and yet, here we all are. It's not just necessity and nest-war which stir people to restlessness; there's something in all of us which acts as a spur, urging us on even when we have no need to look beyond our protective walls. You must know that – and the drones who make plans for you must know it too. These hills around us are full of empty nests, and the summits are beginning to regenerate, but you've no intention of stopping here, have you? You're going to go on with us, into the unknown.'

'We cannot stay here,' Metra told her flatly. 'We must go on.'

'Why?' Lucrezia demanded, although she knew full well that she wouldn't get a sensible answer.

'Warriors may eat the flesh of warriors,' Metra replied, 'and queens may be born again in the bodies of living queens – but not in the rotting corpses of the dead. This is polluted earth, poisoned against us. We must go elsewhere, and we know it. We are all of one mind.'

'Is it really necessity, or merely custom?' Lucrezia asked curiously, although she wasn't at all sure that Metra was in a position to judge.

'While there is life in any one of us,' Metra said, 'and a single egg remains, the queen is mother to us all. We know what we must do; if you do not, what kind of humans are you?'

She was developing a certain subtlety too, for she must have known that Lucrezia would remember the words she had used earlier to describe those humans not bound by ties of flesh and blood to dragomites: the orphaned and the lost.

Perhaps we are, Lucrezia thought. *If the lore tells the truth, then that is what we all are. We belong to another world, and were abandoned here, to forge what bonds we can with the unearthly. Perhaps, in the end, all humans will have to follow the example set by Metra's kind.*

4

THE DRAGOMITE HILLS ended more abruptly to the south than they had in the north, where they were in constant competition with the trees of the Forest of Absolute Night. Here, the recently fallen empire of the dragomites was bounded by a region of bare and inhospitable rock; the last mounds formed a ragged cliff which fell more or less sheerly for forty or fifty mets to a broken apron of dead ground.

Andris could see that this unusually precipitous formation might be self-perpetuating; water flowing torrentially down the cliff-face during the fierce storms which sometimes afflicted the region probably washed the flat rocks clean of all would-be invaders at irregular but fairly frequent intervals. On the other hand, what had happened to the land beyond the strip of bare stone had definitely been contrived by the hand of man. From the edge of the grey ribbon to the distant horizon the ground was black, and Andris had no difficulty recognising the aftermath of fire. As far as the eye could see the earth had been scorched. The blackness was utter; it was obvious that the scorchers had returned in the recent past to make sure that no regeneration could begin.

Andris didn't need to confer with Jacom Cerri or Jume Metra, who were riding close behind him, to decide the reason for this desecration. It had been done to make a clear and absolute boundary between the land of the dragomites and the lands cultivated by men – and to make it more difficult for dragomites to cross that boundary.

While he directed his mount to a precipitous pathway which ran parallel to the river, Andris's mapmaker's eye took a certain clinical delight in tracing the countless meandering cracks which scarred the region below, even though he knew full well that they would make its passage awkwardly inconvenient for horses and wagons. Some of the tortuous channels might possibly extend all the way to the Soursweet Marshes in the west, although the majority would eventually link up to swell the waters of the great river whose course the expedition had been following for some considerable time. The flow of the river was so unsteady, by virtue of the unevenness of the rain, that the slope of the cliff was considerably eased to either side of its main channel, but it still posed awkward problems for the two wagons. While Carus Fraxinus and Aulakh Phar were busy supervising the delicate descent, Andris and Jacom had ridden ahead with Jume Metra to see what further problems might await them on the flatter ground.

As his mare picked her way carefully down the slope, Andris had plenty of time to scan the distant horizon and the blackened ruin which lay before it. Its flatness was as depressing as its blackness; there was not a tree to be seen anywhere, nor even a charred stump of one. Andris had grown used to the alienness of the terrain through which he had recently passed, but he had long looked forward to his emergence into a land fit for the use and habitation of men, and it was disappointing to find that this did not look like a land fit for men at all.

There was just a hint of vivid colour to be seen at the limit of vision on his right hand side, where there was a thin green ribbon which presumably marked the ragged edge of the marshland. He knew from his map that the habitable land to either side of the river formed a narrow strip, bounded to the east by the Spangled Desert and to the left by the Soursweet Marshes, and he had hoped that the strip might be crowded with farms and villages, but the scorched plain was as devoid of dwellings as it was of trees. There was no unambiguous sign of human workmanship to be seen from Andris's present vantage-point, although there were two points which drew the eye by contrast with the stubborn dullness of their setting.

The nearer one was an anomalous patch set against the near-uniform grey of the rock at whose far edge it stood, separated as much by virtue of its lustre as its colour. It had stood out more ostentatiously when viewed from higher up than it did now, but he could still see it, and he concluded that it was no mere discolouration of the rock but something which had shape and form. The other was a slender column which stood up vertically on the horizon, which might or might not be a watch-tower set at the far edge of the fire-obliterated region.

'It can't be a natural pillar of rock,' Jacom Cerri had opined, before they separated into single file. 'The plain seems barren, but it must be paradise for half a hundred breeds of stonerot. That thing has to be a sentry-post.'

'We know nothing of the creatures which live hereabouts,' Andris had replied. 'There might be one which builds needles of rock in much the same spirit that dragomites raise mounds.' But he too thought it more than likely that the thing was man-made. He thought it more than likely, too, that what might conceivably have been paradise for one kind of stonerot would likely be a hellish battleground for half a hundred, but the stolid soldier was not the kind of man with whom to discuss such hypothetical matters; it was the sort of thing better mentioned to Aulakh Phar, or even the princess, if it were to be mentioned at all.

Andris was glad, when he finally reached the level ground, that it seemed easy enough to steer towards the nearer of the enigmatic features. It was temporarily obscured from view, but he was navigator enough to know approximately where it lay. It seemed, in fact, that the easiest route across the problematic rocks headed straight for it.

While he led his companions along that route – still on foot, leading their mounts by the reins – Andris searched the ground for evidence of other users who might have begun to etch out a track, but he could see no hoofmarks even where the rock had been softened by corruption, and there was no litter of the kind which humans left behind on every route they travelled frequently. Rot and running water were clearly more than equal to the task of keeping the place clean.

Such were the gentle undulations of the pitted rock that the entity for which they were headed did not come into view again until they were close, and then it loomed up with startling suddenness. Andris knew immediately that this was no accident, and he was readily able to understand why it had been positioned so that it stood squarely across the nearest thing to a natural road the region had.

'We're obviously not the first travellers to have come this way,' he said sourly, as his two companions drew level with him.

'Nor were these expected to be the last,' Jacom Cerri added.

As usual, Jume Metra said nothing, although she had every reason to be far more distressed by the sight that met their eyes than either of her companions.

What was set out before them was a carefully arranged display. Andris might even have judged it an admirable work of art had it not been so vividly macabre and so obviously threatening. The barricade – which curved away for thirty mets and more to either side of them – was constructed out of the exoskeletons of at least two hundred dragomites and the bones of twenty or thirty human beings, carefully commingled. These relics had been arranged in a semicircular concave arc like a bent bow, whose arrow was the route which the great majority of refugees from the hills would have found it easiest to take.

Because dragomites were so much bigger than human beings, and because their body parts were in a considerable majority, browns, blacks and dark greens almost eclipsed the pale colours of the sun-bleached human bones; it was only at close range that it became obvious that the latter had been very carefully placed. This message was aimed primarily at human eyes.

Andris wondered whether the people who had built the barrier believed that dragomites which had not lived in close association with humans in the so-called Corridors of Power were less dangerous, or simply that they didn't possess the kind of intelligence that could take heed of warnings. Andris was fairly sure that Metra and her companions weren't the kind of people who *would* take heed of warnings, but he could understand the thinking behind the display.

'The men who made this sign have gone to some trouble,' he said to Jume Metra. 'The battles whose casualties these were must have been fought further to the south; to bring all this material here must have cost a considerable effort, and it involved a measure of sacrifice. Dragomite chitin must be a useful resource in this region – all the more so if Princess Lucrezia's account of the Eblans is reliable as an indication of extreme metal-poverty. This warning doesn't simply say: *Go no further in this direction, lest you die*; it also says: *We have such an abundance of dragomite body parts already that we can well afford to be wasteful in their disposition*. Your queen isn't the first to have sent her sisters this way in the hope of finding a new nest-site, nor the first which had a mound-queen to serve as her human voice. The people who live along the river's banks intend to make very certain that no new hills are raised in territory they think of as their own.'

Jume Metra didn't answer. Instead she walked her horse forward so that she could inspect the display more intimately, removing her ornamented helmet so that she could see more clearly.

The eyeless skulls of humans and dragomites had been placed on poles carved from the longest dragomite leg-sections. Behind them, forming a dense and deep thicket, was a vast tangle of crested carapaces, belly-plates and lateral plates, spiced with human long bones and the occasional rib-cage. Some of the skulls were cracked, and where the remnants of palps and antennae hung from the heads of dead workers they were invariably broken. More than a hundred jaws taken from warriors were laid out before the thick wall, to emphasise the fact that the workers could not rely on their usual protectors when they left the hills.

It would only have taken a few minutes to clear a gateway through the centre of the arc, but the mound-woman didn't bother to do so. She contented herself with staring contemplatively at the relics of the dead, occasionally reaching out to touch one or other of the skulls with the tips of her thin fingers.

'We don't know that the human remains are those of mound-women,' Jacom said to Andris, in a low tone, 'and we have every reason to believe that the great majority of the dragomites which have been so easily slaughtered must have been sick and starving. All this may be mere bluff.'

'I think we can be reasonably sure that those are the bones of mound-women,' Andris contradicted him. 'We can be equally certain, I suppose, that the companies which attacked them sustained heavy casualties of their own, but we ought to assume that they will have treated their own dead more respectfully than to leave them here like this. Perhaps the dragomites whose relics are strewn hereabouts were sick and starving, but let's not underestimate the power and determination of those who stood against them. However exaggerated it may be, this must be an honest declaration of intent and ability.'

'I'm not so sure,' Jacom retorted stubbornly. Andris knew the man well enough by now to expect that kind of mulishness, but he also knew that the one-time captain of King Belin's citadel guard was not quite as pig-headed as he seemed – it was just that his mouth tended to lag awkwardly behind his intelligence.

'If the mound-women hadn't attached themselves to us,' Andris added sombrely, 'we might have found a welcome in these parts. While we have such companions, though, we can expect nothing but implacable enmity.'

'The dragomite warriors are getting weaker,' Jacom said, in an even lower tone, 'but still they're too big and too many for our depleted arms. We can't turn against them, however carefully we might design and execute our rebellion. Effectively, we're still their prisoners, but the time might yet come when . . .'

Jume Metra had turned back now, and Jacom had to let his treasonous words fade away. Andris thought it best to make no audible reply, nor did he nod his head to signify that he had made the same calculation, although he had. He was well aware that neither he nor Cerri had any authority over their fellows that would allow them to construct and guide any kind of conspiracy; only Fraxinus commanded sufficient respect to formulate and actualise any scheme which relied on the co-operation of all the members of the ill-assorted party. Andris had not talked to Fraxinus about the possibility that they might be able to make an alliance with the people of this region against their inconvenient escort, but he trusted the merchant to make all the necessary calculations of risk. He was ready to act, if a plan were put to him – and ready to do nothing if nothing were what Fraxinus considered it wisest to do.

'This is bad,' said Jume Metra, shading her eyes from the sun as she looked up into Andris's face. Having spent the greater part of her life underground she still found daylight difficult to bear; she was certainly not lacking in courage and determination but she gave the impression of being near to the limit of her endurance.

'We might turn westwards,' Andris said unenthusiastically. 'Perhaps we could skirt the marshes, staying on the outer margin of the cultivated land. Perhaps we could even go into the marshes.'

Metra shook her head. 'Too much water,' she said, meaning that the dragomite workers and warriors would find it too difficult. Horses and men could swim as well as wade, but the six-limbed monsters couldn't, and the mound-women had almost certainly never learned. It would be just as difficult for the wagons. There was no possibility of escape in that direction unless the wagons were to be abandoned.

'If the people who live in these parts do mean business,' Jacom put in, 'they'd never let us get away with skirting the marshes. They'd simply see it as an outflanking manoeuvre. They'd chase us into the marshland and keep chasing until they'd seen us sink in the mire. It wouldn't help to cross the river, even if we could find a ford – we could see from the cliff-top that the belt of scorched earth extends as far as the eye can see in that direction too.'

'We must cross this barren ground to the land beyond,' said Jume Metra firmly. 'Your queen promised ours. All of you must now make good her word.' She didn't sound optimistic, but she did sound determined. Andris couldn't believe that the mound-women and the dragomite drones really trusted Ereleth, or believed that she could deliver on the promises she had made to them under the duress of her brief captivity, but they definitely intended to hold her to the bargain. He figured that they, like Ereleth and Fraxinus, were in this alliance because they thought it was the only hope they had. He also figured that would make them all the more desperate not to let go.

'You're absolutely right,' Andris said, to humour the mound-women. 'It's time for our noble queen to prove that she's entitled to take charge of this affair – to prove that she really does have knowledge and cleverness the rest of us lack. We'd better report back, as soon as I've been up that shallow rise over there to see if I can get a better view of the other thing we glimpsed from the cliff-top.' He climbed back into the saddle, patting his faithful mare on the neck by way of apology for inflicting his weight on her tired back, and walked her along the barrier so that he could steer around it.

Jume Metra replaced her helmet and mounted her own horse. While Andris moved away to the right she continued to stare gravely at the makeshift barrier. Andris took the mare up to the top of a hummock which was situated a little way beyond one end of the barricade. It wasn't much of a rise, but there was no better vantage-point within two or three kims. When he stood up in his stirrups the tiny spike on the horizon stood out clearly enough against the cloudless sky, but it was impossible to make out any detail. Aulakh Phar had a spy-glass which would have helped considerably, but Phar didn't like to lend out his precious instruments. Andris wondered whether the man on the watch-tower – assuming that it *was* watch-tower, and that there *was* a sentry on duty there – had a similar spy-glass of his own. If so, he would now be clearly visible.

It hardly matters whether he can pick out the wagons on the slope, he thought, as he glanced back. *They'll stir up enough dust to give themselves away as soon as they're on the burnt ground. We'll be visible soon enough.*

He rode back to his companions, shrugging his shoulders to indicate that he still couldn't be sure what lay before them.

'What's the betting that the people who live along the river are every bit as fearful of Serpents as they are of dragomites and humans who keep company with dragomites?' Jacom said.

Andris shook his head, but it wasn't a denial. He didn't suppose for a moment that the presence of the Serpents would make any difference to their reception. He urged the mare to retrace her steps towards the place where the wagons were making their slow and painstaking descent.

None of them glanced back until they were halfway up the slope again, with the descending wagons less than thirty mets away. Then Jacom Cerri leaned across to touch Andris on the arm, and pointed at the horizon. There was now a thin plume of dark smoke extending from the tip of the distant tower.

'They know we're here,' the soldier said dolefully. 'They probably don't know who or what we are, but they know we're on our way, and they're making preparations to receive us.'

'We'll have to face them sooner or later,' Andris said. 'I only hope Fraxinus can make the most of his merchant's art. We can't force a way through, but we might just be able to buy a safe passage.'

He was trying to be cheerful, but in the privacy of his own thoughts he couldn't shake the anxious suspicion that their crossing of the blighted hills, uncomfortable as it had been, might yet prove to have been the easiest part of the long and arduous journey to which he had committed himself.

5

LUCREZIA HAD HOPED that travel would become more comfortable once the hills had been left behind, but the midday sun burned just as brightly above the plain. The stone shelf which extended from the foot of the Dragomite Hills became so hot beneath the blaze of noon that it could burn bare flesh. The hooves of the horses and donkeys had to be wrapped in cloth, and the four darklanders who had stubbornly gone barefoot while the caravan crossed the hills were at last persuaded to put on shoes. By the time the sun was halfway to its zenith all the humans except the mound-women had retired to the shade of the canvas-covered wagons, and the Serpents had retired with them. Even the warrior-riding mound-women carried parasols made of thin sections of dragomite chitin. The only members of the ill-assorted party which sought neither shelter nor protection were the dragomites.

While they were in the hills it had been easy for the dragomites to be discreet. Whenever the expedition stopped the majority of them had retreated into tunnels let in to the derelict mounds, and even while the column was on the move it was only in rare moments that all twenty of them – there were twelve warriors, six workers and two drones – had been visible at the same time. Now, their presence was all too obvious, for they had taken much closer order with the wagons and the horses, arranging themselves in equal ranks on either side of the column, no more than twenty mets away. Here they were able to march with mechanical efficiency, all in step, and that somehow made their presence seem much more threatening.

Lucrezia had wedged herself in a corner at the back of the big wagon, making room for the three adult darklanders to play some convoluted gambling game with worn stones in the narrow space beside her. She had now been watching the steady tread of the warriors for an hour or more, with very mixed feelings.

In recent days the dragomites had begun to show some slight signs of distress, but they never wavered in their purpose. Lucrezia assumed that they must be just as uncomfortable in the midday heat as she was, if not more so, given that they were used to living underground and foraging more by night than by day, but their resolution seemed absolute. In a way, Lucrezia wished that she could be more like them: utterly determined and relentless, perfectly sure of her objectives. Her own condition was little worse now than it had been for thirty days and more but she feared that her resolve was subject to a steady attrition which was weakening it by slow and inexorable degrees. It seemed to require increasing efforts of concentration to maintain her once irresistible curiosity.

The simple fact is, she told herself, *that I'm afraid. That encounter with the rogue shook me up more than I was prepared to admit to Andris Myrasol or Jacom Cerri. I've begun to notice my hunger again, too, now that we're coming into a region where we might hope to find better food. That's why I'm uneasy.*

She had, in fact, been so ill-fed for twenty days and more that the notion of eating for enjoyment and sipping fresh wine had become quite bizarre, while the notion of being entirely free of aches and pains was an impossible dream.

The wagons slowed to a stop, and she saw Checuti, who was driving the smaller one, wave in response to Fraxinus's signal. The darklanders immediately abandoned their game and moved to take care of the horses.

The riverbank was less than forty mets away, but the horses were reluctant to move that way while the dragomites formed a line along the column's flank, and it was not until the warriors had separated, taking up new stations before and behind, that the animals consented to be watered. Afterwards they were fed, after a fashion, although there was little enough nourishment in what the darklanders had to offer them.

As soon as she had taken her own share of the meagre meal, swallowing the mouthfuls of roasted dragomite flesh as quickly as she could in order not to be discomfited by the vile taste, Lucrezia went back to the smaller wagon where she normally slept. Silence reigned, the other inhabitants having already bedded down. Lucrezia knew that they were right to sleep while they could, knowing that trouble might be lying in wait for them a few kims ahead, but when she laid herself down in her accustomed place she couldn't even begin to settle. She felt so restless, in fact, that she was tempted to go to Aulakh Phar and ask for one of his potions, but she knew how reluctant the old man was to deplete his stocks and she didn't want anyone to think that she had been so pampered as a princess that she was now incapable of coping with the rigours of real life. She decided that she must lie down with her brooding anxieties and pretend to sleep, even if the actuality evaded her.

Her determination to lie still lasted more than an hour, but her restlessness would not let up, and in the end she came to feel that she could not tolerate stillness a moment longer. She put on her hat and boots and stepped down from the wagon into the blaze of noon, then looked around for somewhere to go.

There were only three other humans up and about. One was a tall darklander posted as a sentry a hundred mets in front of the lead wagon, whose eyes were fixed on the distant watch-tower, where the ashes of the beacon fire were still smouldering, sending a slender trail of grey smoke into the sky. One was a mound-woman keeping the separate vigil which Jume Metra's people always maintained, presumably out of mistrust of their reluctant allies. The third was Hyry Keshvara, who had gone to the riverbank to set out hopeful fishing-lines, using tackle which Phar – always a great improviser – had rigged up from his supplies.

Hyry had tried catching fish several times before, with very meagre results, but she was not a woman to give up easily. Lucrezia went to join her, and found her wedged into a shady crevice. A huge-brimmed hat at least twice as large as Lucrezia's own provided further shelter from the sun.

'You should get some sleep, highness,' the trader said, when she saw who was approaching. 'We don't know what we might run into before the midnight.'

'I have a better idea than anyone else,' Lucrezia pointed out, in a tone that was only faintly aggrieved. 'I've seen and talked to men from this region. I shall certainly be one of our ambassadors when the time comes to parley.'

'Ereleth won't like that, highness,' Hyry pointed out, carelessly repeating her crime in spite of the grievance in Lucrezia's voice.

'Ereleth has no authority to make decisions on my behalf,' Lucrezia retorted. 'The fact that she was once a queen in Xandria has no more relevance here and now than the fact that Andris Myrasol was once a prince in some primitive nation of the far north.'

'Have you told her that?' Hyry asked, knowing full well that Lucrezia had not. Ereleth was fully determined to play the part of a queen, and would tolerate no denial of her right to do so.

'I'm not Ereleth's pawn, no matter how certain she is that I ought to be,' Lucrezia said, as steadfastly as she could. 'She may believe that she understands what it means to have Serpent's blood – as even your Serpent friends concede that I have – and what her secret lore instructs her to do with me in consequence, but I'm free to come to my own conclusions and make my own decisions. My destiny is my own to seek – and, if possible, to create.'

'For the time being, highness, I'm far more concerned with day to day survival than ultimate destiny,' Hyry told her tiredly. 'I'm content to accept the Serpents as friends – all the more so because I owe them my life – but our other monstrous companions are not to my taste. I wish it were true that Mossassor's kin had the power to command them, but I fear the dragomites consider that the boot is on the other foot. The drones are the ones calling the tune, for now, and it seems that we must dance to it until we drop.'

'We've been glad of their protection so far,' Lucrezia said. 'We may still have cause to be glad of it.'

'You saw that barricade,' Hyry countered bleakly. 'We're now in a place whose inhabitants don't like dragomites, or humans who keep company with them. The darklanders are already whispering about the politics of defection and the possibility that the Eblans might be able to relieve us of the dragomites' problematic presence.'

Lucrezia looked back to see where the mound-women's sentry was. Her station was a comfortable fifty mets away. 'The darklanders will stick to Fraxinus,' she said, although she knew that Hyry was a better judge of that than she. 'They don't know what kind of a welcome they'd receive from the river people. I don't know about Checuti, though.'

'It's Ereleth I worry about,' Hyry told her, keeping her eyes hidden beneath the brim of her hat. 'I've been dealing with her as long as I've been dealing with Fraxinus and Phar, but I don't *know* her at all. I only know that she and Fraxinus are at odds – and that's bad.'

Lucrezia wished that she were in a position to say that she knew Ereleth very well indeed, but it wouldn't have been true. 'Fraxinus is an honourable man as well as a careful one,' Lucrezia observed, fishing for confirmation of her opinion. 'He'll try to honour his promises to the Serpents and the mound-women, won't he?'

'He'll try,' Hyry answered, stressing the second word very faintly in order to imply that trying might not be enough. 'Unfortunately, Jume Metra and her companions will be on the lookout for treason even if Fraxinus is reluctant to consider the possibility. Mossassor seems determined to maintain the alliance, but his friends seem to think that he's leading them to disaster. Ssifuss still thinks humans are a disease contaminating his planet.'

'They're not *he*,' Lucrezia reminded her, ungrammatically. 'They're *it*.'

'I know,' Hyry said, 'but it's such a clumsy way of speaking.'

'The rumour in the Inner Sanctum,' Lucrezia recalled, 'was that Serpents are hermaphrodites, and that they have their reproductive organs in their mouths instead of their hind ends. If they were hermaphrodites they'd be he *and* she.'

'And if they had pricks in their mouths they'd probably be able to cut their esses short and say thanks without thlurring,' Hyry replied. 'If you want to know where little Serpents come from, I don't know. Ereleth already asked me. So did Fraxinus. Mossassor and I only talked about mythology while we were in the forest. Neither he nor his cousins ever suggested that we play conjugal games, so I don't have the least idea what they'd have wanted to *do*.'

'There's no need to be so defensive about it,' Lucrezia pointed out, trying not to make it sound like a complaint. 'I don't suppose they understand our reproductive processes any better than we understand theirs. Even if they'd caught a glimpse of

Andris and Merel getting carried away they wouldn't know that it had anything to do with babies.'

'It doesn't,' Hyry said. 'Always provided that Phar's supplies of contraceptive remain equal to the demand.'

'They ought to,' Lucrezia was quick to put in. 'Unless, of course, you and Checuti . . .'

'Why Checuti?' Hyry asked. Her eyes were visible now, seeming even narrower than usual. She didn't know whether Lucrezia was being serious or not.

'Why not?'

Hyry decided that it was a joke, and laughed. 'I'll trade you Checuti for your young captain,' she said, taking pains to make it clear that she was *not* being serious.

'He's not mine,' Lucrezia said.

'Oh, he's yours, highness,' Hyry said, reclaiming the conversational initiative, 'whether you want him or not.'

Lucrezia said nothing in reply to that, partly because she couldn't think of anything clever enough and partly because she felt that they were straying from the point. She tried to remember the purpose she had had vaguely in mind when she came out to talk to Keshvara. 'I think we have to stay with the dragomites,' she said eventually 'If we really are going to go all the way to Chimera's Cradle, the warriors might be very useful to us. It's not just making a virtue out of necessity – I made promises to the mound-queen myself.'

'Under duress,' Hyry pointed out. 'You said what you had to, in order to save your life. And in the end, it was the Serpents which saved you, not the mound-queen.'

'Even so,' Lucrezia said, 'I meant what I said to her, and to Jume Metra. It's far better for us to find a way to live alongside one another than to waste our resources in perpetual war. If we can persuade the Eblans of that . . .'

'That won't be easy,' Hyry opined. 'Remember what Jume Metra's warrior women did to Djemil Eyub's men.'

Lucrezia remembered it all too clearly; it had not been a pleasant thing to see, and she had had no alternative but to watch.

Hyry stared out at the grey water and the gently bobbing floats which supported her baited hooks. If there were fish in this stretch of the river, they obviously didn't find the bait very attractive. Lucrezia couldn't blame them for that.

'We're all on the same side now,' Lucrezia said. 'We have to be. As long as we can preserve the alliance . . .'

'In an ideal world, things might work out that way,' Hyry replied, in an ominously quiet tone. 'But then, in an ideal world the fish would leap out of the river straight into the frying pan. Perhaps you ought to try persuading Checuti that we're all on the same side.'

It was Lucrezia's turn to say 'Why Checuti?'

'He's been quizzing Aulakh Phar about the exact contents of the expedition's stores, with particular references to plastic.'

'Plastic? You mean plastic explosive?'

'That's right – the stuff that got you into this mess in the first place by blasting open the door of the Inner Sanctum and creating chaos in the grand courtyard. Checuti made the petards his men used that day, and he seems to think he knows all he needs to know about the delicate and dangerous art of causing explosions. I shudder to think what schemes he might be hatching, but he hasn't chosen to confide in me even though he owes me at least one favour. I suppose he's more likely to choose Myrasol as a partner in crime.'

'*Has* Aulakh Phar got any plastic in his stores?' Lucrezia asked.

'Aulakh always has *everything* in his stores,' Hyry told her, 'but he's careful to make sure that only he can read his labels – or remember what they said when they decay into unreadability. Plastic's far too unstable to keep, but he'll have the yeasts which manufacture it and the means to stimulate their performance. If there's any bomb-making to be done, though, I hope he'll do it himself and keep a very careful guard on his produce. Checuti may have a certain charm, but he's not the kind of man I'd trust with toys of that kind.'

'You think Checuti might try to blow up the dragomites?' Lucrezia couldn't believe it. 'All twenty of them? All at once?'

'He stole every single newly refreshed coin in your father's treasury the day before Thanksgiving – all at once. Only a man with delusions of extraordinary competence would have dared to dream of it . . . so Goran only knows what he might come up with, given the chance. I wouldn't want to be around the day one of his grand plans went wrong.'

'He let me live when he had every reason to think I'd be safer dead,' Lucrezia reminded the trader. 'I don't owe him anything any more, since I killed the worm Ereleth used to enslave him, but I can't help feeling a certain prejudice in his favour. He may be a slightly hazardous ally, but I'm not sorry he's around.'

'That's up to you, highness,' Hyry admitted, 'but if I were you, I wouldn't encourage him to play with anything dangerous. Just remember that he's on no one's side but his own . . . unless you count that pet monkey of his, and I'm pretty sure he'd sell that for a handful of beans if he were hungry enough.' While she said this she tugged gently at one of the fishing lines, as if she hoped that jiggling the bait might make it more attractive. It didn't.

'You shouldn't be so gloomy,' Lucrezia said. 'We're out of the blighted hills now, and the horizon's showing a hint of green. We'll be out of the scorched earth and into fertile land by sundown – *earthly* land, at that.' She observed Hyry's tolerant smile, and realised that it was she who was supposed to be the anxious pupil in such matters, and Keshvara the reassuring mentor. She couldn't help blushing slightly.

'You've grown older all of a sudden,' the trader said, not unkindly. 'Whatever the dragomites did to you in the forest and the depths of their nest, it's obviously left no lasting scar.'

'No it hasn't,' Lucrezia said, knowing that she ought to be profoundly glad of it. 'And having survived all that, what can I possibly have to fear from the metal-starved rabble who are masters of this narrow land? What can I possibly have to fear from *anything* I might meet this side of Chimera's Cradle?'

'I don't know, highness,' Hyry admitted, the smile dissolving from her face again to leave her looking as haggard and as tight-lipped as before, 'and neither do you.'

6

CARUS FRAXINUS WATCHED the darklander scale the watchtower, marvelling at the man's agility. There was no apparatus in place to facilitate the climb – if, as seemed probable, the sentry-post had been abandoned once its beacon had been lit, the watchmen had taken the ladder with them.

If only I had a dozen more like him, Fraxinus thought, *instead of the ill-assorted rabble of outlaws and petty royalty which clownish fate has seen fit to foist upon me instead.*

He knew, however, that he couldn't be any surer of the loyalty of his three remaining darklanders than of anyone else. He strongly suspected that if they'd ever taken the trouble to learn to ride they'd have disappeared with their golden fellows and Jacom Cerri's guardsmen when the dragomites had swarmed around the stranded wagons during the battle for the Corridors of Power. Nowadays they seemed to spend more time talking to Checuti than to him, helping to swell the undercurrent of rebellious anxiety that afflicted every aspect of the expedition's routines.

Fraxinus presumed that Checuti was making plans of his own now that the hills were behind them, and looking for allies wherever he could. Even Ereleth had gone into a huddle with Checuti shortly after the midday – a queen of Xandria, reduced to plotting with a notorious thief! How was it possible that such a well-planned endeavour could have collapsed into such an utter shambles?

He sighed, but took care to hide behind a hand which he touched to his sweating forehead. This was all so very different from the glorious adventure of his dreams, which would have set the seal upon a thoroughly successful life. Who would ever have anticipated that so trivial a matter as hiring a mapmaker would prove to be so fraught with difficulties? And who could ever have imagined that the attempt to do so would entangle him inextricably with his present company: a sour queen whose head was filled with mystical lore of which she would not speak; an unruly princess whose reckless hero-worship of Keshvara was almost as ridiculous as her propensity for being kidnapped; a vainglorious thief reduced to vagabondage who played host nevertheless to absurd delusions of cleverness; an oversized northern barbarian who kept a severed head as a souvenir of his journey into the hidden depths of a dragomite hive; and an ex-captain of Belin's citadel guard whose dullness of wit was compounded by his insistence on thinking himself the unluckiest man in the world. He still had Phar and Keshvara, of course, but that advantage seemed horribly slight when counterbalanced against the necessity of a treaty with twenty dragomites and eight of their subtly inhuman nest-companions.

Fraxinus had always prided himself on being a man who could cope with any situation and find opportunity in catastrophe, and he had tried with all his might to see his present situation as a supreme test of his mettle, but he could not resist the gloomy suspicion that it was nothing but a hideous mess from which there might be no escape.

We should not need to search for Chimera's Cradle, he thought, as he leaned to one side so that he could look around the wagon's tattered canopy at his followers. *Taken as a whole, we are surely the strangest chimera this ingenious world of ours has ever produced.*

Swinging from the top of the tower with an altogether unnecessary flourish, the darklander waved his arm to signal that the sentry-box was empty. The tower creaked and swayed as he did so, and he quickly steadied himself. He came down much more carefully than he had gone up. He was accustomed to climbing the living trees of the Forest of Absolute Night, whose decay was compensated by virility; it had not become obvious to him until the edifice trembled that dead wood was infinitely less reliable.

There was another watch-tower visible in the far distance. No smoke ascended from its apex now, but Fraxinus didn't doubt that it had been fired before the midday. The people of this region knew that they were coming, and they had already had more than twenty hours to make what preparations they thought necessary.

The wagons had come within sight of a few lonely homesteads by now, but it had been very obvious that the buildings were derelict and that the fields which had once been marked out around them had not been under cultivation for at least two years. A few more widely scattered buildings were presently visible on the green horizon, but it was impossible as yet to tell whether they were occupied, or whether the surrounding land had been planted with crops.

'It's of little consequence how fast and how far the news was transmitted,' Ereleth told him. 'An army can't be raised overnight.'

Nowadays, the queen often sat by Fraxinus's side, whether he rode in the body of the wagon or took the horses' reins. So intense had the contest of their authority become that she was reluctant to let him out of her sight unless she were in secret conference with someone else, lest he somehow steal a march on her. Had she been better-looking or better-tempered the proximity would have been easier to bear, but she had eyes like an angry hawk's and a forceful thin-lipped mouth. She reminded the merchant of his mother, who had been a notorious scold.

'Had you inspected those relics by which we camped this midday,' Fraxinus told her dolefully, 'you'd have noticed that a good few of them were fresh. The barricade had been renewed and reinforced within the last few days. If the men of the river towns have raised an army to take care of invading dragomites, I doubt they've yet disbanded it.'

'The blight in the Dragomite Hills began at least two years ago,' Ereleth countered. 'Dragomites must have been coming south ever since, but they can only have come in companies of much the same size as the one which has us in its grip, or smaller. The drones which serve chimerical queens are intelligent after a fashion, but they're bound nevertheless by the instincts of their kind. Abandoning a nest is a last step, not taken until all else has failed. Had the dispossessed groups been able to combine forces they'd have made a formidable force, but nature designed the nests as fierce competitors incapable of any greater union. That's why the darklanders, having banded together, were able to defeat such dragomites as they met.

'According to the princess, the human lands into which we are now moving are by no means rich, and they couldn't sustain a standing army of any real size for two months, let alone two years. The logic of the situation must have led them to form relatively small and fast-moving companies little more than a hundred strong. Given agile horses, long lances and a moderate skill with bows and arrows, such companies would soon learn the arts necessary to conduct a war of attrition against a platoon of dragomite warriors, whether or not such warriors were accompanied by mound-women. We, on the other hand, have horses of our own, a good handful of trained fighting men armed with reasonably unrusted steel, and a giant.'

'None of which will make the inhabitants of the region pleased to see us,' Fraxinus observed.

Ereleth ignored the objection. 'And Checuti is right, is he not?' she added. 'Phar does have the means of making plastic secreted somewhere about the wagons. We can defend ourselves against people such as these – if we have to.'

Fraxinus sighed again as he urged the horses forward, heading directly for the next tower. Ereleth was a queen of Xandria and it was perhaps understandable that her notion of strategy and tactics gave a high priority to the stern logic of imperial intimidation and military threat. Her first impulse in any situation was to get her own way by bullying. It would do no good to tell her that a monarch without a kingdom was a head without a body, or that the primary objective of merchants like himself was always to establish the harmonious and friendly circumstances within which honest trade could take place. She had her own opinions as to the proper role of merchants, and would consider herself every sem a queen until she had not a single person about her to whom she might hope to give orders.

'According to Andris Myrasol's map,' Fraxinus pointed out, in a carefully neutral tone, 'the river extends for the best part of five hundred kims before it curves westwards towards the Lake of Colourless Blood. Salamander's Fire is at least three hundred kims further to the south. Given that wagons can't move as directly as birds can fly, we shall have a good thousand kims to traverse, most of it through land inhabited by humans – nomad herdsmen if not agriculturalists. We could not *fight* our way to Salamander's Fire, majesty, even if we had fifty barrels of plastic and a way to make perfectly certain that it would always blow up our enemies rather than our own possessions.'

'I have no intention of fighting if fighting can be avoided,' she informed him, acidly, 'but even you must understand that it's best to negotiate from a position of strength, and that it's sometimes politic to make clear to one's adversaries the power one has in reserve.'

'We only know that these people are metal-poor,' Fraxinus said, doggedly. 'They might well be past masters in the art of causing explosions. As I told Checuti when Aulakh warned me about his inquisitiveness, plastic is a double-edged weapon in more ways than one. Once it is brought into play, the possibility of making peace is usually lost for ever. If we're to achieve anything at all we must do our utmost to persuade the people of this region that we mean them no harm, and that the Serpents and dragomites accompanying us are no threat to them. We must be prepared to accept whatever compromises are offered to us.'

'And if none are offered?' Ereleth was quick to ask.

'Common men are traders at heart, not warriors,' Fraxinus said, repeating a point of faith which had sustained him through a long and successful career. 'They're always open to offers of compromise. If it were not so, human society would be impossible, and all collectives would resemble dragomite hives, united by mechanical instinct.'

She did not raise the objection that not all dragomite hives were so restricted, because she knew full well that it would prove his case. It was because the hive whose warriors marched with them now had been chimerical, and had entertained a human society of sorts, that its survivors had been able to make a compromise with the humans, brokered by the Serpents. Compromise was what bound the ill-assorted company together, and compromise had so far saved its various parts from annihilation.

Fraxinus felt that he had spent a great deal of time and effort trying to reach a compromise with Ereleth, with far too little reward. Although she was now ready to take a part in the discussions which he and Phar had concerning the implications of what little they had learned from Mossassor, she was still careful to protect the details of her secret commandments. She had consented readily enough to the establishment of Salamander's Fire as their immediate destination, but if she knew anything about what might be found there she was keeping it to herself. In spite of having Andris Myrasol's map to guide the expedition, Fraxinus felt that he was still operating as blindly as Myrasol's unfortunate beggar, who might well have been Xandria's last custodian of the dubious lore called the *Apocrypha of Genesys*. He wished he knew whether Ereleth's reluctance to add anything substantial to his attempts to interpret that lore was the result of ignorance or meanness of spirit.

Because he was looking sideways at the queen rather than at the way ahead, it was she who first caught sight of the company which came to meet them.

'There,' she said, pointing into the distance ahead of them. 'There is your army, come to meet us.' She spoke the word *army* with naked contempt, for it was obvious even at this range that the men who had ridden into view upon a shallow ridge were no more than a dozen in number.

It was obvious that the distant riders had exposed themselves deliberately, for they stopped where they were upon the skyline, all in a huddle, as if they were content to let the wagons and the dragomites come towards them while they waited. Two or three minutes went by – by which time everyone in the column had received word that the riders were there – while Fraxinus pondered the logic of this move, and what it might imply.

Perhaps, he thought, *they are equally uncertain. Perhaps they want to study us carefully, before deciding what to do next.*

'We should have made a white flag,' he said, 'to signal our desire to talk.'

'We're not in Xandria now,' Ereleth growled. 'We can't be sure that a rabble like that would know the meaning of a flag of truce.'

Fraxinus couldn't help feeling a slight thrill of delight as she was immediately proved wrong. No sooner had she finished speaking than the huddle broke apart, and one of the riders raised a pole from which flew a makeshift flag. It was by no means pure white, but the intention seemed clear enough.

'Perhaps they think the same of us,' Fraxinus said. He reined in, and stepped down to the ground, signalling to the driver of the second wagon to stop. Six riders detached themselves from the group on the horizon and moved slowly forward while their companions stayed where they were. Jacom Cerri and Princess Lucrezia had already ridden forward, and now Jume Metra and Mossassor were hurring forwards on foot. Fraxinus ran to meet them, and put his arm out to soothe Lucrezia's horse as it shied away from him uneasily.

In the west, the sun was standing just above the horizon, while the eastern flamestars already shone boldly and brightly. The warm evening air seemed oppressively heavy.

'Princess!' Fraxinus said urgently. 'Go to your house-mother and find some finery in her luggage – something that will make clear to uneducated eyes that you are a person of rank. Mossassor, you must make certain that the dragomites are perfectly quiet. I'll ride out to meet these ambassadors with the princess.'

'I shall come too,' Ereleth called after him.

'No, majesty, I beg you,' Fraxinus was quick to say, as he turned to face her. He tried with all his might to make it sound like a plea and not an order. 'We dare not risk too many. Jume Metra may come with us, to hear what we say, but no one else.'

He turned to Metra as soon as he had said this, adding: 'Put on your armour, by all means, to display very clearly what you are, but I beg you to make no hostile move of any kind, and I must ask you to say nothing at all, unless I call upon you for an endorsement of what I say. I assure you that any lies I might tell will be calculated to your advantage as well as mine. Will you agree to that?'

Metra nodded, rather sullenly but without hesitation. Fraxinus had not expected enthusiasm, and was content with her agreement.

The princess had already dismounted and was now climbing up to where Ereleth was. The witch-queen was about to argue, but Lucrezia distracted her, saying: 'Show me what you have, majesty. You must help me choose something suitable.'

The approaching party had covered half the distance separating the two parties by the time Lucrezia appeared again, dressed in an ornately embroidered golden yellow gown, with a jewelled head-dress concealing the lank and unwashed state of her hair. The riders came to a halt, but they kept the white flag carefully upraised while they waited.

Fraxinus watched patiently while Ereleth helped Lucrezia with her fastenings and the princess tried to clean her face as best she could with a damp cloth. She certainly didn't look as if she had just stepped out of her royal apartments on her way to some formal ceremony, but she did have the bearing of a person of quality to go with the borrowed clothes.

'How many more men are waiting beyond that ridge, do you think?' Jacom Cerri asked anxiously.

'None,' Ereleth said scornfully. 'They will doubtless pretend to have an army at their backs, but they're nothing but a band of roving brigands.'

'We can't take that for granted,' Fraxinus was quick to say. 'The fact that they want to talk is excellent news, and gives me hope that we can settle this affair like civilised men. We are emissaries of Xandria, and we shall request an appropriate welcome. Remember what we agreed, Princess Lucrezia?' He wished, as he said it, that he and she had had more time for discussion, and had settled matters in much finer detail, but he was reassured by her calm nod.

Metra had gone back to the place where the dragomite workers had paused, but she was hurrying forward again now, having put on one of the masklike helmets her warrior-women wore in combat. Its freakish design was intended to make her face look like a dragomite's, and Fraxinus wondered whether it might have been more diplomatic to ask her to go bareheaded – but it was obvious enough what she was, and there was nothing to be gained by seeming to be apologetic about it.

Fraxinus looked up at Ereleth, very warily, but she had decided not to offer any further challenge to his authority for the moment. Perhaps, he thought, she was awkwardly conscious of the fact that she had no idea what to say to the men who had come to meet them, and had only protested in the first place on a trivial point of principle.

By now, Checuti and Andris had run to join the group, both eager to volunteer their services. The other Serpents were coming too, although the far-striding Dhalla was just overtaking them.

'No,' Fraxinus said to Checuti, before the thief could open his mouth. 'We can take one other with us, but it must be Dhalla.' He knew that he didn't have to instruct Dhalla to stay silent.

Dhalla wouldn't speak unless the princess told her to. Of all the members of the expedition, she was the only one whose loyalty was both absolute and absolutely clear.

'There are six of them,' Jacom Cerri pointed out.

'Exactly,' Fraxinus said. 'One of the things we must make perfectly clear is that mere weight of numbers is not an issue here.'

'If you can persuade them of that,' Checuti said, 'you're a far better man than I am. Whether they have an army waiting beyond the ridge or not, they have a whole nation further behind them – and we shall have to pass through the entire length of its territory even if we stay clear of the cities strung along the river. They must know full well that if numbers are all they need to destroy us, we're as good as dead.'

'That's exactly why we must persuade them to make us welcome,' Fraxinus said, 'no matter how difficult the task may seem.'

7

LUCREZIA FELT VERY uncomfortable in her borrowed gown. She had taken such trouble these last few days to tell everyone that she was no longer a princess that she now felt like a masquerader. She had always felt uncomfortable in this sort of regalia, even when she had been required to wear it for formal occasions in the citadel. Her sisters seemed to love all kinds of decoration just as they loved all manner of petty luxuries, but Lucrezia had stubbornly resisted such absurdities. She had never conceived of herself as a plaything to be decorated and displayed, and her training as a witch had provided a context in which she could cultivate different pretensions.

She had tried to object when Ereleth had told her not to replace her belt about her waist but Ereleth had insisted that she leave it behind, and had promised to guard the armoury of poison-filled pouches very carefully. Lucrezia had grown so used to the comforting presence of all that witchery that its absence seemed like a yawning gap in her being, but there was no time to worry about it; Fraxinus was impatient to be on his way. By the time Lucrezia had been helped into the saddle – a simple task made rather more complicated by the gown – Jume Metra was already armoured and mounted; Dhalla had saddled her horse and was leading it forward.

When the four of them set off, excitement drove out discomfort – but while they rode sedately across the space which separated them from the waiting riders that excitement was gradually clouded by doubt: doubt that she could play her appointed part, and doubt as to what Fraxinus's intentions actually were. It occurred to Lucrezia that she had no idea whether he really intended to honour the bargains she had made with the dragomite queen and Mossassor, or whether – like almost everyone else – he was secretly desirous of finding a safe way of winning free of those obligations.

'It's a very hopeful sign that they've come to meet us, isn't it?' she said to the merchant. 'It must mean that there's scope for negotiation.'

'It is and it must,' the merchant replied. 'That wall they built across our route looked fearsome, but they'd not have taken the trouble unless they'd far rather have their enemies turn back than have to fight them. At the very worst, their conduct now tells us that they'd rather frighten us away than risk their lives in a pitched battle. Metal-poor they may be, but they're not primitive in their thinking and they're not fools. I think we can strike a bargain which will give us safe passage through their land, and perhaps allow some mutually beneficial trading. That would be best for everyone.'

Lucrezia was reassured by this, as Fraxinus had doubtless intended that she should be. She told herself that he was right. She could not believe that flags of truce had previously proved useful in the Eblans' dealings with dragomites and mound-women, so their use of one now was evidence of their awareness that this was an unprecedented situation which required careful consideration. As Fraxinus said, they could not be fools and they were plainly capable of curiosity. They must feel that it was greatly in their interests to learn the meaning of the new wonder which confronted them.

Fraxinus had turned to Jume Metra as soon as he finished talking to Lucrezia. She was not very comfortable in the saddle, but she was keeping in step.

'I ask you again to bear with me no matter what I might say. I don't know yet what compromise I might be forced to make, but if you wish your queen reborn, you must trust me.'

The mound-woman's eyes were invisible within her helmet, but she nodded in reply and the nod seemed meek enough.

How human is she, behind that mask? Lucrezia wondered. *Is she human enough to keep her own fears and plans secret? Is she human enough to nod assent in spite of fearing betrayal, while having every intention of committing treason of her own, if she thinks it necessary or politic?*

The remaining distance between the two groups was swallowed up in half a minute, and there was no space for further talk.

All six members of the waiting party were dark goldens of much the same hue as Djemil Eyub. They all wore grey jackets and trousers without any overlaying armour. Two wore peaked caps, although the sun was too low to be bothersome; the other four went bareheaded. The sleeves of their jackets were ringed above the elbow with coloured bands, and Lucrezia was quick to notice that no two of them had the same combination of colours. Four of them had six-pointed stars stitched on the breasts of their jackets, and these four hung back, suggesting that the stars were emblems of the lowest rank represented in the company. One of the remaining two had decorated epaulettes and a second set of colours instead of a star on his breast but it was the other who was the leader. He was a lean man with a lantern-jaw and slightly sunken eyes, and he was the only one of the six whose hair had gone grey. His uniform was the plainest of all – even the colours which showed on his sleeve were discreetly inscribed by comparison with those of his followers – but his jacket was cut in a different fashion and its cloth was of better quality. His horse, by contrast, was more brightly dressed than those his companions rode, having a bright blue hood with blinkers that looked as if they were made of dragomite chitin, silver clasps on the bridle and an intricately ornamented saddle.

Lucrezia made careful note of the fact that the lances which the four star-men carried were tipped with some non-metallic substance that looked rather like glass. Three of them also had crossbows dangling from their saddle-bows; the bolts in the accompanying quivers seemed to be expertly fletched, but it was impossible to tell whether they had metal tips. Only two of the six, including the leader, had daggers in their belts; both blades were rather thin, supporting her expectation that these people would be metal-poor, but the leader's was almost long enough to qualify as a rapier. The horses the six men rode were all small of stature, even by comparison with her own modest mount, let alone the huge animal that Dhalla rode.

As the newcomers reined in, the man with the hooded horse moved three mets clear of his companions, clearly intending to act as spokesman for the group. All six of the men were studying Lucrezia's party just as curiously as she was studying theirs, but none spared her more than a brief and very unflattering glance.

They were far more preoccupied with the sight of Dhalla; it was plain that none of them had ever seen a giant before.

'What manner of men are you?' the grey-haired man demanded, looking directly at Carus Fraxinus. 'Have you made beasts of burden out of dragomites and freed the nest-slaves which the dragomites once kept?' Lucrezia noticed that his unsteady eyes, which might at that point have flickered in the direction of Jume Metra, actually glanced uneasily at Dhalla.

'My name is Carus Fraxinus, sir,' the merchant replied, in a voice which seemed perfectly serene, 'and I am a merchant of Xandria. This is Princess Lucrezia, daughter of King Belin of Xandria, and this is Dhalla, her attendant. The fourth member of our party is Jume Metra, sister of the mound-queen of one of the oldest nests in the Corridors of Power. Have you, perchance, seen and talked with men of our company who rode on ahead of the wagons – a party of some fifteen men, all golden but for an amber boy? We are anxious for news of them.'

'No such company has been sighted,' the other said, smoothly enough. 'No true humans have come out of the hills within living memory.' He stressed the word *true* to emphasise that he did not mean the kind of humans who usually travelled in the company of dragomites – but Lucrezia took heart from the implication, because it meant that the grey-haired man was in no doubt that she and Fraxinus *were* true humans, in every sense of the word.

'I am sorry to hear it,' Fraxinus said, for all the world as if he meant it. 'It seems, then, that we must introduce ourselves. Xandria, as I am sure you know, is a great city in the north, whose empire extends from the fringes of the Forest of Absolute Night to the northernmost shores of the Slithery Sea. King Belin's subjects number seven millions in all. We bring you Belin's warmest greetings.'

Lucrezia noticed that the estimate of Xandria's population which she had given Djemil Eyub while he held her captive had expanded by a further two millions in Fraxinus's account, although she had certainly not sought to minimise it. If Fraxinus was hoping to startle his adversary with this information, however, he was disappointed. The other raised his eyebrows slightly, but he was obviously a disciplined man.

'I am General Shabir,' the soldier said. Lucrezia was glad to hear it, for if appearances were anything to judge by, an army which had generals like this could not be a very awesome force. After the briefest of pauses, the general continued. 'This is Colonel Obran, commander of the Sabian contingent of the army of the Nine Towns. These are Captains Semadin, Kahan, Burak and Joakim, who are members of the Tovalian, Antiarian, Mugolian and Ketherian contingents. The army has been in the field for two full years, defending the Alliance against invasion from the Dragomite Hills. The defence has been totally successful; no new nests have been established within the lands of the Alliance, and thousands of dragomite egg-carriers have been killed.'

Lucrezia noticed that the general emphasised the word *totally* as carefully as he had earlier emphasised the word *true*. Who, she wondered, was he trying to convince? Had he brought five men representing five different contingents of his so-called alliance in order to display the unity which was supposedly his strength, or was there something else to be read in the confusion of colours?

'Our understanding,' Carus Fraxinus said carefully, 'is that Ebla is the largest of the Nine Towns. Are you, by any chance, from Ebla, General Shabir?'

That caused a slight stir of surprise in the other company.

'What does Xandria know of Ebla?' the general asked cautiously.

'We have met men from Ebla,' Fraxinus said, deliberately leaving it there in order to tantalise them a little.

Shabir's reaction was not what Lucrezia expected. 'I am empowered to speak for the Convocation,' he said, in what seemed to her to be an over-punctilious fashion, 'and thus for the councils of all Nine Towns. I speak for all, not just for Ebla. What men from Ebla have you met?'

That was for the benefit of his own men, not Fraxinus, Lucrezia thought. *Perhaps his company has its covert rifts, as has ours.*

'A company led by a man named Djemil Eyub,' Fraxinus told Shabir. 'A brave man, who led his followers across the Dragomite Hills and into the Forest of Absolute Night, extending the hand of friendship between your people and mine.'

The slight stir of surprise was much magnified by that, and the four captains exchange meaningful glances.

'I have heard of this Djemil Eyub,' Shabir was quick to say, 'and I know men who would be grateful for news of him, but I have to tell you that he is an adventurer, who is not entitled to speak for the council of Ebla, let alone the Convocation. We are the voice of the Alliance. I ask you again, how do you stand with the dragomites which march alongside your wagons? Are they your slaves, or are you theirs?'

We are the voice of the Alliance! Lucrezia repeated. *How like a mound-woman he sounds, insisting that he and those whose representative he is are all of one mind!*

'These dragomites are our allies,' Fraxinus said, in a deliberately off-hand fashion. Without hesitation, he said 'Princess, I beg you to give this man the news of Djemil Eyub which his friends might seek, and explain your mission here.'

Lucrezia took a deep breath, but dared not hesitate. She knew there was a risk in assuming that Shabir was telling the truth about the men who had fled Fraxinus's company in the heart of the hills, but it was evidently one he thought worth taking.

'I bring the greetings of King Belin of Xandria to the people of this region,' she said, as grandly as she could. 'Hearing that a plague had come to the Dragomite Hills, I set out in the company of one of my house-mothers and a company of Belin's loyal subjects to discover what implications the occurrence might have for the empire, and to see whether a route might be found to the lands mentioned in the lore of Genesys, which Xandria has conserved with the utmost care for a thousand years and more.

'While traversing the Forest of Absolute Night, which some call the Darklands, I met Djemil Eyub and fourteen others, who had come safely across the Dragomite Hills. He told me that his native town, Ebla, might have much to gain from communication and trade with the empire. I assured him that when I reached the land south of the Dragomite Hills I would do my utmost to complete a link of friendship with his people.

'While crossing the hills we discovered for the first time that there were nests in which human beings lived in productive harmony with the dragomites, and we made haste to offer the friendship of Xandria to these people also. We found them in difficult straits, and were able to help them, with the result that they sent emissaries of their own to join our company. We have also been joined by a party of Serpents, who are likewise curious to investigate the legendary regions of the Navel of the World. Our immediate destination is a place called Salamander's Fire, whose name is inscribed on our maps and preserved in our lore. We would be greatly obliged for any information you can give us regarding the present state of affairs there and the road which will lead us to it. I fear that we cannot linger long in your land, but we shall be very grateful for any hospitality you can provide.'

What a fine story! she thought, when she had finished the carefully rehearsed speech. *If only it were all true! What a sorry thing the confused and akward truth of the matter is, when compared to such a noble fantasy.*

She knew, of course, that there was a risk involved in saying all this. She hadn't actually lied about Djemil Eyub's fate, but she had carefully left out any account of the condition in which she had last seen him. If Sergeant Purkin and the other men who had deserted the caravan *had* joined forces with the army of the Nine Towns they might have offered a fuller and far more ominous account of her meeting and its unfortunate aftermath.

Shabir showed no sign that his mood had been softened by her friendly manner. He didn't look round at his companions, but Lucrezia formed the impression that he might be refusing to do so lest one or other of them should say something he did not want to hear. The princess looked at the captains, who were still exchanging uneasy glances.

They are not natural allies, she thought. *Eyub implied that the river towns are usually at odds. Perhaps this so-called general is not as free to negotiate terms as he would wish. This Convocation of which he speaks may be a very difficult master to serve.*

She didn't know whether these speculations ought to make her optimistic or fearful, but she was in no doubt about the import of the general's next speech.

'The dragomites must turn back,' he said. 'We have fought long and hard these last two years to keep dragomites out of our lands, as generations of our forefathers fought in their turn. If you care to come forward without your companions, princess, we will make you welcome, but if the dragomites do not immediately return to the hills we will fall upon them and kill every last one of them – and if you choose to stand with them, we will kill you too.'

8

BY THE TIME the unconvincing general delivered this ultimatum Fraxinus had taken the measure of the man – or so he thought. In his estimation, the unease which possessed Shabir was no ordinary fear, but a kind of defiant desperation. This was a fighting man who had been too long at war with an enemy which kept on coming, never in force but in a relentless, corrosive trickle.

It was easy enough to figure out what must have happened hereabouts when the dragomites were forced to forsake their nests by the plague and their own internecine squabbles. The hills stretched for more than five hundred kims to the west before they petered out in the Grey Waste, and the greater part of that range was bordered to the south by the Soursweet Marshes, where dragomites had difficulty moving about and couldn't possibly establish new nests. They did not stretch as far to the east, but the greater part of that range was bordered by the Spangled Desert, which was probably little more hospitable than the marshland. The narrow land to either side of the river, which had been settled by the humans of the Nine Towns in days when expeditionary dragomites were rare, now comprised a bottleneck into which dragomites had poured from either direction.

Perhaps, if they had been allowed to pass through, those dragomites – especially the ones associated with mound-people – might have consented to seek new nesting-sites in the far south, but it was understandable that Shabir's people had been unprepared to take that chance. In trying to kill any and all dragomites coming this way they had followed a long-established and long-successful policy, but these last two years must have put a terrible strain on their resources, and they must now be close to cracking under that strain.

In such circumstances, Fraxinus thought, they must be ready to compromise, if only they could do so without losing face.

'These dragomites are not like any you have faced before,' he said calmly. 'Thanks to the Serpents who are travelling with us we have established a firm friendship with them. We understand that you consider the mound-people to be your enemies, but they are human, as you and I are, and they know what it is to make and honour treaties. I assure you that we have no intention of troubling you in any way; we only seek safe passage to Salamander's Fire. We ask you this in the name of King Belin of Xandria, and we offer you the friendship of Xandria in return for your help.'

The four captains, who had been nudging closer to one another for some time, now exchanged a few whispered remarks. Fraxinus couldn't hear what was said, but there was no mistaking the anger on the face of Colonel Obran as he turned to silence them with a glare.

'The Alliance of the Nine Towns has nothing against the people of Xandria,' General Shabir said, uneasily but with studied coldness, 'and we welcome your king's offer of friendship. You must understand, though, that the dragomites and their nest-slaves have been our deadliest enemies for centuries. In the last two years more than a hundred swarms have moved southwards from the blighted hills, warriors and warrior-women escorting workers carrying eggs cemented to their backs. Their intention has always been to burrow out a nest in some hidden corner of our realm, there to nourish a new queen and multiply. We understand this – they are, after all, no more than monstrous lice blindly following their instincts – but their success would lead inevitably to our extinction. You may take your wagons across our territory if that is your wish, princess, but you cannot and shall not bring dragomites into the vicinity of the Nine Towns. The dragomites and the mound-women must go back the way they have come, or face destruction. There is no alternative.'

Fraxinus didn't look around to see how Jume Metra had received this ultimatum. He didn't want her to think that he might be wavering in his resolve. His own conviction was that Shabir didn't want to fight, and that he couldn't be sure of the unity or the resolve of his weary patchwork army. There had to be room for a merchants' bargain, in which both parties would consider that they had avoided a loss.

'Xandria has lore which has been forgotten in Ebla and its neighbouring towns,' Fraxinus said, as equably as he could. 'By way of compensation there are doubtless things remembered here which we have lost, for which we could pay in good metal and the means of maintaining it against the ravages of corrosion. There is much that your people and mine might learn from one another. It has always been our way to make peace with others, whether they be humans of our own kind, or giants like Princess Lucrezia's attendant, or Serpents, or the nest-companions of dragomites. We hope, in due course, to meet and make friends with the Salamanders who live at Salamander's Fire. Believe me, general, you need have not the slightest fear of these dragomites. They will not hurt you, and they have no intention of trying to establish a nest within the boundaries of your union. Jume Metra is not their slave, and she can guarantee their meek conduct while we pass through your territory. Is that not so, Jume Metra?'

'We are bound for Salamander's Fire,' Metra promptly said, her voice slightly muffled by her headgear. 'We mean you no harm.'

'We ask nothing but a guarantee of safe passage to lands further south,' Fraxinus said swiftly, 'although we would be very glad of the opportunity to trade with your merchants while we are passing through. We have been subject to many privations while crossing the blighted hills, and we have a long way yet to go. There is much that we should like to buy, and we have the means to pay.'

'We cannot allow it,' the soldier said flatly. 'If you send the dragomites back to the hills, we will gladly treat with the emissaries of Xandria, but the security of our land is at stake and we cannot tolerate the presence of dangerous enemies. You have a simple choice: abandon the dragomites or go back with them to the land from which you came. We have the strength to enforce our instruction; if you proceed in the company of the dragomites we can and will destroy you all.'

Still he sounded like a brave man making a great parade of his bravery, reluctant to let his underlying reasonableness show too soon – but Fraxinus was still certain that he could get past the performance to real negotiations.

'We have not the slightest wish to test your strength,' Fraxinus said. 'We are a civilised people by nature, whose first desire is always to make peace. Xandria is renowned throughout the world for its military might, but its people know the value of friendship and trade, which are the only progenitors of wealth and prosperity.'

Pompous ass! he chided himself, as he said it; but he felt that a certain pomposity might be appropriate to the occasion.

'I don't doubt your empire's renown,' Shabir said, with the slightest hint of a frosty smile. 'But you have not brought Xandria's military might with you. You have not sufficient men to defend you from a company of dragomites, let alone the army of the Nine Towns.'

Fraxinus had no difficulty taking the implication that Shabir was wondering whether he and his people were captives of the dragomites. He couldn't blame the general for entertaining the suspicion – which was, after all, closer to the truth than he cared to admit. The grey-haired man might well be fishing for some indication that he and his fellow Xandrians might welcome help in obtaining release from that captivity, but Fraxinus dared not give him any such indication.

He doesn't believe me, Fraxinus thought, *but I think he would like to believe me, if only I can persuade him. Whether his men have the stomach for a fight or not, he must know that they can't attack our entire company without suffering heavy losses. He must be acutely aware of the burden of responsibility that rests on his shoulders.* 'We have no wish to fight,' he said aloud. 'We have come a long way, and we have a long way yet to go. We need rest, good food, and good ale. Is there nothing that Xandria has to offer the people of the Nine Towns?'

The general's features were set as in stone, but the speculative expressions on the captains' faces told Fraxinus that there were some in this company who might be very interested indeed in the friendship of Xandria and the possibilities contained therein.

'You do not understand how things are in this region,' the soldier said, accurately enough. 'We mean neither harm nor offence to the people of Xandria, but we cannot and will not tolerate the passage of dragomites across our land. I say again, the dragomites and their nest-slaves must go back or perish; if you choose to come forward between their ranks, you must be prepared to perish with them.'

'I think that your attitude is unreasonable,' Fraxinus said mildly, 'but I believe there is a way out of the impasse. If you will not tolerate our passage through your lands, will you let us go round their edge? It is impossible for us to skirt them to the west, where the marshes are, but there must be a strip of barren land in the east where your cultivated land borders the Spangled Desert. Will you let us make our way there – under escort if you wish – so that we may go to Salamander's Fire without causing any alarm?'

Fraxinus suppressed a smile of triumph as he saw the general hesitate, uncertainty clouding his eyes. The princess must have seen it too, and she was clever enough to guess what it signified.

'We could not go back through the blighted hills even if we wished to, general,' Lucrezia put in, larding her gentle tone with all the hauteur she could master. 'There is not enough food to be found there to keep a pack of rats alive, and we have used up all our supplies. We are the kind of people who honour our treaties, and we have made a treaty with Jume Metra's nest to see her and her companions safe to Salamander's Fire. Our dearest desire is to find friends in these lands, for ourselves and for Xandria, but we must cross them nevertheless. You must know by now that the sickening of the Dragomite Hills is but one aspect of a great change which is overtaking the world. It will require the forging of unions far greater than the one which binds your Nine Towns together, if human communities are not to be swept away for ever.'

The last point, Fraxinus saw in his adversary's eyes, was an unexpected hit. Either Shabir had heard something of that sort before, and believed it, or he actually knew of other considerable changes which were stealing upon his world. Fraxinus wanted to ask about that, but thought that this wasn't the time. Shabir, on the other hand, seemed glad of the distraction, as an aid to his procrastination.

'Is that why you have joined forces with Serpents?' the general asked, trying to sound derisive but not succeeding. 'Have they told you tales of the coming end of humankind, when they shall inherit the world which they consider to be theirs by right?'

'Serpents have never been enemies of humankind,' Carus Fraxinus said, ready enough to take up the cue. 'They do not desire our extinction, and have proved themselves willing to join forces with us against the threat of disaster. Dragomites are also very capable of living in fruitful association with human beings, and have done so for thousands of years in the Corridors of Power. We seek and intend to make friends with any creature which might be our ally in the war against the one enemy we all have, and which now threatens the world entire: the chaos which would be the final victory of corruption and corrosion. I ask you again, in the name of Xandria and the good of humankind, to grant us safe passage around your lands if you will not let us pass through them.'

'Only abandon the dragomites and you may have our friendship,' the general replied. 'That is all we require. If you will not, or *cannot*—'

'We *will not*,' Fraxinus was quick to say, 'and you have no right to demand it of us. These dragomites are not mere lice and the humans who have long lived among them are human beings like any others, with whom treaties can be made – and must be made, now that the order of the world is under threat. You must deal with us as a company, for we are united in our purpose. None of us has the slightest desire to hurt you, but we are bound for Salamander's Fire, and we must ask you not to stand in our way. If you are determined not to let us go south, you must guide us to a place where we can cross the river, so that we can go east to the borderlands of the Spangled Desert.'

'You should have come down from the hills directly into those borderlands,' Shabir said. 'You should never have set foot on our land.' But this was mere prevarication, and Fraxinus knew it.

'We did not know how unkindly you would receive us,' Fraxinus retorted, 'and we could not cross the river before, because there are no bridges in the Dragomite Hills. All we ask of you, if you are determined to offer us no more, is the use of a bridge. Only give us that, and we will go east until we find a way to Salamander's Fire which does not trespass on your precious land.'

After several seconds of angry staring – during which it seemed to Fraxinus that everything hung in the balance, waiting for the implacable force of gravity to tip the scales in the direction of common sense – the general made the diplomatic decision.

'There *is* a bridge . . .' he said.

The moment he said it, Fraxinus breathed an unconcealed sigh of relief, believing that he had won a victory of sorts – and that he had made the best bargain they could have hoped for, all things considered.

9

JACOM LEANED BACK in the saddle and looked up at the night sky, whose light was dwindling to a grey blur as the clouds gathered and thickened. On any other night Carus Fraxinus would already have brought the column to a halt, on the grounds that the darkness was so deep as to make it dangerous to continue, but the merchant had effectively surrendered the prerogative of that decision to the group of mounted men who were leading the wagons southwards along the bank of the river. Three of the men had lanterns, and must have known the terrain very well, but Jacom suspected that what kept them going in spite of the deteriorating conditions was simple fear; neither they nor their commanders wanted the dragomites on their land for a minute longer than was necessary.

Jacom had no lantern of his own but he was close enough to the big wagon to share the glow emitted by the one which Fraxinus had hung from the right hand side of the driver's station. The path along which they were moving certainly didn't warrant description as a road, but it didn't seem very hazardous. Even so, he would have preferred to ride inside one of the wagons and leave his horse to take its own chances, had not Fraxinus asked him to remain armed and armoured, ready to act swiftly should anything untoward occur.

'It's not that I don't trust the general to keep his word,' Fraxinus had said – although he was doubtless less certain of that than he thought it politic to reveal – 'but it's as well to emphasise the fact that we're a disciplined company, willing to defend ourselves should the necessity arise and capable of inflicting a great deal of damage on anyone unwise enough to attack us.'

Jacom could see the logic of that argument, but he could also see its essential weakness. The darkness made a convenient cloak for the gradual massing of the Eblan army – or the army of the Nine Towns, or whatever other title it might prefer to adopt – but there was no mistaking the fact that this General Shabir wanted to put on a display of his own. With that object presumably in mind, the general had ordered his cavalrymen to carry far more torches than they actually needed, and those flickering flames now delineated a long wall of stern light which seemed to rim the western horizon for a considerable distance. Jacom didn't doubt that the riders were spread very thinly, but in the gloom they gave the impression that they could close in upon the column at any time and overwhelm it.

While he was preoccupied with these gloomy ruminations another rider came up behind Jacom and moved his horse into step with his own. It was Checuti, looking every inch the military man in his borrowed armour. He had even condescended to carry a half-pike, although Jacom had heard him express the opinion that such unwieldly weapons were only fit for dolts and simpletons.

'Have you counted them, captain?' Checuti asked. 'Have you measured the enemy's strength with the precision befitting a master tactician?'

'I only know that they're too many,' Jacom replied stiffly. 'If they're all experienced dragomite-fighters, they have the numbers they need to defeat our twelve warriors, with a great many to spare.'

'I'd reached the same conclusion,' Checuti agreed, in a more amicable tone. 'They already number at least five hundred, and I think it very probable that they are still gathering further reinforcements to secure their show of strength. Given another two days, and the assumption that they still have substantial reserves available within ten or twenty kims, they might indeed have cause to feel invincible. Might we be going meekly into a trap, do you think?'

'We might,' Jacom said drily. 'But what alternative do we have? Fraxinus is right, is he not? If they will not let us through their lands, we must go around them.'

'But what shall we eat in the fringes of the Spangled Desert?' Checuti complained. 'Even if they keep their word to guide us safely there, how shall we survive?'

It was, Jacom thought, a very good question. Fraxinus was

still hoping to trade with the farmers whose produce supported the Nine Towns, but Jacom couldn't believe that they'd be anxious to bring their goods to a marketplace ringed by dragomites.

'Do you have an alternative suggestion?' he asked, looking furtively around and dropping his voice to a near-whisper because he had a reasonably good idea what Checuti's reply would be.

'Don't be nervous,' Checuti said, in a moderately low tone. 'I've noticed that it's only when more than two of us come together that one of the mound-women drifts into earshot. They seem to work on the principle that it takes three to make a conspiracy – which is, I have to admit, a sensible judgment.'

'The problem,' Jacom said, 'is that the dragomites and the mound-women have a greater advantage over us than the Eblans have over them. Even if you could recruit everyone else to a conspiracy of rebellion – which, having talked to Fraxinus and the princess, I doubt very much – we'd stand no chance at all unless we could somehow persuade the Eblans to weigh in on our side at exactly the right moment. I think Fraxinus is right – while there's a chance of avoiding a fight, we have to take it.'

'The *real* problem,' Checuti retorted, 'is that we're growing weaker with every day that passes. We need food, and there'll be no more dragomite rogues from now on. Once we're in the desert we'll quickly run out of water too. We *have* to get away from the dragomites, or we'll become so weak that the wagons will be too tempting a target. It's a long way to Salamander's Fire, and we'll be closely watched at least for the next two tendays.'

'It's easy enough to talk about getting away from the dragomites,' Jacom countered gloomily, 'but not so easy to do. We'd have to get rid of the Serpents too, and we've no guarantee of finding a hospitable welcome among these folk even then. This general claims that he knows nothing about Purkin and the other men who ran southwards from the nest-war; if he's not lying, Purkin must have thought it politic to avoid making contact. Either way, it doesn't bode well for the prospect of friendship. Anyway, Fraxinus doesn't seem in the least inclined to betray the dragomites. How does Ereleth feel about it?'

'Ereleth is a realist,' Checuti said – which seemed to Jacom to be a conspicously evasive answer. 'So is Keshvara.'

'But Phar won't make a move without Fraxinus,' Jacom pointed out, 'and the princess is solidly behind Fraxinus too. Dhalla's loyalty is to the princess, not to Ereleth, and she's worth eight or ten men in any kind of close fight. Without her, we wouldn't stand a chance. Forget your scheming, Checuti; if we're to survive this mad adventure we all have to stick together, and if that means sticking to Fraxinus's plan, that's what we have to do. Has it occurred to you that the dragomites might be very useful allies to have once we're beyond the territory inhabited by people who are paranoid about them?'

'What did they do to you down in the depths of that nest?' Checuti asked quizzically. 'Familiarity is supposed to breed contempt, not contentment.'

'They didn't do anything to me,' Jacom told him coldly. 'What I saw down there certainly didn't make me like them any more, or fear them any less – but any attempt we make to break the pact the princess made would probably get some or all of us killed. Have you considered that once we're in the desert it's not just us who'll be getting weaker? The dragomites are close to exhaustion too. Our best chance of winning free of them, if that's what we need to do, is to take them to the limit of their own endurance. Fraxinus might have that in mind.'

'Have *you* considered that the proximity of the river might be our biggest advantage?' Checuti riposted. 'You and I can swim – dragomites can't.'

'In case you hadn't noticed,' Jacom said, 'the dragomites have been careful to keep at least half their number between the wagons and the river ever since we came down from the hills.'

'If we could contrive a substantial diversion,' Checuti said doggedly, 'it might be possible to persuade the dragomites to redistribute their warriors. As to whether the Eblans would help or welcome us – that would presumably depend on what we had to offer them . . .'

'I'm not interested,' Jacom said, thinking that he had heard quite enough of what seemed far too fanciful to be called a *plan*. 'I have to stay with the princess, as a matter of duty as well as practicality. She won't ever agree to be part of the kind of mad scheme you're trying to dream up, and neither will Fraxinus. I'm with them – and I advise you to make the same decision and the same commitment.'

As he spoke he felt the heavy splash of a raindrop on the crown of his bare head, and he looked up at the sky again. The grey pall obscuring the stars had deepened until it was almost black. More heavy drops began to fall, and the sound of their splashing on the ground quickly grew to a clatter which drowned the murmurous sound of their argument.

Fraxinus appeared at the front of the big wagon, peering out from behind the darklander who was driving it.

'Take shelter, Checuti!' he called. 'No sense in getting wet. Jacom, will you ride forward to the men who are leading us, and tell them that we'll have to stop?'

'I'll try!' Jacom shouted back, immediately urging his horse to a trot. Checuti did as he was bid and turned aside, but he made no move to fall in behind the big wagon and seemed to be intent on waiting for the smaller one, which Phar was driving in rear.

As he moved forward away from the lantern on the leading wagon Jacom felt that the darkness was swallowing him up, but the lanterns which Shabir's men carried had quickly been hooded and they were in no danger of being extinguished by the downpour. Within three minutes Jacom was close enough to be able to see the ground beneath his horse's feet again.

'We'll have to stop, Captain Burak,' Jacom said to the one man whose name he had been told. 'We simply can't keep going through this kind of murk. I'm sorry.'

'The road's good,' one of the other men replied, with reflexive stubbornness. 'We've had our orders. We're to keep going, no matter what.'

'If we're to reach the bridge tomorrow afternoon there's no time to waste,' added another.

Burak didn't seem glad of their advice, and Jacom noticed that the colours they wore on their sleeves were not the same as the red and white that Burak wore.

'It's too dark,' Jacom complained, still addressing himself to Burak, 'and the rain makes matters worse. One of you must ride to your general for new orders. Our horses can't see the ground beneath their feet. It's too dangerous to carry on.'

The two men who had spoken exchanged uneasy glances, but neither of them voiced a further opinion; they were waiting for a decision to be made. Jacom knew from experience how much easier it was to stand aside and criticise than to take responsibility for an action.

'Let me go with you, Captain Burak,' Jacom said. 'I'll talk to the general.'

The captain was quick enough to reply to that. 'No!' he said roughly. 'You stay with the wagons – all of you. I'll go to the general myself, and he'll send someone to give you his decision. You must go back now – go back and stay there.' If he knew Jacom's name he was refusing to use it.

Jacom shook his head to show dissatisfaction, but he knew that he had no alternative but to do as he was told. He was feeling distinctly uncomfortable now that the rain had soaked through his leather armour and his jacket. His red skirt was clining soggily to his thighs and his socks were wet through. He rode back to Fraxinus's wagon.

'They're sending someone to talk to the general,' he called – adding, because he knew that they could still hear him: 'They're only common soldiers, frightened to make decisions.'

'You can't blame them for that, Jacom,' Fraxinus called back, in dutifully diplomatic fashion. 'We'll keep going a little while longer. Climb aboard before you get soaked.'

This advice, unfortunately, came too late. His belongings were stowed in the small wagon so he waited for Phar to draw alongside and come to a temporary halt before he moved in behind it. While he was busy hitching his horse to the backboard and taking off his saddle he got even wetter. The road was already so miry that his boots became filthy and the bare calves which his uniform left exposed were spattered with glutinous mud.

Andris Myrasol reached down to help him up, and then tried to make as much room for him as was possible while he cleaned off the worst of the dirt.

'The princess isn't certain that this General Shabir has much of an army to command,' Merel Zabio was saying. 'It might be a lot less numerous than we think. Anyway, we've no reason to suppose that they'd welcome us as friends and offer us their protection.' Checuti had obviously taken up his private crusade where he'd been forced to leave off by Jacom's lack of sympathy. Jacom looked around to make sure that no mound-women were sheltering in the wagon. In spite of the fact that four people were now gathered here – five, if Phar were counted, although he was probably unable to hear what was being said over the drumming of the rain – none of Jume Metra's warrior-women had come to listen. Presumably they too were finding the rain a very inconvenient distraction.

'Merel's right,' Andris said, surely to no one's surprise. 'Anyone who jumps ship might be leaping out of the cooking pot into the fire. If these people hate dragomites as much as they seem to they might not bother to discriminate between us and the mound-women.'

'You're the one with the head of a human drone tucked away in his luggage,' Checuti said sourly. 'Are you telling us that you take this pact with the dragomites seriously – that you think we should stand with them against the Eblans if it comes to a fight?'

'What I'm saying,' the amber told him, in a tone which was patient but stubborn, 'is that we wouldn't have any reason to expect the Eblans to welcome us with open arms if we ran away from the dragomites. In Ferentina we have a saying: *better the rot you know than the rot you don't.*'

'And you know the dragomites, do you?' Checuti said. 'You've been to the very heart of a nest, and you've seen the dragomite queen at work, and you've passed the time of day with something growing out of the wall that claimed to be a human being, so you think you know everything there is to know about dragomites. Personally, I think I know people – *real* people, that is, not dragomite-born imitations. I know generals and I know soldiers and I know thieves.'

'Especially thieves,' Merel put in.

Checuti rounded on her. '*You* know what I'm talking about, sailorman,' he said. 'You've been around the shores and islands of the Slithery Sea, keeping close company with men from anywhere and everywhere in the crew's quarters. You don't have to study them to know what the men of Ebla are like; they're like men everywhere. They talk bolder than they are, and they're thieves through and through. We can deal with men like that, you and I. We know how. We can't deal with dragomites – not even the ones which look like human beings. No matter what pacts we think we've made, they're our enemies.'

'You didn't come down into the nest,' Andris pointed out.

'Jacom came in your place. He and I know more about dragomites than any other human beings in the world, with the possible exception of Princess Lucrezia. I think that counts for something.' Jacom observed that in spite of what he was saying, and in spite of allowing the half-human drone to call him *brother*, Andris didn't seem to be counting the mound-people as human beings.

'It doesn't count for much,' Checuti said. 'Believe me, it doesn't count for anything at all.'

'This is all pointless,' Jacom said wearily, feeling that it was time to take the conversation on to new ground. 'Whatever we do, we have to do it together, and we really don't have any choice. That includes you, Checuti. You're in this with the rest of us, whether you like it or not.'

Checuti reached up to stroke the fur of his pet monkey, which had been quick to take its usual perch on his shoulder as soon as he came in out of the rain. Jacom supposed, uncharitably, that the thief-master's principal reason for keeping the monkey was to have someone to turn to when everyone else was set against him.

'I understand your reluctance to leave the princess, captain,' Checuti said, in a tone that had more tiredness than contempt in it, 'but if I were you, I'd think very carefully about sticking too close to her. There are fates far worse than permanent exile from Xandria, and Princess Lucrezia is the kind of person who could very easily lead you to one. And if it's love rather than homesickness that's keeping you one step behind her, forget it. She's poison, just like the potions in her belt.'

'That's not fair,' Andris said, in the curiously punctilious fashion he sometimes adopted. 'Jacom's talking about all of us, not just the princess. We're all supposed to be on the same side, remember? What chance have we got of getting to Salamander's Fire – let alone Chimera's Cradle – if we can't pull together?'

'If I remember correctly,' Checuti retorted, 'it was the princess who told us that we were all on the same side – by which, I think, she meant her side. But what, exactly, is her side? Does she know herself? Does she have the slightest idea what she's about? I see no evidence of it. Is Carus Fraxinus on her side? Is Ereleth? We're trapped in a pit of blind snakes, my friend. We have to look out for ourselves, because no one else will.'

Jacom couldn't help but remember that he had entered into tricky negotiations with Checuti once before, and had come off second best. Checuti had run rhetorical rings round him on that occasion, and he was trying to do the same again. Jacom didn't doubt that Checuti's clever tongue was moved by a clever mind, but he wasn't at all sure that Checuti was trustworthy. What was he, after all, but a thief who hadn't managed to spend the proceeds of his one great coup? Carus Fraxinus was the more reliable man by far, and that was all there was to it.

'We can't escape the dragomites,' Jacom said, taking great pains to make sure that what he said was incontrovertible. 'I don't care what kind of diversion you create – it wouldn't be enough to let more than a handful of us get away, and you'd leave the remainder in greater trouble than before. We couldn't get the wagons away either. It's just not possible. I think we have to stick together, and follow Fraxinus's lead.'

'And I think we need contingency plans,' Checuti said. 'I also think that Fraxinus would want us to make contingency plans, just in case his own go awry.'

'We can't,' Jacom said unhappily. 'There are too many contingencies, and there's too much we don't know.'

'That's not good enough,' Checuti said.

'Perhaps it isn't,' Andris put in, 'but it's the way things are. You and Phar can make as much plastic as you like, but as far as I can see, it's much more likely to blow us all to smithereens than it is to deliver us from our enemies.'

They never found out what Checuti would have said in reply, because at the very moment the amber pronounced the word *enemies* the wagon lurched horribly to the left, and the floor on which they had been sitting abruptly developed a steep slope, sending them all sprawling in a heap.

Jacom knew immediately that one of the rear wheels had collapsed, and the whether General Shabir and his advisers liked it or not, there was no possible question of going forward another sem until it was replaced. He remembered, too, that they had used their only ready-made replacement two days before descending to the plain. That Aulakh Phar could build a wheel he had no doubt – he had seen him do it – but he knew that it was the kind of work which took a long time even in daylight and dry weather.

'Oh, filth!' he heard Merel Zabio say. '*Now* we're in trouble.'

It was a sentiment with which no one could possibly disagree.

10

ANDRIS RAN FORWARD through the driving rain, trying as best he could to shield himself with a cloak clutched in his right hand and held above his head. He dared not use his stride to the full lest he encounter some patch of ground as treacherous as that which had shattered the wagon's wheel, but he hurried nevertheless to tell Fraxinus what had happened. Two of the guides appointed by General Shabir arrived alongside the team of horses that had been pulling the big wagon at the same time as Andris, so he was able to report to them too. They seemed extremely displeased, but there was more frustration than anger in their displeasure; they knew perfectly well that the matter was beyond anyone's control. They knew full well how fragile cart-wheels could be when rot was given time to work on them.

Andris could see that Fraxinus was exerting all his powers of diplomacy as he apologised profusely to the guides and begged them to convey the same apologies to their leader.

'You must stay exactly where you are,' one of the lantern-bearers said, exaggerating the necessity in the faint hope that it would make him seem more competent to command. 'You must replace the wheel as quickly as you can.'

Given that Fraxinus would have dearly loved to do exactly that, there should have been little room for disagreement; alas, Andris took it upon himself to break the news that they had no spare. Fraxinus was quick to declare in a loud and painstaking manner that Aulakh Phar must work as fast as possible, in spite of the rain and the darkness, to repair the wheel that had broken, and that Andris must help him in every way he could.

'I fear that it's beyond repair,' Andris reported dutifully. 'Our only hope of getting under way again is that General Shabir might be able to find a wheel of the right dimensions among the carts carrying supplies for his men.'

'Is there any hope of that, Captain Joakim?' Fraxinus enquired. Even in the near-darkness, Andris could see that Captain Joakim was not at all glad to be asked.

'Go on, Andris,' Fraxinus said. 'Tell Aulakh to make a start.'

By the time Andris got back to the place where the smaller wagon had been brought to a standstill Aulakh Phar was inspecting the damage by the light of a hooded lantern. Merel was standing nearby with Jacom Cerri and Checuti, who had all dismounted from the wagon in order to lighten the load and were now huddled together under the inadequate shelter of a single sheet of canvas.

'How bad is it?' Andris asked.

'It could have been worse,' Phar reported, with a heavy sigh. 'Considering the ample opportunity which corruption has had to extend its empire within the fabric of the wagons since we left Khalorn, and the limited nature of the repairs I was able to make while we were stuck in the Dragomite Hills, I'd say that we've escaped rather lightly. I wish we could have escaped for a day or two more, though.'

'That stretch of stony ground beneath the cliff shook the wheels up very badly,' Andris said, expressing a similar sigh in sympathy with the old man. 'Something like this was bound to happen sooner or later.'

'Let's just be grateful that the damage to the wagon itself is slight,' Phar said. 'At least we only have to find a new wheel. Has Fraxinus sent a message to Shabir telling him what kind of wheel we need?'

'Yes, he has,' Andris said, 'but I don't know what our chances are of getting one. I don't have the faintest idea how many carts Shabir has, or what size they are, or where they're lodged. I dare say he'll do his best to find one. He'll be as anxious to get us moving as we are.'

'You can't be sure of that,' Checuti called out. 'This might change everything' – but there were anxious mound-women within earshot now, and Jume Metra had come to see how bad the problem was, so the scope the thief-master had for sowing further seeds of dissent and dissatisfaction was severely limited. Andris was glad about that – so far as he could see, Checuti's bomb-making schemes were a complication the expedition could well do without.

'It's all right,' Andris said to Jume Metra. 'We can fix it, given time. Your people had better take shelter, though – the dragomites and the Serpents too. It'll take a while.' He knew that the advice wasn't worth much – the big wagon was already crowded enough, so the only obvious way for the mound-women to hide from the rain was to crouch beneath the bodies of the dragomite warriors.

'We do not fear rain,' Jume Metra told him, which he took to mean that they would accept the unfortunate necessity of getting wet.

Andris turned away from the wagon as a group of riders bearing lanterns came out of the darkness which lay around them like a great stifling blanket. They were Eblan soldiers, but they had avoided riding through the line of six dragomite warriors which was established somewhere out to the right of the column and were approaching from the van. Fraxinus was walking alongside the mount of the leading rider, and Andris was mildly surprised to hear him say: 'You see the situation, General Shabir. We have no choice.'

Andris studied the man on the horse, unimpressed by his size, his dress or his manner.

'It's most unfortunate,' Fraxinus went on anxiously, 'but it can't be helped. It won't take long to fit a new wheel if you can provide one, but if you can't do that we'll have to build one. We have the necessary tools, but it's a long job. The night was becoming very dark in any case – had we tried to continue there'd have been more accidents. You shouldn't begrudge us a chance to rest – your men must need sleep almost as badly as we do.'

Andris expected an argument, and judged from the anxiety in his voice that Fraxinus expected one too, but in fact the general made no immediate reply. He seemed to be pondering the situation.

His men are probably in even greater need of rest than we are, Andris thought. *And they've little more shelter than we have, unless the darkness is hiding a small town. Rain dampens everyone's spirits – perhaps it's all for the best.*

In the end, though, Shabir said exactly what Fraxinus must have feared. 'Leave three or four men here to mend the wagon. Take the rest of your people and all of the dragomites, and make what speed you can towards the bridge. I give you my word that the men you leave behind will not be molested, and that the wagon will join you on the far side of the river within hours of your having crossed.'

'That's not possible,' Fraxinus replied swiftly. 'We can't go on in darkness – it's too dangerous. Even dragomites can't see in this kind of gloom; their tunnels are lit, albeit dimly, and they have other senses to guide them within their nests. We all have to stay here until the sky lightens. There's no question of any of us going on.'

The general pondered the matter again, his dour face eerily lit by a lantern carried by one of his men. 'It is very dark,' he finally conceded. 'Even the dragomites are blinded, you say?'

'They normally retreat from the rain into their nests,' Fraxinus said. 'It's far safer to let them rest where they are than to leave them blundering about in the murk.'

The threat was a very subtle one, but Andris was quite certain that the general would not overlook it.

'You may stop here,' Shabir eventually said, grudgingly. 'I'll try to find you a wheel, but it won't be easy. We have no carts nearby, and it's an awkward size. You'd better start making one, just in case – but as soon as the wheel is fitted you must be ready to move on, whatever the hour may be and whatever the weather.' He turned his horse away as soon as he had spoken, heading back towards the big wagon. Fraxinus followed him.

'If they had not planned treachery before,' Checuti muttered in Andris's ear, having presumably come forward for exactly that purpose, 'the temptation will surely become irresistible now. Darkness like this spawns fanciful thoughts in the minds of anxious men.'

'They won't attack while they can't see,' Andris murmured in reply, feeling fairly confident that he was right. 'They must have a very healthy dread of dragomites – even blind dragomites. It requires a brave man to charge a warrior by day, and I doubt that a general as shabby as that one will have any brave enough to sally forth against twenty of them in the dark.'

'Don't just stand there,' Phar called out, as the soldiers' horses turned away. 'Let's get busy.'

'Once I was a prince of thieves,' Checuti said, still muttering so that no one but Andris could hear him. 'Now I'm supposed to serve as a wheelwright's labourer. How are the mighty fallen.'

Andris forbore to point out that he had once been a real prince. He had yet to find anyone outside Ferentina who was in the least impressed by the fact – and had he stayed in Ferentina, it would probably have been his death-warrant. He had long since decided that being a wheelwright's labourer, or some equally humble thing, wasn't such an appalling station in life as those who occupied it made out – except, of course, when such men had to do their work in darkness and in heavy rain, with a hostile army close at hand. He went reluctantly to help Phar, although he had no intention of trying to lever the wagon up until Dhalla put in an appearance; that was the kind of work far better done by authentic giants than men who merely looked as if they had a slight taint of giant blood.

It wasn't long before Dhalla did, indeed, report for this duty, although she was not in the best of humour about it. There was a darklander with her, and they now had more than enough willing arms and strong backs to lift the fallen part of the wagon and provide a makeshift support for it. This they did, and Phar promptly disappeared underneath to make sure that the floor of the wagon would hold together once a new wheel could be fitted. Jacom Cerri had unhitched all the horses, but he tethered them close by, so that they could be put back in harness quickly as soon as the wagon was capable of rolling again.

Phar had laid in a good stock of fresh timber while they were in the Forest of Absolute Night, and he had more than enough on hand to rebuild the wheel and replace the axle. Fortunately, the jolt which the body of the cart had received when the wheel split had not broken any other planks outright, although the whole structure now seemed less than sound to Andris's doubtful eye. Phar climbed aboard, taking the lantern with him, and the crowd began to melt away in the direction of the big wagon, in search of shelter.

'It's as well we've consumed all our reserves of food,' Phar commented to Andris rather drily, as he brought out an assortment of tools. He laid them out in the shelter of the wagon.

'It's a good thing that we've become so thin ourselves,' Andris added. 'Had we been fully laden when the wheel gave way the whole thing would have come apart.'

Phar disappeared into the back of the wagon for a second time, again taking the lantern with him. This time it proved more difficult to search out further materials that he needed. Andris could hear him cursing the disarray caused by the accident. Everything which had not been fully secured had been spilled on the floor.

'You'd better go to the big wagon,' Andris said to Merel, who had not yet followed Checuti, Dhalla and the darklander. 'I'll stay with Phar – we'll call you if we need any more help.'

He didn't anticipate that Phar would need any more help imminently, but he felt that he ought to stand by just in case. Somebody had to.

Merel hesitated. The rain had plastered her hair to her skull and was running in rivulets down her ill-lit face. She didn't want to leave him, but the rain was unbearable. When she'd gone, Andris was quick to duck under the belly of the wagon. Within two minutes Phar had joined him, bringing the lantern with him.

While the old man set up the apparatus necessary to bend a rim for the the new wheel, Andris peered out into the gloom, wishing that he knew more about the lie of the land around them. They had passed a number of homesteads, including one entire hamlet, but the land lay derelict and it was obvious that the buildings were now being used as billets for soldiers. The men who had worked the farms must have sent their women and children to the towns while they joined forces with Shabir – whether as volunteers or as conscripts – to fight the dragomite invaders. In a way, he supposed, this land had been as badly and as comprehensively blighted as the hills themselves, although earthly grass and earthly weeds still sprouted in profusion and the occasional earthly tree still put forth its hopeful leaves.

How they must yearn to have this whole business over and done with, Andris thought. *But it might not be over and done with, even though the plague has run its course in the dragomites' nests and the slopes of their mounds. If, as the queen and the princess seem to believe, the plague is merely a symptom of some greater upheaval . . .*

'That wheel might be a symbol of the whole world,' he remarked to Phar gloomily. 'Can we really hope to maintain the forms of civilisation against the corrosions of nature? The rot's bound to win in the end. Nothing can stand against it. Not flesh, not metal, not stone.'

'Strictly speaking,' Phar told him, 'stone doesn't actually rot. The processes we carelessly group together as corruption and corrosion aren't as similar as our habit implies, although they all involve invisible organisms.'

'Everybody knows that,' Andris replied, a touch resentfully. Phar was always trying to educate the members of the expedition in his eccentric lore, and he was overfond of addressing them as if they were stupid apprentices.

'Everybody knows that there are corruptions, and that there are corrosions,' Phar admitted, 'but how many of the people who use the words as curses really understand or care about the difference?'

'Not many,' Andris said, carefully refraining from admitting that he was none too clear about it himself.

'Life is more various than most people realise,' the old man went on serenely. 'Plants extract carbon dioxide from the air and turn it into oxygen. Animals eat the plants and breathe in the oxygen, recombining the two. It's a cycle, you see. Decay is just another form of life, a further phase in the cycle. Deep down, that kind of rot is just oxidation: a long, slow burn. Rust is oxidation too, and lustrust is just a hastening of it – but stonerot is something else entirely. Rock, you see, is mostly oxides already, like the carbon dioxide in the air, so breaking it down is a very different process.'

'Like plants using the stuff in the air,' Andris said guardedly. 'A different part of the cycle.'

'Well, yes, in a way,' Phar said. 'But then, in another way, no. With rock, you see, you have to take crystallisation into effect, because rock has an innate structure. That's why it's solid. Stonerot isn't so much a chemical process as a physical one, which has more to do with structure-breaking than chemical conversion. Which is why it's better to think of it as corrosion rather than corruption, because the organisms which do it aren't doing at all the same thing as the plants which break down atmospheric carbon dioxide . . . except, of course, that in a way they *are*, because just as plants build their own bodies out of the carbon, the organisms which corrode stone build their own bodies out of *their* substrate . . . but it *is* different. I'm not making this very clear, am I?'

'That's all right,' Andris assured him. 'I understand the basics, and I don't think I need to know much more than that.'

'I know you don't,' Phar said crossly. 'I really think you ought to try, though. We all need to understand the world we're in as well as we possibly can, or the rot will win, in the end.'

Andris had stopped listening to him. He peered out into the darkness, trying to see through the curtain of rain. 'I can hear noises,' he said. 'Someone or something is moving out there.'

Phar didn't reply; he obviously felt that there were plenty of good reasons why someone or something might be moving around in the vicinity of the stricken wagon.

Andris wriggled forwards, steadying himself against the props which had been set to hold up the wheelless corner of the wagon. The noise of the old man's patient labour was all he could hear now. The rainfall was still very heavy and the darkness seemed absolute. 'It's probably one of the dragomites,' he said.

He had just convinced himself that this must be the case when he heard further movements. He reached back to pull the lantern to his side, taking care not to obscure Phar's work. A hawk-moth, drawn by the light and desperate to get out of the rain, fluttered past his face. It was a strangely welcome visitation; there was a measure of reassurance to be obtained from the fact that they were now in a region where there were insects of an earthly kind and an appropriately modest size.

It was not so comforting, though, to feel the ground beneath his feet softening into slimy mud. Huge puddles had formed on top of the saturated earth beside the wagon, and his boots – overstrained by too much walking – were leaking. His limbs, cramped by his crouching position, were beginning to ache. Deciding that he was too wet already to be intimidated by the rain, he stepped out from underneath the wagon and stood up, still peering out into the darkness in the direction from which the mysterious sounds had come.

Something that was not a hawk-moth flew out of the night and struck him in the chest. It was needle-sharp, and he felt the point penetrate his flesh. For one horrid moment he thought that it might penetrate his heart too, but the fact that he had time to complete the thought was evidence enough that it had stuck in the superficial tissues. He felt surprisingly little pain as he lifted his hand to the point of impact, intending to pluck the thing out and throw it away.

Absurdly, it was not until the second missile hit him in the neck, to the left of his voice-box, that he suddenly realised that he was under attack.

He jerked reflexively as his hand collided with the first dart and twisted the point in his flesh. He tried to turn around but his foot skidded and he fell, striking his head against the side of the wagon. He was not stunned, but something very peculiar seemed to be happening to him as his senses reeled. He tried to get up, but he couldn't do it; suddenly, his limbs felt terribly heavy. He tried to call out, not just to Phar but to everyone else, to warn them that the column was under attack, but the words remained stuck in his throat.

What's happening to me? he thought, and would doubtless have followed the thought with more pointless questions, had he been able to form them into words.

He was vaguely aware of the fact that running men were hurtling out of the night, laying rough hands upon him from behind. He tried to lash out at them but his hands were leaden weights which he could hardly lift, let alone thrust out. He opened his mouth again to cry for help, but no sound emerged.

He felt himself being lifted up, and then he felt no more.

11

LUCREZIA HAD SURFACED from a light sleep as soon as the big wagon stopped, fearing that something was wrong. By the time Fraxinus brought word back that the second wagon had broken a wheel she was wide awake. It should have been easy to go back to sleep once it had been confirmed that General Shabir had given permission for the caravan to stop, but she couldn't do it. She lay perfectly still, with her eyes closed, listening to the rain beat upon the canvas which sheltered the wagon's cargo, but sleep would not return in response to the invitation. When the alarm was raised, she sat up immediately, her heartbeat accelerating.

She could hear shouting, but the voices were muffled by the rain and the words were indistinct. The warning cries grew to a veritable cacophony as they were taken up and repeated by more and more voices, some of them much closer than the first, but still she had no idea what might be happening. Within seconds the wagon was lurching alarmingly as those who had recently crowded into it leapt to action, hurling themselves this way and that in search of arms or armour, slamming into one another in hopeless confusion. Lucrezia, whose station was well forward of this turmoil, was quick to pull on the boots she had set beside her. She had to grope about for her jacket, but found it easily enough.

'Take up your weapons!' Carus Fraxinus called out, taking care to sound calm. 'Douse that light! Captain Cerri – run back to the other wagon to see what's amiss, but keep your head low!'

Lucrezia could hear Checuti saying: 'I told you so! They couldn't resist! Fraxinus should never have told them that the dragomites were blind!'

Lucrezia knew that the criticism was unfair. The experienced dragomite-fighters of the Nine Towns must have known perfectly well that dragomites didn't like rain, and that they were apt to huddle down and close their eyes if they couldn't take shelter. Even so, she couldn't understand why the Eblans would choose to launch an attack. The dragomite warriors might be unready, but that wouldn't stop them going into action with all the force and fury they could muster – and Shabir's men would be just as blind as they were.

Chaos is come! she thought. *They must be mad!*

Lucrezia heard scratching beneath the place where she lay as someone scrambled underneath, taking up a position behind the wheel. The candle which had been burning in the back of the wagon had already been blown out, in response to Fraxinus's cry; the darkness seemed absolute from where Lucrezia sat, although she knew that there must be some light outside, no matter how heavy the rain was.

'Hold your positions, everyone!' Fraxinus said, his voice now close at hand but lowered to an urgent hiss. 'Let's not invite attack. And for Goran's sake make sure that anyone you strike is an enemy.'

Lucrezia could smell the damp on the merchant's clothing as he moved past the place where she crouched. She felt a hand on her shoulder, and knew it for Ereleth's.

'Who shouted first?' the princess asked, keeping her voice to a whisper.

'Not one of ours,' Fraxinus replied quickly. 'The dragomites must have caught someone close by who had no right to be there. Almost immediately, Phar called out to Andris Myrasol, but I heard no reply. Then the mound-women began calling, to rouse their whole company. If the Eblans really are attacking, they're insane – the warriors might have been quiet before, but they'll run riot now.'

There were more cries emanating from the direction of the other wagon, and Lucrezia recognised Aulakh Phar's voice. She strained her ears, trying to catch what he was saying, but his words were interrupted and overlaid by harsh cries of anger and anguish from way over to the right, where half the dragomite warriors had been stationed. The strident wails of terror and confusion were loud, but they were brief. She heard no names and no comprehensible commands.

Lucrezia held her breath, waiting for something more, but

there was nothing. Phar had fallen quiet; he too must be listening. If Shabir's men really had decided that the moment was ripe for a sneak attack, their plans must have gone badly awry, for no arrows had hit the wagon and no running spearmen were splashing through the mud towards it. The shouting had died away now, and for a few moments there was no sound at all save for the relentless torrent of rain.

'It's not an attack!' Lucrezia said sharply. 'It can't be!'

'Hush!' said Ereleth urgently – but Fraxinus said: 'You're right, highness! The dragomites caught someone, and perhaps two or three, but it can't have been an army, or they'd be all around us now and the dragomites would be slaughtering them by the score.'

Might it have been some small rebel company, Lucrezia wondered, whose mutinous captain thought Shabir's pact an act of treason? Had they retreated as soon as it became obvious that their attempt to sneak past the dragomites had failed? Was it possible that the would-be marauders had nothing to do with Shabir's militia at all?

She heard someone outside curse the darkness, but someone else was quick to silence them with a sharp word. Everyone wanted to listen; everyone wanted to know what was going on. There was no way for Lucrezia to tell whether Jacom Cerri had obeyed Fraxinus's command to go to Phar and find out what the commotion was. She wondered whether it was time to delve in the pouches at her belt in order to anoint her fingernails with poison, but her once neat nails no longer had their carefully manicured points, which had been broken and eroded by the travails and tribulations involved in crossing the Dragomite Hills.

'Patience, daughter,' Ereleth murmured, as if she had read the thought in Lucrezia's mind. 'Let us—'

She broke off because she was interrupted by a loud cry, which came from the direction of the other wagon. 'Andris! Andris! Answer me!' She recognised Jacom Cerri's voice, and knew that he had obeyed the order, and that he had received bad news from Phar.

There was no reply.

'What's wrong?' demanded a tremulous voice much closer at hand – Merel Zabio's voice.

'Quiet, child!' That was Checuti, who doubtless wanted to give Andris the chance of being heard were he able to reply – and inclined to do so, if he could.

Has he deserted us? Lucrezia wondered, but she knew immediately that any such suspicion was ridiculous. The big amber would never have left Merel behind, if he had taken it into his head to go – which meant, given that Jacom Cerri had called out and received no reply, that he must have been killed, or knocked out . . . or taken. Perhaps, she thought, the invaders had contrived to avoid the blinded dragomites on the way in . . . but not on the way out.

More cries could now be heard, but they were very distant – they came from far beyond the line formed by the dragomite warriors. She couldn't make out any words, but she knew that it must be Shabir's men calling to their own.

'What mischief have they done?' Ereleth demanded, making no attempt to keep her voice down. The way she pronounced the words made it clear that she expected an answer, and expected it from Fraxinus, but he was not yet in a position to tell her.

'Perhaps nothing,' Fraxinus muttered. 'Perhaps they merely sent forth spies, who were rudely sent back . . .'

Lucrezia could hear the hopefulness in his voice, and the corrosive doubt which lay behind it. Then she heard Jacom Cerri speaking, in a kind of exaggerated whisper, asking to see a light so that he might climb back into the wagon. Someone struck a match and groped around for the candle, lighting it at the second attempt, but hardly any of its light filtered back to the place where Lucrezia lay; there were too many barrels and boxes in the way.

The captain scrambled up into the wagon, breathing heavily.

'Well, man?' Ereleth snapped impatiently. 'What's happening?'

'I think they've gone,' Jacom said, as he squeezed his way through the cluttered cargo to the front of the wagon. 'They rushed the small wagon, it seems. Aulakh Phar was underneath and out of reach, but Andris had stepped out for some reason. Phar heard Andris fall and shouted a warning. The mound-women relayed the alarm around the whole perimeter. Then someone else started yelling – he must have been caught by a dragomite, and he wasn't the only one. By the time Phar thought it was safe to come out of hiding Andris had disappeared – seized, he says, though I don't see how he can be sure. The new wheel's hardly begun, but Phar's working again, more urgently than before – three of the mound-women are standing guard around him. Is Andris here, by any chance?' It wasn't until he spoke the last words that he let a quaver of anxiety creep into his voice.

'No,' Merel Zabio was quick to say. 'He must have been taken.'

'Unless he's lying dead in a puddle somewhere out in the darkness,' the captain said, displaying a marked lack of tact.

'We'll have to send men out to search with lanterns,' Merel said fearfully. 'We have to find him.'

Given the circumstances, it wouldn't have surprised Lucrezia to hear this suggestion greeted with open scorn, but Fraxinus was infinitely more diplomatic than Jacom.

'We'll do the best we can,' he said swiftly, 'but the dragomites and the mound-women are better able to search than we are. I'll find Jume Metra.' He struck a light, and looked about for a lantern. It was only then that Lucrezia saw his face, and Ereleth's. Their expressions were very anxious, and for once the two of them looked very similar – as if events had finally forced them into a community of feeling. She could see the faces of Jacom Cerri and Hyry Keshvara too; they were equally haggard and equally haunted. Lucrezia wondered if her own could be any more serene. She began to scramble to her feet, but Ereleth's hand immediately seized her arm, applying urgent restraint.

'Where are you going?' the queen demanded.

'To help,' Lucrezia replied tersely. Jacom Cerri and Hyry Keshvara still had their favourite blades, and they looked as if they were contemplating going out into the rain.

'You can help by staying where you are, highness,' Fraxinus said. 'The same goes for the rest of you. If Andris is within the dragomites' cordon, they'll find him easily enough. If he's not . . .'

Reluctantly, Lucrezia consented to be still. She realised that the almost painful urge bidding her to action was simple fear. She was mildly surprised by the strength of her reflexive reaction, but she knew that her conscience regarding the fate she had once planned for the big amber had been fully assuaged, and that the person she was really afraid for was herself – and herself alone.

Another face appeared in the lamplit crowd as someone else clambered over the back of the wagon; this one was unhuman.

'Iss not good,' the Serpent said, in a tone which was presumably mournful. Rainwater glistened on its scales, catching the yellow lamplight in such a way as to heighten the natural lustre of its skin. The markings which served in better light to distinguish it from its fellows in human eyes were unclear, but Lucrezia knew that it had to be Mossassor. Neither of its companions would have condescended to bring news.

'What isn't?' Hyry Keshvara demanded.

'Three sstrangerss dead,' Mossassor reported. 'Andris gone. Musst have been sseissed – iss what ssey came for.'

'Why?' Lucrezia asked, of no one in particular. 'What do they want with Andris?'

'Don't know,' Mossassor said.

'He doesn't mean that they came for *Andris*,' Checuti put in. 'He means that they came for *someone*. It was a raid, not an attack.' Nobody bothered to point out to Checuti that Mossassor was an it, not a he.

'Information,' Ereleth opined. 'That's what they came after, under cover of the dark. They wanted to spirit someone away for interrogation. They need to know exactly what risks there'd be in attacking us, because they still don't know what to do about us – the offer to guide us to a bridge over the river was just playing for time. Exactly what lies did you tell them, Carus Fraxinus? How many of them will Myrasol contradict, if he's fool enough to talk at all?'

That must be it, Lucrezia thought. *They didn't believe what we told them while Jume Metra was listening. They want to know if we're prisoners, and whether we'll turn on the dragomites if we get the chance.*

'He's not a fool, majesty,' Fraxinus said, leaving unspoken the *but* which was clearly implied by his anxious tone. It might have been better, Lucrezia thought, had someone who was actually present while Fraxinus was spinning his web of tactful deceptions been taken – but given that no sane kidnapper would have tried to take Dhalla prisoner, the only plausible candidate would have been herself. How much, she wondered, had Andris heard about what Fraxinus had said to Shabir – and how fully had he understood whatever third- or fourth-hand account he had obtained?

That, she quickly realised, was only the beginning of the problem, given that Myrasol's own objectives, if he were to be imprisoned and perhaps tortured, could no longer be assumed to coincide with those of Fraxinus and Ereleth, let alone those of Jume Metra and Mossassor. In fact, she concluded, were it not for Merel Zabio's presence here, the temptation might be very strong for Andris simply to switch sides. But Merel was here, and while her fate hung in the balance Andris would surely be careful.

Even in the uncertain lamplight, Lucrezia could see that similar thoughts were going through every other head in the company. For a few moments, the relentless drumming of rain on canvas seemed very loud indeed, as if its volume were rising to echo the uneasy beating of their hearts.

It was Fraxinus who brought the uncomfortable interval to an end. 'We're no worse off than we were an hour ago,' he said, but as if to give him the lie, Merel Zabio's voice sounded yet again.

'They've got Andris,' she wailed. 'We have to go after him. We have to get him back!'

'I'm afraid we can't do that,' Fraxinus said quietly. 'We have to wait until Shabir comes back to us – and then we have to be very careful and very clever.'

'It seems,' Ereleth said ominously, 'that you might have been mistaken in your estimation of the situation – and the breaking of the wheel increases our danger threefold. We really do need to make contingency plans.' As she spoke her claw-like hand tightened again about Lucrezia's forearm, but this time the gesture was an instruction to be silent.

Lucrezia felt mildly insulted. She knew perfectly well what the phrase *contingency plans* was meant to signify, and why Ereleth was speaking obliquely. *Fraxinus is too hopeful*, she thought. *We're a good deal worse off than we were an hour ago – and Goran only knows what the light will bring when it finally condescends to return.*

'You have to do something,' she heard Merel saying to Fraxinus. 'You have to get him back.'

'I know,' Fraxinus replied, with all apparent sincerity. 'But we can't do anything yet. They won't hurt him, and they've no reason to keep him indefinitely. I'll do everything possible to get him back, Merel – I promise you that.'

'I'm going after him *now*,' Merel answered stubbornly. 'Alone, if I have to.'

Lucrezia judged that Fraxinus must have seized Merel's arm as forcefully as Ereleth had seized hers. 'No!' he said sharply. 'Ask yourself, Merel – what would Andris expect of you? What would he expect of any of us? Would he ask us to take up our arms and attack an entire army, knowing what chaos that would unleash? Or would he ask us to be patient, and give him time to play his own diplomatic game? He'd expect us to trust him, wouldn't he?'

He probably would, Lucrezia thought. *He does have a tendency to lunatic optimism.*

The princess shook off Ereleth's commanding hand and moved to a position where she could confront Merel Zabio. 'Fraxinus is right,' she said to the distraught woman. 'For the moment, your cousin is the one man within ten kims of here who's in no danger of being involved in a pitched battle as soon as the sun comes up. We can't get him back by force – but if he keeps his head, it's still possible that we'll all get out of this alive.'

'They shouldn't have take him!' Merel Zabio objected. 'You said they offered us safe conduct!'

'They came so stealthily,' Fraxinus was quick to point out, 'that they must have been ashamed of their own treachery. Perhaps we should be glad of that, at least. There may be some among Shabir's ranks who hold to the opinion that any trickery might be justified simply because we're keeping company with dragomites and Serpents, and we can only hope that he is man enough to keep his word in spite of that. If Andris has the wit to fuel their doubts and nourish their anxieties, this trick of theirs might well work out to everyone's advantage. He may be able to complete the work I began, and make them see that they should let us alone.'

'We can't bank on that,' Checuti complained.

'But they might torture him!' Merel objected simultaneously.

'They may be barbarians,' Fraxinus countered, 'but they're not fools. They must know that torture is only useful when questioners know exactly what information is to be elicited. It can shake loose a name, or some other vital datum, but it can't help to clarify a situation as confused as this. Don't be afraid, Merel. I think Andris can take care of himself – and there's a chance he can take care of us too.'

Lucrezia could see that Merel wasn't satisfied. How could she be? But this wasn't the first time she'd been separated from her lover – indeed, she'd had a hard time clinging to his side for ten consecutive days since coincidence had first thrown them together. He'd been kidnapped by Checuti's men, pressed into service with Ereleth and spirited away into the hidden heart of a dragomite hive. This adventure would probably seem to him to be mere child's play by comparison with the last.

'We'll get him back if we can,' Lucrezia said to her, meaning the half-promise honestly, 'but we'll have to do it by guile, not by force. Although we have his maps, we still need him – there's not a single person here we'd be content to lose, but he's worth two of most of us when it comes to heavy work and fighting, and we certainly won't let him go easily.'

That drew a sharp look from Ereleth, who was watching her from the shadows, but Lucrezia had ceased caring about Ereleth's sharp looks. Ereleth might be absolutely determined to play queen, house-mother and mentor, but she had no real authority in any of those capacities and Lucrezia understood that as well as anyone else.

'Sleep would be useful now, if we could only get some,' Fraxinus said, soothingly. 'If we can't, let's at least conserve what vestiges of strength we have left. When the rain stops and the sky clears it will all begin again, but let's be quiet now. We'll be more use to Andris if we're as fit as we can be to meet tomorrow's challenges, whatever they might be. The dark-landers will help Aulakh with the wheel, although our best hope of getting under way immediately when the sky clears is that Shabir's men might come up with a usable replacement.'

It was obvious that he was right, and Lucrezia saw Merel Zabio accept it at last. 'I'm going back to the other wagon,' she said sullenly, 'to my own place.' All the rebellion had gone out of her now. She didn't wait to be invited or instructed to stay; she vaulted over the backboard and went back out into the sodden night.

Lucrezia couldn't help feeling a pang of pity for her, even though she was no worse off than anyone else.

'We really are in trouble,' Checuti opined.

'Yes we are,' Fraxinus said. 'But anyone who thinks we can blast our way out is an imbecile.'

Fraxinus was too far away from Checuti to decipher the reply which he muttered beneath his breath, but Lucrezia guessed what it was.

What Checuti had said was: 'Who's *we*?' Only a few days ago he had agreed with Lucrezia that they were all on the same side, but it seemed that he was now having second thoughts. Lucrezia wondered whether Ereleth had had the right idea after all in feeding him the worm that had made him her unwilling slave. For the moment, though, it wasn't Checuti's loyalties that mattered; it was Andris Myrasol's.

12

ANDRIS WAS DREAMING, but he knew that he was dreaming. Indeed, he felt more lucid than he did while he was awake. He felt that he was more conscious now than he had ever been before, even though he knew perfectly well how absurd that was. He felt that he was somehow enlarged, not physically but mentally – as if his intelligence had somehow been enhanced by new perceptions and new subtleties.

At the same time, however, he knew better than to trust the flattering illusion. He knew that it was just a dream.

He dreamed that he was back in the dragomite nest, lost in the labyrinthine guts of the dragomite queen with nothing but a severed head to guide him. He knew that he wasn't really there, but there was nothing reassuring in that knowledge; although he knew he was asleep he could muster no sense of certainty that he would ever wake up again. He was afflicted by a curious gnawing suspicion that he might be here for ever, and a peculiar conviction that in some sense he might already have been here for ever. It was ridiculous, but he couldn't shake off an uneasy feeling that everything he remembered of a life outside the dragomite's capacious womb might be the product of a mere delirium which would be utterly lost if he ceased to keep it constantly in mind.

'It's not so bad,' the head informed him. 'It really isn't. Once you get past the idea that it's unnatural, you'll see that it's perfectly all right.'

'Easy for you to say,' Andris replied glumly. 'You never had legs. You've always been one hundred per cent dragomite below the waist. All you've lost is a heart and a pair of hands that you never used for anything much except scratching your nose with.'

'I had balls,' the head informed him. 'Don't suppose that I never had balls, because I did.'

'Of course you had balls,' Andris said. 'How else would you have fertilised the dragomite queen, so that she could produce all those sweet little mound-women? But where, exactly, *were* your balls? Inside the body of the dragomite queen, that's where. You never had a *prick*, did you? You never had any *fun*. You might have had a brain and a way with words, but when you come right down to it, you were just a boil on the dragomite queen's bum, and you weren't even on the outside of it.'

'We were intimate,' the head confessed. 'But so what? What makes you so great? You're not so very different from me. You're just a walking sperm-factory. So you have your own injector-mechanism – how much of a difference do you think that makes? We're the same, you and I. We're just accessories to the wombs which eggs use as factories to make more eggs. That's all any individual of our kind is – just a clever device worked up by eggs for the purpose of making more eggs. At the end of the day, it's all about eggs – and one egg is as good as another. You know that, don't you? You've seen the produce of the dragomite queen, and you know that an egg is just an egg, whether it carries instructions telling it to develop into a dragomite warrior, or a mound-woman, or . . .'

'Or a Serpent or a Salamander,' Andris finished for him.

'Well, not exactly,' the head said. 'You haven't been listening to Uncle Aulakh, have you? Eggs make Serpents, but Serpents aren't just one more way of making eggs, are they? It's more complicated than that.'

'According to rumour,' Andris told the head, 'they have reproductive organs in their mouths.'

'Maybe so – but they don't get pregnant by kissing. They don't get pregnant at all. There's more than one way for eggs to make more eggs, you see, and the simple ways aren't always the best. You might think that the ways dragomites go about things in the Corridors of Power is bizarre, but there's sense in it somewhere, just as there's sense in the production of giants and all kinds of creatures even stranger than you.'

'I'm not strange,' Andris said.

'You're stranger than you think, *brother*,' the head replied. As soon as the head had said this, Andris realised that there must be something in what it said. He was, after all, lost in a dream that was like no dream he had ever had before, and while he was in it he wasn't entirely himself – or, rather, he *was* entirely himself, and a little bit more as well. It was as if there had been something lurking inside him since the day of his birth which had only now acquired the strength or won the freedom to reveal itself.

'Perhaps I've got Serpent's blood,' he said to the disembodied head which floated in the darkness before him. 'Perhaps I'm just like Princess Lucrezia.'

'Perhaps you haven't,' the head retorted. 'Perhaps you're something quite different.'

'Perhaps I really am half giant,' Andris speculated. 'Perhaps I can feel Salamander's fire burning in my heart.'

'Perhaps you aren't,' the head replied. 'Perhaps you can't.'

Andris was sure that he could feel something. Even though he was dreaming, he was sure that it was something real. Even though it was something he'd never felt before, he was sure that it had always been there. It was a part of him. In fact, it was *him* . . . but he wasn't quite what he had always seemed, even to himself, to be . . .

He struggled to get to grips with this strange new consciousness, but he couldn't. If there was any enlightenment to be found in this inner darkness, he couldn't yet make it flare up. Whatever was in him hadn't yet acquired the power to possess him. He didn't know whether he ought to be sorry about that or not, but it certainly didn't make him feel glad. In fact, it made him feel empty and hollow. He'd never felt empty and hollow before, not even when he was hungry and lonely and utterly desolate. He'd always known who and what he was, and he'd always been full of *himself* . . . but he'd been wrong, in some subtle but nevertheless vital sense, and now he knew that he'd always been empty, and always hollow.

When the dream died, he didn't feel any tremendous relief. He felt, instead, that he was losing something . . . something that he might never regain.

He would have stayed asleep if it could have done any good, but it wouldn't have. The dream was gone.

Andris opened his eyes – not without difficulty, because they were horribly sticky. His head was aching dreadfully and he felt exceedingly thirsty.

Someone must have known that he would wake up thirsty – and, more to the point, must have cared – because a mug full of water was thrust into his hand while he was still fighting to unglue his eyelids, and clever hands helped him guide it to his lips.

He blinked away the stickiness and squinted into the yellow lamplight, trying to identify the face that was staring into his own less than two mets away. He had seen it before, but he couldn't put a name to it.

'Seth?' he asked. Seth was the name that the severed head had given him, before it cut off its own wind – but the face that was staring into his was attached by a perfectly ordinary neck to a perfectly ordinary body.

He felt his body slipping, but the clever hands grabbed him again, and held him until he was able to adjust his position on the chair in which he had been placed. He lurched forward as the cup was taken away, and found a table on which he could prop his elbows.

'You're quite well,' the face assured him. 'The drug will wear off in a minute. There's food on the table when you want it, but you'd better eat it quickly. The general wants to talk to you.'

Mention of the general reminded Andris where he had seen the face before. He had seen it among General Shabir's retinue when the commander of the Eblan army had ridden up to inspect the damage to Phar's wagon. He tried to say something, but his lips were stuck as firmly as his eyelids had been.

'I'm sorry they had to use a second thorn,' the voice said. 'When they saw how big you were, they weren't sure the first would knock you out.'

They haven't the slightest idea, Andris thought, *how big I really am*. But by the time he could speak, he had forgotten what the words meant – if, indeed, they meant anything at all.

13

ANDRIS SAT BACK in his chair, feeling slightly strange but not unduly discomfited. The after-effects of whatever they'd dosed him with had died away to a kind of mild intoxication that was not even unpleasant, and the meal he'd just eaten was by far the best he'd had in some considerable time. It had been a luxury simply to be able to sit at a table, eating from a plate. There had been bread that was no more than two days old, and some kind of pickled vegetable, and some kind of soft cheese whose aroma suggested that it was no more than a day or two past its optimum. There had been a stone jug too, full of water far fresher and tastier than the river water he'd been quaffing of late; he'd already downed two cupfuls, and was nursing a third.

He knew, though, that generosity always had its price, and that he was about to be asked to settle his account in full. 'General Shabir,' he said to the man who had just taken the seat on the far side of the table, to let the grey-haired man know that he was in full possession of his wits. He looked curiously at the two men who had taken the seats to either side.

Shabir was quick to take the hint. 'This is Tarlock Nath,' he said, pointing to his left at a golden some three or four years younger than himself, 'a councilman of Antiar, serving with the Convocation.' Andris took this to mean that Tarlock Nath was a man of some importance – as much importance, at any rate, as a general. The man's clothing was functional, but it was well-tailored and his beard had been recently trimmed by a good barber.

'And this,' Shabir went on, indicating the bronze man who had taken the chair to his right, 'is Amyas, an emissary from lands which lie in the south, beyond Salamander's Fire.'

Shabir was making every effort to speak in a neutral tone, and very politely, but Andris got the distinct impression that the last thing in the world the general wanted was to have these two onlookers present. The way he pronounced the word *emissary* suggested that he was using the word as a diplomatic substitute for something else, but Andris had no idea what Amyas might really be as well as or instead of an emissary. The bronze had the darkest eyes Andris had ever seen, and his gaze was as hard as jet. He looked like a fighting man – in fact, he gave the impression of being engaged in a fight of sorts right now.

Tarlock Nath wasn't so easy to weigh up, but Andris couldn't help wondering whether he too would rather Amyas had stayed in the south, beyond Salamander's Fire. Andris also couldn't help wondering whether a man who had travelled from beyond Salamander's Fire might be a man well worth knowing – if he and the other members of Fraxinus's expedition could contrive to extricate themselves from the trouble they were evidently in.

'My name is Andris Myrasol,' he told them in his turn. He didn't bother to tell them that he came from Ferentina, because he thought it entirely probable that they had never heard of Ferentina.

'So we understand,' the general said, deliberately withholding any explanation of how he had come to understand it.

As Andris took a last draught of good water, he carefully took note of his surroundings. There were four other men in the room apart from those seated at the table, all stationed with their backs to the wall and all dutifully standing to attention. They all wore the same colours as Shabir. They were armed with short spears, much lighter than Xandrian half-pikes, tipped with some glassy substance. Three of them also had metal-bladed knives, but they looked more like eating knives than weapons.

The walls of the room in which the company was assembled had once been painted and mounted with hooks and shelves, but they were in a poor state of repair. There were two doors, one of which presumably led to another room. Andris guessed that they must be in a derelict farmhouse which the Eblan army had commandeered for a temporary headquarters. Daylight shone through the poorly glazed windows but it was very grey, no brighter than a cloudless night. The rain was beating on the roof of the building as relentlessly as it had beaten upon the canvas of the wagon where he had first taken shelter from it. It was difficult to guess how long he might have been unconscious.

'That was some narcotic,' Andris observed, trying to sound courageous. 'I'm a big man – it takes a lot to knock me out.' *Or it used to*, he added silently. *It seems to be happening far too often of late.*

'The Soursweet Marshes are full of poisons,' said Tarlock Nath. 'They come ready mounted in good stout thorns. One has to be careful collecting them, of course, and one has to know exactly what to look for, but bitter necessity has forced us to become familiar with the hostile territories which surround our own narrow land. You haven't thanked us yet for contriving your rescue. You haven't even thanked us for the food – and when one has an army to feed, provisions are very precious.'

Andris set his cup down. He looked at Tarlock Nath warily, then flicked his gaze sideways to take in Shabir and the bronze. 'I'm grateful for the food,' he said, making it clear by his tone that he had chosen the words carefully.

'The cost of bringing you here was three dead men,' Shabir observed acidly. 'I hope the sacrifice was not in vain.'

Andris half-remembered hearing a scream. 'What happened to your three men?' he asked.

'They were killed by dragomites,' Shabir told him.

'If you wanted to talk to one of us,' Andris observed, 'you had only to ask. To send men sneaking through the dragomites' line in the dark and the rain was inviting disaster.'

'The man who spoke to General Shabir the day before yesterday would doubtless have been glad to repeat himself,' Nath said, seemingly enthusiastic to seize the conversational initiative, 'but we thought that it might be more revealing to speak to someone without a dragomite nest-slave in attendance – someone who might tell us the truth. I say again, you do not appear very grateful, although we have rescued you from your monstrous captors.'

What am I supposed to say to that? Andris thought unhappily. *Should I tell them what they want to hear?* He knew that the fate of the expedition might well depend on what he told those people – and that the truth might not be the best available option. Unfortunately, he didn't know how to choose between the many lies that might be offered instead.

'You must forgive me if I seem rude,' Andris said, very carefully indeed. 'My reaction to your drugged dart was doubtless exaggerated by tiredness and hunger. We haven't had a great deal to eat during the last thirty days except for the meat of dragomites.'

'We've eaten plenty of that ourselves,' Shabir growled.

'Our friends,' Nath said, without giving any indication that he meant anyone sitting at the table, 'have told us that the ambers who live in the Forest of Absolute Night have much in common with us, because their land also borders the Dragomite Hills. They are hereditary enemies of the dragomites, as we are. We understand that you are not a darklander yourself, but you will understand in your turn that we find it very surprising that men of your colour are keeping company with dragomites. We concluded that you had no choice in the matter – that the ambers among you, at least, must be prisoners. Were we wrong?'

How does he know that I'm not a darklander myself? Andris wondered. 'I'm a mapmaker from the far north,' he said. 'I was hired by Carus Fraxinus to guide his wagons to Chimera's Cradle, by way of Salamander's Fire. I'd never seen a dragomite until we came into the hills – they're not *my* hereditary enemies.' He glanced at Amyas when he mentioned Salamander's Fire but the bronze did not react at all.

Shabir had grown impatient with evasions. 'Are you or are you not prisoners of the dragomites?' he demanded.

Andris was uncomfortably aware that much was at stake, but he didn't know how to place his bet. He hesitated, but he knew that he couldn't put the matter off. 'No,' he said eventually, on the grounds that the truth would be easier to sustain under prolonged examination. 'We're not prisoners. Our alliance with the dragomites was forged under awkward circumstances, but it's an alliance nevertheless.'

'Dragomites don't make alliances,' Nath said contemptuously. 'Apart from their nest-slaves all humans are their enemies.'

'I think you mistake the relationship between the dragomites and the mound-people,' Andris said, as calmly as he could. 'The mound-women aren't slaves.'

'We've fought the human mound-warriors many times before,' Shabir told him, in a tone edged with subdued anger. 'We knew of the mound-women's existence long before this blight began driving them out of the hills. Slaves or not, they're allied with the dragomites against their own kind, and whatever tie binds them to the creatures seems to be unbreakable. If they had their way they'd help the dragomites establish new nests in our fields, and then defend the mounds. They're traitors to their own kind.'

'Perhaps you didn't know this,' Tarlock Nath added invitingly. 'Perhaps the mound-women have tricked you into some kind of alliance by misrepresenting themselves. If so, your friends stand in desperate need of our aid, for they will certainly be killed – or worse – when they have served their purpose.'

The trouble is, Andris thought, *that he might be right. They're certainly using us, but* . . . He dared not even attempt to explain to folk like these what he had discovered in the depths of the dragomite hive, or the peculiar debt that he owed to a severed head which was not entirely dead. 'That's surely our problem,' he said aloud.

'While you're within our estates,' Nath said, 'we're forced to consider it ours too.'

'When we've crossed this bridge to which the general's men are directing us,' Andris countered, 'we'll be outside your estates, and it'll be ours alone. As I understand it, Carus Fraxinus agreed with you that your soldiers should escort us to the edge of the Spangled Desert so that we could go around your lands. A bargain was made, which you must honour.'

He felt the stares of the three men boring into him. Shabir's disappointment and frustration were almost tangible – he, at least, had hoped to hear a different story. Nath and Amyas were giving little away, even to one another, but Andris got the impression that Amyas might actually be amused by all of this.

'Are you telling me that everyone in your company will take sides with the dragomites if the dragomites are attacked?' Nath asked carefully. 'Even against their own kind?'

'We don't want to fight anyone,' Andris said, although he knew that the simple truth would be construed as an evasion. *Perhaps he's right*, he thought. *Perhaps the sensible thing would be to agree that if he and his men attack the dragomites from the front we'll assault them in the rear. Checuti would say so were he here in my place, and do his best to make it true once they released him – and the darklanders, at least, would surely go along with the plan . . . but it would be an open invitation to disaster nevertheless. What could possibly follow except chaos and confusion? I have to persuade him to grant us the safe passage he promised to Fraxinus, if I can.*

'Nor do we,' the general said. 'But it's sometimes necessary to fight, lest we be destroyed by cunning and deadly enemies. The dragomites are using you. If you can't understand that, you're utter fools. Don't you see that we're your only hope of escaping them?'

'Is it the Serpents who are in control?' Nath asked. 'Are they the ones giving out orders which you dare not disobey?'

'It was the Serpents' intervention which saved us when we were in grave danger in the Corridors of Power,' Andris admitted warily, 'but I don't think they can actually command the dragomites. They certainly haven't issued any orders to us. It's simply that we all seemed to be headed in the same direction, with the same ultimate objective, so we joined forces.'

'What ultimate objective?' Nath demanded.

'We're going to Chimera's Cradle, by way of Salamander's Fire,' Andris repeated.

'But why?' Nath asked, as if it made no sense at all for men to entertain such a desire.

'Because Carus Fraxinus thinks we can,' Andris told him. 'Xandria has been cut off from the regions south of the hills for centuries, and when Fraxinus heard that a way was now open he was seized by a powerful curiosity to see what remains of the places mentioned in the lore of Genesys.'

'Then he's a fool,' Nath said contemptuously. 'You're madmen, to think of making such a journey, out of mere curiosity, and to choose dragomites and Serpents as travelling companions. It's impossible to pass through the Silver Thorns, and I doubt that it's possible to get that far. The southlands are in turmoil – isn't that so, Amyas?'

'My own people are experiencing great difficulties,' the bronze said, speaking for the first time. 'Great enough to bring me to the Nine Towns in search of aid. Our fields are under constant attack by all manner of unearthly creatures, and I fear for our very survival. Even so—'

Nath cut him off abruptly. 'We too are under attack by unearthly things,' he said. 'You must understand how utterly determined we are to preserve our territory against invasion. *We cannot allow the dragomites to enter our lives.*'

Andris didn't doubt that he meant it, and that Shabir was even more determined. He suspected that the strength of their conviction was unlikely to be shaken by mere reason.

'We have some cause to think that there is a way to reach our goal,' Andris said defensively, although it was mere procrastination. 'Last year, one of our company bought certain goods in the Forest of Absolute Night which were said to have come from Chimera's Cradle.'

'*Said to have?*' Nath echoed derisively. 'What goods? Bought from whom?'

'Exotic seeds,' Andris said stiffly, 'including some which grew into poisonous thornbushes when rooted in human flesh. They were sold to a trader named Hyry Keshvara by bronze men, of whose origins your friend here is likely to know far more than I do.'

He was perversely glad to see the astonishment written on the faces of his three interlocutors, and the look of doubt and distress which Nath darted at the mysterious Amyas.

'Not my people!' Amyas was quick to say emphatically. 'Such tainted things were rooted out of our fields when the land was first settled, as they were rooted out of yours. If some madman really did carry such things across the hills, they must have gone westwards around the marshes, through the Pillars of Silence.'

'This is irrelevant,' Shabir said. 'The real question remains. Will your fellows help us against the dragomites when we fall upon them, or will they fight for them? If your friends fight with us, our own casualties will be minimal and most of them will survive, but if they fight with the dragomites we could lose ten times as many and all your companions will be killed.'

Silence fell while Andris hesitated yet again over his answer. He wished that Shabir had said *if* and not *when* – and, for that matter, that he had said *you and your fellows* instead of *your fellows* – but he could no longer cling to the hope that Shabir had the slightest intention of honouring the pact he'd made with Fraxinus, even though he now knew that Fraxinus had not been acting under duress. 'I beg you not to do it,' he said doggedly. 'Fraxinus has given his word that we will go around your land, even if it means that we must cope with the hardships of the

Spangled Desert. If you attack us, you'll lose a great many men – and my fellows would almost certainly wind up dead, whether they fought with the dragomites or against them. Why can't you just let us go, as you agreed to do? Does your word mean nothing?'

'Bargains made under false pretences need not be honoured,' Shabir said angrily. 'Your leader told me lies, and his word means nothing.'

'What lies?' Andris riposted, although – assuming that the third-hand account he'd received of Fraxinus's representations was accurate – he knew perfectly well what lies.

'You don't seem to have any idea how foolish you are,' Nath put in, when Shabir seemed disinclined to specify the lies to which he had referred. 'Surely you don't trust the Serpents? Why do you think they helped you when you were threatened by the dragomites? Don't you know that they want to see humans exterminated, so that they can reclaim the world that once was theirs?'

Andris wondered, unhappily, whether they might possibly be right about that too. According to rumour within the camp, at least one of the Serpents thought that human beings were a kind of disease afflicting the world – but Mossassor had saved Hyry Keshvara's life in the forest, and had saved his own in the depths of the dragomite mound. Mossassor seemed to think that humans had a crucial role to play in countering some terrible threat which both species had to face. 'They have their own reasons for wanting to go to Chimera's Cradle,' he said eventually. 'They sought human allies because they knew they would have to make their way through human lands. They saved our lives, although they certainly had no need to, and then they helped us make a pact with the dragomites because they believed such a pact would be to everyone's benefit. So it would prove, I think, if you will only let us pass unmolested. We have no intention of helping the dragomites to found new nests within your estates – and while they are with us, we have the power to stop them making any such attempt. Were you to attack us, and be defeated, I can't say what the dragomites might do thereafter.'

'They'll rot where they fall,' Shabir said. 'Make no mistake about that. There's no question of defeat – and if you and your companions won't help us, you'll all be killed: every one of you, human and Serpent alike.'

He spoke very insistently, but Andris knew that there was doubt behind the mask – that Shabir was by no means certain of victory if – or when – he attacked the dragomites.

'If I were you,' Andris said, trying to match the calculated menace in the other's voice, 'I'd be careful about making threats. We're not all common men, and we can defend ourselves more cleverly than you think.'

'Oh yes,' Shabir spat back at him, 'you have a giant, have you not? And a half-giant too – except, of course, that *we* have the half-giant now. We are brave and clever fighting men, Andris Myrasol, and we have had abundant opportunity to school ourselves against dragomite warriors. Can you not see that unless your friends fight with us they're all going to die?'

Andris swallowed, and fought to remain calm. 'I don't doubt your bravery for a minute,' he said, after a judicious pause, 'nor do I doubt your skill – but I do understand, as you surely must, that if you carry through this mad plan blood will be shed in torrents, yours as well as ours. Perhaps you can slaughter us all – but at what cost, and for what gain? *We mean you no harm!* We pose no threat to your people or your estates. All we want is to pass quietly by. Watch us every sem of the way, by all means, but let us go about our business, I beg of you.'

'You really would stand with the dragomites?' Shabir said, as if it were beyond any comprehension. 'Freely, and of your own will? You really are their friends, and not their prisoners?'

'I have no particular liking for them,' Andris admitted, 'but Fraxinus and the princess have struck a bargain with them, and I don't think there is one among us who would break the bargain.' He said it unhappily, because he had reason to think that it was a lie, but he said it positively, because he believed that it was what he had to say if there was to be any chance of averting disaster.

Shabir looked away, shaking his head. It was Tarlock Nath who turned to one of the patient soldiers and signalled to him. The man opened the door to an inner room and beckoned to others who were waiting there. Three men came in, two of Shabir's troopers flanking a man who wore a rather different uniform. The third man was limping slightly – from an injury which Andris had once been accused of inflicting.

Andris's heart sank as he realised how Shabir had known that he was not a darklander, and why Shabir had thought it likely that he and his companions were prisoners of the dragomites, desperate for release. Even so, he said: 'I'm very glad to see you alive, Herriman. We feared that you had perished in the hills.'

'We nearly did,' Herriman replied gruffly. He looked around anxiously, his eyes flickering from one face to another. 'What's wrong?' he asked uneasily.

It was Tarlock Nath who answered. 'Everything,' he said.

14

Carus Fraxinus and Ereleth walked with Jume Metra and Mossassor to the place where the two dragomite drones were waiting. Fraxinus tried hard to compose himself; he knew that matters of life and death hung in the balance, and that it might be more difficult to negotiate with these friends than with their enemies.

There was a gnarlytree growing by the riverbank which must have been there for forty or fifty years. Its trunk was extraordinarily thick and seemed more than usually twisted, and its branches formed a dense tangle whose interior was clogged with dead leaves. The heavy rain had released a strange musty stench from that dark heart which Fraxinus found distinctly unpleasant, but the two drones, whose heads were almost touching the lower branches, seemed quite oblivious of it. They seemed to prefer the shade, even though the morning sunlight was very weak. The rain had stopped an hour ago, but the sky was not yet clear of cloud.

The drones had reared up, as they always seemed to do when addressing human beings; they were standing on four legs while their forelimbs hung down like arms. Their heads were tiny by comparison with the huge-jawed warriors, but their eyes were nevertheless enormous by comparison with human eyes, and Fraxinus knew that the soft palps which dangled from their mouths like the tentacles of a squid concealed a sting which could put a human being into a trance for days on end. They were unhuman and they were dangerous; the fact that they were intelligent made them no less unhuman and even more dangerous.

They know the psychological value of great height, Fraxinus thought, as he looked up into the mournful-seeming eyes of the drone that was standing to the left. *How much else do they know about us? Do they know enough to make them confident that they can trust us – or enough to be confident that they cannot?*

Jume Metra took up a position between the two drones, facing Fraxinus and the queen. The drones lowered their antennae so that their tips rested on her shoulders, as if they had some means of transmitting instructions directly into her flesh. Mossassor remained beside Fraxinus, standing to his right while Ereleth stood to his left.

Fraxinus didn't wait to be asked a question. 'Aulakh Phar has counted the Eblans as best he can with the aid of his spy-glass,' he said. 'We can't be sure what strength they have further to the south, but we estimate that they have at least four hundred men surrounding us. General Shabir demands that we get under way immediately, and that we continue without pause until we reach the bridge. He refuses to admit that Andris Myrasol is his prisoner, and insists that the men who broke through the cordon last night were not acting under his orders. He's probably lying, but there's no way to be absolutely certain. He says that he'll do everything in his power to find Andris, and return him safely to us once we've crossed the river.'

Fraxinus presumed that the drones were capable of understanding his speech, even though they couldn't mimic it, for there seemed to be no obvious process of translation going on. It was, of course, Jume Metra who replied.

'We do not want to fight,' she said. 'If we can pass unmolested through this land, that is what we must do.'

'We certainly don't want to fight,' Fraxinus said. 'I hope that Andris Myrasol has done everything within his power to convince them of that, if he is indeed Shabir's prisoner.'

The trailing antennae stirred then, and Metra reached up to touch her fingers to their tips. 'They want him to fight for them,' she said, after a brief interval. 'They went all of you to fight with them, against the nest and the Serpents.'

Fraxinus glanced sideways at Mossassor. 'Andris won't do that,' he said, trying to sound as if there could be no possible doubt about the fact. 'He'll do everything he can to rejoin us. He and Merel Zabio are lovers . . . do you understand what that means?'

'Ssink sso,' said Mossassor, very dubiously. Aulakh Phar had tried to explain human reproduction while attempting to gain information about the Serpents' methods of procreation, and had probably succeeded in giving away far more information than he'd obtained in return.

'No,' said Jume Metra, on behalf of the drones. It was ironic, Fraxinus thought, that the drones – who were males, and thoroughly familiar with the concept of sexual differentiation – should be less able to comprehend his meaning than the sexless Serpent.

'It's like being nest-mates,' Fraxinus said, hoping that the word would carry the right implications. 'It means he'll do everything he can to be reunited with her, and to make sure that no harm can come to her.'

Metra had to look up, and she raised her hands a little higher to caress the fast-moving antennae in a fashion that Fraxinus couldn't help but think of as *loving*.

'The man who was taken is one of those who came into the nest,' Metra said. 'He was the one who spoke to a human drone.'

Fraxinus couldn't tell whether she was saying that because the drones approved of the fact, or because they didn't; he could only hope that it was the former.

'He did what the human drone asked of him,' Fraxinus said. 'The drone called him brother, and he answered. He promised to keep the head of the drone, and to revive it if ever he found a way. He'll try to honour his word – that's another reason why he'll come back if he possibly can. He understands that we're all in this together, humans, Serpents and dragomites alike.'

'Will the horsemen attack us?' Metra asked, her voice softening just a little. 'We must decide how to prepare.'

'I honestly don't know,' Fraxinus said. 'If they're honourable men, they'll keep their word. If they're reasonable men, they must be able to see that the best outcome for everyone is that we be allowed to go peacefully on our way. Unfortunately, they're frightened men, and their fear might be great enough to overrule both their honour and their reason.'

The antennae danced, and Jume Metra's face darkened ominously.

'Iss not enough,' Mossassor hissed in Fraxinus's ear. 'Droness musst know how to prepare warriorss.'

'I'm sorry,' Fraxinus said again. 'I can't tell whether they'll stick to the agreement or not. I honestly don't know what instructions you should give to your warriors.'

Life must be simpler in the Dragomite Hills, he thought. *There, it's a simple matter of who's part of the same nest and who's not. The only other issue to be settled is the rules of engagement. They've probably never been in a situation where they couldn't make a straightforward distinction between the nest and everything else. That's what's really upsetting their calculations. It's easy enough to tell the warriors how to act and react to Shabir's men – what's proving difficult is instructing them how to act and react to us. They don't want to categorise us as nest-mates if we're likely to turn against them, but they saw that barricade and understood its meaning. They know that their chances of getting out of this predicament and keeping alive the possibility of founding a new nest somewhere else are very slim if they have to do it without our help.*

'If we have to fight,' Metra said, 'we must all fight together: all of one mind and all of one purpose.'

'Yess,' said Mossassor quickly. 'Iss true. All musst fight, including serpentss. Iss time. Cannot go back. Musst ssearssh for garden.'

They're all frightened, Fraxinus thought. *Serpents and dragomites alike. And why not? How could they be incapable of fear, given that they're reasoning beings? They're in search of reassurance; I only wish that I had some to offer. I doubt that they'd thank or forgive me for a smooth lie.*

Fraxinus looked at Ereleth. He knew that he could depend on her to echo what the Serpent had said, with proper alacrity, but he had no idea whether he could depend on her to mean it. She was, after all, a queen – and a witch-queen at that. He didn't suppose that Mossassor had any more confidence in Ssifuss and Ssumssarum – but they hadn't attempted to go back either, even though they were the only ones who might be confident that they could cross the hills safely.

'We're all in this together,' Ereleth said, on cue, looking up into the faces of the drones. 'You're right – if we're to survive, we must be all of one mind and all of one purpose. Instruct your warriors that we are nest-mates, and that we'll fight alongside them, all for one and one for all.'

She understands what this is all about, Fraxinus thought.

Thus far, the warriors have been instructed to protect us, but not to treat us as nest-mates. They have been ready to act against us if ever we should appear to be threatening their interests. If there is to be a pitched battle, though, there can be no more ambiguity; they must either trust us or treat us as enemies. But if they trust us, they render themselves vulnerable; they know it, and they're afraid. What would their reaction be if they knew that Aulakh Phar is mixing plastic even as we speak, and that Checuti is using it to make bombs? What would they do if they knew that Ereleth has given her blessing to it, and that I have not done all I could to forbid it?

'What we must all remember,' Fraxinus said carefully, 'is that no one wants a bloody battle. The general may well have summoned more men to ride northwards and swell his forces, but even if he were to amass a thousand men by tomorrow noon he couldn't come against us without incurring heavy losses. He must understand that there is no need for that – that all he has to do is keep pace with us for four or five days, and see us safely into the fringes of the Spangled Desert. He can then set a few dozen scouts to patrol the eastern marches and make sure that we don't return. I hope he will do exactly that – but if he breaks his word, we will honour the promises which the queen and the princess gave to your queen; we will fight alongside you to preserve the egg-carriers and the nest.'

To himself, meanwhile, he said: *I mean what I say, because I have to. I have no choice. I only hope Ereleth can see that as clearly as I do, and that she can keep Checuti under control.*

The dangling antennae were still moving furiously; the drones' eyes looked even more mournful than before.

'That is good,' Jume Metra said, without a trace of joy or satisfaction in her voice. 'We will go forward now. You have our word that we will do everything in our power to defend you, if the need arises. Until the dragomite queen can be reborn, we are all of one purpose, all of one will.'

'Yess,' said Mossassor. 'Iss good. Iss nessessary. Iss time.'

Fraxinus looked up at the staring eyes of the two drones, and nodded his head, as if an unbreakable bargain between the three species really had been sealed.

What a wonderful world it would be, he thought, *if such speeches really could mean something – if we really could communicate with one another despite our different languages and all the imperfections of translation.*

15

ONE OF SHABIR'S men ushered Andris and Herriman down an unrailed flight of steps into a windowless cellar hollowed out beneath the farmhouse. Andris felt his feet squelching uncomfortably inside his boots as he descended. He must have been inside for at least ten hours but his clothes were still damp and the chill of the cellar seeped through them in seconds.

By the light of the soldier's candle Andris saw that the cellar was smaller by at least a met in each dimension than the room above – a useful precaution given the friability of the stone which was the favoured building material hereabouts – but it was still reasonably capacious. The soldier hesitated for a moment but eventually passed the candle down for Andris to take. Andris accepted it, and studied his surroundings carefully. The litter on the paved floor was evidence that it had recently been packed with supplies of various kinds, but everything had now been cleared save for a few empty sacks. An army on the move required its food, spare clothing and ammunition to be close at hand and easy of attainment.

'Stay here,' the soldier said, as he turned to go up the stairway while Andris and Herriman stepped down to the floor. 'The general will send for you if he needs to talk to you again.'

Andris didn't bother to ask whether he was a prisoner. Unshackled he might be, but it was patently obvious that Shabir had not the slightest intention of letting him return to the beleaguered wagons. Small trickles of dust were falling from the ceiling, dislodged by the booted feet tramping back and forth on the floor above.

'It seems, sir, that we're fated to be at cross purposes,' Herriman said, with a sigh. 'I swore to those men that you must all be prisoners of the dragomites, desperate for rescue. You've sorely disappointed them – an' me too.'

'Where are Purkin and the others?' Andris asked, as soon as the retiring soldier had closed the trapdoor that gave access to the cellar. 'Have they joined Shabir's army?'

Herriman barked out a short laugh. 'Not us! We only just got out of one army – Purkin weren't about to volunteer us for another. We had a nasty meetin' with a big team of dragomites just as we reached the end of the hills – fourteen warriors an' a dozen workers. Had to run into the marshes to get away. Bad place, the marshes – everythin' seems to be poisoned, an' your skin starts crawlin' within hours. Horses hated it. Made our way out when we thought it was safe, an' then we all but met the dragomites comin' the other way, with that lot upstairs in hot pursuit. None of us wanted to be drafted, so we faded back into the marshes until we'd skirted their positions. They don't keep watch on the marshes. Purkin wanted to go a long way south before cuttin' in to one of the towns, but once we were on a real road it weren't long before we bumped into *him*.'

'Him?'

'Tarlock rottin' Nath. He had a handful of armed men with him, but not real soldiers – servants, I'd say. An' that bronze with the snaky stare. Purkin figured they couldn't take us, so he tries to find out how the land lies – an' before you know it, Nath's volunteerin' to hire the lot of us. Sent Purkin and the lads on to some place called Antiar – next town south of Ebla I think, fourth or fifth in the string. Brought me on with him to tell Shabir what had happened in the hills. Wanted Shabir to bail you out of trouble – which is what Shabir wanted too, until you blew it. That is, he wanted to bail Fraxinus and Ereleth out of trouble. Don't suppose he cared one way or the other about *you*.'

Andris didn't suppose so either. 'I suppose you told them about Djemil Eyub's men being slaughtered by mound-women?' he said tiredly.

'Didn't see any reason not to. How was I to know Fraxinus had given Shabir a different story? Didn't seem to care much, mind – no love lost between Eyub an' Shabir, it seems, even if they do come from the same town. Gave me a filthy shock when they brought you back, I can tell you – I thought you were dead and gone, an' there you were, jabberin' away in your sleep like somethin' demented. How did you get out of that rottin' nest? Did you really make a deal with those filthy things?'

'What choice did we have?' Andris countered sharply. He wished that he didn't feel so cold and wet. 'It was deal or die, so we dealt. We tried to do the same with Shabir, but it looks as if it's all gone wrong. They're going to attack, aren't they?'

Herriman shrugged. He tested the floor with his hand. It was evidently dry enough to suit him, because he immediately sat down, placing his back against the wall and stretching his legs out. Andris set the candle-tray down on the floor and joined him, although his wet trousers felt very uncomfortable. The sound of booted feet had died away now; it was silent up above.

'Look at this way,' Herriman said. 'Whatever happens, you and me're out of it. Maybe you can make a deal with Nath like the one Purkin made, but even if that goes sour, what can happen? We can get drafted, we can get thrown in jail – but nobody'll be comin' after us with spears or jaws. I been in jail before, an' so have you. Even in the army or in jail we get fed, an' the food's not bad. Could be a lot worse.'

'Merel's back there with the wagons and the dragomites,' Andris said bluntly. 'Anything that happens to them happens to her. If she dies . . .'

'What're you goin' to do?' Herriman asked scornfully. 'Take on the whole rottin' army?'

Andris didn't dignify that with a reply. 'What kind of deal did Purkin make with Nath?' he wanted to know. 'And where does the bronze fit in?'

'Don't know about the bronze,' Herriman replied negligently. 'Nath don't seem to like him much – which is odd, seeing as they're ridin' together – but I don't know where he comes from or why he came. No love lost between Nath an' Shabir – this place is a real pit of snakes, if you know what I mean. Seems like nobody likes anybody, although I dare say they get on all right when they're not so scared. I don't know what they're scared of, but I think bad things are happenin' down south an' every southerner in Shabir's army wants to go home. Nath says he speaks for somethin' called the Convocation, but if you ask me he's playin' strictly for himself. He hired us because he's shoppin' for good strong men who know how to handle themselves an' don't have any divided loyalties. I should've deserted in Khalorn with the rest of 'em – but how can you tell, hey? My leg still hurts, you know.'

'It wasn't me that broke it,' Andris reminded him. 'If it gives you any comfort, the last time I saw the man who did he'd just been floored by a giant. It's anyone's guess whether he ever got up again. Is there a chance that the army will fall apart rather than follow Shabir into battle? Is the pit of snakes that close to utter confusion?'

'No idea,' Herriman said. 'But this place isn't an empire like Xandria – it's some kind of *democracy*. Which means every man for himself unless he can see a bloody good reason for helpin' somebody else. Whatever's happenin' way downriver, it's stirrin' up some disturbin' rumours.'

'At a guess,' Andris said thoughtfully, 'I'd say that under normal circumstances the Nine Towns are in conflict with one another – not war, exactly, but not-very-friendly rivalry. Like the dragomite hives, I suppose. When everything's going well it's your immediate neighbours you see as your competitors. At present, things are definitely not going well, and the rivals have all been forced to band together to stop the dragomite invasion. The Convocation must be a kind of super-council made up of men from the town councils, and the military units that normally serve particular towns have been combined into a makeshift army . . . with all the fellowship and harmony you'd expect. Does that fit in with your observations?'

'Sounds about right,' Herriman admitted. 'Wouldn't like to be in Shabir's shoes if this all blows up – he's the one who'll have to stop the rot.'

'No wonder he didn't like what I had to say,' Andris mused. 'I really did disappoint him, didn't I? He was desperate for better news. But I've never been a clever liar – haven't had enough practice, I suppose. And what good would it have done to tell him a pack of lies?'

'None,' Herriman assured him. 'If you'd told him what he wanted to hear, we'd still be in the thick of it. Like I said, things could be a lot worse. Count your blessings. Your girlfriend ain't dead yet – maybe you can still get a happy endin'.' He didn't sound confident about that; in fact, he sounded like a liar who hadn't had enough practice.

'I've got to get out of here,' Andris said, rising to his feet again. 'I've got to get back to the wagons.'

'No chance,' Herriman said. 'There's a whole rottin' army between here and there – an' another war to fight if you got there. Nothin' we can do. Pity about the princess, though. She was cute.'

Andris ignored the clear implication that Merel wasn't cute – or, at least, not cute enough for a man of such refined tastes as Trooper Herriman. 'There are times,' he muttered, 'when a man has to make his move, no matter how bad a liar he is. I've got to try to stop this farce.' While he was speaking he rose to his feet, moved to the steps and began to climb them two at a time. Herriman didn't say a word.

When he got to the top of the stairway Andris shoved the trapdoor, but he wasn't in the least surprised when it didn't budge. He looked down at Herriman, who hadn't moved. 'Well?' he said. 'Are you coming or not?'

'It's locked,' Herriman pointed out.

'No it isn't,' Andris told him. 'It hasn't got a bolt on it. They've just moved something heavy on top of it.'

'They're still up there,' Herriman complained, looking up at the silent boards from which dust had now ceased falling. 'They've gone outside, but they haven't gone away. Not all of them.'

'I know,' Andris said. 'That's what I'm counting on. Coming?'

Herriman shrugged and got to his feet. Andris braced himself on the stone steps, set both his hands upon the trapdoor, and heaved with all his might. The table whose leg had been placed on the trapdoor was solid enough, but Andris was a strong man. The table tilted and fell; the trapdoor splintered in his hands.

By the time Andris had risen to his full height – with his feet still on the steps – three of Shabir's soldiers had raced back into the cottage to confront him. One carried a spear, one had a two-met bow with an arrow ready notched, and the third carried a curious object which Andris identified as a miniature crossbow. It was the man with the crossbow whose eyes he met, because it was easy enough to guess what kind of darts the weapon was designed to fire.

'Wait!' he cried, raising his arms high above his head. 'I have to talk to the general. He's making a terrible mistake.'

While the three soldiers thought about it, Andris lifted his legs clear of the trapdoor and stepped back against the wall, with his arms still upraised.

'It's a trick,' opined the man with the spear. 'Kill them now and get it over with.' Herriman, who had poked his head out of the hole, immediately ducked down again, but he needn't have worried.

'No!' cried the man with the crossbow, with genuine urgency in his voice. 'Orders!'

'Orders said not to let 'em escape,' said the man with the longbow, although he was clearly hesitant.

'I don't have time for this,' said Andris, kneeling to pick up the table which was now lying on its side. It took no more than half a second to position it before himself as a shield, but it was as well that it took no longer than that. The bowman's arrow thudded into the wood mere sems from the protective edge, while the drugged dart from the crossbow glanced off the corner.

Andris charged. The man with the spear stood his ground but he had no chance against the hurtling table, which knocked him flat. The other two had turned to run, but the table caught them in the back before they reached the door, and sent them both spinning into the wall, which they hit with bone-bruising force.

Andris had to drop the table to get out through the door, and he wasn't in the least surprised to find that there were more than a hundred men within bowshot of the cottage, all of them busy loading carts, saddling horses and putting on armour, most of which was made from dragomite chitin.

Andris put his hands to his mouth to form a trumpet and yelled at the top of his voice: 'General Shabir! There's something you ought to know!'

More than a hundred pairs of eyes were instantly turned towards him. Andris drew himself up to his full height, and let his shirt fall open at the collar to expose his amber chest. It was obvious that few of the watchers had ever seen an amber, let alone one of his impressive size. He held his breath for a second or two, fearing that an arrow might come whizzing in his direction, but none of the soldiers moved – they hadn't been set to guard him, and most of them presumably hadn't known that he was a prisoner.

'No,' he said at the top of his voice to the nearest of the

watchers, as if the slack-jawed man had spoken to him. 'I'm not the giant. The giant's twice as big as I am, and a lot nastier – but she isn't the one you ought to be afraid of. She's not the one that'll kill you all.'

He could see that he had their attention.

'Shabir!' he yelled again. 'There's something you have to know before you lead these men to certain death!'

It would have been convenient had Shabir been out of earshot. That would have given him time to make a long speech to the entire throng – and hence, indirectly, to every single man in the ramshackle army. But the general was not out of earshot and he was hurrying back, with his own sword drawn and a company of officers behind him.

Shabir was no fool. 'Get back inside!' he howled. 'Now! Or you die!'

Andris stood where he was, trying not to flinch. The general was still ten strides away. 'If you kill me before you hear my warning,' he shouted, 'you'll regret it.' He felt a distinctly ungentle prick in his back, and knew that the spearman he had bowled over had recovered his feet and his weapon, but not necessarily his temper. Within a further two seconds the point of Shabir's own narrow blade was at his throat.

'Anything you have to say, half-giant, you can say inside,' the general told him. Both points had already drawn blood, and Andris had no doubt that he was far too close to death for comfort.

'All right,' he said, in a slightly more moderate tone. *It doesn't matter*, he told himself. *In fact, it's better this way. Rumours thrive on uncertainty. If the general stifles reports of what I actually say, there'll be speculations aplenty to fill in the void.*

He stepped back into the cottage. All three of the guards were on their feet now. None had been seriously injured but they were all in a violent mood. There was no sign of Herriman, who had obviously made a tactical retreat to the cellar.

'What are you trying to do?' Shabir hissed, as he tried to close the door behind him. 'What trick are you trying to play?' Andris was glad to notice that it hadn't closed; the crowd without was too eager, and the officers who had scuttled in Shabir's wake were more enthusiastic to find out what was going on than to shoo the men away.

'It's not a trick,' Andris lied, with all the conviction he could muster. 'It's an honest warning. Did Herriman tell you, perchance, that Ereleth is King Berlin's witch-queen, and that Princess Lucrezia has been her lifelong apprentice?'

'Do you take us for superstitious fools?' Shabir snarled, seemingly taking greater offence at that insinuation than at Andris's violence towards his men. 'Do you think us so uncivilised as to be afraid of *magic*? We have no queens in the Nine Towns, but we are by no means short of witches. We have our hagwives and our hedge-riders, our brewers of aphrodisiacs and poisons. We know exactly what magic can do – and what it cannot.'

'And in Xandria,' Andris told him, with what seemed to him to be a very creditable sneer, 'they know that the lore extends far beyond the mental horizon of hagwives and hedge-riders. In Xandria, they know that there is a magic fit for queens and the maintenance of empires. In Xandria, the secrets of the most powerful poisons of all have been jealously guarded. Xandria is famous for its walls, but its best defence is the citadel within the citadel, where the ultimate weapon is kept – or was, until Lucrezia was carried out of the citadel by reckless robbers, and Ereleth came to find her. That ultimate weapon is now in Carus Fraxinus's wagons – and if death threatens either the witch-queen or her apprentice, it will certainly be unleashed.'

'I have told you,' Shabir said, with very convincing contempt, 'that we are not the kind of fools who fear magic. We may have less metal than the men of the north, but we are civilised and knowledgeable men.'

'You might be right to doubt the power of magic,' Andris said, carefully laying out what he thought was his trump card, 'but dare you doubt the power of plague, when you have seen what has happened to the Dragomite Hills? Ereleth and Princess Lucrezia bear about their slender waists the seeds of a disease which could wreck the Nine Towns as comprehensively as the hills have been wrecked. They are trained to release that plague if and when their defenders are destroyed. If you attack the wagons, you have far more to fear from victory than defeat.'

'You're lying!' Shabir said immediately.

'I'm not,' Andris retorted, although he knew that the general knew perfectly well that he was. He also knew that the general knew perfectly well that it probably wouldn't make any difference whether Andris was lying or not. If the rumour was put about, the mere possibility would be enough to make his men think twice about launching themselves into a closely fought contest with a will to win.

'You'll regret this foolery, Andris Myrasol,' the general said, in a calmer tone of voice. 'I promise you that. However the coming battle goes, you'll regret this stupid intereference for the rest of your short and miserable life. You were safe until you opened your mouth, but now you've sealed your own doom. Give me that!'

The last words were not addressed to Andris, but to the man with the crossbow, who had recovered his dart. The man handed it over. Andris saw that it was no more than a weighted thorn, carefully fletched to fly straight.

Shabir's slender fingers clenched about the fletchings, crushing them. He held the thorn as if it were a tiny dagger, and he thrust it into Andris's belly with all the force he could muster. If Andris hadn't folded up reflexively, it could easily have punctured his gut. Because he flinched, however, it didn't go in as deeply as it might have done. Even so, Andris gasped and clutched his stomach.

As Andris had previously had occasion to observe, the narcotic was very powerful. Less than five seconds passed before he felt his head swimming and his limbs turning to water.

As he crumpled up, falling to his knees and then tumbling sideways, he heard Shabir say: 'We'll collect you when it's over. When all your friends are dead, we'll send you to join them.'

16

THE BRIDGE WAS not what Lucrezia had expected or hoped. It was not a single span extending from one bank of the river to the other but had three separate sections, each of which could be reckoned a bridge in its own right.

The fact that the river was here divided into three channels by two wooded islands had doubtless made it easier for the men of the Nine Towns to construct a crossing at this point, but it made it virtually impossible to see from one bank to the other. A few red-tiled roofs could be glimpsed through the trees that crowded the islets, but the further spans were quite invisible from the stone quay to which Shabir's men had led the wagons.

The nearest of the three bridges was the only one which Lucrezia could see clearly from the shore; it was further divided by a central column of stone blocks which had presumably been placed in the stream by its builders. The tree-trunks which had been used to construct the bridge itself looked reasonably sturdy, and they provided a platform wide enough for a wagon, but Lucrezia knew how deceptive such structures could be. The evil workings of corruption and corrosion were always enhanced by the erosions of flowing water.

The far bank of the river was not nearly as empty of trees and bushes as the nearer one, so it was difficult to judge whether the rooftops were those of a fair-sized hamlet or merely a cluster of cottages built about the bridgehead. There was such a cluster on the bank where they were, but the houses were all derelict. It was difficult for Lucrezia to judge whether those on the far bank were in a similar condition. There was no smoke rising from their chimneys, but that meant nothing.

It was well-nigh impossible to gauge what potential there might be for soldiers to lie in wait beyond the buildings on the far bank, and Lucrezia knew that there was cause for anxiety in that. Crossing the bridges would be a slow and awkward business, and while the caravan was engaged in that process it would probably be easy enough for Shabir's soldiers to contrive a deadly trap, were they so minded. The men set to guide the wagons had dropped back before the column reached the bridge, but Lucrezia knew that there must be several hundred men set in various positions to the south and the west. If there were hundreds more on the far side, the logical time for them to attack would be while the wagons were making the crossing and the company of dragomites divided.

The same thoughts had evidently occurred to everyone else. 'There might be a hundred men hiding on each of those islands,' Dhalla observed dolefully. She was standing to the left of the larger wagon, while Ereleth and Lucrezia sat side by side on the driver's bench. The queen was holding the reins.

'We'll have to send a party in advance to search them,' Ereleth agreed. 'We should do it now, while Fraxinus is still away.'

Fraxinus had ridden off with Merel Zabio and Jume Metra to make one last demand for the release and return of Andris Myrasol. It was a bold move, for there was a chance that they too might be taken prisoner, but if Fraxinus had not agreed to go Merel would certainly have gone alone, and once Fraxinus had agreed Jume Metra had insisted on going too. Although the dragomite workers and warriors had now been instructed to treat the members of the expedition as nest-mates there still seemed to be a margin of trust lacking between the drones and Fraxinus.

Aulakh Phar and Checuti walked forward to join Dhalla. They had dismounted from the smaller wagon, which had now pulled up behind the larger one. It looked very rickety in spite of the sterling work Phar had done – in exceedingly difficult circumstances – by way of adapting the spare wheel which the Eblans had belatedly provided.

Jacom Cerri rode up on the other side. He seemed more doleful than anyone.

'It would be best to send a handful of dragomite warriors ahead to flush out any treachery,' Aulakh Phar said, obviously of the opinion that in Fraxinus's absence the power of decision rested with him and not with Ereleth, 'but we shall need Metra to organise it for us. Her sisters seem to be incapable of making any positive move without her.'

Lucrezia had not had much to do with the other mound-women who accompanied the dragomites, but she had observed that they were markedly reluctant to display the slightest initiative. 'We are all of one mind here,' the mound-women had continually assured her when she was a captive in the nest – but what they meant by that was that everyone there looked to a higher authority to instruct them what to do. In the absence of a human queen, authority over her sisters had evidently devolved to Jume Metra, the mouthpiece of the drones.

'If there's a second army waiting on the far bank,' Checuti said, 'we'll be like ears of wheat caught between two implacable millwheels. If they're planning treachery, now is the time they'll show their hand.'

'Let's hope that they have better sense,' Lucrezia said, fearful that such talk might easily get out of hand.

'There are no boats waiting where the river narrows,' Phar pointed out, 'and nothing upstream at all. They might hope to box us off on the bridge, but they couldn't attack us there without boats.'

The three Serpents had been walking alongside the dragomite drones away to the left of the column, but now Mossassor came to talk to the humans. 'Iss good,' it said, in an earnestly sombre tone which belied the optimistic judgment. 'All iss well – sshall find thingss eassier on far sshore.'

'Riders approaching!' Hyry Keshvara called out. The trader was stationed some way behind the small wagon, watching the expedition's rear. A few moments later, she added: 'Fraxinus is with them, but they're at least ten in number. Can't see any ambers among them.'

Lucrezia jumped down to join Dhalla, Phar and Checuti. They went together to the place where Keshvara's horse was standing. The dragomites to either side of them had needed no command to draw themselves into a careful formation; the egg-carrying workers and the drones were now guarded on every side by alert warriors. Ssifuss and Ssumssarum continued to keep close company with the drones.

It was easy to see, as the riders approached, that Carus Fraxinus was not a happy man. He was hollow-eyed and tight-lipped, and Lucrezia judged that he was seething with suppressed annoyance. The Eblans had obviously refused to set Andris Myrasol free, at least for the time being. Merel Zabio looked even less happy; she was making not the slightest attempt to control or conceal her ire. Jume Metra was as expressionless as ever. Lucrezia observed, however, that the soldiers grouped about their brave general, serving as an escort for the entire party, looked no happier than anyone else.

Fraxinus didn't dismount in order to make his report; he clearly intended his words to be audible to everyone.

'General Shabir insists that he is unable to secure Andris Myrasol's release until we have crossed the river,' he announced. 'The general has given his word that he will do all he can to find Andris and to send him after us with all possible speed. I have talked with a man named Tarlock Nath, who is a member of the elected council which rules one of the Nine Towns and a delegate to the Convocation which binds the towns together; he has given me the same assurance. It doesn't seem to me that there's any point in creating a deadlock by refusing to move until Andris is returned, so I've agreed to begin moving across the river. Jume Metra or one of her sisters must take an advance party of six dragomite warriors to make sure that the far end of the crossing is secure; then Aulakh Phar must examine the bridges themselves, to make sure that they'll bear the weight of the wagons.'

While Fraxinus was speaking Jume Metra had ridden to the place where the drones were and had dismounted from her horse. As soon as Fraxinus was finished she and two of her sisters moved away, leading three warriors. They were joined by three from the second formation. The remaining dragomites moved nearer to the wagons, coming as close as they had ever been throughout the time they had kept pace with Fraxinus's expedition.

Lucrezia watched Metra's advance party cross to the first island. They didn't pause to make a thorough search of the trees which grew there, but Lucrezia knew that the dragomites had a keen enough sense of smell to detect any humans riding close by.

When the warriors had passed out of sight Lucrezia turned back again to watch Shabir and his men. They were holding their positions, although some of the spearmen looked as if they would far rather have retreated.

Perhaps we should seize Shabir as our hostage, Lucrezia thought, *and take him across the river with us, only giving him back when his friends send Andris to join us*. She knew, though, that any hostile move might bring down a full-scale assault. That was presumably why Fraxinus was biding his time.

'Shall I start checking the timbers now?' Phar asked. 'There's surely no need to wait for Metra to report back before I begin.'

'If you wish,' Fraxinus said, speaking as much for Shabir's benefit as Phar's. 'Take care.'

The latter remark was accompanied by a meaningful look directed at Jacom Cerri, who nodded to show that he understood. The captain drew his sword as he too stepped out on to the bridge behind Aulakh Phar. When Phar knelt down to test the solidity of the timbers making up the bridge Jacom remained standing, darting his eyes rapidly to either side.

Merel Zabio got down from her horse and came to join the waiting crowd. Her expression was thunderous. Lucrezia guessed that she had come to the very brink of mutiny, and now held her peace only because she trusted Fraxinus not to abandon Andris. Lucrezia moved to the girl's side, and murmured: 'Don't despair. Treachery would serve no one's purpose now.'

'They've already proved themselves treacherous,' Merel retorted, not without reason. 'Who knows what their true purpose may be, or how they'll serve it?'

'Unfortunately,' said Checuti, who had also moved close in order to lend her moral support, 'we no longer have any alternative but to wait until they actually launch an attack before taking action of our own. It's best to hope that they're men of their word, even though we cannot quite believe it. I don't know why they risked a raid to kidnap one of us, but I suspect that they didn't get the news they were looking for. Andris is no use to them, Merel – they've no reason to keep him.'

'They had no reason to take him,' Merel said, 'and I've no reason to believe their filthy general when he says he doesn't know where Andris is.'

'Checuti's right,' Lucrezia said. 'We have to hope, while there is still a chance that everything might work out.'

'What do you care?' Merel snapped, in a manner profoundly unbefitting her station. 'You don't care about Andris.'

'Yes I do,' the princess replied evenly. 'We need him. We're too few to regard anyone as expendable. He has the strength and the luck of two ordinary men. We all want him back.'

'I'm not sure he'd agree about the luck,' Checuti murmured wryly. 'He'd certainly prefer it if you'd said *the wit* – although, of course, I'm the only man here with wit enough for two.'

Lucrezia was glad to be able to smile, albeit thinly. She had learned to appreciate the relief that humour provided in fearful situations, and when it came to that kind of black-edged wit Checuti was well enough endowed for three, let alone two.

Aulakh Phar and Jacom Cerri had moved out of sight now, but Jume Metra came back into view, hurrying without actually breaking into a run.

'There's no sign of any men waiting on the far side,' she reported. 'Not within bowshot, at any rate. The houses are half-ruined. The islands are clear, but the rain has made them very muddy – worse for wagons and horses than the timbers of the bridges.'

It was, Lucrezia thought, as satisfactory a report as they could reasonably have expected – but the fact that no men were waiting within bowshot of the distant bridgehead didn't mean that no men were waiting a little farther beyond, ready to move forward.

'We'll wait just a little while longer,' Fraxinus said, raising his voice so that everyone, including Shabir's party, could hear. 'When Aulakh says it's safe, we'll begin to move across. Who'll steer the larger of the carts?'

'I will,' Ereleth was quick to say. Fraxinus nodded immediately.

'I'll drive the smaller one,' Checuti volunteered. Fraxinus sanctioned that too, with a wave of his hand.

'Everyone else who can ride should be mounted,' Fraxinus said. 'Jume Metra and these dragomite warriors will remain at the end of the column to guard the rear. The workers and the drones will cross after the second wagon. Is that agreeable to everyone?' He glanced down at Jume Metra so that she could confirm the arrangements. She did so. 'The donkeys had better cross between the two wagons,' he went on. 'Merel, can you and

Aulakh ride alongside with the darklanders, keeping them together?'

'Yes,' said Merel tersely.

Lucrezia went to saddle her horse. Dhalla followed her, staying within half a dozen mets, and began to saddle her own gigantic mount. Shabir and his escort were moving away now, but they took care to remain within sight. The vanguard of their company was no more than a hundred and fifty mets away, arrayed in such a fashion that they could mount a cavalry charge immediately the order was given, if they had a mind to. Lucrezia hoped that it was merely a precaution, although every instinct told her that it wasn't.

By the time she had mounted up Aulakh Phar and Jacom Cerri had returned. They confirmed what Jume Metra had said – that the bridges themselves seemed sound enough, but that the islands were very boggy and that there was some danger of the wagons becoming enmired, even though their loads were less considerable now than at any other time since leaving Khalorn.

Mud seemed a trivial enough challenge by comparison with those they might have encountered, and Lucrezia could see that Fraxinus was becoming more hopeful by the minute; he, at least, was a natural optimist who had faith in the fundamental reasonableness of his fellow men. She watched Ereleth urge the horses that were harnessed to the large wagon to bestir themselves. The sight still seemed incongruous to her, although she had seen its like a dozen times before. In spite of being a queen of Xandria – of perhaps because of it – Ereleth liked to be in command of the larger wagon, and had established a good rapport with the animals who usually pulled it.

'Will you follow her, Dhalla?' Fraxinus said. 'If there's a problem, that giant beast of yours might have to use its pulling power.'

Dhalla glanced at the princess, who immediately waved her away. Ever-reluctant but ever-obedient, the giant nudged her horse forward so that it fell into step with the wagon. Merel Zabio had already moved towards the donkeys, which were being soothed by the patient ambers. Aulakh Phar joined her as soon as he was mounted. Hyry Keshvara went to accompany them, after glancing back at Lucrezia to see whether she was following Dhalla.

Jacom Cerri was back at the saddle now, and everyone seemed to be ready to take up his or her position in the column.

'You'd better go now, Fraxinus,' Lucrezia said. 'If there's a problem, you'll be needed up front.'

Fraxinus hesitated, and looked about him, but he eventually condescended to move off. Checuti moved the second wagon in behind the donkeys, and Lucrezia directed her mount to follow it, with Jacom Cerri now at her side. Mossassor and his fellow Serpents led the dragomite workers on to the bridge behind them, with the drones waiting to follow. Jume Metra and the warriors moved into tighter formation at the bridgehead, while General Shabir and his cavalrymen looked on from a respectful distance, without relaxing for an instant.

The expedition's progress across the series of bridges was painfully slow. The big wagon did indeed become temporarily bogged down on the first island, and it required all Dhalla's strength and all Fraxinus's ingenuity to coax it on to the second span, while everyone else waited in the rear, some more fractiously than others.

The second wagon became stuck while it was still on the first bridge, but two of the dragomite workers came forward to push. In the meantime, Lucrezia and Jacom Cerri moved out of the way into the trees. Lucrezia knew that the critical moment was now upon them; if nothing happened within the next ten or fifteen minutes, nothing would. She found that she was holding her breath, and had to make an effort to let it out. Three minutes went by, then four.

Jacom Cerri suddenly leaned across and touched her arm. 'Highness!' he said uncertainly. 'Do you see that?'

He was pointing through a gap in the trees at the main channel of the river, which flowed between the two islands. The current was very strong, and it was carrying a good deal of debris, presumably because the river had been fed to excess by the recent rains. The sun was shining brightly on the swirling water, and it was very difficult to make out what the captain might be pointing at.

'What is it?' she asked.

'I saw a swimmer's head,' he told her. 'I'm sure of it. Look!'

For a moment, it did seem that a human head was visible above the rippled surface, but if it had been a swimmer he had been concerned to disappear again as soon as he had gulped a breath. Lucrezia wasn't certain – but she was certainly afraid.

'It's treachery, highness,' Jacom said fearfully. 'I'm sure of it.' He sounded anything but sure, but there was no mistaking the note of fear in his voice, and Lucrezia knew exactly how he felt.

But what treachery? Lucrezia thought. *What good will it do them to set swimming warriors about the islands? What weapons can they have, and how do they expect to make good use of them as they emerge dripping wet?*

Even so, she quickly became convinced that there *were* swimmers in the water, because another head briefly broke the water, very close to the single stone column which supported the middle of the centre span. She moved her horse closer to the shore of the island, moving further away from the glutinous path which connected the two bridges in order to have a clearer view. There was definitely a man under the bridge, in the shadow of the stone support – in fact, there were at least two.

'What are they doing?' she asked, as Jacom Cerri stood up in his stirrups, craning his neck in the hope of getting a better sight of them.

'I don't . . .' he began, but then he changed his mind. Lucrezia could tell from the expression on his face that he did know – or thought he knew. 'Get down, princess!' he said, panic infusing his voice. 'For Goran's sake get down!'

Then, and only then, did the captain do what hindsight must have told him he ought to have done immediately. He raised his voice to its limit and yelled: 'Look out! They're going to blow up the bridges! *Get off the bridges!*'

Lucrezia was in no position to see what effect his words had, although she had not done as she was told and got down from her horse. Nor was there time to get into position, for the warning had come too late. Within seconds of Cerri's warning shout, the air was rent by an almighty explosion.

Great gouts of water and huge shards of timber went flying everywhere, and Lucrezia's horse – which had always been very docile before – reared up in panic, throwing her back over its rump. While she was still falling she heard the second and more distant explosion, and as she landed she thought she heard a third – but that might simply have been the shock of the impact as her head hit the muddy ground.

Had the ground been solid, she'd have been knocked unconscious immediately, but the place where she landed was so nearly liquid that her senses merely reeled in horrid confusion. She could see nothing but a kinaesthetic display of angry light, but she had time to remember that this was almost exactly how her grand aventure had begun, when Checuti's petards had set in train the ridiculous chapter of accidents which had removed her from the citadel of Xandria and set her on the long, hard road to Chimera's Cradle . . . a destination which was surely now beyond her reach.

17

JACOM'S HORSE WAS citadel-trained, and it made no attempt to throw him off when the explosion sounded. Splinters of wood from the broken bridges behind and ahead of him rattled in the leaves, and he ducked low – but as soon as the hazardous rain of debris ceased he stood up in the stirrups again, craning his neck to see what the situation was.

The worst destruction had been inflicted by the bomb which had split the middle span – the longest of the three. The bridge had been packed with donkeys and horses, attended by seven people: Merel Zabio, Hyry Keshvara, Aulakh Phar and four darklanders, one of them a mere boy. At least half the animals had been killed or badly hurt; the rushing water in the middle of the stream was red with blood. Two of the donkeys were screaming horribly as they thrashed in the water, but they were already being carried away by the rapid current. Jacom could see the broken body of one darklander lying on the stump of the span, and the boy had been thrown up into the branches of a tree, where he hung limply, blood running in a steady trickle from his dangling right foot.

Jacom could see three human bodies floating inertly in the bloody water, but he couldn't tell whether they were alive or dead. Someone was swimming strongly towards the nearest one with the apparent intention of rendering aid; Jacom recognised Hyry Keshvara, and saw that the man she was striking out for was Aulakh Phar. Further downstream another golden was moving in the water, but far less strongly, as if trying desperately to keep afloat while dragging the dead weight of an injured leg; that was Merel Zabio.

On Jacom's other side, rather less damage had been done. The back wheels of the small wagon had still been on the span, and the explosion had wrecked them, but the horses had contrived to pull the body of the cart ashore even as it shattered and spilled its load. Checuti didn't seem to be hurt, but the thief had jumped down from his station and thrown himself flat on the ground, with his hands about his head. Jacom realised that he was expecting a further explosion, and guessed that the plastic he and Aulakh Phar had made must be somewhere in the small wagon. His heart gave a slight lurch as he realised that if the bridge had blown up a few seconds earlier Checuti's stock of plastic would certainly have been triggered, and would have blown all of them to smithereens.

Rather more damage had been done to the company which had been on the bridge behind the wagon and on the shore. Two dragomite workers appeared to have absorbed the full fury of the blast, and had been literally blown apart. One of the Serpents was nothing but raw red meat, and one of the drones had lost its head. Only Jume Metra and the warriors, who had constituted the rearguard, seemed relatively unscathed – although the expression on Metra's face showed that she understood the magnitude of the disaster; not one of the egg-carriers was uninjured, although three of them were still alive, having now retreated to solid ground.

Jacom dismounted, and ran to the fallen princess. Checuti looked up, evidently relieved to find himself still alive, and then came slowly to his feet, wiping mud from his face and looking down in disgust at his filthy, sodden clothing.

Jacom bent over the princess, shielding her from the frightened horse.

'I'm all right,' she assured him, although the thickness of her tone suggested that she was lying. Her clothes were as dirty as Checuti's but the mire was concentrated behind rather than in front. Jacom helped the princess to her feet, but she must have risen too quickly; no sooner was she upright than the colour drained from her face and she fainted. Jacom caught her and held her up, looking wildly about for help – but Checuti had gone to the place where the wagon had spilled its load, intent on recovering something from the chaotic mess of broken jars and split sacks.

Jacom looked around to see whether there was any more help to hand, and saw that one of the Serpents – he could not tell which – had struggled out of the water on to the island. The creature was obviously dazed, and its scaly skin was flecked with shards of glass which must have been blasted out of the rear end of the wagon; it fell to its knees as it tried to support itself by clinging hard to a tree.

By now Checuti had scrambled up on to the wreckage of the wagon to get a better view. He looked down at Jacom and said: 'Is she dead?'

'No,' Jacom told him. 'She's only fainted. What's happening on the far side?' Although the trees growing on the second island completely obscured his view of the third span he could hear shouting coming from that direction as Carus Fraxinus bawled out orders to all and sundry.

'The farthest bridge isn't broken!' Checuti reported excitedly. 'Not entirely, at any rate. I think Fraxinus is still trying to bring the big wagon safely to shore. If we can only . . .' He stopped then, having realised – as Jacom already had – that although it would probably be easy enough for those trapped on this island to get back to the western bank of the river, crossing the wide and fast-moving central stream would be infinitely more difficult. Jacom could hear shouting from the other direction now, and he knew that Shabir's cavalry were launching their first assault. The last place he wanted to be was the western bank, but he moved that way nevertheless, half-dragging and half-carrying the princess, so that he could see what was happening.

Another worker dragomite was struggling out of the water on to the shattered stump of the bridge, but only four of its legs were functional. Jacom saw a second Serpent clambering out of the muddy water at the southern tip of the island, seemingly no worse off than the first. *The island can only offer us temporary salvation*, he thought. *We can neither quit it safely nor defend it – unless . . .*

The first Serpent to climb out of the water went to help its companion, but soon turned to run back to Jacom.

'Iss very bad!' it hissed hoarsely, immediately revealing itself as Mossassor.

'Is rotting terrible,' Jacom agreed, as he held the dead weight of the princess tight to his bosom. 'Those filthy bastards planned this all along! We've been played for fools – and now they're coming to mop up.'

He craned his neck to look for the swimmers he had seen in the water, and was not heartened by what he saw. Hyry Keshvara had reached Aulakh Phar and she was keeping his head out of the water, but while she was thus burdened she could make little or no sideways progress, and the current was bearing her rapidly downstream. Another human head – Merel Zabio's – was still visible even further downstream, but she too seemed to be helpless to do anything but drift with the current. There was no sign of the men who had set the charges, but they had presumably swum clear as soon as the fuses were lit and were now well out of sight.

While Jacom's anxious gaze swept back and forth it was caught by someone moving between the trees on the other island. There was no mistaking the giant as she emerged on to the broken bridge and took three hesitant steps in his direction. Checuti waved to catch her attention, and Dhalla cupped her hands about her mouth to shout over the fast-diminishing racket of the screaming animals.

'What damage?' she yelled, her voice booming over the water.

'Wagon ruined,' Checuti yelled back. 'Dragomite warriors under attack. Cerri and two Serpents fit and well. Princess Lucrezia hurt but alive.'

The last item of news was the vital one so far as Dhalla was concerned. The giant didn't hesitate before leaping down into the water. She was wearing no armour, after the habit of her kind, but the huge spear she had in her hand would doubtless make swimming awkward and Jacom watched her progress with avid interest. He knew that if Dhalla couldn't make the crossing neither he nor Checuti had any chance at all.

He saw that even the giant wasn't tall enough to touch bottom once she was eight or ten mets from the broken end of the bridge, and that her swimming strokes, though awesomely powerful, couldn't easily counteract the current. She made good progress through the water, but she drifted far off line and was soon some distance to the south, swimming almost directly upstream in the attempt to reach the island where Jacom waited.

In the end, the giant succeeded in bringing herself to shore, but the way she floundered in the mud thereafter testified to the effort she had been forced to make. Jacom knew that it would be extremely difficult for him to make the same crossing in reverse even if he discarded his armour and his weapons. He had no way to judge whether or not the horses would be able to swim across.

Dhalla strode towards Checuti with a thunderous expression, and Jacom wondered whether she had drawn the wrong inference from what had happened. 'It wasn't Checuti's plastic!' he called to her. 'It was the Eblans. They did it!'

It was only then that Dhalla saw Lucrezia, and she immediately changed direction.

'She's not hurt,' Jacom assured her. 'She's only fainted.'

The racket on the shore had grown in volume to the point where he could barely be heard, and he turned his head just in time to watch the first wave of lancers sweep down on the warrior dragomites. The warriors could have gone forward to attack them, but they hadn't budged. Jume Metra must have been as anxious as anyone about what had happened on the bridges, but now she was facing the enemy, standing firm with her alien company. The surviving drone and the four workers were behind the warriors' line.

The tight defensive wedge into which the warriors had formed gave them very little room for manoeuvre, but the charging horsemen had little enough room themselves; the ruined cottages to either side of the bridge approach forced them to attack in a relatively narrow column, and the infantrymen who were moving upstream along the riverbank in support also had to come through a narrow gap.

Jacom watched, sick with alarm, as the mounted lancers hurled their mounts forward against the dragomite warriors. Bowmen had also moved into position both upstream and down, and arrows were beginning to rain down on the patient monsters, but for the moment it seemed quite impossible for the attackers to prevail. The warriors were simply too big, and their murderous jaws went to work with marvellously efficient brutality. Jacom knew how absurd it was, but he couldn't help the surge of immense satisfaction that filled him as he saw men and horses broken and cut apart by the scything jaws.

Although Jacom knew that there was no earthly point in shouting advice, an inner voice set up a strident clamour inside his head. *Move into the cottages! Use what shelter there is! Get the workers under cover!* But the dragomites weren't human, and they had their own theories of warfare. Without exception –

for the moment – the arrows were bouncing harmlessly off their exoskeletal plates. Missiles could only constitute a very minor nuisance unless a lucky shot happened to catch a big black eye or one of the narrow gaps where the neck-plates slid over one another. The dragomites kept their attention fixed on the array of Shabir's cavalry, carving the air with their awesome jaws, against whose might the rank of glassy spears suddenly seemed very feeble.

Checuti was rummaging again among the debris which had spilled far and wide from the broken wagon.

'There's a sword for you,' Jacom said, nodding his head clumsily because he couldn't point with his finger while he was holding the princess. Checuti shook his head impatiently and Jacom realised that he was looking for the bombs he'd made with the plastic Phar had mixed for him – but who, Jacom wondered, did he intend to use them against?

'Don't go to sshore,' advised the Serpent which still stood close by. 'Sstay here, while warriorss do their work.'

'If you think the warriors can win this fight,' Jacom replied, more tautly than he intended, 'you're no good judge of odds. But you're right about staying here, at least for the time being. Three of us might hold this island against hundreds, given the cover provided by the trees, the floodwater and the mud. If Checuti can gather his grenades, we might stand off a thousand.' He spoke very loudly, so that Checuti could hear him, in case the thief-master had a different notion of whose side he was on.

'What good will it do to hold the island?' Checuti demanded, although he didn't pause in his search. 'Can you swim that river, captain? Can you, Serpent?'

Mossassor nodded uncertainly. 'Maybe,' it said. 'But Ssifuss and the prinssess . . .' Jacom presumed that Ssifuss was the other surviving Serpent, and that it wasn't a particularly good swimmer.

On the shore, wave after wave of Shabir's cavalry clashed furiously with the dragomite warriors. They were ragged and inelegant, but they were very determined. The warrior dragomites ranged against them looked even more inelegant – and Jacom knew only too well how close they all were to the limit of their strength and endurance. Even so, the defenders met the assault with fearsomely mechanical efficiency. The war cries of the Eblans were already turning into a great cacophony of anger, hatred and distress. There was no empty space left on the bank now – just an infinite sea of confusion. The bowmen were no longer shooting, because the foot-soldiers were now too close to the dragomites.

Jacom had never seen such fast and furious destruction. He had watched dragomites fight one another a dozen times while the expedition crossed the hills, and he had thought such battles very fervent, but this was more violent still. He remembered that on the chaotic night when Checuti had raided the citadel of Xandria not a single life had been lost: all that noise and confusion had been on the surface. This was as different as anything could be. This was all whirling blades, thrusting spears and smashing bows, all kill, kill, kill. Horses were going down by the dozen, spilling broken riders everywhere; their thrashing hooves were as dangerous as any of the relatively feeble weapons the Eblans carried.

For a few moments it seemed to Jacom that the dragomite warriors might after all be invincible, able to defy the appalling odds. It seemed that their massive jaws might simply shatter all opposition – but that was a false impression. There were only six sets of the huge jaws, and although their thrusts could not be parried or turned aside they could be dodged. At close quarters the Eblan army suffered swift and heavy casualties, but the men who were not struck down knew exactly what they were about. For every spear that clattered harmlessly to the ground two or three were driven home into the monsters' eyes or necks.

Jacom saw that whenever the warriors reared up on to their four hind legs, freeing their forelegs for use as extra weapons, they exposed a greater expanse of vulnerable breast; when they elected to stay low, chopping with their blade-like jaws at the horses' legs, their eyes were quickly ruined.

Lucrezia stirred in Jacom's arms, and she took her weight upon her own feet, freeing his hands – but he wouldn't let go of her, and when she looked up into his face with a puzzled expression he continued to look over her head at a scene of carnage more appalling than he had ever imagined possible.

Forty or forty-five seconds must have gone by before the first warrior collapsed, but once one had gone down others followed at intervals which seemed to Jacom to be tragically short.

'Retreat!' Jacom shouted, as loudly as he could, startling the poor princess, who was struggling against his grip in order to turn and see what he was looking at. He meant the plea for the mound-woman, but Jume Metra never turned her head. The workers and the drone were in the thick of the fight now; more men and horses were going down, but the sheer weight of numbers made effective defence impossible.

Jacom could understand now why Shabir had been hesitant when Fraxinus talked to him. If his vanguard had shirked this business – if its members had been even a little less than totally committed to the forward press – they might have been turned and routed, for there was not the slightest question of any lack of commitment on the part of their adversaries. It would not have taken much in the way of uncertainty or cowardice to make the attack fall apart under the pressure of such heavy casualties – but the men of the Nine Towns had done this work before, and they knew full well that they must not weaken under the pressure of risk. They had turned their fear of dragomites into implacable hatred, and they pressed forward with all their might.

One by one, the dragomite workers went down. Only then did Jume Metra condescend to retreat, with the drone, to the shattered stumps of the timbers that had composed the bridge, which now projected raggedly into the water, sloping downwards to the surface.

The lone dragomite worker which had hauled itself stickily on to the island now launched herself back into the water, intent on joining her fellows in their last stand. She floundered in the water, having neither instinct nor experience to tell her how to swim, but sheer determination carried her across to the stump of the pillar which had supported the middle of the span, and from that way-station she was able to set off again to bring herself to the battle.

Jume Metra stood defiantly with her sword in her hand, the drone to her right and the worker to her left, while the remaining Eblan lancers urged their horses over and through the mass of gargantuan corpses which now formed a barrier between themselves and their remaining prey. Suddenly, they did not seem to be so many in number, and for the first time Jacom could see the expressions in their eyes.

There should have been no doubt at all in those expressions, for the job was nearly done and the last part of it by no means the most difficult – but Jacom saw that doubt was flaring in those eyes as they looked beyond their immediate quarry for the first time, and saw that there were people still on the island. Even then, Jacom couldn't understand why they were suddenly fearful, until he looked sideways and saw what they were seeing.

Dhalla didn't bother to pause at the broken end of the bridge – this stream was shallow enough, and the current weak enough, to allow her to wade. She surged across the open water with her right arm upraised, bearing aloft her unnaturally huge javelin.

Behind the giant, Checuti had moved to the very edge of the broken timbers. He made no move to jump into the water, but he flexed his throwing arm and measured the distance with such clinical precision that the watchers could not have the slightest doubt of his ability. He had hesitated to begin with, wondering whether he ought to use his bombs against the dragomites rather than the attackers, but that moment had passed. Jacom knew that he had accepted the pressure of inevitability. There was only one enemy in his sights now.

For a second or two Jacom couldn't quite figure out why Dhalla and Checuti were placing themselves in obvious jeopardy, in support of two dragomites and a mound-woman whose fight was already lost, but he only had to consult his own feelings to reason it through. Like him, they were seething with resentful wrath and a determination to make Shabir's men pay for their treason. Even Checuti – who was as careful and as skilled as any man in the arts of self-preservation – apparently could not readily abide any treachery but his own. They intended to take a heavy toll of the half-victorious army.

Jacom let go of the princess, intending to jump into the water and follow Checuti, but the Serpent grabbed at his arm and held him back.

'Only get in way!' Mossassor said. 'Bombss firsst!'

Jacom could see the sense in that, but he wasn't about to stand and wait. He ran to Checuti's side. 'I can throw!' he said, meaning that he had been trained to use a javelin. Checuti didn't bother to argue, pointing to the plastic-filled pipes rooted out of the wagon's spillage, which he had heaped up beside the place where he stood.

'Bite the fuses, captain,' Checuti said, offering him a match.

'Leave as little as you dare – and if you see that imbecile Shabir, blow him to bits!'

If the Eblans had imagined that their greatest enemy had already been felled and trampled underfoot, Jacom thought, they had a shock in store. He took one of the fuses in his mouth and bit it in half.

Then he struck the match.

18

CARUS FRAXINUS WATCHED from the island as the big wagon cleared the last few mets of the third bridge and rolled on to the grassy shore. Ereleth immediately got down and came to look at the timbers she had just driven across. The outer ones were still holding, although a hemispherical section had been ripped out of the stone column supporting the middle of the bridge. The two central logs, their pinnings sheared through, had fallen out of the structure and were drifting away downriver.

'Get a rope!' Fraxinus shouted. 'We have to get it over to the other island – the current's too fierce for swimmers unless they've something to hold on to.'

Ereleth held up her hand to indicate that she understood. When she had fetched a rope from the back of the wagon the three mound-women came with her, skipping nimbly along the divided span. Behind them the six dragomite warriors were moving restlessly about, as if they yearned to find some enemy on which to unleash themselves. No enemy was visible this side of the river – not yet, anyhow. Fraxinus suspected that it might not be long before enemies appeared in plenty.

By the time they had carried the rope to the far side of the islet Dhalla had already crossed the intervening water; anxiety for Lucrezia's safety had not let her wait. Fraxinus could see Checuti's head but Jacom Cerri and the princess were invisible. Fraxinus called out to Checuti but if the thief could hear him over the rapidly increasing noise of battle he had more important things to do than respond.

Fraxinus studied the fast-flowing stream anxiously. There was no sign of anyone in the water now – any survivors of the blasts that had demolished the crowded centre span must have been carried so far downriver as to be out of sight.

'It's useless for you or me to try swimming aginst that tide,' Ereleth said. 'Checuti or Cerri might get across once, but even they wouldn't have strength enough to get back again with the rope in tow. Dhalla's our only hope.'

'Can you swim?' Fraxinus asked the nearest of the mound-women, but he knew as he said it that it was a foolish question. What chance had they ever had to learn to swim while they dwelt in the Corridors of Power? The mound-women were every bit as agitated as the warriors on the eastern shore, knowing that their sisters were faced with a fight to the death but having no possible way of lending aid.

'Is the princess there? Is she alive?' Ereleth demanded of him.

'Checuti shouted to Dhalla before she swam across,' Fraxinus told her. '*Hurt but alive*, I think he said. Dhalla wouldn't have gone otherwise. She should have waited for the rope regardless – but she'll come back for it, if she can. Aulakh was washed downstream. I think Keshvara went after him, but she'll need all her strength to fish him out even if she isn't badly hurt. If she can only get him to the eastern bank . . . but there'll surely be men downstream, waiting. The swimmers who set the charges . . .' He trailed off, knowing that speculation was futile. He had to concentrate on his own situation.

First, the rope had to be fixed across the river's central stream. Then they had to bring as many people across as they could, with whatever portables they could salvage from the second wagon's load. Always assuming, that is, that there would be anyone to bring across once Shabir's army had done its work – and always assuming that they would have the time to do it before more attackers moved in on this side of the river.

'Is there a bow in the wagon?' Ereleth asked. 'If we could attach a light cord to an arrow, and shoot it across, we might then be able to attach the rope to the cord, so that Checuti or Cerri could drag one after the other.'

'Yes,' Fraxinus said. 'There's at least one darkland bow there, and cord aplenty. I'm no archer, but I can hit an island.'

He went to fetch the bow himself. He had to be careful on the divided bridge, but the remaining timbers seemed solid enough and he silently thanked the man who had set the charge so badly that it left its work less than half-done. As he moved on to the shore, though, an arrow thudded into the ground near his boot, and he had to dive for the cover of the wagon in a most ungainly fashion.

There had been no men close by when Jume Metra had first brought the dragomite warriors across, else the wagons would never have moved on to the bridge, but Shabir had obviously sent some of his soldiers across the river before he had sent out the artillerists who had fixed the plastic to the bridge. Now they had moved up from their hiding-place to an attacking position.

From the partial shelter of the wagon it was easy to see where the archers had stationed themselves. They had hastened to the one place where the dragomite warriors could not easily reach them, and were now perched about the chimney-stacks of the derelict houses which had once formed a hamlet around the bridgehead. Fraxinus counted six, but he was certain that there must be more – perhaps dozens, maybe hundreds. Those he could see had two-met bows; he knew that if they couldn't be dislodged and disposed of by the warriors, or tempted to use up their ammunition, they would be able to pick off the human members of the expedition as they tried to make their getaway. They had not so far fired at the team of horses that was hitched to the wagon – perhaps because they intended to claim them as plunder, but more likely because they were conserving their arrows – but they could easily do so if and when Fraxinus's party tried to move off, because the only clear path away from the bridge ran straight between the houses.

Ereleth emerged from the trees to see what was happening.

'Stay out of range!' Fraxinus called. Ereleth showed no inclination to disobey the instruction but the mound-women were in a very different frame of mind. They immediately ran past the queen, ducking low but loosing their crude swords for ready use. They were avid to get into the action, and Fraxinus didn't envy any man who had to face them hand to hand.

The height which the bowmen had was a great advantage, but if they thought it made them perfectly safe they were wrong, as Fraxinus quickly saw. If a dragomite warrior raised the forepart of its body while supporting itself on its four hind legs it could grip the edge of a house's roof, and once that grip was secure it could move its middle legs up. The creatures were so heavy that it was a very awkward way to climb, but climb they certainly could, for these were creatures well used to operating on the sometimes vertiginous slopes of the Dragomite Hills.

The six warriors lost no time in separating so as to assault all four of the houses where Shabir's snipers had set themselves, and the bowmen quickly stopped firing as they realised their peril – but they were not unprepared, for they had lumps of rock at hand, and tiles, and even the chimney-pots about which they clustered, to use as missiles. Such crude weapons could do little damage to a dragomite in themselves, but all that was required of a well-thrown shot was that it should catch a warrior off balance and tip it backwards.

This, it quickly transpired, was not so very difficult to achieve. Worse than that; Fraxinus soon saw that if a dragomite fell on its back – as it was very likely to, given the manner of its climbing – it required several seconds of furious thrashing before it could get purchase enough to right itself, and in that interval its softer underside was vulnerable to attack. Arrows could pierce the exoskeleton here, although they could not go deep enough to cause much physical harm – but the men on the rooftops had other weapons for the purpose which could go deeper if flung with skill: stout javelins with metal tips.

Fraxinus had now seen at least eight more men, but he was relieved that they did not seem to be an army. Shabir presumably had not anticipated the possibility that the third span of the bridge would remain unbroken, but he must have reasoned that the dragomites would be more easily defeated if he attacked them six at a time. The men he had stationed here probably constituted a diversionary force. Their task would be to harass the dragomites and then to retreat, keeping track of them while Shabir's fighting men crossed the river at the next bridge southwards and regrouped for a new attack. For the moment, however, the bowmen showed no inclination to make good their escape.

When he saw the first two or three javelins hurled from the rooftops, Fraxinus thought that they could not possibly be adequate to seize any permanent advantage, but he saw one spear become securely bedded in a warrior's abdomen, and when the creature finished the job of righting itself the spear was pushed more deeply in, making the wound worse. The monster had insufficient flexibility in its limbs to pluck the javelin out, and its attempts to do so drove the head further and further in. Even so, it came to its feet and resumed climbing. Fraxinus knew that the dragomites were near to starvation and exhaustion, and he feared that any injury was very likely to lessen their chances of long-term survival considerably, but he judged that the advantage still lay so completely with the dragomites that the bowmen ought now to flee for their lives.

For whatever reason, they did not. They were determined to stay until they had launched every last arrow and every makeshift missile.

From the far side of the river came the sound of an explosion; then another; then another.

Fraxinus could only hope that it was Checuti who was responsible, not Shabir's men – and that Checuti was using his bombs to support the dragomites rather than to destroy them. He rummaged about in the wagon until he found a darkland bow and a supply of arrows. He immediately moved to the front of the wagon and attempted a shot at the nearest of the Eblan soldiers, hoping at least to provide a distraction.

The arrow missed, but it gave the soldiers on the nearest roof some cause for alarm and they immediately gathered behind the chimney-stack to take advantage of what shelter there was. It was a bad move, for all their antics had severely weakened the roof and the chimney itself must have been rotten at the core. The whole structure caved in, pitching the howling men into the dark belly of the building. Two of the mound-women went in through the open doorway to finish them.

If Fraxinus had still harboured doubts as to the dragomites' intelligence the next few minutes would have settled them. The warriors immediately ceased their cumbersome climbing and set about using their brute strength on the walls of the other buildings, tearing great chunks of stone or timber away from the windows. The men on the chimney-stacks now tried – very belatedly – to retreat, but they had left it too late. The dragomites were quick to cut them off. There were horses galloping away, for Fraxinus could bear the drumming of their hooves, but they belonged to men who had never taken up positions on the rooftops – they too, it seemed, had become impatient with their fellows' lunatic heroism.

Within three or four minutes a second cottage collapsed, then a third, spilling men inside and out. It didn't matter where they came down, or whether they were still in a fit condition to stand and fight: the warriors and the mound-women attacked them furiously. Fraxinus nearly turned away then in order to return to his own task, but Ereleth hadn't shouted to urge him to hurry and he couldn't tear himself away.

The last of the the four houses occupied by the attackers must have been far less troubled by decay than the others; although two dragomites worked away at it with all their strength it simply would not cave in. The missiles launched from its makeshift tower began to have some effect, felling one of the mound-women and reducing one of the dragomite warriors to near-helplessness.

Fraxinus fired three arrows at the ebullient men, one by one. The last of them hit one of the soldiers in the chest, and he rolled down the tilted roof, falling over the edge. It was not until all other matters had been settled, however, that the whole company of dragomites was able to come together around the building. It was then that Fraxinus saw that only one of the mound-women was still standing, and that only one of the dragomite warriors was entirely unhurt.

The six sets of jaws worked away. They would have completed their task in no time had it not been for the fact that four of them were direly enfeebled, but as things were it took a further five minutes to bring the roof down, and perhaps five more after that to dispose of the fallen bowmen.

Any other Eblans who had been sheltering in the trees were long gone by now; the skirmish was over. At last, Ereleth had begun to call after Fraxinus, telling him that she had the cord and that he must bring the bow without further delay.

We won! he thought, as he turned away. *In spite of everything, we won.* But he knew what a pathetically silly thought it was, and that such a battle as this could have no victors at all. He had survived, but the chances of bringing his expedition to a profitable conclusion were surely as negligible as the chances of the dragomites' egg-carriers founding a new nest.

19

WHEN ERELETH HEARD the series of explosions which sounded on the other shore she quickly made her way to the jutting remnant of the bridge which had connected the two islands, but there was no one on its counterpart to relay news to her of what was happening. She knew that it must have been Checuti's bombs which made the noise, but she had no idea how they were being deployed; the trees on the other island formed an effective shield against her curiosity.

She knew that she ought to be paying attention to what was happening on her own side of the river – which events would, after all, settle her own immediate fate – but Lucrezia was on the far side, and so was Dhalla. So, for that matter, were the three Serpents. Without them, there was little or nothing she could do by way of following the secret commandments entrusted to her by her mother.

She was still a little astonished by the feverish pitch of her own anxiety. She had given the secret commandments little or no thought during the first twenty years of her life, and had certainly never taken the view that her life would have been wasted had she never done anything more with them than pass them on to her own heir – Lucrezia, in the absence of any natural daughter. When she had left the citadel of Xandria to go in search of Lucrezia she had been intent on rescuing her from Checuti, and it was only by degrees that her attitude had changed. It had gradually become clear to her that something very strange was happening, and that the bush sent to Xandria by mysterious bronzes had been intended as a kind of signal or lure. Not until the descent into the dragomite nest had she been entirely convinced, but what had happened there had triggered the realisation that this was indeed the time of trouble and terror of which the secret lore spoke: a time when the whole world would be consumed by a crisis which might alter it out of all recognition. However slow she had been to accept that fact, she now knew perfectly well that she could never go back to Belin's Inner Sanctum, and that her commitment to her mission must be absolute. Were Lucrezia to be lost now, everything would be lost, and that seemed a profoundly horrible thought.

She had counted the explosions, and fretted all the more when she had counted four and no fifth came. She knew how many bombs Checuti had made, and she knew that the bulk of his supply remained unused. Why had he stopped? Was it because his objective – whatever that might have been – had been easily attained, or was it because he had been struck down? Time went by and no answer became evident.

She could see men on the far shore, to the south of the part that was obscured by the other island. Some were mounted but many more were on foot, and all of them were moving at their best pace. They seemed to be fleeing in great disarray, but she couldn't be absolutely sure that the retreat was total and disorganised. She looked downstream, but there was no sign of anyone in the water now and the water was uniformly grey as far as the eye could see, with not a hint of red. She could still see the darkland boy, though, hanging in the branches of a tree, all the delicate amber of hs skin turned raw red.

Even the running men were disappearing from view now, and an ominous quiet had descended on both sides of the river.

'What's happening on the other shore?' Carus Fraxinus called to her. She looked round, faintly surprised that he had the leisure to do it.

'I don't know,' Ereleth replied – but as soon as she said it, the situation began to change. 'Wait!' she added. 'I can see someone now. It's Cerri! He's signalling. One way or another, it's all finished. Bring that bow and the cord, quickly!'

While she waited for him to obey, Ereleth craned her neck to see what had become of Fraxinus's companions. She could see at least three dragomite warriors moving about, but the way they were moving suggested that all three were injured. A lone mound-woman was going from one to another, apparently checking their condition. The mound-woman looked round once, and caught Ereleth's eye, but the dark expression on her face didn't change at all. There was no accusation in the glance, no judgment passed on her and Fraxinus for bringing them to this.

Carus Fraxinus brought the bow and the cord at last, and quickly fastened one end of the cord to an arrow. Ereleth watched impatiently as he uncoiled the cord and tied its other end to the rope. By the time he was ready to shoot, Jacom Cerri had seen what he was doing and understood.

'Shabir's men turned tail!' Cerri called over the water. 'The dragomites killed more than a hundred, Checuti's bombs killed half a hundred more, and Dhalla killed at least four score. Their resolve melted away, and they panicked, running south and west in great confusion. Dhalla took an arrow in the thigh and several spear-wounds, but she frightened them more than Checuti's plastic. They could have killed us all had they only had patience and a reasoned strategy, but fear got the better of them. Dhalla won the battle for us!'

For us! Ereleth thought. However frail and hypocritical the promises Fraxinus had made to the drones had been, events had borne him out. His entire company really had acted, under the pressure of necessity, with one mind and one purpose . . . except, alas, that the company was now rent in two, with a torrent dividing the parts.

Fraxinus went out as far as he could on the broken bridge and fired the arrow. Weighed down by the cord, it only flew halfway across the channel before falling in the water. Ereleth cursed beneath her breath. She knew how vital it was to get the rope across; Dhalla might be able to cross without its aid, but no one else would.

Fraxinus cursed out loud, and dragged the arrow back again. The second time, he bent the bow as far as he was capable, and pointed the arrow further upwards, but still it only flew two-thirds of the way. He cursed again, and pulled it back yet again. Ereleth's spirits fell further. *Where is Dhalla?* she wondered. *How bad are her wounds?*

As if in response to her silent question the giant appeared on the far stump of the bridge, thrusting Jacom Cerri rudely out of the way. He didn't protest. Dhalla wasted no time in stepping down into the water, although she was plainly uncomfortable. Ereleth could see that she was bleeding badly from at least four wounds, the ugliest of which was on the upper part of her bare leg, where she must have pulled an arrowhead out of her flesh. Even so, the giant was moving with furious determination. Her eyes were glazed, as if the concentrated exertion of her will left only the merest space for thought and sensation.

Ereleth watched anxiously as Dhalla waded out into the stream, slowly but purposefully, until she was nipple-deep. The water where the giant stood became discoloured with her blood, and Ereleth guessed that she was more seriously wounded than she could admit to herself. Was it this kind of fortitude, she wondered, that gave rise to the saying that giants had Salamander's fire burning in their hearts? How, if so, did it come about that there was also a place called Salamander's Fire? The fact of her ignorance annoyed her; she was a witch, after all, and witches were supposed to know the answers to any questions brought to them by common men – or, at least, to be able to invent answers which would serve the purpose of reassurance.

'Aim upstream of me!' Dhalla called to Carus Fraxinus, in a rasping voice which hardly needed to be raised above a whisper now that everything was quiet at last. 'I'll catch the arrow as it drifts past.'

Again Fraxinus bent the bow with all his might, and let fly. For a second or two Ereleth wasn't sure that even Dhalla's long arms would be able to reach the arrow as it floated downstream, but she clenched her fist exultantly as the giant's fingers caught the missile at full stretch. Dhalla immediately began moving backwards, drawing the cord ashore. Once she had handed it on to Cerri – who had now been joined by Checuti and two Serpents – it became a simple matter to pull the rope across behind the cord. They secured it easily enough.

'Is the princess able to come across?' Ereleth immediately called to Dhalla.

The giant, who was still waist-deep in the fast-flowing water, shook her head. 'She can stand and speak, but she's as limp as a rag,' she answered. 'I'll carry her when the time comes. Who's first?'

Ereleth saw Checuti look at Cerri and Cerri look at Checuti, each one evidently standing back to let the other go first – whether out of politeness or because neither wanted to be the one to test the holding power of the rope it was impossible to judge.

In the end, it was one of the Serpents who took hold of the rope and cautiously lowered itself into the water.

It was immediately apparent that crossing the fast-flowing stream, even with a rope for support, would be a very tricky business. The Serpent – which Ereleth identified as Mossassor when she could see its markings more clearly – had a considerable struggle. Its scaly skin seemed to have shielded it from the worse of the blast, but it was by no means undamaged and it arrived in some distress, quite breathless after the effort. Fraxinus knelt down to help the creature climb on to the ragged timbers, and it seemed to Ereleth that without such help it would not have had the strength to pull itself clear. She knew that Serpents were stronger than their slender frames implied, and she wondered whether Checuti would have strength enough to haul his considerable bulk all the way from one islet to the other.

Dhalla pushed Cerri on to the broken end of the bridge. Ereleth could see yet another figure moving behind her now; there was a mound-woman with them. Ereleth guessed that it was Jume Metra, although she had lost track of the disposition of the mound-women and had no idea how many of them might have been hurt or killed.

Cerri moved out into the stream, clinging hard to the rope. He began making his slow way along it, pulling himself arm over arm. He seemed to be gaining confidence as he came, although the swirling current was obviously very troublesome. Ereleth began to relax, thinking that all would be well and that the entire endeavour might now be completed successfully.

Then confusion came again, threatening chaos.

A swimmer, who must have come from some considerable way upstream, suddenly reared up out of the water where Cerri was, carrying a horribly long knife. Cerri instantly let go of the rope with one hand in order to grab the arm which held the knife, but in the flurry of splashing which followed he lost his grip entirely. Wrestling with his adversary, he was carried downstream with remarkable rapidity. A second swimmer had already reached the rope and grabbed hold, bringing up a knife of his own to saw away at it.

Dhalla, who was still in the water, hurled herself towards the Eblan. Alas, such was the distance between them that it seemed to Ereleth that she had little chance of reaching the man before he severed the rope. Carus Fraxinus dived for the bow, which he had set down, and the two remaining arrows. Before he had even got an arrow notched, however, Ereleth groaned in dismay.

Dhalla had almost reached her target, but she was just a second too late. The rope had parted, and all that was left for her to do was reach out to seize the man who had cut it. He stabbed at her with the knife, but his real intention was simply to steer clear and the blade scored her skin instead of cutting deep into the flesh. Even so, a long ribbon of blood spouted from a line drawn from the giant's ear to her shoulder, and Ereleth cursed again, knowing that even a giant could have little enough blood to spare after taking so many wounds.

Dhalla grabbed hold of the Eblan, and Ereleth heard the crack as the arm which held the knife was unceremoniously broken. The man was still trying to get away, but he had no chance now that Dhalla had him securely in her grasp. The two of them were borne away downstream as rapidly as Jacom Cerri and the man with whom he had been struggling, but soon parted company again. The dead Eblan drifted on downstream while Dhalla tried with all her might to swim against the current, hoping to get back to one or other of the islands.

'We have to get away from here!' Checuti shouted out. 'They may have withdrawn in blind panic, but they'll be as determined to destroy us as they ever were if their officers can only collect them. I still have plastic, but they have hundreds of fighters still alive and armed. We have to run for it now. Go quickly! Flee for your lives!'

'You *must* send the princess,' Ereleth shouted back at him, but she knew as she formed the words that they were all hope and no substance. There was no possible way for the princess to cross over now, unless Dhalla could contrive to reconnect the rope – and the chances of that were obviously negligible.

Slowly but surely the giant had made headway against the current, bu the effort had proved unsustainable and she was now beginning to drift again. She tried to strike out laterally, aiming at first for the western bank, where she had made her stand against an army. It was by no means the closer of the two shores, and it was immediately evident that she was in trouble. As loss of blood finally took its toll she floundered, and the current began to carry her downstream again. For a moment or two Ereleth thought that she would be swept away as casually as all the others who had been delivered into the water had been swept away, but then the giant began to swim again, albeit in a laborious and very ungainly fashion. This time, she swam diagonally towards the nearer shore: the eastern side of the river. Ereleth judged that she would make it to the bank within a few hundred mets, but what condition the giant would be in when she arrived there she dared not guess.

'Checuti's right,' Fraxinus muttered, as much to himself as to Ereleth. 'If we all stay here while Shabir makes haste to regather his forces, they'll be able to pick us off. We have to move, as far and as fast as we can. May they rot and decay, the cowards! Why in the world could they not let us pass through?'

'Were they merchants at heart, they'd undoubtedly have done so,' Ereleth told him acidly, 'but they were not. You should have listened to me, Fraxinus.'

Carus Fraxinus shot her a glance which told her that he thought the last remark monstrously unfair – as even Ereleth knew it to be, in the secrecy of her soul – but the merchant didn't want to waste time in argument. He cupped a hand beside his mouth so that he could shout across the water to Checuti. 'Save yourselves!' he cried. 'Get away, and avoid capture! Go west, as fast as you can, into the marshes. Hide there, and make your way to Salamander's Fire as and when you can. If it's humanly possible, we'll meet you there.'

'Protect the princess at all costs!' Ereleth shouted, although she had little hope that any of them save Jacom Cerri would take the plea seriously. 'Defend her with your lives.'

'Iss bad,' said Mossassor, as Fraxinus turned away. 'Iss very, very bad. Iss very long way to Ssalamander'ss Fire.'

'I know,' Fraxinus said, between gritted teeth. 'And we've not a warrior of any species in any condition to provide us with a good measure of protection. Can we rely on the surviving dragomites at all, now that we no longer have the drones to act as go-betweens, and they no longer have egg-carrying workers to defend?'

'Warriors will defend uss,' the Serpent reassured him. 'Are nesst-matess now.'

Ereleth felt an unexpected pang of sympathy for the merchant. In all his long life he could never have been in such desperate straits as he was now. The feeling of being engaged in a great adventure – which had easily sustained him throughout the long trek across the Dragomite Hills – could hardly seem adequate now to counter the bitterness in his heart. He had nothing but tarnished dreams to sustain him.

It was Mossassor who led the way back to the wagons and it was Ereleth who took the reins to urge the horses southwards. Her first objective was to recover Dhalla. She had been in close company with giants for most of her life, but she had little idea how resilient they were; their duties in the Inner Sanctum rarely extended to violence, and she had never been forced to exercise her healing skills on one who was sorely hurt.

Fraxinus belatedly pulled himself up to join Ereleth and Mossassor. 'We have to reach the Spangled Desert before Shabir's men get to us,' he said. 'We must assume that his main objective is to destroy the remaining dragomite warriors. After that . . .'

'We have to cross the desert,' Ereleth finished for him, 'to Salamander's Fire.'

'Who has the easier part, do you think?' he asked her, in a strange tone which mixed dire anxiety with grim resolution. 'Is the desert worse than the marshes, or are the marshes worse than the desert?'

'We have the right part,' Ereleth told him grimly. 'The dragomites will fare far better in the desert than in the marshes, if they can find enough water to sustain them, and provided that their wounds will heal.'

'Iss very long way to Ssalamander'ss Fire,' the Serpent said again, more guardedly than before. 'Iss bad – but iss not impossible.'

No, Ereleth thought. *It's not impossible. It can't be. It has to be possible for us, and for the princess too. If it isn't . . .*

She had to let the thought trail away into silence. Her secret commandments only told her what to do if and when the order of things was upset; they didn't tell her what might happen if their instructions proved impossible to carry out.

20

LUCREZIA WAS ANNOYED with herself, and more than a little ashamed. She had now been involved in two battles – she didn't count the battle between the dragomite nests of which she had been a disinterested observer – and she had not yet been able to lift a finger in her own defence. When Jume Metra's warrior-women had slaughtered Djemil Eyub's men she had had the legitimate excuse of being securely tied up, but this time she had simply fainted, in the most revoltingly feminine fashion imaginable. Her mind was no longer the mind of a princess, but her body evidently had convictions of its own as to her nature and status.

It was obvious that none of her companions bore a grudge against her on account of her failure to make any contribution to their narrow victory, but that only seemed to her to demonstrate how little they had expected of her. They seemed to expect little enough even now, while they rummaged hastily through the goods scattered about the ruined wagon, trying to decide what was salvageable and what was not – and what, out of all that was salvageable, was essential to their future progress. This was not an easy task; although the blast which had destroyed the bridge had shattered a great many of Aulakh Phar's bottles and jars and had sent the shards hurtling in every direction there was still an enormous heap of litter aggregated beneath the tattered canvas which had covered the vehicle. It was almost as if the explosion had increased the wagon's burden rather than merely spreading its debris around.

'A good kettle is an absolute necessity.' Checuti was busy advising them all, while he threw sacks and boxes from side to side with reckless abandon. 'So is fire-making equipment, and a good sharp knife apiece – not inconveniently long, but sturdy. I wouldn't bother with that if I were you.'

That was a bow and a quiver of arrows which Ssifuss had picked up. The Serpent ignored Checuti's judgment and carefully secured the weapon to the pack which it was making up to carry on its back. Checuti looked as if he were about to make some further comment, but he was distracted by Jume Metra, who had armed herself with exactly the kind of knife he had recommended and then had left the foraging party to leap into the flowing stream, floundering towards the bank with her horse in tow.

'We haven't finished yet!' Checuti called after her. 'We've one horse left to load. There's no time for playing games.'

They had four sound horses between the four of them, but Ssifuss would not be riding, so they had one to use as a beast of burden. Dhalla's mount – which could have carried twice the load of any other – wasn't among them, but Andris Myrasol's stolen mare was, and she was capable of bearing more weight than the average animal.

'She has priorities of her own,' Lucrezia said to Checuti, as Metra made her awkward but determined way to the corpse of the worker dragomite which had been the last to fall. When Checuti saw what the mound-woman intended to do, though, he made a disgusted noise.

'Doesn't she realise that it's over?' he complained. 'Surely she can't intend to start a new nest on her own?'

While Lucrezia sorted through the wreckage in her own fashion – which was rather more meticulous than Checuti's – she watched from the corner of her eye as Metra removed eggs from their gelatinous encasements on the dead worker's back, exercising the utmost care as she did so. 'If Metra thought that,' she said, 'she'd give up. She's part of the nest, or she's nothing. However hopeless things might seem, the fact that she's bearing a handful of eggs will give her a reason to go on, a reason to fight – and a reason to join forces with us. Let her follow her own priorities. The time might come when we need her to stand with us.'

Checuti made another inarticulately dismissive sound, but it was muted.

'Shabir's men will be back soon enough,' Lucrezia added, although she knew that she was talking for her own benefit, trying to calm the anxiety that was building in her breast. 'If they catch sight of the four of us, with no giant to tilt the odds in our favour, we'll need every scrap of motivation she can muster.'

'I only hope the damn things are edible,' Checuti muttered. He hurled away a waterskin that he had just picked up, having found on closer inspection that it was holed. He was still moving at a furious pace, and Lucrezia realised that his flesh too must be all acrawl with fear and uncertainty, no matter how determined he was to seem business-like. 'Then, if things get really tough . . .'

'We can eat your stupid monkey,' Lucrezia finished for him. The thief-master's pet had disappeared into the trees when the explosions began, but it had returned now, and its tiny hands were sorting through the wreckage as enthusiastically as any of the larger pairs.

'If it comes to the point where it's a choice between eating him and starving,' Checuti said grimly, 'he's meat. All I ask is that the rest of you are as reasonable as I am. We need another lantern, and all the oil we can find, if there are any unbroken jars – look there! – and a good rope, too. I wish I knew more about Phar's pastes and potions. There's much scattered hereabouts that might be invaluable, if only we knew the lore of it.'

'I've gathered one or two useful medicines,' Lucrezia told him. 'My lore overlaps his to a small extent.'

'Naturally,' Checuti said, curling his lip in what might have been intended as a half-smile. '*Poisoner, save thyself* – isn't that the saying?'

'I believe you're thinking of *Physician, heal thyself*,' she told him, keeping her own face straight. 'Is that cooking pot too heavy to take, do you think?'

'Yes it is,' he said, as he moved to Myrasol's mare and continued making up the load balanced on her back. 'Cooking pots are fine if you have a cart, but a good kettle will do well enough for men on horseback fleeing for their lives. I've just about finished here – can you get that bag of bones across to the shore?' He was referring to Lucrezia's horse, which had been relatively slight of build even before the long trek through the Dragomite Hills.

'He won't want to stay here any more than I do,' Lucrezia assured him, although that wasn't entirely obvious, given that the gelding was busy cropping the best grass they had encountered for thirty days and more.

Ssifuss had picked up a long spear which had been cast at them from the shore during the battle, although the way it tested the tensile strength of the shaft suggested that it was thinking more in terms of a walking-stick than a weapon. Checuti made no comment or objection, but simply said: 'Can you get to the shore unaided?'

The Serpent weighed the pack it had made up – which seemed heavy enough, considering the slenderness of its arms – then moved its head from side to side as if to clear some slight stiffness from its long neck. Its hood inflated for a moment or two, so that its head appeared to be set against a huge saucer. Finally, it said: 'Yess.'

Unlike Mossassor, Ssifuss had always been reluctant to use human language, although it seemed to understand nearly as many words. Lucrezia was slightly surprised that the Serpent intended to stay with them given that it was said to believe that human beings were a disease afflicting a world which rightly belonged to Serpentkind, but she supposed that it was a case of any port in a storm. A lone Serpent would stand no chance against the least remnant of Shabir's army, but a party of four, mounted and well-armed, would be treated warily by any group less than a dozen strong.

'Right,' said Checuti. 'Let's go – as far as we can as fast as we can.' His eyes were still on Ssifuss, and Lucrezia knew that he must be wondering how fast the Serpent could run. According to Hyry's testimony, though, the Serpent was unlikely to prove to be the slowest member of the convoy. An unladen horse might be faster over a short distance, but when it came to stamina Serpents were hard to match.

They all knew, although they had wasted no time in lengthy discussion, that there was only one way they could go: due west, heading as straight as an arrow towards the Soursweet Marshes. Lucrezia knew that they couldn't hope to get there in a day, and perhaps not in two, but they had to get there as soon as they possibly could. If the Eblans regrouped their forces and contrived to intercept and capture them, they would all be killed. The marshes were their only possible refuge. Lucrezia had no idea what conditions they might find there, and she was certain that Checuti and Jume Metra were as ignorant as she was, but whatever dangers the marshes held would have to be faced. There was no alternative.

Ssifuss looked at Lucrezia, darting its eyes back and forth in a silent invitation to go on ahead.

'No,' she said. 'You go first.'

The creature hesitated, then looked the other way at the mess that had spilled from Phar's wagon, which was now scattered more widely still by their furious rummaging. Lucrezia followed the direction of the glance, but it wasn't immediately obvious what the Serpent was looking at – or looking for.

'What . . . ?' she began, and then her curious eyes picked out the relevant item. 'Is that important?' she asked. 'If you want to pick it up, you don't have to do it in secret. Do you really think there might be some good in taking it? Metra doesn't want it.'

The Serpent looked at her, with its bulbous head tilted slightly to one side; its hood was still slightly inflated. Lucrezia wondered what expression was showing in its features, which seemed at that moment to be more rubbery than scaly.

'Well,' Lucrezia said, 'if all else fails, it might be reckoned meat.' She didn't know whether Serpents had a sense of irony, although Mossassor's speech often seemed to have a touch of whimsy about it.

'Promisse,' Ssifuss said, according to its uncommunicative habit. Lucrezia presumed that it meant the promise which Andris Myrasol had made, although she hadn't been aware that the Serpents knew about it, let alone that they cared.

Without further ado, Ssifuss went to fetch the bag in which Andris Myrasol had hidden the severed head of the dragomite drone. Lucrezia shrugged her shoulders after exchanging a brief glance with the impatient Checuti. 'Given the pressure of necessity that faces us,' she muttered, as she coaxed her gelding into the water, 'it might be convenient if you could school yourself to be a little more elaborate in your explanations.' Ssifuss wasn't out of earshot, but it gave no sign that it had heard what she said.

After water, food and good metal, Lucrezia thought, *the most essential thing in the world is understanding. Once we're safe, we have to get back to the task of figuring out what's happening.* This too was a gesture of self-distraction, made necessary by the horrid dampness that was invading every stitch of her clothing. So fast was the flow of the river that it was only slightly fouled by rotted produce of the Dragomite Hills, but she couldn't entirely escape the notion that she was wading in the blood whose odour filled the air. *But what help can the head be?* she continued doggedly, knowing that once she and the gelding came ashore they really would have to wade through a swamp of bloody flesh, and that she would be in far greater need of distraction than she was now. *Even if it really is alive, our chances of rousing it to consciousness are negligible – and even if we accomplished such a miracle, what could it tell us? It knows no more than we do, and probably far less. What particular wisdom was there to be cultivated in the depths of a dragomite nest?*

Ssifuss moved into the water behind her, swimming in a peculiarly sinuous fashion, using its body and tail rather than its limbs. Checuti mounted his own horse and took the leading reins of Myrasol's mare and the horse Jume Metra was to ride. His monkey clung hard to his neck. The thief-master urged the horses forward, and they went readily enough. Lucrezia looked back as her own gelding moved briefly out of its depth, half-expecting trouble, but all the expedition's horses had been schooled in Xandria, and they moved through the shallow water with practised efficiency and stubborn determination.

For once, Lucrezia was glad that the sun was high in the sky and that the clouds had cleared; she knew that they would dry out quickly, and that the ointments they were using to counteract the effects of lustrust on their blades would not be overtaxed.

On the shore, Jume Metra had finished her work and now stood waiting. Lucrezia could not tell how many eggs the mound-woman had shifted into her pack, but there could not have been space for more than eight. Metra was surrounded by red-drenched corpses, but they were dragomite corpses, and the red was ichor rather than blood. The stench was appalling but the sight of the dead warriors was not particularly disturbing to Lucrezia. The real challenge to her courage lay beyond, where the men slaughtered by the dragomites' jaws and Dhalla's sword lay in obscene profusion. The redness which ornamented their bodies was human blood for whose spillage Lucrezia couldn't help but feel partly responsible.

Why in the world did they do it? she asked herself fiercely, as she followed Ssifuss into the heart of the silent battlefield. *Why did they insist on death when they only had to wait and let us pass? Why did they hurl themselves at the dragomites' jaws in such a passion of madness? Why did they invite the wrath of Dhalla's spear and Checuti's bombs?*

She wondered, while she stacked these unanswerable question about her consciousness like a barricade, whether the real enigma was why the attackers' resolve had broken so swiftly and so absolutely, and why they had fled in such awful disarray, but it seemed to her that the answer to those questions was uncomfortably near to her reasons for subjecting herself to the internal barrage. They had fled, she supposed, because it had all become too much to bear: the blood, the broken bodies, the terror, the horror, the sheer enormity of it all . . .

The battlefield, she reluctantly realised, wasn't completely silent. Not all the fallen men were dead. Some were moaning in pain while others called out for help. It was impossible to guess whether they didn't know that the shadows passing over them were the shadows of their erstwhile adversaries, or whether they were simply too desperate to care.

Ssifuss – who was, after all, an unhuman creature which thought humans were a disease – made not the slightest response to any of the appeals; the Serpent simply strode on in implacably resolute fashion, stepping over bodies when there was no space to go round. Lucrezia and Jume Metra followed on behind, keeping in step.

Lucrezia knew that Jume Metra had no more reason to be inclined to compassion than the Serpent, but she was possessed by an uncomfortable feeling that her own excuses weren't in such good order. She kept her eyes firmly fixed on the back of Ssifuss's head, refusing even to turn her head in response to the sounds which seeped from the ugly morass of death, but she couldn't approve of herself for so doing. Even though she had been a princess, and still was a witch, and even though these wounded men had done their utmost to secure her death less than an hour before, she simply couldn't suppress the instinct of self-hatred which rose into her throat like a choking hand.

The stink of it all was abominable, but she even hated the reaction of disgust which the reek provoked. It would have been easier to bear if the stink had just been blood, but it was not.

If all dead men lose control of their bowels, Lucrezia thought miserably, as her wall of calculated indifference crumbled, *even heroes must die without dignity*.

When they were clear of the battlefield – and the crossing took only a few minutes, although they seemed unnaturally long – no one looked back and no one spoke. Lucrezia had not looked down into the staring eyes of a single corpse, and she suspected that Checuti had refrained from so doing in exactly the same cowardly fashion, for exactly the same cowardly reason, but she knew better than to ask him. Nor did she ask him whether braver people might at least have paused to cut the throats of the wounded, to put them out of their misery. If Jacom Cerri had been with them, she might have asked him such a question, but she couldn't ask it of Checuti. The four of them kept on going, with their eyes fixed on the ground ahead, refusing even to look at the blood which clung to the horses' feet.

The track beyond the battlefield had been churned up by hundreds of racing hooves and turned into a muddy mire, but the further away from the river they went the better the going became and the faster their mounts were able to move. The horses gradually advanced from a walk to a trot, but Lucrezia made no attempt to go any faster. This wasn't because Ssifuss would not have been able to keep up, for he was moving very easily, but because she knew well enough that they had to hold something in reserve in case they were challenged and chased.

They moved in silence for a long time, until Lucrezia thought it was both safe and necessary to begin glancing behind and to monitor the southern horizon. For more than an hour the fear of seeing a company of Shabir's cavalry hastening to their pursuit remained acute, but Lucrezia found it paradoxically comforting in its acuity. For the time being, at least, she didn't want to relax. What she had been through was too terrible to be set aside abruptly.

In fact, though, they saw no one in the east or the south, and Lucrezia gradually became confident that there was no one to see. Eventually, she became convinced that they really had made their escape, and that the battle was over and done with.

Eventually, she was able to start thinking more reasonably again, and wondering what lay ahead of them. It was a long way to Salamander's Fire, but it seemed possible that they might still make it, and that if and when they did Fraxinus, Ereleth and Dhalla might be waiting for them. Eventually, she allowed herself to rest a little easier, and didn't feel too badly about the fact that she was able to do it.

In the meantime, the sun slowly sank before her, until it stood upon the hazy horizon like a great blood-red beacon beckoning her on into the great unknown.

Part Two

Following Divided Paths, United by Courage and Conviction

The people of the world were soon estranged from the people of the ship, and began to ask questions of their forefathers which the forefathers could not easily answer. So it is with every generation, that sons turn to their fathers and daughters to their mothers and say: 'Why have you brought us into this world? Why have you taught us this and not that? Why do you expect this of us, when we might desire something very different for ourselves?' It is in the nature of such questions that their answers never seem adequate to those in search of explanations.

'Why did you come here at all?' the people of the world asked the people of the ship. 'If we are the produce of another world, what business have we in this one? Why do you abandon us to the empire of corruption and chaos, when you prefer to remain cocooned in the ship, where all is serene and incorruptible? By what right do you keep a long and trouble-free life for yourselves while condemning your children to a life which is brutish and short? Why did your own forefathers build ships to cross the vastness of the void, when they had a perfectly good world of their own in which to dwell, and every reason to believe that it would be more hospitable to their species than any other?'

This is the answer which Goran the Forefather gave to the people of the world:

'Everywhere in the universe there is life. From every point of origin life spreads out, encountering other kinds of life. Wherever life exists there is competition for resources; the fundamental logic of life is reproduction and reproduction is innately competitive. Even if there were only one kind of life, this would still be true; the fact that there are many kinds of life merely complicates matters.

'Humans are alive, and by virtue of that fact are in competition with all other living things, including one another. Humans are alive, and by virtue of that fact are ambitious to expand their dominion. Were we to lose our ambition we would sacrifice our role in the unfolding scheme of things; were we to lose our sense of adventure we would prepare ourselves for extinction.

'It is because humans are alive, and capable of building ships to cross the dark void, that we have built ships to bring our children to all the other worlds where they might live. It is because humans are alive that each of those ships go on into the

void when its people have done what they could to prepare the way for the children which they leave behind.

'No place is entirely hospitable to life, nor can it be, for the essence of life is competition. The ship is no more a paradise of ease than the city called Idun, or the garden which came after it, or any of the multitudinous cities and gardens which your descendants will build and cultivate.

'Wherever there is life there is competition, and wherever one kind of life encounters another competition is intensified – but wherever there is life there is also collaboration, for every species which exists is directly and indirectly dependent on a thousand others. Collaboration is as much a part of life as competition, and whenever one kind of life encounters another the intensity of the competition which ensues can also give rise to new kinds of collaboration. Such new collaborations, when they arise, are rich and strange – all the more so if they are planned by no one, expected by no one, and subject to no one's control.

'This is the nature of life, in this world and every other; there is no way to avoid it but death and extinction. Should that be your fate – which is certainly possible – life will go on without you, careless of the fact that something has been lost; it is better far to live, and to live as boldly as you can, thus to take a proper part in the great adventure which is the universe of life.'

This answer did not satisfy the people of the world, but they promised to remember it, at least until the day when they could offer better answers to their own children.

The Apocrypha of Genesys

I

WHEN JACOM FIRST got to grips with his would-be assassin he thought that it would be an easy fight. His assailant was a much smaller man than he, and ought to have brought himself to the edge of exhaustion by swimming. Jacom was also confident that his own training in the Arts Martial must have been more extensive than the other's.

Unfortunately, the matter proved to be less simple than that. Jacom's training had not covered the skills involved in fighting while out of one's depth in a fast-flowing river, and whatever advantage of strength he had was offset by the fact that he was wearing much heavier clothing – including the greater part of his leather armour, which he had been reluctant to shed before entering the water.

It only required a few seconds of panic-stricken grappling for Jacom to realise that he was nearly as close to exhaustion as his opponent, even though he had taken no active part in the battle at the bridgehead save for the lobbing of a few bombs. He found that he had to concentrate his entire attention on the single problem of keeping his opponent's knife away from any part of his flesh. While he was doing that he suffered a variety of kicks and buffets, which hurt him in spite of the cushioning effect of the water. He also took several capacious mouthfuls of river-water, which tasted a good deal fouler than riverwater had any right to.

If only Jacom had been able to force his assailant to drop the knife he might have been able to bring the conflict to a conclusion quickly enough, but he couldn't do that while he couldn't spare either of his hands. His sword was still tightly bound to his belt, and he had no chance of bringing it into play. He had no alternative but to try to use his bulk to force the other man's head under the water, hoping by that means to drown him

– a difficult endeavour, given the way that they were rolling in the grip of the current.

Oddly enough, it wasn't until the soldier started yelling 'Truce!' that it occurred to Jacom that any such move were possible. As soon as he realised that the option was open, though, he saw its wisdom. The only thing which prevented him letting go immediately was the suspicion that his enemy might not be trustworthy. When he relaxed a little, though, the small man made no attempt to strike out at him, and so he relaxed a little more. By slow degrees their struggle to the death was transformed into mutual support, and when they finally let go of one another it was to strike for the nearest solid ground – which, as it happened, was the western bank. Once they had made that decision, though, their struggle became a race; Jacom knew that the first man to get clear of the water would have a considerable advantage, and he feared that a truce forced by necessity might not survive the temptation to seize that advantage.

Jacom didn't find it easy to get to dry ground even though he now had freedom of action. His limbs were like lead and his breathing was so laboured he feared that he might lose consciousness. The shallows were full of densely packed reeds, and the bank beyond was heavily wooded – there was obviously a considerable margin between the river and the road at this particular phase of its meandering course. The race turned out to be as near a dead heat as made no difference.

When Jacom and his erstwhile adversary had pulled themselves through the reeds to a grassy space beneath the boughs of a thick-boled tree, it quickly became clear that neither of them had enough energy left to continue the fight. They collapsed side by side, and lay there panting for what seemed like an age. When Jacom finally felt able to sit up the other was desperate to follow his example, but all they could do immediately thereafter was eye one another warily.

'It's no use,' Jacom said, in the end. 'Can we continue the truce indefinitely?'

The smaller man seemed very relieved to hear the proposition. He nodded, then brushed the back of his right wrist over his forehead to clear wet hair from his eyes. He was still holding tight to his knife, but now he tried to put it back into the scabbard at his belt. He was so weak that even such a simple task as that proved difficult.

'I'm Jacom Cerri,' Jacom said, when the other eventually succeeded in putting away his blade. 'Sometime guard-captain in the army of Xandria, lately in the employ of Carus Fraxinus, merchant-adventurer.'

'Munir Zanarin,' the other replied hoarsely, turning his arm so as to show the muddled red and white colours on his arm. 'Potter's apprentice in Mugol, conscripted into the army of the Nine Towns a year ago to fight invading dragomites and their nest-slaves.'

'I'm not a nest-slave,' Jacom said wearily.

'You fought with the dragomites,' Zanarin pointed out. 'Does that make you a fool or a traitor to your kind?'

'Merely a party to a strange alliance,' Jacom retorted. 'One that would have brought you no harm, had you only let us be.'

'The general gave you every chance,' the Mugolian said coldly. He was still panting, but it seemed that he had breath enough to make a speech. 'He took a risk and lost good men to get one of your people away from the dragomites and their warrior-women, but all he got in return was the news that you would defend the dragomites of your own will. If that isn't treason, it's certainly idiocy.'

Jacom wasn't certain that he could deny the charge with the vehemence it required. He wondered what he should do now. Zanarin couldn't possibly have seen him throwing Checuti's bombs at Shabir's shock troops, but it was entirely likely that some who had would be nearby, and well able to recognise him. It was too late now to claim that he had been nothing more than an unwilling captive of the dragomites. Instinct told him to get up and run, but he still didn't have the strength, and he knew that he had nowhere to run to. He had no idea how far south the river had carried him, but he had every reason to expect that the stretch of riverbank which separated him from Checuti and the princess would be crawling with Shabir's retreating forces.

'You lost a great many more men by attacking us,' he pointed out to the Mugolian, speaking very warily. 'All you had to do was keep company with us, to make certain that we crossed your territory and left it behind us. Now, you've ruined everything. We would have traded with you as friends if you'd only let us.

Blowing up the bridges was a vile trick – and cutting the rope while we were trying to regroup was just as bad.'

'Orders,' Zanarin said tersely. 'Divide and destroy. Keep as many of you as possible this side of the river, that's what Captain Burak said – that's why we were stationed upriver, as a rearguard to the men who set the charges that destroyed the bridge, waiting to see what would happen. I was glad to be there, certain I'd escape the whole fight. I couldn't believe it when I saw that there were people still alive on both sides. Were the rumours true, then?'

'What rumours?' Jacom asked.

'The word went round like wildfire that the amber we snatched had told Shabir that you had some secret weapon – something to do with witchcraft. I heard that Xandria was ruled by witches, who'd tamed the dragomites by magic. I didn't believe it at first, but . . .' He trailed off.

Jacom didn't knew whether he ought to contradict this bizarre statement or not. He had to think of his own advantage now, and if he were to end up a prisoner with Andris Myrasol – as seemed only too likely – it might be better if they both told the same story, even if it were a pack of lies. 'We had the giant,' he said evasively. 'Be glad that you came for me instead of her. If your captain had any sense, he wouldn't have wanted to keep the giant on this side of the river – he'd have been only too glad to see her get away.'

'What makes you think that the people on the far side will get away?' Zanarin asked scornfully. 'Divide and destroy – those were the tactics. Shabir will take his main force across the bridge at Tovali as soon as he can, and chase down the last few dragomites. If your friends are still with them, they're doomed.'

He didn't see what Dhalla did to Shabir's vanguard, Jacom thought warily, *and he can't know that they turned and ran in such awful confusion. How much do I tell him? And what do I do next?* He was breathing much more easily now, and thought that he might have enough strength to stand up – but the little man's right hand was hovering suspiciously close to the hilt of his recently sheathed knife. The two of them continued to watch one another in silence; Jacom knew that Zanarin too must be wondering what to do for the best.

'What now?' Jacom asked eventually, thinking that it was

best to bring the matter out in the open. After all, he was the one in direr need of finding a quick settlement of the matter.

'You'd best surrender to me,' Zanarin suggested. 'You can't get away.'

'And what would happen to me then?'

'No harm would come to you,' Zanarin said, confidently enough although he was presumably improvising. 'We're civilised folk – we don't slaughter prisoners of war. You'd be taken to Tovali, then to one of the bigger towns – Sabia or Ebla. The Convocation meets in Ebla.'

'What do you do with prisoners of war?' Jacom wanted to know.

Zanarin hesitated, as if he were trying to work out an honest answer. 'The Convocation would probably want to know why you were with the dragomites, and why you fought with them against us. If you could explain . . .'

'Somehow,' Jacom said drily, 'I suspect that they'd be just as difficult to convince as your general was. In Xandria, we put our bondsmen to work on the wall which surrounds the city – I dare say you have some similar way of making sure that they labour hard and long to make up for their transgressions.'

Zanarin shrugged his shoulders. 'What alternative do you have?' he asked.

'It wouldn't do either of us any good to start fighting again,' Jacom observed, 'whichever one of us won. Why don't we just go our separate ways?'

'You don't have anywhere to go,' Zanarin pointed out uneasily. 'Even if you manage to join up with some of your friends, you'll all be captured soon enough. We drifted a long way downriver, and there'll be a lot of our soldiers between here and the broken bridge. You might as well give up now.'

Jacom had an uncomfortable feeling that the man was right, but he wasn't in a mood to give up so easily, at least while he lay in such a sheltered spot, safely screened from the enemy. He knew that there was a good chance that he could kill Zanarin now, if only because he had by far the bigger blade and the longer reach. He knew that Zanarin must have made the same observation.

'Maybe I'll go downriver,' he said. 'One man travelling alone might not attract too much attention in Tovali, or whichever of your Nine Towns I fetch up in. I was bound for Salamander's Fire before, and it's the only destination I can aim for now.'

'You can't possibly get there,' Zanarin told him. 'Your skin might be the same colour as mine, but you're an obvious foreigner. News of the battle will travel much faster than you can, and it'll be horribly bad news to the families of the men who died in it. If you don't give yourself up, you'll surely die.'

'I'm going to Salamander's Fire,' Jacom said, in the calmest voice he could contrive. 'The only way that you and your countrymen can stop me is to kill me.' He put his hand on the pommel of his sword.

Zanarin immediately dropped his own hand on to the hilt of his dagger, but his eyes were on Jacom's blade, and Jacom knew that he could never have seen one like it. The expression in Zanarin's eyes testified to the fact that he was no hero; he had followed his orders to the best of his ability, and he had no desire to die for his cause. 'You're mad,' Zanarin opined, in a lacklustre fashion.

Jacom wasn't sure that the man was wrong, but he was determined. While he was still free and in one piece, he had to keep going. It was a matter of duty. He loosened the knot which bound his sword into its scabbard and drew the first few sems from the sheath to show off its solidity. Zanarin still had the hilt of his knife in his hand, but he had little chance of getting in a telling blow before the fight was rejoined on less than equal terms.

Zanarin shrugged his shoulders again. 'You're right,' he said hoarsely. 'It's best to walk away. You can get yourself captured in your own time – or die fighting, if that's your preference. I wish you luck – I really do.' He lifted his hand from the knife in a calculatedly ostentatious manner, and then he stood up. Quite deliberately, he turned his back on Jacom and began to walk away into the bushes.

He's a brave man, in his way, Jacom thought. *If only they'd all had as much sense as that!*

Jacom had only just relaxed, breathing out in profound relief, when the sound of movement in the tall reeds to his left sent his heart fluttering into his mouth again. He groped for his sword, but had not contrived to draw it when he recognised the person who had stepped out into the open.

'I'm glad you talked your way out of that,' Hyry Keshvara said equably. 'I thought I was going to have to kill him.'

'I could have taken care of him,' Jacom replied affrontedly. 'He knew it too – that's why he went.'

'I wouldn't have taken the chance,' Keshvara told him, in a curiously maternal fashion. 'Not while I had a clear view of his back and a dagger to throw. This isn't a game, you know.'

'No,' Jacom agreed, seeing her point. 'It certainly isn't. Are you alone?'

'Aulakh Phar and Merel Zabio are hidden in the reeds a few hundred mets downstream,' she replied, beckoning him to follow as she began walking. 'They're alive, but not at all well. I don't suppose there's anything in those pouches at your belt worth having, by any chance? Woundglue? Liquor? Money? Anything at all?'

'A few matches, doubtless ruined by damp,' he reported, as he stood up and hurried forward to fall into step with her. 'A razor, further rotted by rust than it was before; soap, probably melted; a couple of candles; needles and thread . . . in a word, nothing very useful, except a little protective cream to spread on my sword, in the forlorn hope of keeping the lustrust at bay. You?'

'Much the same. A little coin, of course – but whether it's spendable in these parts I don't know. These aren't the kind of people an honest trader feels she can easily do business with. We'd better wait until nightfall before trying to move on. We'll just have to hope that Aulakh and Merel will be able to walk by then.' She didn't sound at all hopeful about that possibility.

Jacom would have continued the conversation, but he turned instead as he heard the sound of hoofbeats crashing through the undergrowth. He heard Hyry mutter a violent curse.

He knew even before he saw the fast-approaching riders that they had little chance of defending their ground, and even less chance of running away. Hyry had reached for her knife as he reached for his sword, but they both stopped before bringing the weapons out. There was no point.

There were a dozen riders in all, though two of them were precariously perched on a single horse. The extra man was Munir Zanarin, but he didn't seem pleased to have been given the opportunity to ride. Jacom noted that the colours worn by the other men-at-arms were all alike, and that they were not the red and white of Mugol. He was quick to raise his hands away from his body to make it very obvious that he had no intention of drawing his sword.

'I should have killed him when I had the chance,' Keshvara muttered.

'I'm glad you didn't,' Jacom said. 'If they'd found him dead of a stab-wound in the back, they'd have killed us for sure.' He spoke uneasily because he wasn't sure that the newcomers weren't going to kill them anyway. Perhaps they would have, if they'd been soldiers who had come through the battle at the bridge, but they weren't. Two of them were civilians, and the remainder must have been their escort. They might have watched the battle, but they hadn't been in it. One of the civilians was a man of evident authority, whose clothes were neat and clean; the other was a bronze.

'All right, Zanarin,' Jacom shouted, as soon as he was confident that he could be heard by everyone. 'You win. We surrender.'

'Do we tell them about the others?' Hyry whispered. Jacom felt perversely proud that she was asking for his opinion, instead of making her own decision.

'We have to,' he said bluntly. 'It's their only chance of getting to a doctor, and if they're as badly hurt as you say . . .'

'I knew that it wasn't going to be easy to get to Salamander's Fire,' the trader murmured, as the neatly bearded man in charge of the company instructed two of his men to come forward and collect their weapons, 'but I hoped we might get a lot further than this.'

Trying desperately to find a bright side, Jacom said: 'Wherever they take us, it'll be south of here. It's on our way – and who knows what might happen tomorrow and the day after?'

2

LUCREZIA'S FEAR THAT she and her companions would be seen and chased by a company of Shabir's men gradually faded, although it didn't give way to any positive confidence that they were or would be safe. As the hours passed she slowly sank into a kind of trance; although she remained awake her thoughts drifted into a dreamy passivity and her eyes ceased to register the almost formless landscape.

At first she resisted this peculiar somnolence, but after a while it grew to seem luxuriously comfortable and she surrendered herself to its gentle grasp, and to the seductive governance of the dream. She couldn't remember ever having been in such a peculiar state of mind before, and wondered if it might be some lingering after-effect of the poison which the dragomite drone had injected into her when she had been taken prisoner in the Forest of Absolute Night – but she didn't dream about the dragomite nest, or about anything which had preceded her descent into its depths.

She dreamed, instead, of a warm world that was not a world: a world without sky or surface; a world full of substance and heat. There, it seemed, time was measured in slow and stately pulses which extended throughout the entirety of existence, not merely sustaining but delicately enfevering the rhythms of being.

She dreamed of a great tide which constantly changed colour from blue to red before fading back again: a tide which was never still but always searching, urgently burrowing into every hidden covert of the material manifold. She dreamed of sinuous Serpents and dragomite warriors, and of other things more peculiar still. Some, which looked a little like Serpents but stouter and more sagacious, she identified as Salamanders. Others, which had manlike faces, the bodies of leopards and tails like scorpions with enormous stings on the end, she recognised from nursery tales and fanciful paintings as manticores. There were many others to which she couldn't put names. All of these, for some strange reason, seemed very bulky and lumpen, as if she were looking at them with the eyes of an ant or a mouse.

She also dreamed of much tinier and less distinct but equally alien forms, so near to the limit of human vision that they ceased to be things at all, but became pure movement or pure stillness, complementary spirits of change and stability. She saw all this as though she were looking into some magical-eye device at a drop of water, magnified thereby to show off the complexity which even a drop of water – or of blood – might contain.

Throughout the dream, endlessly repeating like a sonorous chorus supported by the everpresent pulsebeat, a single nonsensical question marched upon her ineffectual awareness, pressing down on her with grave significance and yet leaving no scope or space for an answering guess, or even an analysing interpretation.

Why have I Serpent's blood, instead of Salamander's fire?

The question might have reverberated forever within the exhaustion-dulled frame of her mind, but forever was not available to her. Eventually, some other voice was bound to invade her isolation, and eventually it did.

'Are you ill, princess?'

Her trance might not have been sustainable had she been in the vanguard of the little company, but she had gradually fallen back to the rear. At first, Ssifuss had taken the lead, and then – following the dictates of some unspoken contract – Checuti had gone on ahead for a while. Now, Checuti had fallen back again, and Jume Metra had moved up ahead of Ssifuss.

Lucrezia blinked, and shivered slightly, although the half-bright night wasn't particularly cold and her clothing was now as dry as a bone.

'No,' she said. 'I'm quite well. There's no need to stop yet.'

'There is a need,' Checuti said, but not impolitely. 'Better than that – there's the opportunity. There's evidence that a large party of Shabir's men were camped hereabouts for a while – perhaps as recently as the day before yesterday – but they've sucked the land dry of every nourishment and moved on. I don't think they'll be in any hurry to return, even when they've regrouped and are reprovisioned. I think we can afford to rest a while, and I think we ought to take shelter while we still can.'

She looked up into the starry sky; there was no sign of rain-clouds, but there was an unusually cutting wind blowing from the south-west. 'We haven't much in the way of provisions for ourselves,' Lucrezia pointed out, 'let alone for the horses.'

'If we rest for a while now, and slake our thirst,' he said, 'we'll probably reach the marshes tomorrow. We must hope to find food there, and will certainly find water, even if we have to boil it to make it safe.'

She tried to rouse herself to true wakefulness, but the dream still hadn't quite vanished.

'I'm truly sorry, highness,' Checuti said, in a low and oddly humble tone, 'to have brought you to this.'

She knew that he wasn't speaking that way because she had once been a princess of Xandria, although she wasn't sure that he'd have spoken in the same polite fashion had she been born to Merel Zabio's station. Was this some kind of stubborn gallantry, she wondered, brought to the surface by the conviction that he was now in Fraxinus's place? Was he speaking thus to her because he sought some formal concession of his right to command? Or was he in search of some subtler reassurance?

'You didn't bring me to it,' she told him. 'I ran out and fell into your wagon. Since then, you've done nothing for which I could reasonably reproach you. Rather the reverse, in fact. I've discharged such debts as I owed you, but there's more than debt between us now.'

'That I know,' he said, with a sigh. 'The past is all wiped out, and there's nothing to consider but the future.'

'Our future lies with Ssifuss and Metra, for the time being,' she said, in case he had it in mind to make some secret compact between the two of them, disregarding their unearthly companions. 'We all have to work together.'

'I know that, too,' he said. 'I'd far rather be four against an unknown land than two, and I'm not so foolish as to hate Serpents and mound-women simply because of what they are. Can we rely on them, do you think? Metra will probably stay with us because she has no choice, but I haven't yet begun to understand what the three Serpents were about when they collected Keshvara in the forest and saved the rest of us from the nest-war. They've talked with you, I know – you're the one who's supposed to have Serpent's blood in your veins. Would you care to enlighten me as to your judgment of their purpose?'

'I only know what Mossassor has told me,' Lucrezia confessed, 'and I couldn't make much sense of that. Hyry spent far more time with them than I did, and her judgment was that Mossassor and Ssifuss disagreed on many matters. Ssifuss is the only one who can testify to its own motives, and it's been very uncommunicative so far. Perhaps it'll change its attitude now, under the pressure of necessity.'

'Perhaps it will,' Checuti agreed, without much conviction.

'It shows no inclination to desert us,' Lucrezia pointed out, looking at the back of the resolutely striding Serpent.

'Not yet,' Checuti conceded.

'You do intend to make every effort to reach Salamander's Fire, don't you?' Lucrezia said, well aware that the real point of the conversation had to be the question of which way they would go once they reached the relative safety of the marshes. 'You can't think that you'd be better off staying here, returning to your old profession in one of the river towns. It's a little late to hope that you'd be made welcome, given that you're one of the men who hurled several quarter-kilos of plastic at General Shabir's soldiers.'

'No,' he said grimly. 'I can't think that. I was a prince of thieves, remember – I'm far too old to start at the bottom in a foreign city. For the moment, highness, you're the one reliable friend I have in all the world.' He seemed to mean it, after his own ironic fashion.

'I'm no better off than you are,' she pointed out, implying by her tone that he had the better part of the bargain.

'Maybe not,' he said. He paused before adding: 'I think you might get more out of Ssifuss than I would, and I think we ought to find out what its objectives are, if we can. You're certainly better placed to talk to Metra – and it might be useful to have a more accurate estimate of her state of mind too.'

That's why he's so polite and conspiratorial, she thought. *He requires my services as a diplomat.* But she couldn't help feeling glad that he thought her services worth requiring, and she could see the sense in what he said. Now that they were past the point where nothing mattered but immedite survival, they had to be reassured that they were all of one mind and all of one purpose – or to be forewarned if they were not.

Lucrezia eased her tired mount forward until she came alongside Metra, while Checuti removed himself to a respectful distance. Metra eyed her warily, but she seemed ready enough to talk. 'Can a lone human possibly institute a dragomite nest with a single sackful of eggs?' Lucrezia asked bluntly. There was little to be gained by trying to employ finesse in talking to warrior mound-women.

'Perhaps,' Metra said. 'Will you and the fat one try to stop us?'

The mound-woman was evidently anxious on that score, now that she had not a single dragomite to intimidate her companions; she was just as anxious to know exactly how things stood with the no longer corpulent Checuti. Lucrezia noticed that Metra had not abandoned the first person plural, even though she had lost every last one of her sisters.

'We won't try to stop you,' the princess said soberly. 'You have my word on that. We're precious few as it is – we can't afford to go our separate ways, given that we must all vanish into the marshes before Shabir's men catch up with us. Will Ssifuss stay with us, do you think?'

Metra seemed surprised to be asked that question, but she seemed to be giving it serious and sincere consideration; several seconds went by before she answered. 'The Serpents made sisterhood with the drones,' she said finally. 'They are not sisters themselves, as you and the fat one are not sisters, but they know the worth of sisterhood . . .'

She trailed off, not sure how to proceed. Lucrezia took the inference that in Metra's view Ssifuss was trustworthy – more trustworthy, at any rate, than Checuti and herself. Lucrezia also inferred that Metra stood in dire need of reassurance that she was not entirely alone. Human though she was, she had always been part of a close-knit sisterhood, in which all were of one mind and one purpose – or liked to think so. 'Checuti came to your aid when the battle was almost lost,' Lucrezia pointed out, thinking that it would do no harm to make much of that fact. 'Were it not for his bombs and Dhalla's reach, you'd have died with your warriors. You needn't doubt him now, any more than you need doubt me. If we can have confidence in the Serpent, we are all united in a common cause.'

Metra was obviously in a forthcoming mood, and must have been grateful to Lucrezia for breaking the silence which had consumed the party. 'Ssifuss has not spoken,' she said, 'but we may be sure that it will help us. It must find Mossassor, if it can. There is a matter of obligation.' She stopped, but apparently decided that the time was ripe for unburdening herself. 'There is no reason why it should have brought the drone,' she added awkwardly.

'Would you rather we had left the head behind?' Lucrezia asked curiously. 'I thought you'd approve. It's supposed to be a living thing, after all – part of the nest you're trying to save. Surely you should be glad that Ssifuss picked it up.'

'Not necessarily,' Metra said grimly. 'Cannot be trusted. If ever it speaks, don't believe what it says.'

'I don't understand,' Lucrezia said. 'In the dragomite nest, I was told more than once that you were all of one mind. According to Andris Myrasol, the human drone shared the same flesh as the dragomite queen – he said that they were parts of the same chimerical whole. Why should you warn me against it?'

'Human drones are not to be trusted,' Metra told her. 'It is their nature.' The uncertainty of her manner suggested that she wasn't being stubbornly enigmatic; Lucrezia felt sure that if she had been able to offer a fuller explanation, she would have done so.

'Perhaps your claim to be all of one mind isn't as simple as it seems,' Lucrezia suggested tentatively. 'The lore of Genesys tells us that the essence of life is competition, and that collaboration arises out of that competition. I can't pretend to know what kind of mind your hybrid queen possessed, but to the extent that she was human, she must have needed a measure of competition and opposition, doubt and challenge. Perhaps that's what the human drones were for.'

'Perhaps,' Metra echoed, although it was obvious that the argument had meant little to her; in speaking out against the human drone she was merely parroting a warning that must have been given to her a long time ago.

'Most humans think of any alliance between humans and dragomites as a horrific thing,' Lucrezia went on, keeping a close watch on Metra all the while. 'That horror was what drove Shabir to attack us, even though he must have known that it would cost him dear. Reason would have told him to let us through, escorting us across his little realm to make sure that Fraxinus kept his promises, but he couldn't listen to reason. Had he known what the true relationship was between your people and the dragomite queen his horror would have been magnified even further. Many humans react in such a fashion to the notion of any kind of chimera – and it's hard to blame them when the examples which might be set before them include the Corridors of Power and the seeds Hyry Keshvara sold me, which grow in human flesh and turn people into thornbushes. And yet, the place which the lore bids us to call the Navel of the World and the Pool of Life is also called Chimera's Cradle . . . and if Fraxinus has read the wisdom of lore and legend rightly, it seems that some of those who pass for human, or half-human, are chimeras of a subtler kind. There is something in me called Serpent's blood, and something burning in the hearts of giants which they call Salamander's fire. I wonder whether you and I might be closer kin than either of us has realised.'

In saying this, Lucrezia didn't expect any kind of agreement from Jume Metra. She was, in fact, talking to herself rather than to the mound-woman – but the reply she got surprised her.

'Humans aren't so very different from dragomites,' Metra said. 'They have their nests and their nest-wars. Human drones lie too. The fat one lies all the time.'

'Checuti's not as fat as he used to be,' Lucrezia pointed out, by way of reflexive evasion, 'and I dare say he'll get thinner yet.' What she was actually thinking was: *Do you never lie? Can you possibly think that I never do?* But she was supposed to be a diplomat building bridges, just as she had been when Jume Metra took her down into the dragomites' nest, and she said no such thing. 'You needn't doubt Checuti,' she added, not entirely without sincerity. 'He's an honourable man, in his way. You can trust him. I hope that we can all trust one another.'

She looked up as she spoke. The flamestars shone reassuringly bright, but many of their fainter companions were eclipsed by hazy cloud. There were still several hours to go before the midnight, but Checuti was right; it would be wise to rest before then, even though they had nothing to eat and no great abundance of water to drink. The horses were tired, and Ssifuss must be very tired indeed.

Checuti drew level with them again, his arm outstretched.

'There's a farmhouse away to the left,' he said. 'Shabir's men must have been using it until yesterday, but I doubt that they left anyone behind to guard it. It's just possible that they left some scraps of food behind when they loaded their carts.'

'I doubt it,' Lucrezia said.

'It's shelter nevertheless,' Checuti said. 'The cloud's light as yet, but the wind's blowing so briskly that the weather could change quite suddenly. At least we'd be out of sight there. If we bed down in the open, we'll be more vulnerable.'

'I don't know,' Lucrezia said dubiously. 'If there are Eblans around, they'll know this place is here, and they'll be just as enthusiastic to find shelter as we are. It might be safer to avoid the place.'

Checuti clearly didn't agree with this judgment. He was a man who valued stout walls, and the possibility – however slim – of finding something worth stealing. 'What do you think?' he asked Jume Metra.

'Best inside,' Metra opined. It was only natural, Lucrezia supposed, that she should think of enclosure as a good thing.

The Serpent had come back to join them now.

'Besst insside,' it echoed, adding its own voice to Metra's.

'There are no horses there,' Checuti observed. 'And there's no light inside. I think it's worth the risk.'

I'm not a princess any more, Lucrezia reminded herself. *I'm just a traveller.*

'All right,' she said. 'But let's take a look first, just in case. Metra and Ssifuss can look after the horses until we're sure the place is empty.'

Checuti nodded in agreement.

As soon as they had dismounted Lucrezia took a dagger from her pack. She made no attempt to anoint it with any of the poisons from her belt, but she held it ready for use. Checuti smiled, and armed himself in like fashion. They tied the horses to the stump of a long-dead tree a full hundred mets away from the farmhouse and its derelict barns. Ssifuss and Jume Metra seemed perfectly happy to stand and wait for a signal that would tell them it was safe to approach.

As she and Checuti moved off, it occurred to Lucrezia that the world could rarely have seen such a motley crew as the one which they now constituted. *But what of it?* she thought. *Are we not commanded by our lore to respect all life, and to be generous with all who come to us for aid? The men of the Nine Towns may have forgotten that, but we have not.*

The flamestars didn't seem so bright now that there was a risk to be taken, and the building's interior looked very dark indeed as Lucrezia and Checuti walked towards it. 'I'll lead the way,' Checuti said, as they drew close. 'Stay right behind me – if we do surprise anyone, make very certain it's an enemy you're stabbing, not a friend.'

3

ANDRIS FELT EXTRAORDINARILY well. He couldn't remember ever having felt so well in his whole life. In fact, he had the feeling that he had never before *been himself*, and that now – at last – he had some small inkling of what *being himself* might involve.

Since infancy he had always had a sense of not belonging to the places in which he found himself – a sense which had not diminished in the least when he had exiled himself from Ferentina rather than be caught up in the incestuous conflicts which waged perpetually about its petty throne. He had never felt at home anywhere, not even in the privacy of his own skull, and had just about got to the point where he assumed that everyone must feel like that, all the time . . . but he now knew that he had been wrong. It was possible to feel at home; it was possible to *be himself*. He hadn't acquired the gift as yet, but he had caught a glimpse of the promised land. He knew that true identity awaited him, needing only to be sought out and claimed.

The only problem was that there were people in the world determined to keep him from attaining that goal. There were people in the world who didn't even want to leave him where he was, but wanted instead to drag him back to his previous state of being, in which contentment seemed an impossibility. There were people in the world who wanted him in the world, who wanted to make him a captive of awful reality and tedious wakefulness. There were people in the world who simply wouldn't let him alone, who insisted on shaking him, because they wanted to bring him back from where and what he was to pain and discomfort and anguish and danger and restlessness and . . .

'Stop shaking me like that!' he complained loudly.

That was a mistake. By speaking aloud he had added his own voice to the urgent pressure which was dragging him back from blissful innocence to nausea and aching distress. In actively resisting the hand that was shaking him he shook himself, and sent waves of pain surging upon the strand of his oblivion, which doused his sleep as effectively as a bucket of water cast upon a bravely flickering candle.

'Oh, come on!' said a voice, which was not in the least apologetic. 'We have to get out of here! If you can't pull your rottin' self together I'll rottin' well leave you behind. Wake up, for Goran's sake!'

Andris didn't want to wake up, because he knew that waking up was going to be very uncomfortable, but he couldn't stop whoever was shaking him from doing it unless and until he did wake up. He groaned, but the shaking didn't stop. It continued until he was able to import words into the groan, saying: 'Corrosion and corruption! Let me be! I feel *terrible*.'

'I'm not surprised,' said a voice that might have come from anywhere. 'They must have stuck two or three of those rottin' thorns in you. I'm half your size an' I bin awake for hours. You really annoyed the rottin' bastards, didn't you? You just had to go an' get right up their rottin' noses.'

Andris tried to open his eyes. He thought he'd succeeded but he couldn't be sure. He couldn't see anything at all – not even a severed head. He no longer felt as if he were himself, or as if it were possible ever to become himself. He ached all over and there was a truly nasty sensation haunting his belly. 'It's dark,' he observed.

'That's your fault too,' Herriman told him. 'After you started playin' stupid games, they even took away the candle. We got nothin' – except that they ain't come back to kill us . . . *yet*.'

'How long has it been?' Andris asked hoarsely. He was lying on his back, and he had to use both hands to lever himself up into a sitting position. His head was pounding and his neck was stiff, but he managed to do it.

'Too long,' Herriman said. 'Come on, man – we've got to get out of here. I thought you'd never wake up. I'd've left you for sure if I'd been able to raise that rotting trapdoor, but I ain't got your muscles, an' I got a bad leg too. They could be back any time now – we got to get out. It was really stupid gettin' up their noses like that. At least they'd've left us a candle.'

Andris steadied himself, working his jaw furiously to stimulate the production of saliva, in the hope of restoring a comfortable moistness to his mouth. He clutched his right hand to his grumbling belly, but he couldn't put his left hand to his aching head because he still needed it to support himself. 'Got any water?' he croaked.

'Course not. Like I said, we got nothin'. Nothin' except a chance to run before they come back to finish us off. We have to go.'

'They won't come back just to kill us,' Andris said. *If they'd wanted to do that*, he thought, *they could have done it before they left. Shabir might have wanted it, but Nath didn't – and even though they didn't like one another very much, Shabir daren't kill us without Nath's agreement. He filled me full of that drug, but he didn't cut my throat. Which means, presumably, that he did intend to collect me again – so why aren't they here? Can it be that they really did get routed when they attacked the caravan?*

It was comforting to be able to think coherently, but not nearly as comforting as it had been not to have to think at all. He reached out and rubbed his ankles to help restore the circulation of his blood. Then he touched his belly again, this time feeling for the place where Shabir had rammed in the thorn as if it were a dagger. His shirt was stuck to the flesh by clotted blood, but the wound didn't seem to be too serious. At least one other thorn had been jabbed into his neck, not so very far from where one of the original ones had hit him while he'd been standing by as Phar repaired the wagon wheel. Why in the world hadn't he had the good sense to stay in out of the rain?

'They could be back any time,' Herriman complained. 'We'd've been all right if you hadn't . . . filth, even bein' drafted would be better than this. What're we goin' to do now, hey?'

'I don't know,' Andris said. 'How long was I out before, after I got hit by two darts? Six hours, do you reckon? Ten, maybe?'

'How would I know?' Herriman said uselessly.

'It doesn't matter,' Andris admitted. 'It wouldn't necessarily follow that three would put me out longer. The dosage must be a trifle haphazard. There's no way to tell whether it's day or night, tomorrow or the next day.'

'Just get up,' Herriman said. 'Get up the rottin' stairs and put your rottin' back to the rottin' trapdoor. If you can't shift it . . .'

He broke off without bothering to finish the sentence. Andris could follow the reasoning well enough – if he couldn't shift the weight blocking the trapdoor, it probably wouldn't matter whether Shabir's men came back or not. They had no food, no water and no light.

'It's OK,' he told his companion, trying to sound confident. 'I've broken out of jails before. I might have to stand on top of you to reach the ceiling, mind, if the trapdoor is securely jammed.'

'If it comes to that sort of work,' Herriman said, disgustedly, 'I'll be the one who's standin' on—'

This time he broke off much more abruptly, and not because he didn't care to spell out what he was going to say. He broke off because someone was walking very cautiously across the creaking floorboards of the room above. Andris froze, and tried to count the number of feet involved. He became certain, after a moment's calculation, that there were two pairs of heavy boots – but their wearers were trying to tread very lightly, in the hope of remaining unheard.

Andris remembered that Tarlock Nath and the bronze Amyas had been wearing stout riding-boots, just like the ones the soldiers wore, but they surely wouldn't have come here alone, without attendants. On the other hand, soldiers didn't travel in pairs unless they absolutely had to; there was no point in being in an army unless you could turn out in force. Perhaps the two men he could hear were simply scouts, sent on ahead to check the situation before their friends moved in.

'I told you so,' Herriman hissed in his ear.

'If they've come for us,' Andris whispered, as softly as he could, after another pause, 'they're in no hurry to open up that trapdoor' – but even as he spoke he heard a scraping sound, which told him that the people up above had begun moving something from the vicinity of the sealed entrance. There was another faint noise, which he took to be the muted sound of a voice. He couldn't hear what was said, but he was fairly certain that it was a male voice.

'There's not many of them,' Herriman said, still keeping his voice as low as he possibly could by putting his mouth uncomfortably close to Andris's ear.

'But if it's daylight up there, or if they have a candle,' Andris murmured, 'their eyes'll be adapted to the light, and ours aren't. We'd have to come out of the darkness at them, and hit before they had time to react.'

Herriman didn't bother to point out that Andris had neglected to take into account the fact that there was hardly room enough for one of them to lie in wait at the top of the stone stair which led up to the cellar door, let alone two. Nor did he draw attention to the fact that anyone who opened the trapdoor was likely to be armed and very much on the alert. Nor did he volunteer to take the lead.

Andris groped his way towards the flight of steps, thankful that his own boots made very little sound on the dirty floor. He didn't wait to see whether Herriman followed him. In fact, he didn't much care whether Herriman followed him or not.

He heard the unmistakable sound of something very heavy – obviously the table – being dragged away from the corner where the trapdoor was. However it had been wedged, and whatever might have been put on top of it, the table must have been the key element in the barrier sealing the trapdoor; it must now be clear of obstruction, and would only need to be lifted up.

Andris had found the flight of stone steps, and he began to creep up them on all fours, as quietly as he could. The people up above were still moving around with a good deal of discretion, but they were making more than enough noise to drown out the sound of his own movements. He heard more scraping, which he took to be the sound of the table being seized and tipped, so that it might be brought upright. No one had yet set a hand to the trapdoor, and Andris knew that their failure to do so gave him the chance to carry the fight to the enemy, and perhaps take them by surprise. It was possible, after all, that they didn't know he was here, and hadn't come here with the express purpose of killing him. But even if they were just scouts, they might have ten or a hundred fellows waiting within earshot; he couldn't assume that he would only have two adversaries to face.

He paused as he reached the point on the stair at which he could put his own hand upon the trap, and he tested its weight very carefully. His body was uncomfortably cramped, but he was sure that he could move quickly, under the spur of necessity.

He tried to prepare himself mentally. What did it matter that the men above might be armed, he asked himself, given that the Eblans' weapons were so puny and his own muscles so powerful? What did it matter that they might have friends lurking outside, given that they had probably been through a battle and might well be hurt and exhausted? What did it matter what the odds were, when a man had no alternative but to gamble?

The trapdoor couldn't be opened noiselessly because its iron hinges had long since fallen victim to the ravages of lustrust, but Andris was more worried about sight than sound. Assuming that the room above was lighted, naturally or artificially, the light would blind him for at least a few seconds when he hurled back the trap and leapt up into the room. He would have to strike out blindly, at least in the first instance, and to do that he needed to know where his adversaries were. He strained his ears to catch the slightest sound – and then realised that thin slivers of light were now penetrating the trapdoor where its boards had warped. It had been dark up above, but someone had just lit a lantern.

He pressed his eye to one of the cracks, hoping that he might assist his eyes to adapt even though there was no possibility of seeing anything useful through the crack. He wondered whether it would be worth the risk of lifting the trapdoor an inch or two, in the hope that he could look into the room without being observed. He decided, on due reflection, that the risk was too great. He didn't want to give the enemy any warning, lest he lose the one advantage he had: surprise.

He took a deep breath and held it, tensing himself. He felt a sudden panic as he heard the sound of someone in the room moving towards him – or rather, towards the trapdoor. He heard a voice, and although he couldn't make out the words, he knew that they had been spoken by someone who was on the point of reaching down to take the ring set in the trapdoor and lift it up . . .

Having no time left, he threw the trapdoor back, and surged forth into the room, shutting his eyes despite his determination to keep them open against the sudden intensification of the light.

He reached out with his long arms to where he knew the other man was standing, intending to grab and grapple with him, and to use him as a human shield until he could see what the situation was.

He had intended his abrupt appearance to be a shock, and he certainly succeeded in that, for while he was still rising up out of the hole someone mere sems away let out a scream which was positively ear-splitting – and whose naked terror was music to his ears.

4

LUCREZIA COULDN'T HELP the scream which burst from her mouth as the trapdoor was hurled back and the huge form burst forth from the opening, but even as the reflexive yell split the silence asunder she recognised the figure which reached out for her. She would have been able to meet his eyes were it not for the fact that his own reflexive reaction had closed them against the light of the lantern which Checuti had just set down on the table.

The hinges of the trapdoor had broken under the force of Andris's thrust, and the boards shattered as they crashed against the floor. Broken pieces flew in every direction, one long splinter rebounding to stick in the back of Andris's thigh, but the bulk of his body screened Lucrezia from any danger. She leapt backwards as he lurched blindly forwards.

'Andris!' she cried, as soon as she had recovered the breath expelled from her lungs by the scream.

He was already snatching at her body, but he caught himself up. She couldn't be certain whether it was the splinter or the sound of his name which first interrupted him, but once hesitation had him in its grip the danger he had posed evaporated. He let her step clear, and steadied himself, blinking furiously. It was obvious that he was still partially blinded, but he knew now that something had gone amiss with his calculations and intentions, and he froze. He seemed strangely pathetic, standing there in the grip of absolute uncertainty, and she moved forward again, saying: 'It's me! Lucrezia!'

The amber lifted his arms, as if to confess that the situation had moved beyond his comprehension – but then he seemed to realise that a sharp splinter of wood had embedded itself in the back of his leg, and he turned to look down.

'Let me,' she said. 'Hold still.'

Meekly, he did as he was told. She turned him round and knelt down, then yanked the splinter out unceremoniously. He winced, but he didn't cry out.

'Checuti?' Andris said, as Lucrezia stood up, displaying her red-tipped trophy. 'Is that you, Checuti?'

'What are you doing here, you lumpen fool?' Checuti demanded, in a cheerful tone which belied the content of his words. 'You're supposed to be dead.'

'Andris?' enquired a second voice, from a different direction. 'What the rottin' filth's happenin' up there?'

As Lucrezia stepped away from him again Andris drew himself up to his full height, and dropped his arms, briefly making as if to dust himself down. It was a futile gesture; wherever he had been since he had been kidnapped from the caravan he had obviously had ample opportunity to become exceedingly dirty.

'I'm sorry, highness,' he said uncertainly. 'I didn't mean to startle you.' Then, raising his voice slightly, he said: 'You can come on out, Herriman. They're on our side.'

'Herriman?' the princess echoed. '*Our* Herriman?'

'Who else?' Andris said, recovering his wits. 'Do you have any water, perchance? We've been tied up in that dark hole for what seems like thirty hours and more.'

'With the horses,' Lucrezia told him. 'You'd better signal to the others, Checuti – they must be wondering what's going on.'

'What others?' Andris asked, as Herriman climbed up through the open hatchway, limping slightly as he moved to stand by the amber's side.

'It really is you,' Lucrezia said to the newcomer. 'Are Sergeant Purkin and his entire company waiting down there too?'

'Only me,' Herriman grunted gruffly. Lucrezia could see that the familiarity of her address had embarrassed him.

'What others?' Andris repeated, without waiting for the water to arrive. 'What happened? Did Shabir attack you?'

'He attacked all right,' Checuti told him hollowly, from the doorway where he was waving to Jume Metra and Ssifuss. 'The bastards blew the bridge while we were crossing the river – it seems I'm not the only one who automatically thinks of plastic when the need arises to plan treachery. There were two islands in the stream, but we couldn't all make it to safety. We four were stuck on the nearer side, with half the dragomite warriors, facing the whole rotting Eblan army.'

'And?' Andris prompted, when Checuti paused.

Lucrezia took up the story. 'The dragomites did what they could,' she said, 'with Jume Metra fighting alongside them. Checuti pitched in with his bombs, and Jacom Cerri helped him. I only saw the end of the affair, when Dhalla went to help Metra. When the warriors were done for she took over, whirling her spear like a battle-axe.'

'She took at least half a dozen sword cuts and an arrow in the thigh,' Checuti added, having now come back into the room, 'but she didn't even slow down. Maybe if she'd caught a second arrow . . . but the archers were almost useless by that time because too many of their own troops were in the way. If I'd ever seen the like of it before I'd never have dared blow the door of the Inner Sanctum back in Xandria. My darklanders felled her then with darts, but the Eblans didn't have darkland blowpipes at the ready. They came at her twenty or thirty at a time but they simply couldn't get to her – her reach is phenomenal, and that spear . . .'

'She can't have stood off an entire army,' Andris said. Lucrezia was about to say that indeed she could, but Checuti was too quick for her.

'The Eblans must have thought that once they'd got the dragomites it would all be over,' he said. 'They can't have suspected that the worst was still to come. They could have laid her low, given a minute or two more, but their nerve broke. As soon as a few turned tail the rest were off like rabbits. They ran as fast as they could go, in every direction – as much in fear of the ire of their officers, I suppose, as of Dhalla's spear and my plastic. They had us beaten, in spite of all their casualties, but they didn't have the guts to follow through. They broke under the strain, thank Goran.'

'Goran had nothing to do with it,' Andris said enigmatically. 'What then?'

'They scattered, but mostly they went south,' Checuti went on, shutting Lucrezia out yet again. 'The big wagon wasn't destroyed because the furthest bridge wasn't properly broken, and the warriors on that side took care of a handful of Eblans who came against them. We managed to get a rope across, hoping that we could all join up, but Shabir had stationed swimmers upriver with orders to prevent that. We lost Cerri and Dhalla trying. We had to get out while we still could – we were afraid they'd regroup and come back for us – but we haven't seen anyone since we came west. What happened to you?'

Jume Metra and Ssifuss came in then. Andris seemed slightly startled by their appearance, but made no comment. Metra was carrying a waterskin, which Lucrezia took from her and passed to the amber. Andris took a deep draught before passing it back to Herriman.

'Did they hurt you badly?' Lucrezia asked, noting the bloodstains on Andris's shirt. He seemed to have taken wounds in the neck and the belly as well as the back of his leg.

'Shabir wanted to know whether you'd really fight for the dragomites if they attacked,' the amber told her. 'Purkin's men fell in with a man named Tarlock Nath, who brought Herriman with him to see Shabir, adding to the confusion that was already afflicting him. My answers didn't please them at all. I tried using reason to persuade them not to attack, but it was a waste of time. They always intended to destroy the dragomites. Telling the truth only annoyed them, so I tried a few empty threats instead. That annoyed them even more, although I may have weakened the resolve of the men enough to make them turn tail a little sooner than they might have. Shabir threatened to send men back to finish me off, but I think it was just anger talking – he has more important things to think about. We'll have to do everything possible to stay out of the Eblans' way, though.'

'We'd already worked that out,' Checuti said.

'What about Merel?' Andris asked icily. 'What happened to her?'

This time, Checuti was perfectly happy to leave it to someone else to provide an answer. 'She was on the central span when it was blown up,' Lucrezia said softly. 'She was with Keshvara and Phar. They were all thrown into the water. I think Keshvara swam to help Phar, but I couldn't see. Jacom said that Phar looked badly hurt, but that Merel seemed to be alive. He said she was drifting with the current, but that she might have been able to make it to the shore. Could you see her, Checuti?'

'Sorry, no,' Checuti said.

Lucrezia looked at Ssifuss, thinking that the Serpent might

have seen what had happened to Merel before it scrambled out of the water, but it said nothing.

'We'll have to go back for her,' Andris said firmly. 'For all of them, I mean,' he added, after a moment's pause – although it was perfectly obvious that he had said exactly what he meant the first time.

Checuti looked away unhappily, leaving the princess to carry the argument forward.

'We've already been through this, Andris,' she said patiently. 'Our first priority has to be to get away from the Eblans. If they catch us, they'll kill us. We can't go south, not even to look for a crossing-point that might allow us to follow Fraxinus and Ereleth. It's too dangerous. We have to go west, as quickly as we can. We had to stop here to rest the horses, and we hoped that we might find some supplies the Eblans had left behind, but we can't stay long. We have to go into the Soursweet Marshes – it's our only hope.'

'*You* might have to,' Andris said stubbornly. 'I'll take my chances with the Eblans. I didn't fight against them.'

'I've been in the marshes,' Herriman put in dolefully. 'You don't want to go there if you can avoid it.'

'I'm sorry, Andris,' Checuti said again, more unhappily than before, 'but the princess is right. We can't avoid it. You know it won't make any difference to the Eblans that you didn't fight against them. If they'd won, perhaps you could have talked your way out of trouble, but they didn't. They lost a lot more men than they'd expected or hoped. When Shabir pulls them back together, he'll be even more determined to hunt down the people who humiliated him than good King Belin was to find the men who stole his precious Thanksgiving Day coin. They'll come here soon enough – as you must have known when you decided to leap out at us that way. The marshes are our only hope, and we have to get there as soon as possible.'

'Out of the cooking pot into the flames,' muttered Herriman expressively.

Andris didn't say anything. Lucrezia could see that he appreciated the force of Checuti's argument. She couldn't help feeling sorry for him, even though she didn't owe him anything any more. She was still able to feel fortunate that things hadn't turned out even worse back at the bridge, and she knew that

Andris ought to consider himself lucky that he hadn't been there, but she could understand why he didn't.

'If Merel is alive,' she said, 'she'll do everything possible to get to Salamander's Fire. Our one and only chance to meet her there is to go through the marshes.'

'Iss true,' Ssifuss put in unexpectedly. 'Musst hide. Marsshess only hope.'

'You're with us now, are you?' Andris asked the Serpent rather ill-temperedly. 'I got the impression that you weren't too happy before?'

'No sshoisse,' said the Serpent accurately. It was impossible to tell how bitter it might be about the fact.

'What about you?' Andris said to Jume Metra. Lucrezia knew that he was only doing it because he still had bile to spare, and felt the need to let it out. 'Where do you stand, now that you've lost your precious nest-mates?'

Metra didn't seem to be unduly offended or outraged by what she must have recognised as a wantonly cruel remark. 'All is not yet lost,' she replied, with what seemed suspiciously like a slight touch of sarcasm. 'We live; we hope; we fight.'

Andris looked back at Lucrezia. Lucrezia didn't want to hear what he might have to say to her. 'Jume Metra took some eggs from a dead worker's back,' she explained quickly. 'She'll go on till she drops, in whichever direction seems best. It's the only thing any of us can do, Andris. To go south or east from here would be to walk straight into the jaws of death. If Merel did survive she'll head for Salamander's Fire. Fraxinus said that he'd wait for us there, if it were humanly possible. We six will stand a far better chance if we stick together. We brought all the horses we could, including your mare, so one of you will be able to ride.'

Andris met her steady gaze. He must have known that she was right, and that she wasn't trying to give him orders. After all, she was no more a princess now than he was a prince.

'I'm with you all the way,' Herriman said unnecessarily. 'Even if it means the marshes.'

Lucrezia was tempted to point out that if Herriman and the rest of Jacom Cerri's men had been with Fraxinus all the way when he seemed to be in dire peril at the Corridors of Power, the company would have had a dozen extra men to set against

Shabir's ragged army – which might just have provided deterrent enough to discourage him from attacking them. She kept silent, though, telling herself that even if it had been true, which it probably wasn't, it would be far better left unsaid.

'How badly was she hurt?' Andris asked pointlessly.

'We really don't know,' Lucrezia told him, in a soothing tone which rang false even in her own ears. 'It makes no difference. We all have to go into the marshes. To do anything different would be insane.'

'I've been a sane man all my life,' Andris told her resentfully.

'So have I, my pale friend,' Checuti said, with ostentatious irony. 'So have I.'

'So have we all,' Lucrezia corrected him. 'And while we're alive, and sane, we needn't give up hope. We're all better off, simply by virtue of having found one another. Together, we might all stand a chance of getting what we want.'

It was a good speech, although it did beg the question of whether any two of them wanted the same thing. For now, at least, they were bound together by the desire to save their lives. Whether that would be enough to carry them safely through the marshes and out the other side remained to be seen.

5

CARUS FRAXINUS AND the mound-woman – who had recently revealed, under the pressure of enforced social intercourse, that her name was Vaca Metra – hoisted the last of the sacks into the wagon. They were both breathing very heavily as a result of their exertions, but Fraxinus didn't mind that at all. The knowledge that everything in the sacks was edible had made their weight a joy to grapple with. Nor did he mind that Mossassor had remained concealed in the wagon; diplomacy had made him insist that the Serpent stay hidden, even if it meant that they were one pair of hands short while they loaded up. Dhalla was not yet well enough to lend them the benefit of her strength, so it had not been necessary to debate with Ereleth whether diplomacy required that she too remained concealed.

While Fraxinus climbed up into the wagon and fastened the tailboard behind him Vaca Metra went back to the field where the four remaining dragomite warriors were unearthing turnips and wolfing them down. It was not the kind of food that dragomites were used to, but it had nutrition enough to sustain them, and Fraxinus couldn't quite find it in his heart to feel distressed that it was now they, and not he, who had to make do with alien provender. He was, however, prepared to hope that the food would help the warriors recover from their wounds and keep them strong; he had grown confident by now that the dragomites would fight for him as fiercely as they had fought for their human sisters and the egg-bearing workers. Whatever instruction the drones had given them still held – they accepted Fraxinus, Ereleth and Dhalla as nest-mates, with all that implied.

It would, of course, have been diplomatic to keep the dragomites out of sight too, but they could hardly be hidden, and the field where they had been sent to dig was shielded from the farmhouse by a tall hedge.

Fraxinus looked back at the western horizon, and was glad to see no evidence of a dust-cloud there. He knew better than to assume that the pursuit was ended, but he was desperately anxious to maintain a reasonable margin between himself and the army of the Nine Towns until the wagon reached the Spangled Desert.

He glanced at the farmhouse again, but he hardly expected to see the farmer or his children come to the doorstep to wave goodbye, despite his diplomatic efforts and the fact that he had given them a fair price for supplies which Ereleth had advised him to claim as legitimate plunder. He knew that the door would remain firmly barred, and that no one in the house would venture outside until the wagon and the dragomites were long gone. He couldn't blame them for that.

He moved to the front of the wagon, where Ereleth had just finished spooning broth into Dhalla's mouth. The giant was conscious now, but she had been able to swallow food even while she lay for a while in a virtual coma. Her hold on life was exceedingly stubborn.

'I'll drive,' the witch-queen said. 'You rest – but see if you can persuade her to drink a little of this tea. I know it tastes foul, but it will keep her fever under control.' She lifted a pot in which she had just prepared an infusion of one of her many witch's herbs.

'I thought the fever had run its course,' Fraxinus said, worriedly nipping his lip between his teeth as he looked down at the stricken giant, who did indeed seem very flushed. 'She seemed much better an hour ago.'

'It's just the hot food working up a little extra sweat,' Ereleth told him. 'It's not a bad sign. Fever helps to mobilise the body's defences – but it mustn't be allowed to run wild.'

Fraxinus didn't challenge this judgment, although he wasn't at all sure that Aulakh Phar would have concurred with it. It was, he supposed, only natural that Ereleth should consider witchery the highest of the medical Arts, and just as natural that Phar should be as sceptical of its claims as he was of its theories. For the greater part of his life Fraxinus had been a thorough-going pragmatist, only concerned with what worked and what didn't. It was easy enough to fall back on the pragmatism now, even though he had begun to suspect that more fundamental questions about why certain kinds of medicines worked might also have a very significant bearing on the questions which had lately begun to fascinate him – questions regarding the true nature of the mysterious work of Genesys which the forefathers had carried out in the Idun that had first been a city and had then been replaced by a garden.

While Ereleth saw to the horses Fraxinus took up the cup which Ereleth had laid down and sniffed it suspiciously. The smell wasn't particularly unpleasant, but when he took a small sip he realised that the brew was indeed very bitter to the taste. It was the kind of medicine which, in Xandria, a physician might have made palatable by adding a generous helping of molasses. Alas, there was nothing sugary among the foodstuffs which he had bought from the farmer.

Dhalla had closed her eyes briefly, but not to sleep. When he put the cup to her lips she opened them again in sudden alarm. Her pupils seemed incredibly huge as they stared into his face, having expanded almost to the rim of the rust-coloured irises which surrounded them.

'It's all right, Dhalla,' he said, although he was by no means sure that the giant was yet able to understand his words. 'It's some medicine of Ereleth's.'

The giant accepted a tiny spill, but then scowled and reflexively sealed her lips, so that a liberal drop dribbled down her cheek. The resentful expression made her seem oddly childlike in spite of her vast bulk.

'Take it, I beg you,' Fraxinus muttered. 'You have no idea how desperately we need you. I know what a labour it must be to remake the rivers of blood that you lost, but I wish that you could be done with it. If Shabir catches up with us, four dragomites will not be enough to save us from his wrath.'

It was Ereleth, now returned to her station, who replied. 'She'll have blood enough if and when the time comes,' she said, in a grim tone which didn't entirely support the optimism of her words.

The wagon moved off, jolting and juddering more than somewhat while Ereleth guided it back to the road. Fraxinus waited until the going became smoother before he tried again to coax Dhalla to swallow the supposedly magical infusion.

Dhalla kept her mouth shut, but the jolting made her shift about uncomfortably. There was a glimmer of intelligence behind her staring eyes now, and Fraxinus felt more confident about her imminent recovery.

'Come on,' he said to her soothingly. 'It will cool you down a little. You can't be comfortable, hot as you are.'

Mossassor shuffled back to take up a position close to the giant's massive thighs. The Serpent watched Fraxinus lift the cup to Dhalla's lips.

Dhalla had heard and understood what he said, and tried to mutter a reply, but the sound hardly escaped her tight lips, and it remained no more than a tremulous mumble.

'I can't hear you,' Fraxinus said, thinking that he ought to seize the opportunity to force her to take notice. 'Speak clearly – what did you say?'

The giant mumbled again.

'I still can't hear you,' the trader complained. 'You'll have to do better than that.'

She looked at him resentfully, but he was glad when she did indeed try again, this time opening her lips sufficiently to allow him to put the cup to them again. This time, she did swallow a little, and although she screwed up her face, she didn't turn away.

'What did she say?' Ereleth asked. 'I couldn't hear.'

'Nor could I,' Fraxinus told her. 'But if I read her lips correctly, she said *Salamander's fire*. I don't think she was referring to our destination – I think she meant that the heat she's feeling is Salamander's fire. Giants are supposed to have Salamander's fire in their hearts, after all, and I don't think she construes it as a metaphor for courage, no matter what you might say.'

Dhalla raised her head, and permitted Fraxinus to place the cup to her lips again. This time she made an evident effort, and took a considerable gulp.

At first, Fraxinus thought that Ereleth had decided to ignore his sarcastic observation, just as she ignored or repulsed most of his other efforts to get her to talk about what she knew – or thought she knew – about the hidden meaning of the myths relating to Idun and their relevance to the upheavals which had lately affected the margins of their world. In the end, however, she condescended to answer him.

'The Salamander's fire she has in her heart is not a kind of fever,' the witch-queen said, dressing the remark with a theatrical weariness. 'If she thinks it is, she's mistaken. I admit, though, that I was rudely dismissive when I told you that it was nothing but a metaphor for courage. It's more than that.'

'I always thought so,' Fraxinus said, speaking softly, as much for Ereleth's benefit as Dhalla's. He put out a hand to help support the giant's head while she took another draught of the bitter liquid.

'There is a relevant passage in the *Apocrypha of Genesys* which you haven't yet collected,' Ereleth said. 'I can't recite it exactly myself, but what it says, in essence, is that there were no giants in the world before the world, although there were many in its legends, because their hearts could not sustain them. Only in this world, the passage claims, may giants walk – and that they do by courtesy of the gift which Salamanders brought to the garden of Idun. That gift was the source of the fire that burns in the hearts of giants, and of the precious radiance of hope. I don't pretend to know what is meant by *the precious radiance of hope*. Nor, for that matter, do I pretend to know why giants need Salamander's fire to sustain their hearts.'

'Thank you,' Fraxinus said, as much to Dhalla as to Ereleth. The giant had finally managed to drain the cup to the dregs; having done so, she sank down, closing her eyes. After a pause, Fraxinus added: 'I can hazard a suggestion as to the latter question.'

Ereleth didn't turn to look at him, but kept her eyes stubbornly on the road ahead. 'I'm listening,' she said.

'Increasing the size of an animal – or a human – isn't simply a matter of magnification,' he said slowly. 'If you compare the way a dragomite's body is built by comparison with the earthly insects which also wear their skeletons on the outside and walk on six similarly jointed legs, you'll notice that their legs are proportionately much more massive. The same is true of Dhalla – her legs are much stouter than they would be were she simply scaled down to normal height. You can see the same sort of difference if you compare large and small dogs, or large and small horses. The capacity of a leg to bear weight depends on its width, whereas the weight it has to bear depends on the mass of the body. Doubling the dimensions of a body more than doubles its mass, so the legs have to be more than twice as strong. Do you see?'

'Of course I see,' Ereleth retorted. 'I'm not a fool.'

'The same rules must apply to internal organs,' Fraxinus said. 'Specifically, to hearts. I've watched dragomite warriors butchering others of their kind, and I've seen their entrails, which are nothing like the insides of insects. Insects are so tiny that they hardly need hearts or lungs at all – that vital fraction of the air which Phar calls oxygen seems simply to diffuse into their tissues. Dragomites have two pairs of powerful lungs, and multiple hearts, each one as large as a man's. They can breathe in and out at either end, and their ichor has the same redness as our blood – which Phar assures me, on the basis of his lore, has a vital bearing on the working of our every muscle. I suspect that Dhalla is so huge that a heart which was increased in mere proportion to her bulk would not be powerful enough to pump blood to her extremities. I think that some extra element has been added to her make-up which compensates for that deficit. In brief—'

'In brief,' said Ereleth, obviously anxious to support her resentful claim to be no fool, 'you think that although giants are reckoned by tradition to be earthly beings, she might in fact be a chimera.'

'I never was very clear about the distinction between earthly and unearthly life,' Fraxinus said. 'Now I wonder if it makes any sense at all. If Dhalla is a chimera of some sort, by virtue of her Salamander's fire, and Princess Lucrezia is a chimera of some sort, by virtue of her Serpent's blood, and Vaca Metra is a chimera of some sort, by virtue of being hatched from an egg laid by the dragomite queen, how can I not remember that passage in the lore of Genesys which tells us that we are all chimerical beings? The lore itself tells us that the remnant of Idun is called Chimera's Cradle for that very reason.'

As he spoke he looked at the Serpent, who was listening carefully to the exchange, although its command of human language was surely inadequate to let it follow the fine detail of the argument.

'Musst ssearssh for garden,' Mossassor put in defensively.

'Ansswerss there to many quesstionss.' Of that it seemed to be utterly convinced, though it had difficulty explaining why.

'There are said to be no male giants,' Fraxinus added, in a conscientiously speculative fashion, 'but I wonder whether that might be mistaken. An unwary observer might think that there were no male mound-people, but Andris Myrasol seems to have proved otherwise. The human drone he brought out of the nest was certainly a chimera, until it accomplished its own decapitation. It's a pity we don't know more about the home-life of the giants who send their children westwards to serve in Belin's harem.'

The real pity, he thought as he made these observations, was that Dhalla seemed to be as ignorant of the nature of her own species as he was – although that didn't seem so very odd when one bore in mind that Mossassor seemed equally ignorant about the reproductive processes of its own kind. He hoped that Ereleth might respond to his conversational cue. Like the dragomite warriors, she had lost what she was supposed to be guarding, and with it her ostensible reason for going to Salamander's Fire. Perhaps, Fraxinus thought, she might now be tempted to borrow a little of his curiosity, with which to cultivate a new sense of purpose. When it became clear that she was in no hurry to join in, he went on: 'The strangest chimera of all, of course, is surely the one which first involved us all in this affair – the bush whose seed Hyry Keshvara bought in the forest and brought to the Inner Sanctum.'

Ereleth condescended to respond to that. 'I wish now that we had had the opportunity to plant one of those seeds in its proper matrix,' she said. 'It might have been enlightening.'

Fraxinus was quick to take advantage of the opening. 'A bush which grows in living flesh can only be reckoned a clever parasite, even if it puts forth gorgeous blossoms and produces a powerful venom,' he said, 'but ever since Myrasol found that head I've begun to wonder whether those particular promises might have been vulgar lures to attract our interest. How I wish that Keshvara had interrogated her mysterious bronzes more carefully as to their origins and motives!'

Fraxinus had confessed as much to Keshvara only days before. She had agreed with him that she had been foolish, and she had agreed also that the most intriguing property of the seeds which had been entrusted to her might have had nothing at all to do with their ability to produce a powerful poison. The purpose of such seeds, Fraxinus now believed – and in using the word *purpose* he certainly meant to imply design of some sort – was to create a special kind of chimera. The question which now haunted him was: *If the plant had indeed reached its fullest maturity within the flesh of a living, conscious man, what might that man have been inspired to see and to say?*

'It might have been to our advantage to bring the seeds to full maturity,' Ereleth said, presumably thinking along the same lines. 'They were, I think, a message of some kind; we would have done better to hear it in full.'

'Musst ssearssh for garden,' Mossassor said yet again. 'Iss ssummonss. World becomess sstrange. Humanss musst ssearssh too. Iss debt owed to Sserpentss. Ssifuss would not believe, but iss true.'

'Mossassor is right,' Ereleth said, although she didn't seem to relish the fact, or the necessity of expressing her agreement. 'But it's not enough simply to go to the place where Idun was. We need the princess's Serpent's blood, and we need other things too. We must hope that the Salamanders can tell us more.'

'Yess,' said Mossassor. 'Ssalamanderss remember more than Sserpentss. We forget too mussh, becausse we have to. Ssey remember.'

Dhalla made another attempt to say something. This time, she was better able to make actual sounds. 'Salamander's fire,' she said, slurring the first word awkwardly. 'It burns. It *burns*.'

All of these observations, Fraxinus thought, were parts of the puzzle. All of them presumably had some relevance to it. They had not had much relevance to the myriad ways of life followed in the empire, and they had been let lie even by loremasters, unheeded if not actively despised – but now the world was changing, in some still mysterious fashion, and the meaning of ancient myths and ancient sayings was now something that needed to be plumbed. As yet, he had not the means to do it, but he had to hope that the nearer to Chimera's Cradle they came, the clearer matters might become.

'Perhaps, majesty,' Fraxinus said, with a slight sigh, 'we all left our homelands a little too precipitately. It seems that Mossassor and Dhalla have only myths and mysteries to guide them, and I fear that I was in too much of a hurry to see whether it was possible to cross the Dragomite Hills. I began my studies of the *Apocrypha of Genesys* far too late to find a proper understanding.'

'And I,' she said, with an echoing sigh, 'was hastened on my way by a daughter's recklessness and a villain's intemperance. I only hope – however absurd a hope it might be – that the villain can look after the daughter well enough to get them both to Salamander's Fire.'

'If the faint rumours I've heard regarding the Soursweet Marshes have any truth in them at all,' Fraxinus replied, 'it might be more apt to hope that she can look after him. She's a witch, after all – and the marshes are said to be full of poisons.'

6

THE GREAT HAYCART rumbled along the rutted road, continually jarring Jacom's weary bones. He huddled in a corner of the straw-strewn body of the cart, protecting himself against the chill of the night. He knew that dawn would break soon, but it seemed a long time coming; time seemed to have slowed to a crawl since they had been captured.

The main highway connecting the river towns had been far less comfortable than its Xandrian equivalent, but the narrower track along which they were now travelling was an order of magnitude worse. This was hardly a road at all, merely a strip of bare ground worn flat – or nearly flat – by the constant passage of horsemen and rickety carts like the one in which they were travelling. Since he and his companions had been placed in the cart Jacom had not caught so much as a glimpse of anything he could think of as a real road – by which he meant something respectably tarred or carefully gravelled – but nor had he caught a glimpse of anything which counted in his estimation as a town. The largest village through which they had passed had contained less than fifty houses, no more than half of them constructed with decent bricks.

At present, the cart was rolling between high hedgerows which the weak starlight turned into blank and silent walls, but Jacom could only see them if he placed his eye to the cracks in the cart's high side, which he rarely took the trouble to do, given that there was so little to be seen. No birds sang in the hedgerows at present; birds had the sense to wait for the sunrise before stirring themselves to meet the demands of labour and love.

By Xandrian standards of workmanship the cart was a travesty. Had Fraxinus's wagons been as poorly wrought they'd have been lucky to make it across the farmlands south of Khalorn without disaster, let alone the Forest of Absolute Night and the Dragomite Hills. To some extent, the inadequacy of the haywain was caused by the evident rarity of metal pins, but it could not be said that the vehicle gave any indication of adept woodworking.

In one of his less diplomatic moments, Jacom had mentioned the superiority of Xandrian workmanship to Munir Zanarin, but Zanarin's only response had been to sing the praises of the big water-wheels which provided power for the riverside mills, which he regarded as masterpieces of engineering. Having not yet seen one, Jacom didn't know how much trust to put in this judgment, but he suspected a certain degree of exaggeration.

In spite of the constant jarring, Jacom's captivity had not proved unduly uncomfortable so far. They had been fed whenever the haycart stopped – not merely for the midday and the midnight but at reasonable intervals in between – and the barns in which they had been set to sleep at midday and midnight had not seemed particularly dank or verminous. Neither he nor Hyry had been tied up, nor even particularly well-guarded. Either the leader of the party which had captured them – whose name was Tarlock Nath – assumed that they wouldn't try to escape while their two companions were still hovering between life and death, or he judged that their chances of making a getaway while they were in the middle of an unknown and well-populated land were negligible.

As a result of this relatively benign treatment, Jacom now felt less hungry than he had for many days, and his various superficial wounds were healing very well, although he still had some difficulty sleeping.

The cart lurched over a particularly bad pothole, drawing a muffled curse from Hyry Keshvara, who was sitting between the recumbent forms of Aulakh Phar and Merel Zabio. Both of them had been sorely hurt, but the bronze called Amyas had given Keshvara a tub of woundglue and some painkilling powders, while Tarlock Nath's servants had provided clean linen and disinfectant soap, and one of them had set Merel Zabio's broken shinbone as neatly as any qualified surgeon.

With these aids Hyry and Jacom had contrived to make the injured pair fairly comfortable, and Jacom was now confident that both would make a full recovery, given time. Both patients had regained consciousness for short periods of time, but once their most urgent needs had been answered they had lapsed into healing sleep. They had asked few questions, evidently taking sufficient reassurance from the fact that people they knew and trusted were there to tend to them.

Merel Zabio's condition was still the poorer of the two; Jacom suspected that this was not because her physical injuries were any worse – although her broken bone could hardly be regarded as trivial – but rather because she had not had time to absorb the blow of Andris Myrasol's loss before the Eblans' bombs had blasted her into the water. She often moaned and muttered in her sleep, and although no words could be discerned in the stream of sound, the dark melody of lamentation was all too clear. Although Phar was much the older of the two his heart seemed the stouter, and Jacom had no doubt at all that he would make a complete recovery in due course.

'Has your friend Zanarin explained why we're following a winding route through the back of beyond instead of travelling through the river towns?' Hyry asked, in a low voice. They had been given little chance for private conversation during the last two days, but for the moment Nath's men had withdrawn to the far end, where they were gambling in much the same fashion – and with much the same apparatus – as Fraxinus's darklanders had been wont to do. Munir Zanarin was watching enviously, perhaps wishing that he had coin with which to bet. Jacom judged that anything he and Hyry said might be overheard, but it seemed doubtful that anyone was actually listening. Even so, he moved closer to her before replying, placing his back to hers and then speaking out of the corner of his mouth in a virtual whisper.

'Only by implication,' he said. 'He seems scornful of Nath's claim that it's for our safety, lest Shabir's men or the relatives of those who were slain in the battle should try to revenge themselves upon us. He thinks Nath has other reasons for wanting to keep us to himself, perhaps connected with some deal he's made with Amyas. He takes it for granted that Nath's no longer working for this Convocation he's a member of, but purely for Antiar – or, more likely, purely for himself.'

'It does seem that the great Alliance has fallen apart,' Keshvara agreed, 'although I'm not sure why. It's not just that the battle went badly, although the men who were in it are obviously resentful about that. Our captor does seem to be afraid that someone else might try to take us off him; he doesn't want to pass through any town on the way to his own – especially Ebla – lest its leading citizens decide to detain us on their own account.'

'Zanarin's afraid that he might be claimed too,' Jacom added. 'He doesn't want to be redrafted to chase dragomites. He wants to go home, and he's content to travel with Nath because he's headed in the right direction. I think Mugol's the seventh of the river towns, the next but one downstream of Antiar. He doesn't have any recent news from that far south, but he's obviously worried. He won't say much about the rumours he's picked up – he seems to think that spelling them out might somehow add to their authority – but something is wrong. The dragomites aren't the only enemy the Nine Towns are facing, and the southern towns obviously disagree with the northern ones as to priorities.'

'I can't work out where the bronze fits in, though,' the trader said. 'I think he's sticking to Nath because Nath's got us – but what his interest is and why Nath's letting him do it I don't know. I wish they'd just tell us what's what – but Nath's obviously the kind of man who likes to keep everybody in the dark. Petty statesmen always tend to be fetishistic about secrecy and double-dealing.'

'He'll tell us what he wants in his own time,' Jacom opined, with a sigh. 'We have to be grateful that he has reasons for preferring us to be alive, whatever they are. Like Zanarin, we can be content that we're heading in the right direction. This might yet prove to be the easiest route to Salamander's Fire.'

'It always was,' Hyry said glumly. 'If only we hadn't had the dragomites with us, we could probably have come this way at our leisure. Now, alas, any bargaining you and I have to do will be from a position of dire disadvantage.'

'I'll leave the bargaining to you,' Jacom said. 'Whatever the position, you'll be a lot better at it than I am. For the moment, just being alive is breaking even. Anything else we get will be profit.'

'No it won't,' she retorted sternly. 'We've got a lot of recovering to do before we break even in my estimation. They may have us where they want us, but in my accounts they owe us a considerable debt by way of reparation for bombing that bridge while we were on it. Never be grateful to people for helping you up if they were the ones who knocked you down in the first place, Jacom – that's bad business.'

Merel Zabio shifted in her sleep and let loose a sudden volley of incomprehensible syllables. 'She seems to agree with you,' Jacom observed, putting out his hand to soothe her.

'So she should,' said Keshvara grimly. 'She's been as close to death as anyone can be and still get back in one piece, and when she wakes up she'll find that she's lost the love of her life. That's a heavy item to have in the debit column of your private books.'

'I thought you didn't place much value on that sort of thing,' Jacom said. 'The love of one's life, that is.'

'What makes you think that? Just because a trader doesn't let a flicker of interest show doesn't mean she doesn't want to buy.'

'You've never married.'

'I don't make bad bargains. As I said, that doesn't mean that I don't have any interest in the goods. If the price were right . . . but what do you care? Are you still mooning over the princess?'

'Of course not,' Jacom said, too quickly. He felt a shudder in Keshvara's back as she stifled a laugh. He rushed to add: 'She's not dead, you know – not even seriously hurt. If the Soursweet Marshes can be crossed, she'll do it. She's with Checuti, and Jume Metra too.'

'Almost as ill-matched a company as we are,' the trader pointed out, her voice not quite so hard-edged now. 'You forgot the Serpent who thinks humans are a disease afflicting his beloved world. I hope you're right, though. I'd almost begun to like her – Checuti too, for that matter.'

'Pity you got stuck with me, then,' Jacom observed.

'Oh, I always liked you,' Keshvara assured him, with what seemed like flagrant insincerity. 'How could anyone possibly take a dislike to you?'

'Dhalla seemed to,' Jacom said, recalling his failed attempt to persuade the giant that she was duty-bound to help him take the princess back to Xandria.

'Doesn't count,' Hyry replied. 'From a giant's point of view, all men are insignificant little pricks, no matter how handsome, charming and amiable they might be. Ereleth doesn't count either, for much the same reason. Witches are all shrivelled up on the outside, but inside . . .'

'Lucrezia's a witch,' Jacom pointed out.

'So she is.' Again the trader's voice had changed its tone, but Jacom was no longer able to fathom her mood.

The cart lurched horribly again, this time coming to a stop. Nath's men cursed volubly, having lost one of their dice through a crack in the cart's tailboard. For a moment, Jacom thought that one of the wheels had seized up, but then he heard voices from up ahead. At first they were too low for him to hear what was being said, but it wasn't long before they were raised in anger. He heard the words 'no right' and 'demand' echoing back and forth, but the voices soon merged into a clamorous cacophony.

Three of the men at the rear unlatched the tailboard and dropped down from the cart, with their weapons ready in their hands. The fourth came forward with Munir Zanarin to where Jacom and Hyry were rising uneasily to their feet. He showed them the blade which he held, but didn't make any obvious threatening gesture as he carefully stepped over the two recumbent bodies to peer between the slats of the cart's high wall.

'What's happening?' Jacom asked.

'Nothing,' the man replied negligently. 'Be still.' He wasn't one of the men who'd served in Shabir's makeshift army; he was a house-servant brought to provide his master with an adequate bodyguard.

The shouting had died down a little now, but the argument continued. Keshvara knelt down to look at Merel, but Jacom and Zanarin stepped forward to stand to either side of Nath's man, peering through knot-holes.

About a hundred mets away, where Tarlock Nath and Amyas had been riding at the head of their ragged column, there was now a considerable group of horsemen; it was obvious that they had met a party of similar size coming in the other direction, and that whatever pleasantries they had stopped to exchange had quickly given way to a dispute. Nath's men were bunching up behind him, and the narrow road between the hedge was now very crowded. The men who had dismounted from the haywain were running forward to swell the crowd even further.

'There's going to be a fight,' muttered Zanarin, half-gleefully and half-apprehensively.

'No there isn't,' Nath's man retorted. 'Be still and be quiet.'

Jacom glanced back at the rear of the cart, where the tailboard had been left dangling. The riders who had been stationed behind the cart had all overtaken it.

All I have to do, Jacom thought, *is knock this man down and disarm him, using any one of half a dozen elementary tricks, and I could be away. If I could wriggle through the hedge, while the horses had to find a gate . . .*

The flight of fancy was utterly pointless, and he knew it. He turned back to the lackadaisical guard.

'Is it us they want?' he asked. 'Are they trying to take us away from your liege-lord's custody?'

Jacom knew that the guard probably wouldn't recognise the term *liege-lord*, which was alien to the kind of elective democracy which seemingly prevailed in the Nine Towns, but he assumed that the question was readily understandable nevertheless. He wasn't surprised, though, when he didn't get a straight answer.

'These Sabians have no discipline,' Nath's man said disdainfully. 'They supply their quota of men to the Convocation, but they don't pull their weight. They've always thought themselves better than they are, considering their town superior to Antiar just because they're upriver of Ebla and we're down. They've no right to challenge a councilman like that.'

'But what are they challenging him about?' Jacom wanted to know. 'Do they want to take us to their own town?'

The other took his eye away from the crack so that he could turn his disdainful gaze upon Jacom, who likewise turned so that he could meet it. 'You think you're important, don't you?' he said. 'You fight with dragomites against your own kind, and still you think you're entitled to play ambassador. Well, you're not. You're like that rotting bronze – very civilised on the outside, but nothing but slyness and deceit underneath. We should have cut your traitorous throats. All of them.'

Jacom got the impression that all included Amyas and Zanarin as well as his own group – and quite possibly the entire population of Sabia as well.

Nath's man was right, though; the shouting had nearly died away now; the threatened fight seemed to have been aborted. The argument had dwindled into a reluctant agreement to differ.

If the Sabians really had wanted Jacom and Hyry Keshvara for themselves, they were evidently not prepared to risk bloodshed in the attempt to take them.

Keshvara was right, Jacom decided. He shouldn't be prepared to feel grateful simply because he was still alive. These people had tried their hardest to kill him, and they certainly weren't keeping him alive now because they regretted their intemperance. To Tarlock Nath, at least, he *was* important – and he would doubtless find out why in the fullness of time.

'Were you winning?' he asked, with calculated insouciance, nodding in the direction of the place where the gamblers had been playing their game.

'No,' the other relied sourly. 'I left my luck at home the day I was brought forth to join the defenders of our great nation.' He pronounced the words *great nation* as if the concept were an evil nonsense.

'That's a coincidence,' Jacom said softly. 'So did I. But one day, I expect to get mine back.'

7

BY COMPARISON WITH the territories through which they had recently come, the Soursweet Marshes had appeared – at first glance – to be positively hospitable. To Lucrezia, who had spent almost all her life in a citadel within a citadel, even the green fields beyond Xandria's walls had seemed somewhat alien, and the marshes did not seem to her wondering eyes to be conspicuously more strange or unwelcoming. Indeed, the profusion of birds to be seen hereabouts made them rather charming by comparison with the desolate lands through which they had recently passed.

The bushes which grew in great profusion wherever they could find adequate purchase were liberally bedecked with thorns, which presumably had some deterrent function, but there were few large creatures in evidence. The largest Lucrezia had so far seen were huge grey-winged birds with dagger-like beaks and glaring black-rimmed eyes. These were occasionally to be seen flapping lazily overhead, or standing in pools of water watching patiently for fish.

'There's a lot of meat on one of those,' Checuti had said hungrily, when they first caught sight of one of the big grey birds. Since then, Ssifuss has shot arrows at every one which provided an unmoving target, but they were far more agile than they looked. They couldn't take off quickly, but they could duck and dodge. The Serpent had not yet contrived to hit one. The birds didn't hurry to get away even when they'd been shot at, preferring to fix their adversaries with intimidating stares before taking off in their own time, beating their wings in a contemptuously lazy rhythm as they glided away to lose themselves in the great green maze. Although she'd rather have seen one brought down, Lucrezia wasn't entirely sorry to see them go once Ssifuss's arrows had missed; had they been minded to respond aggressively their beaks looked sturdy enough and sharp enough to do a lot of damage.

'We might try to follow one of them,' Andris Myrasol suggested, after the Serpent's fifth failure. 'If we could find its nest, a clutch of eggs might make a very nice meal.' The last of the dragomite-meat they had brought from the wrecked wagon was gone now, and renewal of their food supply had become the most urgent problem facing them.

'We don't know that it's the breeding season,' Lucrezia pointed out. 'Even if it is, a nest built high in one of those big bushes wouldn't be easy to plunder. The thorns get more vicious the higher they're set. Anyway, we'd have no chance of tracking one by night.'

The stars were shining brightly, but the midnight was approaching. They had all reined in to wait while Ssifuss went after its arrow, but Checuti was already looking around for a place where they might camp for a while. Andris was the only one apart from the Serpent who wasn't mounted. He claimed that he was best-equipped for wading by virtue of his height and long legs. He also claimed that he felt very well in spite of the minor wounds he had collected, and the bold way he strode out alongside Ssifuss at the head of the party suggested that he wasn't just putting on a brave face.

'The higher thorns're more than vicious,' Herriman reminded, not for the first time. 'The scratches itch somethin' awful, and no matter how careful you are, they get to you.'

'You have to keep away from those big ones that grow on the bushes with the little pink flowers, at any rate,' Andris put in, 'unless you want a good long sleep and strange dreams, but otherwise they're not so bad. Even the big ones aren't entirely nasty. A mixed curse – if you can have mixed curses as well as mixed blessings.'

'It's not the big ones that're the worst,' Herriman said, in his insistently downbeat manner, scratching his right leg as if by way of demonstration. 'You just haven't felt the worst of them yet.'

'There are hundreds, perhaps thousands, of different kinds,' Checuti observed. 'Given that they crowd every strip of dry land so very ardently, we can hardly avoid contact with them. We'll just have to keep on taking our chances.'

'We have a measure of protection in my pouches,' Lucrezia assured them, scratching an itch on her own arm which seemed to have been brought out by the argument. 'The lore of witchery has nothing specific to say about the poisons of the Soursweet Marshes, but all poisons can be countered, if one has the means and the Art.'

'Does that mean you can identify the dangerous ones?' Checuti asked sceptically.

'Not exactly,' Lucrezia admitted, 'but I ought to be able to recognise the symptoms if anyone does get badly affected, and I might well have an antidote in my belt.'

'*Ought* and *might* are words less calculated than some to build confidence,' Checuti pointed out. 'Perhaps you weren't such a good student as Ereleth believed – or perhaps she wasn't much of a teacher.'

'Magic isn't a simple and straightforward business,' Lucrezia informed him placidly. 'It's not like thievery.'

'If you think thievery's a simple and straightforward business, highness,' Checuti was quick to retort, 'you've led a very sheltered life.' His tone remained light, although there was an element of strain in it which was probably born of hunger.

By then Sssifuss had returned, clutching its unsuccessful arrow, and they moved on.

Where the rocky apron on to which they had first descended from the Dragomite Hills met and merged with the marshes it had been relatively easy to find a safe course into the green maze, but once they had gone a kim or so further there had been no more ribbons of bare rock to be found, and few patches of grassy ground. The horses had learned quickly enough that too close an approach to the thorny bushes was a hazardous business, and their riders hadn't needed to exert overmuch authority to persuade them to wade through the shallow pools and rivulets which soon provided the only significant interruptions to the dense scrub. These had perforce become their way through the vast maze, although their progress was becoming increasingly difficult and much slower.

Andris and Ssifuss, who always walked ahead of the horses, had soon learned that there were very few places where the water pooled to a depth of more than a met. They hadn't been able to go straight, but they'd kept reasonably well to their heading. They'd turned south as soon as they felt that they were far enough away from the edge of the marsh to stay clear of any remnants of Shabir's army.

It hadn't taken long to figure out how the marshes had earned their name. Once they were deep in the heart of the marsh, it had become obvious that Andris and Ssifuss were finding it increasingly difficult to make headway. Lucrezia had only had to scoop up a little of the water in her hand and let it run through her fingers to realise that it was unnaturally viscous, and not by any means as transparent as it should have been. Herriman, on the basis of his previous experience, had declared that the water tasted peculiar but was not wholly unpleasant, but Checuti had not been willing to be reassured.

'The sticky stuff could contain all manner of tiny organisms,' he had pointed out. 'One draught might be perfectly safe, another deadly. Better to boil it first, I think.'

That, alas, had been far easier said than done. The kettle they had was big enough to provide drinking water for six, but building a fire to set beneath it was an awkward business. In the Forest of Absolute Night foraging for fuel had been a mere matter of picking up sticks, but there was no such litter here. The only solid wood available had to be won by hacking through tangled branches whose elastic qualities made them stubbornly resistant to the sharpest blade; bushes which had no thorns at all were rare. Dry kindling was very hard to find, but had to be gathered in adequate quantities lest their precious matches be wasted in futile attempts to light it. Once ignited, the wood was so full of sap that it burned very reluctantly, with an abundance of odorous smoke.

Lucrezia had found her nagging thirst easy enough to bear while they were on the move, but it quickly came to seem unbearable whenever there was nothing to do but wait while her companions struggled to keep a tiny flame alive and build it into an efficient producer of heat. Constant repetition of this ritual didn't make it any easier to bear. It was no more tolerable now than it had been when they had first been forced to enact it, although they had now been in the marshes for days.

'If there's anyone coming after us,' Checuti observed, when they had finally contrived to light an uncommonly smoky fire, which would see them through the midnight but would undoubtedly provide a stern challenge to their mucous membranes while doing so, 'they'll have no trouble finding us. It's perhaps as well we haven't anything left worth cooking – by the time we've boiled water to drink we'll be too exhausted to eat.'

'There's hardly any wind, though,' Andris pointed out. 'The night isn't bright enough to make the smoke stand out like a pillar against the sky. In any case, anyone who was chasing us would have given up long ago. I wish we could find some eggs, though. There are so many birds around that there must be nests somewhere.'

'It's a pity Hyry isn't here,' Lucrezia said. 'This would be a very good time for her to set out those fishing lines of hers.' She felt that it was somehow incumbent upon her to maintain an attitude of calm reasonableness, even though her companions had few compunctions about letting their dissatisfactions show. 'Do you think there are people living in the marshes?' she added, asking the question of no one in particular.

It was the amber who replied. 'Why not?' he said. 'There seem to be people everywhere, no matter how uncomfortable the terrain. It seems hospitable enough, in spite of Herriman's warnings, and there must be food to be had if only we knew how to go about finding it.'

'No humanss here,' Ssifuss contradicted him. 'Ssome in ssouth, by sshoress of lake. Not here.'

'Do you mean the Lake of Colourless Blood?' Andris was quick to ask. His raised eyebrows betrayed his astonishment at the fact that the taciturn Serpent had said so much all in one go.

Ssifuss shook its bulbous head. The names on Myrasol's map meant nothing to Serpents.

'What kind of people?' Checuti asked. 'Fisherfolk? Crop-growers?'

Ssifuss shook its head again. Whatever it knew – or whatever rumours it had heard – had not specified the way of life the men who lived by the lake followed.

'That name no longer seems as inexplicably exotic as it did three days ago,' Lucrezia observed. 'The marshwater has no colour, but it has a thickness which might easily be taken for the thickness of blood.'

'It's more like snot than blood,' Herriman put in, seemingly determined to maintain the fiction that his previous experience still entitled him to be considered an expert. 'We're adrift in an ocean of slime decked out in thorny weed – a real Slithery Sea, not like that fake back home.' He grinned at his weak joke. No one else did.

'The ancient mapmakers were exceedingly fond of high-sounding expressions,' Andris told him. 'They would never have sullied one of their features with a name like the Lake of Slimy Snot.'

'Do you think there's enough nutrition in the stuff to keep us going for a while?' Lucrezia asked, peering at the kettle which Andris was just setting upon the fire. 'After those rotting hills, there'd be a certain relief in knowing that we were wading through an infinite soup-bowl.'

'I doubt it,' Checuti said. 'Too thin.'

'The horses aren't starving yet,' Andris observed. 'They've been grazing, wherever they can find grass, but they seem to be getting some nourishment from the water – and they're drinking it unboiled, too.'

'Well, I'm not,' Checuti said, with a deep sigh. 'Not until I have to. And I have to have something more solid within the next forty hours. If we can't bring down a bird, we'll have to catch something else.'

'Ssnakess and sslithererss nearby,' Ssifuss put in off-handedly. 'Lissardss ssafe to eat too. Big lissards.'

'For Serpents, that is,' Lucrezia added, although she had seen no evidence that the dietary requirements of Serpents were radically different from those of humans, in spite of their unearthliness.

'The idea of Serpents eating snakes and slitherers sounds a little like cannibalism to me,' said Checuti, 'but that's your business. Big lizards wouldn't, by any chance, mean crocolids?'

'Ssimilar,' the Serpent agreed. Lucrezia's heart sank at this admission; she had encountered crocolids before.

'Turtless eassier to catssh,' Ssifuss went on, becoming almost garrulous now that it had condescended to break its long silence, 'but hard to . . .' It failed to find the word it wanted, and made slicing motions with its hands.

'Hard to butcher,' Lucrezia finished for it. She presumed that turtles must be easier to catch than crocolids by virtue of having fewer teeth, but harder to cut up by virtue of having sturdier armour.

They had made their camp on a rare rocky hummock, from which Andris had cleared the relatively puny bushes with a few broad sweeps of his blade. They were surrounded on three sides by dense thickets but there was a miniature shoreline some twenty mets long on the fourth side, with shallows in which a crocolid – or something similar – could easily lurk, with nothing but its dark-adapted eyes showing above the surface. Lucrezia had seen Hyry kill a crocolid while they camped by the river in the Forest of Absolute Night, and it had not seemed overly difficult. On the other hand, she had also seen the scars which a previous encounter had left on the trader's torso.

'We'll just have to improvise as best we can,' Checuti said wearily. 'For now, sleep's the most urgent need, but when we get under way again, hunting and scavenging have to take precedence over rapidity of progress.'

'Is that just starlight reflectin' off the water,' Herriman asked, 'or does that slimy water actually glow? I still can't make up my mind.'

'It's just reflected starlight,' Andris reassured him – but when Lucrezia looked more intently at the water where it pooled most extensively she wasn't entirely sure. The further they went into the marsh, the eerier it became, especially by night.

What *was* obvious, after she'd watched for a while, was that the water was never still. While they had been wading through it themselves they had sent forth sufficient ripples to obscure the fact, but now that she had the leisure to look out upon a relatively calm surface she was able to see that it was constantly stirred by movements beneath. Whatever it lacked in nutrition for human beings, it evidently had substance enough to sustain a crowded community of lesser beings.

It's not much different from the sea, she told herself. *That too is a solution of sorts, full of salts. There are salts in this, but there's something else as well. Something sour, something sweet . . . but if there really were abundant nutrition here for human beings, there'd be humans here to live off it, as tightly packed as the land would permit. There must be something here which makes human habitation inconvenient, if not impossible. And yet, this isn't utterly unearthly in the way that the Dragomite Hills are. At least, it doesn't seem so.*

They drew lots to determine the watches, which they still felt obliged to keep. Even if they were safe from human pursuers, there were Ssifuss's snakes and slitherers to fear, and big lizards too. They could have drawn lots to determine the pairs, too, but Checuti was quick to suggest that – as usual – Ssifuss ought to be matched with Jume Metra. No one had objected to that before, and no one objected now. Andris and Herriman had similarly become accustomed to sharing their term of duty. Tonight, Checuti drew the first watch for himself and the princess. While the others bedded down Lucrezia found herself a station from which she could watch the horses and the camp with equal ease. She was very tired, but she had reasonable confidence in her ability to stay awake and alert. If the rank smell of the smoke didn't assure it, the thought that crocolids might be lurking nearby surely would. Checuti set himself down at a distance which was only slightly less than respectable.

'I'd grown accustomed to a certain level of luxury in Xandria,' he said with a sigh, speaking murmurously out of consideration for the others. 'My poor flesh hasn't taken kindly to the renewal of hardship, and certainly hasn't relished the drastic shrinkage it has suffered these last forty days.'

'It would have shrunk a good deal more had I not relieved you of the passenger my line-mother planted there,' the princess reminded him.

'And I, of course, have known hardship before,' he added sarcastically. 'I know how fortunate I am, highness. I'll be grateful to you till my dying day, as you doubless will be to me.'

'You didn't have to raid the Citadel,' Lucrezia pointed out. 'You could have been living in modest luxury still, but for the over-reaching of your greed.'

'It wasn't greed,' Checuti told her. 'It was lust for glory, which is quite a different thing. All *you* had to do was keep to your bed in the dead of night, and you'd be Queen of Shaminzara by now. You have less excuse than I for having been brought to this.' He had changed his tune since the evening after the battle, whose bloodshed had encouraged an atypical sobriety. Lucrezia knew him well enough by this time to suspect that his present sarcasm wasn't as deeply ingrained as it seemed.

'Agreed,' she conceded, readily enough. 'But I have Serpent's blood in my veins, which would not let me rest easy.'

'Are you sure it was your Serpent's blood, and not your adolescent mind?'

'How can I be?' she answered. 'If there's something within me which is not in other humans, how can I tell what it is? I am myself, and I have no notion of what it might be to be someone else. It was the same with Dhalla, I think, when she spoke of feeling Salamander's fire burning in her heart. It was part of her, as intrinsic as any other. Hyry told you, did she not, what Phar explained to her about our having millions of tiny creatures living inside us, put there by the architects of Genesys – including some which might be capable of metamorphosis, like frogs or butterflies, save only that the final phase of their metamorphosis might only be completed once in a thousand or a million generations?'

'Keshvara told me all of that and more,' Checuti agreed. 'I think she has a soft spot for me, although she pretends to be uninterested in all sexual intercourse. She told Captain Cerri too, but he hasn't my finesse or diplomatic flair and he simply informed her that he had no truck with silly superstitions about bacteria and the like.'

'It was only finesse, then, that prevented you from uttering the same opinion?'

'Oh no. In all matters which I am not competent to decide, I remain content with ignorance. I cannot tell whether that aspect of the lore has any truth in it or not, and I cannot see that anyone else can either, so I let it alone. The mysteries of Genesys fascinate men like Fraxinus and give men like Phar faith in their medicines, but I'm a pragmatic sort. The mysteries which preoccupy me are those which cloud my future. Fraxinus derives pleasure from mere discovery, and values revelation for its own sake, but I'm not so high-minded. When I find something new, whether it be an object, or a trick, or an item of information, I always ask *what might be done with it?* Finesse I have in plenty, but I'm a vulgar fellow at heart. Not like you, I think. There's a lot of Fraxinus in you – or a lot of Ereleth, at least.'

He pronounced the last few words tentatively but teasingly, as if he knew that she might not be pleased to her such a judgment, but thought she should hear it anyway.

'So there is,' Lucrezia agreed, deciding that she too ought to exercise finesse. 'Perhaps there'd be a little more of Ereleth in you, were you the one supposed to have Serpent's blood.'

'Perhaps there would, highness,' he conceded. He let loose a little chuckle which sounded almost plaintive, by virtue of the hunger that underlay and infected it. 'Perhaps there would.'

8

CARUS FRAXINUS STOOD with Vaca Metra at the tailboard of the moving wagon, shading his eyes against the glare of the noonday sun, which was far harsher now than he had ever known it before, by virtue of the eccentric reflective properties of the desert rocks.

Fraxinus had not yet had the opportunity to inspect the rocks closely, because their pursuers were too close and the gap between the laden wagon and the chasing riders was diminishing by slow but inexorable degrees. He could see well enough, though, that almost every ridge scarring the broken landscape was crested with multicoloured crystals and that almost every vertical face exhibited by pit or column carried an elaborately patterned patina.

The trail they had been following had given out twelve or fifteen kims ago, as soon as they had passed the peculiarly sharp boundary which separated the flat fields of the human farmers from the desert. The unevenness was by no means as pronounced as that of the Dragomite Hills, but it promised to be equally troublesome. The ground was inhospitable to horses and wagons alike, and Fraxinus was uncomfortably conscious of the fact that Phar had been the expedition's only competent farrier. Ereleth had so far been very clever and very lucky to find a path through the trackless wilderness that would accommodate the wagon's broad wheelbase, but the pursuing horsemen had the advantage nevertheless, and they knew it. That was presumably why they were still continuing the chase, despite the fact that the wagon was no longer trespassing on their jealously guarded land.

'If only the sun were near to setting,' Fraxinus said. 'If night were falling they'd turn back, I'm sure of it – but we have ten more hours of daylight, and the horses can't possibly keep going through this blistering heat.'

'They have horses too,' the mound-woman muttered.

'Aye,' said Fraxinus, 'and whatever wagons they have to carry their food and water are languishing far behind them. But our horses are hauling a huge weight, and we've no spare animals to share it by turns. They know that time is on their side, for now, and they intend to take advantage of its collaboration while they can. I never dreamed they'd be so persistent – although I must say that they seem noticeably fewer in number now than when we first caught sight of them.'

He clutched the tailboard as the wagon swayed from side to side. The wheels made a curious crackling noise as they ran over the ground with surprising smoothness. The glittering carpet over which they were running was by no means flat even in its most favourable regions, but it was not as hard as might have been expected and the wheels pulverised all but a few of the hummocks and mounds which they encountered as easily as if they had been made of salt. The ruts they left behind were clearly visible. Fraxinus didn't know whether the total absence of any other such signs meant that no one else ever came this way, or that the crystalline structures were constantly re-aggregated somehow.

'We must fight,' Vaca Metra concluded, not altogether glumly. Fraxinus had the impression that she and her sister warriors harboured a good deal of resentment regarding the limited nature of the engagement in which they had been involved at the bridge. She wasn't unduly dismayed by the thought of having a chance to strike back at the people who had massacred her fellows and all but destroyed her own opportunity to assist in the making of a new nest.

'I fear that we must,' Fraxinus agreed soberly. 'Unless, that is, the dragomites will take a turn at hauling the wagon.' It wasn't a joke. Three of the four dragomites were still moving awkwardly by virtue of the injuries they had sustained, but they were strong creatures and they were capable of fast movement.

She looked up at him as if he were quite mad. 'Warriors are not workers,' she said, as if that were the only thing that mattered.

'I suppose not,' he admitted. He might have argued had he

been able to think of a means by which the warriors could be efficiently harnessed, but there was no obvious way to do it – none, at any rate, that could be mastered in the mere minutes that would be allowed. In any case, releasing the horses now would mean losing them, and he needed them desperately. He couldn't help wondering what the chances were of not merely beating off the pursuers but stealing half a dozen of their mounts. It was lunatic optimism to think that he might, but it would require some such donation of wild luck to give him a reasonable chance of crossing the desert with all his worldly goods intact.

He leaned out to see exactly where the dragomites were. They had arranged themselves in pairs to either side of the wagon, and they were effortlessly keeping pace with it.

'Can you communicate with them by signalling,' Fraxinus asked, 'or will you need to ride one in order to command their strategy?'

Vaca Metra looked back at him dubiously, as if she were not sure whether it was her place to command the dragomite warriors wherever she might be stationed.

'Can you at least tell them what we intend to do?' Fraxinus asked.

'What do we intend to do?' she countered.

'The only choice we have left is to select the ground on which to make our stand,' Fraxinus told her grimly. 'I'll tell Ereleth to stop as soon as we see something that looks like a defensible position. She and Mossassor can wield half-pikes, and I'll do my part with a sword. The dragomites must do what they can – or what they please.'

She looked at him dumbly. She knew full well that he'd left out the most important element of all.

'If Dhalla can stand up,' he said, 'she'll doubtless do so. If she can use her spear, she'll do that too – but I don't know enough about giants to estimate her capability. Even Ereleth can't do that – but continuing to run until the last possible moment, when one of the horses breaks a leg or dies of exhaustion, isn't going to make much difference.'

The mound-woman nodded, to signify both understanding and assent. She climbed over the tailboard and waited for a moment or two.

'Slow down!' Fraxinus called to Ereleth.

Ereleth let up slightly, but Fraxinus would have forgiven Vaca Metra had she complained that it was still too dangerous to dismount. She made no such complaint; she simply waited until she had balanced herself, then jumped and landed running. She raced away towards the nearest of the dragomites, which veered to meet her. She swung herself up on to its back, positioning herself between the first two dorsal spines, but any communication which passed between them was invisible and inaudible to Fraxinus.

He lurched through the cluttered wagon, which had now speeded up again, supporting himself as best he could. As he passed along the length of Dhalla's recumbent body she lifted her head, and tried to raise herself on to her elbow. Mossassor was with her, squatting in the peculiar manner Serpents favoured, supported by its curled-up tail.

'Not quite yet,' Fraxinus told the giant, brusquely. He didn't know for certain whether she could stand up, let alone wield her huge spear to good effect, but he knew that any appearance she made must be well-timed. It was possible that if the wagon could find a decent vantage-point on a relatively narrow ridge, with the dragomites to command the slopes to either side, the mere sight of Dhalla stepping down to face them would be enough to deter an all-out attack. She surely had the power to throw a terrible panic into any man who had seen what she could do during the battle of the bridge. He had to hope that the resolve of their pursuers was predicated on the assumption that she was too badly hurt to take them on. The shock of her sudden appearance might crack that resolve as suddenly and as completely as the mayhem she had created on the western bank of the river.

Fraxinus clambered over the backrest mounted on the driver's bench and sat beside Ereleth. It only required a single glance to assume him that their luck was holding. All four of the horses were galloping, none as yet showing any evident sign that it was about to break down. He had to shade his eyes again while he scanned the glittering terrain that lay ahead of them. It was difficult to pick out shapes amid the rapidly shifting pattern of dazzling scintillations. The whole scene seemed to be trembling on the brink of dissolution into multicoloured chaos, but he was able to pick out a hill of sorts. It was not as narrow as he would have liked but it seemed to be possessed of slopes whose relative sheerness, combined with the brittleness which seemed natural to everything hereabouts, would be far more difficult for horses than for dragomites.

'There!' he said to Ereleth. 'Take us as high as you can. Don't be too hard on the horses if they hesitate, but coax them up if they'll consent to be coaxed.'

'I know what I'm doing,' she muttered through tight-set lips. She was already steering for the hill. 'They've worked wonders for me so far.'

Had the high ground which Fraxinus had indicated really been a hill like the kind of hills which could be found in Xandria the strategy would have been sound enough. For the last two hours, though, Ereleth had been steering for the lower and smoother ground, and she had had no opportunity to test the solidity of the occasional hummocks which loomed up like severely pruned dragomite mounds. As soon as she directed the horses on to the slope of one such shallow ridge it became apparent that the mounds were less robust than they seemed. The wheels had been carving out ruts no more than a couple of sems deep, save for crushing the occasional protrusion into sparkling dust, but they were no sooner on the slight upslope than the wheels began to bite deeper and deeper.

So great was the diameter of the wheels that they would probably have been able to keep going for eighty mets or more, but the horses – heavy animals bred for this kind of haulage – found the ground breaking beneath their hooves, and did not like the sensation in the least. It must have seemed to them that they were running on thin ice, breaking through at every step. They were already pulling up before one stumbled; after that, it was a mercy that the ground caught and held the wheels, else the momentum of the wagon might have inflicted fatal injuries on all four of the animals.

'Corruption and corrosion!' Fraxinus cried, in dire frustration, as he clung hard to the timbers behind him lest he be thrown to the ground. 'We're a sitting target now.'

In his mind's eye he saw half the number of the approaching men delightedly reaching for their bows and arrows, while the others made ready with their lances. He stumbled back into the wagon, groping for a sword.

'Let me anoint that with poison!' Ereleth said.

He laughed, without any trace of humour. 'If they get close enough to require poisoning,' he replied hoarsely, 'I'll be as good as dead.'

Dhalla had pulled herself up into a sitting position. The effort brought forth not the slightest wince, but there was a glazed look in her eyes, as if she had only just awakened from a long, deep sleep. She put a huge hand up to her forehead, then stared at the palm as if something might be written there.

'You'd do better to exercise your witchcraft on her, majesty,' Fraxinus said, over his shoulder. 'If you've aught in that belt of yours to fill a half-dead giant full of sudden strength, this is the time to bring it out.'

'I'll do what I can,' the queen replied, scrambling in his wake.

'Iss bad,' said Mossassor. 'Iss bad.' But even as it moaned, the Serpent picked up a half-pike, and clutched the weapon firmly in its slender fingers.

They must be insane to have followed us so far, Fraxinus thought, *but at least we'll make them pay for their insanity. If chaos and corruption have come to claim the whole world, they'll rue the part they've played in hastening its victory.*

9

ANDRIS AND HERRIMAN had taken the last of the three watches. They had found it difficult to keep the fire going, so that they might have the wherewithal to fill a firepot when they set out again and thus preserve their matches, but while Herriman had complained bitterly Andris had simply got on with the job. He had scoured the nearby bushes for any fuel that could be gathered, as carefully as he could, although the scratches inflicted upon him by the thorns seemed far less troublesome than he had expected.

'Have you noticed how hunger grows in the end from ache to agony?' Herriman had asked him, but in truth he had not.

'You're going to regret those scratches,' the guardsman had told him dolefully. 'They might seem trivial now, but your flesh will start to crawl soon enough. I've been much more careful, but I'm beginnin' to itch again all over – and the way that dragomite woman's tossin' an' turnin' in her sleep I'd guess she's got it even worse'n me. Serpent seems to have a hide like armour, though.'

In spite of the care he had taken Andris had indeed accumulated an astonishing number of visible scratches about his huge and slightly clumsy hands. Although they had hardly drawn blood at all, they were etched in bright red where the flesh had reacted to them. He looked at them anxiously, but they really didn't seem to be hurting him.

'I think I'd be willing to walk if only we could eat one of the horses,' Herriman observed miserably, when everyone had been roused and they finally had everything packed. He didn't mean it.

Although the night was tolerably bright Ssifuss had advised – in an abrupt fashion which might have seemed rude had they not had its previous refusal to talk at all for comparison – that it would be wise to wait for daylight before mounting a determined search for food. The princess had agreed readily enough, and no one had objected. In the meantime, they made what southward progress they could.

Andris, who was perfectly content to wade while the others rode, no longer found anything surprising in the fact that the marshwater remained quite warm even though there was a distinct dark-chill in the air. Whatever was responsible for its viscosity evidently had some kind of heat-trapping or heat-generating capability too. The warmth of the water was comforting, and it added to his unaccountable sense of well-being. Nor was he disturbed by the observation that although they could not be more than a few kims from the borderlands which ran along the eastern edge of the marsh, and were trying to follow a parallel course, the marshwater still seemed to be getting more viscous all the time. He couldn't be absolutely certain that the increased viscosity wasn't an illusion caused by the tiring of his limbs, but it seemed real enough.

Presumably, he thought, *the Lake of Colourless Blood will be as warm as real blood, or warmer, and so densely clotted that it'll be more like a gel than a liquid.*

'If we can't look for food yet we shouldn't have started out so soon,' Herriman complained, looking sorrowfully down at him from his position of privilege in the saddle. 'Like the princess says, they must have given up chasing us by now. We should've taken time out to gather ourselves together. Anyway, I don't see why we shouldn't go huntin' by starlight.' Andris inferred that Herriman was uneasy about the evident willingness of his companions to defer to the judgment of a Serpent, although he lacked the temerity to issue a challenge himself.

'Ssifuss is right,' Andris told him. 'Human eyes – even Jume Metra's – don't function as well in the dark as a crocolid's, and we need daylight to see through the water's surface. In the meantime, we have to keep moving. We have to get through the marsh and out the other side as quickly as we can. The sooner we can turn eastwards again the better, but we can't do that until we're well south of the Nine Towns – or so far south that the people don't know who we are.'

Herriman accepted this judgment with a slight shrug, as if to say that Andris must know best – but he dropped back rather than keep company with a man who insisted on correcting his logic.

In fact, Andris had some doubts about deferring to the Serpent, simply because he wasn't sure how good its judgment might be. He was conscious of the fact that the party had no obvious leader, and had no prejudice against the unearthly creature, but he was unconvinced that Ssifuss knew its way around the marshland well enough to secure their safety. But if Ssifuss wasn't equipped to lead them, who was? Had her status in Xandria still carried any meaning, of course, Lucrezia would have had the right of command, but she had made no attempt to exert that right; she was not about to go back on her frequent declarations to the effect that she was no longer a princess. In other circumstances Checuti's natural arrogance might have led him to assume command, but the thief-master was realistic enough to know that his total ignorance of what they might encounter in the marshes and how best to survive there left him ill-equipped for decision-making. It was not clear that Ssifuss knew a great deal, but it did seem to know something. For the moment, at least, Andris decided to let the Serpent lead the way; Ssifuss was, in any case, the one who had to set the pace of the entire convoy by virtue of being the slighter – and hence the slower – of the two who went on foot.

The day, when it finally dawned, was bright and blue. The clouds which dotted the sky were high and hazy, and it was obvious that they would be dispersed before the noonday heat reached its maximum. Andris judged that the heat might well be difficult for his companions to bear, but he still felt so absurdly fit that nothing could intimidate him.

As soon as there was light enough, Ssifuss notched an arrow to its bow, and as soon as it came close to one of the big fishing birds it let fly – but with no more success than on all the previous occasions. The bird seemed so very cumbersome as it took to the air that Andris could hardly believe that it wasn't an easy target, and it added insult to injury by settling again less than fifty mets away, declaring to all the world that it rated the invaders a very minor threat to its well-being. Ssifuss went to retrieve its arrow, hanging its head as if considerably dispirited – but then it suddenly darted to its left, splashing through the shallows surrounding an island which presented a broken wall of thorns, and grabbed hold of something wallowing there.

Andris could not at first make out what it was that Ssifuss had seized; all that was evident was that it was very big and made of something like glass. It was obviously strong, too, for as the creature tried to get away it very nearly pulled the Serpent over. It might well have escaped had not Checuti been very quick to realise that whatever it was, Ssifuss would not be going to so much trouble were it not edible, and jumped down to join it.

Andris tried to race to their assistance, but the water in which he had been wading was too deep to allow acrobatics, and by the time he made it into the shallows the job was half done. Ssifuss and Checuti had the huge creature – it was a turtle at least half the size of the slender princess – by the two front flippers; they were trying with all their might to thrust it up on to a stretch of mud between two bushes.

The turtle's great head whipped from side to side like a club, but its neck wasn't long enough to make such blows count and its horny beak snapped impotently at their fingers. When Andris joined in, lending his weight to the task of pushing from behind, the project was easily achieved, although the turtle turned out to have a glassy tail liberally decorated with jagged spines which whacked him painfully about the thighs.

Once the turtle was beached, it immediately withdrew its head into the shelter of its huge crystalline shell, but that was no defence against a man armed – as Checuti was – with a long stout knife. The thief-master used the broad blade as a lever to pry the head out, and Ssifuss skewered the eyes with its own thinner blade.

The creature continued to thrash about for a good ten minutes, but news of its death eventually filtered through its sluggish nervous system to its every extremity and it became still. Andris was surprised to discover that he could see the red and blue blood circulating in the creature's veins through the almost-transparent shell, while the internal organs were mapped out in a riot of roseate pinks and ochreous yellows. Only the milky flippers were truly opaque.

Ssifuss tapped the vitreous shell to demonstrate its adamantine hardness. It had the appearance of a brittle thing, but Andris tested it himself and concluded that it would be impossible to shatter without the aid of a sledgehammer and an anvil.

'Musst fissh out flessh,' the Serpent declared.

'Or s-sup with a long s-spoon,' Checuti said. Although it was good humour rather than derision which had caused him to imitate the Serpent's speech handicap Ssifuss gave him a sharp and rather baleful look. Andris knew that the thief-master must have been sorely tempted to say 'S-sorry,' but he had the sense to keep quiet.

Andris and Checuti left Ssifuss to begin fishing out the turtle's flesh while they and Herriman went foraging for firewood. By the time Andris returned with a fair-sized bundle their fortunes had improved even further. Jume Metra had gone back to the shallows where they had captured the turtle and had located a clutch of eggs which the creature had just laid. They had been buried in a sheltered spot beneath a seemingly impenetrable thicket of thorns, but Lucrezia had helped the mound-woman to hack a way through to the covert, and the job was quickly finished off by Checuti's blade. They recovered no less than thirty eggs, each one the size of a hen's.

'Sstore eggss,' Ssifuss advised. 'Will keep.'

Andris knew that it was good advice, but it was hard to take, and in the end they settled for storing all but six, so that they might have one each. They boiled the eggs in the kettle while the meat was carefully spitted, awaiting its turn over the fire.

The turtle was indeed difficult to butcher efficiently, but Ssifuss had evidently done some such job before. It had contrived to extract the shell-bound muscles which moved the leathery flippers without reducing them to mere rags, and it had brought out the heart in a single piece. These larger pieces of meat it coated in mud and set to bake separately at the edge of the fire.

The taste of the turtle-meat, when it was finally prepared, was only just on the good side of tolerable, but the egg had served to whet Andris's appetite and he was not about to play the gourmet. He ate his meal with considerable relish – more so, at any rate, than his companions achieved. Jume Metra, whose features seemed to have been set rock-hard for the last two days, seemed to have considerable difficulty chewing the tough meat and forcing it down. She was as restless now that she was awake as she had been while she slept, and Andris guessed that she must be in considerable discomfort.

'Not bad,' said Checuti insincerely, when they had eaten as much as they dared – for they had no wish to make themselves vomit it all out again. 'Not nearly as good as the turtles from the eastern reaches of the Slithery Sea, however. Wouldn't you agree, highness?' While he spoke he fed scraps of roasted meat to his little monkey. It accepted them with good grace and ate with a delicacy that was surprising, considering that it must have been every bit as hungry as its master.

'Unfortunately not,' Lucrezia agreed. 'Much tougher, and not as well seasoned with salt.'

Andris had never tasted any other kind of turtle, and he didn't want to waste time on mere matters of taste. 'I've seen shells like that somewhere before,' he said ruminatively. 'Not as big, but just as glassy. I thought they came from the far east, though, not the Slithery Sea.'

'They do,' Checuti said. 'The turtles of the Slithery Sea are green or grey and very leathery, not at all glass-like. The things you're talking about come from another kind of reptile entirely, and they're scales rather than shells. They're from desert creatures, not swamp-dwellers. Sandskinks and stonemasons. They don't come from the *far* east, unless you count the northern reaches of the Spangled Desert far. They come by the same route as Belin's giant guards – Dhalla would probably know all about them.'

'Cheapskate lensgrinders use 'em,' Herriman put in. 'OK for spectacles if you don't mind the varied tints. Only last for fifty days or so but if you can't afford real glass and the protective fluids to maintain it they'll do the job for you. You just throw 'em away when they're no good any more. In the east they farm sandskinks – not much of a cash crop, but cheap to house an' easy to breed. They say you can feed the things on stones an' garbage, but I wouldn't know if it's true.'

'It's not quite as simple as that,' Checuti said, 'but they're certainly cheap to rear. Slow-growing, though, and you can't eat the meat. It's a business for patient poor people. If Fraxinus and Ereleth make it to the Spangled Desert, they'll probably see plenty of sandskinks and the like.'

Andris recalled that he had often seen sailormen wearing

lenses which must have been made from such scales; he had previously assumed that they were made of some crude kind of glass. The secrets of lensgrinding lore had never aroused his curiosity; his own eyesight was very good.

'They'll make it,' Lucrezia said in a low voice, reacting to a different part of Checuti's account. 'They're better equipped than we are, and they still have dragomites to defend them.'

'If . . .' Checuti began dourly, but promptly changed his mind.

Jume Metra glanced at the thief-master as sharply as Ssifuss had when he had imitated the Serpent's voice. Taciturn though she was, she was no fool. She knew that he had been about to wonder whether the dragomite warriors could be trusted, now that they no longer had egg-carrying workers to guard. 'Our sisters will go to Salamander's Fire,' the mound-woman said colourlessly. 'They will wait there for us.'

Andris wondered whether 'us' meant the ill-assorted party of travellers, or Metra and the eggs which she carried in her sack. Either way, he thought, a little diplomacy wouldn't come amiss. 'This place doesn't seem so bad,' he said cheerfully. 'Nothing's attacked us yet, we've found food to eat, and the few thorns that I've come into contact with haven't even made me itch. I think we can make it to Salamander's Fire – all of us. I really do.'

'So do I,' the princess said. 'We're too resourceful to be stopped by something as ridiculous as a horde of unreasonable barbarians. We'll come out of this stronger than before, itching or no itching.' There was an odd fierceness in the way she spoke, and Andris knew that she was trying to mobilise every last vestige of her resolve and make it active by expression. She didn't seem nearly as comfortable as he was, though; her face was flushed and she was scratching away at her arms and legs at regular intervals.

I hope she's right, Andris thought, turning his head aside to look at the big grey bird which was disdainfully carrying out its own business not thirty mets away. *And I certainly won't be the one to remind her that it's already too late for the dead.*

'Hyry and Merel will make it too,' Lucrezia was quick to add, perhaps having seen the expression on Andris's face as he looked away. 'Somehow, they'll get through. They're infinitely more artful than a nation of brutes and cowards.'

There are times, Andris thought, *when artfulness isn't an advantage*. But he kept the thought to himself.

Ssifuss took the time to clean every last vestige of soft substance from the inside of the shell, parcelling it out very carefully into that which could be eaten and that which – if Andris understood it correctly – it intended to use as bait for 'lissards'. Andris had some slight doubts about the wisdom of rigging traps for crocolids, thinking that such a device might prove to be a little too successful, but he left them unvoiced. It was important to preserve the good mood.

He watched Checuti rake the back of his left hand with the broken fingernails of his right, absent-mindedly. The action brought forth a thin smear of blood. 'Do you want to take a turn riding?' Checuti asked him, as he intercepted Andris's gaze but mistook its meaning.

'No, I'm quite happy walking,' Andris assured the other. 'There's no point in making the old mare carry my weight – she'll hardly notice you, now that you're so much thinner.'

As they set out once again Ssifuss fired an arrow at the fishing bird. It had been standing very still, with its eyes seemingly fixed on the water, but as soon as the arrow was loosed it crouched down and moved its sinuous neck to one side.

The arrow missed by a sem. The bird rose majestically into the air, flapped its wings half a dozen times, then glided out of sight.

'Nearly got him that time,' Checuti said soberly. 'Just keep trying – you're sure to get lucky eventually.'

'Ssoon,' said Ssifuss, as it plodded off to collect its arrow – but it was impossible to tell whether the inflection of the unhuman voice was optimistic or despairing.

10

THE HORSEMEN WERE approaching with alarming rapidity, but as they formed into a line of attack Fraxinus saw, with a burst of exultation, that they were not nearly as many as he had feared. When he had first caught sight of them, against the sober horizon of the cultivated lands, he had estimated that they numbered a hundred and fifty, but if that judgment had been sound they had lost more than half their force. They were no more than sixty now. Given that they must be experienced dragomite-fighters, there ought to be enough of them to overwhelm a party of four warriors, even had the warriors not been carrying injuries, but they would need time to do it – and the ground was against them.

Now that the wagon had stopped, the kaleidoscopic confusion which had made it difficult to judge the lie of the land had abated, and it was possible to get a fair estimate of the unevenness of the sequined terrain. Fraxinus had discussed the tactics of dragomite-fighting with Jacom Cerri and Andris Myrasol while the expedition was still deep in the hills, and Jacom had explained how three horsemen working in close co-operation might wear down a warrior by harassment and attrition, by virtue of the fact that each one only had a single pair of jaws. But the theory of that kind of manoeuvre had relied on the ability of the horses to swerve and wheel about, tempting and teasing the jaws while evading capture. The scorched earth of the region which separated the fields of the Nine Towns from the rocky boundary of the hills was ideal for that kind of agile combat, but the haphazardly aggregated 'sands' of the Spangled Desert were not.

The dragomites were, of course, little better adapted to this kind of surface than the horses which the cavalrymen of the Nine Towns were riding, but that wasn't the crucial factor. Indeed,

Fraxinus decided, the vital element would not be the ability of the horses' hooves to cope with the ground but rather the confidence of the horses. No matter how well trained they had been, they could not possibly be as biddable now as they would have been on familiar ground. But how much difference would that make, when the opposing forces clashed?

'Fall back a little way!' Fraxinus shouted to Vaca Metra. His reasoning was that if the dragomites were within easy bowshot of the wagon, he and Mossassor might be able to offer covering fire; but the mound-woman ignored his call. He hoped she had tactical reasons of her own, and that her decision wasn't a contemptuous reflection of the fact that she had seen him fire a bow before.

While the last two hundred mets separating the galloping riders from the waiting line of dragomites were swallowed up, Fraxinus saw three horses fall, throwing their riders with such force that they had no chance of taking any further part in the fight. He wished that it had been thirty, but it was a sign nevertheless, and he didn't doubt that the attackers must have observed it too and read its ominous message. His heart was racing now, and his empty left hand was tightly clenched into a fist. By the time the cavalrymen actually clashed with the dragomites, they were close enough for Fraxinus to be able to recognise Shabir. The grey-haired general was standing in his stirrups, howling orders to the horsemen who were forming up to tackle the warriors.

Fraxinus was now able to see Jacom Cerri's theory – or a variant of it – in action. The attackers' line broke into four, and each group formed into lesser groups. They came forward not in threes, as Jacom had initially suggested, but in fives. Two lancers came forward to distract the jaws, intending to keep the massive instruments swaying back and forth between one and the other; two men armed with javelins and bows tried to take up flanking positions, aiming their darts at the large eyes set well back on the dragomites' heads and at the places where the chitinous plates overlapped. The fifth man in each group – another lancer – attempted to move to the rear, where he could aim his weapon at the rearmost pair of legs. Fraxinus saw the logic of this move immediately; if the warriors elected to claim an advantage in height by resting on their four back legs while raising the foremost pair to operate as 'hands', the rearmost legs would have to be anchored, and might be badly pricked by a well-aimed thrust of a spear.

This was, of course, a wasteful method of fighting even at the best of times, in that a great many arrows had to be fired and javelins thrown, most of which would bounce harmlessly off the dragomites' armour. Usually, the fives which came forward would have had plenty of support in the rear – not merely other fives to take their place as seamlessly as possible, but armourers' wagons abundantly stocked with extra weapons. That was not the case here; nor was it the case that the dragomites would easily give sufficient ground to let the attackers recover javelins that had once been thrown. On the other hand, the dragomite warriors' wounds had not been given adequate opportunity to heal while they had been constantly on the move.

Had the dragomites been six in number instead of four, it would have been much more difficult for Shabir's men to get behind them, but Fraxinus saw to his dismay that their line was too short. Within seconds of the first engagement the warriors were effectively surrounded. Fraxinus shouted again, but still they refused to fall back – and none of Shabir's men turned aside to come at the wagon; they knew exactly what their priorities were. The only move the dragomites did make in response to the enemy's initial disposition was to draw apart a little. At first Fraxinus thought that this would isolate them, but then he saw that the two outsiders had also moved some way forward, so that the two insiders could provide a measure of protection of their vulnerable rear ends.

Vaca Metra, mounted on the second dragomite from the right, had a bow of her own; it was made of dragomite chitin and had nothing like the range of the attackers' wooden bows, but at close quarters it was an effective weapon, and she was unleashing arrows at the horses with astonishing rapidity.

'They're too clever,' Fraxinus muttered anxiously, as he saw the way the horsemen arranged themselves, and the speed with which they were executing their plan. 'The warriors can't hold them off long enough to make the treacherous ground tell in their favour.'

'Not so!' Ereleth said, in a tremulous fashion which declared that she was just as tense as he was. 'They're not following through, and they're not loosing half the missiles they ought to be.'

She was right. The deceptive ground was already subverting the efficiency of the attackers, and their method of fighting had not sufficient flexibility to allow them to adapt. In spite of having seen what had happened to the wagon and to their fallen comrades, the cavalrymen could make no proper allowance or compensation for the unevenness and brittleness of the crystalline sand which rose in coruscating clouds about their horses' feet.

'That's why they wouldn't fall back!' Ereleth said, pointing eagerly. 'The ground is at its worst there, and Metra knew it! Those flying particles must be stinging the horses' fetlocks; they'll do no real harm, but the horses hate the sensation.'

It was true; the attack, organised with such mechanical efficiency, was already faltering. The formations which Shabir's men had assumed weren't holding, and those arrows and javelins which had been launched weren't finding their marks.

The dragomites, by contrast, seemed to have factored the conditions into their own tactics with surprising facility. As the horses closed in and the riders furiously – but ineffectively – unleashed their armaments, the dance of the dragomite warriors seemed strangely dainty and magnificently graceful. They made no attempt to rear up; instead, their six legs moved with astonishing fluidity as the monsters turned and wheeled on their stations, always steady and always completely in control. They kept their heads very low, and their massive jaws reached out to slice at the legs of the horses. They weren't doing a great deal of damage, but they were feeding the horses' apprehensiveness.

Shabir's riders might have been fiercely determined, but their mounts clearly were not. The animals were as well-disciplined as any Xandrian cavalry horse, but when it came to matters of survival their instincts still came into play – and the horses knew only too well how awkward and how untrustworthy the ground was. Their riders had first to fight them before they could fight the dragomites. To begin with, the cavalrymen fought with all their might; the numerical advantage which had seemed so decisive now seemed rather more marginal, but still it favoured them and they knew it. If only they could settle their horses, they could surely turn the tide their way.

For a full minute everything hung in the balance, and Fraxinus couldn't guess which way the fight would go. If the horsemen persisted, he judged, the battle would be bloodier than they expected, but it would nevertheless be winnable in the end. But if they did not persist . . .

He wanted to yell at them, to tell them to desist, but it would have seemed too foolish. Instead, he clenched his fist all the harder, as if by thus expressing the force of his will he might turn the fight.

For that one long minute, the resolve of Shabir's men held, and Fraxinus came to the very brink of believing that they had sufficient courage to override the reluctance of their horses – but as he teetered on that brink, he saw the attackers falter. It was as if he could feel the draught of their uncertainty cutting through the warm air.

Not for the first time, it was the determination of Shabir's followers that cracked under the pressure of uncertainty rather than the determination of their intended victims. Fraxinus had found it difficult to credit that their general would press the pursuit so far, and he was evidently not alone in that. Had the battle been as easy as mere numbers suggested, the attackers would doubtless have won it, but when they realised how difficult it was going to be, their resolve immediately began to drain away – and they had no more reserves of courage than they had of weapons.

Once begun, the dissolution of the battle into mere chaos was astonishingly rapid. The first spark of panic took no time at all to flare into wholesale alarm. One warrior had fallen by then, but eight or nine of Shabir's soldiers were down, injured or unhorsed. Those which had merely been unhorsed were as useless as those which had been badly hurt, for they had not the slightest intention of going forward on foot against a dragomite's jaws. The remainder were thrown into utter disarray, and the first few cowards were already in full retreat.

For a few long drawn out seconds, Fraxinus watched Shabir howling more and more orders, but they were not obeyed. Then, it seemed, Shabir too cracked under the pressure. Had he had any intelligence at all, Fraxinus thought, the general would have called a retreat and tried to rally his troops at a safe distance, but he was evidently not that kind of man. When his own discipline cracked the result was that he hurled himself into one of the disintegrating formations gathered about a rampaging dragomite, thrusting at its eyes with his ridiculously feeble blade.

Within three seconds the legs of the general's horse had been swept away by a swinging jaw, and he was catapulted over its head to take a bone-jarring fall. He didn't move again.

As soon as the general's fall had been seen, a cry went up from a lone voice, which quickly multiplied into a cacophony of a dozen. The cracking of the cavalrymen's discipline was immediate. They simply turned as one, and ran away at full gallop.

The three remaining dragomites raced after them. At first, Fraxinus was horrified by this intemperance, and he opened his mouth to call them back, but then he saw what they were doing. They made no attempt to catch or kill the fleeing soldiers; instead they went after a handful of riderless horses, intent on steering them in a different direction. The horses were too tired to resist being turned; two of them fled into the wilderness nevertheless, but the remainder were herded back towards the waiting wagon. Five more horses were still down, but they were all injured and useless except as meat. Fraxinus counted eight fallen men, but couldn't tell how many were actually dead.

Fraxinus felt Dhalla's hand on his shoulder as the stooping giant took advantage of what little support he could offer her. He buckled under the pressure, but the emotion jangling his own nerves was so strong that he dropped his sword and put his right hand on hers, gripping it as if it had been the hand of his son Xury.

'No need,' he said exultantly. 'The desert and the dragomites have won the day. We're free!' He had not the slightest doubt that the fleeing men were gone for good.

Fraxinus jumped down from the wagon as soon as his heart had relaxed its pounding. Ereleth followed him. Together they ran to seize the reins of the horses which the dragomites had brought back. It wasn't an easy matter to catch and calm the terrified beasts, but they managed to do it, and eventually contrived to tether four sound animals to the rear of the wagon. By that time, the three remaining dragomites were well advanced with their own tidying up. They had finished off the wounded horses with brutal thrusts of their jaws and were now doing the same for the fallen men.

'Wait!' Fraxinus cried, though not out of mercy or squeamishness.

This time, Vaca Metra heeded his cry, and the warriors paused in their work. Fraxinus ran straight to the place where Shabir had fallen while the dragomites stood still. The general lay side by side with a supine corpse, whose broken neck was all too obvious.

Fraxinus put his fingers to Shabir's neck. He found a pulse, but the general had been knocked out and showed no immediate sign of coming round. Fraxinus checked the stricken man's arms and legs, and found that he had broken none of them; the brittle ground had yielded when he impacted upon it, and that had saved his bones from fracture. He was badly bruised, though, and he was bleeding from numerous cuts, none of them serious. Fraxinus picked a small glass-like sliver from one of the cuts and threw it aside.

'Kill him,' Ereleth advised, having come up behind him while he worked. 'He'll only be trouble if you don't. He's not the kind of man you can reason with, whether he has an army behind him or not. If he were, he'd have turned back five hours ago.'

'Trouble or not,' Fraxinus said evenly, 'he knows more about the Spangled Desert than we do. He can't do us any more harm now, and he might be useful. Check the others, will you?'

Ereleth made no move to obey this instruction, although she did look from side to side, tipping the brim of her hat to shield herself from the blazing sun. 'If it's information you want,' she said laconically, 'you only need one source, and the common soldiers are likely to know even less than their brave and stupid general.'

The general wasn't an unduly big man, but Fraxinus couldn't lift him unaided. 'Dhalla!' he shouted. 'Are you well enough to carry this man to the wagon?'

Dhalla didn't seem to be well enough even to get down from the wagon, but once she had done so she seemed to grow brighter in the hot sunlight, and when she was able to draw herself up to her full height and stretch her limbs she seemed to take on new life. After a pause of three minutes or so she came over to where Shabir lay, and plucked him off the ground as if he were a tiny baby. She took him to the wagon and lowered him over the tailboard with a reasonable degree of gentleness. He didn't show any sign of waking up.

Fraxinus stirred the broken ground where the general had fallen, sifting the scintillant shards with his fingers. 'Have you ever seen anything like this before?' he asked Ereleth.

'You're the great traveller,' she retorted acidly. Her customary bile had evidently returned in full measure under the strain of watching her fate settled by alien sand and dragomite warriors. 'If there were anything like it in the empire, you'd know far better than I. I've got to get under cover again – this terrible light's hurting my eyes and my head's pounding. *Spangled* seems to me to be an entirely inadequate description of the desert's quality.'

As he stood up again and looked around, Fraxinus could see what she meant. Reflected and refracted sunlight seemed to be coming at him from every direction, tinted all the colours of the rainbow, in ludicrous profusion and confusion. He shut his eyes and put his hand over them to shield out the glare that set the insides of his eyelids alight with orange fire.

This is no place for men and horses, he thought. *How many days will it take us to ride around the Nine Towns? How many kims is it to Salamander's Fire?*

When he carefully opened his eyes again the landscape didn't look quite so harsh and alien, but he understood why Ereleth wanted to get under cover. The hours to either side of the noonday were bad enough in these latitudes even at the best of times, and the heat seemed far worse here than it had been in the whited hills. First, however, he had to see to the horses.

From now on, he supposed, the water they had would have to be very carefully rationed. He had no idea how easy it might be to find more, or how frequently it rained hereabouts, but he had a strong suspicion that the answers might be *exceedingly difficult* and *hardly ever*.

He looked around at the other fallen Eblans, but he quickly decided that Ereleth was right. Information was all he needed, and he had already taken possession of the best source; if any of the others were still alive, it was not his responsibility to succour them. They had already done far too much harm to his ambitions and his personnel.

Thirty mets away, the remaining dragomites were now at

work dismantling their dead companion. He admired their implacable efficiency, but he couldn't quite suppress a shudder. *To be reckoned as nest-mates by creatures like these might yet turn out to be a dubious privilege*, he thought – but he knew that he was not so well-equipped with allies as to have the luxury of choice. The thought of butchering the dead horses was nauseating, but he knew that it would have to be done and he wondered whether it would seem unreasonably cowardly to leave the work entirely to the dragomites.

'It's just as well I've turned adventurer in my old age,' he said, speaking aloud although no one was near enough to hear him. 'If I were still a merchant, I'd have to reckon myself heir to an exceptionally poor set of bargains. As things are, I may proceed with all the hope and curiosity I can muster. The only dangers which face us now are those which lie ahead.'

II

JACOM HAD ONLY just managed to get to sleep, after an hour of restless insomnia, when someone shook him awake. He grunted a complaint as he opened his eyes. He could see little more than an amorphous shadow leaning over him. He and his companions had been bedded down in the hayloft of a barn, and the sentry's lantern was on the floor far below, at the entrance to the cattle-stall into which the watchman had retired to rest. The sentry had carefully removed the ladder which gave access to the hayloft, but it had been a token gesture; anyone determined to escape into the night could have climbed down the buttressed pillars supporting the loft. It was evidently just as easy to climb up.

'Shhh! Don't wake the guard or the Mugolian!' The voice bidding him to be silent was very low, but it was recognisable. His visitor was the bronze, Amyas.

'What is it?' Jacom demanded, in some annoyance. He kept his own voice low out of consideration for Hyry Keshvara, Merel Zabio, Aulakh Phar and Munir Zanarin, who were stretched out in various coverts to either side of him, not because he had any ready sympathy with the other's desire for secrecy.

'Be quiet, I beg you,' the bronze said. 'Move right to the back of the loft – we can talk privately there for a while. I mean you no harm.'

The back of the loft was deeply shadowed, but there was a little starlight filtering through a number of holes in the barn's roof. Jacom found his way there easily enough, without making much noise in his stockinged feet. None of the others stirred, and the rhythm of Zanarin's breathing suggested that he was fast sleep.

Jacom had sense enough to realise that this was an opportunity to learn a good deal more about the situation into which he and his companions had fallen, and he knew that he must take full advantage of it. The bronze had no boots on either, and he moved over the faintly creaking timbers with the ease of a man well-practised in the art of covert movement.

'What is it?' Jacom asked, very quietly, as he settled himself against the rear wall of the barn, trying to find a comfortable position.

'I'd have come to you before,' Amyas whispered, 'but I've been as closely watched by Nath's men as you have. He doesn't trust me, although I'm the one who has the greater need, as well as the greater fear of betrayal.'

'I don't understand,' Jacom told him flatly. 'I have no idea who or what you are, or why Nath is so enthusiastic to keep us prisoner.'

'That's why I'm here,' the bronze told him. 'Did you, perchance, look towards the southern horizon as dusk was falling?'

'I did,' Jacom said. 'I could hardly avoid it, given that Nath's men were pointing that way in such evident alarm – but all I could see were a few black dots set against the darkening sky. I asked Zanarin what they were, but he said that he had never seen their like before, and dared not credit evil rumours.'

'*Dared* not is right,' Amyas said. 'The rumours are true, alas; those dots are harbingers of disaster, and the Nine Towns have neither the will not the capability to stand against the invasion they portend. I came here in the hope of finding aid, and found nothing but confusion. If the nations of the far north are no stiffer in the spine than this one, human dominion of this world might indeed be on the point of ending.'

'Things are very different in Xandria,' Jacom replied, as pride required him to do. 'Belin's empire is not the kind to crumble under pressure, and it stands ever-ready to react in a calculated way against any imaginable threat.'

'If it were only imaginable threats we had to fear,' Amyas replied, in all apparent earnest, 'things would not be as bad as they are, and there might be less danger of their becoming ten times worse. I know that your name is Jacom Cerri, and that you were a captain in the army of Xandria. You had command over a company of men, a dozen of whom came here in advance of your wagons . . .'

'So Shabir did have warning of our coming!' Jacom interrupted, the pitch of his voice rising a little in spite of his good intentions.

'Not until the eve of the battle,' Amyas told him. 'Nath took charge of those men too, and sent all but one of them to Antiar. He intends to use them in his own service, but as to how . . . that's a matter on which he and I can no longer see eye to eye. He has made me promises which he probably now regrets . . . but all that's beside the point. You made some sort of blunder, I believe. In the beginning, you brought your men south in pursuit of fugitives, but things went badly awry and now you're cut adrift from your homeland for good and all. That's how things stand with you, is it not?'

Jacom had no idea exactly what Amyas might have heard and understood – presumably from Purkin, but perhaps at second or third hand – and his instinct was to be wary of giving away too much. 'Things haven't gone well for me of late,' he admitted. 'As you can surely see.'

'Your fortunes might yet take a turn for the better,' Amyas said, a little tentatively, 'but you will have to decide whose side to take when Nath finally decides what he will do. Nath was very willing to trade with me while he thought his own situation safe, but things have changed so rapidly that he will soon have no thought in his head but to protect his own security. For the moment, he is no more able to read the portent of the floaters than the Mugolian, and he will not trust my assessment until he hears independent confirmation from Tawil or Sabinal. Only then will he decide whether it is better to run than stand his own ground – and, if he does run, which way he will go.'

'It would be better,' Jacom observed acidly, 'if you were to stop talking in riddles now and gave me the explanation you came here to offer.'

Amyas took no offence at his tone. 'You know, I suppose,' he said, 'that this is a perilously narrow land, surrounded by tainted territories where many kinds of monsters dwell?'

'I've seen a map,' Jacom told him, 'but I know no more than what was written on it.'

'Well, there's good fertile land along both banks of the river which has been given over to earthly crops since time immemorial – but it's not been held without effort. Nath's people have long grown used to the necessity of fighting to defend their fields against alien weeds, but they've also grown used to winning the fight and they've been hard hit by its recent intensification. You might think that their so-called general was wrong to attack your wagons just because you were keeping company with dragomites, but you don't understand the evils with which these people are constantly faced, and the attitude of mind forged over generations by that confrontation.

'The dragomites have always sought to extend the range of their hills by making new nests in the hidden coverts of this little nation, but it's only within the last two years that the Nine Towns have been forced to combine forces and exert themselves to the full in keeping the dragomites at bay. The townsmen have become increasingly desperate in the course of those two years, and the Convocation has had a difficult task to maintain the Alliance. It was difficult enough to persuade the southernmost towns to commit troops to the protection of the northern lands when their own territory was under no abnormal pressure; now that there's an invasion from the south the whole enterprise is falling apart, and the community with it. Were there a king to exercise despotic authority over the whole nation the situation might yet be saved, but these are democratic folk who invest all power in weak and corrupt committees, and the makeshift union they forged two years ago is fast dissolving into anarchy.

'Their problems have never been confined to the north, of course. The fields on the far side of the river are constantly afflicted by pests originating in the Spangled Desert, whose glassy scales provide them with awkward armour. To the west lie the Soursweet Marshes, whose thorny bushes constantly threaten to extend their own tainted empire. Such bushes have to be rooted out before their thorns grow, because they're full of subtle poisons. The work of keeping the desert and the marshes at bay has always been tiresome and never-ending, but those battles never seemed likely to be lost . . . until recently, when the men whose labour kept the fields free of unearthly pollution have been diverted to other tasks.

'To the south of Sabinal, which is the last of the Nine Towns, there's a barren land where nothing earthly has grown for as long as anyone can remember. In normal times it poses no particular threat because its principal inhabitants are creatures with stony bodies which are extremely slow-moving and usually very slow to reproduce. That too has changed within the last few years, and is changing still. When I told the men of the southern towns that theirs was the greatest danger of all they refused to believe me, but I think they will have changed their opinions by now.

'In the distant past there was a considerable human civilisation in the temperate lands beyond the barren region. Its fields were richer by far than those of the Nine Towns, its cities were greater, and its arts were infinitely more glorious – but that civilisation too was rimmed to the east, south and west by unearthly lands. For centuries its boundaries were maintained with relative ease – but then, in the course of a single generation, those boundaries were overrun. We have only legends now to tell us how great the extent of our ancestors' civilisation once was. We cannot tell whether the failure to defend it was an incapacity of artistry or a faltering of resolve, but we know for certain that human beings who cannot and do not stand firm against unearthly invasions risk losing everything.

'My ancestors once used the Silver Thorns as a hunting-ground, and delighted in bringing back marvels from Chimera's Cradle itself. Some among us believe that by so doing they imported deadly blights into their houses and their fields. At any rate, a series of plagues devastated the human population of the southlands some hundreds of years ago. Whatever their faults were, my ancestors paid a heavy price for them – a price which their children's children are still paying. After a time, the plagues abated and a new balance was struck, but we have always known that the balance would one day be tipped again, and not in our favour.

'Even in my father's time, the fields my people cultivated were still greater in extent than those of the Nine Towns, but things have changed since then. The slow invasions which have always threatened to overwhelm the earthly lands have once again accelerated considerably, and new invaders have appeared to supplement their erosions. The dots which you saw in the sky at sundown are the vanguard of one such invasion: spores which are borne aloft like balloons filled with hot air, and drift for hundreds of kims on the wind. Wherever they descend they quickly take root, and the trees which they produce are vilely difficult to displace once rooted. As if that were not enough, other things come in the floaters' wake: packs of dog-like creatures we call hellhounds, lone hunters known as lizardlions, and many other monsters. We have even sighted manticores, which we had long considered to be mythical beasts.

'Nowadays, the territory which remains to us is called the Last Stronghold, and it's bitter necessity which forces us to use such a name. At the heart of our enterprise there is indeed a stronghold, with a wall built all around it as strong as we could make – but we have no way of knowing whether it can be maintained, or for how long. We hope that if we can hold out long enough equilibrium might be restored again, at least for a few more centuries, but we have no idea what pressure we shall have to endure.

'The men of my father's generation were still proud. They still took leave to despise the men of the river towns, thinking them primitive and unruly, always quarrelling with one another – but we have been humbled these last ten years, and we have had to send emissaries forth in every direction, hoping to forge alliances that might help to preserve what little we have left. I don't know what others might have found, but all I have found here is a crumbling society which has no chance whatsoever of resisting the kind of invasions which have all but devastated our domain. I had hoped, at the very least, to hire mercenaries here who might help to defend the stronghold, but there were none to be had while Shabir's campaign against the dragomites continued – and now that it has ended, the army's component parts are scattering. I thought I could rely on Nath to gather a company for me in Antiar, if I paid him well enough, but he fears for his own skin now.

'If tradition can be trusted, we are poorer folk by far than the men who once lived in the southlands, and far less knowledgeable – but we now understand the absolute necessity of defending ourselves against all that is alien, all that is tainted. We know what we must do to preserve what remains of our land, and we are determined to do it, no matter what toll must be paid in blood and sweat.

'Is that explanation enough, Jacom Cerri? Do you understand your situation now?'

There was, in fact, a great deal that Jacom still didn't

understand, but he was grateful for the information which he had been given, and he felt that he understood where Amyas stood in relation to Tarlock Nath and to himself. 'What does Nath want with us?' he was quick to ask. 'And what do you expect of me?'

'I can't speak for Nath,' the bronze said, with studied contempt. 'But what my people need is fighting men: men who are trained and men who are knowledgeable, but above all men who are brave. I need men who believe that this battle against the forces of chaos and corruption might be turned even now, and are avid to do exactly that.'

'Ah!' said Jacom noncommittally. He had guessed, of course, that all of this was an attempted recruitment, but he wasn't at all sure that he wanted to be recruited. Nor was he sure that Amyas was the best master to serve if he had to switch the allegiance he had promised Carus Fraxinus. He wanted time to think about what he had been told – and, if possible, to discuss it at length with Hyry Keshvara and Aulakh Phar. He had no intention of making any promises to Amyas, especially while he was still Tarlock Nath's prisoner.

'Everything I've told you is true,' the bronze said insistently. 'If you think I have anything to do with the bronzes who sold your companion the seeds she brought to Xandria, you're mistaken. There are bronzes living in a certain hospitable part of the Soursweet Marshes, but they are not my people and they have no intercourse with Nath's folk either. My own people live to the east of Salamander's Fire; we are distant descendants of the men who once lived in the fabled Cities of the Plain, but those cities were lost to the great plagues, and the figured stones long ago consumed their walls and their roads.'

'You know Salamander's Fire, then?' Jacom said curiously. 'You know what it is – and what its significance is in the scheme of things?'

'I don't know what you mean by *significance*,' Amyas parried. 'My people have no truck with Salamanders, but there has never been any open hostility between us. They're unearthly, but they seem harmless enough. I've passed close to Salamander's Fire, and doubtless will again, but the figured stones are massed so voluminously about its narrow bounds that no one with feet like a man or a horse dares to approach it too closely.'

Jacom was torn between asking what figured stones were and trying to probe for more information about Salamander's Fire. Before he could make up his mind there was a noise from the cattle-stall down below. The sentry stationed to keep watch on them must have woken up, and he was now bestirring himself slightly, perhaps looking round to make sure that all was well before relaxing again. Jacom had no doubt that he would relax again – Merel Zabio's leg was still in plaster, and Nath's men must be confident by now that it was anchor enough to keep all of them docile in their captivity – but Amyas was quick to seize Jacom's arm and press it tight, urging silence.

They stayed quite still for three minutes, but heard nothing more. Jacom wanted to resume the conversation once he was sure that the watchman had dropped off again, but Amyas obviously felt that he had said and done enough for the time being.

'No treaties now,' the bronze said, in a very faint voice. 'Your friends must recover their strength, and we don't yet know what we'll find in Antiar. Only be assured that you do have choices, and that a man like you always has value, no matter what misfortunes of fate he might suffer. Stay still for a while, I beg of you. When I'm gone, you can make as much noise as you like.'

Jacom might have protested had the other stayed long enough to lend an ear to protests, but Amyas had his own purposes in mind. The bronze let go of Jacom's arm and moved away into the darkness, which was deep enough to swallow him absolutely. He disappeared over the rim of the loft, descending into the barn as nimbly and as discreetly as Checuti's monkey would have done.

Jacom did as he had been asked and stayed quite still for a little while, straining his ears to catch the slight sounds the bronze made as he climbed down from the loft and moved to the door of the barn. If the sentry was still awake – which Jacom couldn't believe – he obviously wasn't sufficiently alert to take heed of any sounds as slight as those. After a further five minutes had gone by, Jacom crept back to the place where he had been sleeping.

Not until he had arrived there, and laid his head down upon the folded jacket he was using as a pillow, did Hyry Keshvara lean across to whisper in his ear: 'Plans laid in the midnight dark rarely hatch out in the broad light of noon.'

It was difficult to judge how light her tone was, but he decided to take it as a joke rather than a veiled accusation. 'Silent eavesdroppers rarely thrive on what they hear,' he replied ironically, 'and I dare say that people who are overfond of quoting proverbs rarely benefit from their wisdom.'

'Spoken like a soldier,' she said. 'Just be sure to make a full report when the midnight's done.'

12

BY THE TIME they were ready to get under way again Andris had become anxious about his state of mind. He was feeling neither hunger nor thirst, and fatigue had ceased to bother him. The only word he could think of to describe his condition was intoxication, but it was markedly different from the diffuse kind of intoxication induced by means of strong drink.

The itching which Herriman had told everyone to watch out for had become noticeable now, in his hands and legs, but it didn't feel unpleasant. His fingers felt rather strange, as if they were bloated, and they had lost some of their sensitivity, but there was nothing intrinsically troublesome about the sensation or the loss. In a way, that was even more worrying than having a perfectly ordinary and conventionally irritating itch; it was obvious to him that his companions were finding the effects of their miscellaneous scratches rather more difficult to bear.

At first, the itches suffered by Lucrezia, Checuti, Jume Metra and Herriman had presumably been ordinary tickling and tingling itches, which they had scratched occasionally but otherwise ignored, but if their responses could be trusted they had grown fiercer by degrees. Lucrezia now seemed to be making a considerable effort to refrain from scratching herself; she was continually wriggling and scowling. The irritation must have spread from her hands and calves to her forearms and thighs, all the way to her elbows and crotch. Only Checuti complained aloud, though, and even he did so in an ironic spirit, dismissing the itching as a minor nuisance.

Forewarned by Herriman, Andris had done his best to be careful of the everpresent thorns, and he was sure that the others – including Ssifuss, who didn't seem to be affected at all – had done likewise, but it was beginning to seem that even the most trivial contact between the thorns and human flesh was sufficient to pass slow-acting poisons into the bloodstream. He couldn't easily figure out why the particular cocktail of drugs which he had imbibed was having a noticeably different effect on him than on his companions, but he remembered all too well that he had been given an overgenerous dose of the anaesthetic which the men of the Nine Towns used, and he wondered whether that had somehow armoured him against the other compounds he was now encountering.

He took some comfort from the fact that the poisons seemed to be relatively slow to act even on his companions, and that their symptoms were not seriously disabling. They showed no sign of fever and the muscles in their limbs didn't seem to be stiffening or weakening, although Jume Metra was certainly holding herself rather awkwardly. What was more worrying, however, was that the horses were evidently feeling the effects of the thorn-poisons too. Their thick coats must have provided them with a greater measure of protection than the increasingly tattered clothing the humans wore, but not as much as the Serpent's scaly tegument. As the day had progressed the beasts became increasingly fractious and resentful, and he wasn't sure how long they would consent to be ridden.

There were distractions from the general misery, though. They had a fright not long after dawn when they encountered a sizeable herd of large animals, whose massive bodies seemed somewhat out of keeping with their long necks, narrow heads and small mouths. Andris stopped dead as soon as he caught sight of them, reaching reflexively for his blade.

'Are those the big lizards you mentioned?' he asked Ssifuss, who had been walking beside him, ahead of the four horses.

Ssifuss shook its head. 'Thosse *big* lissardss,' it said, presumably implying that there was a world of difference between 'big' and *big* in its limited vocabulary.

It was obvious once Andris took the trouble to think about it that the animals were specialist herbivores, and he decided that it was safe to move on. The creatures didn't pause for very long in their grazing to peer at the newcomers, but Ssifuss took care to give them a reasonably wide berth and Andris took the hint. While they remained in view, he kept a wary eye on them, but they made no aggressive moves.

It didn't require much thought to work out the logic of the

beasts' anatomy. They were obviously selective eaters which used their snaky necks to insert their scaly heads deep into the bushes, evading the worst of the protective thorns. Their tiny mouths were thus enabled to pluck the juicy leaves without imbibing too much poison. Andris observed that their smooth grey hides looked very tough indeed, and that the scales decorating their heads gave every appearance of being as hard as the shell of the turtle which Ssifuss had killed. Given that there didn't seem to be very many large predators around of which creatures like these need walk in fear, he could only conclude that the armour they wore was purely and simply to protect them from the deterrents deployed by the bushes on which they fed. The lesson to be learned from that – which, alas, his companions were already in the process of learning by unfortunate experience – was that it wasn't just the biggest and most obviously aggressive of the thorns which had to be avoided.

When they paused again Andris consulted his companions as to the exact extent of their discomfort. Checuti again claimed that the trouble was trivial, but Andris had taken note of the fact that the thief-master's squeamishness had made him somewhat warier of the thorns than anyone else, and that his caution had enabled him to minimise his injuries. Lucrezia admitted that she felt very uncomfortable, but declared that she could bear it. Herriman declared himself sorely tried, displaying his hands and arms by way of proof. Their flesh was reddened by overenthusiastic scratching.

Herriman was the only one of them who complained very stridently in response to Andris's enquiry, but it was obvious that the person who was suffering worst of all was Jume Metra. Although she stubbornly maintained her determination to be uncommunicative she was showing distinct signs of distress and the marks on her arms and legs, which had been made worse by her own scratching, were every bit as red as Herriman's.

'I believe that I can counter at least some of the effects,' the princess said. 'I can't put names to the poisons that have got into us, but I can treat the symptoms. I'll test the ointment on myself, if you're reluctant to trust me, or I can treat your wounds now, if you prefer.'

'I think you'd better use your ointment on Metra right away,' Andris told her, 'and you'd best be ready to treat the horses should they show any further signs of distress. I don't need treatment myself yet – I don't know about Checuti and Herriman.'

Checuti and Herriman both decided that if there was a chance of relief, they'd take it – even from a witch.

The princess looked dubious once she realised the extent of the demand. 'I have only a limited supply of the antidote,' she said, 'and no ingredients with which to prepare more. Without Phar or Ereleth . . .'

'It's lucky that we have anything at all,' Andris reassured her quickly. 'We have to get out of the marshes as soon as possible; hopefully your supplies will last long enough to see us through.'

The contents of the leathern pouch which Lucrezia plucked from her belt were rapidly depleted once she moved on from the people to the horses. Andris noticed that she took hardly any for herself, but it was obvious that she had enough for two more general applications at the most. He knew better than to expect that the salve's effects would last indefinitely, but he hoped that it might last at least a full day, and perhaps two.

'We must avoid the thorns as best we can,' he said, before they started out again. 'Always protect your hands while cutting wood and clearing ground.' No one disputed his authority to hand down such advice, or the need for the instruction to be voiced; the brief elation that they had experienced after feeding on the turtle had evaporated long ago, and they had sunk into a very sober mood. That mood became even more sombre as the ruddy sun sank into the west, at its usual leisurely pace, and the fainter stars came out from hiding.

The night was clear, and the air cooled so quickly that the relative warmth of the water through which he was wading was comforting. The marsh became filled with drifting wisps of mist, although they were thin enough not to obscure the stars. The scattered clouds sparkled with faint but rather eerie reflected light, and their lazy movement lent them a curious semblance of life.

When they stopped for the midnight Ssifuss laid out lures for 'lissardss', and trapped a small crocolid with remarkable rapidity. It didn't seem to Andris that it was an unduly fearsome creature, and Lucrezia confirmed that it was neither as big nor as well-armed with teeth as the crocolid Hyry Keshvara had killed and eaten in the Forest of Absolute Night.

'Are nasstier oness,' Ssifuss agreed. 'Thesse better.'

By the time they had eaten their fill and put the rest in store, Andris was fairly certain that hunger would not be too terrible a threat while they were in the marshes.

Andris and Herriman drew first watch, but when the time came for their duty to begin the glutted Herriman had already fallen asleep. When Andris went to wake him, Jume Metra stopped him, indicating with a gesture that she would take his place.

Andris was surprised by this seeming gesture of kindness; it was the first sign the mound-woman had given that she considered herself a true member of the party rather than someone who merely happened to be going in the same direction. He wondered whether Lucrezia's treatment of her troublesome wounds had awakened some consciousness in her of the rewards and obligations of reciprocal altruism, or whether she had some other motive for wanting to take first watch.

When all was quiet, Andris became uncomfortably aware that he was drowsy himself, presumably by virtue of the after-effects of his meal. He wondered whether he ought to have insisted on keeping the talkative Herriman as a partner – but Metra must have been in much the same condition, for she responded with unprecedented readiness to his conversational overture when he asked after her well-being. Her answers were by no means full, but the fact that she was inclined to answer at all seemed to him to be almost miraculous.

After half a dozen innocuous exchanges Andris' curiosity had been well and truly piqued, and he felt able to raise more intimate questions.

'What will you do if you can't found a new nest?' he asked. He wasn't sure whether or not she understood that her chances of achieving that end must by now have been reduced to negligibility.

'There are eggs still,' she told him. He had expected the evasion.

'I know that,' he said, gently. 'You'll do everything you possibly can, I expect. But if it were to prove impossible . . . can you imagine a different way of life? Could you become an ordinary human, do you think – a creature like me, or the princess?' He was genuinely interested in hearing the answer, although he knew that it was very likely to be another evasion.

She sat quite still, looking out over the faintly sparkling water. 'We are not like the other warriors,' she said finally. 'We have . . . other ways.'

'You mean that you wouldn't just lie down and die, even if the nest were irredeemably lost,' he said.

She didn't reply to that, but her silence was eloquent.

'We're a nest of sorts, I suppose,' he said, a little wary lest the idea seem offensive to her. 'Our little company, I mean. Bound together by circumstance, no matter that we seem alien to one another.'

'Not the same,' she said, but there was an oddly wistful note in her voice that he had never heard before.

'It'll take several more days, at least, to cross the marshland,' he said softly. 'If the princess can't eke out that ointment cleverly enough, you might have to fight the effects of that irritating itch again. It won't be easy. For the moment, the crocolids are our prey, but the tables could be turned if things go badly. We need to pull together if we're to stand a chance of getting through to the other side.'

'We will get through,' she told him. 'We must.' There was little or no inflection in her voice, but it seemed to Andris that she was saying: *I have a goal to aim for. I have something to justify all hardships, to draw me on in the face of adversity.*

'I've been a wanderer ever since I was a child,' he told her. 'It's become a way of life. It's a luxury for me to have any kind of goal at all, even for a little while – but I quite like it that way. I wouldn't want to be part of some larger whole, obligated to direct all my efforts towards ends that weren't my own. I don't suppose you can imagine what it's like to be a free individual any more than I can imagine what it's like to be part of a dragomite nest, but it's what I am and I'm content with it. To me, it seems right and proper and worth striving to preserve. For the time being, though, I'm part of this little group, and I'm prepared to do whatever I can to make sure that we all get through, including you and Ssifuss. You can depend on that.'

'*I* is illusion,' she said rudely. 'There is only *we*, even for you.'

He was used to her habits by now, and he'd already decided not to take offence at anything she said, so he didn't.

'In a way,' he said ruminatively, 'you're right. Individuality *is* an illusion. I was talking to Aulakh Phar once, while we were crossing the hills, about dragomites and nests and what the Serpents might be trying to achieve by securing a deal between you and us. *A dragomite is just an egg's instrument for making more eggs*, he said. *In fact, an entire dragomite nest, with or without human commensals, is just a device made by eggs for the production of eggs. You and I and the Serpents are no different – we're all just clever devices invented by eggs for the purpose of making more eggs. There are different designs and different strategies, but it all comes down to the same thing. That's what Genesys itself was all about: eggs making more eggs, spreading those eggs through the universe, planting them on every world of every star in the bright and blazing sky. We're all just moves in life's endless game.* From that point of view, you're absolutely right. Individuality is an illusion because all that endures is part of the game of life. But I can't adopt that point of view as readily as you can, you see, because you and I are very different egg-made instruments. Although we share the same flesh, the same form and the same language, we're not the same inside our heads. Which makes it all the more remarkable, I suppose, that we can become allies, engaged in a common pursuit.

'I said something of the kind to Aulakh Phar, although I hadn't thought it through then, and I was thinking about the Serpents rather than the dragomites. Phar said: *That's what the lore of Genesys is all about, in my opinion. It's about two different kinds of life coming together, sharing the same world, becoming allied, engaging in a common pursuit. That's what Carus Fraxinus's* Apocrypha of Genesys *is about too, if it's not just something made up and tacked on the lore for no good reason . . . and if Serpent's blood and Salamander's fire mean anything at all, that's what they have to do with*. I think he might be right. If what that old storyteller told me in Xandria meant anything at all, it's something to do with the kinds of life we call earthly and unearthly coming together, the way they do in the depths of a dragomite nest, and producing something new. Chimera's Cradle; the Pool of Life; the Nest of the Phoenix – all the names are tied together by the same thread of meaning. Fraxinus wants to find out how and why, and so do I – just as soon as I've found Merel again.'

While he delivered this speech Andris had avoided looking directly at Jume Metra; instead he had stared out into the swamp, watching the wisps of mist swirling like languid dancers. Now though, he looked back at her face. He was mildly surprised to see that it wasn't expressionless. She had been listening to him intently, whether she could follow the argument or not, and whether she agreed with it or not.

'Merel and Aulakh were hurt,' Jume Metra said, with what almost sounded like sympathy. 'We must all hope that they did not die.'

'Yes,' said Andris, feeling an odd thrill of gratitude as well as a faint sense of achievement. 'We must, musn't we? All of us.'

13

CARUS FRAXINUS KNELT down in the pool of shadow, where the ground was cool enough to touch with bare hands, and carefully scooped up a handful of the glittering 'sand' which had accumulated there. He had to take care because some of the fragments had not yet been ground down to inoffensive smoothness, and the tiny splinters could easily become embedded in the flesh beneath the skin. During the previous midnight Vaca Metra had come to Ereleth complaining of a sore hand, whose cause had turned out to be a shard of natural glass which had worked its way deep into the flesh under the pressure of the mound-woman's labours. Ereleth had excavated it with the aid of a scalpel, but the work had required minute care and the pallor of Metra's skin had testified to the effort required to bear the pain of it in silence.

When Fraxinus brought the handful of coarse dust out of the shadow into the morning sunlight it seemed to catch fire as the multitudinous particles threw back the light, tinting it with innumerable glints of red, yellow and blue. It was not the first time he had seen such an effect. In the eastern parts of the empire it was possible to buy glass vessels of various shapes and sizes in which this kind of 'jewel dust' was sealed. The smaller ones were usually sold as amulets while the larger ones were marketed as household ornaments, but they were not expensive and were thus regarded by the aristocrats of Xandria as vulgar gewgaws unworthy of serious attention. He knew that the dust distributed in the vessels was really a waste-product, the original material having been very carefully sifted in order to remove any particles which were of value in themselves, such as the tiny diamonds which were used in drill-bits. He had always known that such produce originated in the Spangled Desert, but he had never realised that here too it was a waste-product: the debris of scaly skins sloughed by animals, and of dead cells shed by the entities which Shabir called gaudtrees and lapidendrons under the pressure of the hot, scouring winds.

It was a close-knit group of gaudtrees which cast the pool of shadow from which he had plucked the crystalline dust. They did not, in fact, resemble trees very closely; an observer disinclined to romance might have been more inclined to liken them to miniature dragomite mounds. Their basic shape was that of a slender cone that had been unceremoniously crumpled by the brief grip of an enormous hand, but at the apex they sprouted dense clusters of dark spikes, as if each one were crowned by an open sea-anemone whose tentacles had been turned to glass. The gaudtrees had no branches, as such, but each 'trunk' bore a series of tumorous growths arranged in a spiral. These rounded growths varied in texture and appearance from something not unlike the skin of an orange to something more like a pineapple, but the outer tegument – which was relatively soft by the standards of the desert – always overlaid a much harder vitreous dermis, which was often raggedly exposed where the outer layers had been plundered by the indigenous fauna.

Fraxinus could not tell for certain what function the spiky 'tentacles' had. They might, he supposed, function like the leaves of ordinary plants, using the energy of sunlight to manufacture their own substance, but he was reluctant to take it for granted. Their colour was much darker than the greens and purples of the Forest of Absolute Night. Many of the other immobile organisms which grew in the desert had nothing resembling the crown of an earthly tree even to this extent. The lapidendrons had the branches which the gaudtrees had not, but they seemed to be purely structural: mere stalks for the large beads which they bore at their extremities.

To Fraxinus, the lapidendrons looked like half-melted candelabra whose multitudinous 'arms' ended in socketed 'eyeballs' – 'eyeballs' which were also to be found in the marketplaces of the eastern empire, remounted in ornate bezels as brooches or pendants. He could see no evidence of any apparatus which might do the work of leaves, and it was impossible to uproot the things from the hard ground to see what their nether parts might be like.

He had tried to question Shabir about the strange stony life-forms of the desert but the general had been unable to offer any interesting information beyond a few names. To him, the desert was simply a bad place, a source of evils; he had no interest in the home-life of the creatures which lived there or the manner in which its vitreous plants created food on which the local animals might survive and thrive.

Except for sluggish sandskinks and their serpentine cousins – which Shabir called gemsnakes and tinselworms – the desert fauna was not much in evidence by day, but at night it was possible to catch glimpses of nimbler creatures whose surfaces were not nearly so inclined to glitter, and to hear the flickering wingbeats of huge ghostly moths. Not all the creatures of the region were as resolutely sturdy as the gaudtrees and lapidendrons; tinselworms were very delicate and even their more robust cousins the gemsnakes were brittle enough to be breakable if one could avoid their needle-like fangs long enough to hit them hard with something solid.

The place where the wagon had paused for the noonday might almost have qualified as a gaudtree forest had the entities in question put out lateral branches, but because they did not it seemed to Fraxinus that the scene was more reminiscent of a fleet of fishing-boats moored in a bay, with their sails carefully furled about their masts. The desert floor between the gaudtree boles was split by countless narrow cracks and crevices, which would have been an unalloyed inconvenience had it not been for the fact that some of them sheltered deep-set pools of water from which they could renew their supplies.

The gaudtrees evidently had need of water, and grew in profusion wherever such underground reservoirs were, with the result that they provided a ready signal for travellers. In consequence of this convenience, the most awkward challenge which had so far faced them was not shortage of water but shortage of fodder for the horses. Their flight across the fertile fields had been all too brief, and the supplies which they had bought had run out far too quickly for comfort. They still had supplies of horsemeat, which provided sustenance for dragomite warriors as well as humans and the Serpent, but the animals towing the wagon had already grown thin during the passage of the Dragomite Hills, and the two remaining out of those

Shabir's men had obligingly provided were even wirier. They were badly in need of authentic earthly vegetation, or some acceptable substitute, but there was none to be found.

Mossassor, who had climbed the flanks of an unusually squat crystal-tree in order to get a better view of the terrain ahead, leapt lightly down and walked to where Fraxinus was still studying the grains of dust that lay in his hand.

'There iss a sshange near the ssouthern horisson,' it reported. 'No more sspikess – but all sstill glissterss, many colourss.'

Fraxinus sighed. It was no more than he had expected, but it would have been exceedingly pleasant, for once in a while, to hear better news. 'No more sspikess' meant no more clumps of gaudtrees – which probably meant no more water-holes.

'We'd better fill every vessel we have,' he said. 'It might be a long way to the next oasis.'

Mossassor probably had no idea what an oasis was, but it understood the first sentence. It nodded in agreement, licking its lips with its forked tongue. Fraxinus wondered whether draining the reservoir would cause injury to the gaudtrees; if so, they must have been drawing a long line of death or debility across the trackless wilderness as they moved from water-hole to water-hole, plundering their closely guarded treasure.

'Iss bad, issn't it?' Mossassor said. Although Fraxinus still couldn't read the subtle expressions that flitted across the Serpent's relatively immobile face, Mossassor had learned to read his own moods reasonably accurately.

'Yes,' he said, 'it's bad. We've been lucky so far, but we're likely to lose at least one more horse before nightfall. This isn't the kind of territory we can walk through. How are the dragomites?'

'Not well, but sstill sstrong. Can keep going.'

'But can they pull the wagon?'

'No. Can carry uss on backss if all elsse failss.'

Fraxinus couldn't muster a laugh, although the thought of the three dragomite warriors carrying two riders apiece across the desert sands was surely absurd enough to warrant one.

'I'll have another chat with the general,' Fraxinus said. 'It must have sunk into his thick skull by now that if we die, he'll die with us. If we have to turn west and go back into the narrow land . . .' He left the sentence unfinished because he wasn't sure that they could get back to the cultivated lands of the Nine Towns, and he didn't think that Shabir would be disposed to be reasonable if they did.

'Iss very unanxssiouss to help uss,' Mossassor observed, by way of confirmation. 'Sseemss to want to die.'

It was true; Shabir's stubborn refusal to talk to them in any but the curtest fashion seemed to be symptomatic of a perverse determination to suffer, thus to reap the bleak harvest of his failures. Fraxinus could have understood the general's attitude a little better had he seemed to be consumed by hatred for the enemies who had twice defeated his men and then subjected him to ignominious captivity, but he gave little evidence of active hostility; his disinclination to communicate was not maintained by fierce defiance but rather by a deep depression. His lack of gratitude for the treatment which Ereleth had administered to his injuries did not seem to be born of resentment of his dependence on someone he had tried to slaughter, but rather of a complete uninterest in the possibility of putting his bruised limbs to any future use.

'He might be feeling better today,' Fraxinus said, with a sigh. 'At least, we must hope so.'

He let the remaining sand drain from his palm on to the ground, brushing the last of it away very gently lest he drive a sharp spicule into his own flesh; then he looked pensively around at the gaudtrees. 'I wonder if it's worth breaking through the outer walls of those things if we can find a way to do it,' he said. 'They're living things, and they must have softer flesh within. Perhaps there's something at the heart of them that the horses can eat.'

'No musst,' Mossassor said, shaking its head regretfully. 'Ssome living thingss have no ssoftness at all. Ssiss iss Ssalamander land, where flowing sstoness live. Not good for Sserpentss, let alone humanss.' Fraxinus noticed that the Serpent didn't seem completely certain; it was repeating something told to it, not something of which it had personal experience.

'What are flowing stones?' he asked.

'Will ssee,' Mossassor said, not bothering to add any qualifying phrase to the effect of *if we get that far*.

'These gaudtrees might be more like the Dragomite Hills than we suspect,' Fraxinus said hopefully. 'Myrasol told me that each mound was merely the outer layer of a vast creature whose main bulk lay deeply buried – that the mound was, in a sense, the body of the queen rather than a mere container. I can't help wondering whether these clumps are really groups of separate individuals, or whether they might be the spiny projections of some even vaster entity whose bulk lies below ground.'

'Might be sso,' the Serpent said, with devastating common sense, 'but makess no differensse. Can't dig in ground like ssiss.' It turned away and walked back towards the wagon. Fraxinus followed.

Dhalla was standing beside the horses, soothing the leader of the team by ruffling its mane with one of her capacious hands.

'What of the portent in the sky?' she asked. 'Does it spell danger?'

'What portent?' Fraxinus asked, abruptly looking up into the dazzling blue vault to see what she meant.

The sudden onset of brightness as the brim of his hat tilted backwards forced his eyes to close reflexively. After a moment or two he was able to open them, gingerly, but he had lowered his gaze again. He peered through half-closed lids at the giant and the Serpent in the hope of less painful enlightenment.

The hatless Mossassor had looked up too, but its eyes were no better adapted to the task than the merchant's and it had been forced to shade them with its scaly hand.

'Not there,' Dhalla said wearily. '*There*.'

The wind, which was usually at its harshest during the midday, was beginning to pick up from the south-west; it was in that direction that Dhalla's 'portent' could be glimpsed. Fraxinus was not surprised that Mossassor had not seen them from its coign of vantage on the gaudtree, for they were high above the horizon and the Serpent had been intent on inspecting the terrain which lay before them. He couldn't judge exactly how high they were because he didn't know how large they were; to the eye they were mere dots, but there was no way to guess whether they were large and very far away, or small and fairly close.

Because the sun was still in the south-east the glare of the celestial background was not as intense as it might have been, but it was sufficient to inhibit his stare and he looked away before he had contrived an accurate count of the floating dots.

'There are many,' Dhalla informed him helpfully. 'Perhaps half a hundred – and there might be thousands more behind.'

'If there are, and if the wind continues to blow, the sky will be full of them by the afternoon,' Fraxinus observed. 'They can't be birds, for they seem to be helplessly adrift. What can they be? Ereleth?' The queen had just poked her head through the canvas awning that sealed off the interior of the wagon.

'I don't know,' Ereleth said. 'Can things get any worse?'

Fraxinus shook his head, admitting that they couldn't. 'I doubt that they'll trouble us whatever they are,' he said. 'They'll probably pass overhead, unless the wind drops and leaves them becalmed. I rather hope it does – it would be interesting to find out what they are.'

He heard the sound of another voice within the wagon, and knew that it must be Shabir speaking, but he had to wait until Ereleth relayed the words because they were muffled. He saw the queen look back contemptuously; when she turned to face Fraxinus and Dhalla again her eyebrows were still raised.

'He says he's never seen their like,' she told them, 'but that if the reports he's heard are true, they're the agents of doom, which will obliterate all earthly life from the world, and reclaim it for Serpents, Salamanders and dragomites.'

It was the longest speech Shabir had made since falling into the hands of his enemies, but Fraxinus could understand why the general had thought it worthwhile to abandon his customary curtness. He climbed into the wagon, on the assumption that in support of news as bad as this the man might actually condescend to offer a full explanation of his woeful prophecy.

14

WHEN LUCREZIA APPLIED the last of her ointment to the flanks of Checuti's horse she knew that time was running out. The ointment she was now using was a mixture, made by combining three of the compounds in her portable pharmacopoeia, but the swelling of its bulk had not made it stretch any further.

They had already lost one horse to a marauding crocolid, and had been forced to butcher it for meat – which meant that they were now reasonably well-supplied with food, but ill-supplied with transport. She suspected that the mounts which remained might not consent to be ridden much longer, now that she had no further resources with which to damp down the irritation of their legs and bellies. A heavy rainstorm during the night had allowed them to collect a useful supply of water that could be drunk without boiling, but the limiting factors that mattered now were their ability to carry what they had and the extent to which their bodies and minds could resist the insidious poisons of the marsh.

The fact that the poisons did not seem to be lethal in any direct fashion did not mean that their effects could simply be shrugged off or patiently endured. It had become all too obvious, while she tried to make her limited supplies of the antidote last, that at least some of them were hallucinogenic. At first that effect had been limited to the travellers' sleep, producing vivid and nightmarish dreams, but now their waking consciousness was being significantly disrupted. Jume Metra, who had suffered worse than anyone else from the very beginning, was in such a bad state in spite of the administration of the ointment that she had to be tied to her horse.

On the other hand, Andris Myrasol – who had insisted resolutely that he didn't need the ointment at all – seemed to be in a state of near-delirium; Lucrezia was more worried about him than she was about Checuti or Herriman, both of whom seemed well aware of the extent and nature of their problems. Andris still walked alongside Ssifuss at the head of their little party while they were on the move, striving with all his thick-headed and big-hearted might to prove that he was fit enough and fine enough to be the leader of the company, and his gait was indeed surprisingly steady, but his mind seemed to be elsewhere. Three times he had been bitten by snakes, and had shrugged off the wounds as if they were utterly insignificant, but Lucrezia felt sure that he was in a far worse state than he imagined.

In herself, Lucrezia felt tolerably well – and not because she had retained more than a fair share of her medicine for her own use. She had surprised herself by the manner in which she had become inured to the kinds of hardship which had caused her much distress while she travelled south through Khalorn with Hyry Keshvara. She had found reserves of stamina within her lean frame whose existence she could not have suspected. She was half-inclined to attribute it to the mysterious workings of her Serpent's blood, although Ssifuss had been very dismissive on the one occasion when she had tried to raise that topic of conversation with it.

'Mossassor iss dreamer,' it had told her shortly. 'Iss no ssussh ssing. Iss myss.' By which, she supposed, it meant 'myth'.

'Lots of humans say the same,' she had admitted, hoping that it could understand the irony of humans agreeing with Serpents that there was no such thing as Serpent's blood. 'Every species has its sceptics. Checuti and Jacom Cerri came along with Fraxinus in spite of their unbelief, just as you came along with Mossassor.'

'*Sserpentss* have Sserpent'ss blood,' it had replied. 'Iss knot whissh tiess.' She had taken that to mean that Serpents had obligations to their blood kin, even if their blood kin happened to be crazy – except, of course, that she didn't agree with Ssifuss that Mossassor had to be crazy just because it was a dreamer.

When the anointed horse was quiet again Lucrezia turned to call to Checuti. 'He'll be fine for now,' she told him. 'When he starts acting up again, though, you'll just have to do your best to keep him going with sweet talk or stern discipline – or a judicious combination of the two.'

'It's all I can do to keep myself going with sweet talk and stern discipline, in any combination,' Checuti told her, without the half-smile he usually mustered to accompany such remarks. 'If he goes mad, I shall probably go with him. Pray that we reach the edge of the swamp by nightfall – the dreams seem much worse when the stars are shining.'

They had already debated long and hard as to whether to turn due east towards the southernmost territories of the Nine Towns, but Andris had blithely stated that the southern border must actually be closer now. Checuti, on the other hand, had speculated as to whether they might obtain help from the men who allegedly lived on the shores of the Lake of Colourless Blood, who presumably had their own supplies of magical pastes with which to stave off evil dreams and nasty itches. In the end, it had been far easier to let the lie of the land determine their course.

Because they were now so very enthusiastic to avoid the poisoned thorns the marsh had assumed the character of an enormous maze whose passageways were lanes of shallow water, and it had become increasingly hard to find and follow routes which took them in any precise direction. They moved southwards and eastwards whenever they could, but they were often forced to compromise between the two directions, and sometimes forced west of south instead of east.

It had become increasingly noticeable that the waters of the marsh were not quite still. In the meandering channels that offered them the best opportunity of progress the water was usually subject to a sluggish flow, and insofar as it was possible to judge the direction of that flow it seemed to be tending south-westwards, towards the Lake of Colourless Blood. Lucrezia could see the logic in that; if there was a lake, there must be a pit where deep water could accumulate, and into that pit fluid must constantly pour, to replace the water which evaporated from the open surface.

She climbed back into the saddle of her own mount, soothing the restive gelding as best she could, and looked around at her companions. Herriman was taking his turn to lead Jume Metra's horse, although he looked rather glassy-eyed himself and far less steady in his pacing than Andris. Unlike the amber, who was not particularly hirsute, and Checuti, who kept his own beard trimmed with the aid of a carefully protected razor, Herriman had allowed his facial hair to sprout into a madly tangled mass, and now looked more like a wild man of the woods than a veteran of King's Belin's guard.

'Let's go!' the amber called drunkenly, as he waded purposefully into the viscous water from the grassy bank where they had paused. Lucrezia's mount was understandably reluctant to leave off grazing, but grudgingly responded to her urging. She couldn't help wondering whether a man so obviously deranged should be allowed to take the lead, but Ssifuss seemed content to follow – perhaps because it couldn't tell the difference between a recklessly delirious human and a conscientiously sober one.

Once they were under way again Andris and Ssifuss had no difficulty in finding easy passages which led south. As the bushes grew denser and the streams through which they were wading became narrow corridors, though, they soon found themselves with far less choice of routes to take. In order to have something to take her mind off the insidious prickling of her flesh Lucrezia made constant estimates of the angle of the sun, attempting thereby to keep a closer track of their direction, but it was very difficult to do, especially while the sun was still close to its zenith.

It became easier to judge direction once the yellowing orb had sunk halfway to the western horizon, but by then they had been threading their way through the green maze for hours, and Lucrezia couldn't be sure whether their average heading was west of south or east of south. The only thing of which she was absolutely certain was that they were not heading north.

Lucrezia's continual checking of the position of the sun took its own toll of her well-being. She was, of course, always careful to shield her eyes with her hand whenever she tilted back the rim of her hat, but the surges of fierce light eventually came to them like blows directed to the inside of her skull, stirring up a pounding headache. She had powders to treat such pains in her belt, but that supply was also running low, and she had no means of replenishing it. She bore the discomfort as long as she could, and then took a pinch of one such powder, washing it down with slimy water that was still warm from the kettle, but it was either too little or too late and it did no good at all.

She tried to stop looking at the sun, but that precaution was not so easy to take now that it was dropping towards the horizon, no longer blindingly yellow but the colour of an amber's skin. No matter how she angled her hat the light seemed to chase her eyes, determined to find a way to dazzle her senses and delude her intelligence. It became difficult to look at the light dappling the ripples that spread from Andris Myrasol's striding boots and the splashing hooves of Checuti's horse, and just as difficult to look at the vivid green foliage which now seemed to be reaching out at her from either side.

She felt unreasonably hot, considering that the noonday was far behind them. There was a curiously tinny drumbeat in her ear, which had to be the sound of her own pulse magnified by uncommon sensitivity, but there was a strange cavorting music riding on the drumbeat which was surely the product of deranged imagination.

Lucrezia knew that the thorn-poison must be affecting her senses, and she knew that she had to fight the effect as best she could. No one came to ask her how she was feeling, and she presumed that the others must be disorientated in exactly the same way, lost in their own disintegrating inner space. Herriman had not even taken the trouble to complain that it must be his turn to ride by now, and Checuti's turn to wade.

When the first cry of alarm went up, she couldn't react with any speed or co-ordination; the yell seemed to be nothing more than a further fragment of a developing dream, devoid of all real significance. Even when the second, much louder, cry crashed through the distracting 'music' she couldn't make sense of it, and although she looked up and around, searching with her half-blinded eyes for the source of the danger, she was still unready to react.

When she saw what was coming at her, she didn't know what it was. It seemed for all the world like one of the swirling columns of mist which drifted along the surface of the slow-moving streams by night, all sparkling greyness and uncertain form – save that it was moving very quickly indeed. She realised, though, that it was also solid and substantial.

It was her horse that realised the true urgency of the danger, and it did exactly what it had done before upon such realisation: it reared up on its hind legs, lashing out with its hooves, and tipped her abruptly over its back.

If she had learned anything since the last time it had happened, Lucrezia's near-delirium cancelled out the knowledge – but this time she fell into viscous water rather than on to muddy ground, and there was not the same sickening jar. The shock of the splash served to focus her scattered thoughts, and as she righted herself reflexively, coming to her feet in knee-deep water, she understood at last exactly what was happening.

The gelding's flying hooves saved it from injury from the dagger-like beak which had been aimed at its head. The great grey bird veered away at the last moment, screeching and tumbling. For a moment Lucrezia thought that it would actually fall into the water, but its madly beating wings were far more versatile than they seemed. It flapped away, barely stirring the surface with its pinion-feathers.

Lucrezia had time to see that Ssifuss had thrown itself to one side, while Andris Myrasol had his long dagger drawn and was standing firm, but there was far too much commotion to let her see what was happening to the other riders and their mounts, and there was no time to spare because another of the huge birds was hurtling at her like a living spear, eyes aglint behind its savage beak.

Even as she hurled herself forwards, ducking under the beak's lethal trajectory, the absurdity of it all was strikingly evident. They had seen hundreds of the fisher-birds; Ssifuss had been quick to shoot an arrow at any one of them which would tolerate its close approach. They had always fled, without showing the least sign of aggression. Now, all of a sudden, they had become an angry army bent on attack, and perhaps on slaughter. This time, Lucrezia did not rise to her feet. She remained on her knees, keeping her head low. She saw Andris strike two of the birds out of the air, smashing their wings with a single sweeping blow of his blade.

The only person still mounted was Jume Metra, who could not dismount – but she had been bringing up the rear, and her mount was the only one which had a ready avenue of retreat. It had torn the leading-rein free of Herriman's grasp in order to seize that opportunity.

They had come, Lucrezia now saw, into a kind of star-shaped lagoon, from which there was no exit before them or to either side. For once, the sluggish flow had betrayed them, and brought them to the threshold of a pool – which surely could not be the fabled Lake of Colourless Blood, but was certainly a place where the big birds gathered in force. It must, Lucrezia guessed, be the rookery where they built their nests – which they were prepared to defend as boldly as they could.

She had no time to peer into the surrounding bushes to seek confirmation of her theory. She saw Checuti wave a dagger, rather ineffectually, at a bird which dived to peck at his face. She met his eye for just a fleeting moment, and saw his understanding as he too dropped to his knees, ducking close to the troubled surface of the marsh. The horse he had been riding was splashing after Jume Metra's.

Herriman was already running, as best he could, in pursuit of the fleeing horses. Jume Metra's mount was splashing ahead of him, sending up fountains of spray; Checuti's and Lucrezia's were close behind. Alas, the birds were no respecters of retreating enemies. Lucrezia saw one zoom after Herriman, and she saw its wicked beak strike home at the back of his skull. For a second or two she thought, or hoped, that the bird could not have delivered a very powerful blow. It had, after all, to continue in flight – which it did. When she saw the way Herriman pitched slowly forward to splash face-forwards into the water, though, she knew that he was badly hurt.

It would have been better, in a way, had the water been deep enough to permit swimming, but as things were she had no alternative but to splash through the shallows in the most ungainly fashion imaginable. Checuti was heading the same way, with slightly more efficiency if no more elegance, and Ssifuss was coming up behind them, but Andris had not yet turned away, perhaps beause he no longer had sense enough to know when to retreat. Lucrezia dared not look back to see how he was faring.

She reached Herriman, but just as she did so Checuti howled a warning, and she ducked down, almost submerging her entire body, as a huge grey shape whizzed overhead. Herriman was unconscious and the viscous water was red with his blood, but he had not enough metal about him to drag him under the surface, and she was able to treat him as flotsam, turning him over so that he had at least a chance to breathe. Checuti joined her, and the two of them scrambled further on, dragging the body with them.

One more bird dived at them, but the peck it aimed at Checuti was half-hearted at best, and he was able to deflect it with his forearm; even so, they kept going as fast as they could, until they had put another fifty mets between themselves and the trap into which they had unwittingly wandered. Only then did they look for a space between the bushes, where there might be grassy ground.

Eventually, they found an acceptable covert. They hauled Herriman out before looking round to see if anyone else was following.

One of the riderless horses was still in sight, having found safe ground of its own. There was no sign of the second, nor of the one to which Jume Metra was tied. Lucrezia could hear the big amber's booming voice as he yelled, wordlessly, at the birds which must now be concentrating all their efforts on him. She knew that he couldn't possibly be thinking straight, or he would surely have turned and run by now.

Lucrezia reached out towards Herriman's head, intending to feel for a pulse at his neck, but she caught Checuti's eye and he shook his head.

'Dead,' he said sombrely. 'Probably before he hit the water. The beak caught him where the spine meets the skull.'

That's absurd, Lucrezia thought. *It was only a bird. He came through the Dragomite Hills unhurt, and he's been fishing for crocolids without sustaining a single bite. He can't have been killed by a bird.*

'We have to catch the horses if we can,' Checuti said quickly. 'You go after yours; I'll look for the one Metra was riding – but be careful, highness, I beg of you. We're still too close to the birds for comfort.'

Lucrezia's head was pounding and her vision was blurred, but she knew that the thief-master was right. She plunged back into the water, keeping her head low but refusing to go on all fours. The horse waited in the shelter of the bushes, having neither the will to run nor anywhere obvious to run to. It consented to recapture, eventually, but the terror in its eyes suggested that she would be wise not to attempt to mount it again for some little while.

By the time she had coaxed the animal back to their hiding-place Checuti had disappeared, but Ssifuss was bending over Herriman's corpse and Andris was wading to the shore. In his left hand the amber was half-carrying and half-dragging no less than five dead birds, all of them headless. As Lucrezia came ashore the amber turned to her, his expression very bleak in spite of his feverishly burning eyes. In a curiously childlike voice he said: 'I've brought better meat than we've had for forty days and more . . . but I'll not go back for the eggs, my lady – not for the throne of Xandria, let alone the throne of Ferentina.'

Lucrezia was about to reply, but as she opened her mouth a strange whirlpool of light and sound seemed to spring up out of nowhere, and she swayed under its wayward pressure.

How odd, she said to herself, thinking that she had never before been so astonished as she was now, in spite of all the astounding things that had happened to her of late. *I seem to be falling over.*

15

NOW THAT THE sun had begun to sink into the west it was easier to look up into the great vault of blue, which was now so full of the floating dots as to appear diseased. The wind had dropped and the motes were no longer hurrying northwards. Fraxinus was certain that they had begun to grow in dimension; slowly but surely they were falling.

'Is their descent deliberate?' Ereleth asked. 'If they're borne up by gases secreted into the sacs, they presumably have control over their own buoyancy.'

'I dare say they have some control,' Fraxinus replied. 'To call the descent *deliberate* would be stretching a point, though. Had they any intelligence of what lay below them they'd surely stay aloft. Either they're coming to the end of their limited resources or they're responding to some tropism which measures nothing but the distance they've travelled.' *Tropism* was one of Aulakh Phar's words, and the sound of it renewed his regret that the old man wasn't with them to offer the benefit of his analytical wisdom.

Fraxinus was sitting to the queen's right, as usual, but he was uncomfortably cramped. For once the bench was crowded, because Shabir had consented to come out of hiding and join them. He seemed to be curious in spite of himself; the prospect of seeing something of which he had heard such ominous reports had achieved a perverse amelioration of his listlessness. Mossassor was lurking behind them but Dhalla had elected to walk on the shady side of the wagon, whose narrow interior was not to her liking now that she had recovered her strength.

'Presumably they can't take root here,' Ereleth said. 'The desert is so very wide that it will surely form a boundary to their northward progress.'

'But the narrow land of the Nine Towns won't,' Fraxinus

said. 'If they conquer that territory as easily as the general's informant warned, they'll eventually despatch fresh spores from the scorched earth we crossed some days ago. From such a launching-pad they might well be able to drift clear across the Dragomite Hills to the Forest of Absolute Night.'

'They'll not find it easy to take root there,' Ereleth said confidently. 'I doubt that they could even reach the ground – and the followers of which the general has heard such dire rumours couldn't cross the hills. They pose no possible threat to Xandria.'

'Perhaps not,' Fraxinus mused. 'But . . . tell me more about these followers, general. If the spores really are descending on top of us, we might meet them soon enough.'

'I know no more to tell,' Shabir said, in a voice which carried a healthy measure of disdain and derision in spite of its weakness. 'The bronze called them hellhounds and lizardlions, and also spoke of manticores, although that might have been fancy or exaggeration. The men of the southern towns tell tales of huge dog-like creatures that can sometimes be glimpsed in the barrens, but I'm an Eblan born and bred. Amyas also said that the hills, depopulated of dragomites to the extent that they are, would offer more fertile soil to these floaters than the southlands, which are beset by stony life-forms that grind all manner of rival vegetation to pulp. If the floaters establish themselves in the dragomites' land, the forest will be a mere hurdle. They'll reach your homeland in time – not this year or next, perhaps not for a full decade, but in the end they'll reach it. Then your fabulous empire might be put to a challenge which all the metal in the world might be impotent to meet.'

'We're properly grateful for the warning,' Fraxinus said drily. 'But we'll have to leave it to your own folk to deliver it. I dare say that some of them, at least, will take sufficient heart from our arrival to attempt the crossing in the other direction, following in Djemil Eyub's footsteps.'

'And some of them, at least, will doubtless have no better luck than he did,' Shabir answered morosely. The derision had leaked out of his voice again, and his tone had become grimmer.

'He was unlucky,' Fraxinus agreed. 'Don't forget, though, that he came within a day of safety and a good welcome. If your towns really can't be defended against the combination of misfortunes which threaten them, your countrymen ought to consider the possibility of escaping to the north.'

'Tarlock Nath and his bronze friend were trying to recruit men to go south,' Shabir retorted sourly. 'As if the bronze's fabled fortress were more worth saving than Ebla itself! Antiarians have always made me sick, but I never quite understood why. And then you came. Have you the least idea of the trouble your arrival in our land precipitated?'

'I know that had you let us alone, as we asked, you'd have saved yourselves – and us – a great deal of trouble,' Fraxinus replied, turning to look past Ereleth's bowed head at the scowling face of the grey-haired man.

Shabir had the grace to look away, in a manner which tacitly admitted a measure of shame. 'You don't understand how nearly the balance of our lives had fallen apart,' he murmured, 'or how brutally you contrived to tip us over the brink. You're moved by the kind of blind optimism that makes pacts with dragomites, and you still haven't the least idea what fools you are.'

'Perhaps you'll explain it to us,' Fraxinus suggested, without bothering to control his sarcasm. 'Or have you broken your stubborn silence merely to mutter curses and predictions of doom?'

Shabir looked back at him briefly, before becoming sullen once again. He didn't seem to be much interested in offering the explanation that Fraxinus desired, but he did mutter: 'It had to be done.'

'It didn't have to be done,' Fraxinus said, trying with all his might to emphasise the truth of what he said. 'We meant you no harm. Although I didn't tell you the whole truth, for which I'm sorry, *we meant you no harm*.'

'The harm had already been done,' Shabir told him dispiritedly. 'The harm had been done by wave after wave of migrating dragomites, which sapped the strength of the Nine Towns for two full years. The army had begun to fall apart even before the likes of Nath and his mysterious friend brought forth their cargo of ugly rumours.'

The general paused, but this time Fraxinus judged that the man needed no further prompting, and he was content to wait. His steady gaze was demand enough, now that the dam of

Shabir's frustration and resentment had been conclusively breached.

'It wasn't simply that the men whose fields were affected wanted to return to defend them,' the Eblan continued eventually. 'It was the accusations that arose in consequence. The men of the southern towns had been muttering all along that their conscription by the Convocation was unjust and unnecessary – that the northerners ought to defend their own territory against the dragomites. Now they complained bitterly that the men of the north were unready and unwilling to reciprocate, refusing even to recognise that the south was suffering under an invasion of its own. The northerners reacted angrily to such whisperings, saying that seeds dropping from the sky could not be compared with dragomite warriors on the march, and that men who called for aid to defend themselves against mere plants were cowards. Then, just as the army was in the throes of disintegration, you arrived.'

Fraxinus pondered these revelations for a few moments, considering the question of which point to address first. 'You're telling me that you attacked us because you were trying to keep your army together,' he said leadenly. 'It wasn't that you didn't believe our promises – it was because you were trying to rally your men to a common cause.' He would have been unable to keep the anger out of his voice even if he had been inclined to do so, but he spoke levelly enough.

Shabir raised his eyes again, meeting Fraxinus's gaze. 'I tried to give you a chance,' he said, speaking a little hoarsely. 'I did what I could to discover whether you really intended to fight with the dragomites against your own kind. If that amber had persuaded me that he could organise a common cause between us, or even that he was willing to try . . . but he preferred, in the end, to add his voice to the chorus of malevolent and unsettling rumours – a chorus that was already far too loud. I did what I had to do.'

'And that's also why you chased us so determinedly, in spite of the fact that the main part of your force had already been dissipated,' Fraxinus said. 'You thought there might yet be a chance of turning defeat into victory – of using the news of our obliteration to make the Nine Towns pull together again.'

Shabir contrived an abrupt and hollow laugh. 'It wasn't just the Nine Towns pulling apart,' he said. 'All the old resentments were surfacing: town against town, townsman against countryman, neighbour against neighbour. Even civil war might be manageable by talk and treaty, but not the kind of chaos which will claim the land now. Now, it's every man for himself while the dragomites and the floaters fight for dominion over our abandoned fields.'

There was a brief silence, while Shabir tried to stare Fraxinus down. Fraxinus deliberately looked away, refusing the contest.

'Are the floaters really so dangerous?' the merchant asked, when he thought the pause had lasted long enough.

'How should I know?' Shabir countered. 'I've nothing but the word of a sly bronze to rely on. According to him, they shrink to the size of a man's head as they drift to earth, although they're much bigger when they're aloft. He says that the seeds are like big fat worms, and that they burrow like worms, deep into the soil. If you can't pick them up quickly they're soon out of reach, until they send up shoots. By the time anything shows above the surface, he claims, they've extended themselves sideways for half a kim in every direction. Their progeny are direly greedy plants, which soak up water so avidly that everything around them withers, and the shoots are very difficult to cut or burn. If the bronze's word can be trusted, they're far worse than the seeds which drift into our fields from the Soursweet Marshes – far worse, in fact, than anything our forefathers ever had to deal with. But I only have the bronze's word for that – and his intention was to go south again, to defend his own precious homeland more fiercely and more capably than we were defending ours.'

'You didn't trust the bronze, then?' Fraxinus said. 'You didn't believe these floaters were as big a menace as the dragomites?'

'I believed that whatever perils we had to meet had to be faced by a united front, properly governed by the Convocation,' Shabir replied tautly. 'I believed that our only chance of holding out against the combination of threats was to stand together . . . and I believed that our only chance of maintaining the unity which we were in the process of losing was to win a victory which would make us all comrades again.'

'I see,' Fraxinus said bleakly. He did see, after a fashion. He could understand, at any rate, the kind of pressure the general had been under. 'I can't say I'm sorry that you failed. If it's any consolation, you broke our company apart as comprehensively as you broke your own, and may well have doomed it to failure in consequence.'

'If it's any consolation to you,' the general retorted, 'the disintegration of my homeland may be of little more consequence in the unfolding disaster than the disintegration of your little band of travellers. If the floaters and the things which follow in their wake are as dangerous as the bronze claimed, I doubt that there's any human-inhabited land in the world that can stand against them in the long run. Nothing like this strange invasion has ever been seen before, so far as our lore can tell us.'

Fraxinus looked at Ereleth, who was patiently drinking in every word while she kept her eyes focused on the uneven trail ahead. 'Is there anything in your lore which speaks of things like these?' he asked. 'Specifically, I mean.'

Ereleth shook her head, but not without hesitation. 'I know nothing about such creatures,' she said, 'but that doesn't mean they've never existed before. I suspect the bronze exaggerated, for his own reasons. On the other hand – we are forewarned that times of sweeping change will come, and some have secret lore which tells us how to respond. Why else are we here?'

'What about you?' Fraxinus asked, turning to Mossassor.

The Serpent tried to shrug its ill-adapted shoulders. 'We know ssussh sshangess ssometimess happen,' it agreed. 'Iss preparation made for them – iss what we are doing here. In humanss, iss Sserpent'ss blood and Ssalamander'ss fire. In Sserpentss too . . . iss a *readiness*.'

Shabir made a small sound of disgust. 'Men should not trust Serpents or Salamanders,' he opined. 'The disaster threatens our dominion, not theirs. If we cannot stand firm against unearthly invasions, the Serpents and the Salamanders will reclaim the heritage that was theirs before the lore of Genesys was forged.'

'Iss not sso,' Mossassor was quick to say. 'All in ssiss togesser. Ssearssh for garden togesser. Musst be friendss, not enemiess. Iss very important.'

Fraxinus looked up into the sky, shading his eyes against the insistent light. The multitudinous black dots were noticeably larger; the floaters were definitely descending. Was it possible, he wondered, that they might be able to take root even here, among the gaudtrees and the lapidendrons? Or would they simply provide food for sandskinks and their kin . . . and perhaps for humans too?

Fraxinus turned back to Shabir. 'You should have let us through,' he said, letting all his vitriolic resentment show clearly in his tone. 'Rot you, *you should have let us through*.'

'You came too early or too late,' the unrepentant general informed him sombrely, his despair no longer tainted with any edge of vengeful pleasure. 'If Nath's bronze was right, it won't matter in the long run. Nothing awaits you in the south but death and desolation.'

16

THE TOWN OF Antiar was a great deal larger than any of the villages through which the haywain had passed on its way there, but it seemed to Jacom to be a mean and shabby place.

Having been reared on his father's estates and educated at home Jacom had never actually lived in a Xandrian town, but he had paid regular visits to half a dozen thriving markets and ports, all of which had played host to a constant bustle of activity and excitement. To add to this experience, he had passed through all the towns on the Great Spine Road – albeit at a rather hectic pace – while travelling from Xandria to Khalorn in search of Princess Lucrezia. He now felt entitled to consider himself a very adequate judge of urban pomp and virility, and in his judgment Tarlock Nath's birthplace was a very poor specimen indeed: a sprawling aggregation of mean houses with as much life in it as a filleted fish.

In all fairness, he had to concede that he might have formed a marginally better opinion of Antiar had he arrived in broad daylight, but he doubted whether the place had the capacity to shine much more brightly than it did by early starlight. Although the cart arrived by night, there were several hours to spare before the hard-working and hard-drinking people of Xandria would have considered it appropriate to retire for the midnight, and although the weather was a little cloudy the flamestars were bright enough to illuminate all the forms of social intercourse which normally went on after nightfall. In spite of these provisions, the ill-lit streets were virtually deserted and the great majority of the windows shuttered.

The cart was taken to what must have passed in these parts for the wealthier quarter of town, where almost all the houses were two stories high and most were set in their own grounds. Many were surrounded by walls or by dense, high hedges. Jacom inspected the hedges carefully, remembering a rather dubious theory quoted to him by his father, to the effect that one could obtain a reasonable estimate of the quality of a town's thieves and the morale of its citizens by measuring the length of the thorns on its hedge-bushes, but it was too dark to make a proper estimate of the index in question.

He was not unduly surprised when Tarlock Nath's house turned out to be the biggest one they had seen. It was built of very sturdy bricks whose outer facings seemed to have been unusually well-guarded against corrosion. Even its roof-tiles – so far as Jacom could tell in the uncertain light – had an air of freshness about them, which seemed remarkable given the general level of dilapidation that prevailed throughout the nation. The roof was tilted at an angle which suggested that there was a capacious attic space above its second story. There was a grove of high conifers flanking the drive, whose military bearing compared favourably with every other rank of straight-standing trees he had encountered in the narrow land.

'Civilisation at last,' Keshvara commented, as the cart made its way round to the rear door before easing to a standstill. 'As per usual, the likes of us get referred to the tradesmen's entrance.'

Jacom was tempted to say *Speak for yourself*, given that an officer in King Belin's army never had to use tradesmen's entrances, but he remembered that he was no longer an officer in anyone's army.

By now the cart had only half a dozen men in attendance; most of the men-at-arms who had accompanied it on the long march south had gone to their own homes. The few that remained no longer manifested any aggression at all towards the prisoners; their status had moved by subtle degrees towards that of guests.

'It looks a lot better than the town prison,' Jacom muttered, as he helped Merel Zabio to her feet. She and Phar were nearly recovered now, and the plaster had been removed from her leg, but she was still a little weak. Even the normally talkative Phar had not quite contrived to collect himself, although he was certainly taking notice of everything that went on around him. Jacom was very hopeful that the old man would be back to his calculative best within another forty hours, ready and more than willing to take a full part in any negotiations with their host.

Jacom had one brief flutter of anxiety, when Nath hurriedly disappeared after instructing one of his lieutenants to see to their lodging. He feared that the four of them might be dumped in some dank cellar rather than brought into the house. Once they had relieved their most immediate needs in an outhouse, though, they were taken up the servants' staircase to the attics huddled beneath the roof, where they were each – including Munir Zanarin – afforded the unexpected but welcome luxury of a room to themselves.

Jacom found that his own room, though very narrow, had a pleasant lived-in appearance – presumably because some household servant had been rudely dispossessed of it at a moment's notice. Lukewarm water and soap were brought to him so that he might wash, and a little food. The latter was no more than a token gesture – the bread was stale, the sausage ancient and the broth congealed – but that was no surprise; in Nath's shoes he too would have reserved all the good food in the house for himself and his weary men. He was grateful enough to have pure water to drink.

After he had washed himself thoroughly he regretted the lack of a change of clothes, but Nath's servants evidently hadn't thought of that, so he put his own back on before going to see how his friends were faring. Merel Zabio had managed to eat and drink a little, but she had already taken to her bed and was intent on going to sleep without delay, suitably grateful for the use of mattresses and sheets. Hyry Keshvara was sitting on Merel's bed, and she put a finger to her lips as Jacom came in.

'She'll be all right,' Hyry assured him. 'It's just a matter of getting her strength back.' She accompanied him to Phar's room, where they had to bend their necks to stand beneath the slanting ceiling-beams. Phar was lying down on his bed, with his hands behind his head, but his eyes were wide open.

'This isn't so bad,' Phar said, as his gaze scanned the beams, studying the pallid patches where rot had got to work in spite of the protective tar which had been liberally applied.

'Considering that we might be faced with a show trial and summary execution on a charge of befriending dragomites,' Jacom said, 'it's wonderful. We've nothing to trade but the lore in our heads and the strength of our limbs, but it seems that we're not as poor as we thought we were.'

'*You* seem to have people fighting for the privilege of acquiring your services,' Hyry said. 'I'm not so sure that they're interested in the rest of us – and you might care to bear in mind that people only become desperate to hire trained swordsmen when they expect to find abundant work for trained swords.'

'I have no intention of deserting you,' Jacom told her stiffly. 'If Amyas wants to hire me, he'll have to take all four of us.'

'Spoken like a true captain,' she retorted. 'But what if three out of the four don't want to sign on as mercenaries to help defend some beleaguered petty fortress in the far south?'

'It's a matter of available alternatives,' Jacom pointed out. 'Would you rather stay here and defend this petty fortress for Tarlock Nath? If heading directly for Salamander's Fire without paying heed to anyone else were still an option, it would be number one on my list – but it's not. We've lost everything, and we have no option but to offer our services to someone.'

'We didn't *lose* everything,' Aulakh Phar put in, speaking softly but firmly. 'What we had was shattered by a treacherous blow. We don't owe anything to the people who did that to us – in fact, they owe us all the reparation we can exact. Let's not talk meekly of choosing masters – let's talk about the debts we're owed and how to collect them.'

Jacom was mildly surprised by this speech, which would have seemed far more appropriate to Checuti than the old physician, but he only had to glance at Hyry to see that she agreed with the estimation. His father had often vouchsafed the opinion that traders were thieves equipped with a cloak of respectability, but he had assumed that was the natural bitterness of a man who always had to operate in buyers' markets.

'Antiar's the fifth of the Nine Towns,' Jacom pointed out drily. 'We're as close to the middle of the Narrow Land as makes no difference. Do you really think we're in a position to make our own way south, even if we were able to steal horses from those stables we passed just now?'

'At least he noticed the stables,' Phar said to Hyry. 'He's not a lost cause yet.'

'All right,' Jacom said, trying not to let his annoyance show too obviously, 'what's your plan?'

'I don't have one,' Phar told him amiably, 'and I'd rather you didn't have one either. I'd rather do my own negotiating – with

Nath or Amyas or anyone else with whom we might have to deal – and if you want to make a reasonable deal on your own account, you'd be wise to let me do the negotiating on your behalf too. Even if you are the one with the most marketable skills, in the half-blind eyes of our captors, you're not the man best-equipped to sell them at a decent price.'

The arrogance of this proclamation seemed to Jacom to be breathtaking, although he wasn't entirely certain that what the old man said was false. He wanted to assert that he was a grown man and could look after his own interests perfectly well, but he was awkwardly conscious of the fact that he had only just made a portentous speech about the four of them being an indivisible company whose interests he would protect at all costs. He realised that he too might have struck a more arrogant pose than he was entitled to do. In the end, he settled for saying: 'I'm not a fool,' in as chilly a tone as he could contrive. He couldn't resist adding: 'I'm the one the bronze approached, after all. I'm the one who obtained all the information we've so far managed to gather – including the knowledge that Amyas's beleaguered homeland is almost within spitting distance of Salamander's Fire.'

Phar had made his point and was now perfectly prepared to be gracious. 'That's true,' he said, his voice still amiable. 'We're grateful, I assure you. But *we* hired *you*, if you recall, when you became a captain without a command. I don't say that you owe us much for that, given that you've drawn no substantial pay so far, but you're not in a position to volunteer us to join someone else's army.'

To Jacom this still sounded like rank ingratitude, but he swallowed the wrath which threatened to spill out into his next speech. 'We're all on the same side,' he said, rather hoarsely. 'We all have to look out for one another. That's all I intended to do.'

'That's what we intend to do, too,' Hyry assured him. 'It's just that making deals is a tricky business. We've had practice. It really would be better if you let us handle the likes of Nath and Amyas.'

Jacom had collected himself now. He picked up the candle that had been set beside Phar's pillow and held it aloft so that he could inspect a web of fungal hyphae stubbornly extending itself over the dark barrier that had been set to keep its kin at bay.

'Nothing's incorruptible, is it?' he observed philosophically. 'The rot gets to everything in the end. You just have to stand it off as best you can.' He smeared his finger across the grey mass, which looked as if it might be delicate enough to be cleared away by that means – but appearances were deceptive. The fungus clung hard, and refused to yield to his touch.

Keshvara smiled, in apparent approval of what he hoped was a subtle conversational move. She looked briefly at the closed door, as if she suspected that there might be an eavesdropper posted outside with his ear to the panel.

'If everyday corruption were all we had to worry about,' Phar said, effortlessly taking up the new argumentative thread, 'life would be easy enough. The problem is that every now and again something nastier comes along – something which can tear whole houses down in a matter of days. That's when things get difficult. People's lives get turned upside down, and they don't know which way to turn. A physician has to be a good judge of character as well as a supplier of medicines – healing words can be as vital as healing potions.'

'Let's hope you get the chance to exercise your skills tomorrow,' Jacom said neutrally. 'In the meantime, I need a good night's sleep.'

'So do I,' said Keshvara. It was hardly necessary for Phar to add his own voice to the chorus.

Jacom waited until Keshvara had opened the door; then, in response to Phar's nod, he snuffed out the candle-flame with moistened fingers. The door of his own room still stood wide open, and the candle within cast just enough light into the corridor to guide Keshvara back to hers. He watched the trader open her door and close it behind her, and a slight pang of remembrance stirred up the thought that there was more than one use for a soft bed, but he banged his head with the heel of his hand as if to shake the thought loose and flick it away. He went back into his own room and removed his soiled clothing again before getting into bed.

He lay perfectly still, listening to the muffled sounds of movement in the rooms below, where the entire household was presumably still up and about, celebrating the master's safe return. He wondered what Nath's wife and children thought of his lodging four enemies of the nation above their heads, and what his servants thought of being doubled up in their tiny rooms in order to make space for prisoners of war. He had no doubt that armed guards had been posted at the foot of the stair leading down to the main body of the house, with orders to remain alert to every possibility, but he didn't suppose that would make the servants or the members of Nath's family any happier. Given that the bronze was also here, the house must be overfull.

There was not a great deal of sound to be heard outside the house, and what there was seemed oddly distant and disconnected. The enfolding sheets seemed to Jacob to be a kind of cocoon, isolating him from the rest of the world and providing a cloying kind of comfort which was – in some mysterious fashion he couldn't quite fathom – also a kind of threat. In spite of this unaccustomed comfort, or perhaps because of its perceived strangeness, he didn't drift off to sleep quickly. He shifted his position, and tried to think of pleasant matters, but his mind would not be coaxed into any such safe haven; his train of thought insisted, rather perversely, on veering towards darker memories and doubts as to the uncertain future. Such thoughts eventually led him into shallow but disturbing dreams, which made him squirm restlessly, and although he was certainly asleep he remained half-conscious of all kinds of real and imaginary distress for what seemed like several hours.

When he first heard the soft tapping on the tiny rounded window set into the roof his first response was to wish that it would leave off. He might actually have instructed it to do so, but the message probably failed to reach the surface of the dream. At any rate, it wouldn't stop. Eventually, it was supplemented by a voice.

'Friend Jacom!' the voice said. 'Friend Jacom – are you there?'

He recognised the voice, but he couldn't respond; so far as he was concerned, it was still an element of his dream.

The tapping grew louder, and more insistent, until he could dream no longer.

When Jacom eventually realised that a real voice was calling to him he was momentarily convinced that he had not actually been asleep at all, but when he had to struggle hard to identify the voice – which he had recognised not a minute before – he realised that he really was in need of waking up, and that he had to bring some determination to bear on the task of focusing his wandering mind. By the time he contrived to do that, the voice was becoming impatient, and its faint whisper was rising in naked panic.

'Jacom! Friend Jacom!'

Jacom recognised the voice again, although he could hardly believe it.

'Koraismi?' he said hoarsely. '*Koraismi!* Is it you?'

He rose from the bed and went to the window, pressing his face to the glass. It could not be opened, but he could see a face peering through it, and at this distance he could hear the voice quite clearly.

'Quietly, friend Jacom,' the voice pleaded, fading now towards the threshold of audibility. 'Is dangerous. Your guards are very stupid, very slow – they would not last a day in the Forest of Absolute Night – but we must be quiet. You are not alone, friend Jacom. We are here, and we will make a plan. Only wait and be ready.'

'Who's *we*?' Jacom wanted to know. 'Who and how many?'

'*We* are but ten now,' the boy told him, 'but we have made allies. Purkin is a cunning man, and he has a plan, friend Jacom. Can the girl walk, or must she be carried?'

'She can walk now, just about,' Jacom replied. 'But, Koraismi . . .'

'No time now,' the young darklander cut in. 'We must be very cunning, very careful. Be ready – and be careful. We will come. Be ready.'

Jacom heard a scraping sound and knew that the boy was sliding back down the roof. 'Wait!' he hissed urgently, but it was too late. The boy had done what he came to do, and was now returning to those who had sent him: to Purkin, and the others who had once been his men. Somehow, he couldn't quite believe that their one ambition in life was to be his men again – but they had sent Koraismi to make contact nevertheless. They were men of Xandria, and they knew the meaning of friendship and loyalty. For a moment, he felt proud of them. Then he began to wonder what they had in mind, and why, and what Phar would think of their proposed intervention. He couldn't help but smile at the last thought.

If he and Keshvara will not trust me to make plans on their behalf, he thought, *how would they react to the notion that Sergeant Purkin the deserter is making plans for all of us?*

Was it possible, he wondered, that ex-Sergeant Purkin understood the situation they were in far better than he did? Was it possible that pigs in Antiar could fly?

He got back into bed, pulled the sheets up above his head, and set himself to return to sleep. This time, he had no difficulty at all in getting there, or in staying there.

17

ANDRIS COULD HEAR a whispering voice which said *go with the flow* – or words to that effect – but he couldn't work out where it was coming from. Nor, for that matter, could he work out where it was arriving; his ears, so far as he could tell, were quite uninvolved in the process. It was as if the speaker were located inside his head, addressing some kind of inner ear. That would have been easier to understand had he been asleep and dreaming, but he wasn't. He was awake, and wading. It would have been overstating the case to say that he knew exactly where he was, but he certainly wasn't in any doubt as to where he was in a more general sense.

He was in the Soursweet Marshes – which, for the moment at least, had turned out to be infinitely more sour than sweet.

The midday sun was beating down on his bare head, which was a matter for some concern. Being relatively fair of skin he really ought to have been wearing a hat, but he wasn't. Neither was Princess Lucrezia, any longer – although that didn't seem particularly inappropriate, given that she wasn't wading. For some reason he couldn't quite remember, he had been forced to pick her up and carry her. He didn't mind carrying her – not so much because she was a relatively light burden for a man of his bulk, although she was, but because her weight felt strangely comforting. He had no idea why that was – he knew perfectly well that it would have been absurd to think that he might have floated off into the sky had he not been weighed down – but he wasn't in any doubt about the matter. Perhaps it was simply a matter of balance, the unconscious body in his arms providing a perfect counterweight for the pack he bore on his back.

He still felt surprisingly well, all things considered. Although he was dimly aware that he hadn't eaten for a long time he didn't feel in the least hungry; although he was fairly certain that he hadn't slept for a long time he didn't feel in the least tired; and although he hadn't had any medication at all he didn't feel in the least itchy. He didn't feel as well as he had felt the day before, or the day before that, but that peculiar sensation of well-being had given way to a dreamy numbness which still wasn't unpleasant. His hardly felt limbs were working very well; he knew that he was striding along with mechanical efficiency, in spite of the fact that he was thigh-deep in slime.

He was going with the flow, though, and that undoubtedly assisted his progress.

Because the numbness of his brain and the brightness of the sun were both affecting his sight it was difficult to pay much attention to his surroundings, but there would have been little reward in doing so. Keeping clear of thorns had become a reflex by now, and required no conscious effort, and any hope he might have had of navigating a straight course had evaporated long ago. All he had to do – all he could do – was to follow the sluggish flow of the marshwater.

It wasn't much easier to pay attention to what was going on inside himself than it was to keep watch on the marsh, given that the automatism which had claimed him seemed to have transformed the outer reaches of his flesh into a foreign land, but at least he had his imagination to help him, and his intelligence to guide his imagination.

With the aid of his intelligent imagination he was able to wonder what some tiny entity in his bloodstream would feel – if it were capable of feeling anything at all – while it made its slow journey round his system. Perhaps it, too, would be comfortable with its inability to do anything but go with the flow, in spite of the fact that it must know that the flow would simply take it round and round the same dull course. Or would it? Might there, in fact, be any number of different courses which such a creature might follow once it had passed from heart to lung in order to be charged with vivid redness? Might there be any number of different missions it might undertake: to the brain or the liver, the fingers or the toes, including or excluding the occasional detour to the eyeballs or the testicles?

To some such creature, he thought, even a slender and compact body like Princess Lucrezia's would qualify as a whole world. If what was meant by Serpent's blood was that she had some unique and exotic parasite lying in wait in the depths of her being, which had been waiting patiently for some mysterious summons, not merely for years but for generations, then that awakened corpuscle must now find itself in a situation very like his own. It would discover itself in the process of being borne along through a great maze full of unsuspected dangers towards an unimaginable destination, with nothing to guide it but a vague sense of urgency and need. And what of the similar entity which – if Phar's speculations and Mossassor's insistences could be trusted – might be lurking in the depths of Dhalla's mighty frame? Given that it was called a kind of fire and not a kind of blood it might not be compelled to wander eternally through the mazy corridors of her oversubstantial flesh, and if proverbial wisdom could be trusted it might well be anchored within her heart, but it too must have nothing in place of consciousness but an inchoate sense of mission.

'I think I'm beginning to figure this out,' Andris confided to Lucrezia, although he wasn't sure that she was capable of taking notice even if she could hear him. 'The world, you see, is like a body. It's not that it's alive, in any simple sense – or if it is alive, it's not an individual in any simple sense, like you or me . . . except, of course, that you and I probably aren't the kind of simple individuals we thought we were . . .

'I'll start again. The world, you see – by which I mean the world of life rather than the whole entity . . . the *biosphere*, as Phar's jargon has it – isn't just a collection of disparate things. It's more like a patchwork. That's obvious, in a way – I mean, all living things are dependent on other living things, connected to them in eating and being eaten – but there's something more than that. It's something to do with chimeras . . . which is to say that the idea of a chimera is where we have to start if we're going to get a grip on it at all. When I first found out what was going on down in that dragomite mound I thought the most important discovery I'd made was that the dragomite queen was actually giving birth to the mound-women as well as the dragomite workers and warriors: that although the mound-women looked authentically human – and are, in some sense, authentically human – they were born from unearthly flesh. That's certainly remarkable, and certainly important, but I wonder now whether the more significant thing was the relationship between the dragomite queen *and the mound*.

'When I first saw that cave where the human drones were, I thought it was some kind of ultimate horror: all those people, or bits of people, smeared all over the walls, spread so thin and so mixed up that the drones seemed almost normal, even though they were only half-people, torsos on stalks. By that time, I suppose, I'd already realised that the dragomite queen wasn't just a modified worker with a big belly, like a queen ant or a queen bee, but I hadn't really given much thought to the matter of exactly what and where she was. Built into the walls of the mound, I thought . . . ho hum. By that time, it didn't seem particularly odd or significant that she too was smeared here there and everywhere on the inner surfaces of the tunnels let in to the mound . . . but it might be better to look at it in a slightly different way.

'What, after all, is the dragomite individual? A worker isn't really an individual, nor is a warrior . . . they're just sterile units, more like the cells of a complex body. It's the same with bees and ants: the individual is the hive. But in bees and ants the hive doesn't include the nest. An ants' nest, however complicated it might be, is just the place where the ants live: a house. A dragomite mound isn't like that. A dragomite mound is more like a body, whose tunnels are arteries and veins through which its units circulate, just as the corpuscles of our blood circulate through our arteries and veins. Warriors and workers can go outside the mound, of course, but that just means that the dragomite body isn't as carefully confined as ours is . . . and that lack of confinement, of secure containment, has something to do with the differences between the kinds of life we call earthly and the kinds we call unearthly. It also has something to do with the readiness of unearthly kinds of life to form chimeras – including the chimeras they can and do form with earthly kinds of life.

'All of which, you might be thinking, is just so much rambling irrelevance . . . except, perhaps, for the fact that what we're wading through right now might be reckoned another kind of individual, another kind of massive but uncontained and unconfined creature. Just as we have tinier creatures than ourselves wandering around inside us – assuming that Phar's lore is reliable and not the superstitious nonsense Jacom Cerri thinks it is – so the marsh has us wandering around inside it. Just as our bodies have internal defences against invasion – provided, once again, that Phar can be believed – so the marsh has its multitudinous thorns. Do you see? Do you see what's happening to us?'

It seemed that the princess was capable of listening, and had indeed been listening, for she was able to reply. Unfortunately, her slightly slurred reply was: 'No, I don't.'

It was as if his fantasy had puffed itself up from small and limp beginnings to great and glorious proportions, and then had been pricked by a brutal pin. Within an instant, the sense which it had all seemed to make vanished utterly, and Andris could not begin to understand why he had ever thought that there was some special and vital meaning in it all. He was consumed by a sudden surge of anxiety.

'I'm afraid, highness,' he said, becoming awkwardly conscious of the fact that he had stopped wading and that he was swaying uncertainly from side to side, 'that I seem to be slightly delirious.' After a pause, he went on: 'I think it's the effect of the thorns. Perhaps I should have used your ointment after all. I thought I didn't need it because I felt so well, but there's a world of difference between feeling well and actually being well, isn't there?'

Lucrezia's weight shifted slightly in his arms as she raised her head and tried to look around. She put her arms around his neck so that she could hold her head upright, but there was nothing in the least intimate about the gesture. He expected her to say 'Where are we?' and was already mulling over the pointlessness of replying 'In the Soursweet Marshes', but what she actually said was: 'Where's Checuti?'

Andris's anxiety was confused by a rush of guilt, not so much because he didn't know the answer as because he had been walking for hours without even asking the question.

He looked to the left and the right, and then he looked behind him. There was no sign of Checuti. Nor was there any sign of Jume Metra, or of Ssifuss, or of Herriman.

'Herriman's dead,' Andris remembered. 'The birds killed him – and we didn't even get to raid their nests.'

'Never mind Herriman,' Lucrezia said thickly. 'What about

the horses? What about the kettle? What about . . . ?' She left it there.

Andris managed to stop himself swaying. 'I don't know,' he said weakly. 'It's the rotting thorns. They've poisoned me just as effectively as they've poisoned you. We're as good as dead.' He realised as he said it, however, that the effects of the poisons must be waning, or at least ebbing and flowing, or else they would not have permitted him this moment of relative sobriety. For a moment, hope returned, but then he realised that the moment of sobriety had come far too late. They had become separated from their companions and their remaining horses, and from almost all of the equipment Checuti and Lucrezia had salvaged from the wreckage of Aulakh Phar's wagon.

'We're dying, aren't we?' Lucrezia said. 'We feel drunk and light-headed, but that's just some perverted kind of natural mercy. The thorns are killing us.'

'They haven't killed us yet, highness,' Andris said, wishing that he could summon more defiance into his tone.

'But they've defeated us,' she said. 'We'll never get to Salamander's Fire, or Chimera's Cradle.'

Andris felt a strange flutter inside his head as his bruised and deflated imagination rallied and tried to take flight again. 'We have defences of our own against the defences of the marsh,' he murmured, 'but not to cancel them out . . . there's something inside us which is trying to reach . . .' He trailed off.

'Reach what?' the princess wanted to know.

'I don't know,' he said. 'An accommodation. That's what I was going to say – but I don't know exactly what I intended to mean by it. There's a war going on inside us, but we're not defeated yet, and . . . maybe we won't be. We've got to get out of here if we can, though. Without food, and only the slimy stuff we're wading in to drink, we don't have much time to spare. We have to get to the border of the marsh – and then we have to find help.'

'You'd better set me down, Andris,' she said. 'I think I can walk, if I have to.'

'No, highness,' Andris replied. 'You can't walk . . . and if you could we'd probably get separated. I'm . . . well, let's just say that I'd rather we stayed the way we are.'

'I didn't know you cared,' she said – but her voice was very faint, and he supposed that she knew it was a stupid thing to say. Of course he didn't care – but that wasn't the point, was it? He tried, unsuccessfully, to remember what the point was. Then, he put one foot in front of the other and resumed walking.

Walking felt good. It felt, too, as if the walking was *doing* him good. The rhythm of the movement soothed away the sudden rush of anxieties which had fallen upon him like great predatory birds, interrupting the train of thought which had brought him to the very brink of understanding who and what he was, and why he was doing whatever it was that he was doing.

If only she hadn't interrupted me, he thought vaguely. *If only she'd been content to listen and learn, I'd have got there, wherever there might be. But it's all right; it's not too late. All I have to do is keep on walking.*

Once he was moving again he soon began to feel that he could keep walking for ever. After all, it wasn't as if the world had a sharp edge off which he might fall. The world was round, and gentle, and just as long as its great heart kept pumping and its great lungs kept breathing, all he had to do was follow the flow to the quietude of the Pool of Life and the gently rocking crib of Chimera's Cradle. If he could go by Salamander's Fire, so much the better, but it really wasn't necessary. He only had to go with the flow, because all roads led to the Navel of the World, just as all the roads drawn upon the map of his own inner being ultimately brought each travelling corpuscle back to the muscular chambers of the heart and the delicate membranes of the lungs. If he could only find the right state of mind, the marsh would look after him; the marsh would take him where he needed to go.

All he had to do was to go, go, go with the flow . . . *with* the flow . . . with the *flow*. There was a little voice which said so, somewhere . . . a little voice that would never disturb him as Lucrezia's had . . .

He was as sure as he could be that the little voice knew far better than he did what needed to be said, and what needed to be done, and what needed *to be*.

18

IT HAD BEEN a long time since Hyry Keshvara had slept so well. Even so, she woke up as soon as the door of her room was opened. She stayed perfectly still, but she peeped through the narrow slits of her almost closed eyelids into the starlit gloom and tensed her muscles, ready to spring up if there were any need.

There was no need at all. It was a servant girl, who was careful not to look in her direction. The table beside the bedhead was very small, but the girl contrived to set down a jug of water, two small loaves of bread, and three soft candles. Then she picked up the bowl of dirty water in which Hyry had washed herself before the midnight, thrusting aside the towel which had been draped over its rim, and carried the water away.

Five minutes later she was back, with a fresh bowl of hot water and a bar of dark-coloured soap. She hesitated then, but eventually picked up the filthy jerkin and trousers which Hyry had taken off before climbing into bed, and took them away. Hyry opened her mouth to protest, but thought better of it. There were times in a woman's life when she had to trust the logic of the situation.

The trust was justified; the girl soon came back yet again, carrying a loose bundle of clothing which she cast down on the floor. This time, she looked at Hyry, showing no surprise at the discovery that Hyry was looking back at her.

'Thanks,' Hyry said.

The girl nodded by way of formal acknowledgement, but the expression in her eyes spoke volumes. Hyry didn't mind; she'd been unpopular before. All traders were unpopular in some quarters, and female ones were usually less popular than their male counterparts. In fact, given that she'd never been pretty, Hyry's opportunities to be popular had been strictly limited.

Once she'd risen to inspect the bundle more closely the thanks she'd offered began to seem a little premature. The clothing she had been given – or, more likely, lent – was by no means equivalent to that which had been taken away. It belonged to a person at least five sems shorter, and it included a skirt, which was not the kind of garment she would ever have considered wearing by choice. She left that sort of thing to servants, and to the absurdly kilted soldiers of Belin's army.

When she had dressed herself, she knew that she must look every inch a servant, and an ungainly one at that, but she contented herself with a slight shrug of annoyance. She hoped that Tarlock Nath's laundry facilities were up to the task of removing the dirt from her own clothes without completing the demolition job which time and misfortune had so eagerly begun.

The fresh bread tasted better than she had expected, though, and she ate it all. She had no comb with which to restore order to her hair – which had grown far longer than she liked to wear it during the last twenty-days – but she smoothed it with her fingers. She was glad she had taken the trouble when one of Nath's men-at-arms – looking very much cleaner and much more cheerful than when she had last seen him – came in without knocking and said: 'Come with me.' She glanced at the closed doors of her companions' rooms as they passed down the corridor, but made no objection when he led her down the stairway on her own.

Not unnaturally, Tarlock Nath had taken infinitely greater pains over his appearance. He had had the opportunity to immerse himself in a bath and to secure the services of a good barber before dressing in clean clothes. Nor had he been content with any clean clothes that happened to come to hand; he was no longer dressed for travelling, but had resumed his natural role as a man of wealth, substance and authority. He wore an embroidered jacket so gaudy that it would have caused gales of laughter in any fashionable meeting-place in Xandria, and his fingers were dressed with a vulgar superfluity of jewelled rings.

Hyry was not overly surprised to find that the man sitting beside Nath in the upper room to which the guard had brought her was not the bronze Amyas. Nor was she utterly astonished to see who it was, although she might have been had she not heard the tapping at Jacom Cerri's window the night before, and put her ear close to her own window to discover the explanation of it. Seated at the polished table, wearing a suit far less plush than Nath's but by no means poor, was Purkin, one-time sergeant in the king's guard.

Nath indicated that Hyry should take a seat, and waited for her to do so before he sat down himself. The messenger went out, closing the door behind him. Nath had stationed himself directly opposite her, but Hyry did not immediately meet his gaze. Instead, she looked hard at Purkin, carefully feigning the surprise she would surely have exhibited had she not been forewarned.

Koraismi must be right to call him a cunning man, she thought, *but does that only mean that he is cunning enough to have made a pact with Nath, or does it mean that he has been cunning enough to make pacts with all and sundry, with the intention of betraying every last one of them?*

'I'm glad to see you well, sergeant,' she said. 'We feared, when you didn't return, that you and your fellows might have met with misfortune in the hills.'

'The reason we didn't return,' Purkin replied, readily enough, 'was that we were sure you had met with misfortune. I'm glad it wasn't mortal, although it must have been bad. I told the councilman that you must have been captives of the dragomites, unable to do anythin' but stand with 'em, but he ain't certain of it even now. Fraxinus and that lunatic amber seem to have given him a different impression.'

Nath raised a hand to instruct Purkin to shut up, and Purkin obeyed.

'Have you been brutalised since my men captured you, Hyry Keshvara?' Nath asked abruptly. 'Have you been starved, tormented or raped?'

'No,' said Hyry, without making any strenuous effort to sound grateful. 'But we were betrayed, attacked and harried before we were captured, else we should never have been in need of your kindness.' She stressed the word *kindness* very slightly. From the corner of her eye she saw Purkin suppress a smile.

'If Shabir's men had taken you,' Nath told her, 'you'd have suffered far worse – and I doubt that you'd have had a good welcome in Tovali or Sabia. Some might think that you've fallen into far better company than you deserve.'

'I dare say some might,' she said brusquely, 'and I must suppose that they might be right. Why am I here alone? Aulakh Phar is my partner in this venture, and he should hear what you have to say. So should Captain Cerri and Merel Zabio.' She used Jacom's obsolete title quite deliberately.

'I've taken this man's good advice,' Nath told her, pointing negligently in Purkin's direction. 'He tells me that you're an honest trader – a person who can be trusted.'

You mean, Hyry thought, *he's told you that Jacom Cerri can't go back to Xandria, and that Aulakh is a slippery customer whose objectives are unclear. He's told you to talk to me because he thinks my sole concerns are survival and profit*. 'Aulakh Phar is a honest trader too,' she said aloud, 'and we're partners. Any deal you make has to be made with both of us.'

'Of course,' Nath replied airily. 'I understand that perfectly. It's just that your friend is rather old, and still a little frail. I thought he'd appreciate the rest – and he'll surely trust you to negotiate on behalf of all your people.'

'What do you have in mind?' she asked bluntly.

'I hope you realise,' Nath said, aiming for subtle menace but not achieving it, 'that it will require some effort on my part to keep you safe, even in Antiar. I shall assure my fellow councilmen, of course, that you were not directly involved in the slaughter of General Shabir's men by the dragomite warriors and the giant, but some of my fellows might demand to know how such unhuman creatures were supported with bombs, given that the manufacture of plastic is lore known only to true humans. Purkin assures me that the plastic must have been made and used by a bandit and renegade named Checuti, but—'

'I understand the stick,' Hyry interrupted rudely. 'Where's the carrot? Why don't you tell me exactly what you want from us, as recompense for your generosity and protection?'

Nath didn't seem unduly disconcerted by her directness, although he frowned. 'I understand that you met a man named Djemil Eyub in the purple forest?' he said, after a pause. Obviously, he wasn't yet ready to lay his cards on the table.

'Not exactly,' Hyry answered. 'I was stung by a flowerworm and fell into the river before I had a chance to say hello. I suppose you could say that Purkin met him, but they weren't actually able to talk – were you, Purkin?'

Purkin wasn't smiling any more; the frown on his face suggested that he thought Hyry was handling the situation badly. Perhaps he had told Nath that she would be more pliable.

'Eyub was not even a councilman in Ebla,' Nath said. 'He was an adventurer, with no authority to make bargains for anyone except himself. He didn't speak for his own town, let alone the Convocation of the Nine Towns.'

Which means, Hyry thought, *that no one here really expected him to be able to cross the Dragomite Hills safely – in which presumption they were not entirely wrong*. 'Even so,' she said, suppressing the temptation to make the irony more obvious than it was, 'you'd doubtless have been pleased to welcome him home, had he brought Xandrian emissaries with him, and permanent access to Xandrian metal. If he was acting on his own authority, what has he got to do with this discussion?'

'Rumour has it that the council of Ebla is assembling an official party to follow in Eyub's footsteps and complete his work of forging a firm link between Ebla and Xandria,' Nath said. 'Its members seem to think that his adventure has given them a licence to do that, without due reference to the Convocation.'

'I'm just an honest trader,' Hyry said. 'Politics isn't my business. What do you want from me?'

'I want you to help me to forge a link with Xandria,' Nath said, 'not on behalf of any particular city but on behalf of the Convocation, and the entire population of the Nine Towns.'

On behalf of yourself, you mean, she thought. *The Convocation's already fallen apart, and even if it hadn't you wouldn't give a damn any more than the leading citizens of Ebla do. You just want a bolt-hole for yourself and as much of your wealth as you can carry*. Aloud, she said: 'Why do you need me if you already have the sergeant and his men? They can guide you, if you need guiding.'

'I understand that the sergeant and his men have been exiled,' Nath was quick to counter, having now finished beating about the bush. 'Their captain too. The girl is an outlaw and the old man . . . is something of an eccentric. You, on the other hand, are highly thought of in Xandria and well-known even in the citadel where the king reigns in splendour.'

'As I understand it,' Hyry retorted, 'Princess Lucrezia offered

General Shabir the friendship of Xandria, on her own authority and that of her house-mother, Queen Ereleth. He made an agreement with her, then broke it. For all I know, the princess and the queen might both be dead, and Carus Fraxinus too. He too was a well-liked and well-respected man in Xandria. I fear that forging a link between Xandria and the Nine Towns might require diplomatic talents far beyond mine.'

'As you said,' Nath replied, readily enough, 'it was General Shabir who made a treaty with your friends and General Shabir who then broke it. Geneal Shabir is an Eblan, and it is Ebla which now intends to send emissaries to your king. I doubt that they intend to reveal the whole truth of the matter.'

The whole truth of the matter! Hyry let the words echo ironically in her mind. The whole truth of the matter was the last thing Tarlock Nath wanted to reveal, and they both knew it.

'The Nine Towns need to make contact with Xandria, and need it desperately,' Nath went on, in the same defiantly hypocritical vein. 'For hundreds of years we've been able to hold and work our land, needing nothing but discipline to keep it safe – but we can't do that any longer. We no longer have an army in the north to keep the dragomites at bay, and the southern towns are crying out for help that the Convocation cannot provide. Amyas assures me that matters are even more desperate in the far south – but Purkin assures me that Xandria has the military might to attack the dragomites on their own ground and complete the destruction of their nests, and to open a permanent road to our narrow land.'

'And why should they do that?' Hyry asked, carefully saying *they* rather than *we*. 'King Belin isn't sentimental about helping people just because they're human, nor is he stupid enough to send armies against dragomites just because they're not human. If your people want Xandrian metal with which to defend your lands you'll have to pay for it – and I haven't so far seen any evidence that you have anything worthwhile to put up as a price.'

Nath stared at her stonily, but he didn't seem at all surprised by the brutality of her summation. 'According to Amyas,' he said, 'neither the Dragomite Hills nor the forest which lies beyond them can provide a permanent barrier against the invasions which have destroyed his own nation. If Xandria is not forewarned, it's only a matter of time before its southern provinces find themselves in exactly the same position as the Nine Towns. If the invasions are to be countered, Xandria would be wise to make what provision it can now. Amyas intends to return to his homeland, but he has given me a good account of what is happening in the south – far better, at any rate, than any account the Eblans have. Your king needs to hear what I have to tell him, and it is your patriotic duty to help me obtain a hearing.'

Hyry could marvel at the man's temerity. Patriotic duty, was it? She glanced at Purkin, who had resurrected his smile, and knew that he must have had a good deal to do with this line of argument. Was he trying to prepare the way for his own return to Xandria? Did he think that if he only played his cards cleverly enough, his exile might be revoked? If so, was Jacom Cerri included in the plan, or had Koraismi been sent out – unwittingly, no doubt – to play him for a fool?

'Princess Lucrezia would make a far better ambassador,' Hyry said, fishing for information. 'According to Captain Cerri, she was still alive when Shabir's forces turned and ran.'

'Unfortunately,' Nath said, 'my attempts to locate her haven't yet borne fruit. I sent men after her as soon as I realised that she and her companions must have fled westwards after the battle, and I told them to look out for the big amber too, but I fear they might have gone into the marshes, in which case they're unlikely to come out again. The many poisons which grow there are slow but sure, as the sergeant discovered.'

'I still get the itch occasionally,' the sergeant admitted, obligingly. 'Taj and Mor were sick for days, and Aaron and Fernel still have terrible dreams.'

'What about Fraxinus and the queen?' Hyry asked.

Nath shook his head. 'No news,' he said regretfully. 'Shabir chased them into the Spangled Desert, and he's a stubborn man. If he didn't catch them, you can be sure he'll have forced them deep into the wilderness. Your expedition is finished – you really have no choice but to return to Xandria.' He stressed the words *no choice* very slightly, perhaps still under the illusion that he was being subtle.

'I see,' Hyry said meekly. 'I'll have to discuss the matter with Aulakh Phar and Captain Cerri, of course – Merel Zabio too.'

'No doubt,' Nath said, with some affectation of graciousness. 'I hope it won't take too long. I'd like the benefit of your advice, if you're prepared to offer it – your advice as a trader, that is. I'm a man of some means. If I had sound information about the markets on the far side of the Dragomite Hills, I might be able to assemble goods that would be worth trading there.'

Hyry suspected that what he wanted to buy in Xandria was a safe refuge for himself, his family and a few of his servants, not metal to bring back to aid his people in their continuing battle against alien invasions. All his cant regarding the Convocation and the perfidy of the Eblans was a mere smokescreen, just like his optimistic insinuations regarding Hyry's patriotic duty, but the pretence had to be maintained, at least for the time being.

'I dare say that I could place my expertise at your disposal,' Hyry said carefully, 'if I were given sufficient incentive to do so.'

Nath shook his head wearily. 'I'm not lying to you,' he said insincerely. 'There really are people who want you killed. Not just people in Ebla and Sabia – people right here in Antiar. You need my protection. Tell her, Purkin.'

'It's true, Keshvara,' Purkin said mechanically. 'You know what cities're like. Fear breeds rumour an' rumour breeds fear, an' every reported death adds fuel to the fire. To most of the people on the streets of Antiar, *Xandrian* means *dragomite-lover* now. What happened a few days ago put me in danger, an' all my men, not just you an' Phar an' the captain. You have to do what this man says. I'm helping him as best I can, but I'm a soldier, not a merchant or a diplomat.'

Hyry hoped that it wasn't obvious to Nath that the sergeant's speech was as comprehensively infected with insincerity as his own. In a way, she almost wished it wasn't. At least she knew where Nath stood – but Purkin might well be planning to double-cross Nath because of some other deal he'd cooked up on the sly with someone else. Unless and until she found out what he was up to, how could she possibly figure out what the best next move might be?

'All right,' she said, hoping that she didn't seem too eager. 'I'll talk to Aulakh and the captain. I'll explain it all very carefully – I'm sure they'll see the sense in what you say.'

'Good,' Nath said. He seemed genuinely relieved.

The worst irony of all, Hyry thought, as she was led back to her room, *is that he might be right. Maybe the best thing to do is to forget all about Salamander's Fire and Carus Fraxinus. Maybe the only sensible thing to do is to head back to Xandria, even knowing full well that no one there will feel any necessity to be alarmed, and that no one ever thanks the bearers of bad news anyway. But Aulakh isn't going to see it that way, and neither is Merel – and even Jacom isn't such a fool as to think that Tarlock Nath's an adequate substitute for Princess Lucrezia.*

19

THE SLOW AND erratic descent of the floaters had continued all night, and was now approaching its climax. The further the wagon had progressed the greater the density of the creatures had become, and now they were beneath the core of the 'flock'. Within the next few hours several hundred would fall gently to the earth within a kim of the wagon – and the race would be on.

Fraxinus knew by now that it would indeed be a race; ever since the foraging dragomites had set about hunting the balloonlike plants their riders – Mossassor had gone out with them more than once as well as Vaca Metra – had brought back reports of rivals. Shabir had supplied the names 'hellhound' and 'lizardlion', which he had heard from the bronze Amyas on the eve of the battle at the bridge, and Mossassor had agreed that they seemed apt enough for two of the various kinds of creatures it had observed. This news surprised Fraxinus, in that it implied that the scavengers in question must have followed the drifting spores out of the southlands, drawn along the course of the prevailing wind for hundreds, perhaps thousands, of kims. It also surprised Shabir, more than a little, and Fraxinus realised that although he had been quite willing to recruit any and all rumours to the discomfiture of his new travelling companions, the general had not actually believed the apocalyptic accounts he had heard from the bronze. It was not unnatural that the partial confirmation should be unwelcome to him; he had a family in Ebla.

'It seems perverse,' Ereleth remarked, 'that creatures as big and bold as the ones Mossassor describes should chase motes drifting on the wind for long distances when there must be easier prey close at hand.'

'Perhaps,' Fraxinus replied, trying to work out how Aulakh

Phar might have argued the case. 'It may be that the supplementation of the predators' diet by the new food led to an increase in their numbers which devastated the stocks of their normal prey species. In order to fuel their remarkable mode of reproduction the floaters must have to lay down lavish stores of energy-rich protein – not merely to drive the chemical reaction which produces the gas to inflate their sacs, but also to give their wormlike seeds the strength to burrow down into the earth when they land. If the spores are unusually succulent and nutritious, it's only to be expected that there will always be hungry creatures ready to pounce on them as they descend.'

'And that being the case,' Ereleth countered, to show that she could play the game too, 'the spores which survive in the greatest numbers are those which are the most expert burrowers, and thus the ones which have laid down the richest reserves of all. Each subsequent generation is more succulent than the last, and this makes their predators all the more avid to capture them during the narrow margin of opportunity when they're neither airborne nor underground.' She spoke lightly, as if it were a joke, but Phar would have seized upon it as an excellent analysis, and Fraxinus could see the beauty of its logic.

'It's a vicious circle,' he agreed. 'Vicious enough, at any rate, to encourage the more enthusiastic predators to go to any necessary lengths to secure their reward. The creatures Mossassor and Vaca Metra have described aren't necessarily bold because they're big – perhaps they're big because they're long-legged, and the only creatures which stand a good chance of getting to the floaters in the mere minutes when they remain helpless on the surface are long-striding tireless runners: hellhounds, lizardlions . . .'

'. . . and dragomites,' Ereleth finished for him. 'You might be wrong, general, about the inevitability of the floaters colonising the Dragomite Hills. They might instead be the dragomites' salvation. When they begin to descend upon the mounds, they'll find workers waiting everywhere – and warriors to make sure that any hellhounds stupid enough to follow them into such terrain will simply serve to season the diet.'

'Dragomite warriors aren't invincible,' the seasoned dragomite-fighter had replied dully. 'The creatures facing them here are weakened by thirst and the corrosions of these foul sands, else you might be in danger of losing your escort.'

Given Shabir's testimony that the lore of the Nine Towns preserved no record of the floaters ever having been seen in their fields before, Fraxinus had to suppose that they had never previously extended their range into the Spangled Desert either. It was obvious that it would do them no good at all to do so, because the coruscating sands and the adamantine rocks which underlay them were conspicuously inhospitable. Floaters which drifted over terrain of this kind were doomed to perish, but they could not choose where they would come down. Although they would be easier prey here than in regions where they landed on soft soil, their most faithful followers would gain little benefit from that advantage; they too were ill-adapted for desert life, and they too must be reckoned to have been betrayed by their instincts.

It was ironic, Fraxinus thought, that the only real beneficiaries of this particular phase of the Great Unearthly Invasion were himself and his companions. The damnation of the floaters and their followers would be the salvation of the horses appointed to pull the wagon, and of the people who depended on them. Once the worm-like part of the structure had been cut and crushed by dragomite jaws the things could easily be ground up into something not unlike coarse flour, which the horses found very much to their taste and very adequate to their nourishment. It was good for humans too. Fraxinus didn't doubt that it could have been baked into good bread had they had an oven; as things were, it had to be fried into thin pancakes.

As Ereleth cracked her whip, urging the horses to move a little more quickly as she tried to guess where the richest pickings would be available when the descending floaters hit the ground, Mossassor displaced Shabir and poked its head out from the back of the wagon. It was holding a floater which was still wriggling – the first live one Fraxinus had seen. Fraxinus guessed that it must have been passed to the Serpent by a dragomite warrior, almost certainly at its request. Mossassor had to hold the thing firmly to prevent it squirming out of its grip, but the deflated sac gave its clinging hands extra purchase and it had no difficulty passing the creature on to Fraxinus.

The floater was unexpectedly strong, but such strategy as

there was in its thrashing was not adapted to the purpose of escaping a pair of gripping hands, human or otherwise; it was merely performing the spasmic movements which would have enabled it to burrow deep into the ground had it only fallen on rich moist soil.

'Have you ever heard of such things?' Fraxinus asked Mossassor, while the creature's motions became gradually weaker.

'No,' said the Serpent. 'Nossing like ssem in Grey Wasste or itss borderlandss.'

'Not yet, at any rate,' said Fraxinus softly. 'It doesn't have a mouth, so I suppose it has little or nothing in the way of a digestive system, but do you see these three lateral lines of little pores? Three's an unusual number, is it not? They might have some respiratory function, I suppose – or are they sensory organs like the ones fish have?'

'Perhapss,' Mossassor said dubiously.

The creature seemed to have exhausted its strength, but Fraxinus held on to it tightly in case it had a few last spasms in reserve. 'Look at the veins in the sac. At a guess, I'd say they were part structural and part circulatory. The sap inside them isn't quite colourless, but it's neither the red of blood nor the green of leaves. Are they really something new to the world, do you think? Or is it simply that they've previously been confined to a very limited range, which they've suddenly overshot by virtue of crossing some crucial boundary or undergoing a dramatic population explosion?'

'Musst be new,' Mossassor opined. 'Would be lore otherwisse, human if not Sserpent.'

'Not, of course, that they sprang into being overnight,' Fraxinus added thoughtfully. 'What connection can there possibly be between these things, the plague which obliterated the dragomites' crop plants, and the seeds which Hyry bought from the mysterious bronzes? Their simultaneous appearance can't possibly be mere coincidence, but what kind of common cause can there be for such disparate phenomena?'

There were far too many words in this speech that meant nothing to Mossassor; the Serpent didn't even bother with a token evasion.

'Did your bronze friend tell you what the full-grown trees

look like?' Fraxinus called to Shabir, who was still lurking nearby although the Serpent had dispossessed him of the station behind the driver's bench.

'He was no friend of mine,' Shabir growled. 'He was eager to pass on horrific details. According to him they grow fast and they grow tall. Their saplings are like ramrods, too strong to be cut by our common tools, offering no purchase for climbers. Their huge crowns blot out the sun, so that all low-lying plants – whether they be grasses for feed, grains and root vegetables or fruit trees – wither and die.'

'In Xandria,' Fraxinus said pensively, 'we have steel saws, sharp axes and diamond-tipped drills. No tree has a trunk strong enough to stand up to tools of that kind, and there's no shortage of willing hands to ply them.'

'Even if they *are* cut down,' Shabir told him, 'they still blight the ground, and their roots can't be dug out. All the metal in the world can't help you in the long run, and all the men in the world wouldn't be enough to catch them all as they land.'

Fraxinus knew that the general was only repeating hearsay, and that he was not at all reluctant to exaggerate, but he didn't attempt to start an argument on those grounds. 'What we'd need,' he murmured thoughtfully, 'is an efficient predator. Not the kind which chases them, the way the hellbounds and their cousins are doing, but something that can get inside them – something insidious. A plague upon the plague. Perhaps what's happening here is the reverse of what's happened in the hills. The fungi which the dragomites kept have been wiped out by some new disease. Perhaps a similarly virulent disease, which used to keep these things in check, has somehow lost its efficacy, or fallen victim to some newly evolved defence mechanism. Rots come and rots go, but corruption is always with us – do you have that saying in Ebla? Perhaps it's not quite true. Perhaps, every now and again, one kind of rot disappears without being replaced, and one species or another wins free of corruption, if only for a little while.'

'Fraxinus!' Ereleth exclaimed, in a voice whose raucous stridency would have been the envy of any fishwife. 'Look there! This gathering's more complicated than we thought.'

As he looked up, obedient to the summons, the floater gave one last twist and very nearly wriggled free, but Fraxinus renewed his grip in time, and passed the captive creature back to Mossassor. He saw Shabir's face behind the Serpent's half-inflated hood, and saw a bitter smile hovering at the corners of the general's mouth.

He wants us to run into trouble, he thought. *Because he could not defeat us he wants us to fail.* He quickly turned back to see what it was that had alarmed Ereleth.

The unusually dense flock of floaters which was descending ahead of them, becalmed by the dying wind and at the very limit of their gas-producing capacity, had attracted all their usual attendants and more. The wagon had just begun a long descent into a shallow bowl where there were very few gaudtrees and lapidendrons: a bowl so glutted with glittering dust that it looked like a frozen sea surrounding an archipelago of misshapen islands. Each 'island' was a bulbous outcrop of wind-worn rock, every ridge and angle smoothed by long exposure to the scouring wind, patterned with tesserae of coloured glass and semi-precious stones.

The shaggy hellhounds which had pursued the cloud of spores across the desert sands were not lone hunters like the lizardlions; they worked in packs. There was a pack in view now – the first one of which Fraxinus had got a clear sight in daylight. They were big and they were ugly, and he had to suppose that they had been maddened by thirst and by the pain caused by the dozens of tiny slivers of crystal which must have worked their way deep into their fleshy paws. While they waited for the gift of the skies to descend into their slavering jaws they had found other creatures to chase and torment – creatures which they would not ordinarily have reckoned to be competitors or prey, but which were in the present circumstances too tempting to be let alone.

Fraxinus had never seen a Salamander but he had no difficulty recognising them from descriptions he had heard. They were not as tall as Serpents, and very much stouter. Their heads were big and broad and rounded, and their eyes – which were set much further apart than Serpents' eyes – were black and slit-like, sheltered by huge brow-ridges. They wore clothes of a sort: tattered, sack-like smocks which hung from their shoulders to their massive knees. They carried weapons, too, but only spears and those not metal-tipped. Their hides were as smoothly marbled as Mossassor's, though not as vividly patterned. They didn't look as if they would be easily butchered, even by the kind of teeth the hellhounds had – but that wasn't dissuading a dozen-strong pack of the creatures from laying siege to the glassy islet where four Salamanders were making what use they could of a castellate defence.

Behind the first rank of attackers others waited at a respectful distance – a couple of skulking lizardlions, as suspicious of one another as they were of the hellhounds. They were ready to play the scavenger if the battle between the hellhounds and the Salamanders left corpses strewn around, but equally ready to turn away and dash for the floaters when they finally drifted to the ground.

Fraxinus estimated that half an hour might pass before the batch of floaters that was hovering over the Salamanders' islet actually touched down – time enough for the trouble that was brewing there to boil over. He looked around to see where Dhalla was, and located her readily enough, loping along some ten or twenty mets to the left of the wagon, level with the front wheels. A lone dragomite was thirty mets farther out; the other two – including the one which Vaca Metra rode – were on the right flank.

'Mossassor!' he said. 'Can you communicate with the dragomites from here?'

'Not now,' the Serpent told him sorrowfully. 'Not eassy now.'

Fraxinus had expected the reply, but he cursed anyhow, beneath his breath.

'Drive straight for the Salamanders,' he told Ereleth. 'The only way we can define them as friends is to get as close to them as possible – perhaps even get them on board. If we don't do that, the dragomites will give them no more consideration than the wild beasts. Will the Salamanders recognise us as allies, Mossassor?'

'Ssink sso,' the Serpent replied, but it didn't seem at all certain.

Fraxinus waved to attract Dhalla's attention. The moment she turned towards him he cupped his hand about his mouth and shouted: 'Save the Salamanders! Drive the hellbounds away!'

Dhalla – who was almost fully fit now – had been idling in order to keep pace with the horses while they were trotting, but now she was running full tilt to keep up with their gallop; even so, she lengthened her stride enough to pull slightly ahead.

Ereleth was no longer cracking the whip, knowing full well that the horses would lose their wind soon enough.

The hellhounds didn't wait. Maddened as they were, they were clever enough to know that waiting for the helpless floaters to fall was a much better bet than facing up to a giant, three huge-jawed dragomites and what must have looked to them like a runaway house. They scattered, yowling in impotent rage.

The dragomites weren't about to let the dog-like beasts decamp to any position where they might still be troublesome when the floaters came down; they gave chase, fortunately paying no attention at all to the beleaguered Salamanders. Fraxinus watched in unashamed awe as their huge legs ate up the ground and their jaws swiped at the hellhounds with unceremonious brutality. The shaggy predators abandoned all thought of a mere tactical withdrawal and fled southwards, howling in anguish and terror. The dragomites only caught up with three of them, but those three were instantly disabled, their bones breaking as they were smashed to the ground.

Ereleth was reining in the horses long before they got to the rock where the Salamanders waited, presumably in utter astonishment. For a moment or two Fraxinus thought that they too might flee, but Dhalla had understood what was required of her, and she had hastened to place herself between the dragomites and the Salamanders with her spear at the ready. The dragomites, when they turned away from the fleeing hellhounds, seemed to understand what she was doing, and made no hostile move. Fraxinus was ready to shout out to the Salamanders, to tell them not to be afraid and to wait where they were, but by the time he had filled his lungs he could see that no such injunction was necessary.

The Salamanders were all staring at Dhalla, pointing and muttering amongst themselves. It was difficult to imagine those heavy heads moving frantically, but Fraxinus got the strong impression that insofar as they were capable of excitement the Salamanders were very excited indeed.

'They must recognise a heart where Salamander's fire is said to burn,' said Ereleth, who was rather more agitated than was her own habit. 'They might never have seen a giant, but they have their lore and legends, as have we.' She brought the wagon to a gradual halt, not thirty mets from the Salamanders' station.

The floaters were still falling, and it was clear that the Salamanders had positioned themselves cleverly to take advantage of the fall, had not the hellhounds arrived to confuse the situation. Fraxinus judged that there would just be time to say hello before the race began to gather as much of the bounty of the skies as was humanly and unhumanly possible.

20

JACOM SAT WITH Aulakh Phar and Merel Zabio in the shadow of one of the more venerable trees in the grounds of Tarlock Nath's house. The morning wasn't bright enough for them to need the protection of the tree – indeed, the day was so dull that the place where they sat was positively gloomy – but it represented privacy of a sort. They were not unobserved, of course; one of Nath's men-at-arms was watching them from the house while another had carefully stationed himself at the small gate which was the only means of egress from the grounds on this side of the house.

'It seems to me,' Phar said, 'that you've been too content to be pushed around. You should have asked more questions, and used your eyes and ears a deal more cleverly.'

Jacom was wounded by this uncharitable summation. 'You don't seem to realise,' he said, with ostentatious patience, 'that these people really don't like us. Nath thinks that we might be useful, and he's protected us for that reason, but he doesn't think we're important. If we'd been any trouble, he'd have dumped us without a qualm – and if he'd done that while you and Merel were lying at death's door, you'd never have pulled through. We did our best.'

'Where's Hyry?' Merel asked.

'She's gone to the market square with Nath,' Jacom told her. 'She's giving him advice as to the best provisions to lay in for a journey to Xandria.'

'But we're not going back to Xandria,' Merel said.

'Hyry was hardly going to tell Nath that,' Jacom retorted, more sharply than he intended. 'Until we know what we *are* doing, we have to string everybody along, don't we?' As he spoke he looked resentfully at Phar, who seemed to be blaming him for the fact that they had neither a clear plan of action, nor adequate information on which to construct one.

'I don't understand why Nath's so determined to go to Xandria, either,' Phar said. 'He's obviously one of the richest men in town. Why would he decide to leave all this behind on the strength of rumours about floating seeds?'

'He thinks he has better intelligence than anyone else because he's kept Amyas to himself these last few days,' Jacom said. 'As far as I can gather, he strung Amyas along by promising to raise a company of mercenaries for him – but he couldn't deliver even if he still wanted to, because Shabir's army has disintegrated. Amyas has gone back to his own men in a foul temper, and Nath thinks it's time to get out. It's not just the rumours; the whole nation – if you can call it a nation – is falling apart. This Convocation thing, which is the nearest thing they have to a government, seems to have broken up in acrimony. If they only had the sense to have a king and a properly unified army they wouldn't be in this mess. Listen to that row out in the street now – everybody's arguing with everybody else.'

'What is it?' Merel asked, looking round in the direction from which the distant sound of shouting could be heard. 'What are they fighting about?'

'Anything and everything,' Jacom said, bitterly. 'I believe the centre of town's over that way, although you can't see it from the attic windows.' He pointed past the side of the house towards the gardens that lay in front of it. 'They're always at it – arguing, that is. It seems to be impossible for two Antiarians to pass one another in the street without getting into a row.'

'There are a lot more than two of them,' Phar said, cocking an ear in the direction from which the muffled noise was coming. 'They're still quite a way off. Can you make out what they're shouting?'

'As long as it's not *Death to the foreigners* I couldn't care less,' Jacom said. 'The point is—'

'The point is,' Phar cut in, 'that we're just sitting around waiting while everyone else makes plans for us. Amyas wants to take you, and possibly the rest of us, south; Nath wants to take Hyry, and possibly the rest of us, north; and what your friend Purkin might have in mind we haven't the slightest idea. With all due respect to the sergeant's long experience in breaking up brawls on Xandria's waterfront and keeping the citadel safe from thieves – or not, as it turned out – I have to say that he's not a man I'd trust to plan his way out of a room with three unlocked doors. Now, if—'

'He's not my friend,' Jacom retorted. 'And as far as trust goes, whether it relates to his intelligence or his honesty, I wouldn't trust him as far as I could throw a feather into a headwind, but—'

'They're getting closer,' Merel observed, having evidently decided to give her full attention to the distant noises now that they had been brought to her notice. 'I don't think they're shouting anything about foreigners, but I think I heard Nath's name.'

'It's an easy name to mishear,' Jacom said uneasily. He saw that the man who had been watching them from the house now had company, and that the servant who had approached him seemed distinctly agitated. He saw the man-at-arms point towards the tree, as if protesting that he had a job to do – and he saw that the servant wasn't in the least impressed. After a few seconds, the watcher quit his post.

Aulakh Phar, meanwhile, had been listening. 'Merel's right,' he said. 'That's not some street brawl, it's real trouble . . . and it's heading this way.'

The man who had been guarding the gate had come three steps towards them, but now he looked back, as if he had heard something. He stopped, becalmed by hesitation.

'Come inside!' called the man who was approaching from the house. 'You must come inside!'

Jacom came to his feet, drawn upright by soldierly instinct, but Phar remained where he was and put out a hand to restrain Merel.

'Why?' Phar demanded pugnaciously. 'What's going on?'

'Thieves!' the man said, his face darkening at the prospect of disobedience. 'The mob! We have to go inside.'

Jacom saw that the man guarding the gate was still stranded by indecision, looking one way and then the other. The man who had come to summon them was now beckoning to his companion, demanding his help – but Jacom saw that there was someone beyond the gate now, peering in through the eyepiece.

'I don't want to go inside,' Phar said. 'If there's going to be trouble . . .'

There *was* going to be trouble, Jacom saw. The man who had come from the house wasn't about to tolerate any further argument; he released the long cudgel that was hanging from his belt and weighed it in his hand suggestively. The man who had been stationed at the gate drew his own weapon, which was a knife with a thin steel blade. Jacom felt confident that he could disarm either man – or both – if necessary, but he couldn't see why it was necessary.

'Aulakh . . .' he began, but he stopped abruptly. His eye had been caught by a movement behind the man with the knife. Someone was clambering over the wall. It would have been pleasant to see Koraismi or one of the ex-guardsmen, but it was only an Antiarian youth, who dropped quickly to the ground and went to the gate, with the evident intention of removing the bar that secured it. Jacom felt a warning cry rise instinctively to his lips, but he bit it back.

It was, instead, the man with the cudgel who shouted a warning, but it came too late. The bar was down and the gate was open, and half a dozen angry men were swarming through it.

Jacom saw immediately that this was no organised or planned attack. The men were armed, after a fashion, but not with real weapons. One had an axe whose head was carved from glassy stone; one had a pitchfork; one had what looked like a broken table-leg. Given that the guard who was whirling around to face them had nothing but a knife, however – and that a meagre one – there was no doubt at all as to where the advantage lay. Jacom knew it and the man with the knife knew it.

The guard immediately took to his heels. The man with the cudgel wasn't about to disagree with his judgment; nor was he about to waste any more time dickering with foreigners who weren't exactly prisoners and weren't exactly guests. He ran for the door from which he had emerged, with the knifeman close upon his heels.

Aulakh Phar condescended to stand up at least, and Merel was quick to follow his example. Jacom saw a doubtful expression cross the old man's brow, as if he had begun to wonder whether his stubbornness might have landed him in trouble – but Phar was not a man to waste time with idle regrets, nor a man to freeze under the pressure of uncertainty. He stabbed his outstretched arm in the direction of the fleeing pair and yelled: 'After them! Don't let them bar the door against you! Quickly, you fools!'

Jacom winced at his use of the word *fools*, but the fools in question didn't seem to take it unkindly. The men in the van of the invading rabble had paused, looking at the three unarmed Xandrians as if they'd half a mind to attack them, if only for want of any more convenient target, but Phar's cry transformed their mood on the instant. They raced after Nath's men-at-arms, streaming past Jacom with hardly a sideways glance.

'I don't understand,' Merel complained. 'Who are they?'

Jacom only knew who they weren't. They weren't anyone he knew, and they weren't the people who had been making all the noise. Those, he now saw, were coming through the main gate a hundred mets away, and they too had put a group of men-at-arms to flight. It wasn't easy to see what was happening, because there were half a dozen trees partially blocking the view, but Jacom had no difficulty recognising Munir Zanarin among the fleeing men. There was no sign of Tarlock Nath or Hyry Keshvara.

'It's a revolution,' he whispered numbly. 'They're storming the house – maybe the entire neighbourhood.'

'It's a bunch of wound-up farm labourers,' Phar corrected him scornfully. 'They aren't even drunk. I think they've figured out that Nath's planning to run – I'll bet he wasn't the only one trying to buy up supplies in the market. Maybe they're his tenants, or maybe they're just people who figure that if looting time is here they might as well start with good quality loot. Are you going to stand there all day?'

Jacom looked away from the ill-assorted crowd that was pressing on towards the main door, which was obscured from his view by the angle of the house. Phar was looking the other way, at the now unguarded gate. The men who had come through it were hammering at the door through which the house's defenders had vanished.

Jacom looked down at the clothes he was wearing. It was the clothes themselves that disturbed him, more than the lack of a weapon or pouches full of the kind of things a man liked to carry. They were the clothes of a serving-man. Even as the thought formed in his head, though, he was embarrassed by its absurdity. This was no time to say 'I can't go out like this' – so he didn't.

'Come on,' said Aulakh Phar, plucking at his arms – but he wasn't pulling in the direction of the gate; he was heading for the stables.

Jacom hesitated. 'Wait a minute . . .' he began.

Phar wasn't in the mood for waiting. Jacom knew that the same questions that were rising into his mind must be rising into the old man's, but the latter obviously felt that there was no time to spare for discussion or mature reflection. Jacom could understand why. Two of the men who were laying siege to the back door had already peeled off to run in the direction of the stables, and he had no doubt that others would soon be coming around the house from the other side. If they intended to make good their escape they had to act now.

'What about Hyry?' Merel protested, raising the most obvious of the objections which had occurred to Jacom. 'We can't leave without her.'

'We certainly can't leave *with* her,' Phar said, pulling them both along with him. 'Hyry can look after herself.'

Jacom felt a perverse pang of envy, knowing that he had never been so recklessly decisive in his life. Perhaps Phar had been right to criticise his lack of initiative and his willingness to await developments while various others decided what to do with him. Perhaps Phar was right to seize the moment, careless of such timorous questions as where they were going to ride to, if they contrived to ride anywhere at all. In any case, there seemed to be no choice now but to follow the old man's lead.

As they came to the stable doors, though, Jacom saw with a sinking heart that there was no possibility of their being able to saddle up at their leisure and ride away. As soon as the doors were flung wide by one of the invaders he saw that there were half a dozen Antiarians already inside. Nath's servants had been quite prepared to leave Jacom and Phar to their own devices while they were standing meekly beneath a tree, but now that they were moving in the direction of valuable horses – and there was probably no other kind in a jumped-up village like this – they were instantly reclassified as enemies. These defenders weren't about to let foreign hands touch a single item of tack – and the two men who had come into the grounds with the mob were now hesitating, wondering which of the other two groups posed the greater threat.

'Rot!' muttered Phar, as four pairs of eyes turned in their direction while two other men squared up against the local marauders. 'I'll take the big one; you take the other three.'

For a moment, Jacom thought that the old man was joking – but he wasn't. Phar continued going forwards, two or three paces in front of Jacom, holding out his hand towards the biggest of the would-be defenders as if to offer it in friendship. The man wasn't fooled for an instant, and he raised a stout axe-handle as if he were perfectly confident that the mere sight of it would be enough to make an old man back off; but Phar had picked up a handful of dust before he got up from where he had been sitting, and he threw it into the man's eyes with casual contempt and deadly accuracy, then swung his booted foot up into the man's groin with a grace and purpose that Jacom found hard to believe.

The other Antiarians obviously found it equally difficult to credit, but by the time Phar had deftly plucked the axe-handle from the blinded man's hand and smashed it down upon his skull they were moving to take reprisals. Jacom was greatly relieved to observe that they were moving like men who had never been in a serious fight in all their lives.

Jacom chopped the first one across the throat with his right hand, and lashed out sideways with his left as he kicked away the knife which the first man had dropped. It was only a kitchen-knife, but it looked horribly sharp. His flailing left arm knocked the second man off balance, but did no more than that, and the third was quick to close in on him, wielding a huge pole which might have been a cart-axle. Jacom feinted with his right hand, grabbed one end of the pole with his left, and lashed out with his boot. The kick landed in the pit of the man's stomach and knocked all the breath out of him, but he was a big man and the impact left Jacom floundering as the man he had merely pushed away moved in with deadly intent.

He might have been in trouble had not Merel Zabio moved to intercept his assailant. For a moment he thought that she was being stupidly reckless – especially while she was still limping from her earlier injury – but when he saw that she now held the carving-knife that he had kicked away he remembered that she had lived all her life in the thieves' quarter of Xandria's port. He watched her drive the knife into the man's abdomen, then twist it with all due skill and determination so as to disembowel him. She tried to get the knife out again afterwards, but the man fell forwards and took it with him.

Until he saw that, Jacom had not really thought of what he was engaged in as a 'real fight'. He had thought of it as a struggle between people who might never have been true friends but were not true enemies either – but as soon as he saw the blood and guts come gushing out of the stable-hand's belly he knew that there could be no turning back. Now they had to get away, from Nath's house and from Antiar. Nath's plans were an irrelevance now, and Purkin's too; now it was run or die, and if he had to kill in order to run, he must do it. Phar's precipitousness had committed all of them.

Phar had gone on to grapple with another Antiarian, this one a mere stripling, but Jacom could see that the old man was not as fit or as strong as he probably imagined. Although no one had yet managed to hit him, the exertion of disarming and disabling the man with the axe-handle had taken a greater toll than he had anticipated.

While Jacom parried a pitchfork that was as clumsy a lance as might have been anticipated, simultaneously using the heel of his boot to hammer the shin of someone attempting to get round behind him, Merel had to haul the stripling off and hold him while Phar rammed the axe-handle into his solar plexus. Then Merel had to turn away to wrestle yet another youth. The legacy of her piratical upbringing showed clearly enough in the unceremonious way in which she disposed of him. More people seemed to be arriving by the minute, and Jacom couldn't tell which of them, if any, might be the enemies of his enemies and thus potential allies. Nor, alas, could they.

Jacom dispossessed his own attacker of the pitchfork, and whirled it round in exactly the same way that he had watched Dhalla whirl her javelin. The move did not have anything like the same irresistibility, but it was enough to tumble two of his would-be assailants from their feet. He was now well inside the building, and the stink of horse-shit filled his nostrils, reminding him of home.

'Release the horses!' Jacom howled at Phar, who was limping towards the stalls. His thinking was that a further increase in the confusion could only work to his advantage. For every man he knocked down two more seemed to be springing up, as if out of nowhere, and as he swung the pitchfork back and forth before him in a menacing arc no less than four of them jumped back to avoid the tines. More men were pouring through the wide-flung doors behind him, and he knew that the crowd at the front of the house must have had dozens to spare. No one here was wearing colours, though; every man was likely to be reckoned an enemy by anyone who didn't recognise his face.

Merel came to stand with him, back to back – but whether it was bravery and fellow-feeling that moved her or anxiety that she might be caught by the wild lunges of his pitchfork he couldn't tell. She had a cudgel in each hand now, but she hurled one of them at one of their adversaries, presumably because it was too bulky to be useful to her. It missed – and the dancing men had little difficulty now in avoiding the tines of the pitchfork, having seen exactly what Jacom could do with it.

One of the Antiarians feinted to duck under the flailing implement, and Jacom reflexively followed him – but one of the man's companions was prompt to force the tines right down to the ground, and two of them grabbed at the haft. Jacom had to let the weapon go, but he was nimble enough to kick two of his assailants as he spun away in search of a defensible position and an effective weapon.

His attackers would have cut him down on the instant had they had decent blades, and would have crippled him had they had a quarter of his training, but they had neither. Even so, he knew that his likely lifespan was now to be measured in seconds. Phar's recklessness had led them into a trap from which there seemed to be no escape, and he suspected that there would be no quarter given while there was a man writhing on the ground, still screaming as the blood spurted from the knife-wound that had wreaked havoc in his guts.

There were six men ringing him about now, and Jacom had nothing with which to keep them at bay until Merel pressed her cudgel into his hand. It could not have been enough to hold them back for half a dozen heartbeats – but one of the six was suddenly felled from behind, and then another. Both had been smashed about the head, and they fell so heavily that their companions were instantly convinced that the real danger was now behind them. The four turned as one – and Jacom was on them in a trice, felling one with the cudgel and knocking another to the ground with a kick to the inside of the knee.

There were so many people howling with wrath and pain that the great hollow shed seemed to shake with echoes. Jacom's senses were reeling, although he had no memory of taking a blow to the head. Although his vision blurred momentarily he retained sufficient presence of mind to know that some of the men brawling in front of him must be friends, and must know themselves to be friends, so he suppressed his instinctive urge to lash out at anyone and everyone. As soon as he saw a bronze face he realised how this might be the case; it was not Amyas but he knew that Amyas must be somewhere nearby, and that he must have told his men that not all goldens were alike, and that those who had been prisoners were to be given support. He saw a second bronze face, and a third, and knew that Amyas's entire party must be here, probably every bit as desperate to escape the chaos as he and his companions were.

'Thanks!' Jacom shouted, when he finally picked Amyas out, and was grateful to see a flicker of acknowledgement in the other's dark eyes. He had to grapple with another Antiarian then – a bigger man than most, and one whose obvious terror made him all the more difficult to subdue – but once he had thrown the man to the ground he could find no other adversary nearby.

When the fallen man regained his feet he ran full-tilt for the yawning door rather than take any further part in a fight that was obviously lost, and Jacom had time to turn and take stock. Merel was running into a stall with a saddle over her arm, but Phar had disappeared from view. Amyas came forward with his arm upraised in a gesture of amity.

'No time to talk,' the bronze said. 'Grab what you can and ride for your life. Go south, and don't stop for anything! We'll gather on the road by the inn with the sign of the wide-horned bull – I've men there who can hold it and your sergeant has sent his own men to join them.' He was already running into the gloomy depths of the stable as he shouted the last sentence over his shoulder.

Jacom followed him, thinking that at least he now knew exactly what kind of double-cross Purkin had planned.

Aulakh Phar rode past him as he found a stall whose occupant was not yet being saddled, shouting: 'Come on, you fool! Come *on*!' Jacom couldn't help but take the admonition as a further criticism of his incompetence, and it stung, but he knew better than to pause in order to shout back. He made shift to obey, as quickly as was humanly possible.

When he had finally contrived to get a saddle and bridle on a horse, though, and had drawn the girth-strap tight, he found time to tell himself that, on the whole, he much preferred his own more tentative way of handling diplomatic affairs.

Part Three

Into Unearthly Regions, Urged on by Spurs and Spells

When the ship that sailed the infinite dark made ready to leave, never to return, there were those among the people of the world who became afraid, and said to their makers:

'You might have given us weapons with which to conquer the world in the space of a dozen generations, but you have given us swords and spears instead. You might have built us great cities, but you have destroyed the one which you built for your own use, and left us nothing but a garden. With the makeshift tools you have provided it will take a hundred or a thousand generations for our descendants to fill up the world, and the task of conquest will be a hundred or a thousand times harder than it might have been.'

To these complaints the people of the ship remained deaf, but Goran the Forefather made a reply to those of his companions to whom he trusted the esoteric wisdom.

'You speak of conquering the world,' he said, 'but no such conquest is possible. Some of your descendants will doubtless be ambitious to be emperors, and will not heed the warnings set out in the lore which say that there can be no such thing as an enduring empire, but their dreams will turn to ashes as their bones turn to dust. Again and again your children's children will set forth with armies to subdue and rule their neighbours, and will call themselves conquerors when they do so, but the passage of time will prove them liars.

'Those who invade foreign lands, and who set themselves up as petty tyrants by force of arms, go on to father sons within those foreign lands and thereby mingle their own heritage with that of the people they have conquered; within a dozen generations, the conquerors are no more, for their blood is absorbed, peacefully and unobtrusively, into the blood of the conquered. This is the paradox of conquest: that the heritage of conquerors is always dissolved and dissipated within the heritage of the conquered, to form a new whole.

'It is the same with the world itself. Whether it takes a dozen generations, or a hundred, or a thousand, conquest will turn to dissolution soon enough. The conquest of a world, like the conquest of a nation, is followed as night follows day by absorption and fusion, and the making of a new whole. Conquest and empire are delusions, mere temporary aberrations of the evolutionary process; what endures is what lies on

the far side of conquest, when the differences between the conquerors and the conquered begin to disappear and empires give way to true alliances.

'It would be better by far were the people of the world content to avoid the temptations of conquest, now and tomorrow, for your descendants cannot be conquerors in the fullness of time. What they will become instead cannot be foreseen, for there is no destiny, but they will be far better employed in conserving the wisdom that we leave you than in striving mightily and hopelessly to impose their will upon the world and its indigenes.

'The people of the world owe a debt to Serpents and to Salamanders which you cannot yet repay; the wise among you will cherish and preserve the hope that your remote descendants might be able to make good this debt. If they cannot do that, all their petty conquests will count for nothing at all.'

The Apocrypha of Genesys

I

ANDRIS KNEW AS soon as he woke up that for a long time he had been utterly lost in the vivid wilderness of a wonderful dream, but when he tried to trap the dream in the net of memory it had already escaped.

He remembered instead that someone had told him – a long time ago, before he crossed the Slithery Sea on his long journey to the south – that the human memory actually stored everything, and that it was only the mechanism of recall which was faulty.

'What difference does it make?' his younger self had asked, in that irritatingly brash way that younger selves always had. 'If you can't get it back, it might just as well not be there.'

His elderly informant had replied, in that irritatingly smug way that elderly informants always had: 'It makes all the difference in the world, to the unlucky few who suffer some illness which perfects their mechanisms of recall. *They're* the people who really understand the necessity of forgetfulness.'

Fortunately or unfortunately, his illness had not taken that form, if it had indeed been an illness. He still doubted that, although he was now in a position to recognise that *feeling* well and *being* well were not necessarily the same thing.

He found that he was in a small room, which was brightly illuminated by daylight streaming in through a high window. The walls were neatly painted in pale blue, with hardly a trace of rot in the paint or the plaster. He was lying on a mattress, his naked body covered by a warm blanket. The blanket was one of the best he had ever encountered, woven with great skill and delicacy.

The room had no chair, but there was a strange low stool set in front of the wall opposite the window, to one side of the carefully varnished door. Mounted on the wall above the stool, to the right hand side of the door, was a wooden plus sign half a met across, each of whose arms was ten sems thick. There were words carved into the cross-piece of the symbol and neatly outlined in red; he had to concentrate to bring them into focus, but he only had to read a few before he guessed the rest.

CHANGE AND DECAY IN ALL AROUND I SEE, the inscription said. O THOU, WHO CHANGEST NOT, ABIDE WITH ME.

Deists! Andris though, remembering the building on the outskirts of Khalorn in which he and Burdam Thrid had taken shelter after fleeing from Jacom Cerri's guardsmen – the building which had turned into a trap when Ereleth and Dhalla had found them there, with Checuti, and had made him eat a worm which would have killed him by now if Princess Lucrezia hadn't given him the antidote.

He sat up slowly.

Where am I? he thought. How do I come to be among deists?

He got up from the bed and went to the door of the room, stepping gingerly on the cold flagstoned floor. He didn't open the door more than the tiniest crack, because he didn't want to step outside while he was stark naked. He peeped through the crack into the corridor beyond. There was nothing to be seen except more varnished doors. Some of them stood ajar but not sufficiently to show him anything of the rooms beyond. The corridor was narrow and the only window was at the far end, but there was enough light to show him that its walls were uncommonly well made and well kept.

Andris left his own door ajar and went back to the window. A man of more ordinary size would have had to perch on the stool and then stand on tiptoe to look out, but Andris had no such difficulty.

He found that he was some way above the ground; his was evidently a second storey room. It overlooked a lake, whose waters were not like the waters of any other lake he had ever seen. No waves lapped against its shore, but the waters were not still, and they carried a strange silvery sheen. He knew that this could only be the Lake of Colourless Blood which had been marked on his map. He knew, too, that it was in some peculiar fashion the core – perhaps even the *heart* – of the marsh in which he had been lost for . . .

He didn't know how long he had been lost. He had lost all track of time.

Apart from the waters of the lake there was little enough to be seen. The far shore was a mere green blur, and the building in which he was contained seemed to be set at the very edge of the lake on a promontory jutting out into the water. From this position he could see no gardens, fields or quays. What little he could see of the outer wall of the edifice displayed a rich encrustation of lichens and other parasites which seemed perfectly ordinary, although it contrasted sharply with the rot-free walls within.

The door behind him swung wide open, and he turned, starting with alarm when he saw that the person entering was Princess Lucrezia, fully if rather exotically dressed. He made as if to use his big hands to cover his genitals, but immediately felt embarrassed by his own embarrassment, and contented himself with turning his body back to the wall beneath the window and looking over his shoulder.

Lucrezia was clad in a loose-fitting grey robe tied at the waist with what looked like a piece of silken rope. She was carrying a similar garment over her arm.

'I saw your door open,' she said. 'I thought you might need this.'

She handed him the spare robe, keeping her eyes firmly fixed on his face. The garment was far too small to be comfortable, but once he had the belt secured it served to cover up enough of his body to permit him to turn round. The princess seemed thinner than when he had last seen her – although she had had little flesh to spare even then – but she looked quite well. Her complexion was as rich a gold as he had ever seen, and her dark hair was lustrous and delicately perfumed.

He pointed to the wooden cross and said: 'It seems that we've been taken in by deists.' He felt the need to make it clear to her that he was well-informed as well as mentally capable.

'They found us in the marsh,' Lucrezia agreed, giving no hint as to whether or not she had known what deists were before finding herself here. 'Just in time, they said. I believe them. What's the last thing you remember?'

'I was carrying you,' he said. 'We'd lost the others. I followed the flow . . . the current of the marshwater. I was talking to you –

something about confinement and containment, and how the unearthly ways by which eggs made more eggs were much more complicated and various . . . and then we realised that we'd lost Checuti, and the horses . . . and then . . .' At that point his memory, or its mechanism of recall, failed him.

Lucrezia nodded slowly, as if his vague account matched her own memories well enough. 'They've sent people out to look for Checuti, Ssifuss and Metra,' she said. 'They're not very hopeful. Time's against them, they say, and luck played a considerable part in bringing us to where we were found, even though we were following the current.'

'They?' Andris queried.

'The bronzes,' she told him. 'Ssifuss said there were humans here, remember? They call themselves the Community – which isn't a very helpful description. They all live in this one building. They've some livestock and a few vegetable plots, but they mostly live off the marshes. They say they've inherited an immunity to most of the thorn-poisons from their ancestors, so that they can easily go where other men can't. They seem to think of the marsh as a kind of defensive wall protecting them from the outside world, although it's not entirely clear why they think they need protection. They're pleasant enough, but strange. They say that they're not the bronzes who sold Hyry Keshvara the seeds which she . . . they never leave here, apparently.'

'It seems that all the bronzes we run into deny any connection with Keshvara's seeds,' Andris muttered, although he knew that Lucrezia hadn't yet encountered any others. 'Do they feed us at all?'

'There's a big communal dining-room downstairs,' she said. 'I'll show you.'

He followed her out of the room and along the corridor. The broad staircase which led down to the lower storey was made of wood, which had been as carefully varnished as the doors. The deists seemed to place a very high value on neatness and order.

A bronze dressed in a robe exactly like the one that Andris wore was working on the banisters, applying some kind of liquid with such minute concentration that he didn't bother to look up until Andris and the princess reached the step on which he crouched. When he did condescend to glance up, however, his eyes were possessed by a sudden start of astonishment which Andris found perversely satisfying. Presumably, the man had never seen an amber before – nor, in all likelihood, anyone of Andris's generous proportions. Lucrezia nodded politely to the staring man, but said nothing. Andris glanced back as they reached the bottom of the flight, and saw that he was still looking after them in the same wide-eyed manner.

'He obviously didn't see me when I was brought in,' Andris remarked.

'They've only just got used to me,' Lucrezia said.

'How long have you been up and about?' he inquired.

'Two days,' she replied.

'*Two days*! How long have we been here?'

'They managed to rouse me soon enough after they'd administered antidotes to the poisons I'd taken in,' she said. 'You seem to have preserved me from my fair share of stings and scratches while you carried me, as well as sparing me the exhaustion you inflicted upon yourself. You weren't unconscious when they brought me back to my senses – Venerina said that you probably hadn't slept in three days – but you were out of your mind, muttering away about blood and chimeras and "life's endless game". I thought at first that you might be too far gone for the antidotes to take effect, but . . .'

While Lucrezia had been speaking they had come into the big dining-room which she had mentioned. It was, in fact, a bigger room than any Andris had ever seen before, although he suspected that he might have seen larger ones had his excursions within the citadel of Xandria not been so severely limited. The wooden floor was beautifully waxed, and the surface sheen was in the process of being renewed by a team of three bronzes, one of them an old crone and one of them a boy of some two and a half years. The seven long tables which filled the middle of the room were equally well-kept.

'But what?' Andris prompted, when Lucrezia left off.

She made no attempt to take up the thread of her narration. An old man – even older than Aulakh Phar, if appearances could be trusted – was eagerly scurrying towards them.

'Andris Myrasol!' the old man said, raising his bony hand in what was presumably a kind of salute. 'I'm delighted to see you recovered. Lucrezia has told me so much about you. I'm Philemon Taub. Call me Philemon.'

Andris noted that the old man didn't refer to her as Princess Lucrezia, and guessed that she must be sticking to her resolve to be a princess no longer. He raised his own hand, in an awkwardly half-hearted greeting, and then turned aside as Lucrezia beckoned him to a chair.

'I'll fetch you some water, Andris,' she said. The studied neutrality of her tone suggested that she was not particularly pleased to see the old man, and he wondered what she had been about to tell him when they were interrupted. He decided that it couldn't have been a matter of any real urgency, or she'd have told him when she had the chance. She'd had plenty of time to issue warnings if warnings needed to be issued.

'Fetch wine, not water!' the old man said. 'Tell the kitchen-boys to heat some broth before the fire, and bring some pudding too. The man's half-starved, in spite of all that I managed to spoon into him before he consented to be quiet!'

'I'd like some water as well as some wine,' Andris said, deciding that such generosity would certainly extend a little further. 'Thirst first, taste when haste be done, as we say in Ferentina.'

'Ferentina!' the wizened little man exclaimed, as Lucrezia moved away. 'That's in the far north, isn't it?'

It was Andris's turn to be astonished. In Xandria, which was closer by far to his homeland than this desolate place, hardly anyone had ever heard of Ferentina. 'Do you have mapmakers here?' he asked.

'No mapmakers, alas,' the old man replied regretfully, 'but we do have a few maps, which our copyists take care to preserve. We have very little parchment, unfortunately, but we do have turtle-shells and etching-needles, and we are very assiduous in the preservation of our heritage of inscription. We rarely entertain visitors from the world beyond the marsh, but we maintain our knowledge of that world as best we can. We know where Ferentina is, and Xandria – and Salamander's Fire!'

The old man took the seat next to Andris, pulling it even closer as he sat down. Although they were the only ones sitting at a table with sixteen chairs set about it, Andris felt curiously crowded by Philemon's insistent proximity.

'You must have tended me well while I was raving,' Andris said, flexing his muscles to test the fitness of his limbs. 'I'm hungry, but otherwise very well. The poisons don't seem to have affected me as badly as my companions – I felt drunk but never sick.'

'The syrup of the thorns doesn't always affect human flesh the same way,' Philemon told him. 'Some are resistant to it, some find it not unpleasant. The fools who live in the east think the marsh an evil place, but it can be benign to those who can accept its gifts – as you've clearly begun to do. For those who can understand its call, the spirit of the waters is the fountainhead of revelation.'

'Revelation?' Andris echoed in bewilderment. To cover his confusion he pointed to the huge wooden plus sign which was the dining-room's principal decoration. 'You're deists, aren't you?' he said.

The old man laid a gnarled hand on Andris's wrist. 'We're all the children of God,' he said. 'It's just that some of us find it easier to hear His voice than others. Have no fear, my friend – you're among your own kind now. You've found your destiny.'

Andris managed to prevent himself from blurting out a blunt denial. It wasn't that he thought it necessary to be economical with the truth, rather that he didn't want to disappoint the old man. He couldn't help remembering the strange tale which another old man had told him while he contemplated the various kinds of rot that were devouring the Wayfaring Tree. *There is no destiny* had been that old man's refrain; clearly, the blind beggar and Philemon Taub weren't two of a kind.

Lucrezia emerged from a side door bearing a laden tray. There was a woman with her who looked to be about twenty, but was handsome for her age. Bronze skin didn't seem to show the lines of age as conspicuously as the fairer shades; even the conspicuously white-haired Philemon didn't seem to be as wrinkly as most goldens of thirty were.

'I'm Venerina Sirelis,' the handsome woman said, as Lucrezia laid down the tray. 'I'm glad to see that you've recovered so completely, Andris. You were fortunate not to have been picked off by crocolids or snappers – they don't usually attack moving targets, but if you'd stopped for any length of time while the spirit was upon you – well, it's good that you're such a big man, and so full of courage. God saw the spirit of the waters in you, and He protected you. You, in your turn, saved the lady's life.'

Andris nodded in reluctant acknowledgement of these curious congratulations before draining a cup of water to the dregs. He picked up the wooden spoon which had been set beside a bowl of broth.

'The pudding's coming,' Lucrezia said to Philemon as the old man opened his mouth to protest. 'Even Andris can only eat one thing at a time.'

'It wasn't courage,' Andris said uncertainly, speaking between mouthfuls. 'I can't really take credit for saving Lucrezia's life. I didn't know what I was doing. If I had, I wouldn't have lost the others. I failed them.'

'We have people out looking for them,' Venerina Sirelis assured him. 'If they had the sense to follow one of the main streams, as you did, they'll be coming this way. All the streams north-east of the river lead towards the lake.'

'It was courage,' Lucrezia put it. 'Even if you didn't know what you were doing. I stand in your debt again, Andris – perhaps deeper than before.'

Andris slurped thick broth from the spoon, and wondered whether his poisoned mind had confused the princess with Merel, or whether it had caused him to reach out for the thing that most resembled her. *It could have been worse*, he thought. *If I'd tried to carry Checuti, I'd probably have collapsed long before help reached us*.

'We've come a long way,' he said aloud. 'I suppose I'd got into the habit of carrying on no matter what, through injury and all manner of alarms.'

'Lucrezia explained your mission,' the woman said.

Andris cocked an eyebrow at the princess, in case she might want to warn him with some unobtrusive signal that the explanation she had given was less than honest. Her face remained serene.

'I'm not sure I could have explained it,' Andris said, not because he still had his guard up but because it was true. 'I got caught up in it by accident. Lucrezia's the one with the mission – I'm just a hired hand.'

'That's not so,' Philemon said. 'You're under guidance, just as she is – just as we all are, although precious few of us know it.

Don't fight the spirit of the waters, Andris. It's the most precious thing in the world, to those who can hear its voice.'

Andris looked at him blankly, unable to think of anything to say in reply to that.

'He doesn't understand yet, Philemon,' said the woman gently. 'He doesn't know what's happening, to himself or to the world. It's as well that you came to us, Andris. We can tell you a great deal that you need to know.'

Again Andris looked quizzically at Lucrezia. This time, he was surprised to observe, she looked annoyed rather than serene. She didn't seem to like the way that Venerina Sirelis was talking to him. Was she afraid of something? Or did she resent the implication that he was somehow more important than she was?

'I'm sorry, but I think you're assuming too much,' Andris said, as much to take the pressure off himself as to assauge her resentment. 'I'm not a deist. I really don't have any idea what you're talking about.'

'You'll understand soon enough,' the woman said, with a confidence that he found oddly insulting. 'Whether you know it or not, you're a deist at heart. The day will soon come when the truth will be manifest to everyone. We feel it in the waters, we see it in the skies. The day is coming, and everything is about to change.'

2

As far as Carus Fraxinus could tell, it would hardly have been possible for Salamanders to speak human language even if they had had an opportunity to learn it. Their wide mouths were almost lipless and their tongues were much thicker and much less flexible than Serpents' tongues, so their ability to imitate human phonemes was severely restricted. The sounds which they used for communication between themselves were formed in their throats, which were capable of considerable inflation, and modulated by vocal cords that had little in common with human vocal cords. These meaningful sounds emerged as a staccato series of croaks and clicks, few of which sounded remotely human save for those which seemed distantly akin to laboured snoring.

Having had the opportunity to observe these differences at first hand, Fraxinus soon ceased to wonder why humans knew so little about the lives and folkways of Salamanders. Elementary sign-language would doubtless have served to facilitate barter between human merchants and Salamanders, but it was not obvious that Salamanders had anything much to sell that humans might be interested in buying or that Salamanders had any particular need of what humans had to sell. If a Salamander had indeed brought a precious gift to the makers of Idun, it was difficult to imagine why, although it was all too easy to understand why the literal or metaphorical coin they had been offered in return had been difficult to spend.

The Salamanders which Fraxinus's party had found under threat from hellhounds did not seem at all displeased by the arrival of so many strangers, but they didn't seem profoundly grateful, perhaps being of the opinion that they were not in any real danger and stood in no dire need of rescue. They were ready enough to share the bounty of the fallen floaters with the newcomers, even to the extent of eating from a common pot. Afterwards, they were perfectly willing to head south with the wagon, having been bound in that direction anyway. They were not averse to taking turns to ride in the back of the wagon, thus to rest their huge and heavily armoured feet. When it came to conversation, however, they could hardly be bothered to make any kind of effort.

Fraxinus couldn't altogether blame them for their reluctance. The only possible channel of communication involved Mossassor. Although the Serpent couldn't pronounce the syllables of the Salamander language, nor they the syllables of its, it could decipher some of the meaning of their utterances and they some of the meaning of its. This was not because Mossassor had ever had any extensive dealing with Salamanders in the past, but rather because of some mysterious kinship in the languages themselves which Mossassor could neither specify nor explain. This kinship was undoubtedly fortunate, but Fraxinus couldn't help thinking that it was a mixed blessing, not only because the Serpent and the Salamanders never seemed certain that they really did understand what they were saying to one another, but also because Mossassor's understanding of human language was far more limited than it could have wished.

When they did attempt to talk, while camped for the midday or the midnight, the Salamanders had to address Mossassor in a different – and presumably more restricted – version of their own tongue than they used among themselves, and Mossassor had to do likewise. Mossassor had to translate the Salamanders' statements into its own limited version of human language, and then translate Fraxinus's questions and observations into the restricted version of its own tongue which the Salamanders could follow. It was very obvious that a great deal was getting lost in translation, but Fraxinus tried as hard as he could to be grateful for the little that wasn't.

From the moment he first sat down with them around a cooking-fire – which they had lit, using materials which could not have been easy to find – Fraxinus was able to observe that the Salamanders had a very casual way with fire. They were not at all wary of the heat, and he got the impression that if they had not had their iron toasting-forks they might simply have held their deflated floaters between their fingers and put their hands into the flames. Their outer teguments were obviously as well-armoured against burning as they were against the sharp edges of the tiny sand-particles on which they could walk or sit without the least discomfort.

Perhaps, Fraxinus thought, as he noticed this fact while trying hard to make himself comfortable on the inhospitable ground, *that kind of fire is reckoned by them to be common fire, of an essentially trivial nature. Perhaps the phrase 'Salamander's fire' was invented to describe something different, in degree if not in kind.*

Fraxinus asked the crouching Mossassor to enquire as to where the Salamanders were bound, but if they understood its question it did not understand their answer.

'Perhaps you'd better tell them where we're bound,' Fraxinus suggested. 'Never mind the why of it, for now. Let's stick to simple matters until we've got things going.'

'Yess,' said the Serpent. 'Will do ssat.'

The Salamander spokeman's response to the news that the wagon was headed for Salamander's Fire seemed to go on for a considerable time, and Mossassor did not seem totally confident about its ability to follow it. After a couple of brief exchanges which were presumably attempts at clarification the Serpent turned back to Fraxinus with a slightly quizzical air.

'Ssalamanderss ssay that Ssalamander'ss Fire iss ssafe, itss defenderss sstrong. Ssay ssey ssemsselvess never go ssere, but ssat ssere are Ssalamanderss in Crysstal Ssity . . . not word I know. Like healer, but to do with wissdom. Ssey will assk for uss, I ssink.'

'Do you mean that they'll ask these wise ones to take us to Salamander's Fire?' Fraxinus asked.

'Ssink sso.' The Serpent turned back to the Salamander and made another long speech in its own sibilant tongue. The speech the Salamander made in return was even longer.

'I try to ssay what we are doing,' Mossassor explained to Fraxinus. 'I ssay we ssearssh for garden, need humanss wiss Sserpent'ss blood and Ssalamander'ss fire, need Ssalamander too. Ssey ssay ssey don't undersstand, but have heard wisse oness ssay ssat time of sshangess is near. Time for Ssalamander'ss fire to burn . . . I ssink nearesst word iss *brave*.'

'You mean *hot*,' Ereleth put in.

Mossassor shook its head vigorously. '*Not* hot,' it said. 'Hot ssomessing different. Burn *brave* is besst I can ssay.'

'As you've often pointed out,' Fraxinus reminded her, 'the phrase *Salamander's fire* is used among humans as a metaphor for courage. Perhaps the concept of courage is being employed here as a metaphor for something else.' *But how differently can fires burn, save for the heat they put out?* he wondered.

'What can they tell us about this *time of changes*?' Ereleth asked the Serpent, ignoring Fraxinus. 'Do they have a clearer notion of what it involves than you do?'

Mossassor did not take offence at the references to the extreme vagueness of its ideas regarding the kind of change which had begun to overtake the world. It was probably as anxious as she and Fraxinus were to obtain a clearer picture.

Again, the Salamander's reply to this enquiry went on and on; again Mossassor had to ask for parts to be repeated or rephrased. Fraxinus tried to control his impatience, and conserve his optimism that the end result might be worthwhile.

'Ssalamanderss ssay iss time of emergensse,' Mossassor reported, at last. 'Time when ssings in – not word I know – perhapss risse up. I ssink ssey are talking about Chimera'ss Cradle, but ssey ssay *cradle* iss not right. Not birss but sshangess. Ssay ssome Sserpentss musst go ssee, and Ssalamander wisse oness, and humanss – ssee and learn – but ssay iss very dangerouss. Ssey ssemsselvess will not go to Ssalamander'ss Fire, let alone Chimera'ss Cradle. Ssay . . . very difficult to undersstand, but I ssink time of sshangess alsso time to go down, maybe go under. Ssingss emerge and ssingss . . . what iss oppossite of *emerge*?'

Fraxinus frowned in concentration. 'Are the floaters things which have emerged?' he asked, after a pause. 'Was the blight which destroyed the Dragomite Hills also a product of this unique time of emergence?'

This time the exchange of ideas was not quite so complicated. 'Ssink sso,' Mossassor reported hesitantly, after consulting the Salamander spokesman, presumably intending the affirmative answer to apply to both questions.

'How long is it since the last *time of emergence*?' Ereleth asked abruptly. 'How often do they occur?'

Fraxinus knew that Ereleth must have only a partial understanding, at best, of the secret commandments to which she was heir, but that she must now be trying hard to link the content of those secret commandments to what the Salamanders called a *time of emergence*. Her question was apparently an easy one for Mossassor to translate, but translating the answer back wasn't so easy.

'Not ssure,' Mossassor said. 'Long time, hard to count. Not sso little as eight timess eight generassionss. Eight timess eight timess eight, maybe.'

Fraxinus had already observed that the Salamanders had three fingers and a thumb on each hand, and four vestigial toes on each huge and rounded foot. It made sense that their numbering system would be based on eights rather than tens. 'That's about five hundred generations,' he translated for Ereleth's benefit, after some quick mental arithmetic. To Mossassor he said: 'How long is a Salamander generation in years?'

Mossassor relayed that question back to the Salamanders. Their spokesman seemed to make unnecessarily heavy weather of the explanation, and Fraxinus was not entirely surprised when Mossassor eventually said: 'Ssomessing odd about ssiss. You ssay human generassion iss about twelve yearss, no? Iss time between hatsshing of female persson and middle of range of agess at whissh female persson produssess sshildren?' Fraxinus had previously given Mossassor an elaborate account of human reproductive cycles while trying to obtain information about Serpent reproduction; it seemed that the Serpent remembered what it had been told, but that it was having as much difficulty translating this information for the Salamanders' benefit as it had had in explaining the reproductive affairs of its own species.

'That's close enough,' Fraxinus confirmed, not wanting to get into a detailed discussion of the concept of averages.

'Iss not like ssat with Sserpentss, ass I ssay. Ssalamanderss musst be different too, ssough not sse ssame ass Sserpentss. No ssexess in eisser sspeciess . . . Ssalamanderss not understand your generassionss at all. I ssink time ssey are talking about iss ssomessing like ssixteen yearss, but not ssure.'

'In other words,' Fraxinus said, 'they think that these times of emergence occur every eight thousand years or so.'

'Not ssure,' Mossassor said hesitantly. 'Sssometimess less, ssometimess more, even if ansswer iss near.'

'Ask it if it knows how many times of emergence there have been since humans first came to the world,' Ereleth said.

Mossassor attempted to relay this question. This time, the Salamanders conferred with one another before the spokesman offered an answer, and the reply seemed to be inordinately long drawn out.

'Don't know,' Mossassor finally reported back. 'Ssalamanderss not ass good at forgetting ass Sserpentss, becausse do not have to be, but not sso good at remembering very disstant passt. Ssey ssink not sso many ass eight, but not ssertain. More ssan ssree, ssey ssink.'

'Very helpful,' Ereleth muttered.

'How much does our lore have to say about it?' Fraxinus murmured in reply. He was fairly certain that Ereleth's lore didn't include any clear statement as to how many times the secret commandments had been put into operation before, nor any judgement as to the results of their previous invocations. He had tried to get a coherent explanation out of Mossassor as to why Serpents allegedly had to be good at forgetting, but Mossassor hadn't been able to put it into human words. He didn't suppose that there was any chance at all of getting a fuller explanation of why Salamanders didn't have to, at least from Mossassor. It seemed to be time to return to matters of more immediate practicality.

'Will these Salamanders take us to the Crystal City?' he asked, by way of confirmation. 'Will they speak on our behalf to those who might guide us safely to Salamander's Fire?'

That seemed to be easy enough to get across.

'Yess, ssey have ssaid sso,' said Mossassor. 'Ssey ssee no difficulty. Defenssess of Ssalamander'ss Fire not to keep uss out.'

Fraxinus couldn't resist the temptation to ask who the defences which were keeping Salamander's Fire safe were intended to keep out, but he wasn't in the least surprised when Mossassor had to take a great deal more trouble eliciting a comprehensible answer.

Finally, Mossassor said: 'Iss not clear. Not old enemiess . . . but Ssalamander'ss Fire pressiouss, even when it burns . . . I ssink *meekly*. Ssertainly not *cold*, or *weak* . . . difficult. Anyhow, musst be guarded, in casse of trouble. More difficult to rebuild Ssalamander'ss Fire than regenerate Dragomite Hillss, ssey ssay. In time of sshangess, sstrange ssingss happen. Ssmall ssingss can desstroy.'

Fraxinus could see that it wasn't going to be easy to share the wisdom of the Salamanders who could be found at the Crystal City and might then take him to Salamander's Fire. On the other hand, lack of understanding didn't seem to be hurting his chances of obtaining a measure of co-operation. These Salamanaders seemed at least as friendly as the Serpents Hyry had recruited to their cause – a good deal friendlier, if Ssifuss rather than Mossassor were taken as the standard of comparison.

As he walked back to the wagon with Ereleth, leaving Mossassor behind to continue the discussion to the best of its ability, the queen said: 'At least they're not as slow-witted as they are slow-moving. Perhaps they'll have better translators in the Crystal City.'

'I doubt it,' Fraxinus said. 'But if their wise ones really are wise we may be able to make better use of the one we have. We must keep talking to Mossassor as much as possible, to improve its understanding of our language, but if Salamanders are better at preserving their own lore, for whatever reason, we might find out a great deal more about what's going on, at Salamander's Fire if not the Crystal City.'

'We might,' Ereleth agreed, putting a sceptical stress on the second word. 'But if the wisdom that was handed down to me can be trusted, we still need to get the princess back before we proceed to Chimera's Cradle, and we need help from the right kind of Serpents as well as the right kind of Salamanders. For all Mossassor's willingness, I'm not sure it's the right kind.'

'Until we can begin to figure out how many kinds of Serpents and Salamanders there are, and what the differences are between them, that particular item of arcane wisdom's no more use than all the rest,' Fraxinus retorted. 'In fact, it's difficult to see how it counts as wisdom at all, when a straightforward explanation of what these times of changes involve, and why they're so important, would be infinitely more useful.'

'If a straightforward explanation were infinitely more useful,' Ereleth retorted, 'that's surely what we'd have – always provided that it's possible to formulate one.'

Fraxinus looked at her sharply, but he knew that she must be right. Given that the lore – even the lore of Genesys itself – contained no explicit explanation of the crises which sometimes overtook the world, one of two things must surely be true. Either it was impossible to make such an explanation understandable, given the limits of human language, or there was some reason why such an explanation would be of no practical value at all.

Neither of those alternatives seemed particularly palatable, and it suddenly occurred to him that if the second were the true one, the possibilities which lay ahead of him might be far more horrific than he had previously imagined. Some of Mossassor's uneasily translated words, to which he had not paid overmuch attention at the time, now came back to mind: *Ssay ssome Sserpentss musst go ssee, and Ssalamander wisse oness, and humanss – ssee and learn – but ssay iss very dangerouss. Ssey ssemsselvess will not go to Ssalamander'ss Fire, let alone Chimera'ss Cradle.*

Who, if that were so, were really the *wise ones*? Might it not be the case that the wisest ones of all were the ones who stayed well away from Chimera's Cradle during a 'time of emergence', while those who were determined to head straight for it, whether lured by secret commandments or by mere curiosity, might better be reckoned mad and reckless fools?

3

LUCREZIA FOUND ANDRIS sitting by the shore of the lake, at the junction where the meandering river flowed into it. The river was presumably the same one which had flowed much more vigorously beneath the bridge where Shabir's army had attacked them, but it was much tamer and far more alien here.

Andris seemed much more sober now but he had by no means returned to what was, at least in her inexpert estimation, his normal state of being. His exposure to the marsh and its poisons had changed him, and by some means which they had not deigned to explain to her – and for some reason she could not fathom at all – the deists of the Community had taken great care not to reverse that change. Whatever medicines they had fed him had not had the same effect as the antidotes which they had given her. Unfortunately, she didn't know whether she could explain this to him, or what his response would be, or what his present frame of mind might be.

She sat down beside him, and looked out over the glittering surface of the lake, following the direction of his pensive gaze. While they were in the marshes Lucrezia had never been entirely certain whether the glow which the water manifested at night was anything more than reflected starlight, but there seemed little doubt about it now. The water close to the edge of the lake was relatively quiet despite the river's inflow, and the glimmer which lay upon it was subtle, but out towards the centre it was perfectly obvious that the light mist which stood upon the rippling surface was illuminated from below as well as from above.

'This mist seems to absorb the starlight,' Lucrezia pointed out to him, 'but not the light from below. The starlight diffuses into a crowd of little sparks, but the light from the lake fills the mist and sets its bottom layers aglow. Have you ever seen anything like it on your travels?'

'No,' Andris replied. 'Nothing at all.'

She had expected to find the ground muddy, or moist at least, but it was quite dry and firm beneath her buttocks. 'Has Philemon finally bored you half to death?' she asked. She knew that she must sound slightly resentful, although she had not actually been sent away by the old man. Nor had Philemon made any strenuous attempt to imply that he would rather have Andris to himself.

'He wants to take me out on to the lake in a boat,' Andris told her. 'He wants to show me something – it can only be seen by night, apparently.'

'The spirit of the waters, no doubt,' she said sarcastically.

'I tried to get him to explain that, but he wouldn't,' Andris said. 'He seems to think that it'll become clear to me in due time – that it's something that doesn't need to be explained, and perhaps can't be. Surely you must have quizzed him about it during the last two days?'

'I certainly did,' she told him, remembering her frustrating attempts to extract some sense from Philemon or Venerina Sirelis all too clearly. 'He doesn't seem to expect me to grasp it at all. You're the one who's infected by it, it seems – and I fear that infected might be the right word.'

'What do you mean?' he asked, although he seemed to have his suspicions already.

'You must be careful of these people, Andris,' she said softly. 'They seemed to be searching for signs of some strange enlightenment in your delirium, and I fear that they found them. They seem to me to be more interested in bringing the effect of the thorn-poisons on you to some mysterious pitch of clarity, rather than cancelling out their effects as they did with me. I think they hope and believe that you might join them.'

'There's no chance of that,' Andris told her, though not firmly enough to reassure her as to the strength of his determination. 'I've got to find Merel.'

'There's something very strange about these people, Andris,' she went on, trying to get her point home without any undue vehemence. 'I'm not sure exactly what kind of god they worship, or how, but I'm not sure I can believe their claim to be immune to the marsh's poisons. I think they use them as drugs, and that they're perpetually in a state of stabilised delirium. Andris, you must be careful about letting them feed you more poison. We have to get away from here as soon as possible.'

'What about Checuti? What about Jume Metra and Ssifuss, come to that? It's my fault they're still out there, lost.' His voice was harsh, but she didn't know how to interpret the harshness.

'No it's not,' she told him flatly. 'It's nobody's fault that we became separated. We were all out of our minds.'

'So we were,' he said unhappily.

She wasn't at all sure that she was getting through to him, and she didn't know what to say next. In the end she decided to try to keep things light and neutral, and to observe his reactions. 'Am I invited to see whatever it is you're going to look for?' she asked.

'Of course you are,' Andris said. She suspected that Philemon had issued no such invitation, but she let it pass.

'Philemon seemed to be asking you a lot of questions, considering that you'd just woken up after a very long sleep,' she observed. 'Should I have stopped him, do you think?'

'I can look after myself,' he assured her. After a pause, he added: 'He asked me about what happened in the Dragomite Hills – what I saw in the depths of the nest. I suppose he must have become curious when they found that head in my backpack. Did they ask you about it?'

'I told them where you got it,' she said. 'That's all. Do they know how to attach it to a new body?'

'I don't think so,' he said.

They both continued to stare out over the water. The mist obscured the far horizon, so it seemed that the sky and the lake faded into one another at the limit of vision. The light emitted by the turbid water and trapped by the mist was so bright that it would have been easy to believe – had she known no better – that the sky was a reflection of the lake, the stars mere scintilla flickering in the depths of a dark, curved looking-glass. It was beautiful, and Lucrezia was glad to have the leisure to appreciate it, but she couldn't shake the suspicion that something was wrong and she wished that she were better placed to figure out what Andris might be thinking.

'I meant what I said inside,' she said, in a low tone. 'You saved my life, and I'm grateful – all the more so because of . . . well, you know.'

'I meant what I said, too,' he assured her in his turn, 'but I can't claim any credit for it. As you say, I was out of my mind.' He stressed the word *was* a little too heavily, but that wasn't why the words stung her and intensified her anxiety.

'Does that mean that if you had known what you were doing you'd have dropped me and left me to die?' she asked dully.

'Well, no,' he admitted. She wondered why it was something he had to admit rather than proclaiming it proudly.

She paused for a long time then, hoping that he might say something more, but in the end she decided to try a different tack.

'Everything I know about human males,' she said ruminatively, 'is based on hearsay. When I was growing up in the sanctum, I saw them only at a distance, but they were an obsessively frequent topic of conversation among my sisters and mothers. I was aware of them, of course. I knew that Jacom Cerri and the other guard-captains paused in their patrols at the vantage-points which allowed them to look into my garden – and sometimes, when they looked, I'd look back, across a gap forty or fifty mets wide and six stories deep. The only men I saw at close quarters, before I got mixed up in Checuti's robbery, were a couple of ancient slaves requisitioned by Ereleth for the purpose of making practical demonstrations in the course of my education as a witch. The first living man I ever knowingly touched, except for my father, was Checuti. He saved my life too, you know. He was kind, in spite of the fact that he had every reason to think of me as an enemy.'

'According to Merel,' Andris said, seemingly quite willing and able to indulge himself in idle reminiscence, 'he was always very careful about his reputation. He was always prepared to send Burdam Thrid and his bully boys out to break a few legs or a few heads, but he was very punctilious about letting it be known that he was a fair man, and a man who could be trusted by people of his own stripe. He'd tell you that it was just good business practice, of course – not something he'd claim credit for.'

'But he'd be lying, wouldn't he?' Lucrezia said, carefully refraining from adding: *Just like you.*

Andris shrugged. 'According to Merel,' he said, 'it was all just a game to him. He played hard, of course, and he played well . . . but at the end of the day it was just play. He genuinely preferred not to hurt people. When Jacom's men tried to trap him at that farm, when he risked everything he'd won because he was curious to talk to me . . . even then, he took delight in gambling, in playing Jacom along. Jacom hasn't quite forgiven Checuti for making a fool of him – but I don't think Jacom's ever sat down to consider what the alternative would have been. A lot of men could have ended up dead.'

'After Checuti, of course,' Lucrezia went on, reverting to the original course of her train of thought, 'I was with Hyry until the day before I was stung by the dragomite drone. A brief encounter with Djemil Eyub . . . and then, after the confusion in the nest, I met Carus Fraxinus, and you, and Jacom Cerri, and Checuti again, and Aulakh Phar. To me, you were all as alien as the dragomites – *exactly* as alien as the dragomites. Creatures of legend suddenly revealed in startling detail. Can you understand that?'

'It can't have been that startling,' Andris muttered.

'What I'm trying to establish,' she went on patiently, 'is that this entire adventure has been utterly strange to me – much stranger, I think, than it has been to you. There are so many things that you can take for granted and I can't. Do you see?'

Andris shrugged again. 'So what?' he said.

'So,' she said, in a determinedly level tone, 'I'm a little bit out of my depth here. I don't know what's going on, and there's something about Philemon and Venerina and their Community which makes me very uneasy, but I don't know how seriously I can take my own anxious feelings, or how far I can trust my intuitions. Oh, filth – what I'm trying to find out is whether we're still on the same side . . . and you saying that you don't want any credit for saving my life, and that you only did it because you were out of your mind, and speaking to me all the time as if you're on guard, isn't much help. I know you don't have any cause to like me, and I know I couldn't really blame you after what I planned to do with you when you were thrown in jail back in Xandria, but I do need to know where we stand.'

He had no alternative then but to turn and look at her, and he did. She was glad to see that he seemed perfectly sane, and genuinely concerned.

'I'm sorry,' he said, biting back the word *highness* just in time. 'I didn't realise. You're right – we do need to be sure of one another, although I really don't think these people mean us any harm. As far as I'm concerned, we're on the same side, not just because we happen to be heading in the same direction, but because . . . well, because we *are* on the same side. I want to go to Salamander's Fire because there's a chance – however slight – that I'll find Merel there . . . but I also want to go to Salamander's Fire with you, for your reasons . . . and if and when we get there, we'll decide where to go next together, along with anyone else who makes it. That other business is forgotten. It's behind us; it no longer counts. I can't say that I'm overfond of witches as a species, or with what they do by way of practising their skills, but I don't hold any grudges about nearly being caught up in it.'

Before she could reply, he went on: 'And you're right about our hosts, to some extent. There is something weird about them, and it's not just your unfamiliarity with the world that's making you think so. They did save both our lives, though. I think they're good people. Perhaps they expect something from me which I can't provide, either because I walked so far through the marsh without falling over, or because of something I happened to say while I was raving, but . . . well, they'll be—'

At that moment, Philemon Taub came bustling out of the shadows that surrounded the huge building which housed the Community and Andris immediately fell silent. Lucrezia couldn't be sure whether or not the old man had overhead the last few sentences of Andris's speech.

'There you are!' Philemon said. 'You should be at the jetty, back this way. The boat's ready and waiting.'

'I'm sorry,' Andris said. 'We'll come now.' As he stood up he extended a hand to help Lucrezia to her feet, and she took it gratefully. She noticed that he had carefully stressed the word *we* – but the old man gave not the slightest indication that he would rather have Andris to himself.

Philemon led them around the side of the house to a wooden jetty, where a slender-nosed and shallow-bellied boat was tethered. There was a young man sitting in it, gripping two long oars.

'This is Rayner,' Philemon said.

'I can row,' Andris told him.

'I don't doubt it,' the old man replied, 'but you need to rebuild your strength, and there's a particular knack to rowing in this kind of water. Rayner is good at it, and he's a strong lad. That's right, lady – just step down and take a seat.'

Lucrezia had not waited for the instruction; she had already clambered down. The boat swayed as she took her place, and drifted away from the jetty, but Andris had no difficulty bridging the resultant gap. Once he was safely aboard he reached out to help the old man, and then sat down next to Lucrezia, facing the oarsman. Philemon had no choice but to take the seat behind them. Rayner cast off, and with a few deft strokes of the oar he took them away from the quay and out into open water.

Philemon was right; the youth was good at his job. The boat slid smoothly across the mirror-like surface of the lake, buoyed up by the turgor of the viscous fluid. The mist soon swallowed them up, but it did not seem nearly so dense from within. Once they had left the shore behind it seemed that they were in a circle of clear water some twenty mets in diameter.

Lucrezia looked up at the stars, which shone brightly enough through the vaporous air, although their light seemed remarkably unsteady. There was little sensation of movement as Rayner skilfully plied the oars.

'As above, so below,' Philemon said to her, having noticed that she was looking upwards. Lucrezia assumed that he was referring to the play of the light, and she leaned over the side of the boat so that she could compare the streaming stars with their counterparts beneath the surface of the lake.

From their station on the shore, Philemon's comment would have seemed apt enough, but it did not seem nearly so apt at close quarters. It was obvious to Lucrezia that the light which shone beneath the surface of the lake was far more diffuse than the light of the stars; it was not emitted by point sources but by the entire body of the 'water' – which no longer looked like water at all.

Lucrezia remembered looking into the semi-transparent body of the turtle which Ssifuss had caught, seeing the faint outlines of its organs and the movement of its coloured blood through its veins. It was easy enough to imagine the Lake of Colourless

Blood as a vast organism whose confining shell had somehow been removed, leaving its delicate softness exposed. While riding through the marsh she had been vaguely aware of the currents flowing within it, but she had not been able to *see* those currents even by starlight. Now she could see the movement of fluids within the body of the lake – within the soft *flesh* of the lake, as it seemed from this viewpoint. These streams did not flow within vessels like veins and arteries any more than the lake itself was confined by a crystal shell, but they were nevertheless distinct – and notwithstanding the lake's given name, they were marked out by faint colours as well as by luminosity, limned in very pale pinks and subtle pastel blues.

Lucrezia could see, too, that there were structures in the body of the lake: not solid structures, but structures nevertheless. She was fairly certain that they had the semi-solidity of a gel or a colloid, but she couldn't be certain that they weren't simply entities of more viscous liquid, like droplets of oil suspended in water. The streams within the body of the lake flowed through as well as between these 'structures', but they remained respectful of their integrity.

There were genuinely solid entities in the lake too, but they were much tinier than the vaguer structures, and they too seemed respectful of the organisation of the medium in which they swam. Lucrezia picked out the glassy turtles easily enough, although she couldn't be sure at first which of them were large creatures seen at a distance and which were smaller ones swimming nearer to the surface. She saw brightly scaled snakes too, of a kind which she had never seen in the marshes, and in the murkier depths she caught shadowy glimpses of less translucent things, which she assumed to be crocolids and their kin. But these weren't the only kinds of swimmers, nor even the most common.

The longer she stared into the depths the easier it became to pick out less substantial creatures – which might not have been creatures at all, in the strict sense. There were globular entities and things like uprooted plants, with petal-like tentacles at one end and root-like processes at the other. There were creatures like urns and bottles, some surrounded by cilia and others mounted with long oarlike or whiplike propellers. There were creatures like the heads of mushrooms, trailing vast numbers of tentacles behind and below, which seemed to swim by exhaling jets of water. Many of these were so lacking in solidity as to be as insubstantial as the vast 'organs' of the lake itself.

She tore her gaze away and looked at Andris, who was equally fascinated by what he saw.

'It really is a vast organism,' Andris said softly – to Philemon rather than to her. 'This is what you wanted us to see, isn't it? You wanted us to understand that the lake is like the dragomite queen: that it provides a capacious living environment within which many others individuals live and feed.'

'Keep looking,' Philemon said. 'There's something else you'll be interested to see. It's only a matter of time. Keep looking . . . *there*. Do you see it?'

One of Philemon's aged hands was set upon Andris's shoulder, seemingly gripping it hard. The other was extended, the stabbing forefinger indicating the direction in which Andris ought to look. Lucrezia looked too, trying with all her might to see what he was pointing at.

She caught the merest glimpse of something swimming: something much larger than a turtle, or even a crocolid. It didn't swim as such creatures did, with sweeps of oarlike limbs or lazy waves of an elongated tail; it swam instead with powerful strokes of its flippered legs, like a frog. Lucrezia tried to make out its arms, its features, its huge eyes . . . but she couldn't see them clearly. Perhaps Andris could; at any rate, his gasp of recognition suggested that he knew what it was he was looking at.

'Did you see it, Lucrezia?' he said, this time having not the slightest difficulty in using her name rather than her title.

'I saw it,' she confirmed, as it vanished into the depths.

'Yes, I know,' Andris said. 'But did you see the other one? I can't quite remember whether you were there, when the dragomite warrior cut it in two? It's the same, you see – or very nearly. That's the kind of creature which guided Jacom and myself to the queen's egg-chambers and the dragomite drones.'

Had she seen it? She thought not – not, at any rate, while it was alive. But she had heard Andris tell his tale, and Jacom too.

'I knew it when you told me your story,' Philemon said, gripping Andris's shoulder all the more tightly. 'And I knew what it meant.'

'What it means,' Lucrezia was quick to say, 'is that it isn't only humans that have been conscripted into the Corridors of Power. Dragomite queens can adopt other creatures into their families.'

'Oh, it means much more than that,' Philemon told her. 'When you know what it really means, you will know what kind of Serpent's blood nourishes your own flesh, and what it is that calls you to Chimera's Cradle – and why, if you value your life, you must not go.'

4

JACOM APPROACHED THE inn whose sign bore the image of a wide-horned bull with some trepidation. He had been alone for some time, having been separated from his fleeing companions in the crowded streets south of Tarlock Nath's house, when he had had little choice but to barge a way through as best he could, stopping for nothing lest he be torn down from his perch and left to make his way on foot. Since leaving the outskirts of the town he had met no further trouble, and such people as he had passed on the road had shown little sign of hostility, but he was exhausted and sharply aware of being lost in the middle of a country in turmoil. Night had fallen but the stars were shining brightly.

The inn was some three kims south of Antiar, and it proved easy enough to find once he had located the 'road' on which it stood, which was a meandering cart-track leading into the farmlands. Eventually, he presumed, it must reach Kether, the sixth of the Nine Towns counting north to south, but it obviously did so by a route far less direct than the main highway which followed the near-straight course of the river.

The fields opposite the inn were divided into a complex of walled enclosures where livestock being driven to market could be lodged overnight, but Jacom saw that the few which did contain livestock of some sort were guarded by soldiers, not by labourers, and their colours were not the colours worn by Tarlock Nath's men. Nor were the colours entirely reliable, for Jacom recognised one of the men as Kristoforo, who had once been one of his men. Kristoforo still wore the red skirt of his old uniform beneath a jerkin which, if Jacom remembered the colours rightly, falsely identified him as a soldier of Sabia.

Jacom immediately urged his tired horse into the lane where Kristoforo was stationed, intent on finding out as much as he could before presenting himself at the door of the inn. Two golden guardsmen – one keeping watch on two dispirited bullocks and the other playing shepherd to half a dozen recently sheared ewes – watched him as he passed by, pretending to be relaxed and fearless, although their eyes were sharp and suspicious. Kristoforo turned out to be guarding a little flock of wing-clipped geese, which let off a few token honks as the stranger approached, but were obviously not in the mood for raising alarms on their own account.

'By Goran, sir, I'm glad to see you,' Kristoforo said, as Jacom dismounted. 'When the sergeant sent news that you were still alive I could hardly believe it, an' when he pledged that he'd have you in our company within the fiveday I thought it mere bluster. Are Phar an' Keshvara with you?'

'I was about to ask you the same question, about Phar and Merel Zabio,' Jacom said, extending his hand to the man as though they were equals and good friends. 'You haven't seen them, I take it?'

Kristoforo looked surprised, but he took the hand and shook it, rather tentatively. 'No, sir,' he said. 'They headed here, though?'

'I wish I knew,' Jacom replied, biting his lip. 'I can't think of anywhere else they'd be able to head for, but Phar might not like the idea of being recruited by Amyas. Do you know what agreement Purkin's made with the bronze?'

Kristoforo looked uncomfortable. 'Sergeant said – behind his hand, like – that it might be best to keep our options open,' he said. 'Said the bronzes were the likeliest prospect, bein' strangers in a strange land like ourselves, but to keep a lookout for a better offer. Far as I know, he was plannin' to help this Tarlock Nath lay in wagons and supplies for the long haul to Xandria, then help Amyas steal the lot, but I dare say he hadn't finally made up his mind which way to jump. Rumour has it things in the south're gettin' worse, but how bad they'd have to be before they'd make crossin' the Dragomite Hills an' gettin' home to find ourselves outlaws seem like a good idea I don't know.'

'That's what I thought,' Jacom said. He'd probably have said it anyway, but such thinking as he'd had time to do since being caught up in the brawl at Tarlock Nath's stables had indeed led him to conclude that this was the most likely situation. 'Well, it looks as if there's no scope left for further double-dealing. Nath's exploits in the marketplace must have attracted rather too much attention, perhaps because several of his fellow councilmen had similar ideas, and honest tradesmen of Antiar must have taken exception to the prospect of the town's nobility running out on them in every possible direction. That's the trouble with democracy – the rabble get the notion in their heads that the men who rule over them owe them a certain responsibility.'

'They're not civilised folk, that's for sure,' Kristoforo agreed, with a conspicuous lack of enthusiasm.

The problem is, Jacom thought, *what now? Do we have any alternative but to sign on with Amyas – and if we do, do we do so with the intention of deserting him as soon as we're within striking distance of Salamander's Fire, or do we actually go to this Stronghold of his, and help to defend it against who knows what?* He had a strong suspicion that there might be more than one strongly held opinion among the company he had included in his 'we', and that Aulakh Phar and Sergeant Purkin – to name but two – might have very different ideas as to what was to be done and how.

'How many men are there in the bronze's little army?' Jacom enquired of Kristoforo.

'Hard to say, sir,' the guardsman replied. 'Right now, there's five bronzes an' fifteen goldens holdin' the inn and these pens, but I don't know how trustworthy the locals are or how many more we're expectin' to sign up. I think there's seven more bronzes, includin' Amyas, plus three of our men, includin' Purkin an' the darkland boy. Then there's you – an' maybe Phar an' Keshvara an' the amber's girl.' He ended his count on a questioning note, as if to ask whether Phar, Hyry and Merel were indeed to be expected. Jacom wished that he could offer a firm answer.

'We had to scatter after looting Tarlock Nath's stables,' he said, feeling that some explanation was due. 'I lost Phar and Merel in the streets of the town. Keshvara wasn't with us, and I doubt that she'll know where to come even if she managed to get away. Phar and Merel will be here, provided that they managed to get clear. Actually, I pity anyone that tries to stop them – that girl's a real cat when she's angry, and once her claws are unsheathed she doesn't hesitate about using them.'

'Pirate blood,' Kristoforo said. 'May be no more'n a cutpurse herself, but breedin' always comes out in a fight. Keshvara's tough too.'

'Tougher than me,' Jacom admitted.

Kristoforo responded to that with a knowingly manly grin which implied that he knew chivalrous modesty when he saw it, although he plainly didn't.

'How much do you know about these bronzes?' Jacom asked. 'Amyas gave me an account of himself, but we hadn't much time and there were a lot of questions I didn't have a chance to ask.'

'They look on us as hired hands,' Kristoforo said dubiously. 'Can't tell the difference between us an' the local goldens, an' they could use a few lessons in politeness. They call the place they come from the Last Stronghold, as if it were humanity's last hope hereabouts, but I don't know how much they really know about what lies east, west an' south of them – they don't seem to me to be great traders or travellers, an' their horizons must've been shrinkin' for centuries. They're carryin' a fair amount of good coin but they're very free with promises about treasure-vaults back home that might be lure enough for the bumpkins but don't fool men like us. When they first started recruitin' every able-bodied man – or very near – had been drafted to fight dragomites in the north, so Amyas went up there to see some general named Shabir. Nath tagged along with him, though who was leadin' who an' why by the nose an' who was spyin' on who is anybody's guess. But you probably know all that.'

Jacom nodded; it was evident that Purkin's men were no better informed than he was. He changed tack. 'How do you and the others feel about the situation?' he asked. 'Which way would you rather go from here, if you had the choice?'

Kristoforo shook his head dubiously. 'I've no family in Xandria,' he said. 'No land, no job. If I went back I'd be an outlaw. Been a soldier all my life, sir, an' Amyas's people are real soldiers, if you know what I mean – not like these rotting Antiarians – but . . .' He let the sentence trail off.

Jacom got the drift. What Kristoforo was saying was that there were good reasons why a man in his position might want to take up with Amyas and his bronzes, and that he understood why Purkin might have done just that, but that home was home and that it lay in the other direction. He was certain that Koraismi would think the same. On the other hand, if the one-time guardsmen had the option of serving a Xandrian master, like Carus Fraxinus, rather than Amyas, things might look different. They had decided to stay with the expedition rather than go back to their unsafe home when confronted with the Dragomite Hills – although, if rumour were to be trusted, the southlands might be even more dangerous than the plague-stricken mounds.

'Have to bear in mind, though,' Kristoforo added, as if he were following Jacom's train of thought, 'that the Dragomite Hills ain't as dead as we first thought. Those warriors're pretty fearsome. Then again, they say there're manticores in the south, with human faces an' tigers' bodies an' scorpions' tails. Uncuttable trees an' walkin' stones aren't anythin' much to be afraid of, but these hellhounds an' the like . . . looks like wherever we go there'll be monsters to face.'

'Better the rot you don't know than the rot you do,' Jacom commented, reversing the terms of the common proverb.

'Eh?' said Kristoforo uncertainly.

Jacom wasn't sure what he meant himself, and he embarked upon his explanation in a somewhat exploratory spirit. 'We know what's waiting for us back home,' he said slowly. 'Maybe it wouldn't be so bad, to live on the outskirts of the empire, exiled from Xandria itself. By the time the troubles afflicting the southlands reached out to Xandria, if they ever do, we'd probably be old men. But what pride could we ever have in ourselves, if we did that? It might be better to go on into the unknown, as bravely as we can – don't you think? To Salamander's Fire or the Last Stronghold, or Chimera's Cradle or . . . anywhere, really. That way, we'd be going forwards instead of backwards, making something of ourselves . . . wouldn't we?'

'Ah,' said Kristoforo, achieving a peculiar articulacy by making the syllable express a full measure of disagreement lightly seasoned with implication and insinuation, to the effect that Jacom was either terminally stupid or completely out of his mind. Jacom was rather relieved to hear the sound of multiple hoofbeats on the road, which gave him a good excuse to turn round. He looked back at the starlit road, trying to identify the riders, who were five in number.

He picked out Merel Zabio and Aulakh Phar easily enough, but Hyry Keshvara wasn't with them. Nor were Purkin and Koraismi. Two of the remaining three riders were bronzes, but neither was Amyas; the fifth was a golden wearing the colours of Tovali.

'I'll see you later,' Jacom called over his shoulder to Kristoforo, as he began to lead his dispirited mount back to the road.

'Probably when you take your turn to watch the birds, sir,' the guardsman said. It was impossible to judge whether he was serious or not.

By the time Jacom had crossed the road to the inn-yard most of the newcomers had dismounted and the door of the inn had been opened, but only by the merest crack. The people inside obviously wanted to be sure exactly who they were letting in, and on whose orders. Amyas was not among the riders, and his subordinates were evidently being interrogated as to the status and worth of their companions. Aulakh Phar was hovering behind them, listening carefully to what was said, but he gave Jacom a wave of acknowledgment. Merel Zabio greeted him rather more enthusiastically.

'I knew you'd make it,' she told him approvingly. 'I always had this idea that army officers were no good at fighting – that they just bought their commands and let their men do all the dirty work – but you were as good as any streetfighter I've ever seen.' Jacom assumed that this was intended as a compliment.

'You should have seen me at the battle of the bridge,' he said. 'Dhalla and I saw off a whole army – with a little help from Checuti and his bombs.' He spoke lightly, deliberately making no mention of her murderous instincts.

'I was worried when you went the wrong way, though,' she told him. 'You should have stuck with us.'

'Why am I the one who went the wrong way, if I got here first?' Jacom asked. She didn't bother to argue – as she might have – that staying with one's allies was always the right way, even if the other road proved straighter.

By this time, negotiations at the door had reached a satisfactory conclusion. The men inside had allowed themselves to be convinced that everyone present was now a committed member of the corps which Amyas was assembling. Unfortunately, it turned out that all the private rooms in the inn had already been requisitioned, so Jacom, Merel and Phar found themselves casually banished to the corner of the downstairs room which had been colonised by the Xandrian guardsmen and was currently occupied by Luca, Fernel and Aaron. Jacom observed that they had only two short swords and two half-pikes between them, and virtually nothing else except their uniforms, which were so dirty that the red of their skirts looked like long-dried blood. It appeared that the Sabian jerkin which Kristoforo wore was communal property employed by anyone who had to stand guard in the cool night air.

'Where's all your armour gone?' Jacom enquired, although he wasn't entirely sure that they'd been fully clad when they fled in the face of the dragomite horde.

'Nothin' left, sir, but what we've got on,' Fernel said.

'We're a disgrace to the citadel guard all right, sir,' Luca conceded unrepentantly, 'but there wasn't much we could do. Had to eat. Purkin told us to dicker with the bronzes as best we could an' he'd try to get the stuff back when the time came to kit us out.'

All three of the guardsmen took great care to study Jacom's own costume – which hadn't been the best set possessed by whatever servant they'd been borrowed from – and the one and only weapon he'd bothered to carry away from the skirmish in the stables, which was an axe-handle. Then they looked at Phar, whose rags were even shabbier and who had no weapon at all. Merel was little better off, but at least she'd taken the trouble to appropriate a very serviceable stiletto.

'All in all,' Jacom said ruminatively, 'we don't seem to be worth very much, do we? Soldiers with only the meanest weapons, and a healer without a single pill or potion. If I were Amyas, I suppose I'd have to think very seriously about whether we'd be any use to him at all.'

'It's not the hardware we possess that matters,' Phar told him confidently. 'It's what we carry up here.' He tapped his skull. 'I'm worth a dozen other men, and so are you – and Amyas must know that, after seeing you laying about yourself in the stable.'

'I'm worth at least three,' Merel put in. 'No one from these piddling river towns would last a tenday in the backstreets of Xandria.'

'Don't judge the bronzes by the locals,' Fernel advised her. 'They're hard men. And don't judge the locals by the townies. If you ask me, it's not going to be easy going south if anyone decides to make a serious bid to stop us.' Like Kristoforo, he seemed to be assuming that they had no option but to go with Amyas, but he didn't feel compelled to seem enthusiastic about the prospect.

Aaron, however, struck a different note. 'No one'll try to stop us,' he said dourly. 'They got plenty of troubles of their own, without looking for more. They might not like us, especially if we have to pick up supplies they'd rather hoard for themselves, but puttin' together a force big enough to take us on is way beyond 'em now.'

'The real question,' Fernel countered, 'is what we'll have to face once we get into the bronzes' territory. Don't forget that they came this way looking to beg, borrow or buy help. Ask yourselves – how desperate must they be? And why do they call their home the *Last Stronghold*? We aren't being taken south to fight burrowing balloons – we're being taken south to man a fortress under siege from much nastier things than that.'

'So what's new?' Aaron wanted to know. 'Seems to me it was only yesterday we were bein' taken south to fight *dragomites* – an' not by bronzes offerin' coin an' promisin' more.'

Jacom lowered his eyes, acknowledging the force of the tacit accusation with a gesture that was half a nod and half a shrug.

'Let's not lose sight of the fact that we're going the right way,' Phar was quick to put in. 'Carus Fraxinus still has the big wagon, with its cargo intact, and an escort of dragomite warriors. If he can reach Salamander's Fire, and we can meet him there, we'll have a good fund of equipment to draw on. We won't be the only ones trying. Checuti and Princess Lucrezia will be doing their best, with whatever they salvaged from the small wagon . . . and there's Andris too.'

Jacom wasn't sure whether Phar had added the last name because he really thought there was a good chance that the big amber was still alive or as a sop to Merel, but he felt compelled to nod in agreement. Whatever was to be decided in the fullness of time, there was an obvious need to raise morale as far as it could be raised. 'You're right,' he said stoutly. 'We're temporarily separated from our fellows, but the game's not over. There's everything still to play for.'

'Only problem,' Luca said, in a low tone which took obvious account of the fact that there were a dozen other people in the room besides their own party, 'is that our bronze comrades ain't playin' the same game – an' if they're payin' us a wage, they ain't goin' to be happy about the prospect of us playin' on our own.'

Jacom very nearly said *We'll cross that bridge when we come to it*, but he realised in time what an unfortunate saw it might seem, even to those who had not actually been present at the exploded bridge. Instead, he said: 'Isn't there any ale in this rotting inn? I could surely do with a drink.'

The reply he got seemed somehow rather ominous. 'No,' said Luca. 'Bronze bastards drunk it dry two days ago. They ain't just hard – they're real hogs.'

5

IT WAS LATE afternoon when Carus Fraxinus first caught sight of the Crystal City on the south-eastern horizon. The air was almost still but the darkening sky in the east was stained by a strange radiance – a legacy of the dust whipped up by the wind that had carried the floaters out of the south-west in such awesome profusion.

Such displays were often to be seen in the desert, because there was so much mineral dust ground down to the utmost fineness; the smallest particles were easily picked up by any wind stronger than a breeze, and they rarely had time to settle during the calms between one windstorm and the next.

The particles which were presently catching the reddening light of the setting sun drew a great lilac veil across the emergent face of night. It was not quite sufficient to drown the light of the brightest flamestars but it was adequate to confer a certain twinkling hesitancy upon them. The needle-like towers of the Crystal City seemed to the approaching observers to rise by slow but majestic degrees out of the sparkling carpet of the desert, modestly half-concealed by the trailing edge of the illusory veil. It was almost as if the tips of the towers had snagged the edge of the sky's frail garment and were just on the point of drawing it discreetly down.

Beside the wagon, not three mets from its wheels, the Salamanders marched upon their great lumpen feet, stolidly but tirelessly. The Salamanders had slowed the progress of the company considerably, but they had made up for it in other ways. They did not seem to require nearly as much water as their new companions, but they were expert at scouting for it nevertheless. They knew how to butcher and cook sandskinks in such a way as to make their flesh seem almost delicate – a lesson which Fraxinus thought useful, even though the rich harvest of the floaters had ensured that they were reasonably well provisioned for the time being.

The dragomite warriors had drawn ahead of the wagon. They seemed far less grateful for the sedate pace than the horses drawing the wagon – the horses were not at all impatient, even though they were moving in a leisurely fashion. Fraxinus was pleased with them nevertheless; they had lost only one more animal since the last battle between the dragomites and Shabir's cavalry. Ereleth's witchery had proved more than adequate to the task of healing the minor cuts inflicted on their fetlocks.

Dhalla was marching with the dragomites, in such close company that she might have been taken for their leader – not because she liked them but because her stride was so massive that she found it exceedingly awkward to walk in step with the Salamanders. She had recovered almost all her strength now, and her step was buoyant. Fraxinus was glad to see that, too; he was beginning to suspect that a giant's strength might be very valuable indeed when the time came to leave Salamander's Fire for Chimera's Cradle.

Fraxinus couldn't help regretting that the route they had followed from the Corridors of Power had brought them out of the hills on the western shore of the great river rather than the other. It was obvious, with the aid of hindsight, that the expedition would have fared very much better had it elected to come south through the desert rather than the lands which had seemed – on the surface – infinitely more inviting. Given that they *had* come out of the hills into the Narrow Land, though, and that they had been unable to escape a violent confrontation with Shabir, they were still in good condition. If the party which had been left on the western shore had fared as well, there might still be hope for a welcome reunion at Salamander's Fire. In the meantime, there were the wonders of the Crystal City to behold.

'The resemblance which leads mapmakers to call it a city is very superficial,' Ereleth said, as they drew gradually closer to the gleaming spires – whose gleaming was not at all dulled by the distant sinking of the sun. 'No human builders would bother to erect spires as slender as those.'

Ereleth had only just emerged to sit beside Fraxinus on the driver's bench; she had been taking her turn to rest, although she had spent much of the time in a rambling and not altogether coherent conversation with Mossassor.

'It still lies a long way distant,' Fraxinus said. 'I doubt that they're quite as slender as they seem.'

'In which case they must be taller than they appear to be,' the queen replied, in her usual combative fashion. 'Which makes them even less likely objects of human construction. They must overshoot the tallest towers in Xandria and the Thousand Islands by at least two hundred mets. Not even your darklander tree-creepers could climb so high without fainting in dread.'

'Perhaps it isn't the form of it which inspired the label,' Fraxinus said. 'See how the towers seem to grow brighter as the sky goes darker. I don't think it's just reflected and refracted light, like that which illuminates the skyborne dust. I think there must be internal light-sources of some kind, akin to those you saw in the dragomites' tunnels. Human cities shine by night, thanks to the light of thousands of lanterns and hundreds of thousands of candles, and that could be the parallel the mapmakers had in mind.'

'It's just another kind of forest,' Ereleth told him, stubbornly clinging to her minimising mood. 'A huge stand of something like the things Shabir calls gaudtrees, far taller and somewhat sleeker.'

'Is that true, Mossassor?' Fraxinus asked, hearing the Serpent scramble into a position where it too could look upon the object of their attention. 'Did you get much sense out of the Salamanders?' Mossassor had been making valiant attempts to interrogate the Salamanders about anything and everything, on the grounds that even if it obtained very little in the way of meaningful information it was honing its communicative skills to a sharpness which would be useful when they eventually met the 'wise ones'.

'Don't ssink sso,' Mossassor said, its wary phraseology testifying to the fact that it had little more confidence in its ability to understand what the Salamanders told it than it had about its ability to translate the information into human terms. 'Gaudtreess are like treess but Crysstal Ssity made by tiny ssings, like . . .'

'Lapidendrons?' Fraxinus supplied.

'Yess. Not ssame but ssimilar. Towerss not all alive – more like sshell or sscaless of ssnakess, only not ssame.'

'Perhaps he means something like the corals which grow in the Slithery Sea,' Ereleth suggested.

'Perhaps,' Fraxinus said judiciously, 'but I don't see how the organisms sustain themselves, if so. Coral polyps are trawlers, drawing nutrients from the water. I don't see how the little things that build those needles gain any similar advantage from their uplift – it's not as if the air were full of millions of tiny floaters. They may be more like the yeasts that stonemasons use to cement building-blocks out of various kinds of aggregates, but I can't quite see the logic of the towerlike formation.'

'I wonder why the Salamanders are so interested in the place,' Ereleth said. 'They don't actually live there, do they?'

'Not all time,' Mossassor supplied. 'Not many, anyhow. Often vissit. Need materialiss for toolss – alsso Ssalamander'ss Fire, I ssink. Iss why wisse oness are ssere now.'

Fraxinus had seen the tools which the Salamanders carried with them, and had observed that their bowls and handles were made out of crystalline substances far more sophisticated than those used by Shabir's countrymen. 'What materials does Salamander's Fire require and employ?' he was quick to ask.

'Hard to ssay,' Mossassor replied evasively. 'Iss Ssalamander ssing, no Sserpent wordss. Ssey ssay we will ssee in time. Ssink iss ssomessing to do wiss paedogenessiss.'

Mossassor was fond of the word *paedogenesis*, partly because it had realised after first mentioning it to Hyry Keshvara that it was a part of human language which even most humans did not know, and partly because Aulakh Phar had encouraged its belief that the concept was a vital clue to the nature of the drastic changes which, in its belief, were set to overtake the world.

'According to you, everything has something to do with paedogenesis,' Ereleth remarked drily. 'The question is, *what* does it have to do with paedogenesis – and what does paedogenesis have to do with us?'

'Don't know yet,' was all Mossassor could say in reply.

'It's a pity that Serpents are so good at forgetting things,' Fraxinus observed, knowing exactly what Mossassor would say to that.

'Iss not our fault,' the Serpent replied, on cue. 'Have to be.'

'I have a theory about that,' Ereleth put it. 'I think the reason Serpents have to be good at forgetting things is that they have less memory capacity than humans or Salamanders. If they weren't able to shed their lore along with their skins they'd get full up, and would then have no more room for the produce of today and tomorrow.'

Fraxinus knew that the observation was four parts humour and four parts sly malice, but he suspected that there might be an element of constructive provocation in there too. The close proximity of the last few days – plus the absence of its sterner companions – had obliterated the last vestiges of the awe in which they had once held the Serpent, and they now felt free to tease it with mild insults.

'Iss not ssat,' Mossassor said, giving no indication that it knew that the statement was not entirely serious. 'Nossing sso ssimple. Iss ssomessing to do wiss gift, wiss debt.'

Fraxinus knew that it meant the gift which, according to the *Apocrypha of Genesys*, the people of Idun had accepted from a Serpent – a gift which was not really a gift at all, given that the blind man's recitation had made it perfectly clear that it had been paid for with a promise of some kind, thus creating the debt of which Mossassor spoke.

'In your view, everything is something to do with that, too,' Ereleth pointed out.

'Not jusst Sserpentss,' Mossassor reminded them. 'Humanss forget too.'

'It's right,' Fraxinus said. 'That is a puzzling aspect of the situation. Humans are supposed to be good at preserving lore – our whole way of life is based on the memories of loremasters and their efficiency at transmitting that lore from one generation to the next. If several of these times of emergence have occurred since humans first came to the world, and have had cataclysmic effects, why has no record been added to the lore? I know that loremasters are notoriously conservative, but if these crises threatened to wipe us out they'd surely have made strenuous efforts to produce something more comprehensive than a few secret commandments allegedly formulated by Goran or his companion forefathers.'

'Perhaps the changes aren't as cataclysmic as legend makes out,' Ereleth suggested. 'Perhaps the Dragomite Hills and the

Forest of Absolute Night do constitute an impassable barrier, so that the previous times of emergence only affected the southern hemisphere, allowing the loremasters of Xandria to hand down their wisdom without seeing any need for modification.'

'That's a possible explanation,' Fraxinus conceded. 'Perhaps the forefathers were witness to one time of emergence while they were still working in Idun, and became anxious enough to make precautionary modifications to the Genesys plan. They obviously made additions to the lore they'd prepared – the *Apocrypha of Genesys* and the secret commandments must be two such afterthoughts – but it's not impossible that they were being over-anxious, and that subsequent times of emergence threw up fewer hazards than they might have done. Perhaps their effects were localised, closely confined to the civilisation centred on the Cities of the Plain, from whose remnant Shabir's bronzes came.'

'Go on,' Ereleth said, knowing that all this was the mere prelude to less optimistic speculations.

'Perhaps there's no lore relating to these times of emergence because none of the people who experienced them survived to make it. Perhaps human civilisation in the north *and* the south has had to be rebuilt from scattered enclaves which escaped destruction by going into hiding, and found it enormously difficult even to preserve the traditional lore – much of which might, in fact, have been lost. Perhaps humans are less good at remembering than we think – and perhaps Serpents are good at forgetting because they have some way of responding to these periodic crises which requires them to forget everything they've learned in the interims.'

'But we do have some lore relating to these times of crisis,' Ereleth pointed out, 'and what that lore bids us do is to go to Chimera's Cradle, in alliance with Serpents and Salamanders. It doesn't instruct us to hide ourselves away and wait for the changes to die down.'

'That's what your secret commandments instruct you to do,' Fraxinus agreed, although he still hadn't heard a word for word account of exactly what Ereleth's secret commandments did instruct her to do. 'Perhaps, in some way we don't understand, Princess Lucrezia's Serpent's blood pushes her in the same direction. But most of us have neither Serpent's blood nor secret commandments, and if rumour is to be trusted – which, I'll grant you, it usually isn't – there might well be several sets of secret commandments being handed down by different custodians. Perhaps the others do instruct their owners to hide away, to preserve themselves from all contact with the unearthly, and to wait.'

'One rule for some, another for others,' Ereleth said, with only a touch of scorn. 'But why? Why should the forefathers have embedded contrary sets of instructions in the lore?'

'I don't know,' Fraxinus said, 'but I don't think it's as absurd as you're trying to make it seem. According to Aulakh's account of what paedogenesis is, it sometimes works to the advantage of a species if it has two very different strategies of life. The world before the world, which first gave birth to humankind, presumably produced a single sentient species, but this world produced two, akin but in some ways strikingly different. Aulakh applied the word paedogenesis to tiny things, trying to provide a possible explanation for Lucrezia's Serpent's blood, but perhaps it applies to other kinds of species too.'

'To Serpents and Salamanders, you mean?' Ereleth looked over her shoulder at Mossassor as she spoke. 'You think that's why we can't figure out their reproductive processes, and why even they seem a little vague about them?'

'To Serpents and Salamanders,' Fraxinus agreed, 'and perhaps to some humans too: humans like Vaca Metra and Dhalla . . . perhaps even to us.'

'To giants, perhaps,' Ereleth said pensively. 'As to dragomite-women . . . I don't pretend to know the full significance of what happened to Myrasol and Captain Cerri in the depths of the mound, but I doubt if waving the word *paedogenesis* over Myrasol's head-spore like a magic wand would produce any further enlightenment. You and I, mercifully, are long past any necessity to worry about exotic processes of reproduction in respect of ourselves.'

'Paedogenessiss nossing to do wiss Sserpentss,' Mossassor put in. 'Iss to do wiss gift, wiss ssearssh for garden, but not Sserpentss.' It was difficult to tell whether it found the notion distressing, or whether it was simply trying to clear up a misconception.

'Serpenthood is simplicity itself,' Ereleth commented. 'Unless, of course, the dragomites had mound-Serpents before they decided that mound-people were a better bet. Perhaps there were giant Serpents in the world in those days, too.' Her sarcasm was obvious to Fraxinus, but he feared that it would be wasted on the Serpent.

'No mound-Sserpentss ever,' Mossassor replied. 'Were giantss, ssough likess of Ssifuss ssay not.'

'You mean there actually were giant Serpents once?' Fraxinus put in, to make sure that there was no mistake in translation. 'According to legend, at least?'

'Yess,' Mossassor confirmed.

'And giant Salamanders too?'

'No . . . not in our legendss.' It seemed less confident about this assertion.

Fraxinus paused for thought, but could not see any immediate significance in this revelation – which might, of course, be no revelation at all if Ssifuss's sceptical judgment could be trusted.

'There are too many pieces in the puzzle,' Ereleth said. 'Until we discover how some of them interlock, we can't even begin to unravel it.'

Fraxinus nodded his head slowly, having no alternative but to agree.

The sky had darkened to the point at which the veil of airborne dust had become almost transparent. It was now no more than a faint haze masking the eastern sky, and it no longer seemed to have any connection with the Crystal City, which stood high and proud well within the horizon's compass.

Fraxinus had a sense of being dwarfed by the reach of the biggest spires, although it was obvious that only a few of the towers grew to a vast height, the great majority being less than half as tall as the tallest. It was also obvious that the towers were more widely spaced than they had seemed to be at first, and that the spaces between them were filled with a complicated latticework of rather more diffuse structures. It was as if a host of gigantic spiders had been at work, building webs here there and everywhere between the huge pylons, most of them fairly low down where there were ambulant creatures to be trapped.

The light emitted by the towers did not seem so bright now; it was almost possible to believe that it really was no more than starlight reflected and refracted by a host of curved and brilliantly polished surfaces. Fraxinus was still of the opinion, though, that there had to be more to it than that. The towers really were luminous, and the latticework connecting them also had its points of luminosity.

'Could there be some kind of fungus growing on the spires?' he asked Ereleth. 'Does the quality of the light remind you of the tunnels in the dragomite mound?'

'A tower is, I suppose, merely a tunnel turned inside out,' Ereleth said, with a half-smile. 'Perhaps their walls are like glass, so that the light of fungus growing on the inner surfaces may shine through. On the other hand . . .'

She didn't bother to continue. They would find out soon enough.

There was a new sound of scrambling as ex-General Shabir finally came forward to be close to his captors, at last condescending to join their communion of curiosity.

'It's a bad place,' he said firmly. 'Dangerous.'

'According to you,' Ereleth replied waspishly, 'all places are bad and dangerous except the fields surrounding the river towns – and even the fields surrounding the eight river towns in which you don't happen to have been born are to be treated with some circumspection. Salamanders may be alien, and abominably difficult to talk to, but they're a good deal meeker than you or I, and they seem to treat it as a place of pilgrimage. There can be no ravening predators there hungering for human blood. What would they eat when there were no intrepid explorers to feed upon?'

'You can't begin to understand,' Shabir told her – as he was increasingly ready and willing to do. 'This is not a game. This is the end of the world – and those who cannot or will not defend themselves against the end will be the first to perish. My people have failed, and you have the right to despise us for the craven nature of our failure, but yours will not be far behind, and you are hastening to meet extinction.'

'Whatever is happening,' Fraxinus said, immediately switching into a more hopeful argumentative mode, 'has happened before. Humans are still here, as are Serpents and Salamanders and countless other familiar species. Whatever is happening, we may be sure that it is not some vile conspiracy of fate and fortune intended to snuff us out. It is merely something that is going on, in accordance with its own nature and its own pattern, utterly oblivious of the interests and actions of observers. You should rejoice, general, to be a part of such a company as this, for there is more to be gained in every day of our advancement into the unknown than in a lifetime of hunting down dragomite strays.'

'You might think so,' Shabir retorted, with a haughty stubbornness of which Ereleth at her proudest might have been envious, 'but you are fools, rushing to the end which awaits all fools, and I for one shall not be sorry to see you meet it.'

'You tried to be it,' Fraxinus reminded him quietly, 'and you failed. You'll forgive me, I hope, if I continue to cherish my optimism.'

Privately, though, he couldn't help but wonder whether Shabir might be right, and whether the general's attitude – however unappealing and stupid it might be – was the one best adapted to confront the time of changes which they were hurrying to meet.

6

LUCREZIA HAD BECOME impatient with the polite evasiveness of her hosts, all the more so because they seemed to consider her irrelevant to their own concerns. It was Andris in whom they were interested. It was for Andris's sake that they were laying down their teasing trail of mysterious hints. It was for Andris's sake, too, that Philemon Taub and Venerina Sirelis took them both into the cellars beneath the house, to see the pools and tanks in which they kept various creatures fished from the Lake of Colourless Blood, and the vast arrays of flasks, bottles, crucibles and alembics which they used to distill and separate the drugs which they extracted from the produce of the marsh.

'We are not wanderers in the green maze, nor are we helpless swimmers in its shining heart,' Philemon assured the amber. 'We have learned to take what we need and what we desire from the body of the great being; we have refined its spirit, in order that we may partake of its wisdom while setting aside its pain.'

It was all nonsense, Lucrezia thought, and absurdly high-flown nonsense at that, but Philemon always spoke to Andris as if he expected Andris to understand him, and Andris was strangely reluctant to challenge him. She was reasonably sure that he didn't believe that the so-called spirit of the waters, which had supposedly claimed him for its own, was any more than a lingering delirium induced by mind-altering poisons, but he did seem to be taking the possibility seriously.

She felt helpless, not because she was incapable of intervening in the dialogue, but because she didn't know how to make such interventions effective. Philemon and Venerina always treated her questions and objections dismissively, implying that of course she had not the means to understand such matters, and Andris – perhaps flattered by their assumption that he was infinitely better equipped – seemed to have been sucked into their conspiracy of contempt.

It wasn't until the conversation turned to the deism of the Community that Andris finally began to show signs of a rebellious scepticism, which Lucrezia was glad to see and enthusastic to support. Gradually, she began to repair her faith in the big amber's healthy stubbornness.

'You say that there are deists in Ferentina and in Xandria,' Venerina Sirelis asked him, by way of finding out how and where she might begin her explanation of the Community. 'How much do you know about the beliefs they hold?'

'I never paid them much heed,' Andris admitted. 'I wouldn't have recognised the symbol and the motto if I hadn't had occasion to hide out in a church a while ago. As I understand it, deists believe that the world – and, for that matter, all the worlds which are rumoured to orbit other stars – were created, according to some kind of plan, by an extremely powerful and essentially changeless being called God. They think that the ship which – according to the lore of Genesys – first brought humans to this word was carrying forward God's plan. They also think that there's another level of existence beyond this one, hence the plus sign. They think that we somehow go on to this further level after we die, and that this constitutes some kind of magical reunion with the changeless God. Is that right?'

'In its essentials, yes,' the leader of the Community confirmed. 'The way you spell it out implies that you find it hard to believe. What is it that you find difficult?'

All of it, Lucrezia thought.

'Well,' Andris said uncomfortably, 'it all seems rather absurd. This extremely powerful and changeless being, for instance. Where is it? *What* is it? Why does it have a plan and why does the plan include us? Then again, death's death – we know perfectly well that when we're gone we're gone. It's absurd to think that we might just go somewhere else. I'm not one of these people who won't believe in anything they can't see – I'm perfectly prepared to believe in tiny things like cells and bacteria – but the idea of life after death is just silly.'

Lucrezia saw that Philemon was frowning, but Venerina Sirelis didn't seem in the least offended. 'It's understandable that you should think that,' she said. 'All lore is subject to misinterpretation by those who aren't educated to it. Even mapmakers, I dare say, are misunderstood by those who look for different things in their maps than what is actually recorded there.'

'That's true,' Andris admitted ruefully.

'It's true of witchcraft too,' Lucrezia put in. 'The common view is that it's mostly a matter of curses and aphrodisiacs and telling fortunes, but it's not. Curses don't work unless you have the means of doctoring someone's food or intimate possessions, and procuring abortions is a great deal simpler than conjuring affection where no prior inclination exists. Telling fortunes is just charlatanry. *There is no destiny*. It says so in the lore. The future's unmade, so it can't be foreseen. We can only calculate possibilities.' In saying this she intended to lay down further grounds for scepticism, which Andris might deploy by drawing analogies between deism and fortune-telling. She presumed that belief in a godly plan did not sit well with the lore's bald statement that there was no destiny – but Venerina Sirelis didn't seem put out by her remarks.

'When you have a better understanding of the nature of God,' the woman said, 'it won't seem silly at all.'

'Checuti said that the beliefs deists hold aren't important in themselves,' Andris observed, deftly adding another thread to the argumentative skein. 'He said they were like the rituals of the darklanders' secret societies – more or less arbitrary ways of extending the obligations of neighbourliness over vast distances. I thought that made a lot of sense.'

'It might seem that way to an outsider,' Venerina said patiently, 'but the beliefs we hold are far from irrelevant. In fact, they're essential to an understanding of what the world is all about. Until you can begin to grasp the process of which the everyday lives of human beings are just an infinitesimally tiny part, you can't know who and what you really are.'

'I think I have a fair idea of who and what I am,' Andris retorted, to Lucrezia's considerable satisfaction, 'and I doubt that anyone could possibly have more insight into my own being than I do – not even your immense and incredibly clever God.'

'You mustn't think of God as a human being writ large,' Venerina Sirelis told him, her voice still as mild as milk. 'And you mustn't think that our plus sign refers to some other world like this one but somehow displaced from it, in which your personality becomes relocated after you die. What we mean by God is the sum of all the life in the universe – not merely the life which exists on this world but the life which exists on all the other worlds of all the stars, and in the clouds of dust which lie between the stars where they're not so densely packed as they are in this part of the galaxy. When we talk about God having a plan we don't mean that there's a sentient being somewhere, which made up a plan according to some conscious purpose; we mean that all life has certain basic properties which cause it to spread, to reproduce, and to change – properties that bind the entirety of all living things into a common enterprise which we call evolution, or progress.'

'O thou, *who changest not*, abide with me,' Andris quoted. 'That doesn't sound like life.'

'Change and decay in *all* around I see,' Philemon immediately quoted back. 'That's the whole point, Andris – in spite of all the kinds of change which corrupt and corrode, dissolving order into chaos, there remains something which continues, something which is essentially unalterable. No matter what individual moves are made, the game remains the same.'

Lucrezia saw a sudden startled expression cross Andris's face. She half-remembered something he had said during the rambling discourse which had tumbled from his lips while they were lost in the marsh: something about 'life's endless game'. It had to be coincidence, she knew; it couldn't possibly be the product of some revelation vouchsafed to him by the so-called spirit of the waters. As a trained witch – or, at any rate, a half-trained witch – she knew perfectly well that all magic was a matter of mystique cloaking the chemical malevolence of poisons.

Perceiving that a point had been scored, Venerina quickly took up the thread again. 'What Philemon means,' she said, 'is that beneath the ceaselessness and irresistibility of change, there's a pattern. You understand, I suppose, that all the life-forms in the world are in some sense connected – that every organism is part of a species, that every species depends on countless other species for its food, and provides in its turn food for countless others? Everything that happens to the members of one species has effects on members of hundreds of others, and the chains of cause and effect spread out like ripples through the entire world of life. Can you see that all the life in the world forms a loosely interconnected whole?'

'The biosphere,' Andris said. Lucrezia remembered that Phar had used the word. She also remembered Andris's delirious expansion of Phar's throwaway remark that all living organisms were merely different methods by which eggs manufactured more eggs. Somehow, however absurd the notion might seem, there was an authentic convergence between the content of Andris's delirium and the beliefs of the deists. She could see that it was troubling Andris, and it had begun to trouble her too.

'Within the biosphere,' Venerina continued, 'there are enclaves which seem to be sealed off from the rest, isolated by their surroundings. . .'

'Like islands,' Lucrezia said, drawn into the discussion in spite of herself.'

'Like islands,' Venerina agreed. 'But such enclaves aren't really isolated. They remain part of the whole, at least potentially and implicitly. Even if they're cut off from the rest of the biosphere, they remain part of it – an aspect of the same grand pattern.'

'You're saying that the world is like an island,' Andris said, effortlessly jumping to the conclusion. 'You're saying that it's part of a grand pattern which extends – however tenuously – across the dark between the stars, which links all the life in the universe into a common project.'

'Yes,' said Venerina Sirelis firmly.

'And what you mean by God is the whole pattern of life, of which the world is just a tiny part?'

'What we mean by God,' Venerina corrected him, 'is the momentum which maintains that pattern and drives its evolution.'

There is no destiny, Lucrezia thought.

'I see,' Andris said thoughtfully. 'I can also see why knowing this is supposed to give me a fuller understanding of who and what I am – but I still don't see that it has much relevance to the everyday business of living. So I'm part of a grand pattern – so what?'

'The world is like an island,' Venerina said, favouring Lucrezia with an ironic sideways glance of acknowledgment, 'but it's an island which once suffered a crucial break in its isolation. It's a island to which a ship came, and unloaded a whole cargo of new living things. It was as if two very different islands suddenly collided, and began to merge: two complicated sets of organisms, each with its own web of interconnections, its own near-coherence.

'The world is an island which once had only the kinds of life we call unearthly, which suffered the abrupt importation of all the kinds of life we call earthly. In order to establish their own kinds of life, the people of the ship had to make a perfectly literal plan – a plan whose operation constituted a catastrophic disruption of the life that was already here.

'The ultimate aim of the plan wasn't to obliterate the life-forms which were here already, but to achieve an integration of the two . . . but that was a very difficult thing to plan for, because the life that was here was in some respects very different from the life that the planners imported. There were so many variables and imponderables that it wasn't possible to calculate the long-term effects of the chains of disruption which spread out through the vast webs of interconnections which had bound the two different kinds of life together. That's what the lore means when it says *There is no destiny*. The new and more complicated web of interconnections which began to form the moment the ship touched down couldn't be fully controlled, and its development couldn't be predicted in matters of detail.

'There is, however, one thing of which the people of the ship could be certain, and of which we can be certain, and that is that life in this world is subject to the same fundamental pattern and the same fundamental momentum as life elsewhere. Beneath the chaotic flux of change and decay, there is something which remains constant. There is God, whose plan can be – and needs to be – known and understood.'

'If that's what you call God,' Andris said warily, 'I suppose you have a point – but I don't see that your understanding has anything to add to the kind of understanding Aulakh Phar has of the workings of the biosphere. The idea of God doesn't actually add anything, does it? And I still don't see that it's of much relevance to the way ordinary people live their everyday lives.'

Lucrezia nodded in agreement, although she already had an inkling of the kind of reply that Venerina Sirelis was about to make.

'We aren't ordinary people,' Venerina Sirelis said, with an odd sigh that had little or no regret in it, 'and the time is now upon us when we can no longer live everyday lives. The spirit of the waters is becoming animated, and Serpent's blood is beginning to sing in the veins of those who carry it. We are pieces in the game which life is playing, aspects of a pattern which is in the process of a crucial reformation, *and we are in deadly peril because of it*. We must look to our knowledge of God and our faith in God to provide us with guidance. Without such knowledge and without such faith we could only go blindly to our deaths, but with its aid we might at least hope to play an active and conscious part in the process of evolution.'

If this is nonsense, Lucrezia thought, *it's dangerous nonsense*. She knew as she pronounced the silent words inside her head, though, that there were more ominous possibilities. Even if Andris were right about the idea of God being a superfluous embellishment, the deists clearly understood – or thought they understood – what purpose the Serpent's blood she carried in her veins was intended to serve, and they evidently had no doubt that it was a direly dangerous legacy. Ereleth had assumed that the commandments bidding her to go to Chimera's Cradle were urging her towards some rewarding enlightenment, but there were no real grounds for any such assumption. Might it not be the case that she was being drawn like livestock to the slaughterhouse?

'I wish you'd explain all this more clearly,' she said to Philemon and Venerina, sounding a clear note of complaint. 'Exactly what is it that you think is going on in the southlands?'

'The Salamanders call it a time of emergence,' Philemon replied. 'It is a time when new things spill out into the world, to challenge and perhaps displace the old. It is a time when new chimeras are formed. Serpents, Salamanders, dragomites and manticores all have their own ways of responding to such crises, and so – by courtesy of the Genesys plan – have we. Unfortunately, the interests of individuals and the interests of species don't always coincide, and are sometimes flatly opposed. Death works to the advantage of the species; it is a vital element of God's progressive plan, but individuals would prefer to live for ever. Unlike the spirit of the waters, which might save Andris's life, your Serpent's blood will lead you to destruction if you let it

. . . and I fear that it might do so no matter how hard you fight to prevent it.'

7

Jacom had expected the sojourn at the inn to be a mere matter of waiting, but it turned out to be the most frenzied period of waiting he had ever experienced. Men were continually arriving, bringing goods and weapons. Some came only to sell – and they came in armed gangs, clearly aware of the fact that there was more than haggling involved in making good bargains in *this* market – but others came to sign on as mercenaries. Most of the latter were turned away; it was plain that Amyas's confederates could afford to be selective.

Such new recruits as were accepted did not swell the assembly for long, and the room where Jacom and the other Xandrians had taken their station grew somewhat less crowded as dawn approached. Raiding parties, usually consisting of one or two bronzes and three or four local goldens, were continually being formed and dispatched. The bronzes had a paymaster who held court in one of the upstairs rooms, doling out money to his own people – presumably to be used in buying that which was too well-defended to be easily stolen and as bribe-money to defectors from the local militias. There seemed to be a lively trade in information as well as goods; the raiding parties were always told exactly where to go and what their object was.

At dawn there were three carts in the yard and twenty horses in the stables; by mid-morning this capital had expanded to comprise six carts and more than sixty horses. The carts which arrived part-laden were soon filled. The livestock in the pens showed no such rapid increase, but Jacom suspected that the word must have been passed around the neighbourhood that anyone who still had food animals, of whatever kind, had better hide them or move them as quickly as possible towards some distant market. Observation of the traffic within the inn suggested to Jacom that the stockpile of weapons maintained in the cellar which had once held casks of ale must actually be dwindling, because men going out collected equipment therefrom and any useful items which came in were immediately reissued. It seemed astonishing to Jacom that the Antiarians would tolerate such an operation being established on the very doorstep of their town; it was more eloquent testimony to the breakdown of civil order than the riotous disturbances he had encountered in the course of the previous day.

The bronzes didn't seek to involve any of the Xandrians in their hectic race to bring in provisions, although the ex-guardsmen were expected to take turns making their presence obvious to any visitors or passers-by who might be tempted to start trouble. The road remained busy in spite of the fact that the inn had effectively become foreign territory. Rumour must have carried tales of the innkeeper's fate – which would doubtless whisper of worse things than impoverishment – far and wide, but there were obviously many people on the road who had not heard them.

As soon as he had rested, Aulakh Phar busied himself with gathering what intelligence he could from the bronzes. Such items of information as he was initially able to bring back seemed hardly worth the trouble, though, and Jacom felt no inclination to join in. It seemed a pointless task, given that they would be told everything they needed to know when Amyas and Purkin eventually put in an appearance. Merel Zabio was more inclined to restlessness and inquisitiveness, however, and she soon went off with Phar while Jacom continued to sit with the men he had once commanded. They had long since mastered the patient arts of barrack life and the only discomfort they felt was the dearth of ale.

'The way this is shaping up,' Jacom observed to Luca, when the two of them were left alone – save for Kristoforo, who was sleeping off the burden of his tour of duty – 'we could be in for a replay of the troubles I've already been through. If I remember Myrasol's map correctly, the river swings away to the west in a great arc, so we'll still have a bridge to cross – and if these people intend to loot and pillage as the whim takes them while they move towards the barrens, they're likely to stir up just as much ire as our arrival with the dragomites did.'

'Word is there's no army big enough to attack us in the south,'

Luca told him, 'an' no man with the will and power to gather one. The towns'll simply seal themselves off, holding themselves secure against attack. No one will come out after us. Locals say that the general who attacked you is dead, killed in the Spangled Desert. News comes from men who turned back an' left him to it, but it's probably true.'

Kristoforo stirred in his sleep, muttering some incoherent complaint. Luca took it as an injunction to be quiet, although they were so close to the door which led to the kitchens – where hot food was in constant preparation – that there was more than enough noise to cope with. Eventually, Jacom found the strain of idleness too great, and he got up to take a walk before the noonday heat became too oppressive.

He looked out of the window at the yard in front of the inn, where the carts were being loaded. There was nothing there to engage his interest so he went out by the back way to the stables, where a handful of golden boys were hard at work feeding and watering the horses. A couple of bronzes looked on, joking with one another and occasionally barking unnecessary orders at the boys. They watched Jacom pass by but said nothing; they seemed to have a better idea of how he fitted into the scheme of things than he did, and clearly did not think him important.

It wouldn't be difficult to steal a few horses if we picked our moment, he thought, weighing up the odds. *If there's no one in the south capable of stopping Amyas, we'd be just as safe – and Amyas won't spare the time to come after us. I can't make plans of that kind until Purkin returns, though, and Koraismi. I have to give Hyry Keshvara time to find us, too – always provided that she's managed to give Nath the slip.*

He went on through the stable buildings, past an empty henhouse and out of the inn's grounds through a gateway set in a crumbling wall. There was no guard there, but when he looked back at the inn he saw that there was a lookout posted in an attic window.

A narrow stream ran behind the inn, and Jacom crossed the wooden bridge to the pasture beyond. There was a small wood thirty mets or so away to the left, which offered the only cover to anyone who wanted to move up on the inn unobserved, but the undergrowth wasn't dense and he was reasonably sure that no one was lurking there. He moved along the bank of the stream, looking idly down into the surprisingly clear water, where shoals of tiny fish were visible. The inn's sewer obviously didn't discharge its effluent into the brook.

As he came level with the point at which the rear wall of the inn's grounds ended he was able to see the entire length of the building's windowless and doorless flank. Twenty mets away there was a group of people engaged in a private struggle, out of sight of the watchmen. For a second or two, seeing bronze and gold skins engaged in some kind of tussle, he assumed that an enemy had crept up to the blind side of the inn and was in the process of being seized – but then he recognised Merel Zabio, and realised that he was seeing a rather different kind of struggle.

She wasn't fighting for her life. For the moment, at least, she was merely trying to swat aside a groping hand or two and disengage herself from the ruck forming around her as three men – two bronzes and a golden – closed about her in a manner that was not wholly menacing. Jacom could see, though, that the situation was changing, and that the contest was on the point of becoming genuinely violent.

He had to take two steps back to get an adequate run at the stream, but he jumped it with relative ease. He didn't shout a warning, but the men heard him coming soon enough and one of the bronzes turned. He must have recognised Jacom as one of the men with whom Merel had been sitting during the night, because his expression quickly took on a shadow that was half alarm and half speculation.

'Ah!' he said unsmilingly. 'No trouble here, friend.' His voice was cold; he evidently had as low an opinion of Jacom's worth as his fellows in the stables, but he was conscious of the fact that Amyas might not take kindly to his recruits falling out.

The other two men, taking their cue from the bronze who had spoken, immediately released their grip on Merel's arms, as if to declare that they had merely been involved in innocent conversation – an impression which Merel was quick to correct by bringing her knee up sharply into the golden's groin and shoving one bronze so hard that he cannoned into the one who had turned away.

The knee hadn't quite connected with its intended target, so the golden didn't fall down, but he clutched at himself and let out an angry yelp. The bronze who had been shoved turned on his heel, and his hand went reflexively to his belt, where he had a broad-bladed knife, but the one who had turned to face Jacom, who had been knocked to his knees, was on his feet again in a trice, reaching out to stifle the gesture.

'No, no!' he was quick to say. 'A misunderstanding, that's all!' His eyes told a different story, but his cautious brain had full charge of his tongue.

'Are you all right, Merel?' Jacom asked sharply.

'Sure,' she replied cheerfully. 'I was just explaining to these people that I'd been hired as a fighter, not as a whore.'

'You haven't been hired at all!' the less diplomatic bronze retorted, but his companion was quick to calm him.

'We're sorry,' the other bronze said insincerely, after looking first at Jacom and then at Merel. 'As I said, it was a misunderstanding. We were only trying to find out what the situation was . . . we were a little too enthusiastic. If she's yours, she's yours. No one will dispute it.'

'I'm not his,' Merel objected – but Jacom thought it best to put a different interpretation on the bronze's conciliatory gesture.

'She's one of us,' he said. 'We're all in this together, all on the same side. As your friend says, we're not your hirelings, we're your allies.'

'Some allies,' the golden said, as vitriolically as he could. 'No weapons, no brains. Refuse fished from the river by that scavenger Nath. If they won't serve as whores, what use are they?'

The bronze who had appointed himself spokesman instantly rounded on the man. He was probably glad of an opportunity to discharge a little of his carefully pent up anger. 'Shut up!' he said, spitting the words out. 'Whatever anybody else is, *you're* a hireling and a whore, turned against your own kind.'

Merel, meanwhile, had moved to stand with Jacom, which had the effect that the bronze could address them both at once. 'I apologise, lady,' he said, when he turned back again, in a tone which almost sounded sincere. 'We meant no harm.'

'That's all right,' she said, calmly enough. 'Neither did I.'

The three backed off then, although the two bronzes had to give the golden a shove to hurry him along.

'This doesn't seem to be the happiest company in the world,'

Jacom observed, as soon as the three men had passed out of sight around the corner.

'No, it isn't,' Merel said, with no trace of cheerfulness left in her voice. 'They're all wound up, bronzes and goldens alike – impatient to be under way but anxious about what they might have to face once they are. That wouldn't have come to anything much, even if you hadn't turned up, but it wasn't a misunderstanding or a joke. The golden didn't understand – maybe he did think I'd been taken on for that kind of use – but the bronzes knew well enough what they were doing. What the golden said is what they all think – they only shut him up because they didn't want us told. Still, as travelling companions go, they're a little better than dragomites.'

'That's true,' Jacom agreed, although he couldn't help feeling a tiny prick of doubt. The dragomite warriors had, in the end, been instructed that all their human companions were to be considered nest-sisters. The bronzes were almost certainly thinking of them as mere instruments. The possibility of stealing half the company's horses and making their own way south was seeming more attractive by the minute.

'They do have a point, don't they?' Merel said, looking down at her serving-maid's costume. 'Your men still look like soldiers, after a fashion, but you and I might have to prove our usefulness. Maybe I should have kicked the golden a bit harder – it might have made the bronzes laugh.'

'No,' Jacom said. 'Best not to make any enemies, if we can avoid it. We might need these people as much as they need us.'

'We might not have the luxury of not making enemies,' she countered. 'It might be more a matter of being careful to pick the right ones.'

'Maybe,' he admitted. 'Let's just hope that Luca's right, and that none of the enemies Amyas is making hereabouts can muster the strength to stand against us. Once we're clear of the Nine Towns, and into the wilderness again . . . we'll just have to hope that the bronzes are stronger and braver than the enemies we're being taken to face.' Somehow, he couldn't quite bring himself to take that on trust – and what he'd seen of the bronzes so far, whether as enigmatic observers, paymasters or pesterers of women, hadn't increased his confidence at all.

'I wasn't planning on staying with them that long,' Merel told him. 'I don't know what you plan to do, but I'm bound for Salamander's Fire, with no diversions or digressions. If you want to come, you're welcome, but if not . . .'

'We're all supposed to be on the same side,' Jacom reminded her uneasily.

'So we are,' she agreed, with about as much sincerity as the apologetic bronze. 'Just so long as you remember whose it is.'

Until she said it, Jacom hadn't fully realised that he no longer knew whose side it was that they were supposed to be all on, or whether it made sense to think of a common objective now that their patchwork company had been rudely shattered into disparate fragments. Was there really any point, he wondered, in going to Salamander's Fire? And if not, was there anywhere else that he might rather go instead?

8

IT WASN'T UNTIL the evening meal had ended that Lucrezia found the opportunity to have a private word with Andris. By this time he seemed thoroughly perplexed and had certainly become more anxious – belatedly, in her view – about his condition and the interpretation placed upon it by the members of the Community.

'Something's got into me,' he told her, in a slightly bewildered tone. 'Something alive. I feel quite well, but that doesn't mean that it's not an infection. It's doing something to my mind – feeding it with images.'

'And they want to complete the process,' Lucrezia added. 'They want to secure its empire within your body.'

'Why me?' Andris wanted to know, his broad features seeming strangely innocent. 'Everyone else got sick and itchy – why did it take me so very differently?'

'I don't know,' Lucrezia said. 'That's not the point – the question is, how do you get free of it?'

He didn't seem to be paying attention. 'It started a lot sooner than I thought,' he said reflectively. 'It began the first time I was hit by one of those narcotic darts. I had a dream then – about that head I picked up in the dragomite nest. He – it – was talking about eggs making eggs even then.'

'It doesn't surprise me,' Lucrezia told him, wishing that he could get a better grip on himself. 'Have you looked around at these people when they're all gathered together at mealtimes? Half of them look as if they're sleep-walking. Whatever this drug is, they're all addicted to it. All this mysticism of theirs is an invention to make what they've become seem worthwhile, but it's *not*.'

'That's hardly fair,' Andris countered mildly. 'They don't look like sleep-walkers. Their conversation might not be very lively, and they're well set in their routines, but they're hardly subhuman. They seem clear-headed enough to me.'

Lucrezia sighed. She had been exaggerating, of course, but only because she felt the need to jerk him out of his complacency. She didn't want him becoming more securely possessed by the so-called spirit of the waters than he was already, no matter what insight he might thus acquire into the nature and enigmatic schemes of the Community's God. She would have continued to batter at his defences had she been given time, but Venerina Sirelis and Philemon Taub had found them again, and they were anxious to return to the cellars so that they could continue with their own demonstrations and arguments. For the moment, at least, they were winning – Andris had not yet been won over to their eccentric credo, but he was gradually becoming convinced that what the poisons of the marsh had done to him was indeed to open a portal to some peculiar fount of wisdom.

Lucrezia was tired, but she could see that Andris wasn't. She followed him down the stairway into the cellars, determined to keep her wits about her. The amber had slept for two whole days under the influence of the drug which the bronzes had given him when they first found him but now he seemed – as if by compensation – to be rather more wakeful than was natural. She, on the other hand, was not. She couldn't help wondering how such widely opposed conditions could be after-effects of the same poisons.

She had already made a careful study of the assembly of vessels which Philemon and his associates had accumulated in the cellar. Although it was as neat and as clean as everything else within the Community's lodgings, she knew that it must seem to Andris like some charlatan magician's den, all bizarrerie and strange endeavour. But she could see it differently. It was not unlike the workroom where she had spent many long hours with Ereleth, learning to prepare the instruments of her Art. She saw it for what it surely was: a place where poisons were distilled for the cunning affliction of unready victims.

I am not such a stranger here as he is, she thought, *and I'm still in full possession of my faculties. I can see through the veil of illusion they're spinning around him, and I ought to be able to fathom the truth of these matters they've so carefully mystified.*

'Individuals are born and individuals die,' Venerina was busy informing Andris, with consummate patience. 'Each one can be regarded as a tiny impulse to order, which eventually exhausts itself. But on a larger scale, whole populations of individuals of many different species form systems which persist over much longer periods of time, and which are themselves mere aspects of greater systems. Each system has its own impetus, which is potentially capable of sustaining it indefinitely, though not without change.

'Individuals come and individuals go, populations wax and wane, new species emerge and disappear . . . but the largest systems – the world-systems – move according to more stately rhythms. They change, but they change by measured degrees. The world-system of which we're a part has its occasional upheavals, but there's an underlying pattern which is steadfastly impelled towards greater complexity and more intricate interlinking.

'Sometimes, even world-systems die, and are obliterated – but they too are aspects of a larger pattern, which extends across the whole universe. Even on its vastest scale, the pattern is connected. Worlds aren't completely isolated from one another, partly because there is life of a sort in the spaces which separate them, and partly because one of the consequences of increasing complexity is that some worlds generate means by which their own life can be spread from world to world. Some world-systems can send forth spores, which take root even in ground which is already part of some other biosphere. World-systems can meet and compete, and can sometimes – after much experimentation and negotiation – combine into a new whole, a new system.'

'That's what happened here,' Andris said quietly. 'That's what the lore of Genesys is all about. The ship which brought our ancestors to the world didn't just bring people; it brought the seeds of a whole system of life. The plan our forefathers made was intended to allow the new system to be set up within the one which was already here. It had to be a vague plan, because the meeting of the two systems was so very complicated that they couldn't possibly foresee all its consequences – and because those consequences would extend for thousands of years, long after the ship had gone.'

'It's not just something which happened long ago,' Philemon

put in. 'It's still happening. That's the whole point. It's been happening for thousands of years – nobody knows how many thousands, because we don't have the means to keep an accurate count – and it'll go on happening for thousands more. The people of the ship couldn't determine the final outcome, or even calculate the likely possibilities. All they could do was to set matters in train, and leave the rest to their descendants – and, of course, to God.'

'Something went wrong,' Lucrezia said, to demonstrate that even non-believers could follow such trains of argument and draw conclusions in their wake. 'That's what the lore of Genesys records. Even at the very beginning, something went wrong. The people of the ship built a city, and then they realised that no matter what they did to protect it, the city couldn't endure. They had to change the plan. They had to make something else instead: a garden, in the language of the lore. They had to rethink everything and remake everything. They had to make all kinds of changes they'd never anticipated. That's where the story you heard from the blind man in that waterfront inn comes into it, Andris. They had to take something from Serpents and something from Salamanders to patch things up.'

'We shouldn't think of it as something going wrong,' Venerina said. 'Any such plan would have needed continual adaptation and readjustment. That doesn't matter. What matters, as Philemon says, is that the process is still going on, and that we're all a part of it. We're caught up in it: in corruption and corrosion, destruction and displacement, competition and combination . . .'

'We're invaders,' Lucrezia interrupted, unwilling to let the older woman put her own deceptive gloss on the information without challenge. 'Even though we've been here for more generations than we can remember, we're invaders. Everything that we call earthly is simply an instrument of that invasion. Everything we call unearthly is involved in resistance to our invasion. Every now and again a balance is achieved . . . but it always tips again, and the contest flares up anew. Was the destruction of the Dragomite Hills accomplished by earthly life, I wonder? Was it a shot in the ongoing war that's now bringing forth some kind of backlash?'

'You're carrying the analogy too far,' Venerina Sirelis said sternly. 'Or perhaps not far enough. The competition between the two life-systems isn't like a war, with generals sending out armies to capture specific objectives, and new weapons being deployed. It's not a matter of one system driving the other out of particular territories, although that does happen sometimes. One possible outcome of such an invasion might be the total annihilation of one system by the other, but that's not the end which the forefathers had in mind – not because they knew it to be improbable but because they thought it undesirable. The end which the forefathers had in mind – the only end they *could* have in mind, given that the game they were playing was God's game, according to His rules – is the end to which all life is directed by virtue of its nature and its essence: the forging of a new system, a new whole integrating all the former parts.'

'The forging of chimeras,' Andris said, getting his reply in just ahead of Lucrezia, to show that he too had kept up with the implications of the discussion. 'The making of part-human and part-alien entities like the ones I saw in the dragomite nest.'

'If that's the destiny of humankind,' Lucrezia said quickly, 'I don't want any part of it. If that's what the Genesys plan was intended to bring forth, I don't think much of the plan.'

'Nor do I,' Andris said, with a faraway look in his eye. Lucrezia inferred that he was remembering his adventure in the bowels of the dragomite queen.

'But you brought the drone's head out of the nest, didn't you?' she pointed out. 'You let him call you brother, and you answered his plea. You admitted the kinship between you.'

Venerina Sirelis took up the thread of the argument again. 'What you saw in the dragomite nest is just part of an ongoing process of trial and proof. It's something which goes on all the time among unearthly species – it's a key feature of the system which binds together all the life we call unearthly.'

'Unearthly life lacks containment and confinement,' Andris whispered, with the faraway look still in his eye. Lucrezia guessed that he was now remembering his long discourse in the marshes, racking up yet another point of coincidence.

'That's one reason why Philemon took you out on to the lake to show you the free-living cousins of the other creatures which have found a place in the Corridors of Power. The formulation of chimeras is part of the system native to this world, and it's one of the ways in which that system has reacted to the invasion of a different system; it has an inbuilt impetus towards absorption and accommodation. All the species that were part of the natural order here had to cope, one way or another, with that tendency of absorption. In order to maintain their individuality they had to develop ways of combating or of compromising with it.

'Serpents and Salamanders offered two different models of how such compromises could be accomplished by sentient beings, and that's why the makers of the Genesys plan were encouraged – and perhaps forced – to take or to copy something from each species. They prepared us as best they could for life in the world they found, although they could have no clear idea of what the ultimate outcomes of their preparations would be. I say *outcomes* because there must be many different possibilities, including some which the planners couldn't possibly foresee.

'What's happening to the world now shouldn't be seen as a battle in a war of extermination, even though it might result in widespread destruction and devastation. It should be seen as a temporary fervent phase in a long process of mutual adaptation whose beginnings have become mythical and whose end remains unforeseeable.'

'Unforeseeable,' Philemon echoed, 'but not unimaginable. We don't and can't know in any detail what might be happening in the southlands, but we can and do understand how it fits into a scheme of things which is universal as well as local. What happens here and now, you see, is simply one tiny part of something which is always happening everywhere. It really does improve the quality of life when you can see that, and understand it, and take part in it. The business of living, from day to day, year to year and cradle to grave, is easier and better if you can understand your part in it and God's part in it: if you can see, and feel, that you're part of a great adventure which doesn't simply extend from Xandria to Chimera's Cradle and from one year to another but from here to the farthest star, and from now to forever.'

Andris was frowning, but Lucrezia recognised the expression as a frown of concentration rather than a frown of anger or anguish. Venerina and Philemon had given him plenty of food for thought.

'What is it, exactly, that you expect of us?' Lucrezia asked sharply. 'Once we've acknowledged that you understand these things far better than we ever did, what are we supposed to do? Do you expect us to join your Community, or simply to continue our journey with keener minds and gladder hearts?'

'That's your choice,' Philemon said. 'But what Venerina's told you is just the beginning, the foundation-stone of enlightenment. It's merely what you have to know, before you can begin to see. There's so much more to learn, from the lake and its blood. Andris has caught a glimpse of it already, although he doesn't yet know what to make of it. There's so much more we can show him – so much more that he needs to be shown, whether he knows it or not.'

'*Needs*?' Lucrezia echoed, before Andris could intervene. 'Who are you to say what Andris *needs*? Do I need to be shown as well?'

'Needs vary from one individual to another,' Venerina said, as smoothly as ever. 'Not all humans are alike, you see – and I'm not talking about the lustre of our skins. We may not be aware of it, but we're already chimeras, fused with all manner of creatures which dwell inside our bodies, and there are different chimeras in human form. Some of us are host to Serpent's blood, some to Salamander's fire, and some to the spirit of the waters. People can live or die without ever knowing who or what they really are, but times of crisis require and bring forth enlightenment.'

'What are you saying, exactly?' Andris wanted to know. All his combativeness had returned now, and his voice was sharp. 'What is it you think I need, and what do you intend to do about it?'

'They think you need another dose of poison,' Lucrezia told him, speaking as one whose worst suspicions had just been confirmed. 'A bigger one than before, and a headier mix. They think you can be driven to a special kind of madness.'

'That's not what we mean at all,' Venerina Sirelis was quick to say – but Lucrezia was sure that it was, no matter that the handsome woman would have chosen very different words to describe what she had called *a special kind of madness*.

'But if we're all chimeras,' Andris said, his amber brow still furrowed by an anxious frown, 'what can it mean to be human? And if human form masks many different kinds of chimeras, are we not implicitly at war with one another, whether we know it or not?'

'Not necessarily,' said Philemon gently. 'The divine plan requires collaboration as well as competition – but there are many different kinds of collaboration. The kind which we have forged here works entirely to the benefit of its human members; others might be regarded as fates worse than death. That's why the way to Chimera's Cradle is so very dangerous.' He turned to Lucrezia and added: 'There are many ways to carry forward God's plan, my lady, and I beg you not to attempt that path.'

'Have you been to Chimera's Cradle yourself?' Lucrezia asked.

'No,' Philemon admitted. 'Nor have I spoken to any man who has – but the Community has been here for a long time, and many travellers have passed this way in times long gone. We have our lore to guide us, my lady, and we have our understanding of the divine plan.'

You have heard travellers' tales, Lucrezia thought, *and you have your myths*.

She looked at Andris again, and met his eyes. It was hardly surprising that she could see nothing therein but doubt and anxiety.

9

THE CRYSTAL CITY seemed to Carus Fraxinus to be somewhat less wondrous when seen from within than it had appeared from a distance. The needle-tipped spires were invisible from ground level, hidden by the vast webs which connected them. These multi-layered lattices formed a ceiling almost as dense as that formed by the crowns of the trees in the Forest of Absolute Night, and the lowest-lying – as might have been expected – were in a state of advanced decay.

Like the forest floor, the ground over which they walked would have been committed to darkness, at least by night, had it not been for light emitted by the structures themselves. The quality of the light here was, however, very different from that of the forest. The light emitted by the parasites which clustered about the boles of the vast forest trees had been very wan and white; here the light seemed much more robust, and it shone in a bewildering variety of colours. It was as if the paths followed by the beams of light took them through a kaleidoscopic confusion of variously tilted prisms and variously tinted lenses.

The 'streets' of the 'city' were rather narrow, by virtue of the fact that the bulbous structures which stood in place of buildings were very much broader than the trunks of the forest giants. Perhaps in consequence of their narrowness they seemed much busier than the desolate routes of the forest, or perhaps it was simply that the sparkling gemsnakes, sequined millipedes and crabs whose hyaline shells were studded with baubles had not the same fear of humanoids and humankind that the fauna of the forest had; there were no darklanders here to hunt them and the Salamanders did not bother to trap anything less substantial than the sandskinks which presumably preyed on these lesser creatures. Fraxinus was more astonished, however, by the abundance of flying creatures: little moths with ghostly white wings; huge beetles whose wing-cases glistened with a metallic sheen; dragonflies with jewelled bodies and massive jaws presumably adapted to cut through the very same wing-cases.

Fraxinus was surprised to observe that the Salamanders seemed different in this environment. In the open, whether beneath the sun or the stars, their marbled coats had seemed rather drab, but in the multicoloured half-light of the city their scales came to life, revealing a rich complexity of subtle shades.

A similar complexity was to be observed in the vitreous 'walls' between which they were moving. From a distance, the various components of the vast crystalline mass had looked mirror-smooth – and perhaps the heights which extended above the latticework canopy were indeed as smooth as they seemed – but the faces visible down here were very variable. The smoothest usually had a pale ground colour, streaked with various other hues; many of these presented gleaming 'windows' which shone as if they had been recently polished. Around these windows, however, the surfaces wrinkled like the rinds of dried fruits dusted with sugar and spices. Nor were they merely irregular, for it was easy to make out cracks and rents of every dimension, every one of which attracted the attention of insects and other creatures. Some few of these lesions oozed mysterious fluids, which were even more attractive to those in search of sustenance.

The most remarkable of all these surfaces were those which resembled the intricately carved or carefully etched bas-reliefs which sculptors worked into various public buildings in Xandria. The 'carvings' in question often seemed ill-executed or half-finished, but they nevertheless gave the strong impression that a human – or humanoid – hand had been at work. The figures which stood out more or less distinctly from these complex surfaces were monochrome likenesses of some of the creatures which could be seen wandering in the latticework or flitting through the still air. None of them was ornamented like its 'model', but they all echoed the basic forms of local animal life: worms, lizards and various kinds of flies.

'Could they possibly be carvings?' Fraxinus asked Ereleth, while they had only seen these strange figures from a distance. 'Is this the artwork of Salamanderkind?'

'There are too many,' she replied. 'Is it possible that the

surfaces are capable of trapping living creatures and secreting some kind of skin around them to protect the corpses from other scavengers while their flesh is slowly absorbed?'

Fraxinus would have lent tentative agreement to that, acknowledging it as the most likely hypothesis, had not Shabir been looking out over his shoulder. The general was glad of a rare opportunity to parade his wisdom, and he was quick to interrupt.

'Their cousins, which lie flat upon the ground, are often to be found on derelict land near the southern towns,' he informed them. 'They're common in the barrens. They can be smashed up by strong men plying good sledgehammers, given time, but the men of Tawil and Sabinal prefer to stuff the deeper pits with plastic and explode them. The bigger ones make pitfalls large enough to trap a man's foot but no one with a good pair of boots has much to fear from them. It's said that not all the shapes are in the process of being absorbed, and that the others are creatures in the process of formation, which will eventually be let loose like moths from cocoons, but I don't know anyone who's seen it happen, so it may be a fanciful lie. Some call them flowing stones, others figured stones.'

'You mean that what we're looking at is a kind of parasite overlaying a smoother surface?' Ereleth said. 'It's some kind of animal whose flesh is almost as hard as stone?'

'Not *almost*,' the general said. 'It flows, like molten glass on the point of setting, but it's very hard indeed. It's hard work reducing them to rubble, but it can be done, and the parts can't regenerate if they're reduced to the size of a man's head. Is there nothing like them in the northlands?'

'Not to my knowledge,' Fraxinus told him, furrowing his brow as he tried to assimilate this information and its possible corollaries.

'Your ancestors probably rooted them out for good and all a hundred generations ago,' Shabir said. 'It'd be easy enough, given that you have no shortage of steel tools as well as plastic-making skills. The southland bronzes must have been very careless to let such a simple problem get out of hand. The Salamanders obviously don't pay them any heed at all. With big flat feet like theirs, they can afford to ignore them.'

This was the closest Shabir had come to making a joke since he had unwittingly joined their company, but Fraxinus could see that there might be more wisdom in it than wit. If these things usually lay flat on the ground, they might indeed pose a hazard to horses and humans, but they would be utterly impotent to impede or injure a Salamander.

Fraxinus had presumed that the journey through this new wonderland would be long, and had thought it more than likely that they would see the dawn before the Salamanders rejoined their companions, but in fact they had been barely an hour within the body of the 'city' before they were met by another group of Salamanders. The column paused for only a few minutes while the Salamanders croaked and clicked away – utterly defeating Mossassor's feeble attempts to provide a commentary by translation – and then they were on the move again, with new guides. After another hour, or perhaps slightly less, they came to a place where yet more Salamanders had made a camp.

'Their cooking-fire must be carefully positioned,' Fraxinus said to Ereleth, drawing her attention to the way in which the smoke climbed straight up into the canopy above after coiling around the sides of the cauldron which sat atop the fire.

The queen wasn't in the least interested in such trivial technicalities. Her own bird-like eyes were watching the way the Salamanders who had been waiting here reacted to the dragomite warriors and to Dhalla. They showed no conspicuous apprehension, but Fraxinus got the impression that they were intrigued. The incomprehensible conversation, which had continued unabated since the moment the first newcomers had become involved, now swelled to a virtual babble. It seemed that there was much to be explained, and that the Salamanders here were avid for the explanation.

Fraxinus got down from the wagon and went to stand beside Dhalla, who was at the focal point of half a dozen curious stares. He looked up at her, and said: 'Whether by courtesy of rumour or recognition, they seem to know that you have Salamander's fire burning in your heart.'

'For the moment,' she said soberly, 'I can't feel it burning. Perhaps they'll know when it does burn, but there's nothing in the sight of them which arises the slightest flicker of fellow-feeling in me.' Fraxinus realised that she was anxious; the strange surroundings were making her uneasy, although she surely had nothing to fear.

Mossassor had gone to the thick of the congregation, intent on joining in the conversation, but didn't seem to be having much success as yet. Fraxinus looked around at the clutter of the camp, swiftly passing over the stocks of food, clothing, weapons and tools but letting his eyes linger on other objects which were presumably what the Salamanders had come to gather. There were a great many pieces of crystal lying about, many of them more than a met across. Almost all of them were colourless and more or less round, and although he could see no sign that polishers had been at work Fraxinus guessed that they were probably intended to be ground to glass-like transparency, for use as windows, mirrors or – most likely of all – lenses.

The merchant wondered what intensity of heat might be generated by a lens as broad as a man's double-armed reach focusing the light of the noonday sun, and whether that kind of heat had anything to do with the concept of Salamander's fire.

Vaca Metra came up behind Fraxinus, and said: 'We will rest now. We will take food and water from the wagon.'

'Yes, of course,' he said – but she lingered, as if she wanted him to say something more.

'It'll all right,' he said. 'We're safe here. When I know more about what's going on, I'll tell you.'

'They will take us to Salamander's Fire,' she said; it was a question, although it didn't sound like one.

'No promises have yet been made,' Fraxinus told her, 'but I believe they will. If Jume Metra lives, that is where she will head for.' He didn't like to make any comment about the likelihood of her having been able to reach that destination.

The mound-woman nodded, having made her point, and went to rejoin the patient warriors. Mossassor detached itself from the knot of Salamanders and said: 'Iss good. Wisse oness very eager to talk. Glad to ssee uss. I ssink ssey know much more than osserss.'

That wouldn't be hard,' Fraxinus thought. Aloud, he said: 'We're ready to talk when they are.'

When they were ready – which took a long time, because the slow-moving Salamanders were not the kind of creatures who made haste in such numinous matters as 'becoming ready', the

Salamanders ushered Fraxinus to a place close to the cooking-fire. Although he did not feel the least need of extra heat he sat where he was put, suspecting that it was a position of privilege which it would be rude to refuse. Ereleth was brought to sit a third of the way around the fire to his right, while Dhalla was led with even more ceremony to take a similar position on his left and Ereleth's right. Mossassor was put next to the merchant, but slightly behind, while the spaces in between were filled by Salamanders.

It was very difficult to tell one Salamander from another, and most of the ones who had come with them across the desert had already departed, while the remainder had changed their smocks. Fraxinus couldn't be certain, but he thought that only one of the Salamanders in the innermost circle had been among those they had talked to – or had tried to talk to – after harvesting the floaters.

The Salamander on Fraxinus's right appeared to be the senior 'wise one'. That one, at any rate, was the one who launched into a speech when all the rest had fallen quiet. It *was* a speech, for it lasted a good five minutes, without any pauses for translation. It was not until the Salamander finished, and nodded its huge head, that Mossassor took up the challenge.

'Ssayss welcome,' the Serpent told Fraxinus punctiliously. 'Ssayss will be friendss. Ssayss sso much iss difficult for me, but I ssink iss only Ssalamander way, not being difficult. Ssayss time iss coming when Sserpentss, Ssalamanderss and humanss musst come togesser again, musst be sside by sside in . . . not know word, would be ssomessing like ssissterhood, if Ssalamanderss had ssisterss like dragomitess. I know what quesstionss you have, but I ssink it besst if you put on big sshow, like . . . name iss impossible for humanss, but try ssay *Ixtlplt* if you can.'

Fraxinus would have preferred more actual translation and less commentary, but he was entirely in the Serpent's hands and there was no point in putting further pressure on a situation that was already difficult enough.

'Tell Ixtlplt that I'm honoured and pleased to be here,' Fraxinus said. 'Tell it – I'm assuming Ixtlplt is an it, not a he or a she – that I've come a very long way to find Salamander's Fire, because our lore tells us that it's important that someone should go there, on the way to Chimera's Cradle, when changes begin to sweep across the world. Tell it that we don't know why our lore instructs us to do so, but that we take such things seriously. Tell it that we have endured many hardships and troubles on our journey, and that we're grateful to be among friends at last. Tell it that our lore speaks of debts which humans owe to Serpents and to Salamanders, and that we take that seriously too, even though we don't know exactly what the debts are.'

It took a great deal longer for Mossassor to render this speech into terms which the Salamanders might find comprehensible, and the process required several brief clarificatory exchanges. It also took a good deal longer for it to relay the next speech than Ixtlplt required to make it, even after several more clarificatory exchanges and even though it still appeared to be speaking synoptically.

'Iss ssorry for hardsshipss, and sso on. Iss being very polite. Ssayss will take you ssafely to Ssalamander'ss Fire. Ssayss understandss debt, but can't sspeak of it. Are even wisser oness at home, it sseemss. Ssayss will assk for newss of your friendss, help ssearssh. Ssayss Ssalamander'ss Fire iss ssafe fortress, will outlasst plasse ssouss of here where humanss live. Ssinkss not many humanss left ssere, none at all fursser ssouss, but no Ssalamander hass been to . . . ssink iss what your map callss Ssitiess of Plain . . . for very long time. Ssayss no humanss or Sserpentss in mad foresst . . . ssink your map call ssat Ssilver Ssornss . . . but cannot ssay what might be in osser place . . . not know human words at all. Ssomessing like *breeding-ground* or . . . ssomessing like Ssalamander'ss Fire but not ssame. I try transslate Chimera'ss Cradle, but my transslation meanss nossing to Ixtlplt.'

'According to Andris Myrasol's map,' Fraxinus said, 'something called the Gauntlet of Gladness extends from the Silver Thorns to something called the Nest of the Phoenix, which lies about the Navel of the World – but I don't suppose any of that will make sense to Ixtlplt.'

'Makess no ssensse to me,' Mossassor observed ruefully. 'Could not begin to make Ixtlplt undersstand.'

'Can you ask whether Salamander lore has any commandments like the one you set out to follow?' Fraxinus asked, not bothering to glance in Ereleth's direction.

'Have tried,' Mossassor replied. 'Ixtlplt ssayss can't ssay, iss ssorry. I ssink real ansswer yess; ssink ssey know better ssan we do what iss all about. Ssink ssey will tell uss, but firsst iss ssomessing we musst ssee. Ssight better ssan wordss – problem iss we not know enough wordss, and wordss we have . . . not liess, but not eassy to undersstand.'

Fraxinus suppressed a sigh.

'Tell Ixtlplt we're very grateful,' he said. 'Lay it on as thick as you like. Tell it that if there's anything we have in our wagon that it can use, we'll gladly offer it as a gift. Tell it whatever you think it needs to hear. Tell it we'll be very interested indeed to see whatever it is it needs to show us, before we can begin to understand what it's talking about, and that we'll be absolutely fascinated to see Salamander's Fire burn *bravely*. And be polite. Be very, very polite.'

Serpents had such wide mouths that it was impossible for them to smile, but a slight flicker of Mossassor's forked tongue signified that it was following the tenor of the speech well enough, and that it wasn't oblivious of the irony in it.

It's not so long ago, Fraxinus thought, as Mossassor set forth to execute this commission, *that I thought of Serpents as alien beings with which it was next to impossible to communicate, for lack of shared words and shared concepts. Compared with the Salamanders, though, Mossassor seems like an old and trusted friend. At least they do seem genuinely friendly, and all of one mind. And they are right: why bother with awkward and treacherous words when they can simply show us what they think we need to see?*

10

'DON'T DO THIS, Andris.'

Andris looked at Lucrezia from beneath his lowered eyebrows, wondering why he felt guilty in the face of her disapproval. The tone of her voice was half critical and half pleading, and the expression on her face displayed similarly mixed feelings. He didn't understand why she seemed to be more anxious than he was, given that he'd already proved – at least to his own satisfaction – that the marsh poisons couldn't do him much harm. It was true that he still felt a little peculiar, and he was prepared to admit that the fact that he felt exceptionally well rather than debilitated might be a dangerous illusion, but he couldn't believe that Venerina Sirelis and Philemon Taub wanted to do him harm. Indeed, they seemed more enthusiastic to do him good than anyone he had ever met – including the Xandrian princess who had planned to plant a thornbush in his own flesh, break both his legs and bury him in her garden.

While he hesitated he looked down at the bowl which Philemon had placed in front of him. The liquid contained therein was milky and had a very faint glow; it was more viscous than the marshwater through which he had waded for several days but it wasn't as glutinous as the lake's 'colourless blood'. As he stared at it he could feel a strange kind of thirst exerting a seductive force on his mind, but he assumed that was just a trick of his imagination.

He knew, of course, that Lucrezia had reason on her side in asking him to be wary, all the more so because he was her sole remaining protector in a land far removed from the cloying security of the Inner Sanctum. How wretched it must make her feel to think that her one ally in the world was a man she had conspired to kill – and that the only other who might turn up in the near future was a thief who had kidnapped her by accident and must have come close to killing *her*!

'You don't have to worry about me,' he told her coolly. 'I'm as strong as an ox and my head's so thick it'd take more than a cupful of poison to rot my mind.'

This reply merely caused her to look slightly disgusted. He had observed before that she had a low opinion of bravado; her cloistered childhood had evidently left her with an inadequate appreciation of the obligations and glories of heroism.

Andris was sure in his own mind that he hadn't lost his ability to respect reason or to recognise its force, even though the spirit of the lake's waters had already possessed him to some degree. He felt that he had his own reasons for going ahead with this peculiar trial by ordeal, and that they were good enough. Had he been left alone with Lucrezia for any length of time he would have tried to explain them to her, and he was confident that he would have been able to convince her. He would have assured her that he didn't believe in the Community's God, or that the fundamental properties of life really warranted description as a plan, but even if all the mystical excess were stripped away from what they had told him something remained which warranted investigation. God or no God, plan or no plan, his strange dreams did seem to have some truth in them, some measure of authentic enlightenment. That intrigued him, and he would have thought himself a coward had he not thirsted to know more. If there was wisdom in the spirit of the waters, he wanted it all.

'What, exactly, will it do to me?' he asked the old man, by way of procrastination. 'Will it send me to sleep?'

'No, it won't,' Philemon was quick to say. 'Forget the delirium you experienced while you were trekking through the marsh; you picked up all kinds of different thorn-poisons that way, according to no particular recipe. Every component of this mixture has been measured out with the utmost care, and there's a hundred generations of trial and error behind the formula. I've kept the dosage low, while allowing for your unusual bulk, so the only real danger is that it'll be insufficient to take full effect. Once you've tried it, you'll not be afraid of taking a stronger dose next time – I can guarantee that.'

'It's not just bodily harm you have to worry about,' Lucrezia put in, fighting the case to the bitter end. 'I'm an apprentice witch, and I know a good deal about the multitudinous uses of poisons. There are poisons which leave you physically fit but sap your will, and the way you're sitting there looking down at this stuff leads me to suspect that you might already have had a dose of some such compound. Then again, there are potions which make you feel wonderful, and which tempt you to use them again and again, until they *require* to be taken again and again, at increasingly frequent intervals, leaving you in the end at the mercy of pain and madness. They're already talking about further trials and stronger doses – such adventures could enslave you.'

'We are not addicted to the spirit of the waters,' Venerina Sirelis contradicted her smoothly. 'All the elders of the Community use it, to the limit of their capacity, including Philemon and myself. Those who give up its use – as some eventually do – suffer no terrible discomfort by so doing. Nor does it sap our will. In any case, if you're well enough versed in the Art of Witchery, you'd be able to counter such effects if they did materialise, would you not?'

Andris tried to judge whether Lucrezia's obstinate shake of the head signified that she was not yet fully accomplished in her Art or whether she was trying to deny the whole thrust of Venerina's argument.

'In itself, it won't give you faith in God or an acute consciousness of His plan,' Philemon said, evidently having worked out where Andris's interests lay. 'What it should do is to give you a greater awareness of yourself, and your own place in the scheme of things. It will show you who and what you are.'

'Not everyone can share the spirit of the waters,' Venerina added, taking up her companion's cue, 'and not everyone who partakes of it enjoys the same degree of insight. You've already given evidence of a greater affinity than is commonplace, and it's not impossible that you might eventually obtain a symbiotic relationship with the spirit more intimate than mine or Philemon's.'

'Do you also hope that when he's attained this mystical communion Andris will decide to stay in the Community?' Lucrezia asked sharply.

'Is that what you're afraid of?' Venerina countered. 'Do you fear the loss of the servant who might guard you on your journey to Chimera's Cradle?'

'No, she doesn't,' Andris was quick to put in, by way of soothing the situation. 'She knows that I've powerful reasons of my own for going as far as Salamander's Fire; if you think this stuff will make me reluctant to leave, you're mistaken. What's this talk of a *symbiotic relationship*? You never used the expression before – I've only ever heard Aulakh Phar use it, in talking about the dragomites. *He* used it to mean a mutual dependence of different species – a chimera without any actual union of flesh, I think he said. You're saying that the stuff in this cup is alive, aren't you?'

'The entire lake is alive,' Philemon said quietly. 'You've already seen that. You've already drunk its active plasm while you were in the marshes. What you have there is merely an extract. Our relationship with the lake isn't truly symbiotic, because we make no necessary contribution to its well-being, but we're not its prisoners. It doesn't hold us here, and it won't hold you against your will.'

Andris thought that a cunning argumentative move, and couldn't help but smile. Lucrezia didn't. He wondered whether she would rid herself of her Serpent's blood, were there some device of witchery to achieve its elimination – or whether, if there were some similar device to permit a fuller understanding of what there was within her, she would be eager to use it. The latter seemed the likelier possibility.

If I were the kind of man who walked in fear of the unknown, he thought, *I'd never have quit Ferentina. I'd have fought my brothers for the crown, dicing with death in a game whose outcomes could all be seen, understood, and weighed. I chose exile, like my Uncle Theo. I chose the vast and hostile world, and all its mysteries, in preference to that which I knew and understood too well. I have no Serpent's blood in my veins, but I have the same brave wanderer's blood that Merel has: the blood which made us two of a kind. I'd be a coward if I refused this . . . and when all is said and done, I have a thirst.*

He reached out to take the cup in his right hand. 'Forgive me, my lady,' he said to the princess, although he had never called her that before. He met her eyes as he spoke, though, and saw that he stood in no need of forgiveness. For all her caution, she was as curious as he was. She refused to admire his bravado, but she was interested to know what would happen.

He raised the cup to his lips, and took a sip of the warm liquid.

All of a sudden he heard the distant sound of shouting. It was coming from outside, and he hesitated yet again, wondering whether it was news that Checuti and the others lost in the marsh had been found. Venerina Sirelis had already turned away to the window, to see what it was. Andris realised that it was a westward-facing window, and that any news of Checuti would be far more likely to come from the opposite direction. He also realised that the members of the Community were not the kind of people likely to trumpet such trivial good news in such an excessive manner. The liquid sat on his tongue, slightly briny but not offensively so.

'What is it?' Lucrezia asked.

'I don't know,' Venerina answered. The anxiety in her voice suggested that she too had concluded that it was unlikely to be a trivial matter, but she didn't want to leave the business in hand unfinished. 'Drink,' she said. 'We'll know soon enough what the trouble is, and draining the cup will not deny you the opportunity to hear and understand.'

Andris shrugged his shoulders, feeling now that he had hesitated far too long and made too hearty a meal of Lucrezia's doubts. He swallowed the drop on his tongue and took a deeper draught. There was a certain bitterness in the measure, but it was masked by a compensating sweetness that left a curious aftertaste when he had drunk it down. Such was his accumulated thirst that he had drained the cup to the dregs within half a minute.

There was no immediate effect. The lack of difference in his state of mind seemed somehow insulting, but not particularly disappointing. He started to smile again, but he stopped.

Venerina had got up and gone to the window. She had opened the casement so as to hear and see better, and the volume of the shouts increased. It was clear now that they were redolent with fear and desperation, and that implication was echoed by the woman's sharp intake of breath. The distant shouts were being taken up by nearer voices now, and these had immediately conjoined in a clamour of alarm and arousal. If there was news of some discovery, it was certainly not Andris's recent companions who had been found.

Philemon stood up when he heard Venerina suddenly breathe in, recognising the panic in the reflex. Andris and Lucrezia were not far behind. They all moved to the window to see what Venerina was looking at. Lucrezia squeezed her slender frame between the woman and the old man, but Andris had to stand back, peering over their heads. The night was not as bright as the previous one, and the luminosity of the lake served to shadow rather than illuminate the host that was moving along its southern shore, but there was light enough to show him that the dark ripple extended a long way. If the approaching company consisted of mounted men, there must be hundreds.

For half a minute, Andris was certain that they *were* mounted men; the shadowed movements caught by his searching eyes had that kind of flow. But there were other movements too, which his practised eyes were not as quick to capture and which brought forth no echo of familiarity.

'What are they?' Lucrezia asked, presumably not talking about the humans or their horses but about the others that marched with them.

'I can't tell,' Philemon said.

Some of the people of the Community must have been able to tell, though, for they were fleeing in naked terror, and crying warnings about Serpents. But what, Andris wondered, was so fearful about Serpents? And why were the shadows whose forms he was trying so hard to see so very large?

'Could they be Serpents?' Venerina asked, her eyes having adapted to the light more quickly than those of her companions.

'They're too big,' Lucrezia said. 'They're far too tall . . . unless . . .'

In the hesitation which followed, Andris lost all interest in the ominous possibilities signified by that *unless*, for he suddenly felt exceedingly strange. As Philemon had promised, he didn't fall unconscious and he didn't feel any terrible discomfort, but the quality of the light cast by the stars upon the surface of the lake, and the quality of the lake's own light, abruptly altered in a way he had no words to describe. It was as if the world were undergoing an astonishing metamorphosis into a form which he had hitherto been quite incapable of imagining.

He stepped back, put his hands up to his face and covered his eyes as he clamped them shut. It did no good; the changing light was inside as well as outside, and it filled his head.

He tried to speak, but all he could say was: 'I . . .'

As it transpired, no one was listening. The shouts were even louder now,and their echoes more confused, but they were not loud enough to drown out Venerina Sirelis's horrified whisper, which said: 'They're attacking the house! For the love of God, they mean to kill us all!'

These words caused a curious agitation in Andris's mind, which now seemed utterly possessed by strange radiance.

'The ones that aren't men *are* Serpents,' Lucrezia said wonderingly. 'It's just that they're so much bigger than Mossassor and Ssifuss. They're *giant* Serpents . . . and if they mean to kill us, we don't stand a chance. Look how many they are!'

Andris dropped his hands again, and opened his eyes, as if by the force of his own courage and concentration he could let the imperious light flow away. He was astonished and appalled by the steadiness of his own voice as he said: 'I fear this experiment might have been a masterpiece of bad timing.'

He felt, but could not see, Venerina Sirelis push past him, running for the door. He felt, but could not see, Lucrezia take him by the arm. He heard Philemon Taub saying 'Why? Why? *Why?*' in a plaintive tone which displayed, for the first time, the full extent of his decrepitude.

Andris, to his chagrin, had not even begun to understand anything at all.

11

JACOM'S NEW UNIFORM wasn't a good fit, but he knew as he rode at the head of Amyas's column, displaying it to all the world, that it had utterly transformed him. Its colours might have been stitched on to the jerkin as a belated afterthought, and the captain's star had certainly been added later, but its meaning was perfectly clear. The whole outfit was a shoddy patchwork, but what it made of him was a man of renewed status, renewed importance and renewed hope.

He wasn't quite the man he had been before, of course – his belt and sword were doubtless good enough by local standards, but they were paltry by comparison with those that had been issued to him in Xandria's citadel, and although the coin in the purse was reasonably abundant it was far from fresh – but his fortunes had taken a giant leap back from the brink of desolation, and his attitudes had shifted in consequence. He knew, of course, that what had been given to him had been given in order to achieve exactly that shift, but he felt no ingratitude on that score. It was good to know that his loyalty was a prize worth buying.

Amyas had returned to the inn in the late afternoon, in company with Purkin, Koraismi and half a dozen others – but not Hyry Keshvara. There had been no further delay; Amyas had begun barking orders before he had even dismounted from his horse – and he had dismounted only to give immediate instructions for a fresh mount to be made ready. He had moved through the inn like a human whirlwind, jabbering away at his recruiting sergeant and his paymasters while he walked. The place had never been still, but now it became a hive of urgent activity. Jacom had hardly had time to begin feeling left out before he was caught up in it all, Amyas curtly bidding him to fall into step as he went back out into the sunlight.

The bronze had led Jacom through the yard, jerking his head this way and that to instruct the men loading the wagons to make ready for departure while Jacom's eye was caught by a cloud of dots massing over the south-western horizon, speckling the twilight sky. When Amyas had finally turned to face Jacom, he had seen where Jacom's gaze was directed, and said: 'Aye, that's the vanguard of our enemy – as meek and mild as you could imagine, though they're well on their way to capturing this land. There are much worse things coming in their train. This man says you were his officer, but had no aptitude for it at all. Is that true?'

This man was, of course, Purkin, who had also been trying to keep up with the bronze. Jacom had turned to stare at the sergeant's face, whose golden hue darkened almost to bronze as he flushed with embarrassment.

'He doubtless thinks he's a better judge of such matters than I,' Jacom had replied, as coolly as he could, 'but he's been a sergeant all his life in one of the softest billets in Xandria. His contempt is based on long experience of dodging duties and shirking fights, and he has no knowledge of what I might be capable of.'

He was still proud of his improvisation.

'You're not nobly born, I understand, but well-trained in the Arts Martial,' Amyas had gone on to say, serenely ignoring Purkin's discomfort. 'Your father is a landowner, tolerably well off; he paid for your schooling and bought your commission.'

'That's all true,' Jacom had said, refusing to be ashamed of any part of it.

'Good,' Amyas had replied. 'That's exactly what I need. You're an officer again, Captain Jacom – and this time, I believe you'll have every chance to show us all exactly what you might be capable of.'

It was the last thing Jacom had expected – and it had been the last thing that Purkin had expected too, for the sergeant's embarrassment had turned immediately to resentment. Jacom realised now that Purkin must have expected to be appointed commander of the Xandrian contingent himself, with authority over his former officer, as a reward for the double-dealings he had undertaken in Antiar.

Jacom had contrived to preserve enough dignity to accept the commission as if it were his right, and to avoid asking why.

'Take this man inside,' Amyas had said to one of his bronzes. 'Get him a good, clean uniform with a captain's star, and a good belt with a stout sword. Give him a purse of coin – and make sure that by the time he steps out of that door again, everyone here knows who and what he is.' Purkin had opened his mouth by then, but he had not been given time to say anything. 'Gather your troopers, sergeant,' Amyas had said. 'Make sure you gather every last goose, dead or alive, and every last mutton carcase, into yonder cart, and set two men to keep them safe. The rest of you can ride the left flank.' Then he had stridden off again.

Thus it was that Jacom now rode at the head of the column, alongside the bronze captain who was Amyas's second-in-command, who had been introduced to him as Milkiel. No captain had been appointed among the golden mercenaries who had signed on with Amyas's company; they too had been placed under Jacom's authority.

Things had happened so swiftly that Jacom had not had a chance to confer with Aulakh Phar and Merel Zabio, and he had wondered briefly whether they might have decided to slip away for a while before returning to wait a little longer for Hyry Keshvara. Now that an orderly procession had been formed, though, and was wending its way along the cart-road to Kether, they rode forward to speak to him.

'News of your promotion is causing quite a stir,' Phar observed, with no more than a hint of sarcasm. 'A shrewd move on Amyas's part, I'd say. You have charge of the local goldens, so you'll have to cope with any discontent from that quarter – and you'll take the blame if they foul things up.'

Jacom saw the bronze captain eyeing the old man over his shoulder in a jaundiced fashion and he slowed down, letting the other lead the way in glorious isolation.

'Don't complain,' Merel told Phar. 'Better for us to have Jacom in charge than one of them, or one of the bronzes.'

'Far better,' Phar agreed laconically – but Jacom could read doubt in the old man's eyes. Jacom knew well enough what that doubt was; now that he had consented to be taken into Amyas's service, it might not be so easy to quit it again. The Last

Stronghold lay beyond Salamander's Fire, and in a different direction.

'You're not under my command,' Jacom said to Phar, by way of slight reassurance. 'You're still a free man.'

'I'm thought to be too old to fight, I dare say,' Phar retorted, although he knew full well what point Jacom was making. 'I'll have to lean on Merel's arm, and let her lead me where she will, mere woman that she is. Given that we're just two extra mouths to feed, your friend won't mind if we get lost or left behind. On the other hand . . .'

On the other hand, Jacom knew, Amyas certainly wouldn't want to lose him now that he was a captain. Phar would doubtless have continued – and might have had some sharp questions to ask – had not Amyas chosen that moment to ride to the head of his little army, beckoning to Jacom to come with him. Phar and Merel immediately consented to fall back. They understood the benefits of being out of sight and out of mind – although Jacom judged from the glint in Amyas's eyes that they were not yet out of mind and certainly wouldn't be left out of his calculations.

'Would you rather be on a northward road, Captain Jacom?' Amyas asked, when he had the space to do so in private.

'No,' Jacom told him, honestly enough. 'You've doubtless heard more than one account of the difficulties I'd face were I to attempt to return home without Princess Lucrezia, so falling in with Nath would have been a last resort. Even Purkin must have been glad to have the opportunity of deserting Nath for you.'

'There's hardly an atom of gladness in the man,' Amyas said sadly, 'but he takes a certain pride in his double-dealing. You understand, of course, why I put you over the whole company of goldens?'

'I think so,' Jacom replied cautiously.

'I saw how you handled yourself in that brawl in the stables,' Amyas told him. 'You've clever hands and the power of self-restraint. I have braggarts and bullies enough in my own ranks, let alone the ranks of those who've deserted their countrymen to take our coin; what I need in my officers is a measure of discretion and squeamishness, and an equal capability for talk and action. I want to get out of this misbegotten land, if I can, with all my men and very adequate provisions, and I don't want to have to wade through blood to do it. You're golden and you've at least half a brain; you'll serve as my spokesman with the goldens – not just those in my company but the farmers who must be persuaded to hand over their goods without insisting that we step over their dead bodies to acquire them.' Jacom observed that he didn't bother to ask whether Jacom was willing to take on such a role, or whether he was prepared to fulfil it according to any and all orders he might be given.

'Keshvara might have been useful to you in the latter respect,' Jacom told him, in a neutral tone.

'I'm working in my own interests, not those of the company you were in before. I take you for a man of honour, captain, and I expect you to serve me as loyally and as wholeheartedly as any other master. You're no longer bound for Salamander's Fire – let's be absolutely clear about that.'

It wasn't a question; it was a command. Jacom knew that if he had any objection to obeying that command he must make it known now, surrendering the commission he had so recently accepted.'

'I'm a soldier,' he said, without hesitation. 'I know my duty.'

'I don't doubt it,' the bronze replied, with equal alacrity. His voice softened as he added: 'I know that your companions aren't soldiers, and that they have different objectives in mind. I can see that woman's capable of fighting, and I dare say the old man has knowledge in his head that might be useful to the Stronghold when all this is over and we have to begin reclaiming the ground we've lost, but I'm a generous man. Give me your word that you and your men are with me while the Stronghold needs your protection and I'll look the other way if they decide to make their way to Salamander's Fire.'

Jacom was surprised to have the matter laid out so forthrightly, and he saw no reason to doubt Amyas's estimation of himself as a generous man. He knew that he was being hurried into making a promise that ought to be carefully mulled over – a promise which he would not have dreamed of giving only six hours before – but what was being asked of him didn't seem so very unreasonable. What was he, after all, but a career soldier? It was necessity, and necessity alone, which had made him a merchant's hired sword for a little while.

'You have my word,' he said, after a brief silence in which there was more dignity than doubt.

'You might tell your friends, though, that they might be better off with us,' Amyas added, having heard what he wanted to hear. 'The barrens are more dangerous now than they have ever been. If the wagon that got away from Shabir's army hasn't come to grief in the desert its occupants would be wise to make for the Stronghold instead of Salamander's Fire. It's a safer place for a long wait, in my estimation . . . and you'll appreciate that they might have to wait for a very long time if they expect anyone to make their way there by way of the Soursweet Marshes.'

Jacom thought it best to remain cautious in spite of the pledge he had given, so all he said in reply to this was: 'Is it true that Shabir has been reported dead? Have Carus Fraxinus and Ereleth contrived to give him the slip?'

'It's true that he was *reported* dead,' Amyas answered, stressing the word *reported* to emphasise that he didn't consider the men of the Nine Towns to be reliable reporters of the weather, let alone more important matters. 'If your friends can find water and food, they'll find little enough to threaten them in the desert, but thirst and hunger are deadly enemies.'

'I suppose you haven't heard any rumour concerning Andris Myrasol or the princess?' Jacom asked.

'I asked what questions I could while we were on the road and after we arrived in Antiar, and so did Nath's men. We both wanted the big amber. I'm reasonably sure that Shabir's men didn't kill him. If they went west into the marshes, though, without knowing what they could safely touch . . . I fear that poison is even deadlier in its effect than hunger and thirst.'

'Tell me about the Last Stronghold,' Jacom said, turning to a subject on which the bronze could more easily shed some light. 'What am I being taken to defend?'

'There were barely six hundred of us left when I brought my men away,' Amyas told him sombrely. 'Few enough, I suppose, to have packed up everything we possess and to have marched to the river's bend, had there been any welcome awaiting us on the other side. We'd have done it, too, had I discovered a haven ready and willing to receive us and a position easier to defend than our own – but you've seen for yourself what we found. If any fight's to be mounted against the new marauders, it's the Stronghold which will have to be defended. This land will be carved up between the dragomites and the floaters to begin with – and then, as likely as not, it'll become a battleground upon which all manner of unearthly monsters will fight one another. In the end . . . perhaps the patience of the figured stones will allow them to outlast the more fervent creepers.'

'I'm sorry,' Jacom said. 'I don't know what you mean by figured stones and fervent creepers.'

'Your men made Xandria sound like a pleasure garden,' Amyas commented, turning to look at Jacom with a slightly sceptical gleam in his eye. 'I thought it was a kind of boasting. Don't you have creepers there that wrap themselves around the boles of trees, sucking all the sustenance out of leaves and roots alike, and then reproduce themselves by releasing animal spores: worms and snakes and bat-winged butterflies?'

'Not in Xandria,' Jacom said. 'I've heard of such things, but I was half-inclined to dismiss them as travellers' tales, like firedragons and manticores . . . which I suppose I must also believe in, since you say they too have been seen. Do manticores really have humanoid heads set upon the bodies of tigers, and tails like scorpions?'

'It seems so, from a distance,' Amyas confirmed, 'but I've been lucky enough and careful enough not to get too close to one, so it might be mere appearance, swelled by the exaggeration of tale-tellers. Figured stones are said to reproduce the way the fervent creepers do, but I've never seen them give birth although I've had plenty of occasion to step around them in my time. They look like stone rugs, but they're not as meek and helpless as they seem; they can live in almost any kind of dry land and they're very tenacious. They can be shattered, but the larger fragments regenerate so you have to be careful to pulverise them if you want to fight them for the soil they're sitting on.'

'Are they common in the lands around the Stronghold?'

'Too common for comfort, but they were no trouble compared with the pests that afflict us now. It was the more active vermin, like steelflies and hyenoids, that ruined our ancestors' orchards and began to hedge us about even before the recent escalation of our difficulties. In a way, though, the reduction of our population makes things easier. If necessary, we can grow enough within the Stronghold's walls to feed ourselves almost indefinitely. We might have to surrender all the land outside it, although we'll have to scorch the earth for a couple of kims in every direction to keep the air reasonably free of spores and seeds, but as long as we can protect what we grow inside the walls, and as long as we have enough strong fighting men to hold the walls against hellhounds, manticores and any other monsters that might come our way, we'll pull through. We have good wells and stout hearts, and we have the discipline that the Nine Towns lacked. If bad times have come before, they've also gone again, and our ancestors lived through them. We can do it too.'

Jacom was impressed by the man's determination, but he couldn't help noticing that Amyas had only a vague idea of what his Stronghold might have to stand firm against, and no idea at all how long it might have to stand before the siege relented again.

Amyas obviously thought that he had said enough for now – and perhaps regretted that he had set his own anxieties astir – for he pointed to a farmhouse some way to the west of their course, nestling in the starshadows cast by a stand of tall trees. 'Take as many men as you need,' he said, rather abruptly. 'Find out what they're hoarding, and grab everything that's worth grabbing. Don't kill anyone unless you have to, but if you have to, don't hesitate. I don't want to lose a single man if I can help it.'

Jacom met the bronze's dark-eyed gaze very squarely, and let a few seconds go by before he answered. He knew that it wasn't worth asking about the paymaster's reserves of coin; that phase of the game had ended as soon as the bronzes had gathered their forces and ceased to be a sitting target. From now on, it would be straightforward plunder all the way – and this was a test, of his ruthlessness as well as his diplomacy.

Such, Jacom knew, were the responsibilities of intermediate rank. This was what it meant to hold a commission.

'Don't worry,' he said evenly. 'I'll look after them like a father.'

12

IT TRANSPIRED THAT the promises given to Andris by Venerina Sirelis and Philemon Taub were honest, so far as they went. It didn't put him to sleep and it did give him a greater awareness of himself. Unfortunately, the knowledge that he was wide awake wasn't sufficient to dislodge the conviction that he was living in a dream, and the acute awareness of himself that he had was disturbing and grotesque. In other circumstances the experience might have been fascinating and not altogether unpleasant, but it was not the state of mind in which he wanted to find himself immediately before a battle.

By the time he and Lucrezia had run from the room and stumbled through the corridors to the head of the main staircase – with every corner seeming like a lurching step into a new world – the drug had enlivened his consciousness of himself to the point where his inner being seemed to have expanded to colossal proportions. Although he was a big man he had never really been aware of his bulk; insofar as he had been mindful of his conscious self at all it had always seemed to be an entity of no particular size or mass. Now, he felt that his essential self – the part of him responsible for thought and sensation – was both infinitely large and infinitely heavy. He was perfectly well aware that there was still a universe without the neatly-painted walls which hemmed him in, which must itself be unimaginably large and massive, but it seemed to him that he now existed in parallel with that vast entity, equivalent to it to every dimension, rather than confined to the infinitesimal space within the skull of a single creature inhabiting a single world.

Had he had leisure to lie down and contemplate this miracle of personal metamorphosis, Andris felt that he might indeed have learned something about himself, although whether it would have been what Philemon Taub and Venerina Sirelis wanted him to learn was a different matter. As things were, though, he felt constrained to struggle with all his might against the delusion which held him captive, so that he might fix his attention on the disaster which was overwhelming the Community. He tried as hard as he could to blot out the image of his universal self which pressed with such insistence upon his powers of sight and thought, clinging determinedly to the feeble trickle of sensation which linked him to the world of air and violence.

At the head of the stairway he paused, seized by sudden vertigo, and he clutched at the banister while Lucrezia – equally fearful that he might fall – clutched at him. The sickness clawing at his stomach told him that it was too late; the invaders were already swarming into the huge hallway below.

The Community had no arsenal of weapons to dispense to its members. It kept no substantial stocks of pikes, javelins, swords or bows and arrows. Except for the hunters who made frequent forays into the marshes no one in the Community owned everything more lethal than a knife for use in hand-to-hand fighting. Nor was the house itself designed to withstand any kind of siege. The surrounding marshes were supposed to be an impenetrable barrier through which no hostile company could force a way. What was happening now was virtually inconceivable – but that presumably posed less of a problem to Andris than to any of his companions, in that his borders of conceivability were already in the process of undergoing a radical reconstruction. It was difficult for him to concentrate his attention on what he saw, but to the extent that he could do it he was quite unaffected by astonishment, alarm or outrage.

The people inside the house had not secured the doors because too many of their fellows were outside, but it would have made little difference had they done so. The ground-floor windows were too large and too vulnerable, and the enemy's shock-troops were not in the least reluctant to smash their way in, scattering turtleshell lights in every direction. The horsemen didn't bother to dismount; they simply rode their horses straight through the shattered openings. The horses never flinched, in spite of the fact that they carried no armour about their heads or their flanks. Many were bloodied but none were deterred, and the same applied to their riders, who seemed utterly careless of any possibility of coming to grief.

The hall was full of terrorised screams and shouts, but all the noise was being made by the hapless defenders; the horsemen and their Serpentine allies were silent. It was impossible to judge whether the giant Serpents were masters, slaves or equal partners in the enterprise.

Andris swayed, and felt Lucrezia's tiny hands pushing hard as they tried to hold him up. He felt as if his brain were inflating like a grey balloon, oozing through the seams of his skull. His body felt numb, as though he were anaesthised against pain. He could still feel the ordinary sensations of touch and movement, but the quality of these sensations had been markedly changed, altered almost out of recognition. Although he could see clearly and hear distinctly, provided that he could keep his mind focused on such tasks, sight and hearing didn't feel the way they usually did. Everything he saw was bright and sharp, but alien; everything he heard was clear-out and meaningful, and yet bizarre. He was no longer certain that his thoughts were his own.

The mounted men who were pouring into the hall were goldens, much like any other goldens save for the fact that their stares were fixed and their motions mechanical. Their clothes, however, were like none that Andris had ever seen before; if they weren't actually made of Serpent-skin – and it was difficult to believe that they were, given that they kept such company – they had been very ingeniously contrived to mimic it. The men wore no armour, unless the scales of their jackets and trousers could be counted as such, but they were certainly fighting men. They laid about themselves with smooth-headed maces made of some very dark wood or some unusually malleable stone, and they did so with ruthless efficiency, always aiming for the heads of their victims and striking with calm control. Not one of them had yet been unhorsed. Even without support from monsters, their assault would have been irresistible.

Andris tried to remember whether he had taken the first sip of the liquid before or after he heard the first shouts of alarm, but he knew that it made no difference. He would have liked to think that what he was seeing might be a nightmare – a hallucination induced by poison – but he knew that it wasn't. It was happening.

The only Serpents Andris had ever seen were Mossassor, Ssifuss and Ssumssarum. Ssifuss had been the tallest and heaviest of the three, but it had been no taller than Jacom Cerri – who was not a particularly tall man – and somewhat slimmer. The smallest of the Serpents which had crashed into the great hall – at least two of which had used the windows rather than the wide-flung doors – was a met taller than Andris; Dhalla would only have topped it by a few sems. The largest had the advantage of a further half-met of height. They were, to be sure, very thin, and their forelimbs were very slender. It was only their legs and tails which seemed unduly massive, but it was their legs and their tails which they were using in the fight – particularly their tails, which lashed out as they leaned forwards on the balls of their oddly delicate feet, striking people down with as much force and deadly precision as the clubs of the riders.

Andris felt not the slightest flicker of fear or horror as he looked upon this carnage, but he knew that it was terrible. It was at least as terrible as watching dragomite warriors fight while the legless mound-queen looked on from her lake of blood. 'We've got to get out,' he said to Lucrezia. It did not sound to him like his own voice, nor did it seem to him that the words came from his own lips. Perhaps, after all, it was she who had spoken.

'Why are they doing this?' another voice wailed, in a tone which might have been redolent with anguish. 'What do they want?'

'*We've got to get out!*' Andris repeated, trying as he said it to shove Lucrezia back, away from the stairway. He didn't know whether there was another way down, but he knew that they couldn't go down the staircase. The invaders were already at the bottom of the flight, and more than one pair of eyes was looking up at him. The Serpent eyes he could not read at all, but it seemed to him that there was a remarkable absence of curiosity and astonishment in the human eyes which met his. The marauders seemed to find nothing odd about there being an amber among so many bronzes, and there was not a flicker of assumed kinship in the way these goldens looked at Lucrezia.

Andris stood up straight, relinquishing his hold on the banister. Unafraid now that he might fall he flung his arms wide, as if to invite the attackers to come at him. The men who had not hesitated to drive their horses through intricately glazed windows would not try to force them up the stairway, but the Serpents were not in the least reluctant to face him. Two of the unnaturally huge creatures immediately started up the stairway, which was just about wide enough to accommodate them both. They came quickly, evidently fearing nothing although they were naked and unarmed.

Andris retreated a step or two. He was unaware of making any calculations, but there was no panic in his retreat, and he kept his eyes on the advancing Serpents. The confusion in the hall was greater now than it had been before, because all the bronzes who were coming into the hall from various doorways were carrying weapons of some sort, if only makeshift ones, and they were coming forth with angry determination.

There were twelve or fifteen mounted men in the hallway now, and at least eight Serpents, but they were beginning to get in one another's way even before the bronzes began assaulting the horses with anything and everything they had to hand, aiming for eyes and throats and any other vulnerable targets they could see. The horses might or might not have been trained for combat, but the combination of the crowding and the littering of the highly polished floor with a multitude of sharp-edged shards of turtleshell made them anxious and uncomfortable. It was still a brawl rather than a battle, but the attackers were no longer finding it so easy to bring their enemies down, and they were no longer invulnerable to all reprisal.

Andris reached forwards to grip the banister-rail which ran horizontally along the gallery above the hall. He hauled upwards, fully confident of his muscle-power even though he could hardly feel his arms and legs. The rail came up and away, splintering where it had been softened by internal decay. He plucked two of the banisters thus exposed from their beds, and held them one in each hand, like huge clubs. He could feel their weight, but it no longer felt like weight.

He heard Lucrezia shout 'No!' but the word echoed hollowly in his mind, stirring no vestige of response. He knew what she meant, of course – she was telling him not to go to meet the advancing Serpents – but the plea meant nothing. He didn't doubt that he was in control of himself, that he was doing whatever it was that he was doing, but any knowledge of what it was he intended to do had somehow been set aside, along with any explanation of why he was doing what he was doing instead of something else.

He shouted something in reply, but it wasn't until he heard the words – which seemed to have come from anywhere in the world but his own lips – that he knew what they were. He knew, once he had heard them, that they were quite absurd, but he hadn't time to wonder over that.

What he had shouted was: 'Get the head!' There was no doubt about it, because he shouted it again a moment later, and then again.

Absurd as it seemed, he knew that he was getting excited but couldn't quite connect with his own excitement. Sight and sound blurred as his attempt to focus his senses was disturbed, but he wasn't in the least alarmed. He was confident that he would still be able to see and hear and act even if the world without slipped out of focus. If the men on horseback and the giant Serpents could function as automata, with their minds elsewhere, so could he.

He no longer knew where any of his companions were; although Lucrezia, at least, must be nearby he had lost all sensible contact with them. He had hardly any awareness of his physical surroundings, save for the things in his hands, which weighed so heavily and yet did not seem to weigh at all, and for the two Serpents which were coming after him with what he took to be murderous intent. They had reached the top of the stairway now, and he backed away, beckoning them to come after him.

He laughed when they accepted his invitation, for their giant stature was against them now. In the high-ceilinged hallway they had been able to stand upright, but the corridor into which he was leading them was far too restricted. Nor could they any longer stand two abreast against him, for the space was too narrow. Most important of all, they could not swing the heavy tails that were by far the best of their natural weapons.

Andris laughed in sheer delight as he went forward against them, aiming his twin weapons at their heads and at their eyes, striking with all the precision and deft brutality that their golden allies had used down below. Huge they might be, but they were mortal, and they were frail, and he was exactly the right size to make full use of the confined space.

He broke the neck of the first, then blinded the second.

'You see!' he cried, his voice rising eerily to a falsetto screech of which he would not have thought himself capable. 'It's *not* a game. It's kill, kill, kill! It's *not a game!* Get the head! Get the head! Get the head!'

Venerina Sirelis was screaming something at him, and so was Lucrezia. He could hear the words but he couldn't discern the meaning in them. He was losing his grip on the world now, as the train of his thoughts was gobbled up by the illimitable expanses of his inner space. He couldn't unblur his sight, and he couldn't unmuddle his hearing, and he couldn't bring himself to believe that it mattered. He struggled to remember where he was and what he was doing, and the memories in question leapt obediently to the forefront of his consciousness, but somehow he couldn't fix or register them.

He felt that he was still moving, perhaps more purposefully than he had ever moved before. He felt that for the first time in his life he was moving like the half-giant he was, using his body as it had always required to be used. He felt that he was running, and that his legs were enormously powerful, but not as powerful as his arms, which now had hammers instead of fists: the hammers he had always been intended to have and to use. He felt magnificent, and his magnificence was such that it eclipsed the world.

He felt that he was hitting out in wild abandon, and he felt that he was descending a steep slope, and he felt that he was trampling trivial things that got in his way, and he felt that he was whirling and whirling about, aiming his magnificence at the heads and hearts of men and the scaly skins of unnatural Serpents.

He felt he was beside himself as well as inside out. He felt that the yellow light of half a hundred meagre lamps was blossoming into gaudy fire by virtue of his enhanced perception, and that horses were screaming and people were burning. He felt that there was chaos all around him, and that he was himself an aspect of chaos, an unruly force which would tolerate neither order nor structure. He felt that where there had once been mere confusion there was now glorious catastrophe, and that there was not the slightest point in asking why, even though he felt that all the answers in the world were in his grasp and in his gift.

Chaos had no room for whys and wherefores.

Chaos didn't care.

He felt, eventually, that he was riding a nightmare, riding like the wild wind. He felt that he was riding the tide of time, fleeing from a fate far, far worse than death and crying out all the while, lost in triumph and exultation.

He couldn't hear what he was crying out, but he felt that he must be saying to the world that he was no mere plant, no mere thing of thorns and poisons, no mere flower coloured by vivid blood, no mere smear on the wall of some secret chamber in a dragomite nest, no mere spore swallowed whole by some infinite worm which had the world entire in its languorous coils, no mere cell in the body of some vast and lazy Salamander God which slept in the dark between the stars, dreaming of the day when it might awake and set the universe to order.

He couldn't hear what he was telling time and space, but he felt that he was insisting as hard as any human could that he was still a head, still a head that was not the same as any other head, which had a boundary of its own and a universe of its own, interior but infinite, in which he might be a man and a god and a slayer and a saviour and a prince and a wanderer and whatever else he had been and might yet aspire to be.

He couldn't see himself, but he felt nevertheless that he knew what he was, more accurately than ever before – and that, after all, was all that he had been promised.

13

WHILE THE THREE dragomites and their lone rider were scattered far and wide, foraging for recently descended floaters and anything else that was edible, an eight-strong pack of hungry hellhounds took the opportunity to close in on the wagon. The Salamander escorting them to Salamander's Fire was riding along with Shabir, Mossassor and Carus Fraxinus while Ereleth steered, and all four of those in the rear watched the approach of the baying beasts with some anxiety. Fraxinus had observed that the beasts did not appear to be keen-eyed – although they certainly had good noses – and they had obviously never encountered a giant before, so their intemperance was understandable. He hoped that Dhalla would be able to cope with the attack in spite of being so heavily outnumbered, but he picked up a bow and arrow in case some further defence might be required.

When Dhalla moved to intercept the beasts they were quick to jump up at her, aiming for her throat, but in this their instincts betrayed them. Even the biggest of them – a long-limbed female as massive as Mossassor – could only just have reached the target if she had been given a clear shot; as it was, the prodigious leap which she put in merely served to expose her underbelly to a casual sweep of Dhalla's javelin. The giant knocked two more of the creatures out of the air with similar blows, and had little trouble kicking away the one beast which had intelligence enough to go for her ankles.

The hellbounds must have been angry as well as hungry, because they came again even after their first assault had left three of their number bloodied and helpless. This time they tried to swarm around the giant, three going to the left while two went to the right, but they failed to give her a wide enough berth. Her reach was extraordinary, and she had only to grip the haft of her spear at the very end to extend it by a further two mets. She cut the legs from beneath the nearest dogs, one to either side, and still had time enough to go after the two remaining dogs to her left. The survivor on the right managed to get to the rear of the wagon and jump up at its tailboard, but Fraxinus was ready and waiting for it with an arrow already notched to his bowstring. He was no more an archer now than he had been at the bridge, but he had the patience and the courage to wait until the range was so close that he couldn't miss.

The arrow thudded into the beast's breastbone, inflicting a wound which seemed sure to be fatal, but the creature still had the momentum of its leap, and its mass far outweighed the slender arrow. Its slimy jaws were able to reach out for the hand which clasped the bow and snap at it just once before the beast fell away to writhe in mortal agony.

The dog's fangs ripped the flesh away from the back of Fraxinus's hand, tearing the ligaments which extended from his wrist to his fingers, and bringing forth a gout of red blood. He howled in pain and dropped the bow.

Mossassor was quick to respond. While Ixtlplt and Shabir looked on the Serpent found woundglue and applied it liberally to the back of Fraxinus's hand. The bleeding was immediately stemmed, and Fraxinus gritted his teeth against the pain, which was in no hurry to relax its excruciating grip upon his whole arm.

While he fought for self-control Fraxinus looked resentfully at Shabir, daring him to make some comment as to the inadequacy of his bowmanship, but the general did not seem pleased by his former adversary's misfortune. He even had the grace to look rather shamefaced, as if he were blaming himself for his own reluctance to take up a weapon and employ his proven skill.

'Iss not good,' Mossassor said sorrowfully. 'Bites from ssussh beasstss go bad.'

'Ereleth will be able to treat the infection, if it doesn't heal well,' Fraxinus told it, gasping somewhat but keeping his voice reasonably level. 'It's only superficial.'

As he spoke he tried to flex his fingers, but instantly gave up the attempt when the pain promptly redoubled its intensity. He realised that the threat of infection was not the only legacy that the momentary encounter had left; even if the wound were clean enough to require no further treatment, the hand would be useless for at least four days. It was his left hand, but the loss would still be very inconvenient.

'I'm sorry,' Dhalla said, running up behind the moving wagon now that the surviving dogs had been put to flight. 'I should have been quicker.'

'No,' Fraxinus said, forcing himself to speak calmly, as a leader should. There was now a sick feeling in his head that had as much to do with consciousness of his plight as any purely physical reaction, but he refused to give in to it. 'My fault. Should have used a half-pike. Stupid to think I could shoot the thing in mid-leap.'

He sat down, fearing that he might fall if he didn't. He looked up into the serious eye of Ixtlplt and the concerned face of the Serpent. For once, their expressions didn't seem inscrutable at all. Ixtlplt rattled off a long speech, to which Mossassor listened with its usual scrupulous intensity.

'Ssayss houndss and osser ssings are increasing numberss very fasst,' Mossassor reported eventually. 'Ssayss musst get to Ssalamander'ss Fire ssoon. Time for . . . no word. Like birss, but not ssame. Emergensse perhapss closser.'

For once, Fraxinus had little difficulty suppressing the frustration which inevitably arose from the woefully imperfect chain of communication.

'Will the others be safe?' he asked. A dozen of Ixtlplt's companions were following the hurrying wagon's course at a more sedate pace, carrying almost all the produce of their scavenging in their own hand-carts. Fraxinus had volunteered to carry more, but they had refused.

Mossassor didn't bother to relay the question to the Salamander. 'Can look after ssemsselvess,' it said. 'Sstrong and clever.'

Fraxinus sat quite still, nursing his hand and recovering his wits. He deliberately looked away from his alien companions. Dhalla had moved away after tendering her apology and there was no one now in view behind the wagon. The dead and dying hellhounds were already a long way in the rear, disappearing into the shadows of evening.

In order to combat his discomfort Fraxinus decided to make a concerted attempt to draw up a careful account of his situation and to review in some detail the discoveries which he had made since leaving the Crystal City. Mossassor had tact enough to leave him to it.

The wagon was making good speed in spite of the increasing density of figured stones. Fraxinus could not tell, even with the aid of Andris Myrasol's map, how close they might be to the bend of the river which turned it at right angles from the southward-flowing reach on which the Nine Towns had been built to the westward flow which would take it to the Lake of Colourless Blood. He assumed that it must be within fifty kims, for the land to the right of their course hardly warranted description as desert. Somewhere to the south of their present position, according to a vague wave of Ixtlplt's hand, there were human settlements – but they had been dwindling for centuries and were now reduced to a few thousand individuals, if that. According to Ixtlplt the humans were not good neighbours, and they were careful to keep their distance from Salamander's Fire.

With the exception of the figured stones the vegetation of the region through which they were now passing seemed far less alien than the gaudtrees of the Spangled Desert or the strange gargantuan growths of the Crystal City, but it was unearthly nevertheless. If the land had ever been planted with earthly crops and worked by human farmers – as it might well have been at one time – no trace of that habitation now remained. The rigid shoots of the floater-plants were jutting up in profusion amid the leaves and flowers of many other species, which seemed fated to be displaced, but thanks to the recumbent figured stones there were considerable tracts of land which seemed almost as inhospitable to their invasion as the sands of the desert.

Unlike the ones which thrived in the Crystal City, the stone-creatures hereabouts wore the same green and purple hues that were common to the vast majority of unearthly trees. Fraxinus concluded that they might better be classified as mobile carnivorous plants than as very slow animals, if such distinctions retained any relevance at all. Ixtlplt had demonstrated some of the hazards which such structures presented by poking sticks into the serrated grooves – which then closed like toothy mouths, biting the ends off – but had been dismissive of their potential to do any real harm. The largest ones were, however, perfectly capable of opening pitfalls big enough to trap an unwary human foot or equine hoof, and the wagon's various drivers had to take care to avoid them. Their presence was not unhelpful, though, because it was possible for the horses to ride unscathed over the smaller ones, and they kept the land relatively free of floater saplings, thus providing a road of sorts for hasty travellers.

Although he had not yet seen it done, Fraxinus assumed that any small animal trapped and crippled by one of the grooves or pits would quickly be entombed by some fast-setting secretion and then drawn by patient degrees into the body of the stone-creatures, exhibited as one of its 'figures' for a matter of twenty or thirty days. The creatures were victim to various parasites of their own, both animal and vegetable, but most of those which Fraxinus had studied seemed fairly healthy. Floaters which landed on them could be plucked up by a quick and clever scavenger, but those which were sucked under the surface were so comprehensively crushed in the process that their disappearance was obviously not a matter of routine burrowing. He had never seen a floater-plant protruding from the corpus of a figured stone.

Given that the floater-plants could produce complex spores which mimicked worms, Fraxinus was prepared to believe that some of the figures exhibited by these stony monsters might be spores in the process of extrusion rather than prey in the process of digestion, but he had not yet had the opportunity to witness any such budding. Mossassor, after consultation with Ixtlplt, had assured him that this was indeed one way in which the figured stones reproduced, although they could also do so by simple binary fission. The Serpent had remained uncertain, however, as to whether the spores which crawled and flew merely mimicked other species that were quite independent of the stone-creatures, or whether the 'other species' in question ought to be regarded as different phases in the stony entities' life cycle.

As Fraxinus stared out of the wagon, attempting by the sheer force of desire to damp down the pain in his hand, he tried to focus his thoughts even more intently on the wonder of these stony creatures, because he had jumped to the conclusion that their peculiar way of life might have an important bearing on the nature of Salamander's Fire – and, for that matter, of Chimera's

Cradle. He had not seen the chambers deep in the dragomite nest which Jacom Cerri and Andris Myrasol had visited, but their account of what they had seen suggested to him that the dragomite queen might possibly be a distant cousin of the figured stones, able to do far more with creatures which she trapped than simply digest them, and able to extrude a far greater repertoire of 'spores'. If that were indeed the case, perhaps the arcane mysteries of Serpent and Salamander reproduction hid something equally bizarre . . . and if *that* were the case, perhaps unearthly species were capable of a kind of paedogenesis far stranger than the earthly flies with which Aulakh Phar had associated the word. Perhaps the Salamander concepts which Mossassor translated as 'emergence' and 'birth' were difficult because they referred to some more complex variant of the reproductive process of the figured stones.

As yet, though, it was all speculation, based on hearsay. Until he saw what it was that the Salamanders wanted him to see, he would have no firm evidence to support the network of conjectures.

'Is it still bad?' asked a sudden voice, which broke in upon his reverie so abruptly as to make him start.

He looked up to see Shabir standing over him, with anxiety plainly written on his features.

'No,' he said, realising as he said it that the fire in the wound had cooled somewhat under the benign influence of the woundglue. 'It's better. I'll live.'

Shabir nodded, for all the world as if he had come to think of himself as one of Fraxinus's company.

'If we still have a spare horse when we reach Salamander's Fire,' Fraxinus said, 'you might as well take it and ride back to your own land. Provided that you're careful, you should be able to cover the ground safely. With any luck you might meet your friend Amyas coming the other way.'

Shabir was surprised by this offer, although he tried to hide it. He might have expressed his thanks, but after a moment's hesitation all he said was: 'The bronze was no friend of mine. If I wanted to help defend his land I could ride due south. My concern is for Ebla. No matter what happens to the other river towns, Ebla will stand firm. My people aren't idle Tovalians or stupid Antiarians; they have pride.'

'So I've observed,' Fraxinus replied drily. Now that he was sure he could do so without undue discomfort or too little grace, he stood up and made his way forward to Ereleth's station. He showed her the hand, now reduced to an ugly lump by the solidified woundglue – like something newly captured by a figure stone.

'It might well become infected,' he told her, echoing Mossassor's anxiety. 'I could see the beast's fangs in all their yellow glory, glistening with horrid saliva. Can you treat it if it begins to swell?'

'Of course I can,' she said shortly. She probably resented the implied comparison with Auklakh Phar, who had previously been charged with the duty of treating such infections and had done the job very well. 'I've told you before – witchery is far more than mere curses.'

The wagon lurched as it passed over the edge of one of the stony creatures. An unusually thick patch of vegetation then snagged the skidding wheel. Fraxinus cursed as his hand caught on the back of the driver's bench.

'If Ixtlplt thinks this is a road,' Ereleth said, 'I can only say that Salamanders have direly low standards. No wonder they have such massive feet, and have to draw their carts themselves. It's only a matter of time before we lose another horse. You might not be able to make good that generous offer you made to Shabir – who's surely done nothing to earn your kindness.'

'According to Ixtlplt, the road soon gets a good deal easier,' Fraxinus told her, ignoring her attempt to start an argument over Shabir. 'Humans lived hereabouts in the distant past, and the routes their roads once followed still survive, if not the roads themselves. The Salamanders maintain them as best they can, but it must be difficult in the present circumstances.'

'To judge by our experiences thus far,' Ereleth told him sourly, 'the road never gets easier. We'd be fools to expect that it ever will.'

'On the contrary,' Fraxinus answered. 'Since the fiasco at the bridge the road had been getting easier all the time, and we have every reason to hope that the worst is over.'

He dearly wished that he dared mean it.

14

ONE OF AMYAS'S bronzes found a dozen half-eaten bodies in mid-afternoon. He had been drawn to investigate by a chattering congregation of carrion birds. The man called for help because there was also a pack of hellhounds busy about the corpses, which they dragged together so that they could more easily take what they needed while keeping the birds at bay. The hounds were prepared to defend their meal against a single man on horseback, but when Jacom, Luca and half a dozen others rode to support him, firing arrows as they came, the creatures grudgingly conceded the game and made a temporary retreat.

The birds – sleek-bodied creatures with shiny black plumage and heavy beaks – were hopeful at first that the intervention had come on their behalf, and they crowded in upon the ragged pile, but Jacom unsheathed his sword and laid about him, causing the creatures to scatter in resentful disarray. They squawked and screeched profusely by way of expressing their wrath, but they retired to the same safe distance they had earlier left between themselves and the hellhounds, keeping watch with baleful red-rimmed eyes and strutting back and forth in the grip of fierce frustration. The hellhounds allowed an extra sixty mets, but they too refused to be banished; they squatted down in the shade of a burgeoning floater-plant, licking dried blood from their forepaws.

There was enough skin left on the bodies to make it evident that they had all been goldens.

'Your people,' one of the bronzes said to an Antiarian mercenary, trying manfully to hide the relief he was able to take from the fact.

'Not mine,' the Antiarian replied, pointing to a shred of cloth which displayed the remnant of one man's blue and green colours. 'This one's Sabinalian.'

'We're all on the same side now,' Jacom reminded him sharply. 'It's all of us against the wilderness.' He swept his arm round in a wide arc to take in the vast array of floater-plant stalks that crowded the neighbourhood, their domain unchallenged save for a few middle-sized figured stones and a few bulbous cacti.

'Not quite, captain,' the bronze informed him, pointing laconically at the arrow embedded in the torso of one of the fallen men. 'Whoever they were, they weren't on foot until they ran into trouble, and they must've been carrying more than this.' As he pronounced the last word his stabbing finger picked out what little was left of the unlucky company's packs. Jacom could see what he meant; they had been picked apart by human hands, not the teeth and beaks of scavengers, and what had been left behind was of neither use nor value.

'Filth,' murmured one of the goldens, as his gaze flickered from one bronze face to another.

'We didn't do it,' one of the bronzes was quick to insist. 'We need live bodies, not dead ones. Goods we have – it's strong backs and skilled hands we're short of – the fact that you're here is measure enough of our desperation.'

'That's enough,' Jacom said, taking some satisfaction from the authority which sounded so naturally in his voice. 'There's no point in trying to guess who might have done what and why.'

'Not entirely guesswork, captain,' another of the bronzes called out, having dismounted from his horse some fifteen mets away. 'Ground here's soft. It's churned up, but you can just about see the prints of horses shod like ours – must have been the ones the goldens were riding, or leading – and you can see others overlaying 'em which aren't shod at all. Can't be our people, and whatever else the Nine Towns were short of, they were all supplied with farriers.'

'Can you figure out which direction they came from?' his fellow bronze asked, striding off to offer what help he could in the detective work. After a few minutes the man who had found the prints pointed to the south-west. He seemed uncertain, but Jacom suspected that the estimate was correct. Amyas's column had been travelling from the north-west and the Stronghold lay to the south-east. There was nothing to the north-east but the barrens on the outskirts of the Spangled Desert, while Chimera's

Cradle lay to the south-west. On the other hand, Jacom thought, there were supposed to be no human settlements between here and Chimera's Cradle.

'Which way is Salamander's Fire from here,' Jacom asked the more enterprising of the bronzes, 'and how far away is it?'

The man looked at him sharply, obviously wondering why he had been asked, but he then looked about himself pensively. 'Lie of the land's changed,' he said, 'but I reckon it must be just to the east of south, not more than a day's ride away. Amyas could tell you.'

'I'll check with him,' Jacom said, knowing that he wouldn't. There were questions Amyas didn't want to be asked. He went back to the assembly of corpses and reached down, averting his face in a hopeless attempt to protect his nose from the stench. He caught the arrow by the fletchings and tried to pluck it out of the dead man's rib-cage, but it wouldn't come easily. He continued pulling; he didn't want to break it because he wanted to be able to see the point as well as the fletchings. It turned out to be a sliver of polished stone. The fletchings weren't feathers; they were made of some kind of vegetable fibre. He held the arrow up for his informant to inspect.

'Ever seen one like it?' he asked.

The bronze shook his head. 'Not a Stronghold arrow,' he said. 'Not Salamanders either – nor their style at all. Maybe . . .'

'Maybe what?' Jacom prompted.

The man had only paused for dramatic effect. 'Maybe the Cities of the Plain aren't as dead as people say,' he finished.

'But they'd be a long way to the south,' Jacom said, remembering the points marked on Andris Myrasol's map.

'Not that much further than Antiar,' the bronze said, although he didn't sound too sure. 'About the same distance as the Dragomite Hills, perhaps. Closer than Chimera's Cradle, if only by a hundred kims.' He was guessing, never having been either place, but Jacom's memory of the map backed up what he was saying. Perhaps there were humans in the south, even though they'd had no contact with the Stronghold's people for generations. Perhaps they too had been stirred to exploratory action by the changes overtaking their realm. But why would they fall upon a group of strangers with such devastating effect?

'When will we reach the Stronghold?' Jacom asked.

'Day after tomorrow, as long as we can keep the carts moving,' the bronze told him. 'Probably late evening, early starlight.'

They were already having some difficulty keeping the carts moving, although there was a road of sorts which the floater-trees would not obliterate for some time yet; Jacom and his informant both knew that conditions might get a lot worse. Even so, Jacom contented himself with a nod of acknowledgement. He tucked the arrow into his belt and remounted.

As he and his companions moved away the black birds took off, then fluttered down on the corpses like black rain – but only for a moment or two. As soon as the horses broke into a trot the hellhounds were back on their feet again, charging the crows with slavering mouths agape.

Jacom didn't go immediately to the cart in which Aulakh Phar and Merel Zabio were riding, and he said nothing to Luca about the possible significance of what they'd found. Luca would doubtless offer his own account of the discovery to the other troopers, but Jacom saw no point in trying to manage his reportage.

While the column paused by a sluggish stream later in the afternoon, though, Jacom slipped away to see his friends; he drew them away from the wagon in which they had been riding to the shade of one of the few floater-plants that had yet contrived to put forth a sizeable crown.

'If you're going,' he told them, 'you'd best go tonight, due south unless you can make a better estimate yourselves – but you'll have to take care. There are worse things than dogs and reptiles out there.' He showed Phar the arrow.

'You're really not coming with us?' Merel asked.

'That wasn't the deal,' Jacom told her. 'Amyas is treating me as a man of honour, and I have to live up to expectation. You might do better to stay – you've no guarantee that Fraxinus will make it to Salamander's Fire, and you've no idea what kind of reception you might get.'

Aulakh Phar passed the arrow back. 'You've no guarantee that you'll make it to the Stronghold,' he pointed out quietly, 'nor that you'll ever get out again once you're in.'

'If it's Purkin and the others you're worried about,' Merel said, 'you might remember that they've deserted you twice –

once before the first dragomite attack and again during the second. You don't owe them anything.'

'I owe Amyas something,' Jacom retorted, before turning back to Phar and holding the arrow up for further inspection. 'Anything familiar about it? Shot by a man riding an unshod horse, apparently.'

'Nothing at all,' Phar said. 'Stone arrowheads and unshod horses suggest abject metal-poverty, but that seems to be endemic to the region. Keshvara didn't say anything to me about the weapons carried by her bronzes, or the horses they rode.'

'At least some of the dead men were from Sabinal,' Jacom told him. 'Either they were adventuring like the Eblans the princess met, or they'd heard about Amyas's recruiting and decided to make their own way to the Stronghold.'

'Likely enough,' Phar agreed. 'Merel's right, you know – you don't owe anyone anything for deals made under duress. You could come with us – bring the darkland boy with you if you don't want to leave him behind.'

'I'm surprised you want me,' Jacom said. 'You didn't seem to think that I was much of an asset back in Antiar. In fact, you seemed to think that I'd mishandled everything.'

Phar shook his head. 'I'm an unreasonable man,' he said unapologetically. 'I criticise too much. Always have. Wouldn't want that sly bastard Purkin guarding my back, but I'd let you do it any time. You're a good man, and a brave one. Put you beside the big amber and you even seem moderately clever. You did sign on with Fraxinus, remember, even if he never got round to paying you a wage. Don't feel bound to Amyas because he gave you a clean jerkin with a captain's star and a purse of unspendable coin.'

'I am bound to him,' Jacom told him. 'Not by coin, and not by my commission – by my word. I'm bound to my men, too – including that sly bastard Purkin. I'm their officer – I'm supposed to stop them deserting, not retaliate in kind.'

'So you're deserting us,' Merel said testily. 'You're sending the two of us out into a wilderness full of unearthly creatures, all of which have sharp teeth and nasty tempers.'

'I'm not ordering you to do anything,' Jacom said softly. 'I'm telling you what the state of play is. If you want to go to Salamander's Fire, you can. I can't; nor can my men.'

Merel's lack of sympathy was very obvious. It wasn't just that she was clinging stubbornly to the hope that Andris Myrasol might somehow make it to Salamander's Fire; it was also that she disliked the bronzes intensely. The 'misunderstanding' at the inn south of Antiar had planted the seed of a hostility which had grown apace, with neither side making any frail attempt to heal the breach. The bronzes – with the sole exception of Amyas – still persisted in thinking of her as some kind of camp follower, and the fact that they couldn't follow the fantasy through only made them more determined to make casual references in their speech and to use their gazes as a means of insult. In a way, that made what she now said to Jacom all the nastier, and harder to bear.

'You're a real whore, aren't you?' she said. 'Anyone who'll make you an officer can have your loyalty. Belin the Tyrant, Amyas the Fanatic – it's all the same to you, as long as you can lord it over your men and think yourself a true aristocrat.'

'I'm not an aristocrat,' Jacom pointed out, for what felt like the hundredth time since he had left home. 'My father's a fruit-farmer.'

'Keep your voice down, Merel,' Phar instructed her, 'and keep your tongue under control. Jacom's right. He does owe a duty to Amyas – who isn't, so far as I can tell, any more fanatical than anyone else in his situation would be.'

'He's just like Tarlock Nath and that crazy general,' Merel observed bitterly. 'He knows he's in a losing situation, and he's wriggling on the hook. The trouble is, other people can and do get killed while people like that are wriggling.'

'That's not fair,' Jacom told her. 'He firmly believes that his people have a chance of holding on – and he has a passionate desire to make sure that they do. He hasn't simply conscripted a few dozen goldens as fighting men – he still thinks of them as possible ambassadors. He couldn't persuade Nath or any of the other members of Nath's unsteady Convocation that it might be worth setting up any kind of organised migration in this direction, but he really does believe that if the dispossessed farmers of the Nine Towns moved out this way in force they and the bronzes might be able to hold the territory against the unearthly invaders.'

'Look what happened to the ones who tried,' Merel observed, pointing at the arrow which Jacom still held.

Jacom shook his head, refusing even to reply to that jibe. 'It's not our fight,' Merel went on, although she was now the one who knew that she was in a losing situation. 'You took Fraxinus's coin when it suited you, and even when you were just his friend he told you where to find Checuti. If you hadn't made such a mess of things in Khalorn . . .'

'That's enough, Merel,' Phar said quietly. 'It's the future we have to think about, not the past. Perhaps, if we could get a message to Carus Fraxinus . . .'

'If you're going to go,' Jacom said, 'it's best that you just go. Amyas won't hold that against you – from his viewpoint, you're expendable – but if you try to complicate matters, he might be forced to make a stand. You know where I'll be if things go wrong for you – and the same goes for Fraxinus and anyone else who gets through to the meeting-place. Maybe I'll see you again at the Stronghold.'

Phar nodded again. Merel now seemed to be getting impatient with *him*, but she said nothing more.

Jacom turned to leave, but Phar touched his arm to restrain him. 'Have you looked closely at those creatures that look like carpets of stone?' he asked, pointing in the direction of the one figured stone that was visible, some twenty mets away.

Jacom shrugged. 'Amyas says they're a real problem,' he said. 'As bad as the floaters, in their way. The creatures that emerge from the cocoons in the skin of the stone are all pests, he reckons. Apparently they're far more inclined to devastate earthly crops than unearthly plants.'

'It wouldn't be malice on their part if it were so,' Phar remarked. 'It's just that earthly crops are designed to produce rich foodstuffs, even more so than the floaters. They raise some very interesting questions about the fundamental nature of unearthly life, you know. I've got some ideas . . .'

'I haven't the time,' Jacom said, as the signal-horn sounded to call an end to the rest-period. 'To tell you the truth, Aulakh, I don't much care. Just as long as my horse doesn't get a hoof jammed in one of those traps, the figured stones are OK by me.'

'You should care, Jacom,' the old man chided him. 'Care about all the other things too, by all means, but don't forget that there's a mystery here which requires solution. If Amyas's precious Stronghold is to endure, its inhabitants will need to understand what they're up against. I think I'm beginning to see what's going on.'

'I'm sure that if anyone can work it out,' Jacom said wearily, 'it'll be you. I wish you the best of luck. But to me, all that stuff about the lore of Genesys, Idun, the Pool of Life, incorruptible stone and Chimera's Cradle is just a patchwork of dreams. To me, this is about wild dogs and stray arrows.' He let the phrases fall flatly, to emphasise without actually having to say so that he didn't want to quarrel about this any more than he had wanted to quarrel about the question of their desertion – or, depending upon one's point of view, his.

'What I can't understand,' Merel said, probably just to place herself in opposition to him, 'is that all this unearthly stuff is coming from Chimera's Cradle. If Idun is the place where human beings first came to the world, how come Xandria and the nations north of the Slithery Sea are earthly through and through, while the further we go into the southlands the more unearthly everything becomes? It doesn't make sense.'

'It wasn't always like this,' Jacom said, knowing that he had to make his own view known before Phar began some interminable lecture. 'There used to be an extensive human civilisation here, of which the Nine Towns and the Last Stronghold are just remnants. Unearthly life is fighting back against the earthly invaders who've conquered its world – as it has before, apparently. Human empires have always been fragile – that's presumably why the lore tells us that empires are impossible to sustain. We have to resist with all our might, on behalf of earthly life everywhere. That's what Amyas is determined to do. He and Fraxinus are on the same side, whether they know it or not.'

'It's not as simple as that,' Phar said. 'Jacom, you really should listen . . .'

'I don't have time for this,' Jacom said, as he turned and began to walk away. 'I'm sorry.'

'No you're not,' Merel called after him, wounding him more deeply than she knew. 'You're glad to be with people of your own kind, and gladder still to be rid of us.'

I could have been rid of you a lot earlier, and a lot more easily, Jacom thought, remembering the long days and nights spent in the haywain, when he had done everything he could to nurse the two of them back to health. He wished that they could understand that he was forever conscious of all his duties, and that he was still doing his level best to be derelict in none. In a sense, he knew, she was right; he and they were very different kinds of people, and it was not entirely surprising that they now found themselves bound for different destinations with very different purposes in mind.

15

CARUS FRAXINUS HAD not made very strenuous efforts to find out more about Salamander's Fire while they were travelling through the barren lands on the fringe of the Spangled Desert. Given the distraction of his injured hand and the perennial difficulties involved in communicating with Ixtlplt it seemed simpler just to wait and see. Mossassor had established that it was not a city, nor anything that carried the merest impression of architectural splendour, but by the time it relayed these hard-won items of information back to its human associates Fraxinus was not in the least surprised.

'If I were to guess,' Fraxinus had told his companions, for the sake of having it on record, 'I'd hazard the conjecture that Salamander's Fire is mostly underground: a network of caves and tunnels let in to a very particular kind of rock, not unlike a dragomite nest.'

Ereleth knew how he had reached this conclusion, but she was too wary to add any prophecies of her own. Dhalla and Shabir showed no particular interest in the prediction or the reasoning behind it; nor, for that matter, did Vaca Metra. Mossassor was therefore the only one likely to be impressed if the guess proved correct – and so, eventually, it transpired.

No buildings of any kind loomed up on the horizon as they came close to their destination; all that they could see from a distance was a glint of light as the sun's rays were reflected from something smooth and low-lying, more like a huge horizontal lens than a shallow dome. Nothing more than that could be seen when Ereleth was forced to rein in the horses while they were still half a kim away.

'Well,' she said to Fraxinus, 'it seems that you were right about the figured stones.'

The distant gleam which was all that could be seen of

Salamander's Fire was difficult to approach, surrounded as it was by a vast expanse of living stone. It wasn't immediately clear whether the whole thing was a single unprecedentedly vast figured stone or whether it was a colony of smaller individuals packed so tightly as to leave no gap or evident seam between them, but Fraxinus didn't think the difference was of any real significance. In either case, this recumbent leviathan – which presumably formed a circle a kim in diameter around the focal point which was the 'eye' of Salamander's Fire – was mottled with pitfalls and sharp-edged mazy 'mouths' much larger than those manifested by the 'wild' organisms they had so far encountered.

'Like the domestic animals our farmers keep and the crops they plant,' Fraxinus murmured, 'the things can grow exceedingly fat.'

'A better comparison would be the dogs we breed as guards – or the giants which Belin keeps to stand watch over his precious harem,' Ereleth pointed out. 'Now we know for sure why Salamanders have such massive feet – can you think of any other creature that could walk or slither unscathed across that deadly field?'

While Fraxinus pondered this question he looked for familiar shapes among the 'figures' inscribed on the face of the stone. He could see a handful of wormlike forms, but even these couldn't be safely identified as gemsnakes or floaters; the grosser excrescences were so anonymous in shape they could have been almost anything. Fine detail could be made out only on the smallest scale, where these stones exhibited the same moth-like forms that could be seen in abundance mottling the surfaces of their tinier cousins. There was no evident impression of a Salamander or a Serpent, a hellhound or a human being.

'How are we to cross over?' Fraxinus asked the Serpent, who relayed the question to Ixtlplt.

The answer, as usual, was a long time in the delivery.

'Ssalamanderss will ssend sshoess,' Mossassor told him. 'Ixtlplt asskss how many pairss.'

This necessitated a conference. When Fraxinus, in his turn, explained the situation to Vaca Metra she didn't seem unduly disturbed by the prospect of staying with the dragomite warriors, and Fraxinus – after a moment's hesitation – decided that she could be trusted not to make off with the wagon.

'I can stay too,' Dhalla said, perhaps having observed Fraxinus's concern for his worldly goods.

Ereleth was quick to contradict her. 'You're the one who has Salamander's fire burning in her heart,' the witch-queen pointed out. 'If we're to find out the meaning of that saying, you'd best be with us.'

'What about you?' Fraxinus asked Shabir. 'You have the choice I offered before.' He ignored the dark look he received from Ereleth, who felt that whether Shabir wanted to go or not there was not the slightest reason to give away the last of the spare horses that his cavalry had unwittingly contributed to the expedition.

Shabir didn't bother looking at the circular expanse of figured stone; it was what lay outside and beyond it that interested him. He had been taking careful note of the surrounding terrain for some time, observing the unearthly vegetation that was springing up there, and its menacing inhabitants. He knew that the horses had been very fortunate to have come so far, and he must have weighed up the risks which a lone rider would face as carefully as he was able.

'I won't stay with the dragomites,' he said, in a sulky fashion which implied that he felt compelled to make an issue out of something. 'I'll come with you to the Salamanders' lair.'

'That makes five of us,' Fraxinus reported to Mossassor, including the Serpent as the fifth.

Mossassor passed this information to Ixtlplt, who promptly set off with its companion across the solid moat. They were heading uphill, but the slope was very gentle indeed. Fraxinus watched the creatures plod on, their shambling gait somewhat exaggerated by the care they were taking; even they, apparently, had to exercise a certain amount of caution in their dealings with their huge guardian.

While Fraxinus was waiting he knelt down to examine the outer rim of the defensive formation. 'It's very hard indeed on the surface,' he reported to the watching company, after testing it with the point of his knife. 'It seems odd that such a rigid structure can deform so quickly to spring its traps, but it must have an elaborate internal structure which is quite invisible to us.'

'Hunters make traps of steel, which is just as hard,' Ereleth pointed out. 'What man can do by artifice, nature can also do.'

'Tell that to the man who invented the wheel,' Fraxinus retorted, without scorn.

'If we discovered one thing in the course of our journey,' Ereleth replied, 'it's that unearthly life is more various than we thought. Don't be too sure that it has no use for wheels.'

'As steel has lustrust,' Fraxinus said, having found a softer patch where the point of his knife could penetrate, 'so this is afflicted by its own kinds of rot. I'd like to see what our masons could make of this, with all their ingenious yeasts. Imagine the walls of Xandria remade in figured stone, snaring birds and beggars. Perhaps, given an adequately balanced diet of rubble and compost, the walls could be trained to grow by themselves and maintain their own rigidity, so that we wouldn't need a legion of slaves for their maintenance.'

'But we could still give our felons and petty traitors to the wall,' Ereleth pointed out, 'for its decoration as well as its sustenance.' She smiled the oddly hawkish smile which she reserved for ironically cruel contemplation.

Fraxinus was surprised that it was Shabir who added the next logical stage to the progression of thought, thus revealing that he had paid more attention to the discussions conducted aboard the wagon than he had cared to reveal.

'The real question,' the general said, 'isn't what you'd have to feed such a wall, but what it would put forth – if indeed some of those figures are emerging rather than being sucked in.'

'You're absolutely right,' Fraxinus said. 'That is, indeed, the most interesting question of all. For what it's worth, though, I'm reasonably certain that every one of the figures you see outlined in this great circle is being digested. Times of emergence must by their nature happen at long intervals, just as there are long intervals between the births of beings of our own kind.'

He glanced briefly at Mossassor but he didn't bother to make any adjustment to signify that by *our own kind* he meant humankind. Nor did he say aloud that he was uncertain as to whether to exclude Dhalla as well as the Serpent. Nor did he explain that the *long intervals* he had in mind were – in his estimation – very much longer in the case of creatures like these than they were in the case of human births. He knew that Ereleth knew what he meant.

Ixtlplt did not return alone; it brought a whole company of Salamanders, including a few so small that they too were required to walk – very clumsily – in absurd shoes which had soles the size of cartwheels. Their legs were articulated at the hip in such a way that they could do so without undue discomfort, but they looked very ungainly. Once Fraxinus and his companions had fitted their own booted feet into similar devices, however, they proceeded to set new standards in ungainliness. Fraxinus and Ereleth were the most inelegant of all; Mossassor's legs were articulated like a Salamander's, and its leanness gave it a further advantage, while General Shabir had the advantage of Ereleth in the vertical dimension and was not stout or so stiff as Fraxinus; Dhalla had a better and surer stride than anyone, including the Salamanders.

The walk proved much less comfortable than Fraxinus had hoped or expected, and he found the gentle slope more inconvenient than he could have imagined, but he contrived to stay upright all the way, much to his relief. He was unable to pay as much attention as he would have liked to the living ground on which he walked, but so far as he could judge the larger figures set in the stony flesh were just as anonymous towards the centre as they had been near the edge.

By the time he reached the rim of the crystalline structure which formed the pupil of Salamander's Fire's huge eye Fraxinus had confirmed his early impression that it really was a gigantic lens, far bigger than any artifact of that type than the finest Xandrian artificers could ever have contrived. The lens was outwardly convex, but not so bulbous that it protruded far from the circular rim which encased it. At first glance it looked all of a piece, but Fraxinus quickly realised that it was not. Although there was no latticework in which the individual pieces of polished crystal were set there were in fact thousands of them, slotted together to form a smooth outward curve. If the lens were to be regarded as an eye in itself rather than the mere pupil of a much huger structure, it was more like the compound eye of an earthly insect than the kind of eye that a human or a dragomite had.

It was not until Fraxinus and his companions had stood upon the rim looking out over the unbroken surface for two minutes and more that a section of the lens adjacent to the rim slid silently downwards, opening a shaft into the interior. There was a flight of steps leading downwards: huge steps, broad enough and shallow enough to accommodate the big feet and short legs of Salamanders. Ixtlplt's small companions led the way as soon as they had kicked off their ridiculous shoes. Here Dhalla became the ungainly one, just as she had been inside the dragomite mound; the ceilings had not been set with giants in mind.

The flight curved away, but not into a vertical spiral; by the time they had gone down eighty steps Fraxinus was sure that the steps were leading them away from the centre of the lens and into an extensive underworld arrayed beneath the protective apron of living stone and perhaps cut from its innermost flesh. The stairway was lit from above, and the light continued to shine brightly and steadily no matter which way the flight curved nor how far it took them away from the lens. Fraxinus was sure, though, that the light was sunlight redistributed by an astonishingly complicated and very carefully engineered process of reflection and refraction, not the kind of bioluminescence which lit the Forest of Absolute Night after sunset or the tunnels of a dragomite nest.

'Like everything else in the world,' Fraxinus murmured to Ereleth, 'this pattern of structures must require constant renewal. To maintain the great wall of Xandria must be child's play by comparison, and yet their hands seem so lumpen and so clumsy!'

'It's a strange way to live,' Ereleth muttered in reply. 'Have they many other fortresses like this one, do you think, scattered about the world?'

'I think not,' Fraxinus replied. 'This isn't the way they habitually live. This is a very special place, quite possibly unique. This isn't just a dwelling-place; it's *Salamander's Fire*.'

'But if it is indeed part of their natural reproductive process,' Ereleth replied, 'there must surely be some similar nesting-ground wherever Salamanders live.'

'It's not the Salamander equivalent of a dragomite nest,' Fraxinus said softly, 'any more than the citadel of Xandria is a human nursery. It's an artifact, designed for the purposive perversion of nature. Whatever Salamander's Fire may be, it's the literal fire of the forge rather than the metaphorical fire of fleshly passion . . . but perhaps I should say *as well as* instead of *rather than*.'

When he had first set foot on the staircase Fraxinus had wondered whether he might be descending into a vast cave-system where tens of thousands of Salamanders lived and laboured, and he found no firm proof that it wasn't so, but the horizons of his imagination drew in as he walked through corridors that were both crudely hewn and rather ill-kept. He saw no evidence that there might be thousands of Salamanders here, nor even hundreds, and the chamber into which he was eventually taken was mean enough to make such wild surmises seem absurd. One wall was speckled with crystals which glowed with pale light, but there was nothing very neat or extravagant about the display and the other walls were mute, dead stone without any decoration at all.

There were mattresses in the room, but they had not been used for some time; they were copiously stained and their odour was none too fresh. There was a barrel of cold water and an assortment of bowls and ladles, but little else in the way of provisions. In one corner there was a large piece of unpolished crystal, which looked as if it might have been sliced away from a sphere the size of a Salamander's head, but it turned out on investigation to be a mere cover concealing a drainage hole not very far removed from the sewer to which it was connected.

Fraxinus couldn't help recalling the cell in which Andris Myrasol had been confined in the citadel of Xandria; this was larger, but there seemed to be no other respect in which it was preferable.

'Ixtlplt ssayss we resst here,' Mossassor told them, after their guide had made yet another long speech. After listening a while longer, it added: 'Will ssend ssomeone to uss, sssomeone who . . . ah!'

'What?' Ereleth demanded, evidently unsure whether Mossassor's exclamation signified alarm or delight.

Ixtlplt was already leaving, ushering before it the company of curious observers which had accompanied it to the surface to welcome their guests.

'Iss good,' Mossassor said. 'Iss very good.'

'What is?' Fraxinus asked.

'Are Sserpentss here,' Mossassor said. 'Sserpentss wisser than I, know Ssalamander language better, can help us talk.'

'Serpents who aren't in any desperate hurry to meet and greet us,' Fraxinus pointed out.

'Will come,' Mossassor promised, not to be put off its enthusiasm by mere details. 'Will come ssoon.'

'Are you sure,' Shabir asked Fraxinus, with a touch of malice in his voice, 'that it will be as easy for us to get out of here as it was to get in?'

'We're in no hurry,' Fraxinus told him serenely. 'We promised to wait here for the various companions from whom you parted us, and there's no virtue in camping out in the wagon while something interesting is going on in here. So far, our hosts have been more than sufficiently hospitable – *far* more so, in my estimation, than might have been required to discharge the small debt which their companions incurred in the Spangled Desert. We're not prisoners, general. You're still free to go wherever you wish, whenever you wish.'

'In spite of all your clever deductions,' Shabir replied, just a little too accurately for comfort, 'you don't have the least idea why the Salamanders brought you here, or what role they expect you to play in what they're about to do. We took such care to avoid stepping into the pits let in to the surface of that great wheel of hungry stone, but for all we know we might now be in its belly.'

'You chose to come with us,' Ereleth pointed out to him. 'Either you're as brave as the rest of us, or as stupid.'

'Not at all,' the Eblan replied. 'It's simply that I've nothing to lose.'

'We have little enough ourselves,' Fraxinus told him drily. 'Perhaps the difference between us is that we have much to gain, in terms of understanding what is happening in Chimera's Cradle, and why, and what there is for humans to do about it. If you still harbour hopes of contributing to the salvation of your people, you might be well advised to share in our discoveries.'

Mossassor, meanwhile, had been walking around the room, placing its hands upon each of the walls in turn; it had now completed the tour.

'Iss warm,' it pronounced, nodding its head towards the wall against which it had finished up. 'Iss like tunnelss in dragomite nesst.'

'It's only lukewarm, as yet,' Ereleth said, lacing her own hand beside the Serpent's. 'When the time comes for Salamander's fire to burn bravely, it might get a great deal warmer.'

Dhalla, who was kneeling down in order to avoid bumping her head on the ceiling, put her hand to her breast. 'I can feel it,' she said. 'I can feel it burning inside *me*.'

'Soon,' said Fraxinus, 'I hope to be able to tell you exactly what you mean by that.'

16

JACOM COULD TELL that the region through which they were now passing had been under cultivation in the fairly recent past. Considerable stands of earthly vegetation could still be seen, and earthly plants still commingled with the unearthly species which were displacing them. It was even possible to observe isolated clumps of crop plants maintaining a fugitive existence – not wheat or corn, but potatoes and sugar-beets – although the earthly life-forms which were putting up the most strenuous resistance to the usurpation of their privilege were those the farmers would have considered weeds and those which they used for hedging in their livestock.

It was difficult to estimate how long the land had lain derelict, and Jacom didn't like to ask Amyas, whose face was set firm in a deep frown. He felt slightly ashamed of his ignorance, having so often made a point of being a farmer's son and not a townsman. There was no real reason why a man who had lived all his life on the land should be in a position to judge how long the land required to be utterly spoiled, if the earthly land on which he had lived had never been afflicted by more than a few wholly innocuous unearthly immigrants, but it seemed a sensitive matter nevertheless and he kept quiet.

There were occasional buildings visible by the side of what had once been a better road than the one by which they had left Antiar, but they were all in ruins, collapsed in upon themselves as if the creepers which overgrew them had arrived with the express purpose of pulling them down. Farmhouses and barns could occasionally be seen on the ridges which looked over what had once been terraced fields, but at that distance the immature floater-plants which clustered about them looked like the bars of living cages, into which the last remnants of civilisation had been cast to pine away and rot. Such edifices were in far worse condition than those he had seen in the lands immediately to the south of the Dragomite Hills, but he feared that they might not have been empty for half as long. What he had seen during the last two days made it much easier to imagine what would happen to the narrow land of the Nine Towns now that the avid wilderness was hurrying northwards; the revelation had sobered Jacom almost as much as it had sobered the golden mercenaries Amyas had recruited there.

The road itself and the margins to either side of it had not been entirely taken over by legions of floater-plants. Perhaps the inhabitants had mounted a more spirited defence of the territory closer to the road, clearing away the spores as they fell – but if so, they had merely laid the groundwork for other invaders: unearthly grasses and unearthly thistles, whose native greens – mingled as they were with blues and purples – now seemed to Jacom to be a rude parody of the multifarious landscapes of his father's estates.

Figured stones were still in evidence hereabouts, but they were much smaller and more widely separated than those he had seen in the barrens further to the north. There were spiny cacti decked with tiny purple flowers and strange giant mushrooms whose caps were mottled and streaked with pinks and browns. On the steeper terraces disciplined for the planting of vines there now sprouted a chaotic and remarkably dense undergrowth; the banks of the streams and irrigation ditches which criss-crossed the low-lying pastures were similarly afflicted. Where the old hedgerows could still be seen the individual bushes were gradually being smothered and strangled by the ubiquitous creepers, many of which had put forth bell-like yellow flowers in awesome profusion. Unearthly life of all these kinds evidently relished the work that generations of men had put into managing and maintaining the fertility of the soil.

With the plants, of course, had come an abundance of animals. These included long-necked herbivores and shaggy-coated beasts which looked earthly enough to be close kin to certain kinds of cattle. Jacom didn't doubt that there would be predators moving in to exploit these species much as the scavenging hellhounds chased airborne floaters, but he had not yet seen any; the lush vegetation gave them more than ample cover. He knew that he would be far more likely to catch sight of them by starlight – the great majority would be now in hiding from the hot sun – but that they would be manifest only as slinking shadows, carefully voided of all detail. Birds and insects, however, were everywhere. He knew that some of these were earthly, and it gave him a curious satisfaction to think that earthly life was capable not merely of resistance to the invasion but of exploiting its opportunities. There were opportunist birds which could thrive on the seeds of these unearthly plants, and opportunist insects which could crop their leaves, suck their sap and drink their nectar.

For once, Jacom was disposed to wonder whether Aulakh Phar might be right about there being far more living organisms invisible to the naked eye than were readily perceptible, and even to wish that it might be so. It would have been good to think that the true war which raged across the face of this land was being fought at an imperceptible level, where the advantage lay to the earthly rather than the unearthly, and that in the fullness of time all these conspicuous invaders might be cleared away as casually and as dramatically as the 'fields' of the dragomites had been cleared by rapacious blight.

It was not long after noon. According to the estimate of the bronze to whom he had spoken the day before they might be as little as ten hours from the Stronghold. They had not rested long while the sun was near its zenith, although it shone very fiercely in a virtually cloudless sky. Amyas was very impatient to be home now that he was within a range which did not seem at all remote.

The bronze leader had made a token show of his anger when he discovered – two hours before the dawn – that Aulakh Phar and Merel Zabio had slipped away, taking two horses and a modest quantity of plunder, but Jacom had weathered the storm patiently, knowing that it was far more apparent than real. He knew that the bronze leader must have been secretly glad that the rest of the goldens were still with him, by choice rather than bitter necessity, but Amyas had become broodingly silent of late and seemed disinclined to confide in either of his captains. Jacom was riding with him, but they had not exchanged two words in the last two hours; he had felt all the while that the gulf was unlikely to be bridged until necessity demanded it, and so it proved.

That necessity arrived when Sergeant Purkin rode forward to come abreast of Jacom and Amyas. 'Outrider to the left reports seein' mounted men among the floater-trees, sir,' he said. 'Four, maybe five – on a parallel course, goin' the same way. No body armour at all but wearin' some kind of helmet he'd never seen before.'

Amyas instantly straightened up and looked away to the right. Visibility wasn't good in that direction, not because the floater-plants were too dense but by virtue of hedges hemming the road, whose height had been considerably increased by two years' wild growth and the questing creepers. There was a low hill on that side whose crowning vegetation could be seen, but the margin in between was largely invisible from the road.

Jacom's first thought was, of course, that these must be the riders of unshod horses who had slaughtered the men from Sabinal.

'Who saw them?' Amyas demanded. 'Did they see him?'

'One of the river town goldens,' Purkin told him. 'He's no fool – if he says mounted men, he don't mean long-necked deer – but we have to reckon that if he saw them, they saw him. That don't mean much – could be they've known where we were for a day or more – we ain't exactly inconspicuous.'

'What colour were they?' Amyas wanted to know.

'Couldn't see. Golden, he thinks, but . . .' Purkin shook his head as he left the last words of the sentence tantalisingly unsaid.

'But what?' Amyas inevitably wanted to know.

'Don't know, sir. Said there was somethin' funny about their heads, like they had no faces. He'd have looked at the faces for colour, see – maybe they're masked.'

'The helmets worn by the dragomite mound-women cover their faces,' Jacom put in. 'They look very strange indeed – quite startling to a fleeting glance.'

'He's seen dragomite women,' Purkin murmured, missing the point. 'He'd have known if it were them.'

Amyas looked back, craning his neck so that he could judge the distribution of the carts and their escort. He seemed to find it satisfactory enough. 'Collect four of your men,' he said to Jacom. 'Take Zovar with you. Ride to the top of that hill – and the top of the next if you have to – but don't go too far. Stay together, and come back at the gallop if there's any sign of trouble.' Zovar was one of Amyas's bronzes, who happened to be riding close enough behind them to respond to his leader's beckoning hand.

'Get Luca, Kirn and Kristoforo,' Jacom said to Purkin. 'You'll have to show me where the riders were seen.'

Purkin had expected that, and nodded. It only required five minutes for him to collect the three men Jacom had named, by which time Jacom had made his way through a gap in the hedge to scan the nearer slope of the hill as carefully as his position would permit. There was no indication that anyone up there might be staring back at him with equal curiosity.

Jacom picked out what looked to be a reasonable route to the apex of the hill and led his men that way. Once he was a hundred mets away from the road, however, the route quickly came to seem less reasonable. Awkwardly spiny plants which pricked the horses' flanks seemed to be everywhere, sometimes forming impenetrable barricades meandering along the contours of the land. It took twice as long as he had anticipated to reach the top of the hill – and there was little to be seen on the far side but a long downslope and a further ascent to a more distant ridge. The vale between the two hills was very shallow and the rivulet which wound through it was so narrow as to be no barrier at all in itself, but the area to either side of the stream was heavily overgrown with tangled vegetation.

Jacom led the way downslope, deciding that the easiest thing to do was simply to force a way through the thicket. There didn't seem to be any unusual abundance of thorns or spines to make the passage unduly hazardous.

He found when he got to the bottom of the hollow that he wasn't mistaken in this estimation. Even so, the intricately entwined plants grew so high and so thick that his mount wasn't at all keen to push through. He had to slap the creature twice across the rump to force it into the tangle, and then use his ankles and his reins to encourage it further forwards. He was so intent on this task that he didn't look up until he was almost out the other side, and even then his first thought was to look back and see how his companions were faring.

Luca and Kristoforo seemed to be stuck fast; both were furiously active but making no headway. Purkin and Kirn were almost through, but Zovar still had a way to go. It was Zovar, though, who suddenly looked up and pointed, yelling a warning.

Jacom whirled around, and saw that a company of horsemen were coming over the ridge, riding full tilt towards them. There were eight, and there was an unmistakable hostility about their intentions. Jacom knew that they must be invisible from the road where the main column was, and was not entirely sure that Amyas would have been able to hear Zovar's shout.

'Luca! 'Foro!' he shouted. 'Get back! Now!'

He didn't wait to see whether Luca and Kristoforo would find it any easier to retreat than to advance. He struggled with his sword, trying to get the weapon clear of its scabbard. He knew that Zovar was carrying a spear, and that Purkin had a sword too, but he wasn't sure that Kirn had anything better than a long knife. He scanned the approaching riders quickly, trying to judge the strength of their weaponry, and was dismayed to see that at least five had spears.

As if that were not enough, he saw what Purkin's outrider had meant by 'having no faces'. He realised, with a sudden sick lurch of panic, that his blithe assumption that they were eccentrically helmeted had been mistaken.

He had seen the mound-women in their full regalia, wearing armour which was not only made from dragomite chitin but carefully shaped to reproduce a form akin to a warrior's jaws, and that lesson made him unwilling to conclude too soon that the humanoid figures racing towards him could not possibly be ordinary men in ingenious armour, but no matter how hard he struggled to fit what he saw into some such familiar mould he could not do it. The riders seemed perfectly human from the necks down, and there was nothing particularly strange about the tunics and trousers they wore or the saddles on which they sat, but they had heads which did not belong to any earthly or unearthly species he had ever seen.

A year before, Jacom would have been unable to bring forth any ready-made psychological reaction to such a sight, but he was a much-travelled man now, and he knew that the world was a stranger place by far than he had previously imagined. His panic did not last, because the word *chimeras* sprang into his mind, and even though it explained nothing, and gave him no real basis for constructive action, its expression made him feel that he was not yet out of his imaginative depth – still capable of disciplined and appropriate response.

He was clear of the worst of the clinging vegetation now, and he knew that it would be utterly pointless to turn round and try to force a way through it in the opposite direction. No matter what his orders were, and no matter what the odds were, he had to stand his ground and fight. He had no doubt, as the eight riders hurtled towards him, that standing his ground would mean a fight to the death; there was no question of their pausing to talk or accept surrender.

He extended his sword before him and kicked his horse forwards, aiming for the dead centre of the group. He had no idea whether Kirn and Purkin could get closer in time to charge with him, or whether they would do so if they could, but he saw no alternative for himself.

Jacom could see that the distance separating him from his attackers would disappear in an absurdly short time. He had training enough to know that his greatest peril lay in having to pass between two of the horsemen, both of whom had spears which they would doubtless aim at his belly. He might be able to parry one spear-thrust with his sword, but he couldn't parry both. Whether the horsemen had made the same reflexive calculation or not he didn't know and didn't care; he knew what he had to do. As he urged his horse forward, picking up what speed he could, the line ahead of him broke slightly, so that the gap at which his mount was aimed grew slightly wider. He saw the points of the two spears swing inwards, and it gave him no consolation to note that their heads were not made of metal but of some kind of horny substance.

He suddenly jerked the rein to the right, forcing his horse to swerve; instead of continuing towards the lethally inviting gap he aimed straight for the horse to the right of his course, and he brought his sword across so that he could sweep the point of the threatening spear away to the left, towards its twin. He knew as he did this that the horses were bound to collide, and he had not been able to make any proper estimate of the relative masses of the two beasts, but he did know that his animal was one of those his company had brought from the fortress of Xandria, and he was certain that it would not shirk the collision.

It didn't; indeed it seemed to relish the prospect.

It was immediately obvious that the other mount had not had the benefit of any cavalry training at all. The attacker's horse, betrayed by its own instincts, made every attempt to avoid the inevitable crash. In so doing it comprehensively wrecked its own balance, so that when the impact came it went down in a silly heap while Jacom's horse, though lurching badly, kept its feet.

The second spear – the one coming from the right, which might have spitted him – barely touched his waist as its point whipped by. Before the spearman had time to regret his inaccuracy Jacom was turning away from the fallen horse to go for him. Foolishly, the spearman tried to stop his horse and make it turn to face Jacom's. The ground was too treacherous for that kind of manoeuvre at that kind of speed, and that horse too went down, although no one had touched it.

The other six riders were also reining in, but in a more controlled and sensible fashion. They were arraying themselves in good formation, three against Kirn and three against Purkin, both of whom had now got clear of the tangled vegetation. The attackers were right to judge that Zovar was still stuck, but wrong to conclude that he was therefore helpless and unable to be a factor in the coming conflict. Unlike the guardsmen, who were trained to use half-pikes as lances, Zovar had been taught to throw a spear and throw it straight. The fact that his horse was so nearly still meant that he was steady enough throw it well, and he knew better than to throw it at a rider when a horse was a much bigger target. A third animal went down, spilling the half-man from its back.

This meant that the attackers were now three and two. Jacom had no hesitation in going after the three, and he was able to come in from the flank, so that he only had one man to deal with for the moment. His charge had no great impetus, but Jacom had a good reach and a good blade, and whatever the creature he struck had instead of a human skull he had a backbone like any other man. Jacom slashed him across the spine just above the line his collar-bones made, and he jerked backwards convulsively.

Knowing now how badly prepared the attackers' horses were for this kind of conflict, Jacom urged his own mount forward, using it as a weapon to buffet another from behind. That one didn't fall, but any hope its rider had of using his weapon dexterously was gone, and Jacom had every faith in Purkin's ability to tackle the third of the adversaries who had set out to assail him. Jacom turned his own attention to Kirn, and made haste to gallop to his aid. With reasonable luck he would have been able to do so, but now the bad ground betrayed him. His horse stumbled, and couldn't help but go down, rolling sideways as it did so. Jacom was fortunate, in the end, not to be trapped beneath it.

As he scrambled clear he felt a surge of exultation, for he fully appreciated his good fortune in being able to recover his feet so easily. He still had his sword in his hand, ready for use, but there was no enemy directly in front of him. If only there had been, he might have been better off, for then he would not have had to wheel about so rapidly, desperate to get in a blow at someone.

The ground wasn't only treacherous for horses, and his boot caught in a tangle, making him stagger to the side. Even that wouldn't have been too bad had he not been so close to one of the fallen horses, which was thrashing about in pain. A flying hoof caught the base of his spine, very painfully, and he fell.

He wasn't unconscious, and he hadn't lost his sword, but any advantage he might have had was long gone now, and as he tried to rise again he was struck down from behind, without ever seeing the weapon which struck him or the hand which wielded it.

As his all too human body thudded into the ground, he had time for one last sensation attended by one last thought; he felt a wild flutter of amazement at the fact that the fervent and unfulfilled desire which sprang up instantly and irresistibly, wholly to occupy his consciousness, was the desire to find out exactly who or what he had been fighting – and why.

17

BY THE TIME the news arrived that Aulakh Phar and Merel Zabio had arrived at Salamander's Fire Carus Fraxinus had long since passed through the phase when boredom was a welcome luxury. Even if his surroundings had been a great deal more comfortable he would have found the waiting frustrating, and during his confinement in the dingy chamber the time had begun to weigh very heavily indeed on his active brain. Had Mossassor been able to make more progress in his dealings with the Serpents which were allegedly experts in the vexatious business of communicating with the Salamanders he would have had more to occupy him, but whatever increase had been wrought in Mossassor's own understanding had defeated all its attempts to put it into the human tongue. For these reasons, the news – which would have been more than welcome even at the best of times – was the greatest gift that fate could offer.

At first Fraxinus was determined to hurry back to the surface in order to greet his friends beneath the kindly light of the stars, but Mossassor assured him that it would be better for Phar to be brought to him, in that the occasion which they were awaiting was now no more than thirteen hours away. In spite of the fact that their quarters seemed crowded enough already, Fraxinus allowed himself to be persuaded.

Mossassor went back to its fellows to allow Fraxinus a little more space for the reunion. Meanwhile, supplies of food and fresh water were brought in by half-grown Salamanders in anticipation of the happy moment. In the end, Phar arrived in the narrow doorway, looking about himself curiously, but not disapprovingly.

While the two merchants embraced warmly Ereleth and Merel Zabio stood back, eyeing one another in a much warier fashion.

Shabir, who had stood up awkwardly when the newcomers came in, remained in the corner where he had been sitting alone. He passed unnoticed for a little while, and when Merel first looked in his direction the expression in her eye was uninterested. It wasn't until Aulakh Phar said 'Isn't that General Shabir?' in a tone of mild astonishment that she realised who he was. Once she had absorbed the information, however, she was quick to act. She threw herself at him, slamming him back against the wall, while her hands groped for his throat.

The general was too surprised to react immediately, and when he did realise what was happening he was slow to defend himself. He was much older than Merel and just as lean, but he was taller and undoubtedly stronger; he could probably have thrust her back rudely enough if he had only tried, and could certainly have hit her hard enough to give her pause, but he did neither. It was as if he were waiting to see whether anyone would bother to pull her away – and, if so, who.

Aulakh Phar shouted 'Merel!' and Fraxinus took a hesitant step forward but it was Dhalla, who was still sitting down because there wasn't room enough for her to stand upright, who reached out a long arm and grabbed the back of Merel's shirt, hauling her away in a fashion that was unceremonious without being brutal. The victim of the assault put a tentative hand to his throat to test the bruising inflicted by her angry fingers.

'That's the bastard who took Andris!' Merel explained hotly. 'He broke my rotting leg, burned half the skin off my back and arms and very nearly drowned me!'

'We know,' Ereleth said, with a certain dour amusement. 'We haven't forgiven him either, but we've grown used to his sour face. Believe it or not, he's one of us now.'

Merel seemed almost as astonished by this speech as she had by Shabir's presence. Her surprise reminded Fraxinus that time had passed, during which Ereleth had shed the formal mannerisms of her majesty by slow degrees, until hardly anything of them survived. To Merel, who could not have exchanged more than half a dozen words with the witch-queen before, the transformation must seem a near-miracle.

'Is that true?' Merel said to Fraxinus, evidently willing to make whatever concessions might be necessary to his authority, but not to anyone else's.

'We were fortunate enough to take the general prisoner,' Fraxinus told her. 'Revenge seemed to be a pointless luxury, and we harboured faint hopes that he might be useful. By the time we found out that he wasn't we couldn't quite recover the wrathful impulse required to execute him in cold blood. He still doesn't like us, but . . . well, you probably noticed that he didn't fight back.'

Merel looked at Shabir and the grey-haired man met her stare unashamedly. 'I did what I had to do,' he stated. 'Had I killed you, I'd have no reason to be sorry, any more than your giant friend has reason to be sorry that she mowed my men down like so many cornstalks – but we're both alive, and we might as well be glad of it.'

Fraxinus saw that Shabir's reference to the giant had been much cleverer than he intended. Dhalla had caused Merel dire inconvenience before; Merel certainly didn't think of her as a friend, but she had accepted her nevertheless as a member of the same company.

'We have more important things to talk about than the general,' Aulakh Phar said to Merel, taking her arm and drawing her back to stand beside him. 'Let's not disturb a truce that was made before we came. Have you news of any of the others, Carus – of Andris Myrasol, perhaps?'

Fraxinus knew that Phar had added the name for Merel's benefit, not because of any special interest in the amber's fate.

'No news of Andris, I fear,' Fraxinus said, 'but we know that Checuti, Lucrezia, Jume Metra and the Serpent Ssifuss survived the battle of the bridge. They fled towards the marshes.'

'So we were told,' Phar said. 'Jacom Cerri was with us until yesterday. Without his help, we'd never have come so far so fast, but he and the men in his command were reunited in Antiar and they made a pact with a man named Amyas. Amyas is a bronze who—'

'We know who Amyas is,' Fraxinus told him. 'The general was useful to that extent, at least. Is Keshvara dead?'

'Very much alive when last we saw her,' Phar replied. 'She and Jacom saved my life, and Merel's, and kept us safe while we recovered. She and Jacom made our escape from Antiar possible, but the three of us were separated from Hyry. If she's making her way here alone she might have had to travel more slowly and more carefully than we did, but you know how determined and resourceful she is. She'll be here in good time – I'm sure of it.'

Fraxinus knew that his friend couldn't possibly be sure of any such thing, but he knew what the old man was trying to achieve. 'You're right, of course,' he said. 'Myrasol will make it too – there's nothing in the world can stop a man like that.'

Phar glanced slyly sideways at Shabir. 'The general's loyal friend and ally Tarlock Nath waxed lyrical about the dangers of the marshes and the impossibility of crossing them, but we saw no need to give up hope on that account.'

'Doubtless you think yourselves far cleverer than simple folk like us,' Shabir said, without any trace of venom in his dispirited tone, 'but we aren't fools. We know from long experience that men who go into the marshes often fail to return, and that those who do are often changed – but if anyone can survive there, your intemperate friend the half-giant is the man.'

'Andris and the general had a sharp disagreement,' Fraxinus put in, for Merel's benefit, 'but the general didn't order that he be put to death, and has no reason to think that he's dead. He might have gone into the marshes too.'

'Are we safe here?' Merel asked. 'Will the Salamanders let us stay, to give the others a chance to catch up with us?'

'We're as safe as Salamander's Fire itself,' Fraxinus told her, 'and that's as safe as anything within a thousand kims. The fact that it's marked on Andris's map tells us that it has endured seasons like this in the past, and its users have made us welcome. You've arrived at the most opportune time imaginable: the Salamanders intend to set it to work its magic at noon, for the first time in many generations. We shall be permitted to see that magic at work.'

'Do you know what that magic is?' Phar was quick to ask, stressing the word *magic* to emphasise that it was being used metaphorically.

'The Salamanders have not been able to give us a full account,' Fraxinus said, 'but I think I know what to expect. I can't be sure that I've grasped the secret, but what I've seen in the desert and its borderlands has provided an abundance of clues.'

Phar smiled very broadly at that. 'So you know what to expect?' he said amiably. 'You've seen such an abundance of clues that even a mere merchant may deduce the nature and purpose of Salamander's Fire. I'll match my deductions against yours, Carus, one for one – and I'll wager that my lore allows me to see a good deal more than yours.'

'Who's to judge?' Fraxinus retorted, matching the smile in his own more quizzical fashion.

'I think we can trust ourselves,' Phar opined. 'We've known one another too long to be deceptive in such serious matters.'

'That kind of game's doubtless very amusing,' Ereleth put in, 'but it's wasting time. You only have clues enough between the two of you because I took Jacom Cerri and Andris Myrasol into the depths of a dragomite mound and revealed the possible kinship between the dragomite queen and the kind of living stone which rings this artificial eye. We all know by now that there are kinds of unearthly creature which live deep beneath the surface of the soil, and which have the power to absorb alien flesh, not merely by way of nutrition. We know that at certain times and under certain conditions the process can be reversed, and that what has been absorbed may re-emerge, transformed according to whim or design. Dragomite queens are vast creatures riddled with veins and airways and all manner of internal organs, some among them primed for chimerical association with other creatures, earthly as well as unearthly. Salamander's Fire and Chimera's Cradle are entities of the same fundamental kind. What more is there we need to know before we watch the Salamanders put their own fertile stone to work?'

Fraxinus was in far too good a temper to resent Ereleth's attempt to steal his glory and spoil his competition with Phar. 'Very good,' he said, 'and no mere piecing together of the hints I've dropped. You're absolutely right, majesty – were it not for the news which Andris and Jacom brought back from the bowels of the Dragomite Hills, I'd not have seen the significance of the figured stones so readily. You've doubtless studied them at your leisure, Aulakh?'

'Leisure is something I haven't had in quite a while,' Phar said, 'but I've studied them and learned a few of the lessons written in their sculpted faces. Do you remember what that blind man recited to you about seasons in the rhythm of our being? During the last few days I've wished more than once that I had memorised it.'

Fraxinus had memorised it very carefully, knowing that the parchment on which he'd written it down in Xandria would not endure.

'This world has no changing seasons,' he quoted, 'but there are seasons in the rhythm of our being. The tides which surge in our blood are greater by far than the petty tides which stir our shallow seas. The world's seas are briny, but not as briny as the blood of men. Our blood marks us children of other and unimaginably distant seas, and this is true even of those who have Serpent's blood in them. The world's seas are shallow but the water of our being is deeper by far; it marks us children of a great and unfathomable abyss, and this is true even of those whose hearts are warmed by Salamander's fire. There are seasons in the affairs of men, and always will be, despite that the men who live in the world we know were born and will be born again from Chimera's cradle.'

'Yes!' Phar nodded his head vigorously. 'I knew there was a key in it to help unlock the puzzle. We're the children of *unimaginably distant seas*! In the world from which our remote ancestors came, life evolved in the sea; we were born from oceanic waters and we still carry the echo of that origin in our blood and our being, even though our own species and thousands of its ancestor-species were products of the land, but *here*—'

'Here,' Fraxinus interrupted, 'the seas are shallow and not nearly so extensive. Life here evolved – or, at any rate, first took secure root and began to diversify – beneath the sun-drenched surface of the land. The common ancestors of all unearthly life must have been creatures which had more in common with the figured stones than any other unearthly forms with which we're familiar. Indeed, they must retain more traces of that kinship than we thoughtlessly supposed when we contemplated the trees of the Forest of Absolute Night, or the workers toiling on the slopes of the Dragomite Hills, or the Serpents and the Salamanders. We drew ready analogies between these various entities and products of earthly evolution, and were not inquisitive enough to find out how different they really are—'

Phar deftly took up the thread again. 'Except, of course,' he said, 'that they're not so very different in the common phases of their being. Evolution is a matter of adaptation, and given time enough it produces similar forms to do similar things, no matter what kind of clay it has to work with. From tiny one-celled creatures which crowded little drops of water earthly evolution ultimately produced sentient beings which walked erect on two legs, using two hands for manipulation, carrying big brains mounted within their bulbous heads, behind their curious eyes. Unearthly evolution produced similar creatures in spite of employing a very different route. But there's more to the game of evolution than adaptive design, for the process which drives adaptive progress is natural selection, which is essentially a matter of combining and recombining different sets of characteristics. The most important mechanism by which earthly life achieves that end is sexual reproduction—'

'But unearthly life deploys a very different kind of means to the same end,' Fraxinus said, feeling that his turn had come again. 'Unearthly species – if we can continue to use the word *species* in the absence of the sexual mechanisms whose practicality or otherwise defines the boundaries of earthly species – combine and recombine characteristics by forming chimeras. That's a far more flexible and far bolder method of generating novelties than the mean and painstaking processes of sexual reproduction, but the advantages which stem from that flexibility and that boldness have compensating disadvantages. Earthly natural selection might be unventuresome, but that gives it a very necessary steadiness. Unearthly life has the capacity to take much greater leaps and bounds – but it bears much greater risks in exercising that capacity. To remain effective over very long periods of time the progress of unearthly life had to subject its potential extravagance to some kind of rationing, so that it might have the capacity to conserve its gains—'

'Thus, the production of chimeras isn't something which goes on constantly, year in and year out,' Phar went on. 'It's something which only happens occasionally, in brief explosive bursts. In between those bursts most unearthly species reproduce themselves in a more or less mechanical fashion. The best analogy which can be drawn between the way unearthly species conduct themselves and the vagaries of earthly life is with the earthly insects which employ paedogenesis, reproducing for many generations in what's essentially a juvenile form while conditions are stable and hospitable, but switching to a very different pattern when conditions begin to change and become more challenging—'

'Which unearthly affairs do, apparently, every few thousand years,' Fraxinus said, '*and now is the time*. Now is the time when the great majority of unearthly species change their habits and their way of life. Most do so entirely automatically, but not Salamanders – and perhaps not Serpents, although we're still not entirely clear about that. Salamanders are intelligent, and they're adept technologists. They've been able to achieve some degree of technical control over their own times of emergence, or at least make some kind of constructive intervention in the process – here if not elsewhere. Perhaps the forefathers were able to help them with that, once they'd figured out how different the life-forms native to this world were from those they were trying to import and establish—'

'But in any case,' Phar added, 'the lore assures us that the forefathers learned something very important from the Salamanders and the Serpents, which allowed them to modify the Genesys plan in such a way as to make it possible – or at least much easier – for human life to secure its first foothold here. They're not our enemies, and even though it may appear that there's a kind of war going on here between earthly and unearthly life, it isn't – or shouldn't be – a war of extermination. The Salamanders know that, and some Serpents know it too . . . and so should we, to the extent that we take our lore seriously. What's happening hereabouts might be violent and unpredictable, and it undoubtedly threatens the lives of millions of people, but it's important that some people, at least, don't react by trying to destroy anything and everything that's unearthly, nor by trying to run away and hide until the whole matter's over and done with.'

'And that,' Fraxinus finished off, 'is why we're here. Whether we're motivated by secret commandments or mere curiosity, or by the simple pressure of circumstance, we're here to find out what Salamander's fire can produce from the fertile womb of this stony leviathan . . . and when we know that, we'll have a far better idea of what to do next, and how to bring our understanding to full fruition.'

Having completed the final sentence, Fraxinus favoured Phar with a slight – and slightly mocking – bow. Phar replied in kind.

They had no need to make any formal declaration of the fact that their contest had ended in an honourable draw.

Merel Zabio looked around for someone with whom to share her utter incomprehension, but she didn't care to meet the eyes of the Eblan general or the squatting giant and Ereleth – quite apart from being a queen – had obviously understood the greater part of the argument well enough. It was Ereleth who took it upon herself to ask questions, and Fraxinus couldn't help feeling a slight pang of sympathy as he observed that Merel could hardly understand the questions, let alone the answers.

'Are Serpents and Salamanders like dragomites, then?' the witch-queen demanded. 'Are they hatched from eggs laid by some strange figured stone?'

'I suspect so,' Fraxinus told her. 'Given that Mossassor can't give a full account of its own origins and hasn't yet figured out how to translate the account the wise Salamanders have given it of their affairs, the matter remains clouded with uncertainty.'

'But you're saying that the Serpents and Salamanders we're used to are juveniles,' Ereleth said, striving for clarification. 'You're saying that there's some further phase of development possible in each species, but that the real adults only emerge once in a thousand generations or so.'

'We might have to be careful in applying terms like *juveniles* and *adults* to a situation where they don't really obtain,' Fraxinus observed cautiously, 'but in essence, yes.'

'Why do they know so little about their own life-cycle?' Ereleth wanted to know. 'It's not as if Mossassor is some kind of fool.'

'I've been wondering about that ever since you raised the issue of the blatant failure of our own lore to incorporate this kind of understanding,' Fraxinus admitted. 'It obviously has something to do with Mossassor's assertion that Serpents have to be good at forgetting, but I can't yet see the necessity. Aulakh?'

'I can't answer that either,' Phar said unashamedly. 'But it has occurred to me that humans have something in common with paedogenetic species. The human infant is born helpless, very early in its development, so that it retains a considerable capacity for learning. You could say that we too reproduce and live our entire lives in a juvenile phase. When other earthly animals are born their brains are already fully formed – or nearly so – and they have to make do with a stock of pre-prepared instincts to guide the greater part of their behaviour. We, on the other hand, can feed our brains with our learning, moulding it as we grow. That kind of extended youth is a great asset to an intelligent species – so much so that a species probably couldn't cultivate intelligence without having some kind of extended youth phase. If Serpents and Salamanders were able to develop intelligence because they had the capacity to extend the juvenile phase of their development perhaps they can only hang on to their intelligence and their learning by staying young. Perhaps their adult forms aren't intelligent at all . . . but it's all just conjecture, until we actually meet some adults. If we're right about all of this, that might be what's about to happen – in a few hours, you say?'

'At noon,' Fraxinus confirmed. 'I presume the hour's determined by the necessity of having the sun's rays strike that huge lens at exactly the right angle. We'll know more then – with luck, we'll know much more.'

'But we can't be certain of that, can we?' Ereleth said, in a chillier tone than she'd used before. 'Even if everything you've deduced is correct, the conclusions aren't really cause for congratulation, are they? What is it that we know, after all? We know that some kind of upheaval occurs periodically, which wipes out whole human communities. We know that such upheavals have succeeded, time and time again, in reducing human life to such disarray that the survivors are unable to preserve lore to guide their descendants when the bad times come again, save for a handful of secret commandments and a handful of instruments whose use we can't begin to understand, buried in the veins of those who have a human kind of Serpent's blood and the hearts of those who have a human kind of Salamander's fire.'

She looked at Fraxinus as if she were challenging him to contradict her, but he had no intention of so doing. What she said was true; what he and Phar had deduced must have been deduced before, but it had not been remembered. The most puzzling question of all was: *if all this is true, why is it not part and parcel of the legacy of human wisdom?* Perhaps, even if it were true, it would all count for nothing. Perhaps, even if he were to plumb the depths of all these mysteries, and eventually understand everything, the knowledge would be impotent to save him from certain death, let alone empower him to live a better life.

'It may be that we have a long, hard road to travel yet,' Fraxinus admitted, 'but there is neither glory nor profit in turning back. I, for one, am determined to follow it to the end – as, I think, are you.'

For once, the queen's answering smile was not pinched into insignificance by the meanness of her bloodless lips.

'Oh yes,' she said, in a most unqueenly fashion. 'That surely goes without saying.'

18

ANDRIS COULD HEAR voices. At first they seemed to be distant, but as he tried to make out what they were saying he realised that they were actually close at hand. Until he made that connection he was oblivious of all other physical sensation, but as soon as he had placed the murmurous voices he was able to place himself within the prison of his own flesh, and he began to hurt.

The pain was diffuse but it seemed excruciating; it was as if he had been flayed. He knew that the aura of agony was in some sense superficial – that it did not cut to the deepest layers of his flesh in any mortal fashion – but the knowledge didn't lessen the awful oppression of its tyranny. He might have screamed if he had been able to do it, or at least groaned, but his mouth seemed to be cemented shut and his thick tongue was as dry as a bone. All he could do was stir himself, and he had a nagging suspicion that he wasn't even able to writhe with any semblance of grace or energy.

However incompetently he was writhing, the motion was sufficient to attract attention. The overheard speech which had caused him to begin his distressing return to wretchedness might have been conducted in an alien tongue for all the meaning he had been able to extract from it, but now he heard his name, spoken distinctly and more than once. Then he felt a hand on his arm, whose invasive pressure forced him to realise that what he had taken for illimitable agony but a moment before was in fact a more ordinary kind of discomfort, which was already fading. When he stretched his limbs, trying to will himself back into the empire of his flesh, he eventually won sufficient control of the pain to reduce it to a series of specific and not altogether disabling aches.

Eventually, he was able to open his eyes.

He saw the stars. He also saw Lucrezia. She was bending over him, still repeating his name. The cold light of the stars pricked his eyes, and there was a clammy dampness beneath him, seeping into the back of his shirt as he lay supine upon the ground.

Lucrezia lifted his head and pressed a cup of water to his lips, but his head was too heavy for her to support one-handed, and he couldn't maintain the required angle. He coughed and spluttered as water flooded his mouth and his nose, but his reflexes kept him safe from drowning. He tried to summon strength into his leaden limbs, so that he might use his arms to support himself and force himself up into a sitting position, but his arms were the parts of him that hurt more than any other, and they felt as if they hadn't strength enough left in them to lift themselves, let alone serve as props for the remainder of his awkward bulk. His legs felt almost as bad.

He coughed and spluttered for a while longer, and then drew breath. In the meantime, muddled memories which he must have been keeping at bay for some time began to leak into his consciousness again. He had no idea where he was or how he had come to be there, but he remembered something of where he had been.

He opened his mouth to speak, but that only encouraged Lucrezia to force the cup to his lips, and he had no alternative but to drink. The water was brackish, but it slaked his thirst. By the time he was able to open his mouth again his tongue no longer felt like a desiccated tree-trunk.

'That bastard lied to me,' he mumbled. 'He told me that stuff wouldn't put me to sleep.'

'It wasn't the drug that put you to sleep,' Lucrezia told him. 'If anything, it kept you awake far longer than any human being ought to be able to stay awake. Sheer exhaustion put you to sleep, in the end, and might have served you better if it had done so two days earlier.'

Two days! Andris echoed silently. For the moment, at least, he had lost those two days, and perhaps others. He tried hard to bring some order to his memories, so that he could identify those which were the most recent. He had a vague notion that he had been in a boat, rowing, but he wasn't sure whether that had been before or after Philemon Taub had given him the distilled essence of the Lake of Colourless Blood to drink.

After a brief pause for studious puzzlement he said: 'Did I really kill two giant Serpents with my bare hands?'

'More than that,' Lucrezia replied. 'I think you killed five, but one or two of them might only have been stunned. You were using two pieces of polished wood as clubs, and they weren't well-designed for use as weapons.' She must have guessed from his attitude that he needed more information to help him remember, so she continued. 'It wouldn't have been so easy if they'd got to us once we were in the open, but they weren't as fast as they looked and they weren't good swimmers. Once we got to the boat it wasn't too difficult to steer clear of them, even with Rayner doing the rowing. You remember Rayner, don't you?'

She pointed to her right. Andris turned his head and saw that the boy who'd taken them out to the middle of the lake – how many days before? – was sitting there, huddled under a cloak and seemingly half-asleep. Andris managed to raise his head sufficiently to let him look around, and saw that he was lying on a muddy bank some three mets from the edge of water whose waves sparkled with reflected starlight. There was a rowing-boat bobbing in the water, tethered to a gnarly tree whose earthliness seemed quaintly reassuring.

On his other side, between Lucrezia and the boy, a small fire had been lit, but there was no kettle or cooking pot set upon it. Beyond the fire there was another human figure, completing the company of four. Andris recognised Venerina Sirelis. She was pale and drawn, and she was looking at him without any trace of the avid interest which she had earlier taken in his well-being and his mental adventures.

'We were probably wise to keep going as fast as we could,' Lucrezia added. 'We seemed to lose them soon enough, but we were rowing against the flow, and once we were back in the bushy maze they could have got to within a dozen mets of us without being seen. It made good sense to keep rowing until we'd put a healthy distance between ourselves and any possible pursuit – which is perhaps as well, because there was no way in the world we could have stopped you once you had those oars in your hands. It was as if you'd become a kind of machine, locked into an endless repetition of the same movements, oblivious of anything within or without.'

'I don't remember that,' he said.

'That doesn't surprise me,' Lucrezia told him. 'You didn't seem to be in any condition to notice anything. You got us out of there, though. Without you, the three of us wouldn't have made it out of the building. We lost Philemon – he was knocked down by a blow to the head and didn't get up. Some of the other people from the Community escaped by various exits – others were out of the house all along – but I think they all headed west on foot, in the opposite direction to the one from which the attackers came.'

'Which way did we go?' Andris asked.

'Out into the lake, to begin with. Rayner thought we'd be safe in deep water. After that, due south, or as near to it as we could – as you could, that is. By that time, you had the oars and there was no question of debating the matter. You rowed day and night, without food and almost without water, although I managed to force a few cupfuls past your stubborn lips. By the time you fell asleep I wasn't sure that you'd ever wake up – but you no longer seem to be subject to the normal limits of human endurance, if you ever were. If we're going to head for Salamander's Fire now, we'll have to turn south-east. We've brought the boat as far as we possibly can – a couple of hours will take us beyond the limits of the marsh and into unknown territory.'

Andris used the support of his elbows to lift his head a little higher. Then he sat up. It wasn't quite as painful as he'd feared, but he was beginning to be conscious of his empty stomach.

'What have we got to eat?' he wanted to know.

'Very little,' Lucrezia told him. 'It's not long till dawn – when daylight comes, we'll go foraging.'

This was not a comforting reply. Fortunately, there were other things than hunger to think about. 'Who were they?' he asked wonderingly. 'What were they? Why did they attack the house like that, without warning or provocation?'

'I presume that they wanted the house, and thought it best to take it by storm,' Lucrezia answered. 'I don't know why. I don't suppose we ever will.'

'They will die,' Venerina Sirelis said. Her voice was hollow and hoarse. 'The marshes and the Community will kill them all. They came along the river, from the Pillars of Silence – perhaps from the Grey Waste – but they came too far. The spirit of the waters will punish them for what they did. They will all die, human and Serpent alike.'

Andris met Lucrezia's eyes as they listened to this speech. He read in her expression the news that Venerina had not regained even a fraction of the calm composure that she had worn so comfortably before disaster struck. He also read the awareness that if he and she had come safely through the marsh, from its north-east corner to its southern boundary, it was hardly unimaginable that at least some of the Community's destroyers might also come through it unscathed.

'Did you find the enlightenment you sought?' Lucrezia asked him, in a voice hardly above a whisper. 'Were the promises they made you fulfilled? Has the spirit of the waters taken full possession of you, and granted you access to all its secrets?'

Andris wished that he had a ready answer to that question. He searched inside himself, in case one might be lurking just beyond the immediate reach of his consciousness, but all he could find was a sense of absurdity. Days had passed, apparently, since he had faced those two giant Serpents in the corridors of the Community's wonderfully tidy home – days passed partly in a trance and partly in exhausted sleep. Had he dreamed at all, while awake or asleep? If he had, did any legacy of memory now remain to tell him what he had learned in the course of his dreams?

He remembered an old tale about a man who believed that he had made a marvellous discovery while he was dreaming, and then wasted the rest of his life obsessively trying to remember what it was, having lost it in a single moment of inattention which followed his awakening. He tried with all his might to break the barrier which separated him from the memory of what had happened in the private arena of his mind between his encounter with the giant Serpents and his awakening a few minutes before, and he felt it yield just a little.

He caught the ghost of a strange sensation; a sensation of being free; moving with the relentless efficiency of an automaton, beneath the angry sun and benign stars. He caught the merest echo of the intangible spirit of the waters, which had the form of a great lens which had the ability to focus the perceptive power of his intellect and his imagination to a marvellous degree . . . but he could see nothing through it at present but a tantalising void.

For a moment or two, he felt sick with disappointment and frustration. It seemed, for a few fleeting seconds, as if it had all been for nothing – but then he lifted up his hand and placed it in front of his eyes, so that he could study the open palm and the fingers. The hand was filthy, and there were broken blisters at the base of every finger. He couldn't straighten the fingers out, because there were more blisters on the second joints of all except the little one. The lines engraved upon the palm – where certain charlatans swore that a man's future was written in secret code – were exposed like little rivulets of gold when he stretched the skin to break the scum of dirt.

'It's part of me,' he said finally. He felt that Lucrezia deserved some kind of answer, even if it were not an explanation. 'It's part of me now, and always will be. It doesn't matter that I can't yet put it into words and make it into lore. It'll always be there, and I've all the time in the world to discover its secrets.'

She didn't make any comment.

'You think I'm as mad as she is, don't you?' Andris said, nodding in the direction of Venerina Sirelis. After a slight pause, he added: 'Perhaps I am. Perhaps, without suspecting it, I always was.'

There was a sudden splashing sound nearby, and Lucrezia immediately whipped round to face the direction from which it had come. The panic which swept through Andris at the thought that they were about to be attacked helped to raise him to his feet, but he knew as he fought against swirling giddiness that he was not in any condition to fight. He did his best to assume a position which would at least imply that he was ready and willing to do battle, but he could only hope that it looked more convincing than it felt, and that he wouldn't fall down too soon. He was profoundly relieved when a voice called out: 'Iss good. Iss me.'

He blinked to clear his bleary eyes, and finally managed to focus on the figure that was wading through the shallows, emerging on to the bank. It was, as the sibilant accent had promised, a Serpent. Mercifully, it was a Serpent of a perfectly ordinary size – one of only two that he might have recognised even in a crowd of Serpents, even by starlight.

'Ssifuss?' said Lucrezia incredulously. 'How in the world did you find us?'

'Never losst you for long,' the Serpent said, as it came clear of the water and shook its tail, throwing droplets of water in every direction. 'Alwayss caught up again.' It discarded the heavy pack from its back before flopping down on the wet grass. Andris was quick to follow suit, and Lucrezia sat down too, in a slightly more decorous manner.

'It's all right,' Lucrezia said to Venerina Sirelis and Rayner, both of whom were looking at the newcomer with great trepidation. 'It's a friend. It was in the marshes with us – I told you about it. What do you mean, you never lost us?' The last remark was, of course, addressed to the Serpent.

'You mean that you followed us all the way from the Community?' Andris said curiously. 'And before that, all the way from the place where we were attacked by the birds?

'Yess,' Ssifuss replied blandly. 'Not eassy.'

'Why didn't you show yourself when the people from the Community found us, if you knew where we were?' Lucrezia must have known before the question was complete what the answer was, but she finished it anyway.

'Caussiouss,' Sssifuss said. 'Ssought it besst to hide.' The Serpent's eyes flickered back and forth, keeping watch on Venerina and Rayner, mistrustful even now of their intentions. Venerina was holding herself rigidly, but she made no attempt to move from the place where she was squatting. Rayner remained huddled within his cloak.

'What happened to Checuti?' Andris asked. 'Wasn't he with you?'

'Went after dragomite-woman,' the Serpent replied. 'Never caught up. Not eassy.'

'Did you see what happened at the house by the lake?' Lucrezia wanted to know.

'Yesss.'

There was a pause while they waited for the Serpent to say more, but it didn't. It was Andris who said: 'I never knew there were such things as giant Serpents.'

'Nor me,' said Ssifuss, half-swallowing the words in a manner which was awkward even by its own standards. 'Mossassor wass right. Iss truss in myss. Musst move on ssoon. Are not far behind.'

'Not far behind?' Lucrezia echoed. Andris observed that Venerina Sirelis had stiffened again, after beginning to relax. 'You mean they're still after us? After more than three rotting days?'

'Not chassing,' Ssifuss said, 'but coming ssiss way. Ssought I would never catssh up while Andriss rowing, but sstayed here too long now. Ssey not far behind, even wiss prissonerss to sslow ssem.'

'Prisoners?' This time it was Venerina who echoed the crucial word.

'Yess,' Ssifuss said. 'Many prissonerss.'

'They didn't want the house at all,' Lucrezia said, quick to revise her earlier assumption. 'They only wanted the people. The riders were using clubs, not swords. But what do they want the people for?'

'Don't know,' Ssifuss said. 'Musst move ssoon. Want food firsst?'

Mention of food instantly displaced attention from various other matters on which Andris might have sought further clarification. Even Rayner rose to his feet and moved forward at the thought that there might be nourishment to be had.

While he watched Ssifuss rummaging in its pack Andris felt his hunger grow, alarmingly magnified by anticipation. All that the Serpent produced were a few strips of smoked meat, which would have seemed utterly unappetising at any other time, but none of the four humans hesitated for a moment before setting forth to devour them. It was by no means a satisfying meal, but it was a beginning.

'What's going on, Ssifuss?' Lucrezia asked, curiously forcing her to speak even while she was trying to chew. 'Why are giant Serpents joining forces with men to take other men captive?'

Ssifuss wouldn't meet her eye. 'Don't know,' it said. 'Not real – never ssought sso. Wass wrong.'

Mossassor, Andris knew, had believed that there was a measure of truth in certain Serpent myths, much as Carus Fraxinus had believed that there was a measure of truth in the parts of the lore that other humans thought mythical, but it had never mentioned giant Serpents.

'Is there anything in your myths that might help to explain what happened back there?' Lucrezia asked, obviously thinking along the same lines.

'No,' the Serpent replied defensively. 'Nossing. Wass not Sserpentss' doing, I ssink. Not real Sserpentss.'

'What do you mean, not real Serpents?' Lucrezia said exasperatedly. 'They looked very real to me.'

'Perhaps it means that they weren't *intelligent* Serpents,' Andris said. 'Might it be that they were being used by the humans like hunting-dogs – animals rather than sentient beings. Is that it, Ssifuss?'

'Don't know,' Ssifuss replied warily.

'Human giants are like any other people,' Lucrezia said. 'My mothers and sisters used to call the sanctum guards stupid, but they weren't. *Dhalla*'s not stupid.'

'If they had intellects to match their muscles,' Andris said, after swallowing the last of his ration, 'how come they were serving as house-slaves?'

Lucrezia shot him a glance whose sharpness implied that she had taken offence, but her expression softened soon enough into one of puzzlement. 'I asked her, more than once, why she didn't want to be among her own people,' she said, 'and why, if she had to be among ordinary people, she didn't use her strength to be something more than a servant. She said that wasn't the way things were done. Is it possible that the people who attacked the Community have contrived to domesticate Serpents – to breed them for meekness and obedience as well as size?'

Andris didn't know the answer to that, and Ssifuss remained studiously silent.

'Ereleth never did tell me exactly what her secret commandments required her to do,' Lucrezia added, 'but as well as speaking of a special kind of human being – one with Serpent's blood – they also spoke of a special kind of Serpent and a special kind of Salamander. I assumed that Mossassor was the special kind of Serpent, and Mossassor seemed to think so too. Perhaps we were both making false assumptions?'

'Mossassor knew nossing,' Ssifuss said. 'All sstoriess. If ssome truss in ssem, don't know what.'

'But you and Ssumssarum came with Mossassor anyhow,' Lucrezia pointed out. 'Are you siblings?'

'Not like that,' Ssifuss replied unhelpfully. Andris thought it probable that the Serpent hadn't the least idea what the word *siblings* meant.

Lucrezia wouldn't be put off. 'What *is* it like?' she demanded.

'Are of ssame earss,' Ssifuss said, 'but debt is not to do wiss ssat.'

'Of the same earth,' Andris repeated, not certain that he had heard right, or that Ssifuss had found the right word. 'What does that mean?'

'Ssame plasse,' was all Ssifuss would say.

'I think Serpents hatch from eggs,' Lucrezia said, addressing Andris although she kept one eye on Ssifuss while she said it, presumably looking for a possible contradiction. 'Perhaps the eggs are laid in the ground, like those turtle-eggs Ssifuss found in the marsh when we were desperate for food. Perhaps Ssifuss and Mossassor were part of the same clutch . . . but if so, that's not why it was under an obligation to Mossassor. Perhaps that was some kind of debt of honour.'

Ssifuss was deliberately looking the other way now, pretending to watch Rayner finish off his makeshift meal. The boy was obviously discomfited by the Serpent's stare, but he made no protest and Ssifuss eventually condescended to remove its disturbing attention.

'Need more food,' Ssifuss said. 'Can't wait for daylight. Will find.' It had all the hallmarks of an excuse, but no one was about to object. They all watched the Serpent wade into the water, heading for an islet covered by one of the dense thickets whose thorns seemed to make little or no impression on its scaly hide.

'Don't look so disapproving,' Andris said to Venerina Sirelis. 'He's useful, and he becomes friendlier with every day that passes. He could have gone his own way – I don't know why he followed us, but I'm glad he did.'

'It's an it, not a he,' Lucrezia reminded him. 'And I doubt that it's doing what it's doing out of consideration for us, or because it wants to meet up with Mossassor again.'

'As far as I'm concerned,' Andris said amiably, 'he's now a he. He might have no balls, but he's not an object and I refuse to keep on talking about him as if he were. And whatever his motives are, he's welcome to travel with us. Maybe he's coming round to the idea that you really do have Serpent's blood, and that it really is important.'

'Perhaps it wants to know what the spirit of the waters has to tell us, when you can get around to telling us,' Lucrezia retorted – but she didn't sound as if she were making a joke. 'Or perhaps it wants to know what your severed head will say, if ever you can find it a new body.'

That remark brought forth an echo in the recesses of Andris's consciousness. *Get the head!* he had shouted – but he no longer knew why. He looked at the boat, where the head was presumably stored along with whatever worldly goods they had managed to salvage during their flight.

'Perhaps he does,' Andris said. He wished, somewhat perversely, that he still felt the kind of intoxication that had possessed and deranged him before. Perhaps it would have buoyed him up, or at least distracted him from his many discomforts. For now, at least, the spirit of the waters was quiet; he had no way of knowing if or when its co-existence would again become clamorous.

'It's all part of God's plan,' Venerina Sirelis said. It wasn't easy to judge who she was talking to, if she was talking to anyone other than herself. 'The Community will continue; nothing will be lost. There is a purpose in this, and no need for despair.'

'There's no need at all for despair,' Andris agreed, wishing that he could inject more conviction into his voice, 'but we have a long way to go, and it seems that we still have to make what haste we can.' He looked down at his injured and enfeebled hands, wishing that he could use them to rub away the ache in his arms.

At least I'm fit to walk, he thought. *For the time being, I'll have to be grateful for that. Perhaps the marshes were the worst of it, and there's no significant hindrance to be found between here and Salamander's Fire*. He didn't bother to add the words: *and perhaps not*. They were too obvious to need saying.

19

JACOM HAD BEEN awake for some time, but he was pinned down by a heavy weight and he had not yet found the strength to shift it. He had let himself lie still while he collected himself, carefully taking stock of his inner resources. Alas, he had found no real cause for congratulation in his accounting.

His head ached terribly – and would probably have ached all the more, now that his eyes were open, had the night not been so hazy. As things were, even the flamestars shone discreetly. He had no idea what the hour was; it could have been midnight or just before the dawn. His arms and legs were heavy, but attempts to move them no longer brought forth savage surges of pain and he no longer feared that one of them might be broken. The only thing that was still preventing him from sitting up and throwing aside whatever had pinned him down was a general weakness of the flesh and of the spirit.

He knew, though, that he had to overcome that weakness. Every now and again, he could hear the sound of screaming. It was coming from a long way away, but it was undoubtedly the sound of a human voice and Jacom knew that he couldn't continue to ignore it.

He managed to keep his head fairly still while he heaved upwards with both his arms, and he succeeded in rolling the stifling weight from his belly to his thighs. Once there, it wasn't so oppressive as to prevent his wriggling free, one leg at a time.

When he was free it became a simple matter to change his own position and look at the thing which had been pinning him down.

From the neck down the dead creature seemed human enough, but from the neck up it was something else entirely. Jacom didn't know how best to characterise the 'something else'. The head didn't resemble the head of any species, earthly or unearthly, to which he could put a name; the nearest comparison he could draw was with the little monkey Checuti had kept as a pet, although the cast of the features wasn't particularly simian. The dark brown face was fringed with coarse hair in much the same way that the pet's had been, although its forehead, cheeks and chin were hairless. Its wide-open eyes were black and the teeth peeping through the thin black lips to either side of the hoggish snout were orange, more like a rat's than a monkey's. It looked like some kind of travesty – a make-believe monster created by the absurdly simple method of putting on a mask – but it wore no mask and it wasn't a creature of make-believe.

Jacom was neither as surprised nor as horrified as he would have been had he encountered such a being a year before. He had seen half-men in the bowels of the dragomite hive; he already knew that part-human chimeras could be produced by unearthly entities like the dragomite queens of the Corridors of Power. This was merely one more of the same kind, birthed by some alien mother. Why should it astonish or alarm him, given that the region from which all these new and dangerous things seemed to be coming had borne the name Chimera's Cradle since time immemorial? On the other hand, it was clothed and armed, and it had been part of a company whose immediate reaction to the sight of him had been to charge with murderous intent – all of which facts hinted at further dimensions of strangeness and mystery.

The half-man had been killed by a spear-wound to the chest, but that must have been administered as a finishing blow; he had also taken a terrible slash-wound which stretched from his waist to his knee, ripping his clothing and most of the underlying flesh. Jacom could see the white gleam of the hip-bone. This wound had bled in great profusion, and a good deal of the blood had been absorbed into the cloth of Jacom's jacket and trousers. The blood was still slightly sticky where the overlying body had not given it a chance to dry out. The mess was terrible.

Somewhere away to Jacom's right, behind the ridge of the hill, another scream sounded. The screams were more widely spaced now. He had no doubt that the man who was crying out was dying; they were howls of agony, not cries for help.

Jacom found it easy enough to come to his feet now that he

was free of the dead thing. He found his fallen sword and picked it up. Once he was standing he could see the true extent of the damage which the skirmish had inflicted on the contending parties, and he took a careful count of the casualties.

Kirn was dead, his body lying not five mets away beside the body of a horse. Zovar had never made it through the weeds that grew beside the stream; his blood had reddened a huge pool of water which had accumulated behind the dam formed by his corpse. There was no sign of Purkin, Luca or Kristoforo.

The dead half-man who had fallen on top of Jacom – perhaps saving his life by obscuring the fact that he was not dead – was not the only loss the attackers had suffered. There were two others lying dead, and one more dead horse. Jacom took no comfort from the fact that the body-count was even; his own trained men should have killed at least twice as many.

He rememberd shouting an order to Luca and Kristoforo to go back, and he looked across the stream for evidence that the fight had continued on that side. He made out the shapes of three more dead horses, one of them half-obscuring a body that might have been a man or a half-man. He couldn't be certain that there weren't more, hidden by the tangled strip of unearthly vegetation on the far bank of the stream. He was about to cross the stream and check, but he paused before taking the first step and looked down again at the body of the half-man.

He knelt beside the supine corpse and took the torn cloth of the half-man's trousers between his thumb and his forefinger. Carefully, he peeled it back from the edge of the slash-wound, pulling it clear of the creature's groin. It came away more easily than he had anticipated, because this blood, though clotted, had not hardened.

The half-man wore no underclothes; Jacom was able to see his – or, rather, its – groin. There was a tiny aperture which he took to be the equivalent of a urethra, but there was no sign of a scrotal sac or any genital apparatus whatsoever.

It took a little longer to peel away the relevant part of the creature's shirt, but when he had done so Jacom wasn't in the least surprised to find that the creature had no navel.

Why should it? he asked himself. *Has it come from the Navel of the World? Perhaps it sprang full-grown from the Pool of*

Life, or perhaps it hatched from some marvellous egg, laid by a mother whose body is a hill, or a tree, or . . .

His imagination failed him then, and he knew that there was no point in extending the list. There were more important questions, and he had no difficulty in summoning a few of them to mind.

Why is this happening? Why have alien wombs, of whatever form, begun to spew forth progeny whose forms are unrecorded in lore and legend alike? Are they intended to swarm across the face of the world, destroying everything that men have built? Is this the race destined to replace humankind?

He looked more closely at the clothing which the half-man wore. Then he went to one of the dead horses, which had not been one of those his own men had ridden, and examined the bridle and saddle. He found a broken spear of the kind the half-men had carried lying nearby.

The saddle was so similar in workmanship to the one his own mount had carried that it was unlikely to be a coincidence; the tackle had probably been made by true humans, probably in one of the Nine Towns. The clothing was lighter than his own but it was tailored in much the same style – a style quite distinct from that of Kirn's Xandrian uniform.

'All stolen, it seems,' he said aloud. 'The horse, the saddle, the weapon, the clothing . . . and the flesh itself. Something alien has stolen the semblance of men, and sent its creatures forth to supplement that semblance, by usurping the habits and tools of men. But why place such a strange head upon the body, given that even a dragomite queen could produce something as perfectly human as the mound-women – not to mention that awful head which called Myrasol *brother*?'

It made no sense, so far as he could see – no sense at all. He wondered what kind of brain was lodged inside the alien head. Could it think like a man, using the words that a man would use? Or was that where the true difference lay? Myrasol's aspirant brother had most certainly talked like a man, using the words that a man would use, but this creature might be different. He wondered where the two races of unearthly humanoids which shared the world with humankind fitted into all of this. Were they somehow *behind* it all, or were they too in danger of being swept aside and replaced? One thing that seemed certain was that neither the dragomites nor their own half-human associates were anything but victims. So far, they had been punished more harshly than any other species.

In the distance, the wounded man screamed again. This time, unhuman voices screeched in reply. Scavengers were waiting, impatient to claim their prey.

Jacom turned his back on the dead half-man and walked quickly to the stream. It took him five minutes and more to force his way through the densely packed weeds, even though he had the sword to help him, but he didn't pause. On the far side he found one more dead half-man which had previously been hidden from view. The dead man half-obscured by the horse turned out to be Kristoforo.

Jacom cursed beneath his breath, but he took care to remember that Purkin and Luca had survived this particular encounter. Luca, at least, must have managed to return to the main column. But what had happened when he got there?

As soon as he reached the brow of the shallow hill Jacom knew the worst. The ragged hedges prevented him from making any proper count of the broken wagons or the goods they had spilled or the men who had died trying to defend them, but he knew that the situation was bad. The only thing he could be sure of was that the column hadn't stopped. It had kept going forward, although attackers must have come at it from both sides in considerable numbers. He knew that the wreckage must spread over at least a kim, and probably more. He would have to walk a long way before he could measure the full extent of the disaster, and only then would he know how many of the riders had fled to the fortress which Amyas called the Last Stronghold . . . which might already have fallen, if the worst had come to the worst.

Another scream told him where the dying man must be lying. There was no answering jeer from the hellhounds this time; they must have found readier carrion to occupy their teeth and tongues. There was, however, a ceaseless chattering noise made by dozens of black birds as they quarrelled over dead flesh and all manner of spilled produce.

Jacom forced his way through the hedge as close to the screamer's position as he could. From where he stood he could see four recumbent bodies, but three of them were half-men; the battle had evidently been fierce. Hellhounds were busy about these three corpses; they looked up at him with red and glaring eyes but refused to move away. He kept a wary eye on them while he went to the fourth body: the one which still had life in it.

The man was one of Amyas's bronzes. He had taken a bad belly-wound, which had bled copiously but was bleeding no longer. In Jacom's judgment, there was no possibility at all that the wound might heal; the gut within had been ruptured in several places. The man had pulled himself to the wreckage of a broken wagon, but had not had the strength to clamber into the back.

Jacom rummaged among the wreckage and found a water-bottle. He knelt down and put the rim of the bottle to the stricken man's lips, giving him just enough to wet his lips and tongue. The man screwed up his face, but this time fought against the scream, reducing it by the effort of his will to a strangled groan. Jacom went back to the chaotic mess of boxes and jars, sacks and pouches. After some rooting around he found what he was looking for: a stone jar in which were sealed a generous handful of the anaesthetic darts which his captors had used to ease Merel Zabio's distress in the aftermath of the battle of the bridge.

He took pains to explain to the man what he could and couldn't do. The man was a fighter, who had seen such wounds before and knew the limitations of medical artistry well enough. When he was sure that the man understood him, Jacom made as if to administer the anaesthetic, but the bronze pushed his hand away.

'Hundreds,' the man said, speaking thickly through the agony caused by the acids released from his gut, which were already eating away at his internal organs. 'Amyas . . . get help . . . Stronghold.'

'It's all right,' Jacom assured him. 'There's nothing you need to tell me. You've done what you could. Let me use the thorns.'

The bronze still resisted, because he still thought there was something he ought to say – some warning, plea or instruction that it was his duty to pass on. Jacom paused to give him the opportunity, but it was no use. All the man could say was: 'Not men . . . monsters.'

'I know that,' Jacom told him. 'I killed one myself, and I'll kill more if I get the chance. I have to go now, to make my way to the Stronghold. I'll tell Amyas that you did everything you could.'

He meant what he said, but he realised as he forced the second dart to release its merciful poison that he didn't know the man's name.

There were no more screams and no more groans, but the birds were still bickering and the nearest hellhounds were no more than a dozen mets away.

Jacom knew that he wasn't safe hereabouts, even if he could keep the hellhounds at bay. There was plunder in abundance here, and the half-men would undoubtedly be back as soon as they had left off chasing the riders who had fled the assault. There was no possibility of finding a horse, but he had to make up a pack to carry. He needed clean clothes, and food, and a full water-bottle, and woundglue, and . . .

The bronze was unconscious now, beyond the reach of pain – and beyond the reach of any conceivable salvation. Jacom cut the man's throat, to make sure that he wouldn't have to wake up again to find hellhounds squabbling over his liver and lights.

'I'm sorry,' Jacom said aloud. 'I truly am.' He became acutely conscious of the fact that he and the dead man both reeked of blood, and that they were both stained from neck to knee.

He turned away abruptly, and ran towards the nearest of the corpses, lifting his sword to slash at the three hellhounds which had claimed it. They looked up at him, angry and resentful, and for a moment he was certain that they were prepared to fight – but when he was almost close enough to strike out at them, all three turned tail and ran. Within seconds they had disappeared into the hedge, without uttering a yelp or a snarl.

What cowards! he thought. *They were three against one, and the one a mere swordsmen on foot.* But then he realised that more than three hellhounds had been put to flight, for the two which had been tearing flesh from the next half-human corpse along had also taken to their heels – and all the birds had stopped chattering.

Jacom looked along the road in the direction of the Stronghold, and realised that he could see nothing moving at all. The hellhounds had disappeared into the hedgerows and the birds had taken flight – and it was absurd to think that a single human swordsman could ever have caused them to do so.

He felt a strange prickling sensation at the back of his neck, and he turned round to look back the way he had come.

The man he had killed for mercy's sake still lay beside the wagon, but something else now stood over him – and it was not a hellhound. This was something which could put scores of hellhounds to flight merely by virtue of its presence.

Jacom saw that manticores did indeed exist, and that they really did have the bodies of tigers and the tails of scorpions – except, of course, that no tiger had ever been quite as big as this, and a scorpion would have had to be magnified a thousand times to carry a tail like this one. Most unsettling of all, though, was the manticore's head, which would not have seemed at all out of place on human shoulders, save for its size. It couldn't have been the head of a giant, though. Its features were distinctly masculine. The manticore's face reminded him, albeit faintly, of Checuti's.

It's not so strange, Jacom told himself sternly. *If there are creatures with human bodies and alien heads, it's only natural that there should be creatures with alien bodies and human heads. Chimeras must come in all shapes and sizes.*

He assumed a fighting posture, with his sword extended before him, and waited to give as good an account of himself as he could in a fight which he knew he couldn't possibly win.

'Don't be stupid,' the manticore said, in an accent as closely akin to his own as the ones Amyas and Tarlock Nath had. 'There's only one way you're going to get out of here alive, and that's to throw the sword away and come with me.'

'Where to?' Jacom asked, wondering why the question seemed so utterly ridiculous, and why the creature now seemed more like Checuti than it had before.

'Does it matter?' the monster countered, moving forward with an astonishing grace, making not the slightest sound as its catlike paws rose and fell. 'Wouldn't anything be better than being dead?'

Jacom knew that the answer was yes, but he was in a stubborn mood. He hadn't dropped the sword yet, nor had he come to a decision as to whether he would. 'I think you want to take me to Chimera's Cradle,' he said. 'That's where you came from, isn't it – you and all your kind? That's where you were spawned by some monstrous figured stone.' *How proud Fraxinus and Phar would be if they could see me now*, he thought.

The creature was within striking distance now, had he cared to strike at it; because it went on all fours it didn't loom over him as conspicuously as it might have done, but its magnified features seemed very menacing. There might have been a hint of amusement in its gleaming eyes, but Jacom wasn't sure about that. He met its stare for a moment or two, but he didn't lash out with the sword. Instead, he let the point of the weapon droop until it was directed at the ground.

'Chimera's Cradle is your ground, not ours,' the manticore informed him blandly. 'Are you going to drop the sword, or not?'

There had been a time when Jacom might have refused, but he was a different man now, more flexible by far of mind, emotion and action. He dropped the sword.

'All right,' he said, hoping that he too sounded tolerably casual and confident. 'What now?'

20

THE CURVED OBSERVATION window was only a little broader than a man's head. The crevice which gave access to it was too narrow to accommodate a Salamander, so Fraxinus had perforce to conclude that it had been fashioned for the use of a man or a Serpent. That implied, of course, that others like himself had stood here before him in the distant past: men who had handed down no substantial record of their adventures to those who came after them. He wondered whether they too had been forced to share their stations.

Around the rim of the tubular chamber he could see seven more windows identical to the one through which he was peering. It was impossible to see the observers stationed behind them, but he knew that Mossassor and its fellow Serpents must have the use of at least two, and that Aulakh Phar and Merel Zabio were behind one of them. Ereleth had claimed the right to share his – a claim which he would have resented fiercely were it not for the fact that the mutual hatred which had sprung up between them on their first introduction had been all but obliterated by long proximity and grudging familiarity. The remaining windows presumably had wider cubicles behind them, so that the Salamanders could watch their own work.

Mossassor had assured Fraxinus that there would be abundant opportunities to witness Salamander's fire burning 'bravely' and that it would be far more comfortable were a single person to be stationed at each window, but there were too few volunteers to wait for another day. Among the humans, only Shabir and Dhalla had that much patience.

The windows looked down into a pit about thirty mets deep, whose circular floor was some twelve mets in diameter. At present there was little to be seen, although a narrow line of light-rays was leaking through the ceiling, inscribing a diameter across it and faintly illuminating the structures below. It was possible to make out a conical formation of some kind jutting from the centre of the floor, and Fraxinus could see enough detail in the walls to assure him that they were faced with vertical figured stones recognisably akin to the ones which he had seen in the Crystal City. There were eight such faces, separated by darker bands of rock; their substance was partly translucent and their surfaces were much more highly polished than those of the more familiar horizontal stone-creatures. Their intricately contoured surfaces appeared to be innocent of the kinds of grooves and pitfalls which the 'wild' stones used to trap prey.

Fraxinus was in no position to see whether the attendant Salamanders actually did anything to set the process in train; it might have been that the movement of the sun across the sky was the only signal which the Great Eye still required. The external surface of the lens had been entirely exposed when he and his companions had been brought down into its surrounding orbit – through what he couldn't help but think of as its 'tear-duct' – but Fraxinus suspected that it was not usually left naked; he believed that it was usually covered by lids, as the inner surface still was, by some structure that mimicked the function of paired eyelids.

Knowing this, he was not unduly surprised by the suddenness with which the inner eyelids opened, filling the chamber behind the eye with vivid light. Nor was he surprised by the fact that the cascade of brilliance was brought into focus by the gargantuan convex lens, so that its searing energy was concentrated upon the conical structure set in the floor of the pit. What did surprise him, however, was that the cone reflected the almost focused rays so that the point at which they came together was displaced sideways on to the wall of the chamber, and that the cone immediately began to deform itself so that the point in question moved across the surface of the figured stones. The line it followed was intricately curved; it was as if the glowing atom were the nib of a stylus inscribing a flowing script on tablets of smoked and coloured glass.

'The whole structure's alive,' Fraxinus murmured to Ereleth. 'Artifact it may be, but it's no inert device, like the optical instruments designed and built by our own lensgrinders. It really is the living eye of some monstrous leviathan whose body lies buried in the mantle of the world.'

'An unseeing eye mounted in the surface of a womb,' she whispered in return, her lips no more than a few sems from his ear. 'Imagine a window set in the navel of a human woman, so that the sun's prying light might penetrate the very core of her being. As a means of becoming pregnant it would have aesthetic advantages which the natural method definitely lacks.'

'This isn't conception,' Fraxinus reminded her, although he didn't suppose for a moment that she had overlooked the fault in her analogy by accident. 'Whatever passes for conception here happened a long time ago. This is the moment of delivery, when hundreds – perhaps thousands – of years of gestation finally bears fruit. That dancing finger of light is a summons or an invitation, not some magical sperm.'

Where the vivid point of light passed across the surface of the polished stones it left a legacy behind. Fraxinus had no idea how hot the focused light might be, but he knew that it could not be inflicting an injurious burn while it moved about so determinedly. Even so, it left a trace behind it, as if the surface it touched took something of its fury captive, absorbing the meaning of its patient inscription into the body of the vitreous womb. The translucent walls of the womb were not so solid as to be incapable of any deformation, and Fraxinus could not help but think of them as a kind of flesh not unlike his own. The whirling dance of the light made it very difficult to see clearly but Fraxinus was certain that the walls of the chamber were flowing, as though they were bulging under the pressure of some extremely viscous liquid that was being rippled by all manner of sluggish waves.

Within the walls, illuminated ever more clearly as they soaked up the light of the focused beam, deeply embedded figures began to shift themselves, further stirring their clotted amniotic fluid.

'This fire doesn't seem to be burning so very *bravely*,' Ereleth remarked. 'It appears to me to be a rather gentle process.'

'It isn't like a blacksmith's forge,' Fraxinus told her. 'Salamanders may be uncommonly robust, but they aren't made of tempered steel. If *bravely* merely meant *hot*, they would have used the word *hot* – communication between our two species is difficult enough without employing unnecessary circumlocutions. I can only suppose that burning *bravely* is meant to imply that those creatures waiting to be born are no ordinary creatures of the kind which duplicate themselves generation after generation, with little or no variation. Were this womb in its native state, the things emerging from it now would be creatures so different from their progenitors as to seem to watching eyes to be daring ventures of fate: chimeras designed by some hazardous madness. We must remember, though, that this womb is not in its native state, and that it has been subject to some measure of control. The control may not be absolute, but it's certainly adequate to permit constructive influence.'

The shadows within the eight faces were still astir, and they had now begun moving towards the surfaces from which they would eventually detach themselves. Their progress was very slow, but the medium which contained them seemed so dense that it was a near-miracle that they should be able to make visible progress at all. The active faces were gradually filling up with a strange radiance, glowing purple and green while the dark bands between them remained black. Their surfaces were undulating gently, as if responding languidly and sensuously to the luxuriant touch of the darting finger of light.

'It's certainly related to the dragomite queen, but the kinship seems rather distant,' Ereleth said. She was craning her neck uncomfortably, trying to make fuller use of her half of the window. Fraxinus felt her cheek touch his, and had to consent to the touch lest his own view be spoiled. 'Is there some kind of imprisoned male down there, do you suppose, like the human drone Andris Myrasol found?'

'I suspect that sex doesn't fit in to the Salamander scheme of things at all,' Fraxinus said. 'I don't know whether the dragomites invented sex for themselves or whether they borrowed the device from earthly life-forms for their own particular convenience, but in the full spectrum of unearthly life the role played by sex is peripheral. This kind of reproduction isn't anything to do with the fertilisation of an egg by its spermatic counterpart and the ordered combination of their characteristics; the formulation of chimeras can't be haphazard, but it's much more versatile than anything which commonly occurs in earthly life-forms. Look!'

He had no room to point with his finger, but he knew that Ereleth would have no difficulty figuring out where to look. The first of the imprisoned forms had come so close to the surface of its figured stone as to begin to reach through it, deforming it much more extravagantly than the slow ripples which constantly coursed around the segmented circle, but the moment of emergence wasn't easy to achieve.

Fraxinus had observed the alacrity with which the simpler kinds of figured stones exuded an imprisoning membrane around the creatures which they trapped; the initial encasement was far more rapid than the subsequent digestion. What was happening here was no mere reversal of that process; the last imprisoning membraneous layer seemed to be very difficult indeed to split and cast off. The creature which was emerging by degrees from the light-excited surface of the pit was moving far more insistently than its fully embodied cousins, most of which still seemed to be only half-formed, but the last confining layer was remarkably elastic and seemed intent on maintaining its imprisonment.

Fraxinus could see that the creature which was struggling to be born was no common or garden Salamander, if it could be reckoned to be a Salamander at all. It was far too slender – more slender even than a Serpent, unless its image were greatly distorted – and there was something distinctly strange about its form. It was impossible as yet to identify the precise quality of that strangeness; the parts of its body which were fighting to emerge from the face of the figured stone were the extremities of its limbs – hands whose fingers Fraxinus couldn't count and feet which looked more human than unearthly – and it was the more deeply set parts of its body which seemed confusing.

Fraxinus couldn't believe that the function of the beam of focused light was to energise this process, no matter how hot the dancing point of light might be. The real power, he thought, must be coming from within; it was now being released by some kind of metabolic process, having been stored over a long period of time. The light of the Great Eye must be a signal rather than a power-source.

'I can't see,' Ereleth complained. 'The light's dazzling – and it's shifting so quickly that I can't make out what's happening.'

The play of the light had indeed become more hectic, and the walls of the alien womb were now so radiant that the overall intensity was becoming distressing. Fraxinus could no longer make out the exact shape or dimensions of the first of the forms which was stepping down from the soft flesh of the mother of Salamanders, although he was fairly sure that the restraining membrane had condescended at last to release it. The intensification of his confusion was partly due to the fact that the creature itself was strangely iridescent.

'Its skin is decked with scales,' he said. 'Scales which are mirror-bright, but coloured too. It's as if they're reflecting back the light reflected by that central cone, trapping the light in endless circuits.'

'They're not built like Salamanders at all,' Ereleth observed, using the plural because a second figure was now in the process of emergence. 'They're infinitely more delicate, except for . . .'

Fraxinus couldn't blame her for not being able to find words to describe the exception, which was still half-hidden by the partiality of the figures' emergence. The arms and legs of the creatures had seemed ordinary enough, apart from the play of light upon their vivid scales, and so did their heads and torsos – all of which structures seemed as nearly human as Salamanderesque or Serpentine – but it was the third pair of limbs which marked them out as something different from all their humanoid cousins.

'Wings,' Fraxinus said, as the first of the newborn creatures began to unfurl the massive structures anchored to its shoulders. 'They're wings. These beings are more like Aulakh's exemplars than we anticipated; the adult really is a kind of fly, and the Salamanders we know are merely the maggots.'

'They're more like jewelled bats than flies,' Ereleth said, effortlessly matching his casual refusal to be overly astonished, 'save of course that they stand erect instead of hanging upside-down from their perches.'

Both the creatures within the shaft were free now; no part of their bodies was bound to the wall which had extruded them. They stood quite still, as if they were waiting patiently. Having stretched their wings once they began to fold them again. The eye above them closed as suddenly as it had opened, cutting off the light of the sun, which must by now have been a degree or so past its zenith.

The beam of light which had initiated the emergence was eclipsed, but the chamber was still lit by the quiet radiance of its own walls. The scales of the emergent entities glittered no longer, although they still reflected the calmer glow of the eight great facets set in the circular wall. It was far easier now to study their shape and their colour, and Fraxinus was glad of the opportunity.

'Are they simply the adult forms of Salamanders,' Ereleth asked him, 'or are they complex chimeras? They have something of the Serpent about them . . . and perhaps something of the human too. Are they a compound of all our races, do you think?'

'I don't know,' Fraxinus said.

'They might well be the special kind of Salamander of which my secret commandments speak,' the queen went on, 'but I don't understand why they and not the common kind are supposed to go to Chimera's Cradle. Even if they're not mere animals, as you and Phar have suggested, they're newborn – utterly innocent of all learning. Surely they'll require years of maturation before they're ready to go anywhere.'

The two creatures had completely furled their wings now, and they seemed far less alien and far less glorious as they stood quite still. Their eyes were open, but Fraxinus couldn't tell whether they were actually looking at the surrounding walls. Those walls were still luminous, save for the vertical stripes of darkness which separated the figured stones – one of which, Fraxinus saw, was slowly widening.

Within the translucent crystal, which had hardened again to seeming solidity, the vague forms of as yet unborn creatures had relapsed into immobility. Fraxinus supposed that the ritual would be repeated tomorrow, and the day after, and for as many days as were required for the walls to disgorge their full burden of cocooned individuals. Time would tell whether they would all be identical, or whether the occasional bravery of Salamander's Fire extended to ambitious variety.

The widening stripe in the chamber wall opened like a vertical mouth to expose a corridor which was presumably this strange womb's birth-canal. The winged creatures didn't react to its opening; nothing happened until two Salamanders of the familiar kind came to collect their newly hatched kin, leading them tenderly away into the darkness.

The fissure in the wall closed behind them, and the light within the walls gradually ebbed away, fading to insignificance.

'That's all,' Fraxinus said, stepping back from the window. He was careful to place a polite and comfortable distance between himself and the queen before meeting her eyes.

'What Cerri and Myrasol saw in the womb of the dragomite queen was rather more dramatic, by their account,' Ereleth observed, in a tone tinged with slight regret.

'Only by virtue of being more gruesome,' Fraxinus said. 'I don't think it could have been as beautiful, nor as delicately managed. Dragomites may have intelligent commensals in the form of the mound-women, but Salamanders have intelligence of their own, and a legacy of wisdom accumulated over thousand of years. This was purposive, and the Salamanders must have a clearer idea than we do as to exactly what its purpose was. Whatever is happening to the world, a new phase of the process has just begun – a new phase which we have been privileged to witness, and in which we shall be privileged to take part.'

'I don't doubt it for a moment,' Ereleth replied, lifting her left eyebrow in a slightly sardonic fashion. 'I wonder, though, whether we shall survive the adventure, and whether there will be any calculable profit in it if we do.'

'We're too old to be afraid of death or failure,' Fraxinus told her. 'We never had anything to lose but a few years of dull and comfortable existence in Xandria. There comes a time when calculable profit ceases to be an issue, even for the cleverest merchant in Xandria. I intend to go to Chimera's Cradle, no matter how difficult and dangerous the journey might be. The only profit I need or desire is to discover what's there, and to begin to see the logic which underlies the bewildering confusion of our existence.'

Had he made such a speech twenty days before she'd surely have favoured him with an infuriatingly haughty stare, and affected a kind of contempt that reflected her dual status as a queen and a witch. Now, though, she wore a much more relaxed expression.

'If ever you and I were to feel Salamander's fire burning in our foolish hearts, Carus Fraxinus,' she said lightly, 'it would be burning very bravely, would it not?'

She was confessing, in her own oblique fashion, that they were two of a kind, and ought to be glad of it.

'Yes,' he said agreeably. 'It surely would.'

TO BE CONCLUDED

IN

CHIMERA'S CRADLE